Fab Four FAQ 2.0

Fab Four FAQ 2.0

The Beatles' Solo Years, 1970–1980

Robert Rodriguez

Backbeat Books
An Imprint of Hal Leonard
New York

Published in 2010 by Backbeat Books
An Imprint of Hal Leonard Corporation
7777 West Bluemound Road
Milwaukee, WI 53213

Trade Book Division Editorial Offices
19 West 21st Street, New York, NY 10010

Printed in the United States of America

Book design by Snow Creative Services

Library of Congress Cataloging-in-Publication Data

Rodriguez, Robert, 1961–
    Fab Four FAQ 2.0 : the Beatles' solo years, 1970–1980 / by Robert Rodriguez.
        p. cm.
    Includes bibliographical references and index.
    ISBN 978-0-87930-968-8
    1. Beatles–Miscellanea. 2. Harrison, George, 1943–2001—Miscellanea.
3. Lennon, John, 1940–1980—Miscellanea. 4. McCartney, Paul—Miscellanea.
5. Starr, Ringo–Miscellanea. 6. Rock music—1971–1980—Miscellanea. I. Shea, Stuart. Fab Four FAQ. II. Title. III. Title: Fab Four frequently asked questions 2.0.
    ML421.B4R63 2010
    782.42166092'2—dc22
    [B]
                                                                    2010002244

www.backbeatbooks.com

This book is respectfully dedicated to
William Powell Lear, who, in 1962,
invented the eight-track tape cartridge.

Contents

Foreword

I am always amazed at how much there is to the Beatles. In 1968 during our meetings when we were setting up Apple Records, I remember the four lads talking about the individual roles they would take in the launch of this new and exciting enterprise. A phrase kept repeating itself as each of them entered the conversation until finally I asked them about something I found very amusing in the dialogue. To a man, they never referred to the Beatles in the first person but always as if "the Beatles" was a separate entity from themselves—almost as if they were a band from another planet. When I questioned them about this, they explained that the whole phenomenon had gone beyond them and had actually become more than they could comprehend as a group of guys who made really good music. To look back now on this meeting that took place over forty years ago, it is mind-boggling how they had in essence looked into the future and realized how complex and incredibly astounding what they had created would become.

Because I was in that simple place with them, a place where we thought we were just making music and having a good time, I am astounded to this day by just how much there is and was to them. *Fab Four FAQ 2.0: The Beatles' Solo Years, 1970–1980* expands on how intriguing this band, the greatest event in musical history, is, and continues to offer more details of its depths in a very accessible and enjoyable way. It is put together so you can read for minutes or hours and be satisfied.

If you are a newcomer and are looking to learn more about aspects of their individual paths, then you will be amazed how much there was to it all. If you have been researching their story for decades and are such an old-timer when it comes to the Beatles that you feel you know everything about them and their music, I challenge you to dig in. You will find things you never knew and also gain deeper insight into the things you did know about.

I am not a fact person. I am a feel person. That is why I find this book important. Robert has done the painstaking work and research to bring so many interesting facts to our attention so that people like me can simply enjoy the music and the memories without doing our homework. That fact makes me feel good and adds to the wonder of it all.

He has worked it out. . . .

Ken Mansfield,
Former U.S. Manager of Apple Records and
author of *The Beatles, the Bible, and Bodega Bay*;
The White Book; and *Between Wyomings*

Acknowledgments

After All, I'm Forever in Your Debt

D uring the production of this book I was very fortunate to have met some wonderfully generous people from all over the world, mostly through cyberspace. In response to my requests for certain rare images to share with readers, they came through with their scanners, sending items from their collections for all of us to enjoy.

To each, I offer my sincere thanks for the time and effort. This book would not have been all that it is without contributions from the following people:

Jesse Barron, who supplied the Lennon and Wings promo singles.

Derek Bussen, who donated the September 1972 *Jet* cover image.

Herve Denoyelle, who provided several items, including Ringo's "You Don't Know Me at All" picture sleeve.

Keith Emmons, who gave us the *Sentimental Journey* advert.

Mark Galloway, who gave us the *Wedding Album* and *The Beatles at the Hollywood Bowl*—on eight-track.

GH/Justine Dennis, who donated the "Mind Games" picture sleeve.

Robert L. Hooper, who supplied the May 1975 *Hit Parader* image.

Len Hruszowy, who gave us the Apple Studio promo picture.

J. Larry Kobelt, who provided the unused Wings ticket.

Les Kulik, who contributed the *New York Post* newspaper.

Lyle Nance, who supplied the "Early 1970" sheet music cover.

Kurt M. Rusher, who contributed the unused George Harrison ticket.

Kent Sawyer, who provided the rare "Mother" picture sleeve.

Then there were the efforts of the amazing Kasper Gynther—from far-off Denmark—who possesses a wealth of overseas solo picture sleeves, far more than any one book could contain. Though only three made the final cut—the "True Love" and "Ding Dong, Ding Dong" sleeves, plus Ringo's "You Don't Know Me"—these represent but a sliver of what Kasper was only too happy to share. The entire selection will be posted online; on behalf of myself and fans the world over, my deepest gratitude.

There were several others who responded to my call for images but whose contributions sadly ended up unused. Thanks just the same to Steve

Acri, Dick Moers, and Patrick Nolen. Your images, too, will be put up on the website.

Finally, but not least, David Nagy was, like so many of us, a huge fan with deep knowledge and wide tastes. (The *Meet the Residents* sleeve came from his collection.) Art and music were his world, but unfortunately, his health was not as robust as his desire to express himself. Though David lost his battle with juvenile diabetes some years ago, his passion lives on through the inclusion in this book of something that he loved. Do give a thought to David and others like him, as well as the kindness of his mother, Betty.

The remainder of the images are from my personal collection.

Introduction

I Hope You're Having Fun

Welcome back, Beatle people!

On a late-summer Saturday in 2009, a suburban Chicago neighborhood commemorated the end of the season with a block party. It was an astonishingly diverse gathering; excited children, some with infant siblings, played in an inflated bouncy house under the warm gaze of some residents old enough to have witnessed World War II, all within the afternoon shadows of multimillion-dollar McMansions coexisting alongside teardowns on borrowed time. It was a happy celebration, made all the more convivial by the sonic ambience: *Beatles 1* blasting through a high-wattage system set up in the street. Without giving the matter a second thought, someone had supplied exactly the right touch for connecting the generations.

I realized a lifelong dream in 2007 by, with Stuart Shea, producing a book on the Beatles, one that I had long hoped *somebody* would write—but no one did. With *Fab Four FAQ*, we attempted to present a critical history of the group, offering every facet of their story in self-contained chapters that lent themselves to random exploration. That is, readers were invited to pick up and dig in at any point—not necessarily at the beginning—and see where the story led them. Taken in its entirety, the book was always intended to offer an impressionistic accounting of the Beatles' career that covered just about every aspect that a fan would want to know about.

From exchanges with readers both in person and via cyberspace, as well as reviews, I found that we were successful in our goal. My favorite blurb came from one Ari Spool (who is in no way connected to the authors, by the way) of the *Seattle Stranger*, who opined that "any book that can teach you this much about something you already know a lot about is a very good book." Mission accomplished (to coin a phrase), right?

Well, not really. Because if you are a true fan, the story hardly ends with John, Paul, George, and Ringo clearing out their desks in the spring of 1970 and marching out of Savile Row laden with cardboard boxes containing years of accumulated stuff. Reverberations of their former collective echoed onward for years, while each man individually attempted to reclaim his identity after years of subsuming it to a persona first sketched out in

A Hard Day's Night (and amplified, in America at least, in weekly episodes of the *Beatles* cartoon).

For Beatles fans, the 1970s dawned with the heartache of seeing their beloved group in the throes of a bitter, emotional breakup, one frequently likened to a four-way divorce. Most of the antagonism pitted Paul, recently believed to be dead, against the other three. By taking his former bandmates to court, McCartney took the ugly but very necessary step of freeing himself from the stranglehold of Allen Klein, a man whose divisive tactics helped shatter the fragile relations within the ranks at the very moment when the group most needed to stay united. Macca was falsely portrayed as an ego-driven instigator of the disintegration, when in fact the opposite was true: as he repeatedly asserted, by the time of his public declaration, he was the only Beatle who *hadn't* yet left.

Whatever grief the public felt over this turn of events may have been mitigated by the music produced that year. Whereas 1969 saw one new album and two singles' worth of new material issued by the Beatles (plus assorted experimental excursions from John and George, leavened by "Give Peace a Chance," "Cold Turkey," and *Live Peace in Toronto*), the year the group ended saw a bounty of new material: one new album each from John and Paul, *two* from Ringo, and a stunning triple-record set from "the Quiet One," as well as a final Fab Four release, such as it was. Whatever might be said in mourning their end as an ensemble, lack of productivity was not a valid complaint.

Between 1970 and 1980, the four ex-Beatles went on to release *thirty* studio albums, plus one compilation each, two triple live sets, and enough non-album single material to fill two more long-players—an astonishing amount of music. Naturally, though, as the decade wore on and tastes shifted, the critics found new and timely ways to slam the artists for not producing work that measured up to their former collective. Such assessments were unfair: times had changed and, Paul McCartney excepted, the former Fabs seemed less and less interested in reliving past glories, content to express their artistry for its own sake rather than compete with a ghost. Still, the burden of high expectations was enormous, and if the former Fabs seemed testy about comparisons to their '60s work, one could hardly blame them.

Adding to that weight was the question that dogged them for virtually the whole of the decade: "When are the Beatles getting back together?" Depending upon of whom and when the query was posed, the response could be churlish or sanguine. What seems evident in retrospect is that once the musicians' individuality asserted itself and was validated, and the malignancy of the Klein regime was no longer an issue, very little stood in their way. True, George had some personal and musical issues with Paul that would surface from time to time, but he could also be quite positive if caught in the right mood.

John's take, as always, was the most complex. His emotional investment in the band he had once led and had gone out of his way to shatter ran deep. Though he was quoted describing the Beatle years as an ongoing humiliation, he clearly took pride in the group's achievements and was quick to defend them against detractors. (He was also a world-class collector of Beatle paraphernalia, including bootleg recordings.)

Clearly John's feelings were mixed; though he asserted at length in his final interviews that re-forming the band would be pointless, boring, and like a return to high school, he also swore on record in a court deposition two weeks before his death (as part of ongoing litigation against the producers of the Broadway show *Beatlemania*) that the group were in fact planning to perform a live reunion concert as a finale to the in-progress documentary of their career, then entitled *The Long and Winding Road* (later to emerge as *Anthology*). Ample evidence suggest that, public persona aside, he was far more open to working with Paul again than most people ever knew.

As for Macca, he began the decade a shattered man, pilloried in public as the instrument of the defunct band's disunity while privately sinking his troubles in alcohol before pulling himself together again, finding salvation through reinvention. In a way that even his harshest critics had to respect, he created a new act—Wings—from scratch and ended the decade lauded as history's most successful composer and performer. (The Guinness organization awarded him a rhodium disc in 1979 to honor his achievements.)

While often bearish when urged to put his previous act back together again (famously declaring "You can't reheat a soufflé"), Paul also noted that working with his former bandmates on a loose basis was not out of the question. Ringo, for whom the dissolution of the group was widely believed to be a certain return ticket to obscurity, surprised everyone by establishing a viable solo career, albeit with more than a little help from his friends. Once he began riding high chart-wise, he declared he saw little point in reunions. Like the others, his outlook would also shift with prevailing currents, career-wise.

Seems to Just Follow Me Around

The seeds of this book were sown before Fab Four FAQ was finished. Having relived the Beatlemania of my formative years so deeply while writing the book, I found it hard to walk away, especially in light of the continuing desire to tell what happened next. (Those familiar with the opening scene of Bride of Frankenstein have a pretty good idea of what I was feeling.)

I became a fan during the '70s, at a time when nostalgia for the group was high and all four of its former members were releasing successful albums and singles. It seems an eternity ago: four components of the biggest act of the previous decade could be found with regularity on the airwaves (not as oldies fodder), on television, on magazine covers; even on the big screen. Some folks were even lucky enough to see a real live ex-Beatle in concert, passing through town. I was not one of them, at least not during those years. Still, I was able to buy my first solo album when it was brand new (*Walls and Bridges*), though frankly it took me years to warm to it, it being a far more nuanced record than say, *Venus and Mars* (my second).

It was with the intent of bringing those years back for those who lived them, as I did, or to contextualize them for readers too young to have experienced the decade firsthand, that informed this book. As with the previous volume, I think that understanding the achievements of John, Paul, George, and Ringo apart requires a grasp of their world and how events around them influenced their art. Hearing "Jet" on a classic rock station today alongside "Misty Mountain Hop" or "Another One Bites the Dust" can't convey what a breath of fresh air this track was when new.

I also wanted to show what it was like to be a fan during those times. Even if it was too late to go out and see the group live, there were other options. Midnight screenings of Beatle films were commonplace, while touring multimedia shows like *The Beatles: Away with Words* offered some semblance of an event, shared by an auditorium full of like-minded fans. For that reason, this book is populated with images of tickets, 45 sleeves, and magazine covers. Each in its own way depicts the talismans that were part of our world—and theirs—during those years.

The period magazines I consulted were invaluable research tools, allowing me a window into the times—who was up; who was down—in view of later events. Reading contemporary reports as history unfolded helped strip away nostalgia's clouding haze and show how the ex-Fabs were seen in their day, before legend took hold.

This book also contains eleven yearly summaries covering 1970 through 1980. These sections act as buffers between thematic chapters of data, collecting and laying out the stories contained in a given year that will hopefully help put things further into perspective.

Some Things Take So Long

At the outset of this project, I was seemingly alone in failing to grasp what was obvious to everyone else: that I was taking on no less than a quadruple biography. (Actually quintuple, if one recognizes the specter of the subjects' former incarnation hovering over each member for years afterward as its own entity.) Though I had hoped to have the book finished for a summer 2009 publication date, this was not to be. Every path contained further twists and turns, and though I had things pretty well mapped out at the start, once you fall down the rabbit hole, you simply go where it leads.

Upon what I expected to be the completion of the mission, I was stunned to see that I'd produced a manuscript nearly 50 percent larger than *Fab Four FAQ*—and *that* was a pretty hefty book. So it was in the interest of sparing readers a hernia (and my editor apoplexy) that some judicious cuts were made. (To anyone who comes away from this book saying, "Why didn't he talk about x, y, and z?": Hold your fire.) The results before you are meaner and leaner, but if they leave you still thirsting for more, fear not; all material produced but not appearing in this volume will be made available on the book's website.

Part of the process included listening to every single one of those thirty-plus albums (as well as singles). What I heard was revelatory, for what I recalled as weak tea to my younger ears so long ago is, in several instances, pretty damned good—underrated, even. Without a doubt, it was Ringo's output that suffered the most from unfair, even gratuitous abuse. What I heard upon re-listening was a surprisingly solid body of work, suffering at times from too much slickness and unevenness of material. At no point did I find him completely disengaged, though there were certainly moments that were a little too cutesy for my taste.

Conversely, I believe at least a couple of his albums—*Beaucoups of Blues* and *Ringo's Rotogravure*—stand up better than their lackluster chart performances suggest. The opposite phenomenon occurs with some of Wings' output, with best-selling albums provoking thoughts of "what were we thinking?" upon review. What's been said here of Ringo's lesser works is equally true of Paul's, though at least the latter's prolific work habits tend to make his misfires easier to forget.

John was musically active for little more than half the decade, and surely issued his share of less-than-top-flight material on occasion. That said, given this shortfall as compared to his fellow ex-Fabs, it's remarkable how much classic material he *did* produce, the best of which sounds as though it might have been recorded today ("Instant Karma" being one example). Given his ascent to martyrdom in the wake of his premature death, it's easy to forget that, like Jim Morrison, he was regarded by some during his lifetime as a self-absorbed clown.

Possibly the highest expectations fell upon George in the year after the breakup. Everything about his astonishing debut, *All Things Must Pass*, was mammoth: the scope of the release and its sound; the success of "My Sweet

Lord" (which soon turned sour); and the subsequent humanitarian effort for Bangladesh, which showcased the album before a live audience. Right out of the gate, he set a standard so high that it would have been impossible for *anyone* to live up to it, and a backlash set in soon enough.

Fab Four FAQ 2.0 attempts to present the story of the Beatles during the 1970s—and of the four men who used to be them—with neither blind devotion nor gratuitous revisionism. At the end of the day, I—like you—am merely a fan. I'm neither an insider nor a peer, and can therefore only tell their story as seen through the eyes of someone who has followed their career quite closely, has performed many of their songs, has embedded their music into his DNA through repeated close listenings, and possesses an instinct for what rings true and what rings false. You alone will judge the success or failure of what I've set out to do.

Love Is the Answer

A project like this, consuming so many waking hours, engrossing though they were, could not have been sustained without the love and support of the people surrounding me. My wife has been, as always, the bedrock upon which such dreams are realized. She's offered encouragement when my energies flagged, praise when I was in doubt, and called BS when I went off the reservation. Given all that's on her plate, her strength is almost beyond belief. Though my love and gratitude are never expressed enough, Kati, maybe I'm amazed at the way I really need you

Zane and Zoe have never lived without the music of the Beatles—together and solo—in their lives. To them, the group in all its myriad forms—as themselves, as depicted in the *Beatles* cartoon, as seen in *Yellow Submarine*—has been around them always and is as familiar as any close relative. Of late, my seven-year-old son has discovered variations on the theme, such as the Lego animations on YouTube, while my three-year-old daughter is at the point of distinguishing their individual singing voices. Kids: "All I have is yours / All you see is mine / And I'm glad to hold you in my arms / I'd have you anytime."

To my parents, Richard and Shirley Rodriguez, as well as my immediate family —Rick, Russ, Rozanne, Amy, Melissa—there are no joys to be had in this life without all of you to share them with. Thanks for being there always. The same goes for Bill, Val, Shari, Todd, Amii, Ryan, and Josh, as well as all the wee Hoopers and Hostetlers. Love and thanks to Jill, as always.

Then there are friends who may or may not be aware of what they give just by being. I'm sorry if my time is no longer what it was, but that doesn't mean you're very far from my thoughts. (That means you, Craig and Terry, as well as Lorraine and Barb and far too many more to name.) Thanks to Paul Youdelis for making thirty years fall away.

Thanks too to all my Beatle buddies, including Mike Sekulich, Tom Repetney, David Gans, John Blaney, Joe Garcia, Pat Korman, Pete Pecoraro, Mark Caro, and Bob Purse. Also, big thanks to Mark and Carol Lapidos (Jessica and Michelle, too!), as well as Nancy Andrews. Note to Dogbro: It's not 1996 and turning up at the door isn't the same anymore.

Thanks to Stu for everything, as always. Among the missing (in no particular order): Craig Cermak, Pete Wilson, Ron Paquin, Tom Orr, Dave Duerkop, Ken Pieper, Paula Day, Tim Davies, Dave Molter, Dan Molter, Nick Lewers, Nick Poblador, Josh Siegel, Jeff Paszkiet, Lloyd Hiroaka, Gaby Cifuentes, Keith Hedmark, Keith Becker, Sharon Basso-Meyers, Pat Thomas, the Bauers, and Mike Cotter. You, too, Jenna Young. Also thanks to the PIL gang: Doug Brooks, Dave Hogan, Dave Aretha, Jerry Yamamoto, Jim Slate, Dustin Drase, and Chris Hiltz.

This journey might not have begun at all if not for the seeds planted at Blackhawk Junior High School during our unit on the Beatles, way back when. To Marlene Rohlfing, my long overdue thanks.

To all my radio buddies: a shout-out to Terri Hemmert, Joe Johnson, Chris Carter, Rene Young, Tom Frangione, Mancow, Greg Alexander, and Gary O'Brien. To Dick Biondi and Bob Stroud: Keep on keepin' on.

To all my friends in the bookselling business, including Quinn Moore, Gayle Townshend, Mary Anne Diehl, and all the folks at the Book Cellar (Rebecky included!)—a great big thanks for your hospitality. Let's do it again sometime.

Thanks for the essential contributions to this book from Ken Mansfield and designer extraordinaire (and newly minted daddy) Matt Schwarz. You guys are the best.

Finally, my thanks and appreciation to all the hardworking folks at the Hal Leonard Performing Arts Publishing Group and Backbeat Books, including John Cerullo; my editor, Mike Edison; Bernadette Malavarca; Brad Smith; Aaron Lefkove; Sarah Gallogly; and Diane Levinson. To anyone I may have unwittingly omitted: all I can tell you is, it's all show biz.

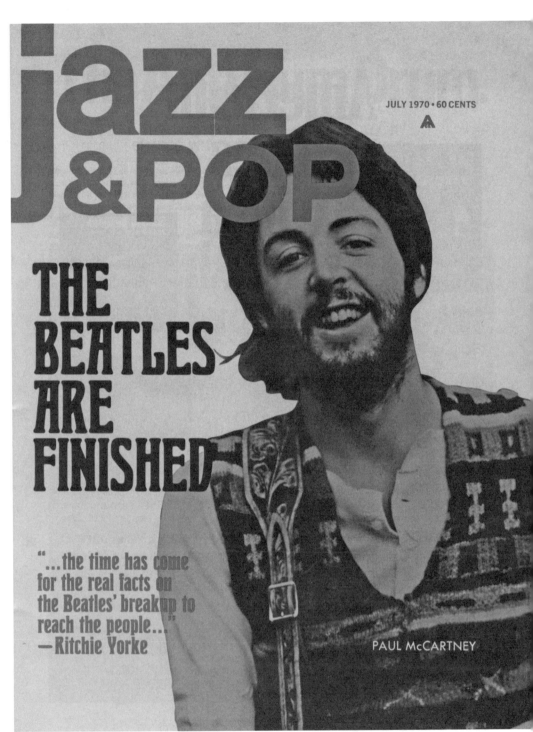

jazz
&POP

JULY 1970 · 60 CENTS

THE BEATLES ARE FINISHED

"...the time has come for the real facts on the Beatles' breakup to reach the people..."
—Ritchie Yorke

PAUL McCARTNEY

Echoing the headline trumpeted in the U.K. press back in April, *Jazz & Pop* magazine let Americans know with finality not to expect any new Beatle product anytime soon.

I Don't Believe in Beatles

In the months following the release of *Abbey Road* in September 1969, the four men who had once thought of themselves as the Beatles stayed busy, each in his individual pursuits. Not long after assisting John Lennon with "Cold Turkey," a chilling account of kicking his heroin addiction the hard way, Ringo Starr began work on an album of Big Band–era pop standards with George Martin at the helm. Could anything have underscored the group's divergent paths more starkly?

On the outs with his bandmates, Paul McCartney holed up at his Scottish farm as rumors of his demise spread like wildfire across America. Though far from dead, he was brokenhearted, shocked, and dispirited at the loss of the only job he had ever known. With the encouragement of his bride, the former Linda Eastman, he gradually began anew with his music, initially using a new Studer four-track tape console to try out some musical ideas. Though he and John had long since stopped collaborating, his work on what would become *McCartney* marked a decided transition into uncharted waters, with only Linda to bounce ideas off of.

The workaholic tendencies Macca was renowned for were also evident in George Harrison after the release of their last group effort. George spent the waning months of 1969 dividing his time between studio work for others (namely Apple signee Doris Troy; ex–Blind Faith bassist Rick Grech; and studio sessionist Leon Russell, soon to be a Harrison fixture), and playing live dates, starting in December with American gospel/country blues rockers Delaney & Bonnie. Their tour took George around England and Denmark; upon his return home, he found time to tread the boards with John one last time as part of the Plastic Ono Super Group at London's Lyceum.

Having turned in his resignation in September, John Lennon hadn't engaged in any serious "Beatling" since the *Abbey Road* sessions, though he did take time out to produce a major contribution to the group's annual Christmas message. While he was still writing songs, his music tended to take a backseat to his political and artistic endeavors, the former typified by the War Is Over (If You Want It) billboard campaign in December; the latter by his set of "erotic lithographs" depicting married life with Yoko Ono, up close and personal. As the New Year began, he busied himself setting up a public exhibition of *Bag One* at a London art gallery before vacationing in Denmark while his three erstwhile bandmates got together to tie up some loose ends.

George's "I Me Mine," first introduced a year earlier during the "Get Back" sessions, was featured in the finished cut of the *Let It Be* film and therefore needed to be on the soundtrack album. Though having long since moved on musically, George got together with Paul and Ringo to record a take for that purpose. It marked their last official Beatle duties together for twenty-four years. In the coming weeks, George and Ringo would separately turn up at EMI's Abbey Road studio to contribute various required overdubs to the project once Phil Spector took over, completing their chores by April.

Paul, meanwhile, returned to the group's former home studio a few weeks after the "I Me Mine" session, laying down more tracks for what would become his solo debut, including "Maybe I'm Amazed." The recordings had begun at home around Christmas 1969 and continued into the next year, eventually moving to London for sessions at Morgan Studios and EMI's Abbey Road facility. Recording in secret, Paul seemed to be making a deliberate shift away from the high production values he'd embraced only months earlier on the Beatles' swan song. In his own way, he was fulfilling the "as nature intended" theme of the aborted "Get Back" sessions, albeit as a one-and-a-half-man band.

John, while not yet ready to tackle a full LP's worth of tunes just yet, awoke on the morning of Tuesday, January 27, with a song in his head, fully realized. He decided to record it that evening, while the inspiration still energized him, and quickly rounded up a cadre that included George, Billy Preston, and Klaus Voormann, as well as Spector to man the board. "Instant Karma" became a smash, giving John even more reason to emotionally separate himself from the band he'd started over a decade before.

Busy as he was, and frankly uninterested, John wasn't particularly following his former songwriting partner's activities. As work on *McCartney* progressed, the public, while accepting of the band's individual projects, was looking forward to the release of the group's long-promised and much-delayed theatrical documentary. To satiate fans in the meantime, Allen Klein conceived *Hey Jude*—a compilation of non-LP Capitol/Apple singles issued between 1964 and 1969. It was released in America on February 23, the same week that Ringo, plugging *The Magic Christian*, turned up on NBC's *Rowan and Martin's Laugh-In*.) "Let It Be," the single, was issued in March, battled John's latest offering for supremacy, then bested it and soared to #1.

That same month, long-simmering tensions between the Fabs reached a peak. Having completed his album, Paul was keen on getting it issued, along with ending the public charade of staying mum on the Beatles' status. Having at last accepted that another group record wasn't going to happen, he saw little point in pretending otherwise. Still, he met with strong resistance to his plan to release his album at the same time Ringo's *Sentimental Journey* and *Let It Be* were due out. Outraged and certain that his former bandmates' obstinacy was motivated by spite, he took out his anger on Ringo, who'd showed up on his doorstep to personally smooth things over. The band, such as it was, was now officially in a three-against-one war.

Though Paul's "I'm doing what you're doing" call to John received a welcome reception, what he did to herald the release did not. *McCartney*, after a compromise that shuffled release dates, was issued in England on April 17. One week prior, promotional copies contained a soon-to-be infamous "self-interview" trumpeting the fact that the Fabs were not getting along anymore and that, further, the artist had a better time with his "family," painting the two commitments as mutually exclusive. With this bit of hype, the word was trumpeted around the world that "Paul McCartney quit the Beatles," signaling their breakup.

John was furious at what he saw as a self-serving betrayal, mostly because it did not serve him. Ringo and George remained sanguine, at least for the time being, publicly staying noncommittal on the odds of the group resuming recording as a collective. For the public, it was a moment of universal shock. Millions had grown up with Beatles (consider what seven years means in the life of an under-twenty-year-old). The prospect of their calling it a day, compounded by the now-public animosity, was a deeply troubling development.

Therefore, the release of both the film and soundtrack *Let It Be* took on the air of an all too fitting elegy. Paul's "The Long and Winding Road" was issued as the band's final single in America: though smothered by strings and choirs, the tune's inherent bittersweetness mirrored the feelings of those mourning the end of the group. As for the now ex-Fabs themselves, none attended the film's premiere, as they had each previous opening. Underscoring his break from the past, George entered the studio at around the same time with Phil Spector—more or less—plus Ringo, Eric Clapton, and a platoon of friends and guests in tow, beginning work on a collection that would astonish the public as much as his peers.

Before Paul's bombshell, John issued an April 1 statement announcing that he and Yoko were undergoing a joint sex-change operation. In reality, the couple began undergoing primal scream therapy, first in London and later in Los Angeles. Pioneered by California doctor Arthur Janov, in

Apple Records

2832

THE BEATLES

THE LONG AND WINDING ROAD

From The Beatles' Motion Picture "Let It Be"

Released one month after Paul's bombshell, "The Long and Winding Road" was the Beatles' last U.S. single issued more or less within the group's lifetime. Its composer's distaste for Phil Spector's arrangement didn't stop it from topping the charts in July.

a nutshell, it advocated stripping away accumulated layers of emotional defenses going back literally to the womb, allowing patients to deal with their ongoing pain after first purging the initial trauma through wordless vocal shrieks. Given the damage inflicted upon his psyche going back to his earliest years, the treatment resonated with John, although he later acknowledged that the hurt doesn't go away—at best, it becomes manageable.

The album he released subsequently, *John Lennon / Plastic Ono Band*, was commonly regarded as his "primal" album, although, truth be told, he'd been expressing himself through screaming as far back as "Twist and Shout" and as recently as "Cold Turkey," both of which preceded Janov. At the time of its December release, the record received terrific reviews, but the public's reaction to the collection of brutally frank vignettes was more restrained; Ringo, who played on the album, chalked this up to its lack of "toe-tappers." In other news that summer, Ringo—taking the briefest of time-outs from work on George's debut—flew out to Nashville to record, in the span of one week, a countrypolitan collection entitled *Beaucoups of Blues*. Though it yielded no hit singles, it was a fully realized effort, showcasing one of the drummer's strong suits: a feel for authentic country and western music.

George's work was momentarily suspended in early July when his beloved mother Louise succumbed to brain cancer—the same disease that would claim him thirty-one years later. Despite the frequent absences of his pur-ported coproducer, Spector, George soldiered on with sessions for what was eventually titled *All Things Must Pass*. Like *Let It Be*, its tone of sad acceptance could as easily be applied to the disintegration of his band (not to mention the loss of his mother) while beautifully fitting the mood of the group's fans. Influences as diverse as Dylan, his Eastern studies, Delaney & Bonnie, and his former organization yielded a sprawling diversity that no single album could contain.

Lest anyone still be holding out hope that the Fabs would put aside their differences and find common ground, Paul put cold water on the notion with a note to England's *Melody Maker* magazine in August when he declared, "In order to put out of its misery the limping dog of a news story... my answer to the question, 'Will the Beatles get together again?' ... is no." The sentiment was seconded with a vengeance by John twice at the end of the year: first on his song "God," which declared, "The dream is over"; then again in an interview given to *Rolling Stone* magazine, which unloaded both barrels on his Beatle past, on being a "working-class hero," and on what he described as the complete humiliation of being a Beatle, underscoring his outrage at Paul at every turn.

As usual, George played his cards close to his vest until he was ready, in his own time, to unleash his weighty opus upon the public. *All Things Must Pass* was nowhere near as directly frank lyrically as John's collection released three weeks later, but the overall impression held by critics and fans alike was: "Where's this guy been hiding all this time?" The sheer volume of high-quality original compositions was revelatory, helping the public to begin to understand that, with a talent this big alongside two acknowledged geniuses, no wonder the group could not remain intact. Though the largely intro-spective collection, spearheaded by two hit singles ("My Sweet Lord" and "What Is Life"), was an unheard-of triple-record set, it became a worldwide smash, putting George's former bandmates on notice that the Beatles' high standards had been maintained.

This most momentous of years, which saw a birth (Ringo's daughter, Lee), a death, and five individual albums (spread over seven platters) issued, ended on an extremely bitter note: on December 31, Paul filed suit in a London court against Apple (i.e., John, George, Ringo, and Allen Klein), all with the intent of breaking his ties to the label that in no small part had been his brainchild. The unfathomably sour turn of events mystified the public and angered much of the ex-Fabs' fan base. Losing the group was a bitter enough pill, but this court action and subsequent public airing of dirty laundry was too much for most fans to bear. The turmoil felt all around was exacerbated in the pages of *Rolling Stone*, with John's staggering and unremittingly bitter interview given to Jann Wenner in December. (It was published in two parts early the next year.) The end of 1970 marked the absolute nadir of Beatlemania—the following year would see a continuation of the infighting, culminating in a musical hit job on John's next album.

Now You're Expecting Me to Live Without You

Pre-Breakup Solo Work

In *Fab Four FAQ*, several recordings issued outside of the group by individual members were briefly discussed. By the time of Paul's April 1970 announcement, seven albums and three singles had been released; of these, only the singles and three of the long-players could be said to contain music (of which, only two actually placed in the Top 10). The rest were experimental doodlings; perhaps it is for this reason that the public didn't regard the long-term future of the group as threatened, with such side projects not exactly competing for the Fabs' share of the market.

The one consistent element to all was the fact that none exactly fit the Beatle paradigm (only "Instant Karma" came close), "Revolution #9" notwithstanding. An interesting observation one can make is that, of the four, Paul alone didn't feel the need to create material outside of the parent group. Could it be that since the Fabs had more or less developed into his baby anyway there was no reason to—that he already had the perfect vehicle for issuing material of his own design?

Both John and George described in interviews how the Beatle brand had become a sort of straitjacket to them; that any material they came up with had to fit a prescribed formula if it were to have a chance of emerging as a Beatles record. But they also seemed unwilling, at least publicly, to completely evacuate the mothership, as it were. Both saw that outside projects could coexist alongside the Fabs; in George's case, as early as the *Let It Be* sessions in January 1969, he talked openly of doing his own album just to record his ballooning backlog of tunes (John enthusiastically concurred).

But upon Paul's declaration that he was leaving the group (to hype *McCartney*, as John bitterly observed)—six months after John had already turned in his notice—there ceased to be a mothership to return to. Each was now forced to strike out on his own, ready or not.

The following records all predated the split as delineated by Macca's April 10 communiqué. (Note: The release dates given are for the U.S., which rarely matched the U.K. dates. In the case of *Sentimental Journey*, its March 24 British release date brings it in under the wire, regardless of when Americans were first able to ignore it.) What *is* worth observing is how the individuals

Newly shorn of their once-prodigious locks, the Lennons spent the New Year with Yoko's ex in Denmark, where the germ of John's near insta-single took hold. "Instant Karma" further validated the notion that he'd outgrown the group he'd once led.

worked toward establishing non-Beatle identities for themselves, and how their subsequent work did or did not follow the preliminary path.

Wonderwall Music—Released December 2, 1968

The first album issued on the Apple label wasn't even originally intended to be. When George agreed to compose the music scores to Joe Massot's *Wonderwall*, he was given a budget of £600—exactly 1% of the film's overall budget. Securing the services of the Remo Four, Eric Clapton, Ringo, Peter Tork, John Barham, and others, plus a host of Indian musicians and travel to India, ended up costing George £15,000 out of pocket (not that he minded). Nonetheless, he expected that the film's producers would buy the rights to the soundtrack from him. They declined, and so an Apple release it was.

The project gave George the opportunity to expand his musical palette in a way that the Beatles never could. Certainly, being given leave to fill an entire LP was novel, though it must be said that necessarily, the compositions were for the most part brief, largely logging in at under two minutes and therefore not really being given the chance to develop. But sonically, the range explored even within the Western cues was astonishing. Upon repeated listenings, certain tracks stick out, among them the piano-based waltz "Red Lady Too" and "Ski-ing," a Clapton showcase. The Indian cuts too were quite varied stylistically, showing open-minded listeners that there was more to the country's music then twanging sitars and thumping tablas. (Years later, an excerpt from the song "Crying" was grafted onto the end of "Save the World" on the *Somewhere in England* album.) By and large, *Wonderwall Music* got the genre out of Harrison's system.

The album, delayed a month after being issued in Britain in November, was packaged with an insert containing the credits on one side and a portrait of George—shot by none other than the former Astrid Kirchherr, now married to Gibson Kemp—on the other. Lacking much in the way of promotion aside from some print ads, the album did not do too badly in the States, peaking at #49. In the U.K., it did not chart.

Unfinished Music No. 1: Two Virgins—Released January 6, 1969

This notorious release caused quite a splash upon its issue, largely owing to the full frontal nudity displayed by still-married Beatle John and his paramour on the sleeve. (It's one of those classic Lennon paradoxes that though he was too shy to employ an outside photographer to actually document the event—Apple employee Tony Bramwell set up the self-timer on the camera and split—John was quite comfortable with sharing the results of that shoot with the world.) Though the release was slotted into the busy month of November 1968, alongside *Wonderwall Music* and *The Beatles*, distribution problems centering on the album jacket pushed its release into the new year, just as the "Get Back" / *Let It Be* sessions were underway. This resulting elephant in the room, along with John's heroin use, could not possibly have lightened the mood among the Fabs one bit.

Those whose blood is brought to boiling at the very sound of Yoko Ono's voice are advised to steer clear of this release. Otherwise, to anyone interested in exploring John's non-pop side, the album comes off like a less focused and detailed version of "Revolution #9," replete with tape loops (some contributed by former Quarry Man Pete Shotton, who is uncredited) and a random assortment of instrumentation. While one could correctly classify that particular "White Album" track as "musique concrète," *Two Virgins* would more accurately be described as an improvisational sound collage.

The album does have its defenders as a work of avant-garde art, though there are an equal number of informed aficionados who say the album is little more than a historic document of the couple's first date and a rather "self-indulgent" one at that (a description applied to their future collaborations to the point of overkill). While John's actual role on the project was decidedly subsidiary, essentially facilitating Yoko on what was largely her vehicle, the cachet being tapped was wholly his own.

One can make the case that the Beatle was trading on his own fame (not to mention ownership of a record company) to act as a patron of Yoko's art—a role he would embrace till the day he died. Take away the cover photo and Lennon's involvement as one quarter of the most popular rock act of the day, and *Two Virgins* would be regarded among the cognoscenti as a solid but unexceptional contribution to the genre—and not the double-fingered salute that it usually is.

Upon its eventual release and distribution, the album actually managed to slip into the *Billboard* album charts and #124 (the same week in March 1969 that the Fabs had *two* albums in the Top 10). In some cities, shipments of the release were impounded on the possibility of violating local obscenity laws. Eventually, its moment of infamy faded and surplus copies could be found quite cheaply. But by the mid-'70s, John—not at all recalcitrant about the artistic statement but nonetheless embarrassed at the execution—sought to buy up all the copies circulating that he could. (There are unsubstantiated reports that hundreds of copies can be found in storage at the Dakota.) The album has twice been issued on CD, first as a budget release of dubious legality, then by Rykodisc in 1997 (though marred by a mastering error that lopped off the last thirty seconds of side two).

Electronic Sound—Released May 26, 1969

During George's trip to Los Angeles in 1968 to work on Jackie Lomax's Apple debut, he made the acquaintance of American Moog synthesizer pioneer Bernie Krause. At George's direction, a brief embellishment was added to the arrangement of "Take My Word." Mightily intrigued by the instrument, George prevailed upon Krause to give him a private demonstration (much in the same way he approached Ravi Shankar upon being seduced by the sounds of a sitar).

Krause, largely known for his electronic recordings in partnership with Paul Beaver (they recorded as Beaver and Krause) was happy to oblige. Following the Lomax session, the two stayed behind as Krause ran through a presentation of the contraption's capabilities. At some point during their get-together, George had the engineer fire up the tape deck and document the proceedings. Krause, in his innocence, showed Harrison what he knew, throwing in some motifs he and his partner were planning to incorporate into their next release. The gathering broke up, with the Beatle inviting the musician to England to provide further instruction.

Some time later, Krause showed up to find an enthusiastic Harrison all set to show off what he'd accomplished with the Moog. Hearing the tape, Krause recognized the very themes he'd demonstrated earlier and demanded an explanation. George blithely responded that he was planning on releasing an experimental album and by the way, how do you like it? Flabbergasted, the musician laid claim to the work as his own and told Harrison in no uncertain terms that if he insisted in issuing it, that they would need to discuss a split. Retorted George, "When Ravi Shankar comes to my house he's humble."

He further told the steaming Krause that should the album make any money, he'd pony up: "Trust me, I'm a Beatle." The resulting release, *Electronic Sound*, contained artwork that appeared to have Bernie Krause's name credited, although visibly whited (well, silvered) out, reportedly at Krause's insistence. The most astonishing thing about this entire episode is not Hari Georgeson's apparent appropriation if another man's work, but that anybody would *want* to take credit for it.

The release consisted of two album-side length "compositions": side one's "Under the Mersey Wall" (so named as a play on a column in the *Liverpool Echo* by another George Harrison called "Over the Mersey Wall") and side two's "No Time or Space." Bizarrely—or perhaps understandably—the two tracks went misidentified for twenty-three years until 1992's CD issue, when the titles were flipped. "Mersey Wall" was credited as recorded at Esher (with the assistance of "Rupert and Jostick, the Siamese Twins") and of the two cuts, it comes off as the more random collection of sounds. "No Time or Space," on the other hand, was taken from the Bernie Krause session (Krause was credited with "assistance"). It demonstrates a comparatively virtuosic touch absent in the other piece (samples of it were mixed in with *Apple Jam*'s "I Remember Jeep"), though a little of it goes a *long* way.

Electronic Sound is the synthesized equivalent of *Two Virgins*. Being a renowned and highly successful musician carries with it a certain expectation from the fans who've given you your position. If you wish to distribute your preliminary sketches, perhaps it isn't entirely sporting to trade on your celebrity in exchange for the masses' hard-earned bread. (Maybe a different handle for such excursions—like Paul's "Fireman"—would have been a more fitting path.) Otherwise, anyone at all expecting to hear a glimmer of something identifiable with George's public musical identity was in for bitter disappointment, though to his credit, he did offer it as a "disposable" Zapple release. (Regrettably, by the time the subsidiary label got under way, the beneath-market pricing concept had been jettisoned.)

Like John and Yoko's trio of initial releases, the album says more about George's apparent belief that anything he committed to tape was worthy of public consumption (or qualified as "art") then it did about the Beatles' traditional handle on quality control. But it should be pointed out that he indulged himself thus only once. The uncharacteristic long-player made it as far as #191, going head-to-head with John and Yoko's sophomore effort. Though *Unfinished Music No. 2* bested it in the end by peaking at a stellar #174, it's a pretty safe bet that, between the two, George's record was spun more.

Unfinished Music No. 2: Life with the Lions—Released May 26, 1969

If *Two Virgins* represented the first act of John and Yoko's courtship, then *Life with the Lions*—decidedly different in tone—shifted things to Act Two: Tragedy. As depicted in the album's sleeve photographs, Eden's innocence had been eclipsed by death (the stillbirth of their first conceived child) and ordeal (their October 1968 drug bust). The couple had committed to sharing their travails with the public, though it's doubtful that they expected things to shift so dramatically for the second installment.

The album's title referenced a British radio show of the 1950s, *Life with the Lyons*, which featured a real life family's adventures, exaggerated for laughs. But there was nothing entertaining about this record's contents. Listeners were instead treated to a harrowing excursion into the duo's public and private lives. Side one begins with a concert recording taped at

Cambridge University's Lady Mitchell Hall one month after the Savile Row rooftop sessions in January 1969.

Yoko had accepted an invitation to showcase her singular vocal stylings well before hooking up with the Beatle. John agreed to appear as her "band," accompanying her on feedback guitar and nothing else. The occasion marked his first public performance outside of the Beatles, though it probably didn't follow the form that most observers might have expected. A review of that day's program described "epic wailing, weird pulses of sound, or cries—almost—of help."

That description wasn't of the John and Yoko show; it was of vocalist Maggie Nichols, sharing the bill. Though few Beatles fans ever suspected that the genre existed, the fact was that such freeform experimental vocalizations did not originate with Yoko Ono. But the public's vilification of her as agent of the group's disintegration and the music's very anti-pop form made it easy for nonbelievers to dismiss and ridicule the artistry behind it.

Side two represented an effort to share with the public the couple's most private pain, a concept that would be fully realized in a musical setting on the twin *Plastic Ono Band* releases. The material was recorded on cassette during Yoko's hospitalization at Queen Charlotte Hospital throughout November 1968. "No Bed for Beatle John" consisted of the two reading newspaper accounts (aloud, Gregorian chant–style) of John's being displaced from the hospital bed he occupied alongside Yoko's when it was needed by a patient, as well as reports on the *Two Virgins* album cover. (Incidentally, a photo taken during the couple's stay at the hospital shows the newly released "White Album"'s giveaway photos of the other three Beatles taped to the wall.)

The most gut-wrenching track follows: "Baby's Heartbeat." Knowing that the fetus was not destined for survival makes the listening all the more distressing, especially when followed by "Two Minutes Silence," exactly as described. (Yoko would later refer to the non-composition, credited "Lennon-Ono," as a tribute to experimental composer John Cage, who'd similarly copyrighted dead air as *4′33″*. Writer John Blaney reports that when musician Mike Batt attempted to pull the same trick on his *Classical Graffiti* release in 2002, crediting the track "Cage/Batt," he was sued—successfully—by Cage's publisher for infringement. One attempts to outwit conceptual artists at one's own peril.

The album closed on a less disturbing note with "Radio Play," another descriptive title covering twelve-plus minutes of someone—apparently Yoko—flipping the tuning dial on a radio (with little "blips" of largely unidentifiable sound flying by) as John, in the background, makes a phone call. Anyone interested in being a fly on the wall in the lives of these two probably found the reality less compelling than it seemed on paper.

Rolling Stone, generally John's biggest supporter, reviled the release in its review, calling *Life with the Lions* "utter bullshit" and "in poor taste." Despite the magazine's status as the arbiter of hipness, they seemed to have completely missed the point, responding not much differently than any mainstream rag would have (but for the language). But with their next vinyl issue, John and Yoko would finally deliver something of musical value, helping to wipe away the growing perception—even from the counterculture—of John's extracurricular activities as evidence that the man had lost his mind.

"Give Peace a Chance"—Released July 7, 1969

The Bed-In for Peace campaign kicked off in Amsterdam during the couple's honeymoon in March 1969. Cannily using the media attention that their nuptials were sure to garner, the two decided that talking peace before the world's press was the best possible use of their celebrity. But the concept was non-renewable—John quickly realized that a more lasting contribution to the movement could be achieved if he'd simply tap his natural gifts as a songwriter.

"All You Need Is Love" had signaled the ability to encapsulate a broad message and present it musically in a universally acceptable way. But he recognized that a new theme, capable of taking on a life of its own (in rallies around the world) was exactly what the movement needed. (Further spurring him on was his own distaste for the shopworn "We Shall Overcome," a song he felt challenged to improve upon as an anthem.)

Failing to get an entry visa to America in the wake of his drug bust, Lennon settled on Toronto as the next-best place from which to broadcast a message of peace to North America. On May 25, the couple, with Derek Taylor and assorted assistants in tow, arrived at La Hotel Reine Elizabeth in Montreal. There, as in Amsterdam, they met the press for Bed-In part two, talking nonviolence to all who met them and frequently invoking the phrase, "give peace a chance."

Whether the song of the same name had already been composed or was contrived just before it was recorded is uncertain; what *is* known is that following a rehearsal involving guests Tommy Smothers (on guitar); Dr. Timothy Leary and his wife, Rosemary; Derek Taylor; comedian Dick Gregory; pop chanteuse Petula Clark (whose prior political commentary was limited to "Don't Sleep In the Subway"); Beat poet Alan Ginsberg; and a host of members from the local Krishna chapter, the song was committed to tape in room 1742 in the late hours of May 31. (Derek Taylor had arranged for the rental of a mobile four-track recording unit.)

Lyrically, the verses were mere throwaways, serving as a rhyming buffer between performances of the chorus. After four such stanzas, the song settled into a repetition of the refrain—its primary purpose for being—punctuated by John's exhortations of encouragement to the largely rank amateurs not accustomed to singing on records ("Everybody now, come on!"). While the last verse stood out for namechecking the notables in the room (though novelist/gadfly Norman Mailer does *not* appear to have been present; his name is likely included simply as a convenient rhyme with "Derek Taylor"), an earlier line drew notice for its use of the word "masturbation." Though the wording of the lyric is clear on the record (and photos of the "cheat sheet" displayed during the session for the benefit of the participants clearly show it), for the purposes of music publishing, John changed it to "mastication"—not wishing to attract further controversy around what was nothing more than a disposable lyric.

Notably, the song was credited to Lennon-McCartney, the latter of whom had nothing to do with the composition. This gesture has traditionally been read as a "thanks" to Paul for helping out on the recording of "The Ballad of John and Yoko" a couple of months earlier. It's unfortunate that decades later, in the wake of the tempest in a teapot between Paul and Yoko over switching the order of the names on certain Beatles songs authored by Macca, that his name was removed from "Give Peace a Chance" by the widow in a childish tit-for-tat that reflected well on no one.

What John conspicuously didn't do was credit the single to himself. Instead, "Plastic Ono Band" became the nomenclature for any group of musicians that he worked with outside of the Beatles umbrella, even if it included (as "Cold Turkey" would) *two* bona fide Beatles on the recording. Keeping with their "conceptual" view of all they did, the band had no fixed membership per se, and through the years would encompass a sizable pool of members. (Lennon would one day remark—fairly accurately—that Wings was as conceptual a group as his own, since the players were constantly changing.)

After some post-production "sweetening" that added a beat to compensate for the rhythmically challenged players, the single became the first commercially viable project Lennon issued as he slowly eased himself into a solo career. In September, it peaked at #14, the same week that the Rolling Stones' "Honky Tonk Woman" was in its third of four weeks at the top, with the Archies' "Sugar, Sugar" poised to knock it off. Even more satisfying to its creator than its chart success was its spontaneous performance one month later in Washington, D.C. at War Moratorium Day, therein fulfilling its purpose.

Abbey Road was released that September, just as long-simmering tensions within the group led to John's privately announced retirement and rumors of Paul's demise. John's choice for the next Beatles single—which, after being voted down, became one more nail in their collective coffin—ended up, by default, becoming the Plastic Ono Band's second release.

"Cold Turkey"—Released October 20, 1969

Having kicked his heroin habit, Lennon was proud of his accomplishment and, as he had set a precedent of doing over the past year, prepared to share his glad tidings with the world. But, as described in *Fab Four FAQ*, his erstwhile bandmates would have none of it. Peeved at their lack of cooperation, he instead recorded "Cold Turkey" with two of his Toronto bandmates—Klaus Voormann and Eric Clapton—plus Ringo. The latter was about to begin work on his own solo debut LP, though, unlike the albums already unleashed by John and George, his would actually contain music.

On September 25, an initial stab at capturing the Beatles reject (which had been premiered in Toronto two weeks earlier in very rough form) was attempted at EMI's Abbey Road facility. Some twenty-five takes later, the evening's efforts were judged a failure, for the ad hoc group reconvened at Trident Studios nearly a week later, this time laying down a satisfactory recording. (One week after this, Yoko miscarried for the second documented time.) Following some overdubbing, the track was completed and rushed into stores in record time.

Following John and Yoko's primal scream therapy treatment under Dr. Arthur Janov in 1970, much was made of the vocal stylings on the *Plastic Ono Band* album, crediting the good doctor as though he'd freed John up to let himself go. "Cold Turkey" provides ample evidence that while therapy might have enabled him to *address* his darker psychological issues, the real inspiration to let loose on record came from his wife. The expressions of agony wordlessly unleashed in the record's final nearly two minutes essentially put to music what "Baby's Heartbeat" only hinted at, a devastatingly vivid nightmare of pain that no lyric (however lucid, as the song's first half was) could ever express. "Cold Turkey" probably represents the first and most successful fusing of the couple's disparate artistic perspectives, melding a soul-deep expression of emotion with a rock and roll sensibility.

Though the song was intended as a cautionary tale to others who might be tempted to follow John's self-medicating example, the lesson didn't take with guitarist Eric Clapton. Having twice performed the song publicly and once on record, making him as familiar with its message as anyone, within a year Clapton too was in thrall to the drug, eventually requiring intervention from Pete Townshend to completely free himself.

Given the subject matter, the brutally cutting twin guitars, and the demonic howling in the song's coda, it didn't stand a chance of getting widespread airplay, being an FM record in an AM market. It performed accordingly, peaking at #30 in the U.S. In the U.K., however, it did substantially better, reaching #12. ("Give Peace a Chance" had made it to #2 in John's homeland, making two back-to-back releases that performed better there than in the States. This trend would eventually reverse itself as his solo career got well under way, beginning in 1971 with the "Happy Xmas (War Is Over)" single.)

Wedding Album—Released October 20, 1969

John and Yoko's romantic (if it could be called that) trilogy was at last completed with the third installment of their "unfinished music," *Wedding Album*, issued on the same day as "Cold Turkey" some seven months after the event. True to their practice of sharing everything with anyone interested, the couple treated purchasers of the elaborately packaged set to a number of artifacts that conveyed the heady whirlwind of their globe-trotting odyssey, including a two-dimensional reproduction of a slice of wedding cake; a strip of photo-booth pictures; their wedding license; posters; a booklet of photos of the wedding; and a collection of clippings from newspapers around the world.

What is most jarringly apparent in those clippings is the unmitigated fury that the relationship sparked in some quarters, with the mainstream media running some unfathomably cruel depictions of the couple as subhuman freaks. One quickly concludes that John's falling in love with Yoko and embarking on a series of high-profile public "happenings" enraged a lot of folks, who apparently regarded his non-Beatle antics as some sort of betrayal.

As for the disc's contents, their audio verité approach at last yielded some halfway engaging documentary listening—at least one side's worth. The album opened with "John and Yoko," some twenty-two-plus minutes of the couple calling each other's names in a variety of styles: screaming, whispering, bleating, braying, snorting, and so forth. By way of rhythm (as this was the work of *musicians*, after all), these myriad pleadings came atop the sound of their hearts beating.

What makes the track intriguing for those intrepid souls who actually gave it a close listen was the way the sounds synched up when the callings were more sedate in emotion, versus the out-of-synch poundings as the voices seemed more desperate—and separated. The exercise might have

For hardcores only: the final installment of John and Yoko's "unfinished music" trilogy was packaged with all the trappings of a real-life wedding, including a "slice" of the cake.

actually been appreciated as the compelling art that it was, had it not arrived as overkill after a year of nonstop conceptual theater (such as the "bagism" demonstrations).

But it was "Amsterdam," the album's second side, that likely spawned more listenings. This sonic encapsulation of the weeklong bedside press conference came replete with supplementary material recorded after the fact, as well as musical snippets (a piss-take of "Good Night" is heard, as well as the chord pickings to what eventually became "Sun King"). Absent and representing a missed opportunity for a public airing was the grilling

John took from reactionary cartoonist Al Capp, who visited during the Montreal Bed-In. As depicted in the 1988's *Imagine* documentary, Capp tried his damnedest to get a rise out of Lennon (resorting to personal insults directed against the couple generally and Yoko especially) and came close to succeeding.

Unwittingly, the Lennon's were one-upped by a reviewer at *Melody Maker*, who was sent a double disc pressing of the album. The record had ostensibly "blank" second and fourth sides, containing only a single test tone (while the actual content was on side one and three). He nonetheless recorded his impressions of *all four sides*, going so far as to note that while sustained listening to sides two and four revealed minor oscillations in the tone, the Lennon's had seemingly intended for listeners to use the sound as a starting point for their own "ragas, plainsong, or Gaelic mouth music." Upon reading the analysis, John played along, firing off a telegram of agreement that read, "Maybe you are right in saying that they are the best sides." Whatever else could be said about their conceptual art, John and Yoko never lacked a sense of humor.

Live Peace in Toronto—Released December 12, 1969

Concerned that recordings from his September 1969 rock and roll concert would fall into the hands of enterprising bootleggers, John took it upon himself to make sure that an audio document of his Beatle-breaking performance in Canada was issued properly. His set was purely ad hoc, assembled on the fly, but left no doubt that, in the words of writers Tony Tyler and Roy Carr, "beneath accumulated layers of bagism and hair, Lennon remained a devout rocker."

Comprised of Klaus, Eric Clapton, and drummer Allen White, the group rehearsed material on the flight from London to Toronto, basically whatever oldies they all knew, plus Lennon's "Yer Blues," which he and Clapton had performed at the Rolling Stones' *Rock and Roll Circus* nearly a year before; the newly composed "Cold Turkey," which had yet to jell as a memorable composition; and "Give Peace a Chance," or, as John noted in his intro, "This is what we came for really." The song was still near its chart peak at the time the ensemble performed their band version, notable for John's complete inability to recall the lyrics to any of the verses (he instead vamped it, letting loose with stream-of-consciousness ramblings that scanned well without making much sense otherwise).

John had absolutely no sense of how well his act would go down before the twenty thousand gathered at Varsity Stadium on that September night.

An attack of nerves, coupled with whatever drug he used to sustain himself before walking out on stage, led to some intense vomiting sessions backstage. But once he appeared, resplendent in white, after the MC's introduction, the thunderous ovation from the gathered faithful helped alleviate any further anxiety. The band tore through several choice oldies and one Beatles tune ("Blue Suede Shoes," "Money (That's What I Want)," "Dizzy Miss Lizzie," and the aforementioned "White Album" track) before launching into the half-baked "Cold Turkey" and "Give Peace a Chance." Overall, despite John's qualms, the band was well received, discernibly growing in confidence as the set proceeded.

Then, in the interest of fair warning, John announced, "Now Yoko's gonna do her thing . . . all over you." The gathered masses who'd bought tickets to a rock and roll revival show could hardly have been expected to anticipate what ensued: the freeform riffing of "Don't Worry, Kyoko (Mummy's Only Looking for Her Hand in the Snow," giving way to the even looser "John, John (Let's Hope for Peace)." It would have been understandable if, after nearly seventeen minutes of warbling, shrieks, and earsplitting feedback, the assembled had hoped for some peace of their own. John later mused that given the similarly mind-blowing experience of their Lyceum show in December 1969 (though he might have been speaking of this night as well), it was entirely probable that some kids in attendance had grown up and formed punk bands, so profound was Plastic Ono Band's sonic assault. More likely, they simply swore off concerts altogether.

Perhaps feeling thrice burned, British record buyers ignored the release. But in America, the set (or at least half of it) represented a return to form, and the album ended up rising to #10 in the charts by early 1970. John had had to fight Capitol tooth and nail to get the album released at all. When they finally relented, it was with the stipulation that this was solo product, as opposed to "Beatle product," for which they were locked into a low royalty rate. When the time came to collect, John found that the label had had a change of heart—possibly owing to the LP's gold record status—and paid at the low Beatle rate after all. (The album's rather sedate cover image, depicting a single cloud against a sky of blue, was shot by Iain MacMillan, who'd photographed the Fabs' last album cover less than four months earlier.)

Now filled with the self-assurance that comes with commercial success, Lennon was ready to issue his strongest solo composition yet. Though as far as the public knew, the Beatles were still together, with a new film and album on the horizon, John knew better and was ready to take his career one step closer to autonomy. His next idea for a single was not even pitched to his fellow Fabs.

"Instant Karma"—Released February 20, 1970

As noted in *Fab Four FAQ*, John had long aspired to get his music to the public as quickly after the moment of its creation as was humanly possible. It's unlikely that he ever again came as close as he did with this release, recorded the same day it was composed and in shops (in England, anyway) within a week and a half.

The Lennons spent the turn of the decade vacationing in Denmark, including some time with Yoko's ex and his current wife. It would be a conversation with Tony Cox and his wife Melinda that initially sparked the phrase "instant karma," an absurdist notion that many naïve young westerners believed was possible. On the morning of January 27, John awoke with a concept for a song inspired by the "instant karma" conversations. He sat down at the piano and very quickly the song came together, words and music.

It's interesting to note that one of the first calls John placed upon deciding to book studio time that very day was to George. Though he'd missed the final Fab recording session (for George's "I Me Mine") due to his holiday on the continent three weeks earlier and, ostensibly, had turned in his notice from his former day job, the ties that bound him to George as man and as musician were still intact. As it happened, George had been palling around London with producer Phil Spector; per George's suggestion, John invited Spector along.

That evening, John and Yoko, George, Klaus, Alan White, Mal Evans, and Billy Preston convened at EMI's Abbey Road studio. But the gathered musicians in the room weren't going to be enough to fulfill Spector's grandiose expectations for the song. Therefore, Billy and Mal were dispatched to round up a group of singers to supplement those present. Per the standard Wall of Sound blueprint, multiple layers of both vocals and piano were stacked atop each other to achieve the unique sound; the icing on the cake was Alan White's nimble drumming, positioned as virtually the lead instrument and presented with just the right modicum of slapback echo. The recording that resulted represented an act of collective genius for all concerned. Not many days in the history of rock and roll proved as everlastingly fruitful.

In America, distribution over a far larger landscape delayed the record's arrival in shops, but within a month, it topped out at #5, falling a little short of its U.K. peak of #2. There, it may have helped that John did something he hadn't done in years (since 1966, to be exact): he appeared on *Top of the Pops*, sort of the English *American Bandstand*. In charting such a smash,

John was simultaneously demonstrating a solo hit-making ability on par with his soon-to-be-former group while setting the bar for his own future work and that of his fellows. Though his capacity for meeting these expectations would diminish over time, on a subconscious level it prepared the public to accept that maybe the Beatles going their separate ways wouldn't be such a bad thing after all.

Sentimental Journey—Released April 24, 1970

It isn't known exactly when the notion to record an entire album of pop standards occurred to Ringo. Perhaps hearing himself awash in orchestration for "Good Night" planted the seed, but by all accounts, his intent was to create a gift for his mother, a former barmaid, and the adults who had raised him. Despite the deprivation he suffered on many levels during his childhood, one thing Ringo never lacked was a musical environment. During the war years and after, those enduring a world gone to hell found music a convenient coping mechanism, and for Ringo, the tunes of that era, the earliest he could recall, evoked happy memories of public sing-alongs. Perhaps the professional turmoil he had become embroiled in of late was reason enough to desire a return to his carefree youth among loved ones. (One can catch a glimpse of the Ringed One's revisiting this pastime in *Magical Mystery Tour*, during the singing sessions held on the bus.)

Whatever the reason, soon after the completion and issue of *Abbey Road*, Ringo booked studio time and the George Martin Orchestra to begin work on a project that saw him tackle a dozen or so vocal hits from his childhood. With Martin at the helm, the drummer also decided that using a different arranger on each track could result in a more interesting mix. Among the talents he gathered were Quincy Jones ("Love Is a Many-Splendored Thing"); Klaus Voormann ("I'm a Fool to Care"); and Richard Perry (on the title track). Perry, of course, would later mastermind Ringo's first "real" album of consequence nearly four years later.

In his first post-Beatles collaboration with Ringo, Paul arranged "Stardust" for the album (which came very close to being titled *Ringo Stardust* before wiser heads prevailed). Overall, the success of the project depends on the individual listener's musical taste and tolerance of Richie Snare's voice. Certainly, the arrangements and musicianship are impeccable throughout, but standouts include Bee Gee Maurice Gibb's arrangement of "Bye Bye Blackbird" and George Martin's "Dream."

Though a promo film (of "Sentimental Journey") was aired on May 17, 1970, on *The Ed Sullivan Show*, no singles were released and the album peaked at #22 in America. Across the pond, it actually hit #7, maybe proving

Mr. Starkey's point that there really was a market for this kind of music, a fact later discovered by Harry Nilsson (*A Touch of Schmilsson in the Night*), Linda Ronstadt (*What's New*), and Rod Stewart (*It Had to Be You*).

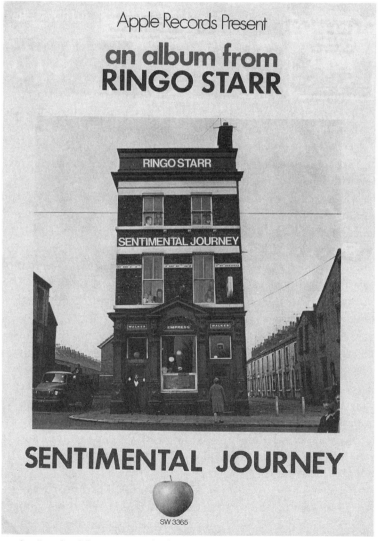

Taking the "get back" concept to its logical starting point, Ringo opted to record an LP's worth of pre–rock era tunes for his solo debut, baffling the public as well as his bandmates.

I Give to You and You Give to Me

Beatles Helping Beatles

Examining who helped whom—and when—provides a pretty good indication of where things stood between the ex-Fabs personal relationship–wise. At the height of their post-breakup antipathies, circa 1970–1971, the clear pattern depicts John, George, and Ringo as fairly interlocked, continuing to collaborate with each other on certain projects, but not with Paul.

To be sure, Paul had his reasons for not soliciting contributions from his ex-bandmates. For his first release, *McCartney,* he took the one-man-band tendencies first cultivated on the "White Album" to their natural conclusion; this was followed by the sheer studio professionalism of *Ram,* wherein he recruited New York's finest session players. (If he had *really* wanted to stick it to his estranged percussionist, he could have hired Andy White, Jimmy Nicol, Bernard Purdie, or even Pete Best for drumming duties. Now *that* would've sent a message!)

Not until early 1981, in the wake of John's murder, did one of his fellow ex-Fabs appear on a solo Macca release (although Ringo had apparently been invited to participate in the Rockestra session). Richie Snare appeared on *Tug of War*'s "Take It Away" and sporadically on subsequent Macca works (notably *Give My Regards to Broad Street*), but George never did. No matter how well they got on as friends—and even to the end of George's days, theirs was a very volatile relationship—between 1970's "I Me Mine" and 1994's "Free As a Bird," the two recorded together but once, and only as a tribute to their fallen comrade.

John contributed to several Ringo albums, but never to Paul's or George's—at least on the record. (Drummer Alan White *insists* that John turned up during the *All Things Must Pass* sessions, contributing guitar to at least a couple of tunes, but this is not confirmed by anyone else.) As for Paul, his contribution to the work of his ex-bandmates was limited to assisting Ringo over the course of several projects, beginning in 1973 (this in itself

In the wake of the group's dissolution, George found an instrumental voice that became his signature sound: slide guitar. His distinctive skills were quickly put to use by both Ringo *and* John on their respective releases.

only came about after John and George had already played on *Ringo* and the drummer didn't want Paul to feel left out), plus the aforementioned cameo for George.

Ringo on *All Things Must Pass*—1970

George's inaugural post-Fabs project was a mammoth undertaking. With a set list of nearly two dozen compositions, he needed to put together a pretty solid crew to build the foundation for Phil Spector's towering cathedral. To that end, he immediately turned to the Beatle he'd been closest to: Ringo. As for the drummer, who had one solo project of his own under his belt, a string of sessions to his credit, and a lot of newfound free time, his involvement was a natural progression, given his ongoing work on several of the projects George had produced for Apple's roster.

Given the latitude and range of the material, it's not surprising that Ringo did not occupy the kit for the duration of the project. (George claimed that Ringo played on nearly the entire album; others say probably about half; Ringo himself professes not to recall.) On some cuts, he opted to play tambourine or other percussion while Alan White or Jim Gordon handled the traps. On others, he double-teamed with one of the aforementioned, helping to build the Wall of Sound Spector was so known for.

It was probably a comfort for George to have Ringo around, given the brave new world he was entering as a solo artist. We now know how it all turned out, but at the time *All Things Must Pass* was being recorded, its universal acclaim was by no means certain. Surrounding himself with friends undoubtedly helped at a time when Harrison's confidence that the public would accept him on his own was shaky.

Ringo on *John Lennon / Plastic Ono Band*—1970

Equally nervous was John, though at least he had enjoyed the support of George Martin during his Fab years. For his first album-length musical outing removed from the Beatles' comfort zone, he too tapped Ringo to act as one third of his band. It would take a few albums before he learned the joys of professional session musicians, but for his immediate needs, John kept things in the family, only using Ringo, Klaus, and, for a cameo, Billy Preston.

In aesthetic and philosophical approach, the two albums could not be more different, though theoretically they had the same producer in common. Whereas *All Things Must Pass* was drenched in instrumentation, John's *Plastic Ono Band* was sparse to the point of skeletal. Never before or

JOHN LENNON/PLASTIC ONO BAND
MOTHER
APPLE 1827

John's landmark solo debut featured a cover shot by Dan Richter, a former mime seen by millions as the "lead ape" in *2001: A Space Odyssey*'s "Dawn of Man" sequence. The otherwise identical cover art for Yoko's companion album saw the couple switch places.

since was Ringo's performance so out in the open, giving listeners a real opportunity to experience his genius as a player (though a rare screw-up is revealed on a take of "Isolation" released on the Lennon *Anthology* boxed set). Especially worthy of notice is the seamlessness with which he and Klaus, who presumably had only played together once before—on "Cold Turkey" a year earlier—mesh on this record. The drumming is, as always, calibrated to the unique demands of each composition.

As much as George, John too needed support from an intimate as he took tentative steps into forging his post-Beatles identity. Furthermore, as he was wont to point out, there was the bonus value of playing with someone who understood your moves and could adjust on the spot to accommodate them. (There's a telling moment in the opening bars of "Remember" where Ringo has to compensate for John's erratic sense of rhythm, just as the singing starts.)

Given the brutally raw emotions expressed in the material, one might have expected that the sessions must have been somber at best, or at least uncomfortable about on the scale of listening to someone discuss his or her psychotherapy treatment. There is no evidence that this was true; on the contrary, outtakes reveal a certain playfulness between takes. As in the well-chronicled *Let It Be* sessions, strolls down memory lane were frequent, including run-throughs of old Elvis and Carl Perkins numbers. (These have been widely bootlegged.)

Also documented was an unexpected in-studio visit from George. As reported by Mark Hertsgaard in the *New Yorker*, unbooted session tapes reveal John warmly greeting his fellow ex-Fab, who had been hard at work down the hall. The "us against Paul" zeitgeist is very much alive in this fly-on-the-wall snippet, as the three display a group dynamic largely absent during an entire month's worth of recorded interactions during January 1969.

George on "It Don't Come Easy" / "Early 1970"—1970–71

The byline crediting Ringo alone for this extraordinary composition has long been believed to be bogus, read as an act of charity by George to jumpstart his friend's recording career. (Years later, Richie Snare would acknowledge that perhaps credit should have been given where due.) Without detracting from Ringo's performance, the gesture stands as a shining example of Hari Georgeson's great generosity. It isn't hard to recognize his desire to give Ringo a proper launch as a solo artist just as he had done for several of Apple's other acts.

The song itself may have been sparked by a Ringo-ism or two, but musically, it has all the earmarks of a Harrisong circa 1970: a signature riff, quasi-philosophical lyrics, an arrangement featuring backup singers and horns, a tremendous solo. (According to Dan Matovina's brilliant Badfinger bio, *Without You*, drummer Mike Gibbins said that George approached *his* band with the song in 1970, but for whatever reason, the offer was turned down.)

In any event, "It Don't Come Easy" was first recorded on February 18, 1970 (five years to the day after the Fabs attempted to nail down a decent take of "If You've Got Troubles," to no avail) during a break in the *Sentimental Journey* sessions. Interestingly, *George Martin* was manning the board for this attempt, at the time titled "You Gotta Pay Your Dues." George directed the "band," comprised of two soon-to-be-ex-Beatles, plus Klaus and Steven Stills (on piano) at EMI's number two Abbey Road studio. It took twenty takes to achieve a keeper before Ringo laid down a lead vocal.

Following work the next day on *Sentimental Journey*'s "Love Is a Many-Splendored Thing," Ringo took another shot at the lead before concluding that "It Don't Come Easy" *wasn't* coming easy and needed a remake. Oddly, George was not present, though at least one source suggests that Clapton—assuming George's position (and not for the last time)—may have been. This second attempt would lie untouched until March 8, when a *third* and final effort was recorded, this time at Trident Studios and with George handling the production—using the same crew as before, but adding Mal Evans on tambourine.

Finishing touches would be added (with an astonishing lack of urgency) throughout the year, with Badfinger's Tommy Evans and Pete Ham contributing backing vocals and the overdub of a horn section. At some point in the track's history, George took a crack at singing lead, delivering a relaxed but energetic performance that in some ways outshone the singing on his own recordings.

This take—believed to be a guide (or scratch) vocal—has been bootlegged through the years and offers a fascinating glimpse into what might have been, had George issued the song himself. There is a repeat of the intro after the guitar break (that was thought better of and duly excised in the finished version), but even more striking is the full-throated exultation of "Hare Krishna!" sung by the Badfinger boys during the solo. It was mixed *way down* in the issued version but can still be faintly heard (at 1:42).

The single was issued in April 1971, well after work had commenced on it. Racing up the charts, by June it peaked at #4 in *Billboard* (the same week the Rolling Stones' "Brown Sugar" topped the charts), besting the chart performances of George's "What Is Life" (#10); Paul's "Another Day" (#5); and John's "Power to the People" (#11), all released within the same two-month span. By any measure, it was a stunning achievement.

Equally noteworthy to the Beatles geeks paying close mind to the singles derby was the song's B-side, unquestionably (given its relative lack of musical sophistication, shall we say) composed by Ringo. "Early 1970" (a title describing the song's theme without actually appearing anywhere in the lyric) gives listeners a crystal clear view of the way things now stood between the ex-Fabs , at least from the drummer's perspective. Each Beatle is depicted: Paul ("Lives on a farm, got plenty of charm"), John ("With his mama by his side, she's Japanese"), and George ("He's a long-haired, cross-legged guitar picker").

This utterly charming tune offers an assessment of his relations with the three: he's unsure if Paul will play with him, while he's fairly certain

This charming Starkey composition served as a tonic to fans distraught over the group's end, as the self-effacing percussionist traded upon his underdog persona to express hope that at least *some* of his ex-bandmates would play with him again.

that John will. As for George (who happens to be contributing a delicious slide guitar part to the track), he's "always" available. After itemizing his own musical limitations ("I don't play bass 'cause that's too hard for me"), Ringo asserts that, come what may, he wants to see all three. "Early 1970" was the perfect tonic for beleaguered Beatles fans wondering if the band would ever, if not get back together, at least achieve some civility. It wasn't too much to ask—was it?

George on *Imagine*—1971

Wishing to return to the world of mainstream pop values (as well as commercial competition with George and Paul, both of whom had scored #1 albums by spring 1971), John set about recording his *Plastic Ono Band* follow-up at his home studio at Tittenhurst. Unlike the previous long-player, this project saw his basic ensemble supplemented throughout by an array of players that came and went, among them Tommy Evans and Joey Molland from Badfinger, the Moody Blues' Mike Pinder, arranger John Barham (who contributed harmonium), Stackridge's Andy (Creswell) Davis, and Renaissance's John Tout.

Also invited along was George. Ringo excused himself early on, due to the shooting schedule of *Blindman* (coincidentally being filmed in the same Spanish locale, Almería, where John had shot *How I Won the War* nearly five years earlier). It is entirely likely that, already having Klaus and Alan White aboard, John was deliberately seeking some Fab magic to add to the mix; it couldn't have hurt that George was the star of the day in his own right, given the phenomenal success of *All Things Must Pass*.

The sessions were extensively filmed, providing a fascinating glimpse into the dynamic at work between the ex-Fabs at that stage. John displays evident glee while introducing his anti-Paul diatribe, "How Do You Sleep?," to an outwardly unmoved George. Whatever his feelings, the guitarist delivered one of the most incisive slide guitar solos of his career, drawing enthusiastic praise from John (who simultaneously rebuked George's perfectionism): "That's the best he's ever fucking played in his life! He'd go on forever [trying to refine it] if you'd let him."

Equally stinging was George's work on "Gimme Some Truth," a similarly acidic attack on governmental hypocrisy that he had actually first heard when John aired it during the *Get Back* sessions a lifetime ago. Less down and dirty was his work on the gentle "Oh My Love" and on the skiffle throw-back "Crippled Inside," which featured him on Dobro. (Perhaps inspired by George's mastery of this rootsy instrument, John would implement it on his topical "John Sinclair" later that year.) The chaotic "I Don't Wanna Be a Soldier" was the final cut containing George's work, though this last recording featured a performance dubbed in after the basic track had been laid down.

John was very clearly delighted with George's contribution to *Imagine*, but the goodwill was not to last. The latter ex-Fab left John's session to begin anew on Badfinger's *No Dice* follow-up before being pulled into the Bangladesh cause. Then, of course, the dispute over John's possible presence (and Yoko's *im*possible presence) dissipated their recent love fest. John and George never again worked together on each other's records, thereafter only meeting in the studio on Ringo's neutral turf.

George on "Back Off Boogaloo"—1972

Largely regarded in America as a one-hit wonder, Britain's T. Rex, fronted by Marc Bolan, was the biggest homegrown rock act of the day (1971–1972), bar none. Inspiring the same swooning hysteria that had defined Beatlemania less than a decade before, Bolan's embodiment of "glam" took the form of crowd-pleasing shtick, danceable guitar-driven grooves, and loads of glitter.

With the exception of 1971's "Bang a Gong (Get It On)" single, audiences in the U.S. failed to see what the fuss was all about.

Ringo had first made the acquaintance of the pre-superstardom Bolan as a regular scene-maker/hanger-on at the office of Apple Films. (As a teenager, Bolan also hung out at the Indica Gallery, another Beatle-related locale.) The two formed a strong bond and spent a lot of downtime together. After one such evening, replete with Bolan's idiosyncratic verbal absurdisms ("Boogaloo" was a pet nomenclature directed at whoever was in his company), Bolan took his leave and Ringo went to bed.

In that twilight between wakefulness and sleep, Bolan's incessant chatter, melded to a musical idea, danced around in Ringo's head, prompting him to get up and attempt to capture the lick by singing it into a tape recorder. The trouble was, each and every device in the house he tried was either broken or had dead batteries. Ringo dashed about, growing increasingly frantic as the tune in his head was fast morphing into "Mack the Knife." Finally, he located a working recorder, captured the tune, and went back to bed—exhausted but relieved.

Soon after, Ringo roped George into helping complete the tune, titled "Back Off Boogaloo." (The self-effacing percussionist would later say that typically, he could come up with a verse or two and a chorus, but still needed George to smooth things out and throw in a few passing chords that would make musical sense out of Ringo's compositions.) Enlisting Klaus and Gary Wright, the group quickly convened at Apple Studios to lay down what looked like a surefire smash.

The song's rather martial-sounding opening was a rare indulgence for the percussionist: a showcase of his own drumming. (Ringo would later claim that song featured him purely on an oversized snare and a bass drum; anyone with ears can tell that this is not so.) Featuring a stinging slide part from George, the song was read by many as a slap at Paul, referencing the rumors of his demise, noting his legal proceedings against the other three, and iterating Ringo's oft-voiced criticism of Macca's post-Fab music as well: "Get yourself together now and give me something tasty / everything you try to do, you know it sure sounds wasted." (That last line may have been a punning reference to Paul's well-documented appetite for weed.) Taken as direct commentary, the song was as damning as "Early 1970" had been conciliatory.

But Ringo has denied this interpretation through the years, claiming that the song was inspired by Bolan and nothing more. Certainly, he would have had his reasons not to reinforce any ongoing negativity toward Macca. (Regarding matters of veracity between Mr. Starkey and Mr. Bolan: Ringo was credited with shooting the cover to T.Rex's *The Slider* LP and has even

Ringo's friendship with Marc Bolan, then the U.K.'s hottest star, inspired him to pen "Back Off Boogaloo," his highest-charting single in his mother country. The two are seen here in a jam scene from 1972's T. Rex documentary, *Born to Boogie*.

described in interviews taking the photo on the roof of Apple. Trouble was, producer Tony Visconti actually did the honors, credit notwithstanding—something that Bolan eventually 'fessed up to.)

Equally contentious is the question of whether or not Bolan himself played on the recording. Persistent rumor holds that he did, but there is absolutely no evidence of his presence on the track, least of all upon a close listening. Far better documented is Bolan's contribution to Randy Newman's "Have You Seen My Baby" on 1973's *Ringo*.

Whether a transient piling on that seconded John's "How Do You Sleep" without being so overtly cruel, or a piece of nothing that just happened to fit perfectly into the "us vs. Paul" mindset, "Back Off Boogaloo" would be Ringo's most successful single in Britain ever, riding the glam rock wave to #2 (while peaking at #9 in the States).

As a footnote, the Ringed One reimagined the song for his 1981 album, *Stop and Smell the Roses,* as a fusion of his past, opening with the "It Don't Come Easy" riff and interweaving snatches of Beatles songs (like "Good Day Sunshine" and "Lady Madonna") throughout. Most people either love or hate the revamping, produced by Harry Nilsson (after his own "You Can't Do That," perhaps).

Ringo on *Living in the Material World*—1973

While Ringo's participation in the sessions that yielded George's *All Things Must Pass* follow-up is well documented, his individual work, as on the previous album, is hard to assess, given his teaming with Jim Keltner throughout. That said, the album contains at least one conspicuously noteworthy percussive moment, on the title track.

The grandiose "Living in the Material World" was a deft blending of Eastern and Western sounds, essentially a sprawling rock narrative with sitar/tabla/flute interludes. In the song's second verse, George recounts how he got there: "Met them all here in the material world / Though we started out quite poor, we got 'Richie' on a tour." Instead of the expected rimshot, Ringo inserted a characteristic drum fill at this point. Cute.

George, John, and Paul on *Ringo*—1973

The *Ringo* sessions got under way in March 1973 in Los Angeles. The stockpile of songs first assembled included one Lennon original ("I'm the Greatest"); one Harrison tune, custom-crafted for Ringo ("Sunshine Life for Me"); one collaboration with the Starr player ("Photograph"); and the one and only Harrison-*Evans* original, ever: "You and Me (Babe)."

Paul offered up a contribution, "Six O'Clock," but his actual participation in recording said song was far from certain. For one thing, he was
having visa issues at the time. For another, if traveling to L.A. would bring
him directly into contact with John or George, just as their primary wedge
issue, Allen Klein, was about to become old news, he would just as soon sit
back until the bone of contention was resolved.

George and Ringo had first made an attempt to record "Photograph"
during the *Living in the Material World* sessions in the fall of 1972, with
George producing. This recording did not take, and so it was revisited five
months later, this time with Richard Perry at the helm. The second approach
proved the charm, resulting in Ringo's first #1—in America anyway. (In
England, it peaked at #8.)

Back in 1968, upon the completion of the "White Album," George
spent some time in upstate New York, visiting Bob Dylan and the Band. The
disenchanted Beatle was smitten with the latter's back-to-basics sound in
particular, and the influence that Robbie Robertson and company wielded
over George became manifest in his compositions over the next couple of
years. However, not until five years later—on, of all things, a Ringo album—
did George get the opportunity to actually record with the former Hawks.

On his own "Sunshine Life for Me," a rustic song demanding a rustic
backing, George drafted Robertson, Levon Helm, Garth Hudson, and Rick
Danko, supplemented by Dylan associate Dave Bromberg, Klaus Voormann
on stand-up bass, and the soon-to-be-ubiquitous Vini Poncia. The resulting
meld of guitars, mandolin, accordion, "fiddle," and banjo made a novel but
utterly fitting backdrop for Ringo's authentically unschooled vocal. (Years
later, Danko was among the first group of Ringo's All-Starrs, not long before
his untimely death.)

The slick "You and Me (Babe)," *Ringo*'s closer, followed a less experimental path, with a marimba being the only really unusual instrumentation.
The collaboration itself had come about by virtue of George and Mal Evans
sharing a house in Los Angeles during the sessions; Mal had essentially came
up with what he called "a meditation song" and asked George to help him
out with the chords. As heard on the album, the guitarist tossed off one of
his sharper post-Beatles solos on what's otherwise a rather syrupy lounge
band impression.

The album's most celebrated moment came with the near-miss Fab
reunion "I'm the Greatest" (covered in chapter 32). Indirectly, though, it
led to Paul's eventual participation on the record. Always sensitive to the
feelings of others, Ringo made it a point to record Paul's song *with* Paul,
flying to England in April (where he was due anyway to fulfill promotional
duties for *That'll Be the Day*).

With Klaus, Vini, and Richard Perry in tow (and Harry Nilsson to follow), "Six O'Clock," a charming Macca ballad, was laid down at Apple Studios. Both McCartney's provided backing vocals, with Paul himself commandeering the piano and synthesizer. As cut, an apparently spontaneous "one more time" coda was performed, to be summarily lopped off the finished album. This "extended version" was inadvertently issued on eight-track and on advance copies at the time; it has since been released as a bonus cut on the *Goodnight Vienna* CD.

"You're Sixteen," covered elsewhere in this book, was likewise committed to tape, providing the icing on the cake to what was undoubtedly a labor of love for all involved. Never again would all four ex-Beatles perform on the same project, but for one shining moment, the *possibility* that the Fabs could be made whole again shone brightly for millions of fans.

John on *Goodnight Vienna*—1974

Now thoroughly living in each other's pockets for the first time since the last Beatles tour, John and Ringo shared a beach house in Santa Monica. There, the nonstop party that was the so-called "Lost Weekend" unfolded. Visitors like Micky Dolenz, Alice Cooper, the Hudson brothers, and Paul and Linda McCartney, as well as the usual suspects—Nilsson, Keith Moon, Klaus, and so forth—enjoyed what may have been the most carefree episode of their entire adult lives. That's not to say that the drugs and drink didn't flow freely and that there wasn't the occasional spot of trouble; but for the most part, no harm was done and productivity was high.

Given the unbelievable success of *Ringo*, no one was ready to tamper with the all-star formula just yet. The trouble was, Paul and the usually dependable George were not available this time out: the former was riding the acclaim of *Band on the Run* while reconstituting Wings, as George busied himself with the start-up of *Dark Horse*: the label, the album, and the tour. (He may also have had reasons to keep his distance, given whatever had transpired between Ringo's soon-to-be ex-wife and himself.)

In any event, the absence of the two ex-Fabs may have been made up for by the addition of superstar Elton John to the mix. The John-Taupin composition "Snookeroo" was a highlight of the *Goodnight Vienna* album (though, oddly, its single issue in the U.K. stiffed). Also in support was the usual Keltner/Klaus/Billy/Vini crew, supplemented by satellites Jesse Ed Davis, Nicky Hopkins, Lon Van Eaton, and others, including guests Dr. John and Steve Cropper.

Having secured John's full attention—more or less—Ringo was able to coax not one but *two* key contributions to his latest effort. The first was an original song, capturing the party atmosphere that permeated much of the ex-Fab existence in 1974: "(It's All Down to) Goodnight Vienna." The phrase, Liverpudlian slang for "let's get out of here," seemed to subconsciously sum up the weariness that the lifestyle was causing them (though Ringo himself was not quite ready to leave just yet).

The song was laid down with John, on piano, acting as bandleader: "One and-a two and-a one, two, three, four—ALL RIGHT!!!" Complete with brass and some full-throated vocal backings, including most of the cast (plus female companions May Pang, Nancy Andrews, and Klaus's squeeze, Cynthia Webb), the song got the proceedings off to a rollicking start, just as "I'm the Greatest" kicked off *Ringo*. Billy's clavinet added a touch of contemporary dance/funk to the track, which, when spliced to the album's coda, was issued as a single (though it barely scraped into the Top 30).

More successful chart-wise was John's arrangement of the Platters' 1955 hit "Only You (and You Alone)." Having created an original yet entirely radio-friendly reworking of the old warhorse, Lennon might easily have benefited by keeping it to himself. Instead, he offered it up to Ringo, providing the album with a worthy leadoff single and Ringo with another Top 10 hit. His generosity speaks volumes about his concern for Ringo's solo viability.

John and Paul on Ringo's *Rotogravure*—1976

Though "retired," newly minted American citizen John Lennon was on hand to assist with the next Ringo project. This time, though, his participation would be limited. As a new father, John set his priorities elsewhere, though he was loath to turn down a request from the Ringed One for help. His input on *Rotogravure* was limited to just one song, the self-penned (and suitably domesticated) "Cookin' (in the Kitchen of Love)." Again John led off an album side—this time two—and played piano, but the song hardly represented his best efforts. Clearly, whether from too many years in the industry or perhaps from having a baby around the house, John was tired.

Far more charged up was Paul. As on the last project, his actual participation in the recording was unexpected, as he was gearing up for his *Wings Over America* tour, but the delay due to Jimmy McCulloch's broken finger gave him unanticipated downtime to come through after all. He'd written a song for Ringo, inspired by Nancy Andrews and entitled "Pure Gold," and turned up, along with Linda, to lay down some trademark Wings' crooning. (The actual backing had already been cut; otherwise he probably would have played on it.)

As for George, he again was tied up: laid low with hepatitis; testifying in court for the "My Sweet Lord" case; and preparing his Dark Horse label debut album, *Thirty-Three & 1/3*. Still, he managed to contribute a tune, one that had been in circulation for some time. George had tried to interest both Ronnie Spector and Cilla Black in the song (originally titled "Whenever" around the time of the *All Things Must Pass* sessions and renamed "When Every Song Is Sung" by the time it was actually copyrighted in 1972), but a successful capture proved elusive. Ringo, already familiar with the tune, placed dibs on it.

Under an even newer title—"I'll Still Love You"—the song was at last recorded and issued. (George expressed relief at the time that he wouldn't have to compose a *new* song for Ringo.) Hari Georgeson's absence on the haunting ballad was scarcely felt, however, as Lon Van Eaton turned in a suitably Harrisonian guitar solo.

Though the ex-Fabs' presence brought marquee value to the project, *Rotogravure* marked the beginning of what would be a long slow decline in Ringo's efforts. Whether it was the partying, putting too much control into the hands of those who did not "get" him, or just a general Fab fatigue in the marketplace, it would be years before the Ringed One successfully recaptured his mojo and began again to live up to the promise of those first few releases.

Ringo (and Paul) on "All Those Years Ago"—1980

After bottoming out commercially and artistically with *Ringo the 4th* and *Bad Boy* in 1977 and 1978 respectively, Ringo took 1979 off—granted, a year that didn't exactly pan out as the opportunity for kicking back that he might have anticipated. Still, by 1980, refreshed, tanned, and relaxed, he was ready to get back in the game. Having tried working without his fellow ex-Fabs on his last two outings (with dire results), Ringo, perhaps recognizing what side his bread was buttered on, put out the call.

First to respond was Paul, who, in a year already showing itself to be full of surprises (see chapter 31), booked time in a French studio and put himself at the drummer's disposal. George likewise agreed to perform and contribute material when he was available in the fall, while John—back in action after an even longer sabbatical than Ringo's—offered up a couple of tunes and a commitment to get together. Also helping out were Harry Nilsson (for the first time since 1974), Stephen Stills, and Ronnie Wood.

Ringo and John met on Saturday, November 15—for the last time—at New York's Plaza Hotel, whereupon John gave him a cassette featuring two original demos: "Nobody Told Me" (though John's own perfectly usable studio take was already in the can, recorded during the *Double Fantasy* sessions) and a somewhat less substantive track entitled "Life Begins at Forty."

The two made plans to get together in January to record the songs. This did not happen.

Only days after their meeting, however, Ringo was back in England, at George's FPSHOT (Friar Park Studio, Henley-on-Thames) facility, laying down tracks that did eventually see the light of day. One, George's "Wrack My Brain," would end up as Ringo's final Top 40 single upon its release in October 1981. Another was a cover of the pop standard "You Belong to Me," perhaps best known by Jo Stafford's 1952 chart-topper.

The third song recorded was another Harrison original, entitled "All Those Years Ago." This final tune would make it only as far as the basic track stage before Ringo decided to take a pass on it, citing the lyrical content and the key it was recorded in as unsuitable. Not at all put out, George took the song back with the intent of saving it for himself.

To this day, the song's original lyrics remain a mystery. Some accounts say that as written, "All Those Years Ago" was a veiled slam at Lennon, given the evident tension between the two ex-Fabs in the final months of 1980. In addition to publicly minimizing the importance of George and Ringo to the Beatles in his September 1980 *Newsweek* interview, John delivered a scathing psychological assessment of George throughout his talks with *Playboy* interviewer David Sheff, centering on but not limited to a perceived snub in George's *I Me Mine* autobiography. (Even Yoko tried to tamp down his tirade.)

We will probably never know what the song's original content was, for George's world—as well as most everybody's—was changed forever just a few weeks after recording began on the song. At some point after the shock of December 8 began sinking in, George's reflections on what John had meant to him and indeed the world began taking lyrical form. As rewritten, "All Those Years Ago" would serve as a communiqué to a grieving world from those who had known John best, featuring George, Ringo, and—per its creator's request—Paul, along with Linda and Denny Laine (who later complained that he was never paid for his contribution).

UNCLE ALBERT/ ADMIRAL HALSEY

Words and Music by PAUL and LINDA McCARTNEY
Recorded by PAUL and LINDA McCARTNEY on Apple Records

NORTHERN   SONGS   PTY.   LTD.
Sole Distributors for Australia and New Zealand

LEEDS   MUSIC   PTY.   LTD.

UNIVERSAL HOUSE, PELICAN STREET, SYDNEY, N.S.W.

50 CENTS

Paul's efforts to establish his bride as his new songwriting partner landed him in hot water with his music publisher, who accused Macca of some unsubtle double-dipping. The dispute with ATV's Sir Lew Grade was settled when Paul agreed to star in a TV special for the mogul.

4

Got to Pay Your Dues if You Want to Sing the Blues

1971

hough the New Year began on a down note, with Paul's litigation against his estranged bandmates, not all was bleak. George's *All Things Must Pass* was topping the charts in America as well as Britain, while "My Sweet Lord" performed likewise. Sadly for George, its very success would draw unwanted scrutiny when Bright Tunes, the publishers of the 1963 hit "He's So Fine" (recorded by the Chiffons) divined a rather unholy resemblance to their song and demanded compensation. In the meantime, George filled his time with Phil Spector laying down tracks on behalf of Ronnie Spector, who was attempting a musical comeback. The one song eventually released from the sessions, George's "Try Some, Buy Some," was not a hit.

Less litigious was his follow-up success with "What Is Life," a joyous riff-driven number that was far less weighty than its ponderous title suggested. It gave him a Top 10 hit in early 1971, while later that year, folk singer Richie Havens enjoyed his biggest chart success (peaking at #16) with a pleasing cover of George's "Here Comes the Sun." George also left his mark on the year's Top 10 with his production of Badfinger's "Day After Day," which—reaching #4—would be their highest-charting single ever. (The Pete Ham composition featured George doubling the writer's slide guitar motif.)

When not consulting with his lawyers or giving depositions, Paul was in New York City, accompanied by Linda. The two were in town to audition musicians for his next album, which would be recorded in the Big Apple. Sessions for *Ram* began on January 10, just over a week before he was due back in a London court. Beatle-watchers were saddened at the unfolding revelations as they heard how Paul had thrown Ringo out of his home, and how the battle between Allen Klein's partisans and Lee Eastman's had irrevocably forced the choosing of sides within the band. It was precisely the sort of situation that Brian Epstein had been so adept at defusing, and on some level, the ex-bandmates must have come to realize how vital their departed manager had been to their success.

John was vacationing with Yoko in Japan when repeated calls from attorneys prompted his return to England to deal with the legal mess. Not at all pleased, he nonetheless managed to squeeze in a recording date upon his return, cutting "Power to the People" one day after meeting with editors of the underground leftist magazine *Red Mole*. The song marked a dramatic shift away from his "Give Peace a Chance"/ "War Is Over" sentiments, but given what was going on in court, brotherhood was probably the farthest thing from his mind.

Ringo dealt with the lawsuit's black cloud by working with Frank Zappa on a film project, *200 Motels*. Playing a version of Frank himself ("Larry the Dwarf"), Ringo took on the first of a string of cinematic releases that kept him busy for the next couple of years. By summer, he would be off to Italy and Spain to shoot the spaghetti western *Blindman*; afterward, he would direct a documentary on England's T. Rex phenomenon, entitled *Born to Boogie*.

In between duties before or behind the camera, Ringo issued his first pop single, the Harrison-produced "It Don't Come Easy," in spring 1971. (Truth be told, to this day it's long been held that the "Richard Starkey" songwriting credit was more a reflection of George's generosity than anything else.) To fans expecting little more than a country-flavored novelty tune, the song was a stunning taste of what a rock record from Ringo Starr could be. On its own merits, it reached #4 on the charts on both sides of the pond.

Paul's solo debut had sold quite well, but the critical reception was mixed. This time out, he made the calculated decision to produce a record that pulled out all the production stops, from a platoon of seasoned session players to full-blown orchestration, utilizing musical ideas too numerous to count. A foretaste of *Ram* came with the issue of the melodic but slight "Another Day" in February. In contrast to John's recent rabble-rouser and George's majestic prayer, it seemed a lightweight piece of fluff, though it charted well. By the time Ram was issued in May, the critics were gunning for Macca, simultaneously calling the album "monumentally irrelevant" (per *Rolling Stone*) and "pretentious" (critic Robert Christgau). Fans thought otherwise: boosted in the States by the release of the *Abbey Road*–like musical collage "Uncle Albert / Admiral Halsey," it was kept off the top of the charts that summer only by Carole King's *Tapestry*.

The legal wrangling from Paul's court action came to a head in March; on Friday the 12th, the judge handed down a ruling appointing a receiver to collect all joint monies, pending the further sorting out of the entanglements binding the four. Ironically, it was Paul who showed up the following Tuesday in Los Angeles to tend to one last bit of Beatles business. The soundtrack to *Let It Be* had received a Grammy nomination for Best Original Score. When actor John Wayne announced the winner, it was Paul—with Linda—who took the stage to collect their Grammy for an album he professed to despise. He limited his remarks to a quick "thank you" before vanishing with the trophies. (No ex-Beatles were present a month later when the album won again at the Oscars—record producer Quincy Jones accepted for them.)

The three other ex-Fabs were fairly united in their displeasure with the outcome of the court case but it was John, as always, who took the lead in voicing that opinion. Though they announced in April that they would not appeal the ruling, John's antipathy found a voice in the track "How Do You Sleep," issued later that year on the *Imagine* album. Featuring a biting lead from George, the song shocked many with its sheer viciousness, escalating a war of words that had already begun with Paul's "Too Many People" on *Ram*. Relations between Lennon and McCartney would be marked by much sniping in the press throughout the year, though by early 1972 they seemed to have finally gotten over much of it.

Between work on John's album and with Apple protégés Badfinger, George maintained a fairly busy schedule while basking in the afterglow of *All Things Must Pass*'s acclaim. He also paid a visit to Ravi Shankar in Los Angeles in June to assist with the sitar maestro's current project. It was then that he became aware of the calamity that had struck Bangladesh. Ravi prevailed upon him for help in organizing some sort of benefit, and from this, rock's first large-scale humanitarian effort was launched. On August 1, the Concert for Bangladesh became the forerunner of the now-commonplace full-scale rock benefit.

That same summer, Paul committed to putting together a new group, rather than employ an ensemble of session men, to take his act on the road. Blowing off George's invitation to perform in New York, he instead recruited drummer Denny Seiwell, who'd played on *Ram*, and guitarist/singer/songwriter Denny Laine, formerly of the Moody Blues, to form the basis of a band with Linda and himself. The fledgling group would stay unnamed until the September 13 birth of their daughter, Stella. Paul later revealed that, as he had prayed during the difficult birth for the safety of mother and daughter, the phrase "wings of an angel" kept popping into his head. Linda's inclusion in the musical vehicle became the subject of much ridicule from fans, critics, and even his peers. (Mick Jagger—who in fact had a past with the former Ms. Eastman—famously declared that he would never go onstage with *his* "old lady.")

After litigation concluded with the Apple court case in March, John and Yoko attended to another legal matter: securing custody of Yoko's daughter Kyoko. Their do-it-yourself attempt to transfer the seven-year-old from her father's care to Yoko's ended badly in Spain in April, when the Lennon's were arrested for kidnapping. Still, by late summer they'd gotten a judge to officially declare in their favor—the only trouble now was finding the child, since Tony Cox had disappeared. The couple decided to move to the U.S. in the hope of tracking down Kyoko. At the time, John's entry visa was limited to six months, but the Lennons hoped that their cause would enable them to prevail against any objections by the department of Immigration and Naturalization.

Not long after they arrived, *Imagine* was released. Like *All Things Must Pass* and *McCartney*, it landed atop the charts, though John was quick to point out its "sugar-coating" as a concession to commerciality. The title song almost instantly became a classic, without actually making it to #1. Though its Utopian politics made it seem like an evocation of the old "All You Need Is Love" / "Give Peace a Chance" sloganeering, John and Yoko would soon find themselves falling in with a notorious pair regarded in some circles as America's most dangerous radicals: activists Jerry Rubin and Abbie Hoffman, formerly part of the Chicago Seven. By year's end, John too had stepped up his political activism, taking part in marches and performing benefits. In so doing, he'd unwittingly placed a big bull's eye on his back, as far as the Nixon administration was concerned.

Ringo's two 1971 films, *200 Motels* and *Blindman,* opened within a day of each other in November (though the latter film wasn't released in America until two months later). Debuting that same week was Wings, at a press reception hosted by the McCartneys at Leicester Square's Empire Ballroom. Though the band themselves did not perform, their newly recorded album *Wild Life* was spun. Intended to represent a back-to-basics approach, it was regarded by most as a major step backward and panned. (In its defense, years later Macca related an anecdote asserting that the release had its fans: "I saw this fella heading for the hills in California holding a copy." What the man likely didn't tell him was that he was going skeet shooting.)

Another premiere held in November was the Ravi Shankar documentary *Raga.* Though it was not officially an Apple film, its soundtrack was released on the label, as was Badfinger's *Straight Up.* Long a fan favorite, it yielded two hit singles: in addition to the aforementioned "Day After Day," "Baby Blue" also became an FM classic. George's nonstop labors resulted in the pre-Christmas issue of *The Concert for Bangla Desh.* His second triple-record set in a row, it too was widely anticipated, bringing the historic occasion into the homes of those who hadn't been able to see the show live.

Rounding out Apple's year-end releases was John and Yoko's "Happy Xmas (War Is Over)" single. Pressed in festive green vinyl, it arrived in shops too late to make much of a chart impression, though it had been recorded in October. In England, it wasn't issued at all for another whole year, owing to a dispute with John's music publisher (who didn't believe Yoko was entitled to co-credit). Nonetheless, it became a holiday staple on radio in years to come, bringing 1971 to a close on a far more uplifting note than the year before.

One year after the Beatles passed into history, their story was taken up for young readers by Margaret Sutton. Famed for her Judy Bolton mystery series, Sutton was nearing seventy when she penned the biography.

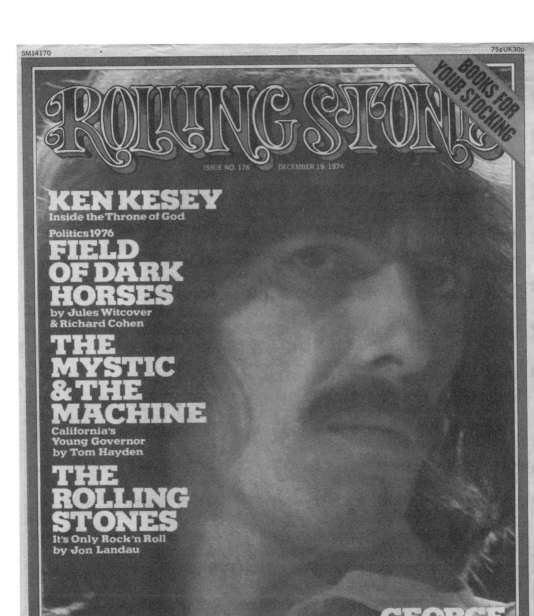

75¢UK30p

BOOKS FOR YOUR STOCKING

ROLLING STONE

ISSUE NO. 176   DECEMBER 19, 1974

KEN KESEY
Inside the Throne of God

Politics 1976
FIELD OF DARK HORSES
by Jules Witcover & Richard Cohen

THE MYSTIC & THE MACHINE
California's Young Governor
by Tom Hayden

THE ROLLING STONES
It's Only Rock'n Roll
by Jon Landau

GEORGE HARRISON
Lumbering in the Material World
by Ben Fong-Torres

Though the *Dark Horse* raga-rock review may have been challenging to some, critical response, as typified in the pages of *Rolling Stone*, was unduly harsh—a far cry from the adoration directed George's way three years before.

5

I Really Want to See You

Some Memorable Live Performances

The logistics of mounting a full-scale tour changed drastically in the '60s, with most of the technological development coming well after the Beatles had quit the road. Innovations like monitor speakers that actually allowed singers to hear themselves, powerful PA systems, road crews that could set up and break down a stage with the efficiency of an Indy pit crew—all of these elements set the table for the '70s becoming the golden era of the rock concert.

The ex-Beatles were not about to be left behind. In their previous collective incarnation, they had built their reputation as live performers well before their songwriting efforts bore fruit. Individually, all of them would eventually rediscover the buzz that interaction with an audience afforded, with each taking tentative steps on his own particular path back to the stage. Ringo, who would distinguish himself with his regular "All-Starr Band" tours beginning in 1989, mostly sat out the decade, limiting himself to rare guest appearances. (He *did* take a curtain call at Paul's final *Wings Over America* show.)

Predictably, it was Paul, well known for his showman tendencies, who took live performing the farthest. While John was the first ex-Beatle to step out on his own, his appearances tended toward unpredictable one-offs, and always for a cause. In between was George, who pioneered the Big Event while remaining self-effacing and conflicted throughout.

Here is a rundown of some notable live performances that marked the decade. Whatever the setting, the in-person appearance of an ex-Beatle always generated electricity.

George: The Concert for Bangladesh—Sunday, August 1, 1971—New York City

Riding high on the acclaim accorded *All Things Must Pass*, George took little time to bask in the glory of his achievement. Though his single "What Is Life" had given him another Top 10 hit in early 1971, George was less concerned with building upon his success than he was with lending a hand to others. That same spring, Apple artists Badfinger had turned in a follow-up to their successful *No Dice* album, produced by Beatles engineer Geoff Emerick. To George's ears, the recordings sounded a little too raw; wishing to present them in a more polished and fully realized form, he offered to re-produce *Straight Up*, a deal that the band actually canceled a tour of Australia to accept.

While thus engaged, George took a time-out, accepting an invitation from John to sit in on sessions for the *Imagine* album at his Tittenhurst Park recording facility (dubbed Ascot Sound Studios, or ASS). But before he could resume the Badfinger project, a call from Ravi Shankar changed George's plans for the foreseeable future.

Shankar was born in British-ruled India in the town of Varanasi (formerly Benares). By culture and blood, he identified with the Bengalese, who were now struggling for their very lives. As Bangladesh (formerly East Pakistan) fought for her independence, genocide on an unprecedented scale was taking place under the heel of U.S. ally Pakistan, with massacres and mass rape claiming up to a million lives. Additionally, the Bhola Cyclone and ensuing floods hit fleeing refugees hard. Upwards of half a million died in the storms, most of them children.

Given the horror of these natural and manmade disasters, Shankar was stunned by the western world's indifference. He believed that by staging a benefit concert, he could draw attention to the crises while earmarking the proceeds for relief agencies. Being inexperienced in the logistics of such a set-up, he turned to George for advice.

Recognizing the scope of the catastrophe, George set aside his Badfinger duties at once and flew to New York. Doubting that Ravi's plan would raise sufficient awareness and aid, he decided that such epic suffering demanded far grander action. (As he later explained, proximity to John Lennon had taught him to think bold.) With the cachet he'd earned as the "ex-Beatle most likely to succeed," George began working the phone lines, calling in chits on those in his immediate professional circle.

Initially, he attempted to recruit his erstwhile bandmates. Paul, unwilling to agree to a display of unity while the ex-Fabs were up to their eyeballs in litigation, was quick to kibosh any happy reunions, despite the gravity of the

ROLLING STONE

No. 90
60¢ UK 15p
September 2,
1971

The George
Harrison
Bob Dylan
Concert

Splendor
in the
Short Grass

As reported in *Rolling Stone*, George's stunning all-star benefit for the suffering in war-torn Bangladesh put the world on notice that altruism and rock music weren't necessarily incompatible.

occasion. Ringo, who'd just begun work on a spaghetti western (explaining his out-of-control beard), was slow to acquiesce; hedging his bets, George secured the services of session ace Jim Keltner.

John Lennon posed his own set of problems. As eager as he was to return the favor of George's help on *Imagine*, he would not or could not see performing without Yoko at his side. But George was adamant: there would be no room on *his* stage for any avant-garde antics. He would happily provide Yoko with excellent seating on the main floor. After pondering George's proposition for a couple of days, John, squeezed between his wife on one side and the chance to contribute to a cause bigger than himself on the other, opted out, flying back to Europe in a huff and leaving both wife and cause behind).

Unfazed, George soldiered on, assembling a team built around *All Things Must Pass* stalwarts Billy Preston and Klaus Voormann, as well as bassist Carl Radle. Ringo came through after all, and, perhaps as a consolation for disrupting his work on their project, Badfinger was invited. (The band's three guitarists would provide "felt but not heard" acoustic support while drummer Mike Gibbins assisted with percussion. When asked if he felt put out giving up his kit, the diminutive Welshman assured George, "I'm only here for the beer.")

At the top of George's wish list was the stellar but slippery Bob Dylan. Though he and George had only grown in closeness through the years, culminating with their collaboration on "I'd Have You Anytime," Dylan was inscrutable. Since his 1966 motorcycle accident, only twice had he disrupted his self-imposed retirement from performing in public.

Though Dylan dutifully turned up at rehearsals, George knew his mercurial nature and regarded his participation as far from certain. (On his handwritten set list, he had scrawled "Bob—?" at the point where he had slotted him.) The ex-Beatle's unabashed hero worship occasionally manifested itself; when he asked Dylan if he would be performing "Blowin' in the Wind," the incredulous troubadour responded, "Will you be singing 'I Want to Hold Your Hand'?"

Equally questionable was guitar slinger and close friend Eric Clapton's commitment. The summer of 1971 saw Slowhand in thrall to a serious heroin addiction, instigated in part (at least according to Eric) by his frustrated infatuation with George's wife. Like Dylan, Clapton had been something of a recluse of late. Despite his expressed interest in helping, he failed to materialize on any of the flights George had booked him on until the last possible minute, precluding any serious rehearsal time.

As with Ringo, George took no chances on Eric's potential non-appearance, inviting Taj Mahal's guitarist Jesse Ed Davis as Clapton insurance. According to Clapton's 2007 memoir, George also had to lure the strung-out guitarist over the sea with assurances of a plentiful supply of his fix, to be delivered to his hotel room—not the hardest thing to find in New York City, then as now. (Once he did arrive, Eric further handicapped himself by foolishly bringing along a Gibson Byrdland hollow body: a *jazzman's* guitar.)

The only open dates on Madison Square Garden's schedule fell on the weekend of July 31 to August 1, giving George less than six weeks to pull the musicians together and rehearse. The addition of George's newest buddy, Leon Russell, helped goose things along, given his industry contacts and multi-instrument abilities. Eventually, nearly three dozen musicians shared the stage, including sax legend Jim Horn and Memphis producer/ songwriter Don Nix. Steven Stills contributed the use of his sound and light system to the cause, then was stunned when George neglected to ask him to play. (He ended up stewing in Ringo's room—drunk—complaining, "Thoosshh asssholes.")

First word of the pending event leaked out via Al Aronowitz—the same journalist who'd witnessed Bob Dylan and the Beatles sharing their first joint in 1964. Later a small blurb appeared in the *New York Times*, announcing "George Harrison and friends." Within hours, twenty thousand tickets had been sold for each of the two Sunday shows (the Saturday show was moved to 2:30 p.m. the next day after tickets were printed). Ticket scalpers did a brisk business, with some $7.50 seats going for as high as *$20*.

History records the performances as a triumph, showing that pampered, doped-up rock stars could put aside their hedonism momentarily for a good cause. The Concert for Bangladesh was a massive success in terms of raising public awareness as well as funds—nearly a quarter of a million dollars overnight. In doing so, it directly set the template for all such rock and roll good works that followed, including Live Aid and Farm Aid.

George sought to sustain the relief through sales of an album and from a theatrically released motion picture. What he 'hadn't counted on was corporate and governmental greed dampening the altruism. First, Columbia, Bob Dylan's record label, would not allow their star's performance to be released through Apple/Capitol. Weeks of unnecessary wrangling eventually saw an agreement worked out, with Columbia distributing the tape issue of the concert while Apple disseminated the vinyl.

Less accommodating was England's Inland Revenue. Despite much pleading by George and UNICEF, the organizing entity responsible for pulling together the event was not recognized by the British taxing office as a legitimate charity, and was therefore liable for taxes on the money raised. Not until George wrote out a check for a million pounds sterling from his personal bank account was the matter considered closed. (Years later, Lennon would dismiss the whole tainted event as "ca-ca.")

Though far from being a seeker of the limelight, in bringing help to suffering Bengalis George solidified his image as a giving, caring man who truly walked the walk, spiritually. Not until 1973 would he be freed of his charitable commitments for long enough to resume his musical career, by which time a seemingly fickle public seemed weary of the ever-serious nature of his work.

John: The Free John Sinclair Rally—Friday, December 10, 1971—Ann Arbor, Michigan

Somewhat smaller in scope but no less a "cause," John's U.S. solo concert debut took place some four months later. (He *had* jammed with Frank Zappa at the Fillmore East in June, but that had been merely a guest appearance.) Now living in New York City and having thoroughly fallen in with the so-called "Radical Left," John found himself caught up in the case of one John Sinclair, former manager of Detroit's political rockers MC5 and cofounder of the White Panther Party.

In July 1969, as the Beatles toiled away at their final group effort, Sinclair was arrested and convicted for selling two joints to an undercover officer. Under the draconian Michigan laws in place at the time, he received a ten-year prison sentence. This heavy-handed punishment stirred outrage among the counterculture, who believed Sinclair had been targeted for his politics. (Indeed, Yippie leader Abbie Hoffman attempted to publicize the case before the Woodstock Festival's half-million attendees. Unfortunately, his half-baked impulse to do it *during the Who's set* only resulted in physical injury from Pete Townshend's Gibson SG for his trouble.)

One week after the release of the "Happy Xmas (War Is Over)" single in America and still basking in the critical acclaim accorded the *Imagine* LP, John was arguably at the zenith of his solo commercial success. With Beatle mystique aplenty and solid peace activist bona fides, he was ready to extend his political reach into uniquely American concerns.

Given his rapport with Hoffman and Jerry Rubin, John's interest in Sinclair was inevitable. As the latter's case wound its way through appeals, a benefit was set up to rouse support. Others on the bill included veteran folk activist Phil Ochs; Commander Cody and his Lost Planet Airmen, soon to enjoy their only hit with a remake of Johnny Bond's "Hot Rod Lincoln"; Detroit rocker Bob Seger, who'd scored a string of local hits without yet cracking the big time; and established Motown star Stevie Wonder, himself transitioning from pure pop to a series of artistically mature releases, beginning with 1972's *Music of My Mind.*

The event was held at the Crisler (*not* Chrysler) Arena before fifteen thousand people. In direct contrast with Bangladesh, an equally ad hoc event that boasted the sheerest veneer of professionalism, the Sinclair concert—or at least John and Yoko's segment of it—looked and sounded like a group of street musicians plucked from the alley and thrust into the limelight.

Headlining the event, they did not take the stage until the wee hours of the morning. At this point, John lacked a backing band; support at this gig consisted of whoever was at hand, which in this instance encompassed the ragtag David Peel and his Lower East Side fellows, as well as Rubin himself.

John's charitable efforts for a local cause took form as the One to One concerts. What no one could have predicted at the time was that they represented the last full-scale solo performances he would ever undertake.

Their "set" consisted of four songs, all of them topical: "Attica State"; "The Luck of the Irish"; Yoko's feminist anthem, "Sisters O Sisters"; and "John Sinclair."

So new were the compositions that John sang them with a lyric sheet atop a music stand. (This charming lack of pretension echoed George's performance of his own "Bangla-Desh" at the benefit of the same name, though he at least had discreetly taped his cheat sheet to the floor.)

Whether due to the power of an ex-Beatle championing his cause, or simply as a result of the judicial process taking its course, Sinclair was sprung from the slammer two days later. Though the concert might rightly have been considered a success, powerful forces were unleashed that night that would dog John for years to come.

Unbeknownst to the Lennons, FBI informants tracking the activities of Rubin and Hoffman, et al. were now alerted to the ex-Beatle's involvement with enemies of the administration. A full report on the event (which included the transcribed lyrics to "John Sinclair") made its way to J. Edgar Hoover himself.

Alarmed at the prospect of a radicalized Lennon leading the newly enfranchised youth of America on an anti-Nixon crusade, North Carolina Senator Strom Thurmond, tipped off by Hoover, notified administration aides of the peril, recommending a full-scale effort to deport the Lennons. With John's visa due to expire early the following year, plans began to be laid to stop the threat of a movement from taking root. Before long, John was made to feel the folly of incurring the U.S. government's wrath.

Paul: Wings Debut—Wednesday, February 9, 1972—Nottingham, England

As the Beatles' career wound down, Paul McCartney, alone of the four, argued long and loud that their inter-band squabbles could be effectively quashed if they would simply "get back" to their club act roots. Chucking the baggage that came with being the most successful rock band in history would be easy, he assured his skeptical bandmates. The Beatles could simply show up at local venues unannounced and play under a pseudonym: say, "Ricky and the Redstreaks." Needless to say, this astonishingly foolish pipedream found no traction among his fellow Fabs, though, in all fairness to Paul, naivety was in plentiful supply during the Apple years. But the romanticism of such an undertaking never left Macca. As soon as he was able to put together a viable act (or, arguably, even sooner), Paul was determined to give the fantasy a proper go.

Having released two commercially successful solo LPs by mid-1971, Paul was now ready to forge a slightly more expansive and enduring setup. The two Dennys (ex-Moody Blue Laine and session drummer Seiwell), Paul, and Linda formed the core of Wings. Only after the addition of Irish-born guitar ace Henry McCullough in early 1972 did Paul deem the new outfit ready to hit the ground running. The method to their madness was simple: load up their gear in a van, drive to any town with a university or venue that they fancied, locate someone in authority, and offer to play. No big buildup, no press, no fuss.

Locales were chosen at something close to random: if any group member was intrigued by the very name of a place, that was reason enough to check it out. While roaming England's East Midlands, someone suggested the Leicestershire town of Ashby-de-la-Zouch (the setting for Walter Scott's *Ivanhoe*). Unfortunately, something about the band of would-be entertainers put off local officials, who declined to take them up on their offer.

Undeterred, McCartney and company headed for Nottingham, where Henry McCullough reported having enjoyed a splendid reception for his Grease Band the year before. His assessment proved correct: the students at Nottingham University were thrilled to host the first public performance of Wings (though one who was there would years later lament, "How were we to know they were gonna end up shite?").

On February 9 around lunchtime, a crowd of less than a thousand queued up at the student' union, located in the Portland Building, paying 50p a head to check out a former Beatle's newest incarnation. Doubtless, many were hoping to hear some familiar classics, though it's unlikely that Little Richard covers and Wings originals were what they had in mind.

What they did see was a group, comprised of four old pros and one rank amateur, that had not yet jelled as a playing ensemble. The band played a few selections from the recent Wings debut, *Wild Life*; a couple of twelve-bar improvisations from Henry; and a few selections going back to Paul's earliest exposure to rock and roll: Elvis's Sun Records treatment of Bill Monroe's "Blue Moon of Kentucky," as well as two from the Richard Penniman catalog, "Long Tall Sally" and "Lucille."

Also performed was his as-yet-unreleased response to the shooting of twenty-six unarmed protestors in Derry, Northern Ireland—half of whom died immediately—by British soldiers a mere ten days before. "Give Ireland Back to the Irish" proved that John Lennon had no monopoly on reacting to events and turning them to song. Before a crowd of starstruck students, Wings previewed what would become their first single banned by the BBC.

John would later express admiration for the way Paul "climbed off his pedestal" to conduct his hit-and-run tour of the U.K.—though he still maintained that for the Beatles to attempt the same trick would have been insanity. Given the less than stellar act that Wings was at this juncture, one must commend Paul on his innate grasp of guerilla marketing. Bypassing the media channels freely available to him, Macca used low-profile concerts to generate buzz and bring the band up to speed organically—a deliberate strategy to set Wings up for long-term viability. Unfortunately, other factors—not least a dictatorial manner that veteran musicians found grating—ensured things would play out somewhat differently (see chapter 14 for details).

John: The One to One Concert—Wednesday, August 30, 1972—New York City

Whatever feelings John may have had at missing out on the outpouring of goodwill following George's Bangladesh concert he likely saw the opportunity to redress one year later. But rather than address a global tragedy, John chose a cause much closer to home—at least the home he aspired to remain in. The Willowbrook State School was an institution for children and adults with mental disabilities, located on Staten Island. The facility had made the headlines when a young investigative journalist by the unlikely name of Geraldo Rivera reported on physical and sexual abuse of the patients, as well as overcrowding and general neglect. The scandalous story stirred community outrage (simultaneously scoring Rivera an Emmy and putting him on the path to bigger things).

Like other New Yorkers, John was appalled by the revelations, but unlike most, he was well placed to put his talents to use toward a solution. Soon enough, he found himself pressed into service by Rivera as the top-billed act at a concert designed to raise funds and awareness of the Willowbrook patients' plight. The show would take place as part of the One to One Festival, so named for a program that sponsored one-on-one mentoring of the patients. (As a footnote, the event was held on the same day that actress Cameron Diaz was born.)

Sharing the stage was singer Roberta Flack, fresh off the success of her duet album with Donnie Hathaway ("Where Is the Love?"), as well as the ever-reliable Stevie Wonder, who would soon have a monster hit of his own with "Superstition." (He'd actually premiered it at the same venue one month before, as a support act on the Rolling Stones' *Exile on Main Street* tour.) As for the headliner's current chart success, ten weeks after the release of *Some Time in New York City*—not so much. Providing comic relief at the event were faux '50s rockers Sha-Na-Na, who had performed similar duties just before Jimi Hendrix's set at Woodstock. Unknown to the public at the time was how close Paul McCartney came to joining John at the gig. An invitation had been extended that Macca was inclined to accept, but the prospect of Allen Klein using the reunion to propagandize himself ultimately kept Paul away.

By now of course, the Nixon administration's campaign to deport the Lennons was in full swing. Justifiably disturbed by the overt actions against him as well as the covert (phone taps, surveillance, shadowing), John was making a conscious decision to burnish his public image, taking a step back from the strident leftist causes that his latest LP championed in favor of charitable work that everyone could come together over.

At last John had an electric backing band, such as it was. Elephant's Memory were, at least, competent and thundering. (*Time* magazine reported the wife of Democratic presidential candidate George McGovern in attendance and asking rhetorically, "Why does it have to be so loud?") Supplementing the ensemble were bassist John Ward and drummer Jim Keltner, the latter enjoying the distinction of being the only musician to play *both* ex-Beatle Madison Square Garden benefits.

As with George's event a year earlier, popular demand forced a matinee performance. Both show's attendees were provided with souvenir tambourines to shake throughout, while film *and* television crews documented the proceedings. Though the event was tainted by the inclusion of so much subpar *New York City* material, the faithful were treated to exactly one Beatles tune—"Come Together"—that made up for the lack. (John's somewhat begrudging introduction: "We go back in the past *just once* . . . .")

The two shows were distinguished by noticeable differences in quality. (As John noted during the matinee, "Welcome to the rehearsal!") There is an overall sloppiness and lack of punch evident in the earlier performance as contrasted with the evening version of the same songs. Nonetheless, it was the *inferior* show that would be issued as the *Live in New York City* album and video in the 1980s, as it was felt that unacceptable levels of noise marred the superior evening show. In time, advances in technology overcame these problems, and a few tracks from the evening performance eventually saw issue on the *Lennon Anthology* set.

Interestingly, in his lifetime John only saw fit to release one tiny sliver from the event. It came as a coda grafted onto the "Happy Xmas (War Is Over)" single as found on the *Shaved Fish* compilation. There, a reggaefied version of "Give Peace a Chance" from One to One's finale can be heard for less than a minute. Only trouble was, the bit John used features Stevie Wonder's impassioned lead vocal—not his own.

The shows represent the last—and only—full-scale concerts that John Lennon would ever undertake.

George: The *Dark Horse* Tour Begins—Saturday, November 2, 1974—Vancouver, British Columbia

Nothing about George's decision to embark on what became known as the "Dark Hoarse" tour in late 1974 makes sense—then or now. To begin with, he was famously the Beatle most eager to quit the road, while also enjoying the adulation of crazed fans the least. To a musician reclusive by nature, the idea of launching a juggernaut that would circumnavigate North America should have seemed positively ludicrous. While there had been talk following the Bangladesh benefit about taking the act on the road, playing two shows a city (one for charity, one for the band), this quickly evaporated once the reality of record company infighting manifested itself.

Furthermore, on a personal level, George had hit an unprecedented low point. Nineteen-seventy-four had begun with his long-troubled marriage to Pattie finally unraveling, as she very publicly took up with Eric Clapton, George's mate. (This after a fling with future Rolling Stone Ron Wood, who also had been become one of George's pals.)

Coinciding with this heartache was the manifestation of something akin to post-traumatic stress disorder in the wake of Beatlemania. The acclaim accorded Harrison's magnum opus *All Things Must Pass* and the subsequent Bangladesh concert now faded, the mystic Beatle had taken up some rather unholy coping mechanisms, partying and hitting the bottle hard. (Both John and Ringo, hanging out together in L.A. with Harry Nilsson and Keith Moon, seemed to be going through the same malaise at the same time.)

Then there was the matter of the tour's ostensible purpose: promoting the *Dark Horse* album. This latest collection of songs had been rush-recorded, and it showed. Any issues of uneven material on the still-unreleased (as the tour began) album aside, the strain of rushing to finish it and rehearse for the tour *simultaneously* left their mark on George's already thin voice, as his vocals were now reduced to a raspy croak. Though George would later attempt to make light of his sound by calling it his "Louis Armstrong period," fans were not amused and critics less so.

The final element of alienation hardwired into the whole enterprise came with George's dogged insistence on placing sitar maestro Ravi Shankar and company front and center with *two* sets of music during the show. At the Bangladesh event, the gravitas of Eastern music served well to set the tone for a serious cause. Three years later, with an audience wanting to see a Beatle, or at least to rock, there was no similar subduing influence to reel in their impulse to jeer.

Purely in a sense of tolerating an errant son's whims did Ravi accept the thankless task, at least initially, until well into the tour when George was forced to rethink the presentation in response to underwhelming reviews. Ravi's two sets were combined, sprawling ragas were ditched in favor of more pop-like offerings, and his act was shifted to mid-set, as sort of a diversion while the scenery was being shifted for the next act.

Brought along perhaps as applause insurance was Billy Preston, always a crowd pleaser. By now, Billy had scored a few hits of his own, among them "Nothing from Nothing" and "Will It Go Around in Circles?" For those seeking a respite from the unrelenting solemnity of George's performances, Preston was a highlight.

Undeniably, many of the faithful in attendance were hoping for some of the magic seen in the Bangladesh film, with Beatles classics like "While My Guitar Gently Weeps" or "Here Comes the Sun" presented in a live setting. What no one counted on was George's perverse penchant for twisting the lyrics to suit his current mood. The former tune was now sung as "while my guitar tries to smile." John's "In My Life," which ordinarily should have been a rare treat, was now recast as, "in my life, I love GOD more."

It is unclear just what George intended in thus setting himself up for rejection. Audiences were being treated to a side well known to his friends: the *grumpy* George. All of his least lovable attitudes—hectoring, intolerant, and condescending—were on full display. Throughout the *Dark Horse* tour, Fab fans witnessed the anti-Paul.

In L.A., where one might be expected to be on one's best behavior (considering who might be in attendance), George was in an especially foul mood. A tepid response to one song prompted, "I don't know how it feels down there, but from up here you seem pretty dead." On another occasion, he railed against those on the floor with their "dirty reefers."

While all these negatives detracted from the high expectations people had going in, there were also genuine highlights that went mostly unreported. Smaller press outlets without axes to grind tended to review the shows the best, whereas rock establishment coverage, such as *Rolling Stone*'s, tended to spin the tour as something close to an unmitigated disaster (something that George never forgave them for).

Once one got past the star's attitude and smoky vocals, the actual music was peerless. To begin with, George had handpicked a well-seasoned lot for his backing. Given a chance to let rip, they acquitted themselves well. Session stars Andy Newmark and Willie Weeks comprised the rhythm section while Emil Richards provided percussion. Jim Horn and Tom Scott added brass, and guitar duties were shared with Joni Mitchell sideman Robben Ford, who gave George a run for his money with dueling leads on some selections.

Though not to everyone's taste, the inclusion of Ravi Shankar represented George's generous attempt at showcasing a brilliant musician to an audience that otherwise might never have experienced what one day would be called "world music." George himself eventually lightened up a bit before the tour ended, occasionally hoofing it up with Billy, or donning outlandish headgear.

In 1974, camaraderie between the former Beatles was approaching levels unseen since 1969. With business entanglements winding to a close, fewer obstacles stood in the way of their collaborating publicly, though the fear of triggering Beatlemania Mark II still tended to inhibit any musical interactions. Nonetheless, John—already having appeared onstage with Elton John (see below)—made it known late in the tour that he would be willing to "help" the struggling enterprise in a similar capacity at the final stop. George accepted the offer, but when John's capricious nature got the better of him before a scheduled business meeting and he failed to show, rage that George had already vented once toward Lennon resurfaced (see chapter 29). He seethed at May Pang over the phone, "Just tell him I started this tour on my own and I'll end it on my own!"

Never again after 1974 would George Harrison mount such an ambitious tour. (Only in 1991, after Eric Clapton practically arm-twisted him into it, did he return to the road at all; unfortunately for most fans, that road was in Japan.) Irretrievably soured, the *Dark Horse* tour validated feelings that had first surfaced back in 1966. The occasional one-off live show in the '80s and '90s served to satisfy any impulse George had to take the stage again.

John: Elton John Concert—Thursday, November 28, 1974—New York City

Throughout 1974, John spent a lot of time in the recording studio, on behalf of himself and others. Temporarily abandoning the troubled "Oldies but Moldies" concept LP, he plunged into work on *Walls and Bridges*, armed with a batch of new songs reflecting on the transition from Yoko to his new love with May Pang. His efforts were boosted when Elton John popped in for a cameo on what John considered to be one of his lesser efforts on the album,

"Whatever Gets You Through the Night." With the addition of a rollicking piano track and harmony vocal, the song bore an undeniable sheen that Elton declared would take it to the top of the charts. John demurred, noting, "I'm out of favor at the moment."

Nonsense, Elton retorted. So secure was he in his assessment that Elton managed to extract a promise from John that should the song make it to #1, he—John—would have to join Elton on stage in the fall for his show at Madison Square Garden to perform it live. Never believing in a million years that it would happen, John agreed.

Not long after their session at the Record Plant, John joined Elton at the Caribou Ranch studio in Colorado to return the favor, playing guitar and singing background on his own "Lucy in the Sky with Diamonds." Come November and against its creator's wildest expectations, "Whatever Gets You Through the Night" knocked BTO's "You Ain't Seen Nothing Yet" from its perch atop *Billboard*'s Hot 100. It didn't take Elton long to call John on his debt. The two quickly found themselves in rehearsal for the event, slated for Thanksgiving evening.

Elton took great pains to make sure that his horn section got their parts down exactly as they were on the record. Performing "Lucy" after "Night" seemed a good combination, but the two artists were stuck for a third to close John's portion of Elton's set. John quickly shot down performing "Imagine," but at Elton's suggestion acquiesced to "I Saw Her Standing There," noting with some amusement that it was a "Paul" song and therefore he'd never sung lead on it before.

Whether through pure rumor or an insider leak, the appearance of John onstage with Elton became something of an open secret. The show was sold out anyway, but anticipation of exactly when the "surprise" would happen kept the audience on the edge of their seats. The electricity in the air was palpable, but when Elton began his introduction about two-thirds of the way into the set ("Seeing how Thanksgiving's a joyous occasion . . ."), the Garden absolutely exploded with a rapturous ovation.

Elton later described John as the most jittery man he'd ever seen in his life; two years after his last live appearance (on this very stage), John was nauseous with nerves before walking out to thunderous applause unheard since the days of Beatlemania. It became an oft-told myth afterwards that he didn't know that Yoko was in the audience, but those in the know at the time dismissed this as disingenuous bull—after all, she'd requested tickets in advance (and then complained about where they'd put her). Furthermore, she'd sent orchids to both John and Elton, which each man was wearing.

The band tore right into a sloppy but spirited version of the hit single (which by then had been displaced from the top slot by Billy Swan's "I Can

Help," later covered by Ringo). Elton's as-yet-unreleased take on "Lucy in the Sky with Diamonds" followed; it would top the charts in January 1975. Upon its conclusion, John stepped to the mic to thank "Elton and boys for having me on," announcing his intent to finish with one more song "before I get out of here and be sick." Elton, many fans, and by her own later account, Yoko, were by this time in tears, caught up in a wave of emotion. John then dedicated their performance of the first song on the first Beatles' album "to an old estranged fiancé of mine called Paul."

As well as being John's final appearance before a paying audience, the occasion was later enshrined in myth as the end of John's public romance with May Pang. Again, self-spawned legend held that John and Yoko met up backstage, where, in a line worthy of an *ABC Movie of the Week* (or an *Afterschool Special*, anyway), an observer is said to have commented, *"There's two people in love!"* The reality was far more complex, of course. But as Carleton Young once famously noted, "When legend becomes fact, print the legend."

Paul: The *Wings Over America* Tour Begins—Thursday, May 3, 1976—Fort Worth

Reminiscent of the Beatles' determination in late 1963 not to tour America until they'd had a hit record, Paul McCartney bided his time before bringing his Wings extravaganza to North America. True, they'd enjoyed numerous hit singles and albums by this time, especially after his breakthrough with *Band on the Run* in late 1973. But as a performing entity, Wings had been something of a revolving door. Not until the addition of American drummer Joe English midway through the *Venus and Mars* sessions did the "classic" incarnation of the group finally materialize.

No fool he, Paul observed and studied reports from the sidelines as both John and George performed their live shows in America, noting what worked and what didn't. (At John's One to One show, for instance, the performance of "Come Together" brought the single biggest ovation of the evening, a point that John felt was lost on George, who performed his Beatle material sparingly and with alterations.) While still somewhat self-conscious about trotting out his Fab past (at least in 1976), Paul was by now secure enough to recognize that he needn't fear that his body of solo work would be eclipsed by tunes he'd written in his twenties.

Band on the Run's follow-up, *Venus and Mars*, had been well received by the public and critics alike. Paul used the success as a springboard for a tour of England and Australia in the fall of 1975. Before embarking on the subsequent European and American legs of the world tour, the band

reconvened at EMI studios at Abbey Road, quickly knocking out the most democratic album of their entire career, *Wings at the Speed of Sound*. Boosted by the strength of two smash singles ("Silly Love Songs" and "Let 'Em In") and the pending tour, it did just fine on the charts, spending seven weeks at #1 in America in the summer of 1976. (Interestingly, more material was drawn from Wings' two previous releases than from their current album.)

Originally, Wings Over America was to start in April, but the day after their last show in Europe, lead guitarist Jimmy McCulloch broke a finger, requiring some healing time before he could resume playing. (Accounts of how the injury occurred varied from a slip in the bathtub to a fistfight with pop idol David Cassidy.) For that reason, some tickets printed up in advance of the scheduled dates bore a line drawn across them and were honored for the rescheduled shows later.

It's not unreasonable to conclude that Paul had consciously been planning years ahead of time for the moment when the house lights would go down, signaling the start to his first post-Beatles show on an American stage. The one-two punch of opener "Venus and Mars / Rock Show" straight into "Jet" set the scene brilliantly. Those in the audience would have been hard-pressed to find the appropriate cue to sit down in the face of such adrenalin-inducing pyrotechnics. Saving his new songs for later in the set, Paul took the audience on a trip down memory lane, beginning with *McCartney*'s hit-that-never-was, "Maybe I'm Amazed." Onstage, it was presented in a slower tempo than the original and featured a new coda. So compelling was the by-now fully realized performance that it was issued as a single in 1977, eventually reaching *Billboard*'s Top 10.

The emotional highlight for most attendees would have been the long-anticipated Beatles sequence. After presenting a generous sampling from his last three albums, McCartney trotted out "The Long and Winding Road," "Lady Madonna," "Blackbird," "I've Just Seen a Face," and what John once called "the only thing you done," "Yesterday." (Macca could count on drawing tears from his audience on that last one.)

For most performers, this showstopping segment would have made everything that followed seem anticlimactic. (In a year that saw his ten-year-old

Revolver track "Got to Get You into My Life" surface as an American hit single, it's worth noting that he *didn't* add that to the mix, though in three years' time he'd warm to the notion). But Paul wasn't finished yet. His staging of the crowd-pleasing "Live and Let Die" was literally incendiary. Throwing in the current hits and album tracks and encoring with the rockers "Hi Hi Hi" (another tune that really came to life in concert) and the unreleased "Soily" brought things to a fittingly bombastic finish.

On every level: critical, commercial, musical—the Wings Over America tour was a smash. The band played to over half a million people over the course of thirty-one shows (with three added to the scheduled twenty-eight). From the wilderness of his first few solo releases to now, Paul had built an entirely new musical paradigm for himself, not dependent upon past glories. In so doing, he at last had outrun the damning title of breaker-upper-of-the-Beatles (more or less abdicating the distinction to Yoko) as he now became known indisputably as the overachieving ex-Beatle, easily eclipsing George's good works (as the latter's post–*All Things Must Pass* output increasingly served merely to type him as an out-of-touch zealot).

With such a pinnacle of success achieved, there was only one place left for the band to go, and that was down. True, the biggest-selling single of their career—"Mull of Kintyre"— lay just ahead, but its geo-specific subject, campfire sing-along refrain, and bagpipes (!) left American record buyers cold. Wings soon fragmented, leaving a middle-of-the-road release (*London Town*) in its wake. By the time McCartney-Laine-McCartney had regrouped, the relevance of Wings had been superseded by disco and punk.

Wings' 1976 American tour proved to be their shining hour. For those who weren't there, the three-record set album of the same name is an essential document.

George: *Saturday Night Live* Taping—Friday, November 19, 1976—New York City

The *Dark Horse* tour two years earlier marked the bottoming out of George's post-Beatles stock before it steadily began to rise. Though he never again would achieve the *All Things Must Pass / Bangladesh* levels of universal acclaim, by late 1976 his "rehabilitation" seemed complete. An album, *Extra Texture*, had been fast-tracked into production in early 1975 to fulfill the same function that *Mind Games* had for John in 1973: to redeem the artist from negative fallout spawned by his last offering. It would be Apple's final release (until being revived in the 1990s, anyway)—fittingly, for George's *Wonderwall Music* had jump-started the label a mere seven years earlier.

His commercial redemption took a huge leap forward with 1976's *Thirty-Three & 1/3*, his Dark Horse label debut. The album received warm reviews, frequently eliciting positive comparisons to *All Things Must Pass* while benefiting from the virtue of two hit singles, "This Song" and "Crackerbox Palace." Any other artist in similar straits might be expected to tour in order to close the deal with fans, but George was in no mood for any such undertaking in support of either his album or his label. Instead, he did a load of interviews, produced music videos, and succumbed to SNL producer Lorne Michael's entreaties, booking an appearance on the then-esteemed late-night show. Paul Simon was on board for his second of twelve hosting stints. (This appearance was the occasion of his famous Thanksgiving "turkey suit" performance.)

Bereft of his usual allotment of facial hair and sporting a striped sweater, George was at his most engaging and accessible. He opened the show with a tongue-in-cheek skit depicting him and Michaels attempting to reach an understanding as to how the $3,200 fee offered would be paid to a *single* Beatle. ("That's pretty chintzy," George is heard remarking.) The same show also previewed the comedic music videos George had produced for the album's two singles (though "Crackerbox Palace" had not yet been issued in that form).

But the highlight of George's appearance came with his musical collaboration with Paul Simon, an artist he had admired from afar but never actually performed with. Simon was still riding high with his 1975 release, *Still Crazy After All These Years*, which featured his own revival of a beloved act, Simon and Garfunkel, on the song "My Little Town." Before a live audience, Simon and Harrison ran through a nearly twenty-minute set a day before the show aired, though only two songs would make it to the actual broadcast.

Given both men's background in singing close harmony, it's no surprise that they chose material that supported such a treatment. Simon's "Homeward Bound," with the two trading off on verses, proved a nice complement to George's "Here Comes the Sun." The performances elicited an emotional response from the audience much as John's appearance with Elton had done nearly two years before.

Also performed, but not broadcast, were the old skiffle standard, Leadbelly's "Rock Island Line," as well as the Everly Brothers' "Bye Bye Love." Considering that George had recorded a bizarre reworking of this last song on the *Dark Horse* album as a kiss-off to Pattie (while giving her and Eric Clapton a tongue-in-cheek performance credit), its public performance must be regarded as strikingly ironic or a completely inadvertent and inappropriate song choice by the well-meaning Mr. Simon.

The appearance marked a return to form for George. Henceforth, slipping back to the sidelines, he would rest securely in his niche as a widely loved and supremely gifted artist, though forever typed as a second-tier ex-Beatle. Overshadowed by Paul the hammy showman and John the charismatic recluse, George was at peace with his position, lacking the taste for the limelight so present in his peers. The public and he seemed to have reached an understanding: if given enough space to go about his business without being bothered to play the game and live up to superstar expectations, he would in turn serve up some engaging Harrisongs as the spirit moved him. It was a good fit.

Paul: Concerts for the People of Kampuchea—Saturday, December 29, 1979—London

In 1978, after *London Town* had run its course, Paul again got the itch to put together a band that would be capable of recording and touring. Through Denny Laine, drummer Steve Holley and guitarist Laurence Juber were recruited. Having sustained a lot of flak for his last album's overall "soft" tone, Macca was ready to rock out again.

He brought in producer Chris Thomas to oversee the project. In the years since Thomas had engineered on the Beatles' "White Album," he had grown to become one of the most successful rock producers of the day, with clients ranging from Badfinger to the Sex Pistols. His collaboration with Wings resulted in *Back to the Egg*, a collection purporting to be Paul's response to punk, but coming off more like an exceptionally muscular album that Wings might have released in 1974.

Still, the band was primed to hit the road by fall of 1979, beginning with some nineteen dates around the U.K. for what was slated to become their first world tour in three years. This first leg ended in Glasgow, Scotland, on December 17. (A live recording of "Coming Up" from this show became a hit single in America the following year.) Next on the itinerary was their first-ever tour of Japan, a country that they'd been banned from heretofore owing to previous drug convictions (see chapter 7 for details).

In between lay a massive benefit to be held over four days at London's Hammersmith Odeon. In September 1979, UN Secretary-General Kurt Waldheim (formerly of Hitler's SA), made a public call for the Beatles to reunite in order to perform at an event to raise money for the refugees whom John referred to privately as "those yachting enthusiasts," the Cambodian boat people. This did not happen, but once Waldheim had caught Paul McCartney's ear, the two did find common ground on a cause that Paul was willing to get behind.

Cambodia had fallen victim to the ongoing Vietnam War during the early 1970s, when U.S. military strikes spread into the country in an effort to eradicate Viet Cong bases. Soon, a civil war erupted between the formerly pro-U.S. government and forces of the pro-Communist despot Pol Pot. Now renamed Democratic Kampuchea, the country became the site of mass killings on a scale reminiscent of Bangladesh, minus the storms. With such large-scale starvation, disease, and refugees struggling for survival, UNICEF was desperate to draw the world's attention while raising some cash.

Paul spearheaded the effort to recruit talent for a four-night benefit, with funds from the shows, an album, and a film going to the cause. Lest anyone get a sense of *deja vu*, why, yes, this was intended to emulate the success of George's event eight years before. Unlike the earlier charity, this one was pulled together in a less ad hoc manner, with some fundamental organizational lessons having been learned along the way.

George was not asked to participate, but given the flavor of the acts chosen, it's hard to see where he would have fit in. Queen, fresh from the success of a U.K. single (the rockabilly homage "Crazy Little Thing Called Love"), performed on Boxing Day, without a supporting act. December 27 saw the Clash headline a bill that included reggae artist Matumbi and Ian Dury.

The third night was anchored by the Who. Just three weeks before, while on a U.S. tour that introduced ex–Small Faces drummer Kenney Jones, the late Keith Moon's replacement, to Americans, eleven Who fans had been killed in a stampede at a show in Cincinnati. Also appearing that night were 2 Tone Ska artists the Specials, and the Pretenders, arguably the hottest act in England at the time.

But Paul reserved the highest-profile slot for Wings, on closing night. Opening acts that night were future McCartney collaborator Elvis Costello, with the Attractions, followed by Rockpile, the Dave Edmunds / Nick Lowe–led combo of rootsy popsters (on this night featuring Led Zeppelin's Robert Plant for a cameo on Elvis's "Little Sister"). Following Wings' set came the all-star ensemble assembled by Paul in a sort of rock and roll emulation of the Big Band era, dubbed Rockestra.

During the *Back to the Egg* sessions a year earlier, Paul had pulled together a number of friends from his musical world to play on a pair of tracks for no other purpose than to have fun and create a massive sound. There were three drummers (Steve Holley, John Bonham, Kenney Jones), a platoon of keyboardists (including Gary Brooker from Procol Harum and John Paul Jones), numerous guitarists (Pete Townshend and David Gilmour among them) and an assortment of percussionists, augmented by a brass section. The resulting tracks, "So Glad to See You Here" and "Rockestra Theme,"

Melody Maker

January 5, 1980   20p weekly   USA $1.25

COLD TURKEY FOR KAMPUCHEA

NO BEATLES REUNION—BUT WHO, WINGS, ELVIS, CLASH, DURY & QUEEN DO IT FOR CHARITY

(p. 20-21)

In what ended up as a fitting send-off (unbeknownst to anyone at the time), Wings presented the "Rockestra" as an encore to five day's worth of benefit concerts for the suffering of Kampuchea.

were, unsurprisingly, so dense with sound that singling out any particular musician was a challenge.

Now, given the array of talent at his fingertips, Paul was not about to let an opportunity for a *live* re-creation pass him by. In fact, most of the musicians on the record were on hand to recreate their studio performances, augmented by the Pretenders' James Honeyman-Scott and Rockpile's Dave Edmunds and Billy Bremner. Of the twenty musicians onstage, Pete Townshend was (to quote Paul) "the only sod" that refused to wear the gold lamé jacket Macca proffered.

Of course, Townshend had a perfectly good excuse: told to show up at eight o'clock for rehearsals that day, he arrived in the morning, only to discover that he had a twelve-hour wait ahead of him. The time was put to good use when he and Ronnie Laine proceeded to drink themselves insensible. Come the Rockestra's set, the decidedly unkempt and beyond-reach Who guitarist spent most of his stage time undermining the bandleader, leering at Paul during "Lucille" and tossing his top hat into the audience at his first convenience.

A specter hung over this evening's performance. Word "on good authority" was that a Beatle reunion, or at least an appearance by John Lennon, was in the offing. Print media fanned the flames, while ABC television offered a bounty of $2,000 a minute for film footage of the Fabs reuniting. Ticket scalpers enjoyed a second Christmas outside the venue, where the precious ducats were being snapped up for ten times their face value.

Of course, it was all hype. No John Lennon—not even in the audience (though Paul *did* teasingly reference him). But what did make the evening exceptional was the fact that, unbeknownst to everyone, it would be Wings' last live performance. Scheduled to fly to Japan in after a two-week break, Paul McCartney was instead arrested on drug charges and thrown into jail for nine days. It was the start of what would be a very bad year.

6

Help Me Cope with This Heavy Load

Some Stellar Sideman

In his 1975 television interview with Tom Snyder, John Lennon explained that one of the primary attractions of pursuing a solo career (rather than carrying on with his previous band) was that he wouldn't be locked into a musical arrangement that had gotten stale. He asserted that after years of playing together, the Fabs had gotten to where they could anticipate any move the others would make.

Why this was a bad thing he didn't explain, since in other interviews, he talked up *the virtues* of bringing Ringo or George into his own sessions, as they knew him well enough to follow his lead. In any case, the three ex-Beatles who *didn't* formally put together new bands shared the same musicians amongst themselves, Klaus Voormann and Jim Keltner frequently being their rhythm section of choice.

The following musicians—some recording artists in their own right; others star players for a host of others—made their mark on the decade in a variety of ways. Here are their stories:

Eric Clapton

The fabled friendship between George and Slowhand went back as far as Clapton's Yardbird days. During the package tours of 1964 and 1965 (head-lined by the Beatles), the two guitar slingers developed a rapport as human beings within the constraints of their respective careers. But not until the former was contracted to compose the score to *Wonderwall* in 1967 did they first collaborate as musicians.

The obvious question—why wouldn't as successful and creative a guitar-ist as George have simply played any needed parts himself?—is answered in the end by considering the man's egoless nature. Though obviously in the wrong profession for avoiding the limelight (and in the wrong band for dodging adoration), George never particularly possessed the drive to enact every aspect of a project himself, unlike, say, Paul. His solo career was defined as much by his willingness to share the spotlight as it was by his own singular gifts.

In any case, George—recognizing the need to assemble a team of western musicians for *Wonderwall*'s score—drew from the talent pool at hand, augmenting the disintegrating Remo Four with guest Monkee Peter Tork (on banjo); Ringo (as Richie Snare) on drums, and Eric Clapton on lead guitar. (Interestingly, Clapper chose "Eddie Clayton" as his pseudonym for the project. It is not clear whether or not he realized that Ringo's first professional gig ten years earlier had been with the Eddie Clayton Skiffle Group, led by a front youth whose birth name was Eddie Miles.)

Clapton couldn't have chosen a project more at odds with his day job. Cream's reputation was built upon a foundation of extended—some might say "self-indulgent"—soloing as each man in the trio sought to outshine the others. As a guitarist whose reputation was defined by lengthy variations upon blues scales, Clapton found himself cast in a project that was its polar opposite, requiring precision and discipline as George literally composed the film cues clocked to their very second of screen time. But Clapton rose to the challenge, with "Ski-ing" (a track notable for its distorted—and backwards—riffing) a particular standout within an eclectic collection of East-meets-West set pieces.

Not until 1972—two years after its initial issue—was Eric Clapton's emotional paean to unrequited love discovered by the public upon its re-release. The decision not to perform "Me and Mrs. Harrison we got a thing going on" at the Bangladesh event was a wise one.

The project arrived on Clapton's doorstep just as he wearied of Cream's approach to music. They would disband by the end of the year, whereupon Clapton would co-found the more focused ensemble Blind Faith, en route to finding his own voice. Nineteen-sixty-nine would conclude with Clapton well integrated into Delaney & Bonnie's act—a happenstance that greatly influenced the future paths of both Eric and George.

For the former, it put him into proximity with the stellar musicians who would eventually defect from D&B to form the nucleus of Eric's Derek and the Dominos. For George, a ready-made house band for the *All Things Must Pass* sessions was at his disposal. Spearheading the group, Clapton was rewarded with some rather high-profile parts on George's solo debut, among them the lead on the collection's exquisite opener, "I'd Have You Anytime," and the blistering riffing on "Art of Dying." Between takes, prodigious jamming took place, some of it documented on the *Apple Jam* disc. Gracious as always, George turned considerable album time over to Eric for the "I Remember Jeep" guitar showcase.

Following the public display of their musical association at the Concert for Bangladesh in 1971, Clapton, occupied with his own rising solo stardom, did not appear on a George Harrison record again until 1979, where he cameoed on the intro to *George Harrison*'s "Love Comes to Everyone." (Yes, he was credited along with Pattie on George's dire take on "Bye Bye Love" for 1974's *Dark Horse*, but only as a sardonic joke.)

Not until George's 1987 "comeback" album, *Cloud Nine*, did he work again with Eric. Clapton supplied leads on some of the album's more uptempo tracks, notably "Devil's Radio." Their professional collaborative resurgence culminated with Eric basically arm-twisting George into giving touring another shot, supported by his own band as they played a string of dates together in Japan. The 1991 dates made for a fitting climax to a musical and personal pairing that weathered drug abuse, career setbacks, and a singular marital drama.

Billy Preston

While the background to Billy Preston and the Beatles' musical partnership is well chronicled in *Fab Four FAQ*, it's doubtful that anyone present at their January 1969 rooftop set could have envisioned how truly intertwined their fates would become in the years that followed. Having earned his MVP stripes on the *Let It Be* project, Preston was awarded an Apple recording contract. As his "sponsor," George immediately took it upon himself to help the fledgling star gain his footing alongside their other acts.

Recruiting an all-star cast that included Clapton as well as Keith Richards, George produced *That's the Way God Planned It* and its follow-up, *Encouraging Words*. Though Billy's Apple releases never quite caught fire with the public in the way that they deserved, the close working relationship between the two proved invaluable as George began to shape his post-Beatle identity as a man who wore his spirituality on his sleeve.

For Billy, proximity to the ex-Fabs made him well-positioned for building an extraordinary resume. He reciprocated George's generosity by providing

Though his pair of Apple releases failed to click with the public, Billy Preston found enduring success upon moving to A&M, where he racked up a string of top-selling singles during the '70s.

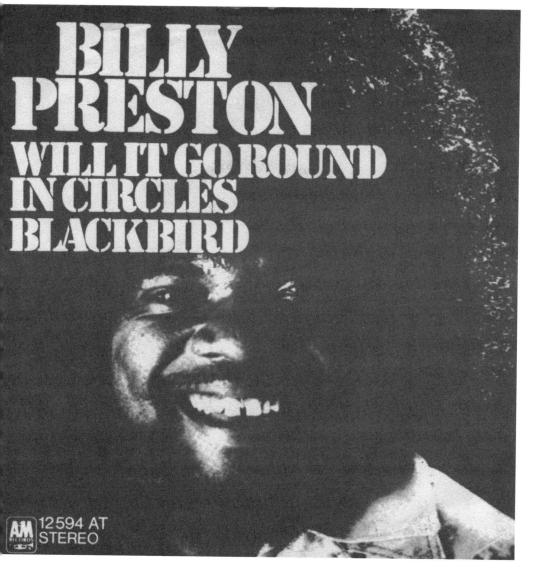

keyboards throughout *All Things Must Pass*. By that time, Billy had himself recorded a pair of songs destined for inclusion on the release: the title track as well as "My Sweet Lord." At around the same time, he sat in with John for "God" on his *Plastic Ono Band* album. (There's an uncredited bit of organ on "Isolation" that might also be Billy.) Earlier that year, he worked alongside both soon-to-be ex-Fabs on John's "Instant Karma."

Despite all the effort put into launching Billy at Apple, not until he moved to A&M in 1971 did he score his first hit single. Though "I Wrote a Simple Song" featured George on guitar, it drew far less attention from DJs than the B-side, a clavinet-driven instrumental. The record was flipped and "Outa-Space" rocketed to #2 on the charts; it also earned a Grammy the following year as Best Instrumental Performance.

In 1973, Billy completed the hat trick by recording with his *third* ex-Beatle, appearing on Ringo's triumphant self-named blockbuster. He contributed to the pop-funk of "Oh My My," while an erstwhile Beatle reunion sparked by the recording of John's "I'm the Greatest" fueled rumors that the threesome were putting together a new band, augmented by Billy and Klaus Voormann. (Preston would never record with Wings, but with Linda around, perhaps he simply wasn't needed.)

The case can be made that when George brought Billy into the *Let It Be* sessions, he probably spared the latter years of toiling away in semi-obscurity. In accepting George's later invite to come on tour with him in 1974, he returned the favor with interest. Given Billy's abundant skills at working an audience (evidenced in the *Concert for Bangladesh* film) in a way that George was never quite able to master, he provided sweet relief from the relentless gravitas that typified "Hari's on tour."

Billy contributed to *Dark Horse* and *Extra Texture* for George as well as *Goodnight Vienna* for Ringo. In between his Fab interactions, he recorded and toured with the Rolling Stones; his organ solo on *Sticky Fingers*' "I Got the Blues" and his duet with Mick Jagger on *Black and Blue*'s "Melody" are highlights. He scored a string of Top 10 hits in his own right, most famously "Will It Go Around in Circles?" and "Nothing from Nothing" during the '70s, as well as penning Joe Cocker's "You Are So Beautiful."

Except for his title role in 1978's execrable Bee Gees / Frampton big-screen debacle, *Sgt. Pepper's Lonely Hearts Club Band*, Billy stayed conspicuously out of the ex-Fabs orbit in the second half of the decade. Not until 1989 when he joined the first All-Starr Band with Ringo did Billy revisit his Beatley past on a grand scale. He thereafter guested occasionally at Beatlefest, where fans (with good reason) regarded him as a Fifth member. In 2002, he turned up at London's Royal Albert Hall to honor his friend one year after his death. At the *Concert for George*, his stirring cover of "Isn't It a Pity" nearly stole the show.

But years of substance abuse problems had begun taking a toll on his health. Just after a celebration in Los Angeles to mark the reissue of *The Concert for Bangladesh* on DVD in 2005, he went into a coma. Before he passed away in June 2006, a set of Beatles covers he'd recorded as a tribute to his benefactors was marketed through his website and the *Fest for Beatles Fans*—a fitting epitaph.

Alan White

The Beatles recording career was bookended by White men on drums. In 1962, it was *Andy* White who occupied the throne for "Love Me Do"—a situation regarded by hapless newcomer Richard Starkey as "Pete Best's revenge." In 1969, as the string had been played out, John Lennon asserted his independence from the group with an ensemble that featured *Alan* White (no relation), a twenty-year-old already possessing a wealth of experience.

Though his professional ascension came well after the Fabs had changed the world, it in some ways paralleled theirs. White actually performed as a member of Billy Fury's backing band—the same Billy Fury that the Silver Beatles had auditioned to back up six years earlier. Additionally, White's career took him through Germany, honing his skills as it had theirs. He followed these gigs with a succession of bands, including Ginger Baker's Airforce and Balls, both of which included Denny Laine. (The two men also participated in a one-off recording project as "The Magic Christians," recording a knock-off cover of Paul's "Come and Get It" purely for the purpose of stealing sales from Badfinger's hit version.) He was in a band called Griffin, managed by former Animal Alan Price, when a call from Apple changed his life.

Having received an invitation to *attend* the floundering Rock and Roll Revival festival in Toronto, John Lennon had accepted an invite to *perform*—and now needed a band. With Klaus Voormann on board, Eric Clapton a "maybe," and Ringo unavailable, the call for a drummer was put out. Supposedly, John himself had seen Griffin performing in a club—a highly unlikely scenario—and had remembered being impressed by the drummer. (More likely, White's presence as a regular visitor to Savile Row left an impression on someone in position to suggest him when the time came; probably Terry Doran.)

In any event, once White got over his belief that someone was pulling his leg and that the offer was in fact legit, the assembly gathered at Heathrow, boarded their plane, and conducted an impromptu in-flight rehearsal—sans drum kit. (White recalled John being adamant about performing "Blue Suede Shoes" with *Carl Perkins'* arrangement—not Elvis's.) Though the musical product amounted to little more than a performance by an above-average garage band, the effect on White's career was incalculable: suddenly he was appearing on an album alongside some of rock's biggest names.

While some accounts incorrectly place White at the studio session for the "Cold Turkey" single not long after (Ringo was on hand), he *did* get the call for the Lyceum's "Cold Turkey" performance in December 1969, alongside George, Keith Moon, Delaney & Bonnie, Jim Gordon, Billy Preston, horn players Bobby Keys and Jim Price, and his Toronto bandmates. By the time this recording was issued in 1972—as a "bonus" disc to the *Some Time in New York City* set—White had joined Yes in time for their *Close to the Edge* tour.

In between came the moments that sealed his immortality in Beatle lore: "Instant Karma" and the *Imagine* sessions. For the first, White was pressed into service on piano as well as kit, adding a layer of keyboard to that being played by John, George, Billy Preston, and Klaus Voormann. The drum sound that gave the song its pulse was arrived at by covering his traps with a towel, providing a dampening that—with Phil Spector's judicious use of reverb—created an unearthly pounding that reverberated within the listener's chest—unheard of on a Beatles record, or anywhere else for that matter.

Proximity to both George and Spector made White a natural for inclusion on *All Things Must Pass*. There, he shared drum chores with both Ringo and Jim Gordon. At this late date, it seems all but impossible to recall with precision exactly who played on what cuts; White believes he played on both the singles "My Sweet Lord" and "What Is Life" as well as "Isn't It a Pity," "I Dig Love," "All Things Must Pass," and "If Not for You."

Following the *Plastic Ono Band* sessions (which featured Ringo) came *Imagine* in the spring of 1971. With the Ringed One too busy to commit, White got the call. He ended up behind the kit on nearly the entire album, with these exceptions: "Jealous Guy" (where he played vibes as Jim Keltner sat in), "It's So Hard" (which featured Jim Gordon), and "I Don't Want to Be a Soldier" (also Keltner). White recalled in an interview years later that John, recognizing the controversial stands the album took both politically and personally, asked his musicians to review the lyrics at the project's onset, lest they sign on to anything they didn't feel completely comfortable with.

These sessions ended White's involvement with the ex-Fabs. George had begun relying upon Jim Keltner, sometimes in tandem with Ringo, while John relocated to New York, also tapping Keltner's services. White stayed in England, eventually joining Yes, which became his musical home off and on for the next several decades. (Though Paul's drummer trouble seemed chronic, White's availability never coincided with those times.)

Jim Gordon

Within the annals of rock lore, few tales of unredeemed tragedy are as staggeringly awful as the story of session drummer Jim Gordon. For a short time in rock's golden age, he had it utterly made, but struggles against the demons inhabiting his head would leave his mother brutally murdered and himself in stir for the remainder of his days.

Gordon's presence on innumerable recordings makes it well-nigh impossible to turn on the radio for any length of time without sampling his work. A complete list of credits would require a book unto itself, but as introduction, here are a few acts he worked with: the Beach Boys, the Monkees (first two albums), Mason Williams ("Classical Gas"), Harry Nilsson ("Jump into the Fire"), Bread ("It Don't Matter to Me"), Joe Cocker (the Mad Dogs and Englishmen tour), Randy Newman (the first three studio albums), Traffic (*Low Spark of High Heeled Boys*; cowrote "Rock & Roll Stew"), Carly Simon (played alongside Klaus Voormann on "You're So Vain"), Gordon Lightfoot ("Sundown"), and Frank Zappa (*Apostrophe*).

Growing restless with the studio work from which he'd made his reputation (as well as above-the-norm session fees), Gordon was seeking a new challenge in 1969. He found it in the eclectic ensemble that was Delaney & Bonnie and Friends. Hearing that the act was about to go on tour in Europe, he made an arrangement with his colleague Jim Keltner to "trade"—he would make the trip, while turning over to Keltner a passel of studio work in exchange. Entering the company of bassist Carl Radle, keyboardist Bobby Whitlock, and, above all, Eric Clapton primed Gordon for his next big career move.

The aforementioned musicians segued from the D&B tour into work with George on *All Things Must Pass*. Early on in the sessions, the group decided on recording an album of their own, under the nomenclature Derek and the Dominos. Feeling burned by the hype surrounding Blind Faith a year before and unsure of the reception awaiting his as-yet-unreleased, self-titled solo debut, Clapton was eager to reclaim some anonymity with his next project. (What was intended as their debut single—"Tell the Truth," backed with "Roll It Over"—was recorded with George and ex-Traffic guitarist Dave Mason sitting in and Phil Spector handling the production. Unfortunately, the band didn't feel that the fast tempo truly represented where they wanted to go and they quickly recalled the release. It was later re-recorded—without George, Phil, or Dave.)

Gordon shared drumming duties on *All Things Must Pass* with Ringo and Alan White. Though his involvement in the Clapton project essentially ruled out any long-term commitment to George, Gordon did manage to squeeze in one more ex-Fab recording date: with John for the bluesy "It's So Hard," cut for *Imagine* in early summer 1971. (Like other D&B personnel, Gordon was also present at the December 1969 London Lyceum performance of "Cold Turkey," billed as part of the Plastic Ono Supergroup alongside drummers Alan White and Keith Moon.) He also played on Ronnie Spector's "Try Some, Buy Some."

All drumming aside, perhaps Gordon's greatest legacy is as composer (actually, co-composer; then girlfriend Rita Coolidge also had a hand in writing the piece, but went uncredited) of the piano-based coda to Eric Clapton's unrequited love paean, "Layla." As originally conceived, the song's opening movement concluded with the incendiary guitar climax powered by the dueling leads of Clapton and Duane Allman. But rather than simply let the recording collapse, someone—accounts differ as to whom—had the bright idea of grafting the piano piece Gordon had been messing around with onto the track. (The tape for this part was sped up slightly, placing the key between C and C-sharp.)

Unbelievably, Derek and the Dominos' album *Layla and Other Assorted Love Songs* went largely unnoticed upon its December 1970 release (around the same time as *Plastic Ono Band* and *All Things Must Pass*). Only when the title track was issued in edited form as a single in 1972 did the release start to get its due, long after the band itself had imploded (and Duane Allman had died in a motorcycle accident).

But while Gordon's career went onward, his slow descent into mental illness began manifesting itself. Complaining of voices in his head nagging at him—principally but not exclusively his mother's—he sought to blot them out through self-medication. The hard-drug-and-alcohol-fueled escapism only intensified his paranoia, until by the end of the '70s, the once-golden boy of L.A. session work was unemployable.

Despite efforts at treatment at various mental health facilities, the sickness reached its climax on the evening of June 3, 1983. Arriving at his seventy-three-year-old mother's apartment, he rang her doorbell; upon her opening the door, the six-foot-three-inch drummer smashed her head repeatedly with a hammer (so that she would not feel what was coming next) before finishing his work with repeated stabs to her chest with a sharpened butcher's knife.

With no one willing to dispute the assessment that Gordon was one very sick man, the state of California has kept him locked up in its Atascadero State Hospital ever since. Now somewhat lucid (due the medication he is kept on), Gordon has expressed his wish to again record with Clapton some day.

Jim Keltner

Perhaps the most lasting reminder of George's tenure with Delaney & Bonnie in late 1969 was the Tulsa-born drummer who, once brought into the ex-Fab's inner circle, would become a mainstay for years. Keltner was an in-demand studio pro by the time he was first tapped for work on Yoko's *Fly* album in 1971. But George had just missed crossing paths with him, as he had drummed on their *Original Delaney & Bonnie: Accept No Substitute* album. (By the time George had joined the D&B tour as they played Denmark and the UK in late 1969, Jim Gordon had taken Keltner's spot, in an amiable trade for studio gigs.)

Keltner got his start sitting in with the T-Bones, a studio band responsible for the Alka Seltzer jingle-turned-hit-single, "No Matter What Shape (Your Stomach's In)" back in 1966. He was later recruited into Gary Lewis's Playboys, briefly occupying the drummer's chair while the group's namesake was otherwise occupied. (This also placed him alongside fellow Oklahoman Leon Russell, another future Harrison satellite.)

Keltner was in London, at work on Gary Wright's first album after leaving Spooky Tooth (entitled *Extraction*), when he first met George in 1970. Both he and John had admired his work with Ry Cooder from afar, and soon the opportunity for him to work with both of them presented itself: on *Imagine* with John, and at the Concert for Bangladesh with George.

The double drumming from Ringo and Keltner at that last occasion sparked a mutual admiration society between the two, as they began pairing up on Ringo's solo albums, first with 1973's *Ringo,* followed by *Goodnight Vienna.* Calling themselves "Thunder" (Ringo) and "Lightnin'" (Keltner), the duo ended the practice in 1976 with *Rotogravure,* but resumed for a few cuts on *Stop and Smell the Roses* in 1981. (On *Ringo the 4th,* the Ringed One double-teamed with session ace Steve Gadd, the drummer most renowned for his signature lick on Paul Simon's "Fifty Ways to Leave Your Lover.")

Meanwhile, work with both John and George kept Keltner busy. In order, he played on *Some Time in New York City, Living in the Material World, Mind Games, Walls and Bridges, Rock 'n' Roll,* and *Extra Texture (Read All About It).* For the latter album, George asked him to overdub a new drum track over Jim Gordon's original performance on "You," the Ronnie Spector castoff first recorded back in 1970. Apparently, George thought that recasting the song's rhythm would enhance its commerciality (an unadorned sampling of the original can be heard on "A Bit More of You").

Keltner was also invited to John's One to One concert at Madison Square Garden in 1972, making him the only musician to play *both* ex-Beatle charity events held at the venue. But his work among giants wasn't limited to

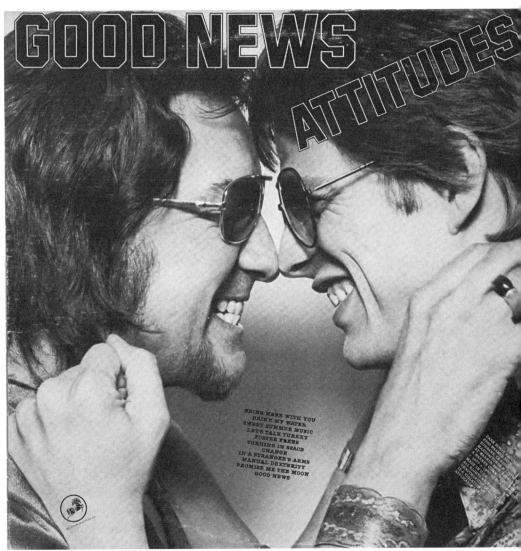

GOOD NEWS ATTITUDES

BEING HERE WITH YOU
DRINK MY WATER
SWEET SUMMER MUSIC
LET'S TALK TURKEY
FOSTER FREES
TURNING IN SPACE
CHANGE
IN A STRANGER'S ARMS
MANUAL DEXTERITY
PROMISE ME THE MOON
GOOD NEWS

Session drummer extraordinaire Jim Keltner (left) was an ex-Fab intimate, appearing on numerous records by George, Ringo, and John. He's shown here with superstar producer David Foster (right) as one half of Attitudes on their 1977 Dark Horse release, *Good News*.

the former Fabs. In 1973, Keltner played on Bob Dylan's classic "Knockin' on Heaven's Door," recorded for the Sam Peckinpah film *Pat Garrett and Billy the Kid*. His work can be heard on Top 40 hits like Bill Withers' "Ain't No Sunshine," Carly Simon's "Anticipation," Arlo Guthrie's "City of New Orleans," Seals and Crofts' "Summer Breeze," Maria Muldaur's "Midnight at the Oasis," Gary Wright's "Dream Weaver," Eric Clapton's "Lay Down Sally," and dozens of other familiar acts.

Perhaps the drummer's first brush with stardom in his own right came as one quarter of Attitudes, the outfit comprised of L.A. session stars signed to Dark Horse. The group released a pair of albums and scored one Hot 100 hit ("Sweet Summer Music") before returning to their day jobs. Though the group folded, the friendship between Keltner and George did not, manifested as it was in a variety of ways.

Early on, George parodied the invitation to join the "Wings Fun Club" advertised on the back of *Red Rose Speedway* with a club of his own: the Jim Keltner Fan Club. On the back of *Living in the Material World*, he advised potential members to send a "stamped undressed elephant" to the address provided. Later, George cast the drummer in the role of judge in his court-room music video of "This Song," the send-up of his "My Sweet Lord" litigation. (Interestingly, though Keltner doesn't appear on the parent album, *Thirty-Three & 1/3*, a song *about* him does: "It's What You Value." In it, George offers his explanation for having paid Keltner with a Mercedes instead of cash for work on the *Dark Horse* tour.)

In 1987, Keltner once again anchored a Harrison album, this time under producer Jeff Lynne for *Cloud Nine*. (It was a digital sampling of Keltner's drumming that became the basis of George's last #1 single, "Got My Mind Set on You.") He also contributed drum overdubs to *Brainwashed*, George's posthumous 2002 release. But between the two releases, Keltner became an honorary member (as "Buster Sidebury") of the Traveling Wilburys, featuring George, Roy Orbison, Bob Dylan, Tom Petty, and Jeff Lynne.

Jesse Ed Davis

It may have been in December 1968—during the filming of the Rolling Stones' *Rock and Roll Circus* television special—that John Lennon first became aware of guitarist Jesse Ed Davis. The then twenty-four-year-old accompanied bluesman Taj Mahal at the event, which—had it aired at the time—would have undoubtedly raised the stellar player's profile immeasurably. But, as it happened, the *right* people witnessed his performance, and that was all that mattered.

Born in Oklahoma (like Jim Keltner and Leon Russell), the nearly full-blooded Kiowa Native American got his professional start with country music star Conway Twitty in the mid-'60s. A stern taskmaster, Twitty was unwilling to stop the van for a bathroom break while traveling to the next gig. Davis saw his employment come to an abrupt end one evening when, having heeded his boss's advice to relieve himself in a jar, tossed the full vessel out the window—without first rolling it down.

Davis then ventured out west to try his luck in the burgeoning rock and roll industry as a session player. Through Leon Russell, he began making a name for himself recording with Gary Lewis before accepting the Taj Mahal gig. The eclectic Mahal gave Davis the opportunity to show off his skills in a variety of idioms: blues, soul, rock, and even a little jazz. After learning all he could from the well-rounded musician, Davis took his leave and settled back into session work.

Between jobs with artists ranging from David Cassidy to Albert King, Davis squeezed in sessions for friends like Leon (for *Leon Russell and the Shelter People*) and ex-Byrd Gene Clark (*White Light*) in 1971. (Perhaps most familiar is his appearance on Jackson Browne's hit "Doctor My Eyes.") It was around the time that George began organizing the Concert for Bangladesh in New York that word began filtering out along the grapevine that Eric Clapton might not be showing up to play after all—leaving George short a guitarist. Taking the bull by the horns, Davis showed up at George's hotel, guitar in hand, and with Leon to vouch for him, landed the gig. (Klaus was deputized to take him aside and bring him up to speed on the set list.)

Though Clapton showed up after all, Davis stayed on and was rewarded for his assistance with the gift of a Harrison original—"Sue Me, Sue You Blues"—for inclusion on his second solo album, *Ululu*, in 1972. (Davis was able to maintain the exclusive for a full year before George recorded it himself for *Living in the Material World*.) Though the two men shared a friendship, George was far less likely to employ Davis than, say, John or Ringo, simply because he never had to look far to find a lead guitarist. That said, he *did* use Jesse quite a bit on *Extra Texture*—for the last time.

For his part, Ringo tended to employ friends like George, Eric, Peter Frampton, or Apple artist Lon Van Eaton for his lead guitar needs. But while the "Lost Weekend" period was in full swing, Davis was along for the ride, participating in sessions for *Goodnight Vienna*, Nilsson's *Pussy Cats*, Keith Moon's *Two Sides of the Moon*, and John's *Walls and Bridges* and *Rock 'n' Roll*.

It was on John's work that Jesse really shone. His guitar style, like George's, seemed to possess less in common with traditional six-string pyrotechnics than it did with an almost human-sounding voice. Given the inherent soulfulness of John's material, it was a fitting match. Davis contributed to only two Lennon albums, but his work stands out as among the finest John ever recorded. One example would be his incredibly fluid lead on "Nobody Loves You When You're Down and Out" from *Walls and Bridges*. Another would be the guitar break on *Rock 'n' Roll*'s "Stand by Me." No matter the setting, Davis's leads projected emotion, underscoring the humanity within the grooves.

Sadly, an all-too-familiar dependency on drugs and drink plagued Davis as the decade wore on. Though still scoring some high-profile gigs, among them Rod Stewart's *Atlantic Crossing* album in 1976 and Neil Diamond's Robbie Robertson–produced *Beautiful Noise*, Davis became increasingly incapacitated by his addictions. By 1980, his A-list projects were a thing of the past, although he was still deriving a great deal of satisfaction from his participation in the Graffiti Band. This outfit paired Davis's music with Indian activist Gary Trudell's poetry.

The final hurrah came unexpectedly in February 1987. The Graffiti Band and Taj Mahal were sharing the bill at Hollywood's Palomino Club. In attendance were George, Bob Dylan, and ex-Creedence Clearwater Revival leader John Fogerty. With little fanfare, the trio joined the ensemble onstage, and for a moment, it was like 1971 all over again. They plowed through an entire set, including "Proud Mary," Dylan's "Watching the River Flow," and, basically, Carl Perkins' greatest hits before ending with a ragged but right medley of "Twist and Shout / La Bamba."

In June the following year, Davis fell over dead at a Venice laundromat. An autopsy revealed an array of narcotics in his system; the gifted but troubled guitarist was forty-three.

Klaus Voormann

When twenty-two-year-old Klaus ventured into a seedy nightclub in Hamburg's Reeperbahn in October 1960 and first cast his eyes upon the Beatles, little could he have dreamed how life-changing the moment truly was. The results of that evening's walk would take him to the heights of rock stardom, from winning a Grammy to performing before tens of thousands at Madison Square Garden to playing on a succession of million-selling singles.

So intertwined were the fates of the Fabs and Klaus that every Beatles book you can pick up will detail his background in some fashion. But we're concerned here with his career during their solo years—a time when, if anything, he was even more in their pocket than before. Their musical association can be traced to the *Live Peace in Toronto* event in September 1969—a seminal date that essentially straddles the Beatles' group and solo eras.

During the months that led up to the formal announcement of the breakup, Klaus functioned as Paul's stand-in on bass, performing on "Cold Turkey," "Instant Karma" (piano as well), and Ringo's "It Don't Come Easy" (recorded before Paul's April 10, 1970 announcement but completed and released the following year). Additionally, he acted as arranger for one tune on *Sentimental Journey*: the Les Paul and Mary Ford hit "I'm a Fool to Care."

In addition, the fact that he was living at Friar Park at the time placed him at hand for virtually every project that George took on as producer.

Klaus's credits as bassist on the ex-Fabs' recordings are well documented. He appeared on (in order): *All Things Must Pass, Plastic Ono Band, Imagine, The Concert for Bangla Desh, Living in the Material World, Ringo, Walls and Bridges, Goodnight Vienna, Rock 'n' Roll, Extra Texture (Read All About It)*, and *Ringo's Rotogravure*—more than any other single musician. Sharp-eyed readers can make a couple of observations: first, he never recorded on a Paul McCartney/Wings album, and second, his involvement with the ex-Fabs' recordings ended after 1976 (though his friendships did not).

Klaus moved to Los Angeles in 1973 and lived there through the end of the '70s. During that time, he participated in hundreds of recordings with some of the biggest artists of the day. As with the others, a complete rundown is well-nigh impossible, but among the highlights are Carly Simon (the opening bass figure to "You're So Vain" prompted her whispered "Son of a gun!"), Randy Newman ("Short People"), Lou Reed (Klaus is credited

George was the only co-owner to show up for the official opening of Apple Studios in September 1971. He's seen here flanked by stalwarts Klaus Voormann (left) and Badfinger's Pete Ham (right). Standing just behind them are Derrek (left) and Lon (right, with beard) Van Eaton.

on *Transformer*, but it is Herbie Flowers playing the signature bass line on "Walk on the Wild Side"), and Harry Nilsson (*eight* albums total).

While he is known to most fans as the artist responsible for both the *Revolver* cover (for which he won a Grammy) and the *Anthology* collage/mural, Klaus's artistic side was in evidence throughout the decade. He designed album artwork for Edwards Hand's *Stranded* (1970), Spooky Tooth's *You Broke My Heart So I Busted Your Jaw* (1973), and Jackie Lomax's *Did You Ever Have That Feeling?* (1974). Even more impressive are the series of pencil sketches—one illustrating each song—that accompanied the *Ringo* album.

Though seldom thought of in his own right musically, Klaus did manage to *compose* exactly two songs. (When one is joined at the hip with an ex-Beatle or two, what's the use?) One tune, "So Far," was recorded by Doris Troy and produced by George. Another, "Salmon Falls," was actually cowritten with Harry Nilsson and released on the *Duit on Mon Dei* album in 1975. Other contributions included the occasional sax part (assisting Jim Horn on *Living in the Material World*'s title cut) and the odd vocal (on *Rock 'n' Roll*'s "Bring It On Home / Send Me Some Lovin'" medley, Klaus can be heard performing the call-and-response with John).

Klaus knew the individual Beatles as well as anyone could have, having shared the Hamburg experience as well as the full flower of Beatlemania and the subsequent years apart. It is probably for this reason that he was well placed to observe when change—not for the better—came over them. At one point, he lamented to *Rolling Stone* that Ringo was not the man he once had been, therein forecasting the problem with alcohol that the drummer would come to terms with in the 1980s.

With George, as close as they were, Klaus found himself witnessing some of his darker moments. Hard partying marred the *Extra Texture* sessions as the musicians found themselves consumed by L.A.'s 1970s drug culture. Recognizing that George was bottoming out from events of the past couple of years, Klaus was nonetheless disgusted by what he saw and minimized his participation accordingly.

By 1979, he had had enough of America and session life. Klaus returned to Germany with his wife to recharge himself, transitioning nicely into a career as a record producer. (He'd had a taste of it in 1973, handling the production for Apple artists Lon and Derek Van Eaton.) In 1980, he made a cameo on the big screen in Robert Altman's *Popeye*, starring Robin Williams and ex-Ringo paramour Shelley Duvall. Scored by Harry Nilsson, Klaus played Von Schnitzel, the conductor.

Since then, he's stayed semi-retired as a musician, though he's been known to strap on the bass occasionally at fan gatherings. He did show up at

Born in Texas (the same day as Keith Richards), session sax man Bobby Keys worked with everyone from Elvis ("Return to Sender") to the Rolling Stones (notably "Brown Sugar"). Like Keltner, Keys was a steady presence alongside three of the ex-Fabs—both recording and partying. This solo single was issued on Ringo's short-lived label in 1975.

the Concert for George memorial celebration in 2002. There, he was slightly put out to find David Bronze (from Clapton's band) playing *his* parts. In 2008, he became the subject of a remarkable documentary, *Voormann and Friends: A Sideman's Journey.*

Nicky Hopkins

In *Fab Four FAQ,* a discussion of this session pianist extraordinaire covered his background and his one-time cameo with the Beatles on "Revolution." But Hopkins' work with the individual ex-Beatles was just beginning. All told, he contributed to five solo albums, most notably to *Imagine.* Additionally, George (with Klaus) returned the favor by playing on Nicky's 1973 solo album, *The Tin Man Was a Dreamer.*

Before he left England for good, John had a recording studio set up in his Tittenhurst Park home. It was here that the *Imagine* sessions took place; rather than revisit the spartan production of his *Plastic Ono Band* debut the year before, Lennon set out to create something with more obvious commercial appeal. To that end, he invited Nicky Hopkins, for whom he'd often expressed admiration, aboard.

Much of the album's work took place before cameras documenting the proceedings. For that reason, viewers of the *Gimme Some Truth* documentary are treated to the sight of John suggesting that Nicky double him on piano for the album's title track, in true Spector style. (As Hopkins doesn't seem to have been filmed much, to see him at all is a treat.)

Hopkins' contributions on the album are many, but standouts include "Crippled Inside" ("Take it, cousin!"); "Jealous Guy," and—on electric piano—"How Do You Sleep?" By the time the two men would work together again (three years later), John had moved to New York. Hopkins' work on the *Walls and Bridges* album is subtler, though no less effective. "Old Dirt Road" is a particular showcase (for Jesse Ed Davis, as well).

Nicky was part of George's handpicked backing for the suitably stripped-down sound he sought for *Living in the Material World*. There, his Floyd Cramer-esque playing provides fine melodic support to George's slide guitar on "Give Me Love." Elsewhere on the mostly somber work, Hopkins shared duties with Gary Wright, another Harrison stalwart.

That same year, George (as "George O'Hara") contributed his usual tasty slide work to Hopkins' second solo effort. Guests included guitarist Chris Spedding as well as Mick Taylor, who perhaps felt honor bound to return the favor of years of Nicky's work on the Rolling Stones' albums. (His Stones credits are incalculable, but for two examples demonstrating his versatility, see "Angie" and *Exile on Main Street*'s "Rip This Joint.") Though Hopkins wasn't much of a singer, *The Tin Man Was a Dreamer* features some fine moments, especially the semi-autobiographical "Waiting for the Band."

The pianist played here and there on a pair of Ringo albums (*Ringo* and *Goodnight Vienna*), but after one final track for George (*Extra Texture*'s "Can't Stop Thinking About You"), his solo Beatles work ceased for over a decade. He did bring some fine touches to a pair of tracks on Badfinger's *Airwaves* in 1979, but health issues left him seriously weakened. His session work continued (as his strength allowed) with artists at a variety of levels (Meat Loaf, Belinda Carlisle, Eddie Money) before he finally recorded with Paul for the first and only time on "That Day Is Done," a collaboration with Elvis Costello recorded in 1989 for his *Flowers in the Dirt* album.

Nicky Hopkins died in 1994 at the age of fifty. At the time of his death, he was working on his autobiography. Undoubtedly, it would have been a fascinating read.

Gary Wright

Spooky Tooth was an English progressive band of whose multiple iterations most Americans remained blissfully unaware. Formed in 1967, the fivesome contained one American, keyboardist Gary Wright. During one of their periodic breakups, Wright found himself pulled into the sessions for *All Things Must Pass*. George and Wright hit it off, and so began a personal and musical kinship.

Not long after his work on George's debut, Wright teamed up with future Foreigner architect Mick Jones and formed a group they called Wonderwheel for the road, though the album they made, *Footprint*, was released in 1971 under Wright's name. George played on several of the tracks (as did Jim Gordon). In November of that year, George used the occasion of an appearance on Dick Cavett's TV talk show to plug Wright's album, sitting in on slide as Wright (playing guitar) and company made their American debut performing "Two-Faced Man."

In 1972, the two traveled to India, staying with Ravi Shankar and sharing a deep interest in spiritual matters. Wright was unique among those whom George worked with, in the sense that he was not yet a household name. Most of George's musical friends were either already-made stars (Clapton, Gary Brooker, et al.), old friends (Billy, Klaus), or studio pros (Keltner, Hopkins). Wright's star was in the ascendant; as he built his own career, he did session work (it's his piano heard on Nilsson's megahit "Without You") while pioneering the integration of synthesizers into analog recordings. After contributing to 1973's *Living in the Material World* and 1975's *Extra Texture*, Wright, following a move from A&M to Warner's (a familiar path) unleashed his monster. It was called *The Dream Weaver*.

George did not participate in its recording, being tied up with his own work, but *The Dream Weaver* did feature a couple of his friends: drummers Keltner and Andy Newmark. The album spawned two hit singles, "Dream Weaver" and "Love Is Alive," both classic rock staples for years to come. Wright toured relentlessly, pioneering that oh-so-'70s stage artifact, the "key-tar," a keyboard worn like a guitar, presumably to enhance the sheer spectacle of the event.

The album played out its string, but follow-up hits were scarce. In the meantime, Wright and George maintained their friendship, pairing up on *Thirty-Three & 1/3* and cowriting "If You Believe" for its follow-up, *George Harrison*. It would be almost another decade before the two worked together again, this time on the Jeff Lynne–produced *Cloud Nine* in 1987. It marked their final recording date together.

In 2008, Wright went on tour again, this time as part of Ringo's Tenth All-Starr Band.

Rick Nielsen and Bun E. Carlos

The idea of John Lennon and a group of possibly his most gifted disciples joining forces proved irresistible to Jack Douglas, who was in position to see what each party could offer the other. Sadly, the musical pairing remains a case of what might have been, despite the recording that actually took place.

Based in Rockford, Illinois, Cheap Trick burst upon the national scene in 1977 with their self-titled debut. Critics were gaga over a band that combined

STOP THIS GAME

Cheap Trick
Cheap Trick

Epic
9071

Power pop rockers Cheap Trick realized a lifelong dream when they recorded 1980's *All Shook Up* with George Martin. Guitarist Rick Nielsen called Martin "the most brilliant producer, musician, and artist I have ever worked with."

the best elements of the Beatles—well-conceived, melodic tunes with superb vocals—with a modern rock sensibility: pounding drums, inventive but edgy guitar, and a unique undercurrent of rumbling bass (courtesy of Tom Petersson's eight- and twelve-string basses). While John had never heard of them, his producer had. Douglas had produced their debut album; in fact, he had helped them get their record deal. In a startling coincidence, just as work was starting up on *Double Fantasy*, Cheap Trick were finishing up their fifth studio album, *All Shook Up*, produced by one George Martin.

At some point in the *Double Fantasy* sessions, Douglas decided that it would indeed be a good idea to shake things up—and he knew exactly who to call: the group's hyperkinetic guitarist, Rick Nielsen, and Bun E. Carlos (née Brad Carlson), Cheap Trick's avuncular but masterful drummer. (In a case of unparalleled bad timing, bassist Peterson had just left the band.) He got hold of Cheap Trick's manager and requested their services on a *John Lennon* recording session. It's doubtful that anything on earth could have stopped them from arriving at the Hit Factory at warp speed, gear in tow. (Rick even received permission from his wife, who had just given birth to their son, Dax, to attend the session.) The two were tasked with contributing to backings for the dark "I'm Losing You," as well as Yoko's "I'm Moving On."

Laying down a ferocious take of John's song, the duo recalled nothing so much as the Plastic Ono Band sound of a decade before. The comparison did not escape Lennon himself, who told Carlos that he wished the guitarist had been around when he cut "Cold Turkey." "Clapton choked on that one," John opined. Douglas saw, as he had predicted, a definite chemistry between the artists. Of Rick, the producer observed, "That's [John's] kind of madman." For his part, Nielsen told John that as unknowns at the time of their 1977 recording debut, they had felt that they had nothing to lose by requesting his services as their producer. They wrote him a letter to that effect, one that he never saw. John expressed his regrets at missing out, telling Rick and Bun E. that he would have loved to have taken the job.

With so much love going around, the enduring mystery all these years has been: why didn't their work appear on *Double Fantasy*? Theories abound: some claim that Yoko told the Cheap Tricksters to take a hike, believing them to be a couple of nobodies who were trying to ride John's coattails to advance their career; according to another notion, Ken Adamany, Cheap Trick's manager, made some unreasonable financial demands that killed the deal. Yet another asserts that the tracks they cut were simply too raw to fit alongside the more polished recordings already in the can.

Perhaps the most compelling reason was one only recently reported. The *Double Fantasy* sessions were intended to be kept secret, with all kinds of subterfuge employed to keep the rock press off John and Yoko's trail until they were ready to announce things in their own way. When John saw a report of the work in progress in *Rolling Stone*'s "Random Notes," he was allegedly livid at the word getting out prematurely and blamed Cheap Trick's people. The band were never asked back, and the cuts found on the album were re-recorded with Cheap Trick's version playing in the musicians' headphones. Rick's riffs and Bun E.'s groove were replicated, in more polished form, for the finished album.

Whatever the truth, the Lennon / Cheap Trick axis represented a lost opportunity. Perhaps if John Lennon had lived, the breach would have been smoothed over and future collaborations would have taken place. *Their* version of "I'm Losing You" was eventually issued in 1998 on the *John Lennon Anthology* box set. Because of the mystique surrounding the never-released but often-discussed track, this version of the song was actually used as a promotional tool, with a new video produced featuring Nielsen, Carlos, and Levin recreating their performances—along with animated line drawings of John. (Apparently, a more finished version of their recording, with an additional overdub of guitar and keyboard, remains in the can. It aired on the *Lost Lennon Tapes* radio show and has been subsequently bootlegged).

Cheap Trick remain fans. As their career trajectory moved onward and upward, they recorded their own tributes, including "Day Tripper," "Magical Mystery Tour," and, most fittingly, "Cold Turkey." In 2007, they hosted a fortieth anniversary of the *Sgt. Pepper* album event at the Hollywood Bowl, acting as house band for a star-studded celebration (since released as a CD and DVD), reprising the event a year later.

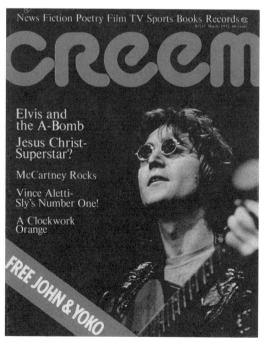

Shown here at the John Sinclair benefit in December 1971, Lennon was becoming increasingly involved with radical chic politics, a development noted warily by rock journalists. Nineteen-seventy-two saw his complete immersion, much to the detriment of his art.

7

What's It All to You?

T he year began on a positive note, with George again enjoying chart success with a boxed set, this time *The Concert for Bangla Desh.* Though bearing a rather hefty price tag—all for the cause, mind you—the release still made it to #2 on the American album charts, blocked only by Don McLean's *American Pie.* Also good news was the meeting over dinner between John and Yoko and Paul and Linda in New York. Though their ongoing row reached a climax in November with a back-and-forth issued in the pages of England's *Melody Maker* (see chapter 29 for details), the two former partners now agreed to stop "slagging off" each other in the press.

Career-wise, both parties had their hands full. Wings installed the final piece of the puzzle with the recruitment of veteran blues-rock guitarist Henry McCullough, late of Joe Cocker's Grease Band. As the self-described "only Irishman to play at Woodstock," McCullough brought superb improvisational and multi-instrumental abilities to the group. (On the down side, at least as far as his Wings career was concerned: he knew his value in the marketplace and was not prepared to be marginalized.) The January 30 shooting deaths of fourteen civilians by British soldiers in Derry, Northern Ireland, spurred the release of the group's first single, the atypically political (for Paul) song, "Give Ireland Back to the Irish."

No less an activist was John. In December, he'd played the Free John Sinclair benefit in Ann Arbor, Michigan, just days before taping a volatile exchange with audience members on *The David Frost Show* (it would air in January). Being an artist who created in reaction to his surroundings, John's new material was exclusively political in nature, a reflection of his immersion in the American agitprop community. Seeing his new role as an observer, reporting on events in song, John hoped to win hearts and minds by trading his Beatle cachet for access to America's heartland. To that end, he and Yoko booked a week of hosting the ultra-mainstream *Mike Douglas Show* in February. It was a unique moment in television history, one that combined music with conceptual art and a forum for counterculture figures to address housewives directly. For whatever might be said about the experiment's lasting effects, it certainly drew heavy ratings for the show.

Their musical performances that week marked the public debut of John's collaboration with New York City activist-rockers Elephant's Memory. Thoroughly steeped in a classic rock and roll vocabulary, their funky sound, distinguished by the sax of bandleader Stan Bronstein, proved a good fit for Lennon's immediate needs, if not over the long haul. The band had already scored one national hit (1969's "Mongoose") when, between backup gigs on albums released by John and Yoko together and separately over the next year—as well as the One to One benefit and an appearance on the *Jerry Lewis Labor Day Telethon*—they released an eponymous LP for Apple.

Around the same time John was on television rubbing elbows with Chuck Berry and Bobby Seale, Paul was launching his first concert tour in over five years. With little more than a road map and a van full of gear, Wings began hitting the road in England, rolling up at universities and volunteering to play (for a modest fee). It was an audacious move for someone of his stature, but a notion that he'd long entertained for his last band. Wings were attempting to jell as a band naturally through much live work, presumably away from the full scrutiny of the rock press. As a formula for laying the groundwork for bigger things, it seemed to work.

George had spent the entire second half of 1971 enmeshed one way or another in the cause of the Bangladesh refugees. After a serious auto accident in February (which left Pattie with a concussion), his musical output was curtailed, at least as far as his own releases were concerned. While penning material for Cilla Black, he also contributed to recordings by Harry Nilsson, Dave Bromberg, Jesse Ed Davis, and Apple discoveries Lon and Derrek Van Eaton. The latter's "Sweet Music" made for a fine Harrisonian-sounding single that spring, although, despite George's efforts to promote the song, it failed to find much airplay.

Far more successful was his contribution to Ringo's second rock single, "Back Off Boogaloo." Inspired by proximity to Marc Bolan, who in that period represented something of Beatlemania's second coming, the song was produced by George and featured some great slide guitar. The tune was seen by some as a slap at Paul, a charge the drummer denied. This time around, few doubted that it was Ringo's own work, therefore making it all the more satisfying when the single hit #9 in the American charts, while peaking at #2 in Britain, blocked from the top position by, of all things, the Royal Scots Dragoon Guards' recording of "Amazing Grace." At this point, busied with film commitments on his T. Rex documentary *Born to Boogie*, followed closely by a key supporting role in *That'll Be the Day*, Ringo limited his time spent behind the kit to helping out friends like Nilsson and the Van Eatons.

Of the four ex-Beatles, only one put out an album that year: John (with Yoko) issued *Some Time in New York City*. Presented in mock *New York Times* packaging, the collection offered commentary on a host of topical concerns

A plum role in *That'll Be the Day* gave Ringo the opportunity to revisit his youth while stretching his wings as an actor.

ranging from women's liberation to the troubles in Northern Ireland. While his commitment to these causes seemed genuine enough at the time, the record's abysmal reviews and commercial failure alienated much of his audience, causing Lennon to later disown the release, Still, releasing such provocative music took guts, especially in the overheated political climate of the time. One incurred the wrath of the Nixon administration at one's own peril, as the Lennons learned that year.

Back in February, a secret memo sent by a Nixon supporter in the Senate strongly urged that the "problem" of a politically active ex-Beatle potentially influencing the presidential election could be defused by simply attacking his vulnerability—in this case, a drug conviction that could be used as an excuse to force him from the country. Thus the wheels were set in motion for what became a years-long effort to throw the couple out. John soon learned the price of speaking out when he discovered that his phone was tapped and that he was under constant surveillance. Even Nixon's re-election in November did not end the campaign to deport him. The pressure brought to bear would profoundly impact his life, his marriage, and his art.

Meanwhile, Apple continued to generate product as though actually attempting to compete with other labels. In addition to Badfinger's recent hits and the Van Eaton brothers' miss, other acts tended to fall into the oddity category, from the western swing of the Sundown Playboys to the street poetry of New York City's David Peel. One of the more interesting signings was Chris Hodge, who scored a near-hit that spring with "We're On Our Way," a glam-like extraterrestrial tale. (Nationally, it peaked at #44, but in some markets—Chicago, for instance—it made the Top 20.) It has been asserted by some that Yoko Ono had a hand in bringing Hodge to Apple, based upon the single being produced by one Tony Cox. Yoko's ex was in fact on the run that year, defying a court order to turn over custody of Kyoko to the Lennon's. That he would take a time-out from abducting their daughter to lend a hand to Hodges, a fledgling second-tier T. Rex act on his ex-wife's current husband's label, staggers the imagination. (The Tony Cox in question was actually the producer of U.K. act Caravan, among others.)

Of similar novelty caliber was the second single from Wings, issued off the heels of "Give Ireland Back to the Irish," which had been banned by the BBC. (Anticipating such a response, Macca cannily issued the single with an instrumental version on the B-side.) While a pleasant enough slice of pop, the puerile "Mary Had a Little Lamb" was read by many—then as now—as being a deliberate gesture of contempt for the powers that be: "Ban this!" But unwittingly, it underscored the schizoid nature of Wings. What kind of band were they? The glorified garage band hitting the U.K. university circuit? The bubblegum lightweights who had produced this record? The answer proved elusive, as Paul's solo voice had yet to be determined with any certainty.

On tour in Sweden that August, the McCartneys experienced the first in a series of events that became almost routine: they (along with Denny Laine) were arrested for possession of marijuana. Police had intercepted what had been a daily mailing of pot and hash to them as they traveled. (They pleaded guilty and got off with a $2,000 fine.) While the event and a subsequent raid later that year after pot was found growing at their farm in Scotland certainly helped to cultivate an outlaw image, Paul still found himself on the receiving end of much scorn from the rock press, mostly over musical matters. He would eventually disarm them as the quality of his releases rose, beginning with a single released by Wings in December: "Hi Hi Hi." Earning a second BBC ban with the tune (as well as underscoring his drug arrests) probably did his career more good than harm.

Nineteen-seventy-two saw the first rumblings of what would become a nostalgia craze the following year as no fewer than three pop idols from an earlier era scored chart hits. Elvis released his final rock and roll single, "Burning Love" that fall, managing to reach #2. Chuck Berry, hot off his appearance with John on *The Mike Douglas Show* earlier that year, actually reached #1 in October with undoubtedly the least worthy single he ever issued, the juvenile "My Ding-a-ling."

Rick Nelson landed a Top 10 single with the autobiographical "Garden Party," his telling of an October 1971 Madison Square Garden rock and roll revival concert in which he performed. After his set ended amidst a barrage of booing (he mistakenly thought it was aimed at him for updating his material; in fact, it was the crowd responding to some heavy-handed actions by security), he described the event in song. John and Yoko were in attendance and were referenced in the lyrics ("Yoko brought her walrus . . ."), as was George, more obscurely ("Mr. Hughes hid in Dylan's shoes. . . ." Hughes was a pseudonym George used while traveling and not Howard Hughes, as is commonly believed.)

Other references to the ex-Fabs issued on vinyl that year were less respectful. The satirical iconoclasts at the *National Lampoon* saw the earnest doings of John and George in particular as ripe for parody. In 1972, the ensemble, which featured Christopher Guest (known better in later years as Spinal Tap's "Nigel Tufnel") and Tony Hendra (seen in *This Is Spinal Tap* as their manager, Ian Faith) issued an album entitled *Radio Dinner*. To Fab followers, the release is noteworthy for several wicked spoofs on the former Beatles.

George got off relatively easy; a response to the Bangladesh benefit came in the form of "Concert *in* Bangla Desh" (emphasis added). On it, a pair of Bangladeshi stand-up comics (Hendra and Guest) entertained a crowd of starving refugees as part of an effort to collect a bowl of rice for George, in order for him to mount a proper hunger strike. (Their hackneyed material was punctuated throughout by a tabla roll instead of the usual rimshot.) Paul's newfound politicization was savaged with a sketch depicting an Irishman in a bar singing "Give Ireland Back to the Irish." The performance quickly ended in a blaze of gunfire.

But the most brutal take immediately followed. Lennon was hoisted on his own petard with Hendra's devastating "Magical Misery Tour" (a.k.a. "Genius Is Pain"). Taking John's own words from the *Lennon Remembers* interview, Hendra (as the artist himself) set them over a Plastic Ono Band–sounding piece of music, proclaiming his own brilliance while asserting his victimhood at the hands of everyone from his Aunt Mimi to his ex-bandmates to the public. After whipping himself into a screaming frenzy by the track's conclusion, à la "Mother," singer Melissa Manchester—as Yoko—intoned, "The dream is over." What the track underscored was the fine line between frank self-awareness and self-parody. It was a line that Lennon—as well as the others—skirted all too frequently.

8

Just Wishing for Movie Stardom

The Ex-Fabs on Film

By the time filming wrapped on the Beatles' first motion picture, it was evident to the studio professionals all around them that their drummer, the newest member of the group, possessed something special. *Help!*, their cinematic follow-up, built a plot line around Ringo, as did *Magical Mystery Tour* (to the extent that there *was* a plot).

This indescribable *something* projected well onto the screen, and before the band's demise, Ringo managed to score a pair of high-profile roles in non-Beatle films, 1968's *Candy* and 1970's *The Magic Christian* (coincidentially both based on Terry Southern novels). With plenty of free time on his hands following the Beatles' dissolution, he went on to expand his cinematic palette to include behind-the-camera work (literally, in the case of *Born to Boogie*, where he served as cameraman as well as director) while tackling meatier roles (*Blindman*, *That'll Be the Day*).

His fellow ex-Beatles were active in film as well, though not to the point of taking scripted roles. With several experimental art films under his belt by the time of the split, John assembled what amounted to a feature-length music video to promote *Imagine*. Not to be outdone, George, in a foreshadowing of his later role as film exec with HandMade Films, debuted as producer with 1974's *Little Malcolm*.

Of the four, Paul showed the least interest in putting something ambitious on film, at least during the '70s. (His reluctance would prove well placed, as evidenced by 1984's *Give My Regards to Broad Street*.) McCartney's forays into filmmaking were limited to documenting himself, both in the studio (*One Hand Clapping*—unreleased), onstage (*Rockshow*), and by fulfilling a commission to pen an original song (1973's "Live and Let Die").

Overall, while none of the ex-Fabs was in much peril of scoring any Oscars for acting, (Paul was nominated for—but did not win—Best Original Song in 1974 for his James Bond theme and again in 2002 for the title song to *Vanilla Sky*), most everything they touched is, at minimum, entertaining; in Ringo's case, at least one film merits viewing by even non-Beatle fans.

Imagine (1971)

When John and Yoko first got together, Ms. Ono was often referred to in the press as an "actress." This shorthand identification, in place of the far more accurate "conceptual artist," likely originated from her starring role in a 1965 exploitation film entitled *Satan's Bed*, wherein she played Ito, the naïve girlfriend of a drug dealer. Around the same time John was jetting around the world trying to elude a gang of Eastern thugs out to claim his drummer's gaudy hand jewelry (in *Help!* of course), his future wife was being brutalized graphically and repeatedly by some no-goodniks. It was an auspicious start to a decade that, for the most part, would end with the couple's every move being caught on film. Though the paparazzi were responsible for much of this, Yoko herself would spend even more time behind the camera creating a series of shorts that served as a natural visual extension of her art.

Her most notorious cinematic achievement was the one commonly called "Bottoms" (in fact a remake of an earlier effort titled *No. 4*), first screened in 1967 and consisting of 365 celebrity rear ends, offered as a statement advocating "peace" (or "piece," as the case may be, all concepts being realized in the mind of the beholder). Once she and John got together and began viewing their lives as their art, it wasn't long before Lennon became drawn into her world, producing films himself. The results of their collaborations ranged from completely self-indulgent (*Smile, Self-Portrait*) to actual thematic statements (*Rape, Ten for Two*).

While most of their celluloid output is only of interest to hardcores, the seventy-minute film produced in conjunction with the release of the *Imagine* and *Fly* albums is the most familiar. Not to be confused with either the 1988 David Wolper–produced documentary *Imagine: John Lennon* or the making-of-the-album documentary *Gimme Some Truth, Imagine* was a series of videos accompanying each track from John's album and three from Yoko's. Everything assembled for this film falls into the classification of "concept video," rather than anything resembling a performance clip, except for "Imagine" itself.

The title song is easily the best-known sequence. In an atmospheric opening, John and Yoko are seen walking up the fog-shrouded driveway amidst the greenery at Tittenhurst Park. The couple reach the doorway and pause a moment before disappearing inside, to reappear in what Jack Bruce might call a "white room," with John at his similarly pigmented piano. There, sporting amber lenses and shoulder pads, he lip-synchs "Imagine" into the

ONE SHOWING - SATURDAY MIDNIGHT
FEBRUARY 12th - ADMISSION $1.50

FILMS BY JOHN LENNON & YOKO ONO
A Genesis Presentation. Produced by JOKO Film Productions.

Well before meeting John, Yoko was an established art-house filmmaker while John dabbled on an amateur level. By the time of this 1972 festival, Yoko facetiously mused that his cinematic talents were threatening to outshine her own.

camera as Yoko throws open the shades, lighting the room. It's a simple but elegant presentation, suitably minimalist for the song.

Shooting took place both at the Tittenhurst Park estate and in New York City. Much of what comprised the remainder of the film was later sliced and diced for projects assembled posthumously, notably 1984's "Nobody Told Me" video. Most fans have seen sequences depicting John with a stethoscope listening to various inanimate objects around New York City and a series where Yoko is escorted into a posh hotel room by various celebs, including actors Fred Astaire and Jack Palance, talk show host Dick Cavett, and George Harrison; these originated with the video accompanying "I Don't Wanna Be a Soldier." "Crippled Inside" depicted John being photographed for the *Imagine* label in front of his home, while the original "Jealous Guy" clip contained the sequence of him and Yoko entering a boat and rowing across a small lake to an island.

The series of short films is visually intriguing, if perhaps a little tiresome after a while, one's enjoyment being predicated on how fascinating one finds the couple. (Reviews at the time were largely scathing, especially in England, where critic Robert Brinton noted that a *Tom and Jerry* cartoon contained more laughs while representing a better investment of one's time.) The production was directed by actor/photographer/mime Dan Richter, who'd shot the cover to the *Plastic Ono Band* LP. (He had also played the lead ape-man—"Moonwatcher"—in the "Dawn of Man" sequence of Stanley Kubrick's *2001: A Space Odyssey*.) *Imagine* aired on American television on December 23, 1972—well past the release of the records it was tied to. (Interestingly, the One to One concert had broadcast just over a week before as part of ABC's *In Concert* series.) This was the only time it was screened on the air intact, as it was trimmed down afterward to under an hour for home video release.

200 Motels (1971)

In late 1970, Frank Zappa and the Mothers of Invention arrived in London, fixing to begin creating a cinematic extension of their recorded work. Conceived as an attempt to illustrate—both graphically and figuratively— how touring could make a rock band crazy, *200 Motels* was certainly ambitious. Along with the inclusion of a number of well-known personae, plans called for a sequence to be filmed at the Albert Hall with London's Royal Philharmonic Orchestra augmenting the Mothers on a composition titled "Penis Dimension." But the production was troubled from the start, and what resulted was a hodgepodge culled from the one-third of the full script that actually ended up filmed.

The entire story of what can be seen as Frank Zappa's *Magical Mystery Tour* (i.e., a highly touted, independently produced rock film starring Ringo that demonstrated the perils of working in medium other than the one you're good at) has become the stuff of rock lore, with Zappa himself eventually producing a documentary called *The True Story of 200 Motels*. For our purposes, here's all you need to know: Zappa was given a modest budget on the strength of an outline and some musical sketches to produce a "life on the road" picture, showcasing his band while offering what could be described as multiple realities within a given circumstance. It gives away no secrets to say that Zappa was an artist with little patience for audiences that couldn't keep up; therefore, the inside jokes and self-referential humor throughout proved a delight to his fans while alienating or baffling just about anyone else, including those working on the project.

One early casualty was bass player Jeff Simmons, whose frustration with his key but incomprehensible role led him to walk out on the eve of the shoot. No problem: ex-Turtles bassist Jim Pons, suggested by singers Howard Kaylan and Mark Vollman (who'd been with the Mothers since their own band's breakup), fulfilled musical duties, while Simmons' speaking parts were to be handled by Wilfrid Brambell—Paul's grandfather from *A Hard Day's Night*. Though it might have been interesting to see Brambell and Starkey reunited on screen, after only a few days the fifty-eight-year-old professional had had his fill of the profanity and chaos and stormed off the set in a rage. Zappa thereupon declared that the next person who walked in the door would get the role. That person happened to be Martin Lickert, Ringo's chauffeur, just returned with some tissues for his employer's cold. ("And he plays bass," Ringo told Frank.)

Keith Moon was cast just as randomly. Overhearing the drummer and Pete Townshend in conversation at London's Speakeasy Club, Zappa invited them both into the project. (Only Moon turned up at the appointed time and place—he was cast as a harp-playing nun.) As for Ringo, he was grateful for a diversion from Paul McCartney's ongoing lawsuit. He accepted the plum role of "Larry the Dwarf"—a Zappa look-alike who fulfilled the latter's speaking parts as the real Frank was seen performing and conducting. Ringo first appears as Larry when he is dropped onto the set (on wires) and explains to the band's manager (played by veteran actor Theodore Bikel) that Zappa "wants me to fuck the girl with the harp" (played by Moon). One immediately sees Brambell's point: *A Hard Day's Night* this was not.

Hired to direct was filmmaker Tony Palmer, who had produced a BBC documentary, *All My Loving*, featuring Zappa *and* the Beatles as well as many other stars of the day. The film attempted to contextualize contemporary (1968) rock music with violence in the world; later Palmer—who seemed to have a predilection for titling his projects after Beatles songs beginning with the word "All"—would produce a mammoth TV miniseries on the history of pop music, *All You Need Is Love*. But from the start of *200 Motels*, trouble brewed between Palmer and Zappa, who insisted on directing himself. A compromise was struck, with Zappa handling the "characterizations" and Palmer the "visuals."

Utilizing an inexpensive method that Palmer had employed on his earlier Cream concert film, *200 Motels* was shot on videotape and only transferred to more expensive film stock after it had been edited and effects added; later, to recoup cost overruns, the studio ordered videotaped out-takes wiped and resold, forever destroying any lingering artifacts of interest. The entire production was set-bound, actually enhancing the overall claustrophobic vision. (The group was denied the use of the Albert Hall after a representative of said venue saw the lyrical content of Zappa's proposed performance and turned them down.) With the project careening out of control, Palmer demanded to have his name removed from the credits, but agreed to reinstate it after he was talked into salvaging the footage.

Though Ringo's role is key in the film, it is hardly a full-blown starring vehicle. Mostly, the film traces Zappa's obsession with groupies ("Every musician wants to find some pussy," Larry deadpans at one point) and the ignorance of small-town Americans, as compared with the relative worldliness of traveling rock musicians. Any non-Zappa fans tempted to check out the film should be aware that unless one has limitless patience for the artist's puerile preoccupations, *200 Motels* is hard going. Though Zappa was notoriously anti-drug, the film has a psychedelic, stream-of-consciousness feel, making it a challenge for all but the most determined viewers—or cultural historians—to sit through.

Blindman (1972)

Ringo had long been an aficionado of all things western, including the cinematic genre. Through a deal brokered by Allen Klein, he was at last able to realize a goal when he was invited by producer Saul Swimmer to star in a western (albeit a "spaghetti" western, so-called for its Italian production team and general B-level aesthetics). Beginning in 1966, Klein had co-produced a series of artless Sergio Leone–type knockoffs featuring American expat Tony Anthony (born Ralph Pettito in West Virginia) as a low-rent Clint Eastwood. Anthony and Swimmer had co-scripted a pair of films in the early '60s; now the confluence of Swimmer, Anthony, Klein, Apple's money, and Ringo's desire to spread his wings as an actor resulted in one of the Ringed One's weightier cinematic projects, the phenomenally un-PC *Blindman*.

To nearly anyone who is not a spaghetti western fan, the film remains an unwatchable time-waster, but aficionados appreciated the film for what it was. While perhaps not up to the artistic level of Sergio Leone's work with Clint Eastwood, *Blindman* boasted a big budget; a fine, effective score by Stelvio Cipriani; first-rate widescreen cinematography; a wry (if violent and sexist) script; and a compelling centerpiece in the form of Anthony's title

Though hardly the lead character in Ferdinando Baldi's *Blindman,* Ringo still offered the spaghetti western certain promotional value.

character. Loosely based on Japan's *Zatoichi* series (which featured a blind swordsman), *Blindman* told the tale of a loner in the Old West who, though bereft of sight, was nonetheless a crack shot. Drifting along in a hostile world, he must rely on his wits and his acutely developed remaining senses to survive; when the opportunity of a lifetime presents itself for a $50,000 payday, Blindman will stop at nothing to collect his due.

His mission is to deliver fifty mail-order brides to some miners in the town of Lost Creek, Texas. When he's double-crossed and a man named Domingo kidnaps the women, Blindman has to overcome any and all obstacles to track them down. Ringo played Candy, Domingo's equally unscrupulous brother. It is said that the best compliment one can give an actor is forgetting his well-known persona completely to buy into a characterization. Such is the case here; Ringo drops his native speaking voice and normal movement patterns to inhabit the amoral Candy in totality. Once one gets past the novelty of seeing Ringo astride a horse, one can easily absorb his performance in a role custom-tailored for him. (Though Domingo, played by Lloyd Batista, occupied more screen time, it was the ex-Fab who received second billing.)

Without spoiling too much of the plot, it can be said that Fab watchers saw a Ringo unlike any other they'd seen on screen before. He was shown, unremarkably for the genre, as brutal, remorseless, and mad, bereft of any of the qualities normally associated with Richie Snare, which was exactly the point. Wishing to depart from the sort of comic relief roles he'd been known for, he found the work exhilarating. "It was the first time that I ever saw what actors could get off on . . . the whole thing takes over your body, and you just get elated with it." Also worth watching, for Beatle spotters, are the cameos in the opening scene, featuring Allen Klein and Mal Evans (the latter of whom was becoming known for such vignettes) as a pair of baddies going up against the title character.

The subsequent success of Ringo's recording career sidetracked what was evidenced here as a most promising film career as a character actor. As John had often noted, there was some sort of elusive star quality projected by the Beatles' drummer that was capable of shining through, no matter what the setting. Ringo would tackle one more substantial film role the following year (in *That'll Be the Day*) before reverting to the sort of comic bit parts (excepting *Caveman*, which was a lead role) that he was usually associated with, having grown weary of the hurry-up-and-wait nature of filmmaking that accompanied a more serious commitment.

For contemporary audiences, *Blindman* remains very much a film of its time, with an anti-authority subtext and much female nudity; Ringo's presence is simply a bonus. Some reviews at the time were scathing (as was usually the case with Tony Anthony's work —undeservedly so), Roger Ebert's, for example. The man who penned the screenplay for *Beyond the Valley of the Dolls* called *Blindman* "a greasy bill of goods," giving it one and a half stars. But to fans of the genre, the film holds up quite well and is definitely worth a look, if one can find a print of it. In English, that is.

The Concert for Bangladesh (1972)

Nowadays, when a major charitable event is being planned to fund-raise for a particular cause, the cinematic documentation intended to keep the cash flowing is well plotted out. Professional film crews are contracted, all logistics are worked out in advance, and all contingencies are planned for. This luxury was not afforded George and the team that worked to put everything in place for his Madison Square Garden concert to benefit the suffering refugees of Bangladesh.

With everything being organized on the fly, George found himself having to work with what was at hand and not necessarily what he might have desired. In this case, that meant booking a crew more accustomed to filming sporting events at the Garden than they were to working with performers. As director Saul Swimmer would later explain, there was no such thing as camera synchronization; for such a massive undertaking to operate under an "every man for himself" system made for nightmares after the fact when the whole thing had to be put together.

As one example, normally cameras shooting a fifteen-minute magazine of film are covered before the point of running out by another camera so that the continuity is maintained. At the Bangladesh concert, so chaotic were the conditions that apparently all the cameras began filming at the same time and therefore ran out of film at the same time, causing gaps in some performances. Ultimately, this was fixed by splicing together performances from the afternoon and evening shows to create a hybrid whole.

Other issues were less easily remedied. At least one camera shot the entire concert out of focus. Another cameraman, so intent on what he was looking at on the stage, failed to notice unsightly cables hanging in front of the lens, marring otherwise good footage. One can get a sense of the limitations watching the film today by observing what is and what isn't seen. For example, Ringo's performance of "It Don't Come Easy" suffers because of a camera angle that for most of the first minute captures more of his microphone boom than his face. On the plus side, the film overall presented more extended shots of the performers than the now-popular quick-cutting editing style would allow today.

In the end, the technical issues were resolved sufficiently to produce a worthy cinematic treatment of a singular evening in rock history. Millions

When two legends meet: this iconic shot capturing George and Bob Dylan during rehearsals for the landmark benefit graced many a dorm room wall in the '70s.

saw the film upon its March 1972 release, and, while it may not have conveyed the same electricity that attendees felt, it also provided an up-close look at something rare: an ensemble of artists coming together in support of something bigger than themselves.

Loads of personality came through, such as when Ravi Shankar took the stage. The hot lights wreaked havoc on the delicate Indian instruments, and so before commencing their set, Shankar and company took a minute or so to re-tune. As they finished, the crowd erupted in spontaneous enthusiastic applause at the apparent "overture" to Ravi's set. Rather than humiliate them for their ignorance, Ravi merely deadpanned, "If you enjoyed the tuning up so much, we hope you enjoy the playing even more."

The audience was genuinely moved at the sight of two Beatles on stage again. Once the initial wave of emotion swept over them, it was renewed when the opening notes of "It Don't Come Easy" wafted into the arena. As a song that many likely never expected to see performed live began, Ringo too was caught up in the moment, visibly touched by the response. He had never expected to have to sing the song again after having laid down his vocal in the studio, but for security's sake, he made sure he had the lyrics with him, out of sight below his toms. Unfortunately, the stage lighting and accompanying shadows rendered them invisible when the moment of truth arrived. He therefore, in a blend of forgetfulness and nerves, mumbled his way through the next three minutes, uttering slurred vocalisms where the actual lyrics eluded him.

George too made sure he was prepared to sing the newly minted "Bangla-Desh," the show ender. (He might have done himself a favor if he'd done the same for "Something," which was marred by his forgetting the opening to the second verse; his amusement at his own confusion is obvious in the film.) Worth noting is his evident plan to escape the stage without having to actually take a bow. Once he'd finished all his required singing on the song, and while the band was cooking behind him in double time, he slipped off his Strat, gave a two-handed wave to the audience, and vanished into the shadows. Before anyone had quite realized what he'd done, he was gone.

Given the inherent challenges that producing such a worthy document of the show had presented, the fact that it stands up as well as it does in the recent DVD remaster is a minor miracle.

Born to Boogie (1972)

Even in the absence of any compelling recording or acting duties, Ringo seemed to have little trouble staying busy. With one foot firmly planted in the film industry and the other in music, he was given the opportunity to satisfy both urges without having to actually learn lines or write a song. It came in the form of Marc Bolan, whose musical career had taken some twists and turns before a succession of reinventions had landed him atop the pop world—or at least the English iteration of it. "T. Rextasy," as the British rock journals of the day would have it, represented the second coming of Beatlemania, wherein hysterical girls propelled a series of singles to the top of the U.K. charts.

Starr and Bolan enjoyed an acquaintance going back at least as far as the start-up of Apple. The audaciously self-important but charming twenty-three-year-old amused the drummer (crowed he: "We've done in a year what took the Beatles four years"), who recognized in Bolan a chance to experience the other side of all the adulation he too had once been subjected to. Ringo had been contemplating putting together a cinematic series of sketches of stars of the day (the Elizabeth Taylor / Richard Burton coupling was one idea bandied about), but Apple Films stayed largely idle. Still, when he learned that T. Rex was due to play a pair of sold-out shows on March 18, 1972 at Wembley's Empire Pool, he proposed that *he* document the event, and from there sprang *Born to Boogie.*

Betwixt the voltage generated by the thousands of screaming attendees and the Electric Warrior onstage, Ringo himself commandeered a camera in the photographer's pit and filmed Bolan's act while supervising a crew. For a relative novice, he did a creditable job of capturing the excitement without resorting to the clichés of the day. Had they left the project at that, it would have made for a nice souvenir of the pop star at his absolute zenith of popularity. But between them, Bolan and Ringo cooked up (or perhaps "half-baked") a series of vignettes, some spontaneous, some scripted, and used these as a bridge to connect concert sequences. Introducing a dwarf with an oral fixation to the proceedings placed the scenes somewhere between *Magical Mystery Tour* and Led Zeppelin's *The Song Remains the Same* on the spectrum of self-indulgence.

Far more compelling was the studio jam sequence (filmed either at Apple Studios or at John's home studio at Ascot—no one agrees). Featuring T. Rex augmented by Ringo (playing his Ludwig Hollywood kit) and one Elton John on ivories, the ensemble smoked through Little Richard's "Tutti Frutti" before gliding into "Children of the Revolution," creating one of rock cinema's finest moments. (Given Elton's well-defined extrovert tendencies, it's interesting seeing him here as foil alongside Bolan's effortless star power.) Also worth mentioning was the "mad tea party" interlude, shot on the lawn at John's Tittenhurst Park estate. (Ringo frequently acted as house sitter before buying the property himself in 1973.) There, accompanied by a string section, Bolan (as the Mad Hatter) performed an "unplugged" set of his hits while Ringo and some nuns (one played by Bolan's then wife, June) had tea. Such were the '70s.

If one can look past the flat attempts at "you had to be there" silliness, a well executed time capsule of post-Beatles hysteria remains. The musical sequences look and sound first-rate, the latter due in no small part to producer Tony Visconti, who never met a well-crafted overdub he didn't like. Said the *Morning Star* newspaper (with tongue firmly in cheek), ". . . this is the best teeny-bopper entertainment since the Beatles succumbed to insecticide." Certainly Bolan was pleased with the results, noting with inadvertent irony: "That was the end of an era for me, that concert." Sadly for him, by the time *Born to Boogie* was finished and ready for release at Christmas 1972, the group's chart supremacy had begun to wane, never to recover. The film never saw release in America, where, despite efforts to replicate the mania of their native land, T. Rex was regarded as little more than a bubblegum act.

That'll Be the Day (1973)

Nostalgia for the pre-Beatles youth culture swept public consciousness beginning in 1973. In America, this longing was largely embodied (if not spearheaded) by the popularity of George Lucas's *American Graffiti*. On the other side of the pond, where the 1950s had been a very different experience, *That'll Be the Day*, scripted by Ray Connolly, fulfilled largely the same role.

The film told the story of Jim MacLaine (David Essex), growing up in an England still suffering from the deprivations of the Second World War. Abandoned by his father as a child, young Jim is restless and determined not to follow the path prescribed by his mother (Rosemary Leach) to enter university and build a conventional existence for himself. Instead, he drops out and falls in with a worldly-wise carnival worker named Mike (Ringo), who in his own colorful way seems to have surrounded himself with all the good things in life: travel, easy women, and rock and roll. Initially naïve but an apt pupil, young Jim soon discovers how to utilize his looks to score big with the ladies, practicing his "art" by cutting a swath through the holiday camp he and Mike alternate seasons with.

Along the way, his native self-absorption only increases, as he casually betrays all who fall into his path, eventually Mike included.

Essex (born David Cook) had first gotten attention as lead cast member onstage in *Godspell*; *That'll Be the Day* represented his first motion picture starring vehicle. The film had come into being when producer David Puttnam suggested to writer Ray Connolly that Harry Nilsson's "1941" might form the basis of a good motion picture. (The autobiographical song detailed his own abandonment by his father at an early age and the repetition of the pattern in later years with *him*; it is not for no reason that Harry, John Lennon, and Ringo Starr bonded so closely, given their respective family histories.)

The low-budget film was financed rather creatively with money being put up by EMI's budget LP division, in exchange for a fifties-era double-album soundtrack that would be marketed on the strength of the film. In no time at all, the investment was recouped.

For Ringo, the film represented a chance to revisit his own youth, particularly the glory days of Butlin's Holiday Camp with Rory Storm. A more tangible tie to the past came with the casting of early '60s idol Billy Fury as "Stormy Tempest," the camp's resident entertainer. Fury, as readers of *Fab Four FAQ* may recall, was the big-time singer whom the fledgling Beatles (pre-Ringo) auditioned to back on tour, ultimately losing out and getting the gig with Johnny Gentle instead. (Rory himself showed up at the audition, merely to get himself photographed with Fury, while Lennon stuck around long enough to secure an autograph for himself.) As Tempest's drummer, "J. D. Clover," Keith Moon had a small role—the band even played the Who's then-unreleased "Long Live Rock."

While playing the part of Mike didn't represent much of a stretch from who he himself had once been, Ringo thoroughly inhabited the character. He's seen as cynical, but not heartless, happy to live in the moment without a care for tomorrow. Only once is he shown reproaching his protégé, after Jim takes advantage of a schoolgirl. Mike's disgust makes it clear that he thinks that there are some lines you don't cross. Elsewhere, such as in the pool room scene, Ringo illustrated why he is so fascinating to watch. It isn't the mere tossing off of lines with conviction, but his array of non-verbal communication techniques that demonstrate a seeming effortless command of film craft. Nowhere else in his cinematic output (with the possible exception of *Blindman*) was he given the opportunity to actually act rather than trade upon his well-known persona. One only wishes he'd been offered more of such quality roles.

The film did a great job evoking the "kitchen sink" British dramas of the early '60s, even without being produced in black-and-white. (The kudos it won for period authenticity were well deserved, except that Essex's hair throughout is strictly contemporary.) The success of *That'll Be the Day* came roughly at the same time that Essex's self-penned single, "Rock On," became an international hit. (In the U.S., the song replaced "That'll Be the Day" over the end credits.) Connolly was asked to craft a follow-up, which he did, entitled *Stardust*. Picking up where the first story ended, it followed McClain's drift into rock and roll stardom. In this film, far more conventional than its predecessor, Ringo did not reprise his role—understandably, given how his own recording career had taken off.

Son of Dracula (1974)

With the success of *Born to Boogie* behind him, Ringo wasn't quite prepared to let Apple Films languish, even as the record label itself headed toward oblivion. A horror spoof script caught his attention, representing for this fan of escapist entertainment a chance to work in a genre he hadn't yet explored. It so happened that Harry Nilsson was likewise a fan: on the cover of his *Son of Schmilsson* album, he featured himself as a vampire in glorious black-and-white. After David Bowie passed on the lead role to what became *Son of Dracula*, Ringo gave the part to his inseparable pal—after first getting Harry's teeth fixed (which Nilsson's mom thanked him for).

Billed as "the first rock and roll Dracula movie," the project boasted a fairly impressive cast. Beyond Ringo as the three-thousand-year-old sorcerer, Merlin, the film featured actress Susanna Leigh as Amber—she'd already starred in an Elvis picture (*Paradise, Hawaiian Style*). Van Helsing was played by Dennis Price. Once considered one of Britain's top film actors (notably opposite Alec Guinness in 1949's *Kind Hearts and Coronets*), he'd been reduced by alcoholism to accepting parts in a stream of increasingly awful horror films, of which *Son of Dracula* would be his last—he died shortly after filming was completed. Distinguished character actor Freddie Jones had scored much acclaim in 1969's *Frankenstein Must Be Destroyed* for Hammer; here he played *Baron* Frankenstein.

Enjoying a preeminent horror career himself was director Freddie Francis. Originally a cinematographer (for which he'd scored two Academy Awards), he'd recently directed 1972's classic *Tales from the Crypt*. It is

What sounded great on paper—two outsized personalities and horror film buffs to boot—fell flat on celluloid. *Son of Dracula*, Ringo and Harry's cinematic collaboration, failed to rise to the level of their musical interactions.

therefore all the more baffling that *this* film is such a mess. While passable enough as cheap drive-in fodder, it displays very little in the way of focus or discipline. A capable actor, given a substantial role, Ringo comes off as barely engaged throughout, as though he realized that the work was a time-waster even as he was filming it. Harry—in life a charismatic, larger-than-life figure—appears fairly wooden on the big screen. His previous film credits had been largely limited to scores; it therefore may have been a bit much to expect him to hold this project together in the lead role as "Count Downe."

The plot was no better or worse than any of the genre: as heir to the throne of all monsterdom, the Count is poised to be crowned king, but learns that he must relinquish eternal life after falling in love with a mortal (Leigh). An operation to end his vampire status must take place, with complications ensuing. Though Harry's character is outshone throughout by those around him, audiences did get an opportunity to see him perform musically throughout, with back catalog material like "Remember," "Without You," and "Jump into the Fire" in the soundtrack. (The onscreen band included Keith Moon and Peter Frampton.) "Daybreak," the film's only newly composed tune, would be Nilsson's last Top 40 single.

The ultimate value of *Son of Dracula* was the fun it allowed Ringo and Harry to have together while filming in England. (Extending the good times wherever he could, the former Fab even hired the estranged Mrs. Harrison, Pattie, to act as official set photographer.) The film had its premier in Atlanta, Georgia, on April 19, 1974, for no other reason than that it sounded like it would be a blast. A huge ceremony greeted them with twelve thousand kids and bands playing, but, as Ringo later noted, "As soon as we left, they took the movie off." It isn't necessarily a sign of sheer awfulness to note that it has never been released on video or DVD; perhaps the best assessment came from the Ringed One himself, who merely offered, "It's not the greatest movie in the world but I've seen worse."

Ringo's film career continued onward throughout the decade, albeit with decreasing returns each time out. Appearing as himself opposite partner-in-crime Keith Moon throughout the Who's 1978 *The Kids Are Alright* documentary, the Ringed One also accepted scripted roles in Ken Russell's star-studded *Lisztomania* (1975) and the cult-trash triumph *Sextette* (1978) alongside past-her-shelf-life cinema legend Mae West. A discussion of the artistic merit of both films is best left for another book. Or pamphlet.

Life of Brian (1979)

George wasn't particularly known for any cinematic aspirations. The process of being an actor in the Beatle films was something he approached with decreasing enthusiasm each time out; that said, he later learned to enjoy making creative musical videos for his songs. Eventually, if a film project drew his interest, involving friends, he might be lured into lending a behind-the-scenes hand if needed. This manifested itself the first time in 1974, when a West End play, *Little Malcolm* (also known as *Little Malcolm and His Struggle Against the Eunuchs*), by David Haliwell, was optioned as an Apple film, starring actor John Hurt in the lead role. George had been drawn into the project by Mal Evans, whose musical discovery, Splinter, had composed a song ("Lonely Man") intended to be the film version's theme song.

Though *Little Malcolm* was not a blockbuster, George's role as executive producer stirred something within him. The next time the opportunity presented itself came some four years later, when his friends in Monty Python were running into some trouble with their third film project (after *And Now for Something Completely Different* and *Monty Python and the Holy Grail*). *Life of Brian* was a satire on Western religion, specifically the drift from Jesus' original message that became twisted by mortal man for various reasons, resulting in something far removed from its original intent.

As for the Pythons' taking on such a weighty theme, the idea came about from a flippant response Eric Idle gave to a reporter asking what their next film project would be. (His answer: *Jesus Christ: Lust for Glory.*) One early idea for a sketch along these lines came from Idle and Terry Gilliam, who conceived of having the cross on which Jesus was crucified be shoddily made and falling apart, prompting the angry carpenter's son to reproach the builders and instruct them on how to do it right. This could hardly fill an entire movie, however, and eventually the Pythons came up with a new main character, Brian of Nazareth, who spends his life continually being mistaken for his contemporary, the Messiah.

The film was to be financed by EMI, who had committed two million pounds to the project. On the Thursday before the Saturday that the Pythons and crew were scheduled to fly out to North Africa to commence shooting, however, they were hit with a bombshell: EMI, on the orders of head Bernard Delfont, was pulling the funding. It seems that someone had finally gotten around to reading the script and was not amused. Stunned, the Pythons began fanning out to scramble for funding to resuscitate the project.

Believing there was no money to be had in England, Idle flew out to California to see what could be found. By sheer coincidence, George was in town. After Idle cried him a river, George offered to help: "When the Beatles were breaking up, Python kept me sane, really, so I owe you one." Not believing what he was hearing, Idle passed the message onto the other Pythons, who were flabbergasted. But George was serious: he *really* wanted to see this

While dining with the Python troupe during the production of *Life of Brian*, George regaled his companions with insights into his fellow ex-Fabs. According to Michael Palin, Harrison described Ringo as "simple" and saw John as reduced to a "housewife."

film. Thus it was that the wheels were put in motion for *Brian*'s bailout, or what became known as "the world's most expensive cinema ticket."

Together with his business manager, Denis O'Brien, George set up HandMade Films. (It was originally to be called "British Handmade Films," after a similarly named paper product George spotted in Somerset, until it was pointed out that anything with "British" in its name invariably lost money.) As a boss, George was content to work behind the scenes while remaining hands-off as far as the actual film was concerned. He certainly had no notion of appearing in the film, but on a trip to Tunisia to check on their progress, he found himself whisked into wardrobe and—before he knew it—garbed in Arab attire, where he was placed in the film as "Mr. Papadopolous," owner of "the Mount," as in the "sermon on."

It marked George's only appearance in the film, and a non-speaking one at that. (Though the character is heard giving a big Liverpudlian "Hullo!" to Brian, the recording of the line was flawed and had to be looped in the studio by Palin, imitating George.) Keith Moon was slated to appear as a prophet in the film; literally, on the night he died, he expressed his excitement about the part to Eric Idle. John Cleese was particularly keen on getting actor George Lazenby (famed for his onetime role as James Bond) into the film as Christ himself, simply to be able to blurb on the posters: "George Lazenby IS Jesus Christ." Unfortunately, he was not available.

The film opened in August 1979 to positive reviews. As fate would have it, George—in New York a few weeks later—happened to run into Lord Delfont at Kennedy Airport. He pulled him aside and asked whether Delfont happened to know that *Life of Brian* had already grossed $1 million. Though he didn't point out that much of EMI's fortune was Beatle money, he *did* thank him: ultimately a $4.6 million investment reaped $35 million in returns, making HandMade Films one of the most successful independent companies in film history.

Rockshow (1980)

Not to be confused with the made-for-TV *Wings over the World* special, *Rockshow* was produced strictly for the theaters. Unlike the earlier document of the same 1976 tour, this was pure performance: no backstage footage, no narration; nothing but straight music. It seems amazing in retrospect that this film took so long to make it to the marketplace: the *Wings Over America* album was out less than six months after the tour ended, while the television special aired about a year and a half before *Rockshow* arrived. By that time, Jimmy McCulloch was dead, Wings was in tatters, and musically, Paul had moved well on.

Still, seeing and hearing the thunder that was Wings' greatest iteration on the big screen was well worth the price of admission. Certainly, a major investment of time had gone into overcoming sonic limitations, enabling venue speakers to pop in a way that simulated the concert hall experience. Indeed, after premiering in New York City on November 26, 1980, the film enjoyed a steady run on the midnight movie circuit before being issued on early home video (in shortened form) in 1981. While it's never been properly reissued on DVD, a handful of songs can be seen on the *McCartney Years* set.

9

Take a Dose of Rock 'n' Roll

Compilations, Reissues, and Rarities

The Beatles renewed their recording contract with EMI in February 1967 for nine years. Once it lapsed, the record company was free to repackage their material any way they saw fit, a task they took on with relish. While the contract was in effect, only once did the label prepare a reissue project for release: the "Red" and the "Blue" compilations that, for many, summed up the group's career. These were issued with the ex-Fabs' blessing (more or less) in response to some enterprising frauds who'd been doing a brisk business via mail order.

Not until the deal had run its course did EMI begin sniffing around for any excuse they could find for assembling packages connected roughly thematically. (The success of the "Red" and "Blue" packages spawned similar wonders from Capitol with their Beach Boys back catalog; the resulting *Endless Summer* double album went to #1 in 1974, followed a year later by *Spirit of America*, which hit the Top 10.) Suddenly, the Fabs' upbeat material was fair game for consolidation (*Rock 'n' Roll Music*), as were their ballads (*Love Songs*).

At least those latter two were collections that *sort of* made sense in the pre-*Anthology* years; less so the depths to which EMI would later sink (*Reel Music?*). Alongside the four distinct solo "best of"s, EMI's marketing strategy meant that fans had no shortage of ways to repurchase what they already owned. Not until 1977's *Beatles at the Hollywood Bowl* album and (marginally, perhaps) *Rarities* in 1980 were fans actually given something of value that *hadn't* been issued to death (except in bootleg form).

The Beatles Alpha-Omega Volume One and Two—Released January 1973

It took a certain amount of testicular effrontery to flagrantly pirate copyrighted Beatles (and solo) recordings, flogging them on television and

Heightened demand for a Beatles live release was finally satisfied by the 1977 issue of the Hollywood Bowl recordings. Despite its success, Apple has indicated no plans to reissue the album on CD.

marketing them as apparently legitimate releases. But this is precisely what Audio Tape, Inc. of Asbury Park, New Jersey did barely three years after the group disbanded. Apparently reading (correctly) that the market was ripe for a definitive review of the Fabs' recording career, Audio Tape issued two separate four-record sets, drawing from the group's Capitol/Apple catalog as well as several solo releases.

In titling the sets *Alpha-Omega*, the compilers apparently meant to offer a representative sampling of the Fabs' work that covered all bases. It is therefore worth noting what the sets did and did not include. To begin with, the songs were not presented in chronological order; instead, they were jumbled about randomly. This may have suggested that the programmers arranged them in a pleasing sequence, like anyone composing a mix tape, but more often than not, the juxtapositions seemed simply arbitrary; for instance, "I'm a Loser" was followed by "Lucy in the Sky with Diamonds."

As the discs were clearly "mastered" from existing vinyl, surface pops and clicks appeared throughout on *every* pressing. Then, too, the compilers must have gotten lazy in a few spots, not bothering to lift the tone arm when they let side one of *Meet the Beatles!* run in its entirety in one sequence. But on balance, *Alpha-Omega* represented a far bolder sampling of recordings than did the official releases that it sparked. For instance, while the "Red" album features nothing but original material, *Alpha-Omega* offers a variety of covers associated with the Beatles: "Twist and Shout," "Roll Over Beethoven," and "Long Tall Sally" among them.

Then, too, there is the solo work thrown in. By placing George's "Wah-Wah," Paul's "Heart of the Country," and John's "Crippled Inside" within the mix, the compilers showed far more imagination than anyone responsible for collating the ex-Fabs' eventual compilations. Still, there are some omissions. Compared side by side, the pirate sets contain all the material released in the "legit" issues, except for these cuts: "Please Please Me," "From Me to You," "Drive My Car," "Girl," "Magical Mystery Tour," and "Revolution" ("Revolution #1" appears instead.)

Once Apple caught wind of what was going on, they moved quickly on two fronts. First, they quickly pulled together their own compilations (see below); next, they slapped Audio Tape, Inc. with a cease and desist order that shut the cheeky entrepreneurs down. Today, *Alpha-Omega* sets regularly turn up on eBay (often in poor condition, given the shorter shelf life accorded box sets). But to fans of a certain age, they remain a fond memory of a time when acquiring a treasury of Fab recordings in one (or two) fell swoop(s) was a real delight.

The Beatles 1962–1966 and The Beatles 1967–1970—Released April 2, 1973

The assembly and rush into production of the "Red" and the "Blue" albums, as they are popularly known, marked perhaps the last meaningful managerial act of Allen Klein on Apple's behalf. To stanch the obvious loss of sales to the upstart pirates from New Jersey, Apple needed to act fast in getting a sanctioned package to market. The haste with which the pair of double albums was prepared became evident over time, once purchasers had the chance to review their contents, but these quibbles stopped no one from purchasing what they'd obviously been waiting a long time for.

To most fans (in America, at least), the chance to buy any Beatles compilation was long overdue. Groups of far less merit had assembled "greatest hits" packages from time immemorial, but the Fabs had studiously avoided being compiled after the low-rent *Collection of Oldies* was issued in England in 1966. (A clause in their 1967 EMI contract enforced their wishes.) After proposing a double greatest hits LP in 1964 (!), Capitol, notoriously quick to milk a buck wherever possible, backed off, collating material only once in

Though brazen and thoroughly illegal, the *Alpha-Omega* collection was far more comprehensive than anything ever released officially.

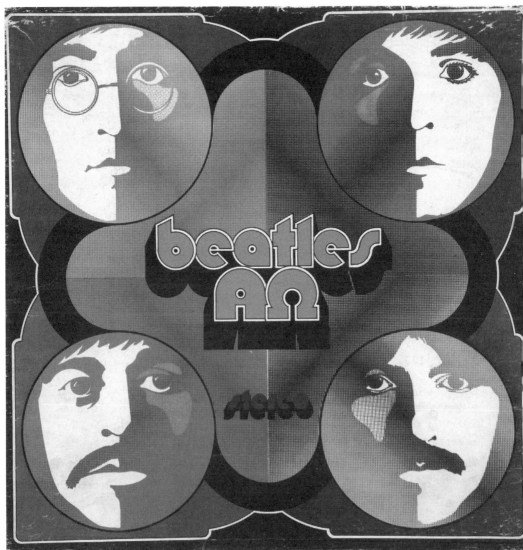

the group's lifetime (per Allen Klein's directive) for *Hey Jude*, an album that made sense as a means of collecting some of the stray singles floating about.)

That the two sets did as well as they did is attributable to attractive packaging, a major promotional push, and canny track selection: all of the hit singles are represented (as along with some album tracks whose radio airplay made them as popular as singles); present too are a handful of significant cuts like "Girl" and "While My Guitar Gently Weeps." Klein had a list of songs cobbled together, intending that the ex-Fabs be given a chance to say "yea" or "nay" on their selection (accounts differ whether John or George ended up doing the honors). Per John's suggestion, the jacket featured the Angus McBean before-and-after *Please Please Me* poses shot at EMI that bookended the band's career.

Some found reasons to take issue with the new compilations. First, given that this was all previously issued material that could have incurred little in the way of new production costs, why the hefty price tag? A $9.98 list at a time when a single album went for $5.98 was deemed robbery. (The year before, *Some Time in New York City* had been marketed as including a "free" bonus live jam disc; in fact, the album's list price was boosted a buck to $6.98, further incensing would-be buyers already upset over the LP's contents.)

Second, within the twenty-six selections chosen for the first volume, why no Harrisongs? Surely there was room for an "If I Needed Someone" or a "Taxman" alongside "Eight Days a Week" or "Michelle." (Or even "Do You Want to Know a Secret?" if preserving the Lennon-McCartney stranglehold was deemed essential.)

Further, the packaging itself was absolutely barren of any useful context. There were no liner notes or in-depth recording details (such as instrumental credits) provided; even the inner gatefold was austere, with a single over-populated image inviting owners to "spot the Beatle" within the gathered throng. While at least two solo Beatles releases had come packaged with posters, and Paul's concurrent *Red Rose Speedway* boasted a booklet of photos, the new compilations offered nothing to justify the price tag. Lyrics were included, but the inserted discography fact sheet (". . . for your information") was riddled with errors. (The Beatles recorded "Thingumybob"? The *Help!* soundtrack included "From Me to You"?—who knew?)

Most jarring of all was the extremely sloppy acquisition of masters. Just as in the group's '60s heyday, if the proper true stereo masters weren't at hand, Capitol/EMI had no problem using whatever was. This made for some senseless inclusions: "Hello Goodbye," for instance, was offered in mono, while "A Hard Day's Night," finally appearing on a Capitol/Apple album in America, came in fake "reprocessed" stereo. A token stereo mix of "Please Please Me" seemed accidental in the face of fake stereo mixes of "I Want to Hold Your Hand," "I Feel Fine" (the dreadful echo-drenched Capitol mix), and "Ticket to Ride"—all of which appeared in true stereo on the English release and elsewhere. (Also in the U.S. only was the "James Bond" instrumental snippet preceding "Help!")

Some songs most definitely did not benefit from a stereo mix. In addition to the increasingly anachronistic '60s mixes that sent the lead vocals out of one speaker and the backing track out the other, there were attempts at stereo for stereo's sake that ended up disemboweling powerful original mixes. John, who evidently did not actually listen to test pressings in advance of the album's release, was irritated to discover that "Revolution," for example, had been ruined. "It was a heavy record," he lamented in 1974, "and they turned it into a piece of ice cream."

Still, for everything that could have been improved, the twin sets did serve the purpose of conveniently bringing together a fine sampling of the Beatles' career to those who wanted to whittle down their LP collections (or to those for whom it served as their introduction to the band's work, present company included). Though lacking the heft of *Alpha-Omega* (whose two four-record sets added up to 120 tracks to *1962–1970*'s total of 54), the "Red" and "Blue" albums were a smash, quickly sliding into *Billboard*'s Top 5, where *1962–1966* peaked at #3 while *1967–1970* topped the charts for one week (before being knocked off by *Red Rose Speedway*).

Shaved Fish—Released October 24, 1975

On the eve of his freedom from any record company commitments for the first time in over a decade, John signaled his retirement from active recording by issuing this valedictory collection of stray singles. Possibly owing to the fact that his contract was still in force, Lennon's involvement was very hands-on: selecting the songs, supervising the edits, approving the cover art.

It had concerned him that EMI was not properly looking after his back catalog; turns out his fears were not unfounded. In preparing the collection for release, he discovered that the master tapes to some of the songs had gone missing—either misfiled or simply vanished—"Cold Turkey" and "Power to the People" among them. As a result, several of the tracks were taken from "dubs," appearing with premature fades compared to the original 45 iterations. (When the album was remastered for CD, EMI went to the trouble of tracking down the proper masters, restoring the running time in the process.)

Shaved Fish ran the gamut of all John's Plastic Ono Band singles from "Give Peace a Chance" through "#9 Dream." The non-original "Stand by Me" was omitted, as was the Lennon composition on its flip, "Move Over Ms.

L." But it was clear to anyone listening closely that the album was intended to be somewhat thematic in its programming, bookended by separate performances of "Give Peace a Chance" while running down Lennon's solo accomplishments, the sweet ("Instant Karma") along with the sour ("Women Is the Nigger of the World," albeit shortened slightly).

Unfortunately for purists, Lennon chose to muddy the waters by featuring the original 1969 "Give Peace a Chance" as a snippet only, leading into "Cold Turkey" and leaving listeners expecting to gather their "Collectible Lennon" in LP form frustrated. Similar disharmony awaited folks expecting to hear the sweet strains of "Happy Xmas (War Is Over)" come to a tranquil ending; instead, the raucous One to One concert-closing performance of "Give Peace a Chance" segued in (and with Stevie Wonder singing lead at that), giving purchasers a distinct sense of "what the hell was *that?*"

Still, any Lennon was good Lennon. The album reached twelve in America, not as high as it might have but still better than solo "best ofs" by his fellow ex-Fabs. In England, "Imagine" was issued as a single (it hadn't been at the time of its original release), bolstering *Shaved Fish* even higher to #8 in the charts. (A sharp-eyed critic in the U.K. noted in *New Musical Express* that production for "Cold Turkey" had been mistakenly attributed to Phil Spector. John wrote back and conceded the point, noting, "There's no echo on it." Still, he asserted that he couldn't be expected to be keeping his full attention on the project when he "was having his baby" at the time.)

Blast from Your Past—Released November 25, 1975

As with his fellow ex-Fabs, Ringo was conscious of the looming expiration of his EMI recording contract. Unlike John, he had every intention of keeping his career going, and given that his long association with EMI was not being renewed, he decided to have a hand in putting together his own "best of" collection before it was done for him. By late 1975, he had—against all odds—racked up a significant streak of hits and therefore, given a pair of non-album singles, could easily justify the existence of such a collection.

Blast from Your Past was a well-assembled collection, featuring not only the obvious *Ringo* smashes —plus "I'm the Greatest"—but also the non-album "Back Off Boogaloo" and both sides of "It Don't Come Easy." (For good measure, his debut single, "Beaucoups of Blues," was thrown in, affording buyers a sampling of his impressive country-flavored album that few had heard.)

There were some omissions, however. John's "Goodnight Vienna" was conspicuously absent; though not a major hit, it was certainly worthy of a second listen (also, the single version, which fused the opening track and its reprise together, did not exist on album at the time. Today it can be found on the *Photograph* "best of" CD). The case could also have been made for including "Snookeroo," the Elton John–Bernie Taupin song that deserved a better airing than it got (having bombed in England as a single), as well as at least two of Ringo's three outstanding non-album B-sides ("Coochy-Coochy" and "Down and Out"). As it was, the collection clocked in at just past thirty minutes, making these absences all the more baffling.

Despite the potential attraction of such a gathering of essential Starr recordings and its holiday release date, the album was a disappointingly poor performer. Barely lasting three months on the charts, it peaked at #30—a shoddy end to the Apple label (which in this case, was a bright red in color) before its rise from the dead in the 1990s. For Ringo, too, it was an early clue to the new direction, portending the southward shift that his recording career would take ever after.

Rock 'n' Roll Music—Released June 7, 1976

With four straight double album repackages having done bang-up business (*1962–1966, 1967–1970*, plus the two Beach Boys two-record sets), Capitol/EMI decided in 1976 to revisit the Fab well. Having done a decent job of re-presenting their hits, both singles and radio-familiar album tracks, the label was now prepared to offer up further samplings of their career, based upon a loose "rock and roll" theme. These were up-tempo songs not used in the "Red" and "Blue" sets—for the most part. (The rule was relaxed for "Drive My Car," the Beach Boys / Chuck Berry pastiche "Back in the U.S.S.R.," and the political screed "Revolution." "Get Back," at least, was presented in the superficially different *Let It Be* version.)

Covers—off limits three years earlier—were offered up with a vengeance, including every Carl Perkins, Chuck Berry, Little Richard, and Larry Williams song the Fabs had ever tackled. As they released nothing not written by themselves after 1965—and of the covers they did record, nearly all originated in the 1950s—the package necessarily took on a nostalgic cast. The creative geniuses at Capitol decided to run with this concept, presenting the album with a sleeve design that left no Eisenhower-era cliché untouched: Coca-Cola, a '57 Chevy, Marilyn Monroe. If they'd conceived the album as a sort of tie-in with the currently popular sitcom *Happy Days*, they couldn't have done a better job.

Ironically, a semi-retired John Lennon had approached EMI, wanting to design a cover himself. His offer was summarily spurned, resulting in a package that disgusted the ex-Fabs. "It made us look cheap and we never were cheap," asserted Ringo. Given that the album's contents transcended '50s-era rock and roll, encompassing the *sturm und drang* of "Helter Skelter,"

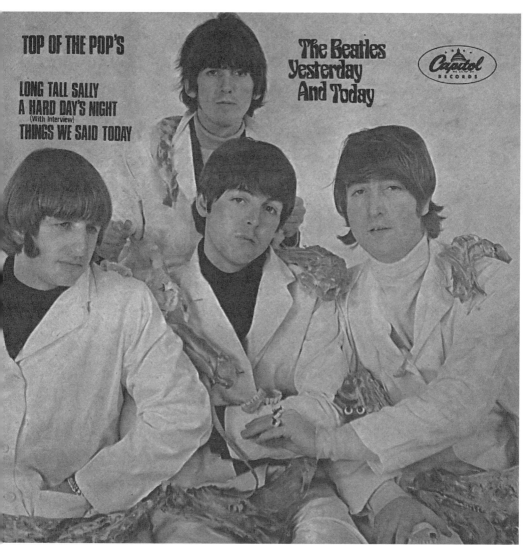

TOP OF THE POP'S

LONG TALL SALLY
A HARD DAY'S NIGHT
(With Interview)
THINGS WE SAID TODAY

The Beatles
Yesterday
And Today

Capitol
RECORDS

Alongside the stream of compilations and repackages being issued throughout the '70s was a thriving underground industry. Some, like this one, titled *Top of the Pop's* [sic], contained recordings that eventually saw legitimate release.

the polemic of "Taxman," and the bile of "Hey Bulldog," a much more canny presentation might have been achieved by offering up images of the band from their leather days as the original punks, simultaneously evoking the *au courant* scene on the ascent in Britain and New York (though Ringo's pre-Beatles visage would have had to have been Photoshopped over Pete Best's).

On the plus side, the masters were subjected to a good hard look for the first time since they'd been recorded. After hearing the mixes prepared for the British release, George Martin was moved to get involved, providing brand new remixes of five early tracks in response to the dreadful attempts at stereo generated from mono. (For some reason, the left and right channels were switched as well.)

Though they hadn't done so with the "Red" and "Blue" releases, EMI broke with precedent and issued a new single to promote the set. In America, *Revolver*'s single-that-never-was-till-now, "Got to Get You Into My Life," was selected, backed with "Helter Skelter." That last selection represented the label's pulling their punches, though only slightly: a popular two-part made-for-TV movie bearing the same name had aired that spring, based on prosecutor Vincent Bugliosi's best-selling account of the Manson Family murders. Though issuing a track that now evoked mass killing would have been tasteless, making it a B-side was less so.

In Britain, "Back in the U.S.S.R." / "Twist and Shout" was released, peaking at #19. "Got to Get You Into My Life" fared better, rising to #7 ten years after it was recorded. It couldn't have hurt that Paul McCartney, the song's author, was currently on tour in America, where his "Silly Love Songs" had topped the charts not long before. *Rock 'n' Roll Music* made it to #2, blocked from the top slot by *Wings at the Speed of Sound* (recalling a similar situation three years earlier).

Despite the packaging, the release represented an attempt to go beyond the obvious in re-imagining the Beatles' work. Credit too must be given for including the heretofore non-album B-side "I'm Down." If the label's overall strategy (beyond putting their top money spinner to work) was to introduce the Fabs' music to a younger audience, then *Rock 'n' Roll Music* was a canny move. But its success in a Beatle-driven year (Macca on tour, *Thirty-Three & ⅓*, *Ringo's Rotogravure*) preordained what the *next* Beatle repackaging would be: the flip side of "rock and roll."

The Best of George Harrison—Released November 8, 1976

In walking away from EMI (until 2002's posthumous *Brainwashed*) in order to start up his own label, George delegated any authority to oversee the repackaging of his past work. This Capitol seized upon with abandon, reasoning that if they were no longer beholden to the Dark Horse, they were free to market his brand as they saw fit. Further, if reissues of Beatle material were doing bang-up business, why not combine the two themes (Beatles and Harrison) all in one package?

Despite suggestions from the artist himself regarding track selection and a title, Capitol ignored his wishes, instead choosing to humiliate George with the implication that as a solo artist, he just didn't have enough "great hits" to fill an entire LP—an insult that not even *Blast from Your Past* had stooped to. EMI chose seven Beatles tracks for the release, forsaking the likes of "I

Need You," "It's All Too Much," "Old Brown Shoe," or anything remotely Indian-sounding for commercial crowd pleasers like "Something" and "While My Guitar Gently Weeps." (Even at this, they could not resist tweaking the sound a little: "Think for Yourself," for instance, was slapped with a dash of reverb—this treatment is absent from the CD reissue.)

The ways in which Capitol graphically promoted the Beatles, as a group and as four solo acts, were endlessly creative, as this collage used in 1977 demonstrates.

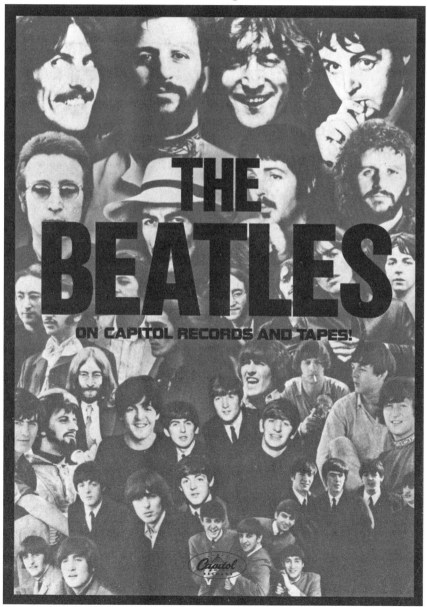

The album did serve the useful function of preserving the "Bangla-Desh" single (it remains the only place the song can be found on CD today), but otherwise offered a predictable roll call of hits. Absent are "Ding Dong, Ding Dong" and "This Guitar (Can't Keep from Crying)"—albeit Harrison's two worst-performing chart singles—while worthy tracks like "Isn't It a Pity," not to mention the three non-album B-sides, were also excluded. Given the decision to give equal billing to the Beatle material, there wouldn't have been room on a single disc anyway.

In the States only, the album was packaged in a bizarre sleeve that placed a rather dour-looking image of the artist, circa 1974 (George was clean-shaven throughout the bicentennial year), upon a backdrop of deep space. Elsewhere and on the eventual CD issue, an equally unflattering shot depicting Hari posing before a vintage hot rod was used. As a final touch worthy of Allen Klein, the album was released less than two weeks before *Thirty-Three & ⅓*, effectively sabotaging the long-awaited Dark Horse debut. (The new album peaked at #11, three places lower than the far less acclaimed *Extra Texture* had done the year before.) As for *The Best of George Harrison*, it eventually did go gold in early 1977, but its chart peak was an anemic #31. Perhaps the public had the good sense to ignore EMI's astonishingly "tacky" (George's description) release.

The Beatles at the Hollywood Bowl—Released May 2, 1977

Virtually alone among their peers, the Beatles during their lifetime had not issued a live album. (While the Who and the Kinks had each released classic concert recordings by 1970, the Rolling Stones' first attempt, 1966's dreadful *Got Live If You Want It!* included a pair of studio recordings dressed up with screaming girl sounds alongside the badly recorded and mixed material that comprised the bulk of the release. They'd get it right with 1970's *Get Your Ya-Yas Out.*) This wasn't for lack of intent: as early as their debut, George Martin had weighed the merits of recording the Fabs at the Cavern; further, a plan to tape their February 1964 Carnegie Hall concert was stymied by union rules.

Labor issues were apparently ironed out by the time the band returned to the States that summer, making possible the documenting of their August 23 appearance at Los Angeles' Hollywood Bowl. There, before seventeen thousand of the screaming faithful, a dozen tunes were recorded by a Capitol mobile team (on a three-track), drawing chiefly from the current *A Hard Day's Night* LP—the British iteration. Though the sonic wash and what was believed at the time to be a subpar performance precluded release of the material, a portion of the opener, "Twist and Shout," was used for the documentary set *The Beatles' Story,* issued by Capitol in November 1964.

A year later, the band's two return shows at the same venue were taped, though the first performance was plagued by technical problems. Again, no one thought that anything other than a historical curiosity had been captured, and so the recordings were archived and forgotten. Not until 1971, after the breakup, did anyone revisit the scrapped effort. At that time, word was that Phil Spector—coming to be a specialist in abandoned Beatles projects—was asked to give the tapes a listen to see what could be made of them. He apparently concluded that no amount of celestial choirs and orchestration would result in a saleable product, and so the matter was dropped.

But things changed in the years that followed. Though Apple made a practice of being inattentive to the demands of the marketplace, EMI did not and began wondering aloud if something could be made from tapes already in hand as a way to both stymie the crop of underground live recordings in circulation and address what quite obviously was a demand from the public for some fresh Beatles. This time, George Martin was pulled into the project on the condition that he be granted veto power if he did not like what he heard. Maybe it was the passage of time and the attendant nostalgia; perhaps it was simply the realization of what 1977 technology could do to bring the flawed recordings up to snuff. But this time he saw the potential in the raw recordings and, with Geoff Emerick assisting, set about getting them into releasable shape.

Their first task was to secure an operational three-track deck with which to play the tapes during the transfer to a modern (for 1977) sixteen-track. As Martin wrote in his liner notes, the antiquated machine kept overheating, until finally they took to blowing cold air over it to cool it. Many hours were then spent EQing, filtering, and balancing the recordings, minimizing the audience sounds while preserving the energy and excitement.

It became clear pretty early on that while Capitol had hoped to get two albums out of the project (or at least one double album), there simply wasn't enough usable material to work with, never mind the repeated songs. The first 1965 show simply had too many problems (the album incorrectly identi-fies this as the source for the some of the material when it actually was the August 30 show that was used alongside cuts from the 1964 performance). Furthermore, George Martin was a "one great single album is better than one so-so double album" kind of guy; remember his attitude toward the "White Album"? Therefore, he decided to select the cream of the '64 and '65 shows and edit them as one continuous performance, even if it meant omitting certain songs ("I Want to Hold Your Hand," "If I Fell," "I'm Down," and so forth).

On the whole, he chose well. The one-two punch of "Twist and Shout" into "She's a Woman" kicked things off with a bang before giving way to Paul's crowd-baiting patter ("Can you HEAR me?") and "Ticket to Ride." The often-overlooked "Things We Said Today" is presented with a rave-up bridge, while Ringo's reading of "Boys" brings down the house. (Curiously, George still has his twelve-string on for that number.) The show ends with Paul's "good night" to the attendees (his comment that "Contrary to public opinion, we've never played any longer than this" was excised) and a solid performance of—for the thousandth time—"Long Tall Sally."

Capitol pulled out all the stops in promoting *The Beatles Live at the Hollywood Bowl*, buying commercial time on television as well as supplying retail outlets with much ephemera. The announcement of the pending release prompted some enterprising DJs to begin airing "exclusive" excerpts from the bootlegged 1964 show, little realizing that "You Can't Do That" would *not* be a part of the album's actual contents. It mattered not; demand being what it was, *Hollywood Bowl* rocketed up the charts, peaking at #2 in the States while topping the charts (for one week) in England.

Responses from the ex-Fabs were mixed. While John—ever the collector of his own past work—was apparently was quite pleased with the album, George remained rather distant from the release. Seemingly unable to distinguish the *Hollywood Bowl* set from the concurrent *Star-Club* release, he dismissed it as only of historic interest, adding that it sounded "just like a bootleg, but because Capitol is bootlegging it, it's legitimate."

Despite the demonstrable desire by fans to see the album reissued on compact disc, perhaps even augmented with leftovers ("Baby's in Black" appeared as the B-side to "Real Love" in 1996), Apple has expressed no interest in ever fulfilling this wish, leaving the job, as always, to helpful bootleggers.

Love Songs—Released October 21, 1977

A scant five months after *Hollywood Bowl*'s release, Capitol again geared up for a major Beatle product drop, this time with a two-record counterpoint to 1976's *Rock 'n' Roll Music*. Rather unimaginatively dubbed *Love Songs* (in hindsight, it would have made more sense to follow precedent and choose an all-encompassing cover song title that described its contents the way "Rock 'n' Roll Music" had done for the last go-round; say "Words of Love"), the album certainly stretched that definition to the breaking point with the inclusion of tracks like "She's Leaving Home" (a ballad, perhaps, but a love song?) while omitting "Don't Let Me Down"—a love song if there ever was one.

This time, the packaging was toned down, even somewhat classy, featuring a faux-leather sleeve lettered in gold. The only accompanying image was the panoramic 1967 Richard Avedon shot (see page 101 of *Fab Four FAQ*), reconfigured to suit EMI's present needs by boosting Paul's image (virtually eclipsing everyone else's) while reducing George's and pushing Ringo's to the side. Included inside was a twenty-eight-page booklet containing the lyrics, calligraphed on what looked like parchment, to the songs within.

What must have sounded like a "can't miss" idea on paper just didn't fly. Despite the evident care put into the presentation and even the mastering ("This Boy" and "Yes It Is" appeared in true stereo for the first time), the album, timed to capitalize on the upcoming Christmas season, didn't perform nearly up to the level expected, as least in America, where it peaked at #24 (in England, it did much better, climbing to #7). Release of a single intended to promote the LP, "Girl" (remixed to center the vocals), backed with "You're Going to Lose That Girl," was canceled—but not before picture sleeves had been printed. (Any vinyl floating about to the contrary is counterfeit.)

With the relative failure of *Love Songs*, the age of double-album Beatles compilations came to an end. Henceforth, any trawling through their back catalog would result only in single-disc releases and more tightly focused themes.

The Beatles Collection—Released December 1, 1978

In 1974—the tenth anniversary of the Beatles' arrival in America—Capitol Records rewarded execs and staffers exceeding sales quotas with a limited-edition box set featuring seventeen American Beatles albums: every Capitol and Apple issue (including *The Beatles' Story*), minus *Let It Be*, which had been distributed by United Artists. It was a handsome set, packaged in a black box embossed in gold with the composite images of the four ex-Beatles that were used in Capitol's promotional materials that year. Today, the set is considered one of the rarest and therefore most valuable of the latter-day Beatle collectibles.

Perhaps it was this one-off project that planted the seeds for what four years later became the most expensive (to date) official Beatle product released to the public. *The Beatles Collection*, retailing at the princely list price of $132.98 in America, gathered together all twelve original Parlophone and Apple releases (minus the '66 *Oldies* LP), plus a "bonus" disc entitled *Rarities*, purporting to contain all of the loose single sides not contained within the British albums. Imagine then, as a purchaser of this rather pricey behemoth, taking it home, only to exclaim (as thousands doubtlessly did): "Where's 'Hey Jude'?"

In the States, the set was issued in a limited edition of three thousand; not so in Britain. But it was this supposed freebie that was the real selling point in the U.K., where many more non-album singles had been issued over the years. The chance to get them (mostly) in one fell swoop seemed valid enough, until buyers realized that they were still well short of having all the Fab recordings; two American compilations, *Magical Mystery Tour* and *Hey Jude,* would be needed to fill in the gaps. Pressure from the public, as well as from retailers who did brisk business selling the unlimited edition piecemeal, forced EMI to issue *Rarities* less than a year later as a separate release, thereby incurring the wrath of all who'd bought the box set in the first place purely to acquire the "exclusive."

Meanwhile, back in the States; Capitol did a curious thing. Instead of simply issuing the box with the twelve British albums, plus the bonus disc, they tweaked it slightly. The U.S. edition of *Rarities* was the same as its U.K. cousin, except for the swapping out of the two German-language Beatles recordings, "Komm, Gib Mir Deine Hand" and "Sie Liebt Dich," for their English-language equivalents, a move that made absolutely *no* sense. To sum up: EMI released a box set of Beatles recordings on both sides of the Atlantic that, differing slightly, managed to alienate every potential and actual purchaser.

The good news for Capitol was that the limited edition, issued in time for Christmas, sold out almost immediately. But the whole exercise left the corporation with egg on their faces; in just over a year's time, they would attempt to set things right with a special U.S.-only *Rarities.*

Wings Greatest—Released December 1, 1978

Among the four ex-Beatles, Paul was easily the most prolific (not that quantity equals quality) and, further, was the keenest on releasing freestanding singles that weren't attached to an album. Thus, by 1978, he had accrued the most "orphaned" material that would have benefited by some sort of collection. Well before the release of this compilation, Macca spoke frequently of collating all the stray material—released and unreleased—and calling it *Cold Cuts (and Hot Hits).* Had he followed through on this, it would have made for a brilliant showcase for his post-Beatles work. But despite efforts throughout the years to bring the unissued tracks up to snuff (as late as 1980), the idea was inevitably scuttled in favor of whatever new material was ready to go at the time. (Accommodating bootleggers have filled the gap along the way, however.)

Instead, Paul issued this collection as a contractual obligation to EMI before splitting for the greener pastures of CBS (in America at least) in 1978. *Wings Greatest* was a compilation that easily could have been a double album. Having issued a triple album (*Wings Over America*) a year earlier, perhaps he was a little reticent to lay another bloated product on the market at holiday gift-giving time. In any event, this package served to collect several but not all of his hits, perhaps consciously keeping the door open for a Part Two.

Given the tracks that were conspicuously absent on the release (the #1 "Listen to What the Man Said," "Maybe I'm Amazed," "C Moon," "Letting Go," and so forth), this may have been exactly the case. What is interesting is that, despite its title, this really was a *Paul McCartney* Greatest Hits, as "Another Day" and "Uncle Albert / Admiral Halsey" predated the formation of the group. By streamlining the collection, Paul might have been hoping to maximize sales. In fact, *Wings Greatest* peaked at #29, a disappointing performance that bettered Ringo's "best of" by only one. Given that Capitol was about to lose Paul to a competitor, maybe their promotional efforts were not all they could have been.

In Britain, the album did much better, peaking at #5 (oddly, since Paul's solo work inevitably performed better in the States than at home). It may have been helped by a TV advertisement depicting numerous "regular people" singing McCartney tunes. The payoff comes when a truck driver, tunelessly bellowing out "Band on the Run" at a traffic light, is told by Macca (in a vehicle beside him with Linda and Denny), "You're a little flat, mate!" The trucker, oblivious to the ex-Fab's identity, looks out the window to see his tires and says, "Funny, I just checked them this morning." Pure comedic gold.

Perhaps the most curious aspect of the release was the packaging. The sleeve was designed by Hipgnosis, the English design firm responsible for any number of iconic album covers throughout the '70s, including Pink Floyd's *Wish You Were Here* and Led Zeppelin's *Presence*. Prominently featured on the front and back cover and on the poster inside was an Art Deco statuette of a winged woman. (A photo of Paul, Linda, and Denny displayed throughout the package originally also depicted Jimmy McCulloch and Joe English. Retired from the group at the time of the release, they were unceremoniously excised from the picture.)

As if to magnify the object's actual size, it's depicted on the front cover in a snowy setting before a mountain backdrop. On the poster inside, it is revealed in its proper scale as a tabletop object. Apparently at great expense, the statuette was actually flown to the Swiss Matterhorn for the cover shoot. It's fascinating that Paul, notoriously tight with a buck, would have splurged on something so completely inconsequential.

The Beatles Rarities—Released March 24, 1980

In 1979, it was announced that the *Rarities* set issued in Britain would be released as a separate album in the States as a part of Capitol's "budget line." This drew outcry from several quarters, if only for the sheer pointlessness of it all. The rareness needs of American versus British fans was obvious to anyone paying attention, and they did not overlap all that much.

At some point, an uncommon event happened: wiser heads prevailed and called a time-out for a rethink. The market showed a clear receptivity to some sort of collection that collated the oddities floating about in Beatledom: rare mixes, non-album B-sides, strange edits, even noticeably different mono mixes. Such a set wouldn't necessarily be pitched toward general audiences, but if done right, it could satisfy the Beatles geeks as well as fans accepting of an eclectic mix of material not bound by a particular stylistic theme.

As Capitol grasped at an understanding of the concept, inspiration from an unexpected source pointed the way.

In Clint Heylin's *Bootleg: The Rise and Fall of the Secret Recording Industry*, the story of "Richard" is told. In 1979, this remarkably astute collector set about assembling an array of issued but rare (at least in America) Beatles recordings, including the Ringo-on-drums single version of "Love Me Do," the promotional version of "Penny Lane" featuring an extra trumpet flourish at the coda, the World Wildlife Fund issue of "Across the Universe," and so forth.

Once a master tape was in place, Richard gathered up an assortment of memorabilia (aided by a collector with an even bigger stash) and shot a cover photo in his living room. As a final touch, he produced a sleeve and labels bearing Capitol's standard packaging of the day, resulting in a forgery that had all the earmarks of a legitimate release. He called the album *Collector's Items*.

When the set hit the streets, the reverberations were felt all the way into the executive offices at the Capitol Tower. Here was some upstart with the cheek to issue a record that looked for all the world like one of their own releases, except that it wasn't—it merely traded on the company's name. Shrewdly taking the hint, Capitol's researchers on the project, which included Ron Furmanek and Wally Podrazik, patterned the newly configured *Rarities* after Richard's model, even duplicating his hybrid "I Am the Walrus," which brought together in one place all the song's stray variations.

Upon its release, *The Beatles Rarities* (U.S. edition) represented the boldest effort yet to satisfy the hardcores, short of raiding the vaults as EMI did later at the time of *Anthology*. Custom-crafted for American audiences, it gathered songs never issued on Capitol ("There's a Place" and "Misery"), mono variations ("Helter Skelter," "Don't Pass Me By"), single mixes and

For neither the first nor the last time, shrewd bootleggers forced the hand of the Beatles' record label by issuing smart and attractively packaged illicit collections. (Note the *Sgt. Pepper's* picture disc, a novelty then in vogue.)

B-sides ("Help!," "The Inner Light"), as well as variants only a true trainspotter would love (the "high hat intro" version of "All My Loving").

Inadvertently, the initial release became something of a rarity itself when it was discovered that the sleeve contained a couple of errors: George Martin's name was accidentally left off as producer, while someone mistakenly attributed the "I got blisters on my fingers!" exclamation from "Helter Skelter" to John instead of Ringo. These were fixed for the second pressing, as the album sold well enough to make it to #21 on the charts—not bad for a collection not necessarily geared to the masses.

The collection has not been issued on CD. Aside from the pirated needle drops found on the 'net, it's unlikely it ever will be, especially in light of the *Anthology* sets.

10

We Fell in Love on the Night We Met

1973

To Beatle-watchers, the expiration of Apple's contract with Allen Klein on March 31, 1973 suggested intriguing possibilities. More than egos, creative clashes, or the advent of Yoko Ono, the injection of the abrasive yet shady New Yorker into the Fabs' business affairs drove a wedge into the group, pitting mostly Paul and John against each other, with George and Ringo accepting the ABKCO (Allen Klein's management company) ride for what it was worth (while retaining personal advisors of their own). Long before Klein's deal with Apple came to a close, each of the three had grown disenchanted with him, George especially over persistent (and well-founded) whispering about Klein's role in Bangladesh profits that had gone astray. To observers, once Klein was gone, what other reason could there be for the four of them *not* to get together?

While on the set of his television special in March, Paul himself explicitly said as much to reporters. With relations between John and him no longer frosty, few opportunities for socializing between the two former antagonists were wasted. That said, Wings' long-awaited full-scale tour of Britain was in the offing, and that at least would keep the four of them from resuming any musical activities together. It was but one of many ambitious professional duties Paul had slated for the year; another included the release of an album that had been in the works for a year, *Red Rose Speedway*. Though much studio work had taken place the year before, the album would mark the first full-length offering from the five-piece band. Reviews were mixed, but the inclusion of a well-crafted ballad, "My Love," drove the album straight to #1.

Its release in spring coincided closely with the first collection of new Harrisongs in nearly two and a half years. Having at last recharged his creative batteries with an extended musical layoff (as well as a trip to India in 1972 with Gary Wright), George released *Living in the Material World*, the long-awaited follow-up to *All Things Must Pass*. The spiritual nature of his Indian visit was evident with the new material, which was possibly even more

You're Sixteen

Words and Music by BOB SHERMAN and DICK SHERMAN

RINGO STARR
on Apple

23|200
Made in England

JEWEL / LONDON

At producer Richard Perry's suggestion, Ringo's cover of this 1960 Johnny Burnette hit paid huge dividends when it became the *second* #1 from one album—a feat unmatched by *any* of his former bandmates.

reflective overall than its predecessor. "Give Me Love," the album's leadoff track, was issued as a single. It followed—and in some cities did battle with—Paul's recent chart-topper for the top slot. Before summer had arrived, 1973 was shaping up to be a good year to be a Beatles fan.

In late winter, a pair of four-album compilations of Beatle (and stray solo) material arrived, pitched to new Beatlemaniacs or older ones looking to replace and streamline their collections. *The Beatles Alpha-Omega* was a pirated collection marketed by mail order and heavily promoted on radio and TV. It's hard to imagine what compelled the manufacturers to thumb their noses so brazenly at Apple and EMI, but robust sales proved that a market existed for such repackages. Apple took notice and, as a weapon to combat the fraudulent release, quickly assembled two double-disc sets of their own, titled *1962–1966* and *1967–1970* respectively, but forever known as the "Red" and the "Blue" albums. While not as comprehensive as the collection that had inspired them, they did have the virtue of not being mastered from vinyl. Both albums sold briskly.

The best-selling releases underscored Apple's status as little more than a clearinghouse for Beatle and ex-Beatle product by that time. Badfinger, the label's one non-Fab signing that showed promise as a viable act, released *Ass*, their final Apple album, in November. Plagued by management troubles and the indifference of their former nurturers, Badfinger's bittersweet departure was commemorated on vinyl with Pete Ham's "Apple of My Eye."

On March 3, the fifteenth annual Grammy Awards ceremony, held in Nashville that year, was broadcast live on television for the first time. Ringo and Harry Nilsson were co-presenters for the Best R&B Male vocal performance. Their appearance took on the air of a comedy skit, with the two drawing laughs for their lighthearted reading of the cue cards. (The award went to Billy Paul—who was not in attendance—for "Me and Mrs. Jones.") Later that evening, the 1972 Album of the Year award went to *The Concert for Bangla Desh*. Ringo collected the trophies in George's absence.

Just two days later, Ringo arrived in Los Angeles to begin work on his first proper rock album. Richard Perry, with production credits that included Carly Simon, Barbra Streisand, and Harry Nilsson, was at the helm. When he had first approached Ringo to be a presenter at the show, the two had gotten to talking about working together. Perry proved to have just the right touch for drawing out the drummer's unique personality while placing him in settings that allowed him to shine. Just as importantly, his relaxed working methods facilitated an easygoing environment, one conducive to productivity that benefited both Ringo and the project.

As it happened, John and George were also in town for business meetings at Capitol. Both were more or less pledged to help out on Ringo's work in progress, but no one planned for both men to be on hand the evening of March 13. On that historic date, the three ex-Fabs laid down the backing to John's "I'm the Greatest," igniting rumors that a Beatle reunion was in the offing. Though spokesmen for all involved sought to tamp down expectations, the fires of Beatlemania were now stoked. By the time the album was released in November, it wasn't quite the Second Coming, but it was close. The fact that *Ringo* happened to be a great album was just a bonus.

Though the odd man out on that particular session, Paul was no longer estranged from the others. His recent drug arrests caused some difficulties getting into the States, but Ringo was happy to bring the sessions to him by relocating to London. With Harry Nilsson in tow, a few more tracks were completed ("You're Sixteen" and "Six O'Clock" with Paul, plus "Step Lightly"), bringing work on the album to an end. In the interim between the album's completion and release that fall, Ringo kept up the pace. After *That'll Be the Day* premiered in April, he quickly shifted gears to begin filming *Count Downe*, retitled *Son of Dracula* upon its 1974 premiere.

Some Time in New York City had been released in June 1972; one year later, John still hadn't gone back in the studio on his own behalf, if only just to create something to turn the page. This marked the longest stretch of time he'd gone between projects in his entire recording career. Yoko had no such problem; in January 1973, she released a two-record set of new material, *Approximately Infinite Universe,* marking the first time in their relationship that John had no musical response to her work. Preoccupied by the continuing efforts to deport him as well as shell-shocked from the lambasting he had taken from every quarter for his last release, John was—to put it one way—in a funk. (Not to read too much into it, but John, notoriously self-conscious about his hairline, shaved his head in June. He would not be the last depressive to do so.)

Elsewhere in Fabdom, a landmark that had served as Ground Zero for the explosion of the Mersey Beat and subsequent British Invasion was about to go the way of the Bambi Kino. On Sunday, May 27, the very last performance at the original Cavern Club in Liverpool took place before its demolition. Each ex-Fab had been invited to come by; all declined. The move, ostensibly to make way for a subway ventilation shaft, proved for naught, as the air system was never built. But it typified an ambivalence felt by the town toward the group that, for most Americans at least, had put the city on the map. Hard to believe as it is now, not until the 1980s would town officials actually start to encourage tourism capitalizing upon their most successful export.

Some Liverpudlians were granted the opportunity to sing their favorite Beatles songs on camera that spring as part of a vignette within the *James*

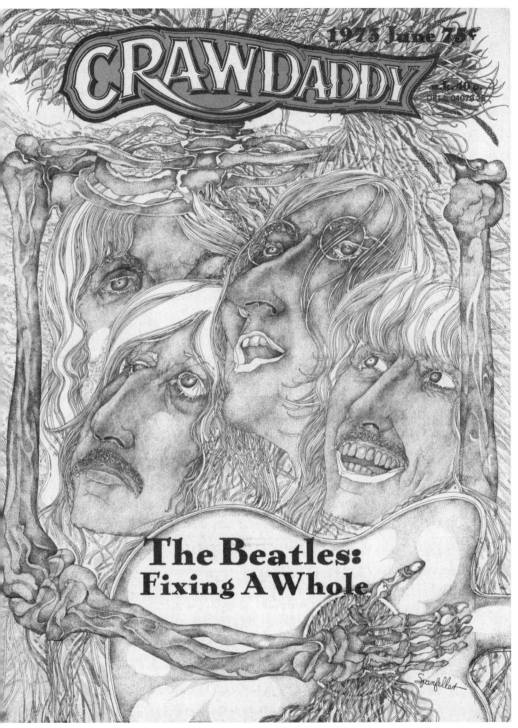

CRAWDADDY

1973 June 75¢

**The Beatles:
Fixing A Whole**

The clamor for the four ex-Beatles to reunite during the 1970s was unrelenting, but *Crawdaddy* was one of the few rock journals to suggest that maybe this wasn't such a good idea.

Paul McCartney TV special, which aired on both sides of the pond in April and May. Taped segments included everything from a pub sing-along to a pastoral interlude to a song-and-dance production number, but what fans might have wanted to see the most—Wings in concert—only really came at the end: too little, too late. Still, it may have primed the pump for the theater tour of Britain the band undertook (with pub rockers Brinsley Schwartz in support). While their new album, *Red Rose Speedway,* wasn't much of a draw unto itself, the McCartney-penned theme to the new James Bond flick, *Live and Let Die,* offered audiences a glimpse of the spectacle that slowly but surely was becoming a staple of their stage act. In about three years' time, they'd have it perfected.

For George, the high drama of a Hollywood film had become part of his daily existence—not in his music but in his personal life. A variety of forces that had come between himself and Pattie had finally reached the breaking point that summer. There were the usual infidelities and drug use, but even the area that had once bound them, Eastern religion and meditation, had become a corrosive force, as George, practicing his faith with the single-mindedness of a monk, had all but frozen his wife out of his life. She in turn found comfort in the arms of his best friend, who had been pitching woo at her for some three years by this point. Eric Clapton's obsession with Mrs. Harrison spawned two immediate by-products: the angst-driven love song "Layla," and a heroin addiction.

An oft-recounted incident occurred somewhere around this time. The degree of salaciousness varies with each telling, but the only certainty is that the two principals at the center of the story are dead. The only witness to the alleged event to publicly recount it is Pattie Boyd; her recent telling is as colorful and elaborate as anything found in a potboiler romance. Without spending a lot of ink on it, the basic plot held that the Harrisons and the Starkeys, as close as two adult couples could be, were in the habit of having dinner together. On one such occasion—out of the blue—George declared in front of everyone that he was in love with Maureen. As reported, Pattie was devastated, Maureen was embarrassed, and Ringo was upset. (More fleshed-out variations have Pattie actually catching her husband in flagrante delicto.)

Beyond dispute is that both marriages essentially ended that year. Ringo was off recording or filming, spending much time away from home and thus effecting a separation. Pattie, after a fling with Ronnie Wood, left George and took up with Clapton by year's end. For both ex-Beatles, the downward slide into serious substance abuse issues began here, a sad irony in the face of the unquestioned career triumphs.

No less unstable was the Lennons' home situation, which, as of May, had relocated to New York City's famous Dakota building. Located at Central Park West, the gothic-looking nineteenth-century structure had famously been used as the locale for the 1968 film *Rosemary's Baby*. No sooner had the couple moved into the apartment formerly occupied by actor Robert Ryan (who soon afterward followed his wife into death by cancer) than long-simmering troubles between John and Yoko came to a head. An undercurrent of hurt and humiliation lay not far beneath the surface of their unified public front (on April 1, they'd called a news conference to declare the formation of a new country, Nutopia, which had no borders or land and existed only in the minds of its citizens), stemming in no small part from John's acting out in front of a group of friends on election night, 1972. The oft-told incident concerned his act of adultery committed before the stunned gathering.

Anticipating where their troubles would lead, Yoko "ordered" assistant May Pang to yield to any advances coming from her husband. In September, John moved out, heading west to Los Angeles soon after—with May. This came just after he'd finally managed to get a collection of tunes together and produce them himself, calling the collection (fittingly) *Mind Games*. While certainly a step back toward the tuneful pop he'd produced for most of his career, the record sounded rushed and somewhat subpar. When the title song performed only so-so on the charts, John recognized his fall from favor with the public, making the blockbuster success of Ringo's album all the more galling. In need of something benign to do, he decided now was the best time to take on an oldies project. On paper at least, returning to his roots with Spector at the helm was a no-brainer.

Indeed, the release of *Ringo* was greeted with rapturous acclaim. "Photograph," the lead-off single, was an elegantly produced ballad with a haunting melody. The ersatz Wall of Sound somehow managed not to swamp the lead vocal and Harrison harmony, while embodying the best qualities of the Beatles' singles: hummable and familiar, yet fresh and enduring. "You're Sixteen," issued as a follow-up, rode the current wave of '50s / early '60s nostalgia; coming just as *That'll Be the Day* was reaching theaters in the States was a masterstroke of serendipitous timing.

Not to be outdone, Paul at last issued the album everyone had hoped he had in him. Under the direst of conditions (which saw two band members quit, a health scare, and an armed robbery) in a foreign land, Paul, Linda, and Denny somehow managed to hold it together long enough to produce what to that time was arguably McCartney's best post-Beatles work, *Band on the Run*. Oddly, while critics were quick to embrace the return of Macca to top form, record buyers were a little slower, waiting until two singles had been issued in the States, and then a third ("Helen Wheels," "Jet," and the title song, respectively) before really giving the album its due, chart-wise. Its release ended the year on a note of triumph for Paul at least, who distinguished himself as the one ex-Beatle whose marriage was still intact.

The Magic That You Do

Their Best Albums

Within this list of fourteen albums lies the case for the genuine artistic greatness of John, Paul, George, and Ringo individually, *after* the Beatles. While as a collective their music was magic, the roughly seven years of togetherness profoundly shaped their individual abilities, all to varying degrees of recognition by critics and the public alike. While none of them needed to imitate their past incarnation to produce worthwhile music, one could make the case that they fell short during the times when they strayed farthest from the built-in quality control that the four of them jointly were able to impose on each other's excesses.

While many of these releases were rightly recognized in their time as special—opinions formed by a nebulous mixture of expectations, context, and whatever else was happening at the time—the quality of others was only evident in hindsight. Conversely, does anyone really believe that *Wings at the Speed of Sound* holds up as a #1 album?

NOTE: Highest U.S. chart positions follow release dates in parentheses.

Beaucoups of Blues—Released September 28, 1970 (65)

As described in chapter 18, Ringo's second straight concept album came about through a series of lucky confluences, centered on the making of *All Things Must Pass*. Suffice to say, the experience was a dream come true for the country-fried Beatle. But for the majority of fans, especially in 1970, the worthiness of a solo recording was assessed in no small part on how much it evoked the Fabs. And an oddly titled album, coming off the heels of a record of big band–era tunes, was certain to raise eyebrows, if it were acknowledged long enough to get any reaction at all. For most of the record-buying public, the idea of Ringo Starr now offering up a country and western set was carrying a joke too far. But those who ignored *Beaucoups of Blues* did so at their own loss.

A successful record of the idiom wasn't necessarily predicated upon tight musicianship per se, although in this case Ringo had at his command some of the genre's top players. In addition to Pete Drake on pedal steel, future Top 40 crossover artist Charlie Daniels was aboard, as was guitar picker par excellence Jerry Reed. A songwriter of no little renown ("Guitar Man," for which he handled lead chores on Elvis's recording, as well as his own release, "Amos Moses"), Reed received a nod to what became his own hit record the following year as Ringo mangled "when you're hot, you're hot" in the fade-out to "$15 Draw." Other Elvis connections included the Jordanaires (on backing vocals) and drummer D. J. Fontana. If making the trip had only resulted in jamming with these legends, Ringo could have considered it a success.

But the album's material was written and pitched specifically with the Ringed One in mind. He chose wisely, with selections running the stylistic gamut from country waltzes to rockabilly to bluegrass, conveying the usual stories of ill-fated romance, dissipation, and, in the case of "Silent Homecoming," a chillingly timely antiwar statement. Four songs apiece came from Nashville stalwarts Chuck Howard and Sorrells Pickard. The late Mr. Pickard recalled the singer as a hard worker whose professionalism and charm made the project a real joy to work on. (He also reported that the album's rather desolate cover image was taken of Ringo sitting in the doorway of genre-busting recording artist Tracy Nelson's smokehouse.)

The "It" factor that made the album work as well as it did was Ringo's voice. While previously regarded as best suited to novelty tunes within the straight rock genre, Ringo's sound lent itself to plain, flat, but eminently authentic readings that on this album proved exceptional. He was able to convey heartbreak or carousing with equal aplomb, and held his own when dueting with country star Jeannie Kendal on "I Wouldn't Have You Any Other Way."

Had Ringo elected to explore the genre more deeply, he could easily have given former Monkee Michael Nesmith, then carving his own country rock path with the First National Band, a run for his money. But Ringo's attentions waned, and he went forward with his film career for the next year or so before returning to the pop/rock sound that had won him his fame. He remains proud of *Beaucoups of Blues,* however, counting it as his first meaningful artistic statement outside the Beatles. That pride is justified.

All Things Must Pass—Released November 27, 1970 (1)

So much has been written and said about the creation of George's staggeringly monumental debut release and the phenomenal success it enjoyed that

Apple

By the first anniversary of their breakup, several classic albums and singles had been issued by the former Fab Foursome, which must have caused at least a few fans to marvel at the variety and quality of material made possible by their dissolution.

perhaps a better discussion can be had by reviewing the album's contents. As early as the post–"White Album" *Get Back* sessions, George—while contributing some stellar leads to the Lennon-McCartney material—seemed intent on moving beyond overtly "poppy" sounds in his own writing, instead emulating the rootsiness of Dylan and the Band with rather straightforward compositions not well suited to the rock concert standards of the day.

To support whatever observational or philosophical points he wished to make, Harrison created melodies rife with diminished passing chords—floating somewhere between majors and minors—giving his material an insidiously haunting quality. Furthermore, the Indian influences he'd absorbed, along with American blues and soul, became thoroughly integrated into his sound, resulting in deceptively sophisticated music. (Nowhere was this more evident than in what became his signature sound: his slide playing.)

Striving for neither McCartney's mass appeal nor Lennon's confrontational posture, George wished to reach listeners on a higher level, seemingly regarding commerciality as an afterthought. Though of course "My Sweet Lord" would prove to be a staggering success (as well as an unholy albatross), the buzz at the time propelling sales of *All Things Must Pass* was less about any individual songs then it was about a major talent unleashed, one who'd been hidden in plain sight all those years. That the "Quiet Beatle" was capable of such range—from the joyful "What Is Life" to the meditative "Isn't It a Pity" to the steamrolling "Art of Dying" to the playful "I Dig Love"—was truly revelatory. After years of being led to believe that with two geniuses in the band, perhaps only one or two cuts per album were all the George anyone needed, the public learned, with these eighteen uniformly brilliant Harrisongs, what they'd been missing.

To be sure, some of his more pious pronouncements might have been out of place on a Beatles album ("Hear Me Lord," for example, was premiered—and rejected—during the *Let It Be* sessions), just as John's stark and deeply personal "Cold Turkey" had been. But there is plenty of material on *All Things Must Pass* that would have worked just fine on a new Fab record. "Apple Scruffs," for example, Harrison's touching paean to the über-fans who camped out on their office doorstep, is easily imagined with harmonies from John and Paul. (Outtakes from the session tape reveal the "hell" it was to record; while trying to tape the harmonica, guitar, and foot tap in real time, George had to wear a Dylan-esque harmonica holder that tortured him relentlessly by ensnaring his prodigious facial hair.)

The album's title song was actually tried out by his former band during the *Let It Be* sessions. A nascent arrangement featuring John on keyboards and layered vocal harmonies was attempted before George withdrew the song—it was never again picked up by the Fabs. (If it had been, we never would have had the majestic Spector-ized version we all know and love.) Thirty-plus years later, Paul ended up singing lead during its performance at the memorial Concert for George in 2002; according to Clapton, Macca was humbled at having to relearn it.

For the legions of Fab-watchers looking for insight into the group's breakup, the album provided much to dissect. While John's concurrent *Plastic Ono Band* release directly addressed issues within and without the Beatles, *All Things Must Pass* did so more obliquely. "Run of the Mill" was a bittersweet commentary on the breakdown of a friendship, while "Beware of Darkness," one of George's finest compositions *ever*, cautioned listeners not to put too much stock in negativity, false leaders, or life's enticing illusions. As explored elsewhere in this book, "Wah-Wah"—inspired by George reaching his limit with the stifling straitjacket his band had become—described how something once sweet had gone sour; he now knew with certainty how his life could improve "if I keep myself free."

The album's religiosity has been rather overstated, and comes up directly in only three songs. Beyond "My Sweet Lord" and "Hear Me Lord" was "Awaiting on You All," an exhortation to chant your Lord's name in order to become free. While not prescribing any God in particular, George did take a swat at organized religion, asserting that "the pope owns fifty-one per cent of General Motors / the stock exchange is the only thing he's qualified to quote us." (This damning characterization of the Catholic Church was omitted from the printed lyric sheet enclosed.)

The unmistakable specter of Bob Dylan hung over the project, though Dylan himself did not appear. First, there was George's fine cover of Bob's "If Not for You"—he and Bob laid down a take in New York before work commenced on *All Things Must Pass*, though *that* particular recording was passed over for release on Dylan's album at the time. George's standout performance (drummer Alan White *swears* that John Lennon is on the recording—a most unlikely possibility) was neither pulled as a single nor showcased at the Bangladesh benefit concert, though it was rehearsed. Instead, newcomer Olivia Newton-John used George's blueprint to score *her* first hit. Album opener "I'd Have You Anytime" marked the first Dylan-Harrison composition, wedding Bob's lyrics to George's seductive music. Then there was the aforementioned "Apple Scruffs"—connected to Bob strictly by influence. But Dylan aside, George managed to weave a unique tapestry from very many disparate threads; the net sum on *All Things Must Pass* was entirely of his own making.

There have been some through the years who have suggested that Hari Georgeson might have done his career more good if he had parceled out the *All Things Must Pass* material judiciously over a couple of releases rather than issuing it all at once with his very own "White Album." While they may have a point in terms of sustaining his chart velocity, in artistic terms, it would have been like standing still. George's next album represented a refinement of the themes expressed the first time around, just as *Dark Horse* marked an advance from *Living in the Material World*. For George, ever the explorer, revisiting a triumph was just not in him.

John Lennon/Plastic Ono Band—Released December 11, 1970 (2)

It's important to note that before *Plastic Ono Band*'s release, John's output on his own was mixed, adding up to three increasingly accomplished singles ("Instant Karma" being the best received) as well as a string of LPs best left forgotten. Still, after Paul threw down the gauntlet with *McCartney* in April 1970, with all due respect to Macca, it wouldn't have taken much to better it so long as John reined in his experimental impulses. Not only did he leave his former partner in the dust artistically with *Plastic Ono Band*, but it took a three-record box set from his former junior partner to overshadow his achievement.

Plastic Ono Band has been called John's "primal" album, as it unleashed a torrent of lifelong resentments and accrued pain with a directness rarely heard in pop music (with the possible exception of Nina Simone's work). He had undergone treatment at Dr. Arthur Janov's center in Los Angeles before work commenced on the album, and the ensuing narrative—then as now—held that therapy "freed" him to strip the scab from his psychological wounds and throw off accumulated layers of coping mechanisms, resulting in blunt truth-telling, bereft of metaphor or poesy. In fact, John was expounding upon an arc that began at least as far back as "Help!"—on his debut, he took it to its natural apex.

At its very best, John's music of the last couple of years had taken his own inner life, be it romantic ("Don't Let Me Down"), self-reflective ("Julia"), or straight-ahead narrative ("Cold Turkey"), and made it universally relatable, soliciting empathy from listeners. Though his own travails were the starting point, John intended for his art to be universal. With the harrowing "Mother," for instance, he began with his own history but crafted the song in such a way that anyone listening could hear his or her own story within (or, as he introduced it at the One to One concert two years later, "A lot of people thought it was about my parents, but it's about 99 percent of the parents alive or half-dead").

John's debut long-player of original material stirs attention today not only for its breathtaking honesty but also for its visceral immediacy. Counterintuitively, he tapped Mr. Wall of Sound himself to assist with the production while seeking a bare-bones, in-your-face listening experience that—even now—could have been recorded last week.

Though drawing upon elements that had made up his musical vocabulary since he'd first stepped into a recording studio (echoed vocals, evocations of '50s records, concise melodic underpinnings), the real revelation was his guitar playing. Without the cover of Hari Georgeson or George Martin's sonic sheen, John's "primitive" (his word) playing served as a second voice, eschewing pyrotechnics for raw emotion that complemented his singing. (The agitated-sounding "I Found Out"—which enumerates the various institutions in life that ultimately disappointed—is a prime example.)

The songs themselves contained a subtext of a new life rising from the ashes of the old, of leaving behind that which is no longer needed and asserting one's own individuality. The aforementioned "Mother," complete with the most chilling vocal Lennon ever committed to tape (during the drawn-out fade), begins with a funereal bell (echoed a decade later on "Starting Over" for *Double Fantasy*) tolling an ending, while "God" enumerates the various past fancies John now knows to be false, leading him to move forward with belief in himself (and Yoko). The album is so rife with a litany of letdowns (within all of the aforementioned titles, plus "Isolation" and "Remember") that they are ironically evocative of *Catcher in the Rye*'s Holden Caulfield, railing against the world's inherent "phoniness." The overall negativity is balanced—somewhat—by the optimistic "Hold On" and "Love," the album's emotional center.

No discussion of the album would be complete without mentioning the musical support provided by Ringo and Klaus Voormann. Again minus the usual array of instruments found on your typical rock and roll record, the sparse but tight rhythm section anchors Lennon's material, whether piano or guitar-based. It's particularly noteworthy that John directed his fellow "primitives" to go for feel rather than precision: that is why, although the record is replete with flubbed notes and at times raggedy performances, the instinctive telepathy between the musicians provides a level of energy and spark that enlivens the songs in a way that perfection would have dampened.

Consensus among rock critics holds that John never bested his debut (according to some, it was a downhill progression ever after) but that is to miss the point. *John Lennon / Plastic Ono Band* represented a one-of-a-kind purging while laying waste to the past; any further revisiting of this approach could only serve to water down the album's thematic power. Though not exactly tailored for pleasure listening, Lennon's debut succeeded in clearing the decks. On his next outing, John could go back to being commercial.

Ram—Released May 17, 1971 (2)

The issue of "Another Day" as a stand-alone single in February 1971 scarcely hinted at the riches to follow. True, the pleasant-sounding ditty was lyrically darker than its whistle-along melody suggested, but at the time, critics carped that Macca was easily being outclassed by the weightier offerings from two of his fellow ex-Fabs. It was strictly an apples-and-oranges comparison, for while John and George produced music with a point, calculated to engage on an intellectual or emotional level, Paul's art was intended to score in aesthetic terms as pure pop. Judged that way, *Ram* was his first masterpiece.

In the same way that *Beaucoups of Blues*, *All Things Must Pass*, and *Plastic Ono Band* captured each creator's respective strengths and presented them fully optimized, so did

Ram offer a graphic depiction of Paul's gifts as master musician, song-writer, and producer. In a marked departure from the homegrown charm of *McCartney*, *Ram* pulled out all the production stops, tapping the Big Apple's finest studio pros along with the New York Philharmonic. (Paul admitted that his approach *was* a reaction to carping that his debut was underproduced, and was therefore chagrined when this LP was equally lambasted.)

It's hard to know where to begin describing the contents of this LP. Tracking all the musical ideas zooming past on every cut is an exercise in futility. One could make the argument that, perhaps realizing that his gifts would never find favor with the rock press in the same way that George and John's had done, Paul served up what had to be a very deliberate return to the polish of *Abbey Road*. Like the Beatles' best work, it possessed a broad stylistic range: from '50s rock and roll (the Buddy Holly homage "Eat at Home") to some down-home pickin' and grinnin' ("Heart of the Country") to acoustic blues ("Three Legs") to some unfinished bits stuck together ("Uncle Albert / Admiral Halsey"). And fully integrated into each song were soaring harmonies, heard nowhere to better advantage than on the *Pet Sounds* pastiche "Dear Boy."

This last song, believed by John to be yet another insult hurled his way ("I hope you never know how much you missed") was actually written about John See, Linda's first husband and the biological father of Heather. See, an anthropologist, saw his marriage break up in 1965 after announcing his intent to move the family out of the country to pursue his career. In 2000, See committed suicide in Tucson. (Said Paul: "He was a nice guy; an Ernest Hemingway type.") Lennon wasn't entirely off the mark, as the album's superb opening number, "Too Many People," *did* contain a bit of provocation directed his way, as did the closer, "Back Seat of My Car." Even without the puerile subtext, Paul chose two extraordinarily strong songs to bookend his sophomore release.

The first featured thundering drums, a touch of brass, and a lead vocal that leaped from the speakers. Like so much great McCartney music, it took some twists and turns, following a logic of its own, before arriving at a cacophonous conclusion that is as stirring as it is chaotic. Likewise, "Back Seat of My Car," a song Macca had been toying with as far back as the *Let It Be* sessions, began as a subdued ballad—possibly overlush (to use John's word in another situation; it did feature a *harp*, after all)—before the brass came in and things picked up. The song thereafter shifted smoothly back and forth between quiet interludes and an insistent refrain: "We believe that we can't be wrong." This was sung with almost mantra-like repetition until 3:42, when—out of nowhere—Paul kicked it up several notches. Whatever he was singing about initially suddenly took on a desperate urgency; keeping in mind that he was battling the other three ex-Fabs in court at this time, his delivery of the line was as emotionally gripping as anything on *Plastic Ono Band*.

Beyond the overall execution of the collection's individual songs, what gave *Ram* its greatness was the overall cohesion. Implementing a trick he'd used to good effect on *Sgt. Pepper's*—reprising a tune to provide the illusion of a unifying concept—Paul tied things together nicely, at once elevating the set to a higher thematic level and giving listeners the sense of being taken on a journey. (He would revisit the gimmick overtly on *Band on the Run* and *Venus and Mars*, and more subtly on *Back to the Egg*.) *Ram* put the public on notice that, *McCartney* notwithstanding, the Beatles' resident crowd pleaser was still alive and well.

And the whole thing's brilliant in headphones.

Imagine—Released September 9, 1971 (1)

Having delivered a cathartic masterpiece his first time out, John was now ready to begin the transition from personal to public politics in his work. Just months after the release of *Plastic Ono Band*, he issued the rabble-rousing stomper "Power to the People" as a single. Donning a Japanese riot police helmet in the sleeve photo, Lennon put listeners on notice that all his "love is all you need" preaching was passé; now, with America ensnared in a bloody stalemate in the Far East, and an apparently fascist government in place, the time had come to get out in the streets and agitate for change *now*. The fact that the lord of the Dakota would repudiate those sentiments by decade's end does not detract from the power of the track: he was simply doing what he'd always done, trying on a new set of clothes and making what he could of the situation before moving on.

Though largely in thrall to England's leftist novelist/activist Tariq Ali at the time, John dialed down the rhetoric with his next political missive, which represented as much absorption of Yoko's art as it did his own evolving worldview. "Imagine" was—like his "War Is Over (If You Want It)" campaign, or even "Give Peace a Chance"—an explicit *suggestion* that listeners reconsider their handed-down values: was any nation or spiritual belief worth dying for? Wasn't peace with your fellow man worth surrendering a little sovereignty or group identification?

Beyond the song's simple melodic beauty was the appeal of a Utopian world where human beings could at last realize the ideal that every belief system promised, achievable—according to John—by dismantling the very constructs humankind has always instinctively built to sustain itself. It was a compelling thesis and one that was far easier to suggest than it was to live up to, as John's detractors were quick to point out. (Elton John, for instance, privately lampooned the Lennons with a parody that went: "Imagine six apartments / It isn't hard to do / One is full of fur coats / The other's full of shoes.")

Imagine—the album—is generally considered to be John's high-water mark as a solo act, especially by people who have never listened to *Walls and Bridges*. True, it contained such radio-friendly fare as "Jealous Guy," "Oh My Love," and the catchy but slight "Oh Yoko!," but the album's real meat lay in the edgier tracks like "Gimme Some Truth," "It's So Hard," and "I Don't Wanna Be a Soldier." Then, of course, there was the character-assassinating "How Do You Sleep," a track that debased its creator more than its intended target.

Unlike the austere sound captured previously, Spector's brass, strings, and layered instrumentation sugarcoated these proceedings, smoothing off the rough edges and giving some tracks a cocooned feel. While possibly enhancing the LP's appeal, Spector's approach also subdued the overall spirit in a way that the production on *Plastic Ono Band* did not. On hand for the Tittenhurst Park sessions were established Plastic Ono Band members Klaus Voormann and Alan White, as well as special guests Nicky Hopkins and George Harrison. The latter contributed some of the album's grittiest playing, especially on "Gimme Some Truth." (Like several songs on the album, this one would have been familiar to Georgeas a Beatles reject dating from the 1968 India songwriting camp. Other "oldies" included "Jealous Guy"—formerly "Child of Nature," "Oh My Love," and "Oh Yoko!"—begun in 1969 but left unfinished until the *Imagine* sessions.)

Like *Plastic Ono Band, Imagine* came fully laden with "finger-pointing songs," accusatory diatribes against the usual societal hypocrites. But perhaps the most affecting was the one in which John turned the tables on himself. "Jealous Guy," nominally an apology to Yoko for crimes past and ones not yet committed, displayed a discernible vulnerability in both the singing and the lyrics, a concession that while he feared he might have lost Yoko's love, Lennon was also being true to his own nature. By reiterating what he'd expressed earlier in "Run for Your Life" ("Well, you know that I'm a wicked guy and I was born with a jealous mind"), he displayed self-awareness that stopped well short of the obvious next step: reforming. Instead, he offered a warning about future transgressions ("Look out, babe"). The song represents a profound moment of facing reality over fanciful idealism.

While the title song did not reach #1, the album did, momentarily renewing John's position in the rock world and within the competition he perceived among his fellow ex-Fabs. Though he would continue to produce material of high quality—sporadically—until his premature death, *Imagine* represented him at his critical and commercial zenith. *Some Time in New York City*, no matter how well intended, irrevocably injured his brand, and though he would achieve another #1 album, never again was he really regarded as one of the top-flight acts of the day. Newer artists emerged who were more relevant, more political, rocked harder, and above all projected authenticity. Whatever brilliance John still had in him would be embraced by his base, but for all intents and purposes, his days as a spokesman for a generation were behind him before he turned thirty-two. None of which detracts from the luster of *Imagine*.

Living in the Material World—Released May 30, 1973 (I)

Just after the Bangladesh benefit, George vented his mixed emotions in a song called "The Day the World Gets 'Round." All the stress and anxiety from weeks of—in a sense—placing the weight of the world upon himself spilled out, resulting in a song that was at once an expression of gratitude to all the good hearts that had contributed to the success of the event and a stinging indictment of those who possessed the power to make things better (i.e., governments) but instead of helping had turned their backs when it suited their ends to do so. (In 2009, the song would be remade by the former Cat Stevens, with Klaus Voormann in support, as a charitable release.) Outrage that the suffering he saw was being ignored by the very authorities who could make a difference resulted in an earnest counterpart to John's "Imagine."

"Jet" (represented here in its rather risqué sheet music form) was classic McCartney: catchy melodies topped with nonsensical lyrics, wrapped in exquisite harmonies over an insistently dynamic performance. Critics and fans alike were bowled over that Paul was at last getting his act together.

The track was issued on the long-awaited follow-up to *All Things Must Pass*, *Living in the Material World*. (Months before its release, it was announced in the press as bearing the title *The Magic Is Here Again*—if this was accurate, George would surely have set himself up for no small measure of scorn with such unintended vainglory.) Comprised in large part of songs that either declared his spiritual goals or decried past and present injustices, *Living in the Material World* was, in its own way, George's *Plastic Ono Band*—a point that did not go unnoticed by Stephen Holden in his review for *Rolling Stone*. (He further called it "miraculous in its radiance" and a "concise, universally conceived work.")

In contrast to John's earlier groundbreaking LP, George—handling the production chores himself—presented his collection in richly arranged settings, though not as densely as Spector might have done. Freed from the tyranny of the Wall of Sound, George's own production gave the tunes breathing space, allowing the instruments to sparkle and his increasingly accomplished slide guitar playing to shine through. This was amply shown to great effect on the advance single, "Give Me Love (Give Me Peace on Earth)." Long laboring in the shadow of his "senior partners," George must have felt validated when the song displaced Paul's "My Love" at the top of the charts in some markets.

The album's relative lack of bulk compared with its predecessor made it easier to streamline a theme, which in this case was the most overt spiritual message of Harrison's entire recorded output. But, in contrast to the dour preacher that George was caricatured as in the rock press, the album presents its message with romanticism, lyrically and especially musically. Nonetheless, packaging the record with enough Krishna paraphernalia to set up a temple in the comfort of one's own home—undoubtedly the artist's intent—George may have unwittingly scared off those otherwise receptive to his message, simultaneously setting himself up for parody.

At this distance, it is easy to judge the album on its musical merits, which are considerable. While not calculated to offer much in the way of instantly catchy ear candy, *Living in the Material World* is rife with thoughtful compositions that grow on one after repeated listenings.

"Who Can See It," for instance, which declared considerable bitterness at Harrison's Beatle past, was a dramatic ballad very much in the style of Roy Orbison. (George got quite bold with his singing on this album, sliding into falsetto on more than one song.) The wistful acoustic ballad "Be Here Now"—with its title taken from the 1971 meditation guide by Baba Ram Dass—was arranged with a nearly imperceptible undercurrent of sitar drone. The album's closer, "That Is All," sums up the journey in much the same way that "Hear Me Lord" did on *All Things Must Pass*, though John Barham's arrangement of strings and choirs is far more subdued than anything on the earlier album.

Lest anyone think that *Living in the Material World* was one long sermon, there were several other tracks that dispelled this notion. "Sue Me Sue You Blues" brought things back down to Earth with its stinging slide leads and bluesy feel while offering sardonic commentary on the litigation-heavy events of the past few years. "Don't Let Me Wait Too Long" was a Spector-esque (in the "girl group" sense) pop confection that came *this close* to being issued as a follow-up single.

George regarded the album's title track as a "comedy" tune, as it pulled out the big production number clichés in a lighthearted look back on how he'd gotten to where he was and what he hoped to achieve in this life. The song's seamless segues between full-blown rock and Indian segments were a production marvel. Lastly, "The Lord Loves the One (That Loves the Lord)" was *not* the sanctimonious rant that some characterized it as but instead a funky, up-tempo piece that revealed George's own inner conflict, reconciling his earthly role as a rock star with its utter triviality in the Grand Scheme of things. Here, as everywhere else, his guitar playing was stellar; it's a shame that the gravity of so much of his material blinded people to his true gifts.

Living in the Material World stands today as that rarest of things: a million-selling masterpiece by an ex-Beatle that's been largely forgotten by the general public.

Ringo—Released October 31, 1973 (2)

There are many folks in this world—the "ignorant," we shall call them—who believe that Ringo Starr's invitation to join the Beatles in 1962 made him the luckiest man who ever lived. This presupposes that talent had nothing to do with it; in fact, as anyone reading this (or *Fab Four FAQ*) already knows, it is beyond dispute that the Ringed One's percussive skills were integral to the Beatles' recording success; this is to say nothing of the less definable "It" factor that added immeasurably to the group's appeal, and so forth. Still, when Richie Snare entered the recording studio in March 1973 with producer Richard Perry, what he emerged with would benefit greatly from a rare confluence of timing, public longing for the old days, and all-around good will projected his way. While under any lesser conditions, *Ringo* might not have become the commercial smash that it was, this in no way detracts from its excellence as a fully realized collection of pop/rock tunes.

Still finding his legs as a songwriter, Ringo had a modest set of original tunes to his credit by the time he and his supporting musicians convened to work on this album. Proximity to and an established working relationship with George produced "Photograph," Ringo's first #1 single and his signature tune as a solo artist. (Interestingly, the two never officially cowrote another song.) His initial writing sessions with Perry protégé Vini Poncia yielded two tracks for the album, "Devil Woman" and "Oh My My," the latter a Top 10 single. On his own, he came up with "Step Lightly," a cute but slight throwback to his pub sing-along days, as well as the meatier "Down and Out," issued as a B-side.

But it would be the assistance he received from his fellow ex-Fabs that really shone a spotlight on the album. Always concerned about their former drummer's career, George and John readily agreed to help out. George donated the uncharacteristic hoedown "Sunshine Life for Me (Sail Away Raymond)," which proved to be a good musical fit with backings from the Band. Assisting the nascent songwriting career of one Malcolm Evans, he also contributed the set closer, "You and Me (Babe)." John gave Ringo a track he'd originally begun for himself before realizing that he could never get away with singing it: "I'm the Greatest." Once word of three Beatles recording together got out, a buzz began building for the album well before it hit the streets. For a brief shining moment, the anticipation was something that resembled the old days.

Paul's involvement was not to be denied. He brought in "Six O'Clock," a catchy ballad that, had he recorded it himself, might have been considered unremarkable, but that in Ringo's hands was stellar. Macca added a touch of synthesizer embellishment to the track, as well as—famously—his saxophone impression on "You're Sixteen." For Ringo, the moment to issue a well-produced oldie as well as an album featuring all three of his former bandmates could not have been better. With a nostalgia craze sweeping the country and renewed Beatlemania being stoked by the issue of the "Red" and "Blue" album sets, it was the perfect storm of opportunity to release a well-crafted album. (Only Elton John's blockbuster *Goodbye Yellow Brick Road* stopped it from topping the charts.)

Ringo proved to be greater than the sum of its parts. With its superb supporting cast, pitch-perfect production, and lavish packaging, it proved to be an embarrassment of riches for the self-effacing percussionist. Though he would never duplicate the scale of its success, he now had a road map with which to plot a winning path as a recording artist. For the public, Ringo's musical offering prompted the question: If they could put aside their differences long enough to produce some fine music, would making the reunion a little more permanent be too much to ask?

Band on the Run—Released December 5, 1973 (1)

With two Wings albums and another four non-album singles under his belt by summer 1973, Paul was ready to produce an album that would finally wow both critics and the public. While *Wild Life* went gold—largely on the cachet he'd earned as an ex-Beatle—and *Red Rose Speedway* did even better, holding the #1 spot briefly, neither release was particularly well received by the same rock press that had lauded the work of the other ex-Fabs. With a stockpile of songs that he was certain would add up to a juggernaut, Macca convened the band for rehearsals at his Scottish farm in July in advance of recording sessions slated for Lagos, Nigeria in August.

These plans hit a serious snag when a long-simmering discontent between Henry McCullough and his boss ended with the guitarist leaving in a huff; drummer Denny Seiwell followed suit days later, literally as the remaining three Wings were headed for Africa. Normally, the decimation of a band on the eve of a recording session would require a serious rethink of how to (or even *whether* to) go forward. For Paul, who had already faced professional adversity in his recent past, the events were a mere speed bump en route to fulfilling his mission. No slouch on lead guitar or drums himself, he simply committed to overdubbing the parts and proceeding as planned, band or no band.

It has been suggested that adversity raised his game and challenged him to kick it up a notch, resulting in what was universally held to be a tour de force. But Paul rejected this assessment (while simultaneously conceding that it was probably right). The end result of the trio circling their wagons and hunkering down was an album that restored Paul's good name and put him back in the game for good, redefining perceptions of who was the ex-Beatle most capable of carrying on their legacy. Until *Band on the Run*, that ex-Fab had been widely assumed to be George.

The first hint of what the sessions produced was a single, "Helen Wheels," released in advance of the album. Despite what anyone might have expected with the band reduced to their core, the song rocked convincingly—no one missed the services of McCulloch and Seiwell. Though it had been intended as another stand-alone single, Capitol persuaded Paul to add the song to *Band on the Run* in America, promising him that they could move another "quarter million units." He agreed, and they did. (A video—directed by the ubiquitous Michael Lindsay-Hogg—was produced for the song, featuring Linda wearing a fur coat. After her commitment to full-time animal rights activism years later, the clip was crudely doctored with a special effect to remove the offending garment.)

Band on the Run dropped just in time for Christmas 1973, one month after the leadoff single. In a reversal of what had been the standard pattern, the sales were good—not great—and the *reviews* were robust. Putting himself out on a critical limb, future Springsteen producer/manager Jon Landau went so far (in *Rolling Stone*) as to call it "the finest record yet released by any of the four musicians who were once called the Beatles." Only after first "Jet" (in January 1974) and then the title track (later that spring) were released as singles did the album climb back up the charts and land at #1. Fans were ecstatic, and at last the band—dubbed "Paul McCartney and Wings" as of

Red Rose Speedway—began to get respect. In January 1975, the album was honored with a Grammy for Best Pop Vocal Performance.

As described elsewhere in this book, "Band on the Run" (the song) seemed to be an explicit exploration of escape and the quest for freedom. Other songs in the collection likewise hinted at that subtext, including "Bluebird" (previewed on the *James Paul McCartney* TV special) and "Mamunia." This alone gave the album some implied unity (as did the arrangement of "Picasso's Last Words," which included snatches of "Jet" and "Mrs. Vandebilt"), heightening it above a mere set of random songs.

But though the usual array of styles was showcased, there was also a definite *je ne sais quoi* captured in the grooves that moved listeners. This wasn't the usual modicum of silly love songs; in fact, the only tune that came close to fitting that description was the Denny Laine cocomposition "No Words," making *Band on the Run* unusual within the McCartney oeuvre. While not exactly as slickly produced as other Wings albums would be, it did maintain a sonic standard worthy of George Martin, with tasteful string arrangements courtesy of Bowie producer Tony Visconti (then married to Apple's Mary Hopkin), while sax was provided by an even older associate, Howie Casey, who, as a member of Derry and the Seniors, had played the same Liverpool-Hamburg club circuit as the Beatles.

Like *Ram*, the new album was all over the map stylistically, sometimes within the same track. "Picasso's Last Words" was another artfully stitched-together Macca montage, inspired by a *Time* magazine account of the artist's death and written after a challenge by actor Dustin Hoffman, whom the McCartneys ran into while the former was filming *Papillon* in Jamaica. Over dinner, the two discussed their respective creative processes, and when the actor doubted that Paul could just pull a melody out of the air, McCartney grabbed a guitar and did just that, before the stunned Hoffman's eyes. ("He's doing it! He's writing it! It's coming out!")

Indeed, Paul had done it. *Band on the Run* satisfied on every level, distilling all the finest qualities of his Beatles music and fusing them with Wings' distinctive identity over the course of ten songs that took listeners on a journey. It was exactly the record fans and critics had long hoped he would make; the challenge now was, as it had been for John, George, and Ringo with *Plastic Ono Band*, *All Things Must Pass*, and *Ringo* respectively: where do you go from here?

Walls and Bridges—Released September 26, 1974 (1)

Attempting to retrieve his good name after *Some Time in New York City* blew up in his face, John entered the studio in summer 1973, determined to simultaneously create a collection of songs without a strident agenda and seize control of his own product. He dispensed with the services of Elephant's Memory (who had recorded *Approximately Infinite Universe* earlier that year with Yoko while John was lying low), instead going with a team of seasoned studio pros, as he would from this point forward. Also, for the first time he took matters into his own hands as a producer. Given a dearth of really strong material and his own haste in the studio, the resulting *Mind Games* album was merely good instead of great—and its chart performance reflected exactly that.

From here, John drifted into the troubled oldies project. Much rock lore originated with this highly combustible re-teaming with Phil Spector. Some reports tell of the party's forcible ejection from A&M Studios after a bottle of brandy was emptied onto a recording console. Without so much as a time-out, the merrymakers resumed the fun at Record Plant West. Harry Nilsson told the story of how Spector managed to tie a barely conscious Lennon to a chair before leaving the studio for the evening; after freeing himself hours later, John had to call a friend to let him out of the locked facility.

The most infamous incident involved Spector's gunplay. Long accustomed to drawing a handgun on those who displeased him, the producer made Mal Evans the recipient of his wrath one hazy evening when the musicians were slogging through Chuck Berry's "You Can't Catch Me"—the object of the Morris Levy litigation. According to those there, Spector pulled the weapon on Evans and the gun discharged, blowing a massive hole in the studio ceiling. Stunned silence followed the deafening explosion, broken by John bellowing: "If you're gonna kill me, Phil, then kill me. But don't fuck with me ears—I need 'em!"

The entire effort finally hit a wall in December when Spector left Lennon a cryptic message announcing that work would be suspended, as the studio had burned down. John easily confirmed that this had not happened, but learned at the same time that Phil had absconded with the master tapes. This left him with nothing to show for two months of work, such as it was, but a tall bill for studio time and session men.

John's ongoing funk reached its lowest depths with the infamous Troubadour Club incident weeks later (see chapter 29 for details). Thereafter, he managed to pull himself together. Work on Harry's *Pussy Cats* album proved just the tonic for shaking off his ennui, while proximity to May, his new love, proved to be as inspiring to him as Yoko had been in 1968. New songs began emerging quickly, marking a return to the self-referential material that had long been his stock in trade. While his personal life had been bruised by suffering and despair during the last year, his ability to organize it and channel it into art proved every bit as therapeutic as primal scream therapy had been purported to be four years earlier.

Walls and Bridges is a much-overlooked release within the Lennon canon. Though, like George's *Living in the Material World*, it went to #1 and spawned a #1 hit single, it has consistently been overshadowed by *Imagine* and even

It took five albums and seven singles before John Lennon scored his first #1 single from a #1 album—an achievement realized but once in his lifetime. Interestingly, *Walls and Bridges* represented the only new material recorded without any input from Yoko, being created during the so-called "Lost Weekend."

From the album "Walls and Bridges" recorded by John Lennon on APPLE RECORDS

LENNON MUSIC/ATV MUSIC CORPORATION
NEW YORK, N.Y.

$1.50

Distributed by

Double Fantasy—a real shame considering that as an album, it is probably second to *Plastic Ono Band* in terms of being a thoroughly cohesive and fully realized collection. Bearing no politics other than the personal, it chronicled in detail not only the travails of the breakup of his marriage, but also weariness at how taxing life can be when one truly reaches maturity, and the doomed exuberance of the attempt to live it up like a teenager at twice that age. In short, while containing moments of high spirits and joy, overall, *Walls and Bridges* depicted the yin-yang tension in striving for healing wherever one can find it ("Whatever Gets You Through the Night") while recognizing that every cure has its cost ("What You Got"). It's a dark theme—and a very adult one.

The undervaluing of the album stemmed in no small part from its creator himself, who—once back with Yoko and crafting a renewed domestic bliss meme—dismissed the release indifferently as the work of a dysfunctional created during a period he disparaged as "the Lost Weekend." One must therefore recognize that, with Yoko beside him and the songs a stark reminder of not only his May Pang interlude, but a painful transition running counter to the then-current "the two of us are really one" message, John wasn't exactly going to go out of his way to praise the material.

However much he resisted revisiting it, what John created in 1974 stands among his most enduring work. While his hit single "Whatever Gets You Through the Night" isn't typically ranked among his greatest tunes, it does offer a snapshot of where he was at the time. Given the disorder of his life, finding any coping mechanism around was the order of the day, and the song's wobbly but driving energy evoked the late-night activity vibe beautifully. More durable was the lovely wistfulness of "#9 Dream." With a string arrangement borrowed from Nilsson's "Many Rivers to Cross" (on *Pussy Cats*), this elegantly produced track was a touching look back at Lennon's past, framed as a somnambulant vision. (As karmic law would have it, it peaked at #9.)

Having honed his production skills since *Mind Games*, John brought a much more focused studio craft to the new album. Gone were the murky mixes of the former album; what's more, with the addition of the Little Big Horns, *Walls and Bridges* featured a sound that was both contemporary and timeless. It was clear that John had been absorbing a lot of current music, as the funky instrumental "Beef Jerky" attested. (It bore traces of the same inspiration that informed the Average White Band's "Pick Up the Pieces" the following year.) The riotous "What You Got," featuring a blistering vocal, blasting brass, and a stellar performance from Jim Keltner, was equally suitable for the dance floor. (It remains a favorite of Paul

Shaffer's CBS Orchestra on David Letterman's show as a play-out during commercial breaks.)

"Going Down on Love" kicked off the album in an arresting manner, with John's voice nearly a cappella, underscored only by subdued guitar and stark congas. It set the scene for all that followed: having lost his love, he's left with no choice but to pursue a path of dissipation to drown his troubles. While "Surprise, Surprise (Sweet Bird of Paradox)" celebrated new romance, John still felt moved to offer a touching sendoff to Yoko with the vaguely Latin-feeling "Bless You." In the past, songs to his wife had taken the form of pure adoration or apologies. On this one, however, John acknowledged that they'd parted, but extended his best wishes upon whoever is "holding her now," and reassured her that "now and forever, our love will remain." For the original Jealous Guy to express such sentiments demonstrated considerable growth.

Each side of the album was anchored by a key track. Side one concluded with "Scared," a blunt self-analysis that sounded like a *Plastic Ono Band* out-take, but for the judicious use of brass and Jesse Ed Davis's usual expressive guitar. With a walking rhythm and bent notes that echoed the lone wolf howl heard at the start, John described the battering life had given him, leaving him frightened, wounded, and weary. Whereas the *Plastic Ono Band* songs tended to assert that hard-earned self-knowledge had armed Lennon to deal with life's struggles, on "Scared" he sounds as though he has no expectation that the outcome will be good; as Pete Townshend would sing along similar lines the following year on "However Much I Booze," "There ain't no way out."

Side two's centerpiece was the equally bleak "Nobody Loves You (When You're Down and Out)." While the old Jimmie Cox blues standard "Nobody Knows You When You're Down and Out" (best known to rock audiences by Derek and the Dominoes' cover) may have inspired the title, the sentiments expressed are as old as popular music. In a weary voice, John expressed what writers Ben Urish and Kenneth G. Bielen described as "the essence of a three o'clock in the morning bleary-eyed, self-pitying, booze-drenched interior monologue." Again he cast himself as one who recognized the false bravado of self-defilement for public spectacle. But in the end, there are no easy answers: "All I can tell you is, it's all showbiz."

Walls and Bridges has gone largely unnoticed by the public and is generally underrated by critics. But seen for what it is and not compared with the music listeners thought Lennon *should* be making, it is a solid song cycle themed on the aftermath of a breakup, a sort of rock recasting of Sinatra's *In the Wee Small Hours*. Perhaps, due to John's penchant for making grand statements with his music, the smaller ones go unrecognized.

Venus and Mars—Released May 27, 1975 (1)

The success of *Band on the Run* sustained the crippled Wings well into 1974. As the album continued to be the gift that kept on giving, Paul hung out with John for the first time in years, probing for an opening to resuming their partnership, if even on a limited basis. Distracted by his immigration battles and the ongoing Yoko-May saga, not to mention his professional commitments, Lennon wasn't biting—at least not yet. Still, by year's end, with his first #1 album in three years under his belt and feeling reconnected with the rock community for the first time in years via associations with some of the era's biggest stars (Elton, Bowie), the timing may have been right to at least *consider* expanding his horizons.

But, as noted elsewhere in this book, plans for him to join the McCartneys in New Orleans in early 1975 failed to materialize. What might have resulted in a major career shift for both men went for naught and Paul, having reconstituted Wings, began laying down tracks. After a false start with drummer Geoff Britton, Joe English became the final piece of the puzzle that set Wings on an upward arc for the next three years. Perhaps having the confidence of knowing that he'd won over skeptics, Paul went into the studio with a strong batch of songs. The result of Wings' collective labors was an album that extended Paul's winning streak while setting the stage for Wings' eventual world conquest.

Credited to Wings (no "Paul McCartney and . . ." this time), *Venus and Mars* was the most overt "concept" album that the group ever made, though what the unifying theme was, no one could say. Perhaps the fact that it was the most conspicuous "group" effort to date, with Denny and Jimmy each scoring a lead vocal, was concept enough. In any event, while not exactly "slick," it held together as a unified whole even better than its predecessor. The "Venus and Mars" motif kicked off each album side (in more fully realized form on side two before segueing into "Spirits of Ancient Egypt").

As an opener, it set up "Rock Show," a fanfare composed to herald the band's concerts throughout the next year. Featuring Allen Toussaint on piano and one Kenneth "Afro" Williams on congas, the song duly rocked while offering a rundown of venues around the world that the band would soon play. The studio recording featured a rather interesting coda that was lopped off when performed live, showcasing Toussaint's playing to good effect as Paul "rapped" a sequence describing getting prepped to go see a concert with his squeeze ("Place your wig on straight, can't be late / C'mon, we got a date").

As this bit of silliness faded into the distance, "Love in Song," a delicate ballad picked on twelve-string guitar, came gently in. Definitely one of Paul's better efforts, it's virtually completely overlooked today. Its appearance also marked the prevailing sequencing aesthetic, where virtually no two songs in a row bore the slightest stylistic resemblance to one another. Fans and his fellow ex-Fabs were all too aware of Macca's penchant for composing ditties that were throwbacks to an earlier era. From "When I'm Sixty-four" to "Honey Pie" and beyond, his innate capacity for crafting pre–rock and roll pastiches was without peer. To some, such whimsy was insufferable, but "You Gave Me the Answer," appearing here (dedicated to Fred Astaire) was actually one of his better efforts in the genre.

The album's release was spearheaded by an advance single, "Listen to What the Man Said," a song that shot to #1 that summer. The two other singles issued from *Venus and Mars* did less well: "Venus and Mars / Rock Show" peaked at #12, while "Letting Go," a strong track topped with a full slab of brass, inexplicably stalled at #39. Later that year and into the next, it would become one of Wings' onstage highlights, as would "Call Me Back Again," a piano-based soul shouter that fully achieved what the Fabs' "Oh! Darling" only hinted at, with a full-throated vocal unheard since the coda of "Hey Jude" seven years before.

What was particularly striking about the *Venus and Mars* album was that of its thirteen cuts (twelve if "Venus and Mars" is counted once), nine of them were on the set list for the Wings over the World tour. In contrast, of the album that actually was released on the eve of the American leg of the tour—*Wings at the Speed of Sound*—only four of eleven tracks were showcased. Thus by Macca's own decision-making can we see the esteem accorded *Venus and Mars* by its creator—a judgment audiences evidently concurred with, even if critics didn't (*Rolling Stone*'s review was particularly scathing, citing the "almost gleeful enthusiasm with which he makes trivial anything meaningful").

Ringo's Rotogravure—Released September 27, 1976 (28)

Ringo's final release of new material for Apple, *Goodnight Vienna*, had been every bit as good as its better-known predecessor, but as George and John had done before him, he soon found that you're only able to re-introduce yourself with a splash once. After the record played itself out, he didn't rush into a new project, instead sitting out most of 1975 musically (he did take a film role, as the pope in Ken Russell's *Lisztomania*). By the time he was ready to enter the studio again, he'd inked a new deal with Atlantic and changed producers. Otherwise, the winning formula Richard Perry had blueprinted was kept more or less intact.

Sessions for *Ringo's Rotogravure* began in April 1976 at Cherokee Studios in Los Angeles. Handling lead guitar chores for most of the album was Lon

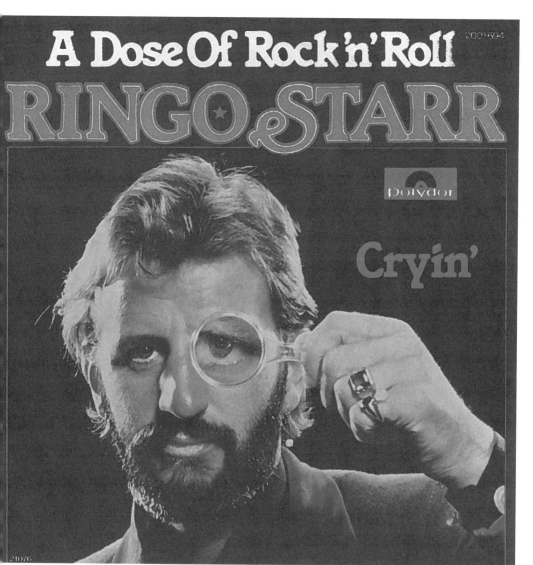

A Dose Of Rock 'n' Roll

RINGO STARR

Cryin'

polydor

Issued as lead single from his Atlantic debut, "A Dose of Rock and Roll" was an anthemic statement of purpose, setting the table for the parent LP's rich array of styles. Unfortunately, the public's acceptance of the Ringed One's less than courant offerings had waned since his last public outing, leaving *Ringo's Rotogravure* sadly ignored.

Van Eaton, whose most recent album with his brother Derrek had been produced by none other than Richard Perry for A&M. Klaus and Keltner were aboard in their usual roles, as was Dr. John. The guest list included a few new names: Eric Clapton, who contributed a calypso-ish ditty entitled "This Be Called a Song"; Peter Frampton, an old friend who'd finally made it big that year with his double live album; and relative newcomer Melissa Manchester on background vocals. A Vini Poncia protégé, she would contribute to both Atlantic releases.

As for the ex-Fabs, George was a little busy, as he had been last time out. Working feverishly to complete his Dark Horse debut, *Thirty-Three & ⅓*, he nonetheless contributed a song that had been around at least since 1972, back when it was called "Whenever." He'd been composing material for Cilla Black at the time (including "The Light That Has Lighted the World," which he ended up recording himself for *Living in the Material World*). Cilla did record the tune eventually, but her issue came long after Ringo's, which was titled here "I'll Still Love You" (after bearing the name "When Every Song Is Sung" for a time). This moody torch song was one of the album's highlights and evidence that when it came to George, Ringo was the recipient of his strongest giveaways.

John—idle from recording since early 1975 (with David Bowie for "Fame")—answered Ringo's request for material with a reggae-light piece of fluff entitled "Cookin' (in the Kitchen of Love)." While not exactly "I'm the Greatest," it was a lighthearted track that grew on one with repeated listenings. In June 1976, he flew out to Los Angeles to play piano on the session, marking his last studio date for four years.

Paul wrote a song for Ringo at the time of the *Goodnight Vienna* sessions (not used at the time) entitled "Pure Gold." Utterly suited for the Ringed One, it was a charming '50s-style ballad. The backings had been cut without Paul, who was not expected to be involved, busy as he was with the Wings Over America tour. But a week after John's visit—during a couple of days off between Tucson and the tour-closing Los Angeles dates—the Macs offered a window to Ringo; after a pleasant dinner, Paul and Linda added backing harmonies to the tune. Days later, Ringo showed up onstage at the Forum near the end of their set and presented a bouquet of flowers before thunderous applause. (He did not, however, "sit in" musically.)

Ringo's Rotogravure yielded two singles stateside and a third in Europe ("You Don't Know Me At All," for which a video was produced). The first was "A Dose of Rock 'n' Roll," written by Ring O'Records artist Carl Grossman (née Groszmann). It was a superb opener, featuring a sing-along chorus (which threw in a snippet of "Hey! Baby" at the end) and lead guitar from Frampton. It was exactly the kind of feel-good celebration of old-time rock that Bob Seger would record a couple of years on; perhaps if the producers of *Risky Business* had been enamored with Ringo's work, the song might have been elevated to the status its anthemic nature demanded. The following track, "Hey! Baby," was the second single and requisite oldie. (It's discussed elsewhere in this book.)

Other songs on the album included the aforementioned "You Don't Know Me At All," a pleasant piece of period pop written by New Zealand folkie Dave Jordan. (The video accompanying this release seemed to be designed for maximum shock value in revealing Ringo's newly shaved bald head.) A Poncia-Starkey composition, "Cryin'," was a well-executed, oddly metered country kiss-off, allowing the Ringed One to explore his traditional strong suit, while "Las Brisas," a romantic ballad co-credited with Nancy Andrews, represented a singular excursion into mariachi sounds.

This most unlikely of idioms strongly underscored where the joy in this release lay: in a game willingness to try anything and not take itself too seriously. While not exactly highly regarded by those whose interest in the drummer's career began and ended with *Ringo*, *Ringo's Rotogravure* holds up surprisingly well.

Thirty-Three & ⅓—Released November 24, 1976 (11)

As noted elsewhere, sometimes the strongest works a recording artist issues are produced in the face of the greatest adversity. In George's case, the *Dark Horse* album was itself part of the problem, since in attempting to juggle recording, producing, label, and tour planning duties simultaneously, he overstressed himself and blew out his voice. Indeed, had the LP been cut months earlier, when he was in much better spirits and shape, the results would have been far less criticized. Song for song, the musicianship was impeccable, most of the material quite strong and less lugubrious than its predecessor, and the overall sound and feel was much more contemporary than the usual Harrison offerings. But *Dark Horse* might just as well have been called *Dark Cloud* for the welcome critics gave it.

Extra Texture merely marked time between the end of Apple and the Dark Horse label start-up. George may have been intending to spend the year recharging his creative batteries, but a case of hepatitis laid him low, delaying work on the next project. By the time he was up and about, he'd fallen far behind on his new label debut; furthermore, things were coming to a head with the "My Sweet Lord / He's So Fine" court battle. So it was in the midst of this ill wind that *Thirty-Three & ⅓* came into being. (The title came from both the rpm speed of a vinyl album and also George's age at the time he recorded it.)

A&M, Dark Horse's distributor, had yet to see a worthwhile return on their investment and, fearing that the delays in George's product being delivered signaled something nefarious, litigious, or sanctimonious, slapped him with a lawsuit to break the deal. Had they been a little more patient, their reward would have come in the form of George's strongest collection in years and possibly most commercial *ever*. Instead, Warner Brothers reaped the benefit of an album that put Harrison back in the game, doing much to erase the bruising his brand had suffered over the last two years.

George implemented some of his touring musicians for the album: Tom Scott on horns, Willie Weeks on bass, Emil Richards on marimba, as well as the ever faithful Billy Preston, just off of a stint recording *Black and Blue* with the Rolling Stones. Gary Wright, then enjoying the biggest year of his career with the success of "Dream Weaver," was also aboard. Conspicuously absent was Jim Keltner, busied with Ringo's session (but invoked in song on "It's What You Value"). Session drummer Alvin Taylor took his place, while Attitude member and future superstar producer/arranger David Foster shared Fender Rhodes duties with session man Richard Tee. The resulting sound was tougher, funkier, and generally more upbeat than anything George had issued before.

The two tracks receiving the most attention were the hit singles, "This Song" and "Crackerbox Palace." The first was a lively send-up of the plagiarism lawsuit, assuring listeners that, whatever else might be said about "My Sweet Lord," *this* song "don't infringe on anyone's copyright." With self-deprecating humor ("My expert tells me it's OK") *and* a snappy arrangement, "This Song" featured succinct Scott and slide solos, as well as a guest vocal from Monty Python's Eric Idle. Any lingering embarrassment George might have felt over the charges of musical theft were adroitly disarmed with the witty track, bolstered by the accompanying courtroom video.

Contrary to any perceptions shaped by *its* video, "Crackerbox Palace" was *not* about Friar Park, George's palatial estate in Henley-on-Thames. It instead concerned Lord (Richard) Buckley, an American comedian/hipster and eccentric of the 1940s and '50s. Owing in no small part to the copious amount of drugs he imbibed, Buckley had a rather surreal worldview as well as a gift for wordplay that made him a darling of the '60s counterculture. A chance encounter with a man who reminded George of Buckley proved serendipitous: it was George Greif, a former manager of the Lord. Greif invited Hari Georgeson to visit the long-deceased Buckley's old residence in Echo Park, which he'd called "Crackerbox Palace." George jotted the name down on a cigarette pack, and from such cosmically divined convergences were great songs made.

Like the two above tracks, George's cover of Cole Porter's "True Love" was issued as a single—just not in America. It too was supported by a humorous music video filmed at Friar Park. Other "oldies" on the album were the opening track, "Woman Don't You Cry for Me," and "Beautiful Girl." The former, a song George had begun writing in 1969, was probably the hardest blues/funk track he would ever record, and its in-your-face bass riffing began the album unlike anything he had ever released or ever would again. The lovely "Beautiful Girl," half finished at the time of the *All Things Must Pass* sessions, featured some twelve-string picking in support of a characteristically fluid slide solo.

"See Yourself" was a song dating to 1967, written in response to the media crucifixion Paul underwent upon "confessing" to having tried LSD. Whereas in the past, George might have been a little more heavy-handed in his criticism of hypocrisy, here he slaps back gently. The album steers clear of any overt devotionals, save for the ethereal "Dear One." For most listeners, one such sermon per album is enough, and that is all George gave them.

Lastly, the album closer, "Learning How to Love You," was a jazzy ballad, perhaps Harrison's finest pure love song since "Something." Untouched by any ambiguities that it could *really* be about God as much as a romantic partner, the track featured a rare picked acoustic solo that must rank among this ex-Fab's Top 5 all-time instrumental interludes. The song's dedication to Herb Alpert, the famed trumpeter who, as co-head of A&M, was currently suing George, was apparently sincere and not intended as irony.

George appeared on *Saturday Night Live* in November 1976 to plug the release; three months later (newly mustachioed and permed), he appeared on German TV lip-synching "This Song." These two dates account for all of the in-person promotion he did for *Thirty-Three & ⅓*. If ever an album cried out for a tour, it was this lively, energetic, and colorfully upbeat collection. It says much for George's disenchantment with the record business that it was enough for him to put out such a strong album and feel no need to flog it.

Wings Over America—Released December 10, 1976 (1)

The Wings extravaganza that hit the States in the summer of 1976 was well documented on both film and tape. A TV special and possibly a feature film were always part of the plan, as was a double live album of the show's highlights. But enterprising bootleggers forced Macca's hand, resulting in the *triple* record set that eventually saw issue by year's end. (*Wings from the Wings* was an underground issue of the entire June 23, 1976 set at the L.A. Forum, recorded the last day of the U.S. tour. It being the bicentennial year, the three discs were issued on red, white, and blue vinyl.) That the album made it to the shops in time for Christmas only months after the tour ended was a bit of a minor miracle in that Paul had to listen to nine hundred hours of tape to choose the best takes—this after spending much of September and October on the road in Europe and Britain.

Given Paul's perfectionist tendencies, a certain amount of "sweetening" in the studio was deemed necessary before the results could be made public, but it would be nitpicking to suggest that the album in any way misrepresentative of the stage act. Given how *de rigueur* live albums were for big-name acts by mid-decade, it was critical for Paul to make sure that his would be exceptional and not simply a bloated, self-indulgent mess. But given the sheer professionalism that typified his stage presentation, it was a safe bet that the music itself would be the last thing to suffer.

Actually, presentation is one of the factors that made *Wings Over America* such an appealing listening experience. Reflecting the tour's set list, the six album sides broke down nicely into thematically arranged mini-sets. Side one was an arresting succession of songs, none more dramatic than the segue from "Venus and Mars / Rock Show" straight into "Jet." Few live albums captured the energy from the venue where they were recorded and projected it through the speakers the way this one did. Even minus the visual, the mental image of Wings at the height of their powers was vivid. Following that powerful opening, Paul shrewdly brought the tempo down somewhat with *Band on the Run*'s Plastic Ono Band pastiche, "Let Me Roll It." (Jimmy McCulloch was unable to restrain himself from embellishing the song's simple, repetitious riffing on the instrumental break.)

The side concluded with the one-two punch of Denny's vocal on the moody "Spirits of Ancient Egypt," followed with little pause by Jimmy's "Medicine Jar"—just as they'd been sequenced on *Venus and Mars*, giving audiences exactly what they were already hearing in their heads anyway. The latter track featured a blistering solo that marked—alongside "Junior's Farm"—the young guitarist's finest moments in Wings. (Though performed on the November 1975 swing through Australia, "Junior's Farm" never quite seemed to jell onstage and was dropped for the 1976 shows.)

Side two kicked off the "piano set," which began with "Maybe I'm Amazed," a crowd-pleaser if there ever was one. On this take, slowed in tempo compared to the one-man-band version cut for his debut, Paul's vocals were as strong as ever and shown to great effect in the added coda. This side also featured the first two of five Beatles classics: "Lady Madonna" and "The Long and Winding Road." (It was here that Macca first reversed the "Lennon-McCartney" credits—an action that conspicuously drew *no* criticism at the time, as compared to much later.) Though not yet ready to pull "Hey Jude" out of his trick bag—that might have been *too* strongly identified with his last band—he did select songs that were calculated to put audiences on their feet. "Live and Let Die" ended the side with its usual explosive drama.

An acoustic set came next, beginning with an abbreviated version of "Picasso's Last Words" segueing into the rather unexpected selection of Simon and Garfunkel's "Richard Cory," sung by Denny. (The song was an adaptation of an 1897 poem by Edwin Arlington Robinson, concerning a much-admired rich man who nonetheless ends his own life.) The earnest tone of the tune was belied by Laine's ad-lib substitution of "John Denver"—a high-riding star of the day—for the title character. Two of Paul's avian-themed songs followed: "Bluebird" and "Blackbird," sandwiching the unexpected Beatles selection "I've Just Seen a Face"—first heard in America as the leadoff track to *Rubber Soul* eleven years earlier. But it was

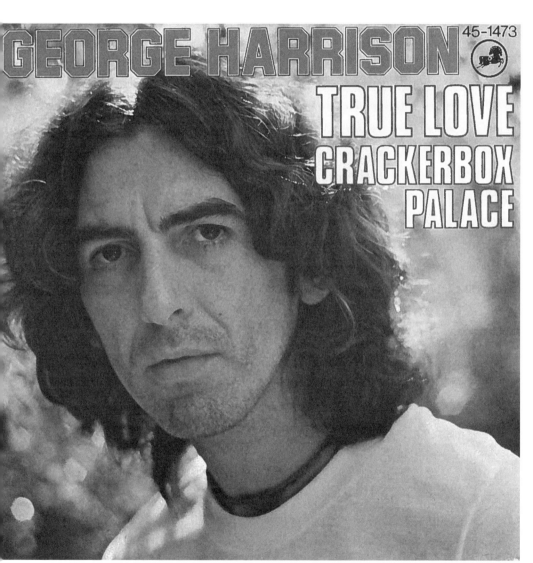

Represented here by its German picture sleeve, "True Love" was the third single released from *Thirty-Three & ⅓*, George's last serious run at competing on the record industry's terms (at least until 1987's *Cloud Nine*).

the side-ending performance of "Yesterday" that had audiences swooning as it closed the Fab portion of the set. With Paul alone in the spotlight with his acoustic guitar, it would have been difficult for even the most jaded of fans not to be moved by the evocation of a more innocent time from their collective youth.

The "piano set" resumed with a batch of newer Wings tunes, encompassing material from *Red Rose Speedway* (thankfully limited to "My Love") through *Venus and Mars* and *Wings at the Speed of Sound*, including the hits "Listen to What the Man Said" and their newest single, "Let 'Em In." (Though the tour ended before July 4, listeners can hear Denny acknowledge the bicentennial year on that side by calling out "Happy birthday, America!") Also performed—during the Los Angeles shows only—was Laine's "Yesterday": "Go Now," the Moody Blues' first hit, on which he sang lead. His *Speed of Sound* track, "Time to Hide," arrived on side five, along with another cut from the same release, "Beware My Love." In the studio, both songs suffered from indifferent production and/or the seeming haste with which they'd been laid down. Onstage, however, the hidden potential in both tracks was unleashed, resulting in sharper and more focused performances that fully demonstrated the band's ensemble capabilities.

Predictably, the set ended with the much-anticipated performance of "Band on the Run," the group's megahit of two years before. In concert, a film of the album cover photo shoot played on a screen above the stage. Macca and crew then left the stage, leaving his audience holding their lighters aloft as they clamored for an encore. Wings did not disappoint: within minutes, the musicians reassembled onstage as their leader sidled over to the microphone and asked, "Fancy a bit of rock and roll?" The band then launched into a rollicking performance of "Hi Hi Hi" that (again) bested the studio recording, before ending the set—and the album—with the unreleased "Soily." Despite their rather lengthy show, the band (including the horn section) delivered the goods, pulling out all the stops and coming off as fresh as if they'd only just arrived. It made for a stunning, powerful finish to an album that must have instilled much regret among those who'd passed on a chance to catch the tour when it came to town.

Wings Over America went to #1, making Paul the second ex-Beatle to top the charts with a three-record set. (Like George's, it too came packaged with a poster, but no lyrics.) Though he's gone on to release several live sets since, this one is required listening for both Macca and Beatles fans, capturing the glory that was the '70s concertgoing experience. It has been available on compact disc since the 1980s, but only the 1999 Japanese issue has been remastered.

George Harrison—Released February 14, 1979 (12)

In the years following the *Dark Horse* tour, George made the slow transition into a private figure who occasionally enjoyed a hit single or two. *Thirty-Three & ⅓* marked the last full-scale media blitz he would engage in to promote a record until 1987's *Cloud Nine*. In between, he gave a few interviews but otherwise steered clear of any TV or public performances (though he would produce music videos). In his own way, he was pulling back to enjoy domestic life, outside the limelight, just as John was. The only difference between them was that George was still under contract, requiring him to sit down and record some tunes every so often.

He was in a good place in his life in 1978. Although his beloved father had passed away in May, he had at last become a parent himself with the birth of Dhani in August. A month later, he married Olivia, and between family life, indulging his hobbies of racing and travel, and his newfound second career as a film producer, George stayed productive, even if he wasn't on the charts. Still, there was more music left in him, and with his own facility at Friar Park, he could record as the mood struck him in a most relaxed setting.

Inspiration reclaimed him during a stay in Hawaii, where the Harrisons had purchased a home. George had started to worry that he might have dried up, since he hadn't written any new tunes at all since 1976. But under the influence of the exotic locale, his peaceful home life, and some psychedelics, the creative juices began flowing again. He soon had a stockpile of material, including a composition written with pal Gary Wright called "If You Believe." To signal that he was in earnest about putting together a solid album, he secured the services of Warners staff producer Russ Titelman for his second Dark Horse release. As if signaling a renewal of his recording career (or a "new phase," if you will), he titled the release simply *George Harrison*.

Though George's choice of producer indicated that he wasn't completely tone-deaf to the demands of the marketplace, the album conspicuously represented almost a complete rejection of current pop trends. (The one exception, "Love Comes to Everyone," featured a danceable tom-tom thump; ironically, as a single it bombed.) Instead, George gave listeners entry into a mystical world of romance and relaxation, where the overall mood generated was as much a statement as the collection's lyrical content. Unique with this particular release was the preponderance of laid-back tunes, the complete absence of his "Lord" (sweet or otherwise) in the lyrics (though a spiritual undercurrent is apparent in a song or two), and a sense of peace with the world that seems as natural here as John's did forced on *Double Fantasy.*

The album's money-spinner was "Blow Away," the first song written. Whether consciously or by accident, George seemed to be restating what he'd first asserted in the title tune to his debut: "A mind can blow those clouds away." This update framed the thesis in an irresistibly seductive melody, as playful as the earlier tune had been solemn. What's more, it successfully competed against the headwinds of disco and new wave in the charts, giving George his biggest hit since the "Dark Horse" single. The aforementioned "If You Believe" was nearly as engaging and might have made a good radio track, had anyone at Warners actually, um, believed.

Critics by nature tended to regard the Beatles' catalog as sacrosanct and didn't take kindly to anyone tampering in any way with the Fabs' musical legacy—not even one of the Fabs themselves. Therefore, just as they had the knives out for George when he altered lyrics of Beatle material on the *Dark Horse* tour, or dissed him for producing a sequel to "While My Guitar Gently Weeps" with "This Guitar (Can't Keep From Crying)" on *Extra Texture*, they could not help themselves when he opened himself up to further scorn by daring to compose a song entitled "Here Comes the Moon," as he did for *George Harrison.*

Those capable of getting past their mental baggage recognized that the seeming rip-off of "Here Comes the Sun" was a sweet companion piece, nothing more or less, and comparisons were unfair. Even had the earlier song never been written, "Moon" would still stand as a lovely, lyrical evocation of the lunar orb and the emotions it stirs. Whereas the *Abbey Road* track contained an escapist subtext, given the Fabs' business troubles, this later song may have likewise held an undercurrent of resentment against the music business as George increasingly absented himself from the grind. As Paul observed about his former bandmate, "[He] didn't suffer fools gladly. He'd just think, 'No . . . [record promotion] is an *unnecessary* evil.'"

An even more direct evocation of Harrison's former band came with the resurrection of a "White Album" reject, the much-fabled "Not Guilty." Though the Fabs' cluttered arrangement—the culmination of *102* takes—finally surfaced in 1996 on *Anthology 3,* the version released here was mellow and jazzy, with acoustic guitar taking the place of the original's gritty riffing and some novel interplay between George's scat vocals and Willie Weeks's bass. With over a decade of perspective to bring to the table by 1979, George managed to turn the bitter sentiments he'd directed at John and Paul back in 1968 into something bittersweet—like fine wine. The results were worth the wait.

One of the album's standout tunes was a song purposely written in the style of an earlier B-side, the melancholy "Deep Blue"; only "Soft-Hearted Hana" was lighthearted in a Jimmy Buffet sort of way. The title was a pun on Hana, an isolated hamlet on Maui, and "Hard-Hearted Hannah," a song dating back to the dawn of the jazz era, revived in 1961 by the Temperance Seven, who scored a hit with their George Martin–produced remake. The lyrics are appropriately psychedelic, given the circumstances of the song's inspiration, while also tossing English rhyming slang in for good measure (a "Richard III" is a "turd"). Given George's affinity for the ukulele, it's somewhat surprising that he didn't employ one on this old-timey tune.

Harrison paid homage to his car racing buddies with "Faster," a song that was as much about Formula One as it was about anyone embarking on a career in the limelight like, say, a rock star. The title had been taken from renowned racer Jackie Stewart's memoirs; in the video, which featured George lip-synching in the back of a limo, Stewart played his chauffeur. Another ode to a real person was "Dark Sweet Lady," an elegant paean to Olivia. Its simplicity and earnest vocal make it especially affecting. (Inexplicably, the album contained no Smokey Robinson tributes.)

The collection lacked much that could be classified as mainstream rock, although the magnificent "Flying Hour" was cut during these sessions and held back for *Somewhere in England*—only to be shot down by corporate shortsightedness. Overall, *George Harrison* is replete with the guitarist's ongoing Santo and Johnny tribute, while hanging together thematically like a postcard from a vacationing friend. *Rolling Stone* described the album as having "nothing at all to do with the '70s"; presumably, this was intended as a compliment.

12

I'm Sorry That I Made You Cry

The Worst

L et's get one thing straight from the outset: "worst" in this context doesn't necessarily mean "execrable" (though in at least a couple of instances, the word may fit). What follows is a roll call of albums that may merely have fallen short alongside some of the more enduring releases issued by the former Fab Foursome between 1970 and 1980. There will doubtless be much here to provoke some argument (*"Red Rose Speedway*! Are you kidding?!?") while other selections are pretty universally acknowledged. But for greatness to be recognized, some sort of comparative measure must exist, so here ya go:

McCartney—Released April 17, 1970

It's interesting to examine the deliberately provocative musical statement Paul was making with his first solo release, in the wake of Lennon's numerous projects as well as *Abbey Road*, the absolute zenith of his collaboration with George Martin. *McCartney* (self-titled, arguably because *Unfinished Music No. 1* had already been used by John) was a collection of musical sketches, only a handful of which qualified as fully realized compositions. For anyone wanting to get to the root of the most common rap against Paul's solo output, look no further: the main complaint against this debut release is not the rough-hewn anti-production throughout—that is the album's charm—but the almost defiant banality of so much of it. To invoke a George Martin observation, Linda was no more a substitute for John than Yoko was for Paul.

As a Beatle, Paul had made attention to detail, insidious melodies that sounded as though they'd been around always, and occasionally wry commentary his musical signature. He could make the most inane statements sound either profoundly romantic or excitingly urgent. And, thanks to the collective weight of his three partners, his worst tendencies were usually curbed, even when he recorded alone. But on his own, charmless ditties like McCartney's "Teddy Boy" (actually attempted—and dropped—during the *Get Back* sessions and later issued—for some reason or another—on *Anthology 3*) were free to be explored, unfettered by the disapproval of his mates. One can readily observe that the same malady that torpedoed this album's shot at greatness was also responsible for the underwhelming offerings of his fellow ex-Fabs: a lack of self-discipline.

What made *McCartney* so frustrating a listen was not the absence of compelling musical ideas; it was the abundance of them. Had melodies like "Momma Miss America" been teased out into compositions with a beginning, middle, end, and point, *McCartney* could have ended up as highly regarded in its own way as *Plastic Ono Band*: a full slate of focused, listener-friendly pop confections that might very well have given fans far less cause for bitterness at the Beatles' breakup. Instead, many were left to wonder whether the most popular and successful band of the 1960s had been sacrificed for *this*.

Wild Life—Released December 8, 1971

Making good on his publicly expressed desire to get a new group together, one that—unburdened by expectations—could go about developing at its own pace while beneath rock journalism's radar, Paul launched Wings as a four-piece in late 1971, barely two years after the Beatles juggernaut had ground to a halt. From the outset, it didn't appear that the group would be anything more than a vehicle to record and play live—Macca (with some input from the Lovely Linda) would be calling all the shots, while the supporting musicians simply did what they were told, more or less.

This was all well and good, though it begs the question: why even give the new outfit a name? Both George and John, who had played live dates (or were about to) and issued albums of original material, had made a point of surrounding themselves with a fairly constant coterie of musicians without contriving a group moniker. ("Plastic Ono Band" as top billing ceased after *Live Peace in Toronto*; thereafter, releases were billed as either John Lennon or Yoko Ono with the Plastic Ono Band and its assorted variants.) For Paul to forge a group identity, specious though it was, was to invite comparisons to his last incarnation.

The newly minted band spent the summer and fall of 1971 woodshedding, something of particular importance to the novice keyboard player. Both Dennys (Seiwell and Laine) were pretty accepting of Linda in the band, Henry McCullough less so. But with the veteran guitar ace aboard, Wings crisscrossed the U.K. in early 1972, debuting with a series of university gigs. This was their equivalent of Hamburg's Reeperbahn, especially for Paul's missus, as they honed their act before a paying audience that stopped just short of clamoring, "Mach schau!"

It is therefore all the more puzzling that Paul decided to introduce the band, not via the low-key gigs, but in the more permanent form of an LP— one issued a scant six months after *Ram*. Moreover, instead of building upon *Ram*'s success, which fans might naturally have expected, *Wild Life* stripped away not only all the production gloss, but also the musical invention that had characterized its predecessor. (The opening "Mumbo," for example, was a cut that began its life as a hackneyed jam, augmented with overdubs and thereby underscoring the LP's caught-on-the-fly flavor.)

While clearly intended to herald the dawn of a hungry, rough-and-ready outfit, most bands fitting that profile did not include one of the era's defining artists as a charter member. Therefore, if Paul was trying to deny what he was by slumming with a pair of journeymen (plus Linda), one has to ask what his point was—simply more diminishing of expectations? (Of course, John was likewise on the verge of recording with the similarly unexceptional Elephant's Memory rather than join the cream of rock's players as George had done. It was as though both men were suffering from a musical inferiority complex that demanded that they play with musicians not quite on their level.)

In any event, had *Wild Life* been kept under wraps as the rehearsal tapes that the collection largely is, McCartney's reputation might have been spared much of the abuse it became subject to over the next couple of years. (And the album would have gone from disappointing waste of time to fascinating Holy Grail, offering a glimpse inside Wings' formative stage. Context is everything.)

Some Time in New York City—Released June 12, 1972

There were some people, Paul McCartney among them, who felt reassured by the hymn-like quality of *Imagine*'s title track. Seemingly a step back from the implied militancy of "Power to the People," the plea for a universal rethink of the man-made constructs that divide people seemed a worthy return to the sentiments of "Give Peace a Chance" or "All You Need Is Love"—very Gandhi-like efforts to win hearts and minds through peaceful means. But if listeners were somehow lulled into thinking that John's statement wasn't political, he made certain with his next release that no one would miss the point.

Having fallen in with some of America's most proactive voices of dissent, John tapped into his own inner anti-authority bent, resulting in a work so spectacularly ill-conceived that he himself disowned it in later years. *Some*

The musical partnership between these two rock legends was highly combustible. Though John opted to drop Phil Spector for *Mind Games* in 1973 after the failure of *Some Time in New York City*, he gave collaboration another shot for the oldies project— a decision he came to regret.

Time in New York City swapped the private for the public, abandoning what had been the trajectory of John's art going back at least as far as 1965 and reinventing him as a town crier, reporting musically on the news of the day with. Though harnessing his sway over young minds to a movement for change wasn't necessarily a bad idea unto itself, his forgetting where his strength lay as an artist—taking his own inner life and transforming it into themes that resonated universally—was a miscalculation that all but wiped out the good will that had taken years to build.

There's little wrong with the album that a complete lyric rewrite couldn't have helped. Musically, John is in top form: his vocals are powerful and impassioned, while his melodies quite fittingly tap the wellsprings of his youth: blues ("Attica State," "John Sinclair"); folk ("Luck of the Irish"); and raucous, sax-driven rock and roll ("Woman Is the Nigger of the World," "Sunday Bloody Sunday," "New York City"). However, the strident, hectoring tone is so alienating a force that even those usually oblivious to lyrical content couldn't help but feel that they were being lectured to (or, as Paul noted the year before with great prescience, "Too many people preaching practices.") Had he integrated his points with the personal voice that was his great gift, say in the manner of Gil Scott–Heron, a contemporary who had produced the groundbreaking *Pieces of a Man* album the year before, Lennon—and his audience—might have fared better.

The other aspect of the album's rejection that can't be overlooked is Yoko's contribution. Aside from the couple's trio of sonic experiments and *Live Peace in Toronto*, their work on albums had been kept strictly separate. Whatever one thinks of Yoko's music, fusing the two distinct styles together was tricky—only once to this point had it been achieved successfully ("Happy Xmas"), and that had been a bit of a one-off. Placing her braying into the mix alongside John's was a tough sell, especially in a climate that resented her generally. That said, at least two of her cuts—"Sisters O Sisters" and "We're All Water"—aren't bad. In any setting other than on a John Lennon solo album, they might even have found praise.

Red Rose Speedway—Released April 22, 1973

In the nearly one and a half years since last heard from on LP, Wings had added a lead guitarist, played numerous gigs, and set about doing some prodigious recording. Some of the results were quite good ("Little Woman Love," "Hi Hi Hi") and some were dreadful (take your pick), but at least the band showed that they were capable of playing in the big leagues. "Live and Let Die," the George Martin-produced James Bond theme, had set them up for making 1973 a memorable year, but getting a strong new album together would be key to fulfilling their goal of taking the act to America.

A bounty of material had been recorded over the past year to flesh out a double album as Wings' sophomore effort. But EMI was quick to quash the grandiosity of those plans, justifying their decision with an array of reasons including the commercial failure of John Lennon's most recent release. (Still, they did spring for a gatefold sleeve, a booklet of pictures, and a Braille imprint on the back that read, "We love you, baby"—a message to Stevie Wonder.) One might therefore conclude that Paul, restricted to just two album sides, would have made good on George Martin's wish for the "White Album"—pare down the material in order to "have yourself a really super album." Only thing is—he didn't.

There was no denying the potency of "My Love" as a chart hit and McCartney's first post-Beatles evergreen, a "standard" calculated to spur versions by other artists. Beyond this lay a wildly uneven assortment of songs. Two of them, "Get on the Right Thing" and "Little Lamb Dragonfly," were *Ram* outtakes; unsurprisingly, they are among the album's stronger offerings. Another, opener "Big Barn Bed," was actually previewed on *Ram* as the coda to the "Ram On" reprise. Here, presumably fully fleshed out, it reveals itself as merely a repetitive set of licks strung together, unable to rise above its utter insipidity.

Little else on the album recommends itself. "Loup (1st Indian on the Moon)" is, to its credit, an uncharacteristically wordless experimental number (resembling *Meddle*-era Pink Floyd) that unfortunately rumbles on well past the patience of most lucid listeners. Side two concludes with a medley, but, unlike its more famous cousin on *Abbey Road*, the fragments comprising it aren't merely half-finished—they're half-assed. In the '60s, the Beatles decried the prevailing practice of constructing an album by surrounding one smash with a bunch of subpar filler, instead priding themselves on issuing LP-length collections of potential hit singles. With *Red Rose Speedway*, Paul seemed to be returning to a standard in pop music that he himself had helped eradicate.

What made the situation even less explicable was the known quantity of top-flight recordings in the can. Some were songs already road-tested during Wings' hit-and-run touring of the countryside, "Soily" and "1882" among them. Then there were the cuts that surfaced as non-album B-sides: the excellent "Country Dreamer," as well as "I Lie Around." Denny Laine's "I Would Only Smile" and Linda's "Seaside Woman" would have made nice contributions, breaking up the continuity of nonstop Macca lead vocals. "Tragedy," a cover of Thomas Wayne and the De Lons' 1959 hit, was also committed to tape but did not make the cut. Given what did, the real tragedy was the missed opportunity.

Extra Texture (Read All About It)—Released September 22, 1975

The period of 1973 through the end of 1975 represented something of a golden era for the ex-Fabs. Each delivered at least one thoroughly terrific album (*Living in the Material World; Band on the Run; Ringo; Walls and Bridges; Goodnight Vienna; Venus and Mars*) as well as a few near-greats (*Mind Games; Dark Horse; Rock 'n' Roll*). This hot streak was bound to end eventually, which it did with the arrival of George's rushed follow-up to *Dark Horse* in the fall of 1975.

With less than nine months separating it from its predecessor, *Extra Texture* at least maintained the outer appearance of being an up-tempo, fun listening experience. The "OHNOTHIMAGEN" marketing angle played up the meme of the irrepressible but beloved ex-Fab's return, as though the irritable, gravel-voiced mystic on tour the previous year had been but an illusion. Purchasers taken in by the spirited Ronnie Spector outtake "You" were no doubt dismayed to discover that what spun on their turntable, instead of more of the same, was a collection of languorous dirges, bereft of joy or even a particularly uplifting message.

To be sure, *Extra Texture* boasted several fine cuts (see chapter 27) plus the two singles issued, but the remainder of the collection was almost entirely weary in tone, amounting to a prolonged buzz kill. Tracks like "World of Stone" and "Grey Cloudy Lies" were every bit as downbeat as the titles suggested, while "Can't Stop Thinking About You" was an R&B-style weeper. Isolated from the morose surroundings on this LP, it could have really shone, but here it simply prolongs the tedium.

The album did conclude with an upbeat attempt to dispel the gloom of the long misery-fest that preceded it. But instead of redeeming *Extra Texture*, "His Name Is Legs (Ladies and Gentlemen)" was a self-indulgent in-joke. Musically off kilter, this murky mix of muttered asides attempted to offer homage to Harrison buddy and renowned "zany" Larry Smith of the Bonzos; instead, it proved one stick-in-the-eye too many, with most listeners

Apple Record's inexorable descent into obsolescence was explicitly depicted on George's penultimate single for the label. All but entirely eaten away, Apple would cease operations for the next sixteen years until being reconstituted for the CD-reissue era.

too bummed to play along by this time. Coming off the heels of so much bad press the year before, George seemed to be doubling down on efforts to alienate his audience. His next outing, the vastly superior *Thirty-Three & ⅓*, marked the return of the George fans had been hoping to see for the last several years. For much of the rock press, however, it would be too little too late.

Wings at the Speed of Sound—Released March 23, 1976

With two critically acclaimed and wildly popular Wings albums in a row under his belt, by the fall of 1975, Paul was at last ready to take his new band on the road outside of Europe. In November they toured Australia; a planned visit to Japan was aborted due to—of all things—Paul's record for drug arrests. With the following year's planned jaunt across the United States, Macca believed it would be a wasted opportunity to make the trip in so large a market without *some* new product to promote.

To that end, the band convened at Abbey Road studios in January and February 1976 (before more dates in Europe) to put together *Wings at the Speed of Sound*. Bolstered by two hit singles, "Silly Love Songs" and "Let 'Em In," as well as a year of great hype and accolades, the album duly went to #1 in the States. Its commercial success had much more to do with the transient circumstances than it did with the quality within.

Bearing a title that served as a fitting description of its creative gestation, *Wings at the Speed of Sound* bore all the earmarks of being a rush job. Neither as inspired as *Band on the Run* nor as cohesive as *Venus and Mars*, the album marked a return to the *Red Rose Speedway* template: take one (or in this case, two) well-conceived hit singles and build an album around them. Aside from the crowd-pleasing "Beware My Love," no Macca composition on the record rises to the standard of the originals issued on either of its two predecessors.

(The hackneyed "She's My Baby," for example, must earn some kind of honor for sheer awfulness—and given its author's prolific tendencies, that's saying something.)

The one aspect of *Wings at the Speed of Sound* worthy of commendation was its first—and only—attempt at full group democratization. *Each* band member took a turn in the vocal spotlight (though not all composed what they sang). The results were fair to middling: having scored with a first-rate anti-drug song on the last album, Jimmy McCulloch stuck his hand into the medicine jar one more time and came up with "Wino Junko"—not horrible, but definitely the lesser of the two songs. Linda McCartney was justifiably proud of her culinary skills, but "Cook of the House"—a '50s-sounding piano-and-sax number penned by her husband—is enough to make one lose one's appetite.

Denny Laine fared well with the "I'm a bad man on the run" number, "Time to Hide," a song that really came to life on *Wings Over America* later that year. (His decision to cover the old Simon and Garfunkel song "Richard Cory" onstage suggests that he was a fan. Certainly, "Time to Hide" seems to bear more than a hint of inspiration from S&G's "Somewhere They Can't Find Me.") Lastly, Joe English handled vocal chores on Paul's "Must Do Something About It," contributing needed authenticity to a light R&B number for which Macca's voice may not have been convincing enough.

The album concluded on a decided downward slide. "San Ferry Anne" contained the germ of a good idea, augmented with some jazzy trumpet, but somehow misfired, while "Warm and Beautiful" failed to reach the level of romantic poignancy that its composer usually reached effortlessly. Lines like "Sunlight's morning glory tells the story of our love" sounded every bit as forced as "my love does it good" rang true. All in all, a recipe for an eminently forgettable listening experience.

Ringo the 4th—Released September 26, 1977

Simply put, had *Ringo's Rotogravure* not underperformed chart-wise, there's little reason to think that Atlantic would have altered the formula so drastically for the follow-up. But underperform it did, and though it represented an LP's worth of fine music that more or less adhered to Richard Perry's blueprint, those in the corporate boardroom were more than a little concerned that their sizable investment was in danger of going south. Therefore, in an effort to keep current, the goofy but beloved uncle persona was jettisoned, to be replaced with the suave romantic and streetwise man of the world. Though this characterization wasn't all that far removed from reality, it also didn't necessarily translate into good music. And there's where *Ringo the 4th* went horribly wrong.

The ill-conceived decision to cover Joe Simon's "Drowning in a Sea of Love" is discussed elsewhere in this volume. Though just one slice of the pie, it was a big one, being the leadoff track and a single besides. But other songs that followed further amplified not just the dance club motif, but also the perception that the album was being narrated by someone you'd want to avoid at a party: inebriated, loud, and full of himself. "Tango All Night" might have been halfway passable, but Arif Mardin's practice of dousing the tracks with shrill vocal backings (begun on the preceding album) is continued here, as though he felt insecure about the Starr's ability to hold his own.

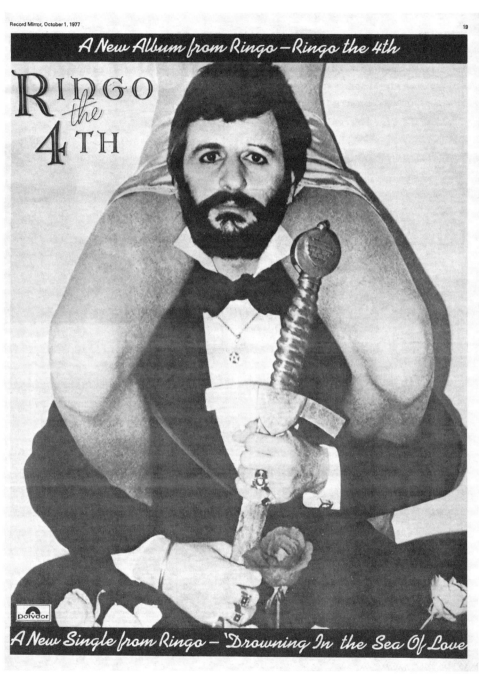

Record Mirror, October 1, 1977

Bearing a cover photo shot by Nancy Andrews in a closet at New York's Plaza Hotel, Ringo's second album for Atlantic left most fans bewildered and not a little disappointed.

The leering "Can She Do It Like She Dances" only reinforces the obnoxious lush theme. It was cowritten by Steve Duboff, discoverer of the Cowsills and writer of "The Rain, the Park, and Other Things" as well as Crispian St. Peter's "Pied Piper." For some reason, the compilers at Rhino bypassed superior material, choosing *this* for *Ringo the 4th* representation on *Starr Struck: The Best of Ringo Starr Vol. 2.*

New Orleans legend Allen Toussaint was a Ringo favorite ("Occapella," "Lipstick Traces"). On this release, he was represented by a song first recorded in 1974 as the title track to singer Robert Palmer's debut album, "Sneakin' Sally Through the Alley." It's a fair attempt, but again, overpowered backing vocals threaten to swamp Ringo's lead. For sheer bizarreness, "Out on the Streets" is worth mentioning: here we have the Ringed One as tough guy, engaging in a spoken monologue at the song's end with a would-be street thug who wants to steal a watch. Ringo sings "Well, you watch this, cause I'm gonna stomp on your fuckin' head!" (Ironically, this same song of New York City street violence namechecks the Dakota.)

Though none of his usual gang of enablers was present on *Ringo the 4th*, the lineup of studio pros was impressive: David Spinozza, Tony Levin, Steve Gadd, David Foster, and, in vocal support, Melissa Manchester, Bette Midler, and Luther Vandross. Clearly, lack of talent was not the album's fatal flaw.

Bad Boy—Released April 21, 1978

The biggest difference between *Bad Boy* and any other successful Ringo album was the absence of any truly top-drawer material. Despite several strong tracks (described in chapter 24), unfortunately there were too many stinkers in the collection to really rate it as a keeper. A more artful producer might have been able to transform the songs alchemically into something more distinctly "Ringo" while maintaining the requisite commercial gloss, but Vini Poncia was not that man. His production was workmanlike without being overtly offensive, resulting in a less uneven album than *Ringo the 4th*—no small feat—but one that also managed to make listeners wish for a few higher highs to balance out the lowly lows.

Like its predecessor, *Bad Boy* boasted solid musicianship in the form of Ringo's Roadside Attraction; indeed, for the first time on one of his solo albums, he was the sole drummer. (Derrek Van Eaton reports that Richie Snare involuntarily squeezed the last recorded sound out of one of his Beatle-era Zildjian cymbals on the record—it's the last thing heard on *Bad Boy*.) Another commonality with the preceding LP is the absence of big-name guests. Given the continuity of the same players throughout, they are hardly missed.

Sadly, an inability to distinguish the really worthy from cringe-worthy doomed the project. The title track, for instance (a cover of the Jive Bombers' 1957 near-hit) is plagued by the continual stretching out of the word "boy" into "boy-oy-oy-oy-oy-oy-oy. . . ." What might have been an OK '50s-style ballad is needlessly marred by this annoying distraction. "Monkey See—Monkey Do" is likewise irritating, as is the supremely poor choice of "Where Did Our Love Go."

The album ends with a reworking of a song Ringo had already recorded for a U.K.-only release. In 1977, he had lent his vocal talent to a project conceived by actor Donald Pleasence, an animated film entitled *Scouse the Mouse* (a sort of antecedent of *An American Tail*). The Ringed One was cast as the lead rodent, hinting at a future in kids' entertainment. (Later, of course, he hosted a season of *Thomas the Tank Engine*.) The soundtrack album, largely featuring his lead vocals, was issued as the third contractually due album in his deal with Polydor outside the U.S. When the hastily recorded *Bad Boy* ran low on material, they simply retooled the finale from the *Scouse* album, "A Mouse Like Me," and recut it, adjusting the species along the way.

As John once said to Ringo in a different context, "Who'd have thought it would come to this?"

"Wonderful Christmastime"—Released November 20, 1979

Holiday music is a genre so vast and so lucrative that one would be hard-pressed to find a single successful recording artist who hasn't taken at least one stab at it, if not an entire album's worth. That said, it's a deceptively tricky idiom to master. The holiday discount bins are littered with offerings from artists that aren't exactly well suited to "peace on Earth" sentiments (Billy Idol, to name one) and one-offs from acts that hit the jackpot just once (Patsy and Elmo, for instance). Then too there are the attempts by some to craft a *new* yuletide classic: some successful (the inexplicably popular "This Christmas" comes to mind), others simply bizarre ("Christmas Shoes," anyone?).

Lying somewhere between the extremes was this frothy confection, recorded in July 1979 during sessions for what became *McCartney II*. (Despite the appearance of the last iteration of Wings in the video, Paul has no one to blame but himself for this record.) It is difficult to believe that the annual popularity of John and Yoko's "Happy Christmas (War Is Over)" wasn't a *little bit* on the composer's mind when he began to write what was undoubtedly expected to likewise become an evergreen. Unfortunately, there is much to take issue with in this recording. It's probably for the best that when

McCartney's legacy is assessed, this composition's existence likely won't be held against him.

For starters, there was the incredibly dated-sounding instrumentation. Employing the late-'70s work horse, a Prophet-5 synthesizer, so prominently throughout instantly dates the song to the era in which it was recorded—few McCartney recordings are so marred. (Not to belabor the "Happy Xmas" comparisons, but at least Phil Spector had the good sense to steer clear of wah-wah pedals and electric sitar.) Then there are the lyrics, which bear all the characteristics of having been hastily scribbled down as placeholders that their author simply forgot to amend. ("The word is out about the town / to raise a glass, ahhh don't look down.")

Paul's attempt at creating a holiday perennial (like John) fit the mold of much of his work: largely loved (or at least accepted) by the public while loathed by critics.

But perhaps being catchy in that maddening Macca way and projecting good cheer was good enough. Though "Wonderful Christmastime" continues to alienate (in 2006, Retrocrush.com deemed it the "Worst Christmas Song of All Time"), it also has its fans. In an interesting contrast, the single peaked at #6 in Britain upon release, while in America it failed to chart at all. Nowadays, however, it has at last reached the status of perennial classic on the airwaves. Love it or hate it, few songs within the McCartney oeuvre have provoked such strong reactions

Double Fantasy—Released November 17, 1980

Of fans who can remember 1980, separating *Double Fantasy* from any lingering emotional resonance is nearly impossible. First, there was the half-decade wait for some new Lennon music. As each year from 1975 onward came and went without so much as a one-off single, anticipation built, until by the turn of the decade, expectations fueled by nostalgia made legions of fans delirious with joy once John's return was announced. Then, within three weeks of its release, the tragedy came. Many fans hadn't yet heard the entire work, save the lead-off single; as product by the truckload flew off record store shelves that sad Christmas season, indelible memories of their initial exposure to the music became inextricably intertwined with profound grief.

For that singular circumstance, *Double Fantasy* occupies a unique position within the Lennon canon. The release was new enough that some reviews—mixed or negative—that hadn't yet gone to press were pulled, and eulogies took their place. Had John lived to build on this renewed career, doubtless he would have produced something a little bolder than the rather safe material he presented here upon reentering the marketplace. But for the timing, any honest assessment of the album must conclude that the final release within John's lifetime became exalted far beyond what the music warranted.

Adding to the difficulty in assessing *Double Fantasy* was Yoko's participation. Then as now, a robust segment of the population was not too kindly disposed toward the woman who "broke up the Beatles." Even had they managed to suspend their judgment, Yoko's musical stylings were far removed from the traditional tastes that her husband had helped to shape. No matter how much time Jack Douglas spent hammering her material into something resembling standard rock formats, it was only the most open-minded and nonjudgmental of listeners who could embrace the duo on their own terms—and this was but a minority.

Mostly, fans considered *Double Fantasy* to be half an album. Mourning John made them perhaps a little more receptive to Yoko's contributions than they might otherwise have been, but this sentiment seems to have faded through the years. Certainly, AOR radio has not supported what many (then as now) judged to be the album's fresher-sounding tracks. Yoko's compositions displayed a range absent from her husband's work: less rooted in the past ("Yes, I'm Your Angel" notwithstanding) and decidedly more complex in their themes, encompassing alienation ("Give Me Something," "I'm Moving On") as well as ambiguity ("Every Man Has a Woman Who Loves Him," perhaps her strongest track).

The pop/rock world of 1980 was far removed from the one John had turned his back on five years earlier. Disco, then on the ascent, was definitely on the downswing while an edgier brand of rock, usually dubbed "New Wave," had first taken root overseas, then in America. Had he chosen to compete directly on those terms, John would certainly have been expected to have something to bring to the table, being the man who indirectly blueprinted the sound with tracks like "Instant Karma," "Cold Turkey," and many *Plastic Ono Band* cuts. Instead, it was *Yoko* who seemed plugged into current trends, while John kept working the same vein of nostalgia he'd mined for much of his musical life.

Compositionally, he seemed to be directing all of his musical energies toward sledgehammering home the narrative of marital love taken to its hyperbolic apogee. "The two of us are really one," John sang in the Buddy Holly-esque "Dear Yoko," expressing a point of view more suited to adolescent naiveté than the nuanced perspective expected from someone entering middle age. Paul at his most saccharine had never quite made the same claim for Linda and himself; instead, he merely lived it.

Of John's seven compositions on *Double Fantasy*, "Cleanup Time" and the aforementioned "Dear Yoko" are undoubtedly the weakest. The first track featured an instrumental backing so slick that listeners could have mistaken it for any of the bland "light rock" permeating the MOR airwaves. But it was the lyric, with its smugness in nursery rhyme form, that really grated. Continuing to advance the happy househusband narrative with a vengeance, Lennon sang of the purported bliss that came with being a "king" blessed by "angels." What he described as "the magic ship of perfect harmony" sounded like a disturbingly isolated life ("No friends and yet no enemies").

Throughout his solo career, from *Plastic Ono Band* through *Walls and Bridges*, John was routinely far more convincing than this in portraying the ups and downs of his daily existence. "Cleanup Time," like so much of *Double Fantasy*, sounds like he's trying too damned hard to sell us *something*. (Likewise with "Dear Yoko," which similarly evoked the blessing of "the gods.")

"Watching the Wheels" was a cut above most of his new material, being a workmanlike treatise on the artist's five-year absence from the public eye.

Though the backing was competent to the point of anonymity, it was John's soulful vocal, particularly at the end, that gave the track its emotional pull. "I'm Losing You" (watered down though it was compared to the Cheap Trick recording) likewise packed more of a punch than any other Lennon cut on the album; not coincidentally, it conspicuously didn't push the marital bliss narrative.

What's inescapable to any objective listener is that the album's "heart play" dialogue concept between the two artists was impossible to sustain over an album. John's effortless commerciality was at cross purposes with Yoko's accessible but edgy (if not downright cacophonous) approach. What *Double Fantasy* unwittingly revealed were the same fault lines that had artistically fractured the Beatles. An album simply wasn't big enough to contain the separate and musically divergent talents.

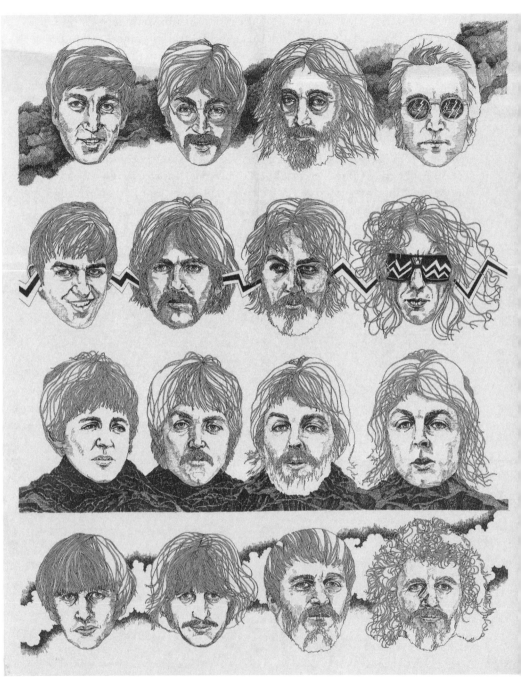

Capitol wasted no opportunity to promote the tenth anniversary of the Beatles' arrival in America. Having all four ex-Fabs on their roster and each one enjoying strong current as well as robust back catalog sales certainly helped.

13

Baby, It Looks Like I've Been Breaking Out

1974

February marked the official tenth anniversary of the Beatles' arrival in America to perform on the *Ed Sullivan Show*. To commemorate the occasion, Capitol Records launched their "Decade" promotion at the beginning of the year. The logo featured a composite graphic of all four ex-Beatles in their current iteration, fused together as if still a group. The entire back catalog and all in-print Capitol/Apple Beatle and ex-Beatle product were heavily pushed, with displays and posters (including a set illustrated by Keith McConnell—the same artist responsible for the cover art on the two Beach Boys double-album compilations—depicting each Beatle as he looked circa 1964, 1967, 1969, and 1973). Adding to the campaign's sizzle was the fact that each ex-Beatle had a new album in release or due out that year.

Ringo was riding high as the year began, as the second single in a row from his eponymous long-player hit #1 in America. "You're Sixteen" was also the second track issued to feature input from one of his ex-bandmates, in this case, Paul. "I'm the Greatest" was passed over for a follow-up, though John himself pushed for it. Instead, the infectious "Oh My My" became the third and final single pulled from *Ringo*; it peaked at #5, besting every Lennon single's performance since "Imagine," three years before. With considerable wind at his back, the drummer had at last established a viable career as a recording artist. His fortunes outside the group had been an ongoing concern held by both John and Paul. Four years after the split, they could rest easy.

Paul himself was at last enjoying the fruits of his well-planned labors with *Band on the Run*'s chart-topping success, en route to the ultimate goal of launching a full-scale U.S. concert tour. That ambition had to wait a couple of years for fulfillment, but building a solid, crowd-pleasing body of work was something he took very seriously. Barely two years into Wings' existence, critics remained capricious, while the band itself was shaky beyond the commitment of the McCartneys and Denny Laine. Still, despite Wings' up-and-down progress, Paul expressed openness to making music with his ex-bandmates repeatedly throughout the year. While stopping short of calling for a permanent reunion, Paul was quoted in *Melody Maker* as opining, "I'd like to see us work together on a loose basis."

His comment echoed sentiments from John that same year. Though less sanguine than his former songwriting partner, John showed an open-mindedness that made a refreshing change from the hostility queries about reuniting usually prompted. As his newest album was about to drop in September, he told radio listeners, "Why not?" when asked, seconding the notion on national television in December when interviewed on, of all things, ABC's Monday Night Football by Howard Cosell: "You never know, you never know. It's always in the wind. . . ." (George's position was more ambiguous. While enthused to play with John, he was less favorable towards Paul. Still, he was quoted as saying, "I'm ready for the Beatles to reform and kick down some doors!")

Nineteen-seventy-four saw more physical proximity between the Fabs than at any time since 1969. Though visa problems and assorted business responsibilities precluded all four from being in the same place at the same time, gatherings of any three occurred throughout the year. Perhaps the most storied near-reunion came in Los Angeles in the spring. With John and Ringo palling around with an ensemble of hearty partiers calling themselves "the Hollywood Vampires" (members included Nilsson, Moon, Voormann, Mal Evans, Alice Cooper, Micky Dolenz, and other transient participants), Paul and Linda McCartney were moved to pay a visit as sessions began for Harry's *Pussy Cats* album, produced by John. (Ringo just missed him, having left once recording wrapped up for the night, though the three would converge within days.) Though conditions were hardly optimal, John and Paul, along with the others, jammed in the studio. It was the last time the two were caught together on tape; the results were comparable to their first recorded performance, the Quarry Men's 1958 recording of "That'll Be the Day."

The year saw John hard at work in the studio: in addition to Nilsson, sessions included Ringo, Elton John, and Mick Jagger; furthermore, he completed two albums on his own behalf. Thus, despite the period away from Yoko being characterized as "the Lost Weekend," his musical output was formidable, besting that of his former bandmates. Still, the separation became largely defined by the drunken incident occurring on March 12 at L.A.'s Troubadour Club. Just one year after recording "I'm the Greatest" with Ringo in the same town, John's Nilsson-enabled escapade cost him much public sympathy, between his brawling with customers and heckling the Smothers Brothers. Perhaps unfairly, one evening's Brandy Alexander–fueled revelry became fixed in legend as the height of debauchery, though by the standards of the Who, the Stones, or Led Zeppelin, it was nothing more than amateur night.

Making hay while the sun shone, Ringo took full advantage of the acclaim his album generated by reentering the studio in August with the same producer and some of the same supporting players. Augmenting the previous project's cast of John, Klaus, Jim Keltner, Harry, and Dr. John, Elton John joined the festivities as *Goodnight Vienna* was being recorded in L.A. Though the novelty of such a strong collection from Ringo had dimmed a little, the album matched its predecessor in overall quality. A remake of the Platters' "Only You" and Hoyt Axton's "No No Song" became Top 10 singles, marking the Ringed One's last such superlative showing.

Beyond his albums and session work for others, further evidence of Ringo's talents was manifest that year. Both *That'll Be the Day* and *Son of Dracula* made their stateside debuts, for better or worse. Even more intriguing were the projects that didn't come to fruition. A film combining live action and animation entitled *Ringo and Harry's Night Out* was apparently started and never completed; reportedly, it was a takeoff on the duo's notorious nightlife. Monty Python's Graham Chapman and a young Douglas Adams, later renowned for *The Hitchhiker's Guide to the Galaxy,* crafted a sci-fi fantasy television script for Ringo, riffing off of *Goodnight Vienna*'s *The Day the Earth Stood Still* jacket art. In it, Ringo traveled through time and space, accompanied by a robot and meeting a character that was to be played by Keith Moon. Several songs from the album were to have been worked into the special, but sadly, the script (described frankly by Chapman as "too rude") was rejected by the networks and abandoned.

The eventual wind-down of Apple was not far from each of the ex-Fabs' minds. Paul was already cutting a deal with Capitol for future releases: his October 1974 single, "Junior's Farm," would be his last on the label he'd played so critical a role in conceiving. George had been looking ahead for some time to his future professional home. Having taken a bit of a break from recording, at least for his own benefit, he spent much of the first half of 1974 setting up his own label, Dark Horse. In May, the company officially opened for business, having inked a distribution deal with A&M Records and signed an artist roster comprised of Ravi Shankar and an English pop duo called Splinter. Bill Elliot, one half of the act, had already worked with a Beatle, recording John's "God Save Us" in 1971 as a benefit for the underground magazine *Oz.*

While not carousing, John, seen here with Harry Nilsson (left) and New York DJ "Cousin Brucie" Morrow (with microphone) often turned up at charitable events. This April 1974 March of Dimes Walkathon in Central Park featured the two singers serenading the assembled with an impromptu performance of Fats Domino's "I'm Walking."

Splinter's sound, achieved with production and musical support from their boss, was reminiscent of George's old protégés, Badfinger. The ex-Fab was also deeply involved with the production of Ravi's Dark Horse debut, an album that strove to bridge the gap between East and West. The resulting *Shankar Family and Friends* release was an ahead-of-the-curve effort, applying Indian classical instrumental and vocal elements to a pop template.

George was very keen on exposing rock audiences to what for him was a life-changing, transcendental experience through chanting, meditation, and Indian music. To that end, he decided to fuse Ravi's offerings with his own show, one heavy on newer solo material; Beatles classics, not so much. With Tom Scott's L.A. Express (fresh from supporting Joni Mitchell) backing him and Billy Preston along for the ride, the *Dark Horse* tour promised to be a one-of-a-kind roadshow. In the push to get the album finished and the ensemble rehearsed, however, George's voice—never the most robust of instruments—suffered a severe strain that left its mark on both the accompanying record and the critics' impressions. Chafing at what they saw as the mystical Beatle's inherent preachiness, reviewers savaged the tour. George was already under enormous business pressures as well as personal travails; what began with the best of intents ended up traumatizing him. It was the first—and last—full-scale continental tour George would ever undertake.

Watching from the sidelines was John. Having bottomed out with the Troubadour incident, he managed to bounce back through work. *Pussy Cats*, while not exactly a blockbuster, was an important step toward his musical maturation as an artist and craftsman. Work on the oldies project he'd begun the previous fall had been suspended after Spector, in an instance of increasingly erratic behavior, absconded with the tapes. Therefore, John felt he had no choice but to start from scratch, crafting a new set of songs as his muse reawakened. Though still coping with a personal and professional malaise, he had managed the tricky balancing act of channeling his suffering into art that was universal and accessible without being maudlin and defeatist. In July, he began work on his most focused musical statement since *Plastic Ono Band*; it was called *Walls and Bridges*.

Well aware that he was on the outs with the record-buying public, he cannily made good use of Elton John's eager input, tapping him for a very upfront musical (and vocal) contribution to "Whatever Gets You Through the Night," a song that briskly nailed the stay-out-all-night milieu. Essentially a duet with the most popular pop star on the planet, the song couldn't miss—and didn't, landing on the top slot of the charts for exactly one week in November. As fate would have it, this timed out beautifully to pay off the debt incurred when Elton wagered that it would hit #1. The payoff: an onstage appearance with Elton at his Thanksgiving evening Madison Square Garden concert to sing the song live. Not only did John fulfill the bargain, but he threw in a bonus performance of Paul's "I Saw Her Standing There"—a sort of blown kiss to "an old estranged fiancé." (When in town, Paul and Linda had of late been gathering at the apartment shared by Lennon and Pang; the residence was also the scene of visits from Mick Jagger and David Bowie, among others.) Contrary to self-generated myth, John and Yoko did not reconcile backstage that night.

That year saw the opening of two separate theater projects that attempted to stitch together story lines from the Beatles' songs. The first was a West End show penned by Willie Russell entitled *John, Paul, George, Ringo . . . and Bert*. This clever musical comedy told (fictitiously, of course) of the band's rise

The reconstituted Wings scored a follow-up to the success of Band on the Run with "Junior's Farm," a tough rocker that fully displayed the talents of new members Geoff Britton (holding cards) on drums and guitarist Jimmy McCulloch (with cigarette).

and fall through the eyes of a fifth Fab who didn't last, due to his own musical shortcomings. It was a clever, insightful tale, making good use of Beatle material throughout, although George hated it enough to pull permission for the use of "Here Comes the Sun." Paul objected to what he believed—erroneously—was his characterization as the instigator of the breakup.

Far less nuanced was *Sgt. Pepper's Lonely Hearts Club Band on the Road.* This off-Broadway monument to excess featured a plot line even more rooted in fantasy. It didn't actually tell the Fabs' story at all, but was instead a sort of "good vs. evil"–themed fairy tale, using the Beatles' music as a unifying device. Both shows were produced by the Bee Gees' manager Robert Stigwood, who four years later adapted the second property to film, resulting in one of the biggest box office turkeys of the '70s.

On the subject of films, Paul would produce a behind-the-scenes look at Wings called *One Hand Clapping*; dissatisfied with the results, however, he shelved it. George's initial toe-dip into film production came that year with *Little Malcolm*, predating HandMade Films by four years. Mostly, his year climaxed with the rather personal *Dark Horse* album, a project so misbegotten that it wasn't even released until midway through the tour. Still, the title song seemed to actually benefit from Harrison's diminished vocal abilities; it peaked at #15. Less successful was his holiday tune, "Ding Dong, Ding Dong," which barely made the Top 40. (The rarely screened video is a hoot, showing George garbed in his many iconic Beatle suits, including 1963's collarless jacket and his Sgt. Pepper costume.) Even with a tour to draw attention, his commercial success was now decidedly far from a given—quite a fall in less than four years.

The year ended on a bittersweet note when all four signed the legal papers dissolving the Beatles' partnership. John's was the last signature, coming in the rather surreal setting of his hotel room at Walt Disney World in December, where he, May, and Julian were vacationing (along with Mal Evans). It would be the last such gathering, as drastic change was on the horizon.

14

There Is No End to What We Can Do Together

The Wing Men

While his first album outside the Beatles was largely a one-man-band affair, Paul knew that at some point he would have to recruit a supporting cast if he were ever to enact his fantasy of playing live again. With the meticulous step-by-step approach that typified his songcraft, he didn't rush into casting new bandmates, waiting instead until he'd released a pair of post-Beatles albums before seeking something a little more roadworthy.

With the exceptions of longtime mainstay Denny Laine and Jimmy McCulloch (and, to a lesser degree, Henry McCullough), his choices tended to be drawn from the ranks of seasoned *studio* professionals, as opposed to road-tested musicians who'd had a bit of fame in their own right. (Though Henry had backed Joe Cocker at Woodstock, his fame was arguably less than that of Jimmy McCulloch, who had the novelty of his age to draw attention.) All protests that Wings was a democracy aside, Paul made sure that no one ever upstaged him or demanded a greater share of the spotlight. (For proof, note that *none* of Wings' alumnae parlayed the high-profile gig into solo stardom.)

One might assume that for a working rocker, the offer to become band-mates with an ex-Beatle would be the dream of a lifetime. The reality was somewhat different, as Wings never managed to sustain stability much beyond two years at a time. Once inside the group, members found the creative atmosphere restrictive, chafed at being kept in a subservient position, or took exception to being in the same band with someone still in her learning curve. Despite record sales in the millions, the revolving door of membership reinforced the notion that Wings was never a true band of equals, but merely Paul and some backing musicians—the same description that John Lennon applied to the Beatles during their final years.

Though they became a hit-making machine as the decade unfolded, Wings were never well regarded by critics. Paul's most inane tendencies were often cited as proof of who the *real* talents in the Beatles had been, while his defensive posture (exemplified by "Silly Love Songs") won him few positive reviews. But the band was not entirely without fans, among them Pete Townshend, who often expressed his counterintuitive view that *Linda* was the band's secret weapon, giving Wings a *je ne sais quoi* that defined their sound.

Still, with the Beatles legacy to live up to, Wings were doomed to little respect—even by their own members. Linda McCartney herself—rather gracelessly—let slip in a *Playboy* interview (outside Paul's hearing) that "we just picked the wrong people." Her bandmates in Wings were "good, not great," as though their mediocrity that had held Paul McCartney back from rising to the level of his talents. Rightly or wrongly, it was an opinion that few argued with.

Denny Seiwell—Drummer (1970–1973)

Upon landing in New York City in late 1970 to begin work on his second solo album (technically credited to "Paul and Linda McCartney," drawing derisive snorts from Paul's music publisher, to say nothing of the rock establishment), Macca set up shop in Manhattan, in a locale described as "the basement of a burned-out warehouse." The seedy surroundings were evidently part of the screening process, as the more timid musicians tended to stay away. Present in said basement was a battered drum kit; it was in this forlorn setting that one of most successful artists in rock history tested the mettle of his next Ringo from among the ranks of nine studio pros.

Not yet a superstar in New York's session circuit, Seiwell possessed experience principally in jazz, although straight after *Ram* he played on Billy Joel's 1971 debut, *Cold Spring Harbor*. For reasons best known to themselves, the McCartneys were deliberately cagey about their intentions during the audition process. Seiwell was contacted, ostensibly to work on a demo for an unnamed artist. When a scheduled jingle gig canceled, he shrugged and went to check out what otherwise might have barely registered on his radar. The surprise presence of an ex-Beatle in the least likely of environs gave him slight pause, but the command to "play," unaccompanied by even a single guitar, daunted him not. Going straight for the toms, he banged out a suitable rhythm that impressed the Maccas, no less than his straightforward persona and no-nonsense work ethic.

He got the job, first on *Ram*, then as a charter member of Wings later that year. Like Paul's previous drummer, Seiwell made himself invaluable with a laid-back drumming style and easygoing personality. (As would be the case with other session drummers working with the ex-Fabs, the order to "play like Ringo" dictated his approach.) Given the chronic chaos that typified Wings' beginnings, the drummer's flexibility and ready willingness to go with the flow made him the ideal musician in Paul's eyes.

Seiwell's work can be heard on several singles, including "Another Day," "Live and Let Die," and "C Moon"—the latter track featuring him on cornet—as well as three albums: *Ram*, *Wild Life*, and *Red Rose Speedway*. Though these didn't exactly represent the cream of Paul's post-Beatles work, Seiwell was apparently satisfied with the music and with Paul's efforts to build Wings from the ground up, working their way through college gigs before graduating to traditional venues. But other issues rankled.

The drummer grew increasingly disenchanted with the lowly wages ($175 a week), as vague assurances of a more lucrative future stayed chronically unfulfilled. As pre-production rehearsals for the *Band on the Run* album began at Paul's Scottish farm, it became clear that this album had the makings of a monster. Yet the McCartneys gave absolutely no indication that they were prepared to follow through and formalize a legal agreement that gave non-writing members of the group their due.

Also coming to full boil were the long-simmering tensions between Henry McCullough and the head Wing. With the guitarist splitting on the eve of the band's scheduled departure for Lagos, Nigeria, Denny saw trouble ahead. The band was in disarray, and with nothing but another McCartney pipe dream and empty promises to look forward to, Seiwell phoned in his notice, hours before flight time.

Paul apparently took this second resignation in three days with good grace, not entirely displeased at the prospect of handling the skins himself. (Denny later noted—with some annoyance—that Macca duplicated drum parts on *Band on the Run* that *he* had worked out—without credit or thanks, of course.) Having had his fill of travel, Seiwell went back to New York, resuming his session work with a passel of Wings hits beneath his belt.

Through the years, Seiwell has stayed busy, recording with artists ranging from Art Garfunkel to Donovan, along with soundtrack scores for both film and television. (He also managed an on-camera cameo in Emilio Estevez' *Bobby*, appearing as the bandleader.) When Mary McCartney began assembling footage for the 2001 documentary *Wingspan*, Seiwell's 8mm home movies proved priceless.

David Spinozza—Guitarist (1970–1971)

On Paul's shortlist of musicians to recruit when putting his *Ram* team together was a twenty-one-year-old session *wunderkind*. David Spinozza was well known in New York studio circles; despite his youth, he'd proved as adept at pop as he was at jazz, funk, and Latin fusion. By the time the McCartneys first approached him, the guitarist had completed a pair of albums with the Cuban percussionist Candido Camero—whose composition "Jingo" was popularized by Carlos Santana—as well a jazz funk album with the legendary flautist Herbie Mann. (*Push Push*, produced by future Ringo collaborator Arif Mardin, featured a stellar lineup that included bassist Donald "Duck" Dunn, keyboardist Richard Tee, and drummers Al Jackson and Bernard Purdie.)

Spinozza received a call from Linda in late 1970, summoning him to meet her husband—he assumed—for a recording session. Turns out that what they had in mind was an *audition*, a situation he felt himself beyond. (He would also later learn that their first choice, Hugh McCracken, was busy with an Aretha Franklin session in Florida.) But Paul liked what he heard: a player who could handle anything you threw at him.

As a trio, Spinozza, Seiwell, and Macca began laying down the basic tracks for the *Ram* album, an experience that the guitarist felt was a little odd in that Paul never recorded his bass parts in the first go—he always tracked them later, preferring to play guitar or piano initially. In a workmanlike fashion, the trio cut the following tracks: "Another Day," "Oh Woman, Oh Why," "3 Legs," "Eat at Home" and "Get On the Right Thing"—the latter abandoned at the time but later salvaged for *Red Rose Speedway*.

Spinozza's employment with Mr. McCartney came to an abrupt end mid-sessions over a basic philosophic disagreement: Paul (with Linda as his mouthpiece) demanded absolute availability from his sidemen, despite disruptions in the work schedule owing to trips back to England to handle business. Being the professional that he was, Spinozza was in constant demand; given any break in the *Ram* sessions, his calendar quickly filled, not exactly placing him at the McCartneys' beck and call: "I said I could make two of the days, but not five, and Linda got very indignant."

Without missing a step, Paul again reached out to Spinozza's colleague, Hugh McCracken, who this time was available, to complete the album. (The latter would later work on *John's* final recordings, alongside Bowie sideman Earl Slick.) As for David, he too kept busy, cutting "Me and Julio Down by the Schoolyard" with Paul Simon, "Right Place, Wrong Time" with Dr. John, and the *Moon Shadow* album with LaBelle, among many other recordings.

Spinozza's ex-Fab working experience might have ended there, but for him, lightning struck twice. In 1973, he found himself again summoned to a New York recording studio, this time on behalf of the Lennons. Upon the recommendation of Hugh McCracken, he was asked to join sessions for *Mind Games* and Yoko's *Feeling the Space*. It was unclear to Spinozza whether or not John knew that he'd already worked with Paul, but, given what he believed to be the unmitigated animosity between the two ex-Beatles, he kept his mouth shut, fearing he'd be fired on general principle. Once his past did leak out, John merely observed that Paul "knows how to pick good people."

The guitarist's skills were put to good use on John's album with a cracking band that included Jim Keltner, Sneaky Pete Kleinow on pedal steel, and saxophonist Michael Brecker, among others. (Spinozza's superb extended solo on the Tex-Mex "Tight A$" is a particular standout.) But his rapport with Yoko on *her* album soon blossomed into something more.

Just two months after their debut long-player was issued, the touring lineup for Wings jelled, with the addition of veteran guitarist Henry McCullough. Despite the occasional onstage memory lapse by their novice keyboard player, the band developed a solid act fairly quickly.

In the fall of 1973, John and Yoko separated, with John heading west to L.A. accompanied by the Lennon's (very) personal assistant, May Pang. Not to be outdone, Yoko took up with an employee herself, the young but worldly guitarist. (Unsubstantiated scuttlebutt has it that Yoko informed John of the relationship via phone, further reporting that they'd consummated their affair on her birthday in February 1974. John's purported reaction was to retaliate by publicly planting a sloppy wet one on May before a crowd of paparazzi, assuring that Yoko would see it in the papers.)

Spinozza contributed mightily to Yoko's next album, *A Story*. Coproducing the project, he spearheaded a platoon of professionals that featured much of the *Mind Games / Feeling the Space* crew, including McCracken. The album included the first recording of Yoko's "Hard Times Are Over," a song that was resurrected as the finale to *Double Fantasy* six years later. (This version features a slide guitar lead that sounds as though it was played by George himself.) Though *A Story* went unreleased until the 1990s, one track, the startlingly prescient "It Happened," was issued, with Spinozza's permission, as the B-side to "Walking on Thin Ice" in the wake of John's murder in 1981.

Although Spinozza served as bandleader for Yoko's October 1973 stint at the famed Greenwich Village club Kenny's Castaways, and rehearsed the band for her 1974 concert series in Japan, their personal relations were somewhat rocky. The constant stream of phone calls between the Lennons tended to undermine the here and now, causing the guitarist to at last sour on the relationship before the Japanese tour began.

Though he never again worked with any ex-Beatles, Spinozza's career trajectory continued upward. He went on to work with other notables throughout the decade, including Gil Scott-Heron on "The Revolution Will Not Be Televised" and with James Taylor, producing the ex-Apple artist's 1974 album, *Walking Man*.

Henry McCullough—Guitarist (1972–1973)

Of all the musicians to pass through Wings, Irish-born guitarist Henry McCullough was perhaps the most prototypical journeyman rocker. Not for him the life of a studio professional—McCullough was a gritty man of the streets, equally at home playing in a seedy local as he was performing before a half a million in upstate New York.

Though familiar to most readers of this book primarily for the work he did during his twenty-month stint with Paul, McCullough is equally renowned around the world for playing in the Grease Band, which backed Joe Cocker on several albums, including *With a Little Help from My Friends* and 1969's *Joe Cocker!* The latter album—which included Paul's "She Came in Through the Bathroom Window"—featured two musicians soon to be familiar to other ex-Fabs: Sneaky Pete Kleinow and Leon Russell.

After Cocker moved on to another band for the Mad Dogs and Englishmen tour, McCullough briefly joined prog rockers Spooky Tooth for one album, *The Last Puff* (which featured their take on "I Am the Walrus"). He also found time to contribute to the original recording of *Jesus Christ Superstar*, foolishly turning down royalties for a flat fee in the belief that the album was doomed to obscurity.

It was Denny Laine who first brought McCullough into contact with Paul. After *Wild Life* was recorded, with the fledgling band facing upcoming live dates, Denny decided that he wasn't really cut out to sing *and* play lead guitar after all. After three days of jamming, on oldies and new material, Paul popped the question and Henry acquiesced. He quickly found himself thrown into the deep end of controversy when Wings' debut single, the politically charged "Give Ireland Back to the Irish," stirred sectarian violence in the homeland. McCullough's brother actually suffered a beating when Henry's role in the recording became known.

For the first year, Henry's input brought the band a quantum leap forward from their somewhat ragtag beginnings. Linda's instrumental shortcomings were easily masked by Henry's prowess, but aesthetically, there wasn't much he could do with offerings like "Mary Had a Little Lamb" (beyond adding a folksy flourish of mandolin). Still, his presence in live situations helped establish the band's rock credibility when he performed a twelve-bar blues piece (usually called "Henry's Blue," a shape-shifting workout that varied from performance to performance) in their early sets. His freewheeling spontaneity and jamming capacity served the band in good stead when new material was in short supply.

Probably McCullough's shining hour with Wings was the guitar solo on "My Love," a contribution that received universal kudos for elevating to greatness an otherwise potentially mawkish McCartney valentine. The song sparked a moment of unintended hilarity when, for a television appearance, an overabundance of oil-generated effects smoke caused Henry to vomit after the song concluded. "Hi Hi Hi" likewise offered him a rare showcase (on a Paul McCartney record) for some adroit slide guitar. ("C Moon," the flip side, saw him make his recorded debut on *drums*.)

Equally deathless was McCullough's cameo on Pink Floyd's *Dark Side of the Moon* album. During its recording at EMI's Abbey Road studios, Roger Waters prepared a series of questions on three-by-five note cards, and then recorded the responses from a variety of participants. Working on *Red Rose Speedway* at the same facility, some Wings members found themselves roped into the project. While Paul and Linda's answers didn't make the cut,

HENRY McCULLOUGH

Mind Your Own Business!

Whether as a deliberate provocation to his former bandmate or simply an attempt to bolster his label's roster with available talent, George signed ex-Wings guitarist Henry McCullough to Dark Horse in 1975.

Henry's did. He was first asked when he had last been violent. The follow-up, "Were you in the right?" elicited the following reply: "I don't know—I was really drunk at the time."

Despite his integral role in the band that Wings had become, McCullough's tenure was marked by an undercurrent of unease; the guitarist never seemed to get a good read on where the bandleader was coming from. In the press, he opined that, despite his and his fellows' commitment to their group's success, Macca's loyalties were stronger to his former band than to his present one. For his part, Paul saw Henry as less of a team player than others in the group, and it vexed him.

Ultimately, low pay, resentment at being a seasoned pro forced to share a stage with an amateur, and the dictatorial demands of the bandleader took their toll. Matters came to a head in August 1973, during the *Band on the Run* rehearsals. Poised for a trip to Lagos, the band were working on a Denny Laine song ("No Words," perhaps?) when came a guitar line that Paul insisted Henry play. McCullough, equally adamant, balked, saying it could not be done. Upon this, the guitarist departed, confirming his resignation by phone the next day. (Three days later, Denny Seiwell did likewise.)

McCullough didn't stay idle long, working first with Donovan on *Essence to Essence* before reuniting with Joe Cocker for 1974's *I Can Stand a Little Rain*. The latter album featured Joe's smash cover of Billy Preston's "You Are So Beautiful," reinforcing the fewer than six degrees of separation running throughout the Beatles' extended family. These ties were drawn closer when, in 1975, McCullough released his first solo album, *Mind Your Own Business!* on Dark Horse. Said Henry of George: "We found we had an awful lot in common."

Geoff Britton—Drummer (1974–1975)

Wings' drummer issues, momentarily punted when Paul commandeered the throne for *Band on the Run*, were at last settled with the addition of Geoff Britton in April 1974. Unlike everyone else recruited to this point, there had been no referral or personal acquaintance involved: Britton came in cold, one of about fifty prospects that auditioned at the Albery Theatre in London. Though he had a bit of showbiz notoriety, having played in the British group East of Eden in the late '60s, he also came with a rep guaranteed to win respect: Britton was a championship-level karate black belt, a point that Paul and others wasted no time exploiting as his defining trait.

"He'll be able to whip the band in[to] shape" was Macca's facetious way of introducing Wings' newest member. By this time, the auditioning process had gotten more elaborate. Britton was initially disappointed to find that he was expected to play a few numbers with hired session men as Paul, Linda, and Denny watched. Only after making it to the final five did he actually get to play with his future bandmates, having beat out, among others, Jimi Hendrix Experience drummer Mitch Mitchell and Liverpudlian Aynsley Dunbar, newly landed from a stint with Frank Zappa.

Once the decision was made, Paul himself made the phone call, cruelly teasing out the answer Britton was nearly frantic to hear. The newly anointed percussionist, late of Wild Angels, quickly found himself flown off to Nashville, where the group, with the addition of Jimmy McCulloch on lead guitar, began laying down tracks. The first product of their labors was the stylistic throwback single, "Walking in the Park with Eloise," released under the nomenclature "The Country Hams" The song itself had been composed decades earlier by Paul's father and recorded as a sort of gift—the seven-inch equivalent of Ringo's *Sentimental Journey*.

Wings Mark IV made their vinyl debut on the pounding rocker "Junior's Farm," backed by the country ballad "Sally G." The record, representing the only new material issued by Wings in 1974, landed at #3—a promising beginning for the fledgling lineup. But before it had even been issued that fall, turmoil within the ranks was trumpeted to the outside world in England's *New Musical Express.* An August headline announced "Wings Upheaval," reporting a split between the McCartneys and the two new members, along with stalwart Denny Laine.

Hyperbole notwithstanding, it would appear that while in Nashville, long-awaited contracts binding the musicians together were presented for signing. Rather than the smooth business agreement anticipated, a heated discussion ensued, with a consensus voiced among the non-McCartneys that they were being pushed into something they didn't really feel comfortable with. Ultimately, Laine declared that he, for one, didn't need a piece of paper to assure his commitment—exactly what Macca wanted to hear—while conversely, a Wings spokesperson told the press, "Wings members are free to pursue their own musical careers." The statement did nothing to reassure the public of the band's stability.

Whatever business concerns troubled the outfit, they were soon papered over, and Wings' latest iteration made the rounds to promote "Junior's Farm" before beginning work on the follow-up to *Band on the Run.* Recording commenced in November at EMI's studios, to be completed in New Orleans early the next year. But after cutting just three songs ("Love in Song," "Letting Go," and Jimmy's "Medicine Jar"), Geoff Britton abruptly quit.

Chronic tensions between Wings' two newest members could no longer be ignored. It would appear that, in addition to the ten years in age separating them, Geoff and Jimmy were locked in a lifestyle and personality clash. The ultra-health-conscious jock Britton could not abide the adolescent antics of the hard-partying Scotsman and was not bashful about telling him so. (As he explained later to *Melody Maker*, "They say I hate Jimmy McCulloch's guts. What I really said is that he's a nasty little cunt.") Additionally, the upheaval of Britton's sudden ascension to rock royalty (and the travel his new position required) put a strain on his marriage. Given the choice between Macca and his wife, Britton chose to honor the latter commitment, making his the briefest tenure of all the Wings men.

After fulfilling some martial arts–related duties (a tournament here, a spaghetti western there), Britton quickly settled in as drummer with Rough

Diamond (a band fronted by ex–Uriah Heap singer David Byron) before moving on to Manfred Mann's Earth Band (for the *Angel Station* album). Though only briefly in the eye of Wings' storm, Britton summed up the "madness" thusly: "No matter how good you are, you are always in the shadow of Paul"—an observation that no one could disagree with.

Jimmy McCulloch—Guitarist (1974–1977)

Though all the Wings men were seemingly chosen in part for their very utilitarian facelessness, guitarist Jimmy McCulloch perhaps came closest to becoming a '70s rock god. Blessed with talent, charisma, and good looks in equal measure, the youthful Scot (he was all of twenty-one when he joined, but looked younger) was a veteran professional by the time he was recruited.

Born in Glasgow, the gifted guitarist formed his first band, the Jaygars, with his brother Jack in 1964, at the age of eleven. After a name change (to One in a Million), the group released a pair of singles and even opened for some top-flight talent in their native Scotland, including the Who. Meeting them proved to be Jimmy's lucky break, for in 1969 he was recruited by Pete Townshend to handle guitar in a band built around an ex-Who roadie, singer/songwriter/drummer John "Speedy" Keen. Named for their boogie pianist, Andy "Thunderclap" Newman, the band scored a #1 in England with the classic "Something in the Air." (The song was originally entitled "Revolution," but a group from Liverpool beat them to the market with a song by the same name.)

Though Thunderclap Newman released a critically acclaimed album, *Hollywood Dream*, the complete lack of personal rapport between the band members as well as the inability to score another hit doomed them to obscurity ever after. But young McCulloch's burgeoning career continued, boosted by the exposure the hit single provided, as well as the limitless support given by his parents. (They had moved the family to London to aid Jimmy's musical progress.)

McCulloch next enjoyed a stint with the venerable John Mayall's Bluesbreakers, following the well-traveled path blazed by Eric Clapton, Fleetwood Mac's Peter Green, and the Rolling Stones' Mick Taylor—all in all, a prestigious gig for someone not yet twenty. This preceded a stretch with Stone the Crows, a Scottish band fronted by Maggie Bell (known to most Americans as the backing singer on Rod Stewart's "Every Picture Tells a Story") and singer-guitarist Les Harvey, brother of Alex. After Les was electrocuted on a Swansea stage in 1972, the young McCulloch was deputized to take his place, completing tracks on the unfinished album, 1973's

'Ontinuous Performance. The band split later that year, freeing Jimmy to take work where he could.

He entered Paul's orbit quite by accident, while recording a solo album at London's Kingsway Studio in the fall of 1973. Paul was engaged in a three-day mixing session for *Band on the Run* when, during a break, he happened upon the young guitarist layering slide guitar parts. Liking what he heard, Macca asked if Jimmy would like to go to Paris to work on some material Linda was recording. McCulloch put aside his own project to work on the song "I Got Up" (eventually issued on Linda's posthumous release *Wide Prairie*) and soon after found himself on board Mike McCartney's *McGear*—an ad hoc Wings album fronted by Paul's brother. (The former had taken on the pseudonym so as not to appear to be riding his Beatle brother's coattails when he began making music himself, as part of Scaffold, back in the '60s.)

Not until the conclusion of the *McGear* sessions in the spring of 1974 was McCulloch formally asked to become a member of Wings. The ambitious guitarist expressed his glee in joining the major leagues thusly: "I want to get something down on record that's going to be appreciated." With the addition of Geoff Britton, Wings was now fully operational for the first time in nearly a year.

The Nashville sessions proved productive with the recording of "Junior's Farm." The solid-rocking number did much to reassure those convinced that McCartney had lost his way. Given the chance to let loose ("Take me down, Jimmy!"), McCulloch turned in a blistering solo that ranks among Wings' more shining moments. Moreover, his natural ability to steer a band his way rather than simply blend in proved mutually beneficial to Paul, whose hipness quotient went measurably upward with the new addition.

Not everyone was ready to embrace the hyperkinetic upstart, however. The Cockney karate pro, Geoff Britton, found himself harnessed to a band-mate whose juvenile antics he found insufferable. Recognizing his social shortcomings, McCulloch conceded, "Sometimes I really blow it and get on people's nerves." But Macca, perhaps feeling that a gifted lead guitarist was rarer than a good drummer, tacitly sided with Jimmy and did nothing to discourage Britton's departure.

Indeed, Jimmy's song, "Medicine Jar" (cowritten with his Stone the Crows bandmate Colin Allen) was among the first tracks recorded for *Venus and Mars*. An anti-drug rocker—ironically, as it happened—it soon became a highlight of the Wings tour in the fall of 1975 and in America the following year—quite a coup for a new member. (The similarly themed "Wino Junko" would grace the hastily recorded *At the Speed of Sound*, with lesser results.)

The Wings Over America tour proved Jimmy's crowning moment. As documented in the films *Rockshow* and *Wings over the World*, McCulloch showed himself to be every bit the equal of anyone sharing Paul McCartney's stage. His incisive playing proved to be just the tonic to provide an edge to songs that might otherwise drift into soft rock territory: his work on the live version of "Maybe I'm Amazed" being but one example. (Additionally, the youthful panache with which he presented himself proved a *visual* spark plug alongside the group of thirtysomethings surrounding him.)

But following over a year of such highs, Paul elected to mellow things out. With Linda pregnant and a passel of equally laid-back tunes prepared for their next long-player, Jimmy was afforded less of an opportunity to do what he did best. He gamely took part in the maritime sessions aboard the *Fair Carol* in the Virgin Islands, but a characteristic restlessness soon came over him. He found side projects: White Line, with his brother Jack, and Hinkley's Heroes, an aggregate of "celeb" rockers, including Maggie Bell and Mitch Mitchell. But mostly, he found drugs.

This Jekyll-and-Hyde persona, divined early on by Geoff Britton, began surfacing with regularity, alienating his bandmates. His welcome worn out, in September 1977 Jimmy turned in his notice. (Though he was present on *London Town*, his departure before its release insured his absence from the packaging.) Officially, his leaving was ascribed to a desire to join the re-forming (minus Ronnie Line) Small Faces, though an equally disenchanted Macca is said to have phoned Steve Marriott and told him, "You can have him."

McCulloch provided his usual superb instrumental and vocal support on tour and on the album *78 in the Shade*. But despite a successful 1976 U.K. reissue of the Small Faces' 1967 hit "Itchycoo Park" that momentarily renewed interest in the band, the reunion came a little late and the public had moved on. Jimmy's downward slide had begun.

His next project looked a little more promising, on paper at least: the Dukes, a hard pop outfit fronted by Miller Anderson and featuring ex-Be Bop Deluxe bassist Charlie Tumahai. (Anderson had been a member of the Keef Hartley Band, which had performed at Woodstock—as had Henry McCullough. Hartley, in turn, had gotten his big break in 1962, replacing Ringo in Rory Storm and the Hurricanes. As always with the Beatles, six degrees. . .).

While possessing considerable potential, the band was almost doomed from the start. They recorded an album for Warner Brothers in the summer of 1979 with some really strong material on it (and well worth seeking out), but without a champion within the corporate structure, support was virtually nonexistent. Jimmy, meanwhile, was deteriorating rapidly, becoming difficult to work with and surrounding himself with exactly the wrong people. When the end came of a drug overdose in September 1979, the only wonder was that it hadn't occurred sooner.

Jimmy McCulloch's tragedy resulted from pushing away anyone strong enough to save him from himself. By the time any one of his previous sponsors might have thought to help him, he was beyond reach.

Though a rather unlikely collective, Thunderclap Newman left their mark with a single LP, produced by Pete Townshend in 1969 and containing the classic "Something in the Air."

Joe English—Drummer (1975–1977)

In early 1975, Wings did not have the luxury of conducting a drummer hunt at their leisure. They were well into recording a new album and had an upcoming tour looming, meaning that whoever they accepted would have to be available immediately, a quick study, *and* ready for the big time practically overnight. Rochester, New York native Joe English fit the profile beautifully.

English got the call from trombonist Tony Dorsey, one quarter of the horn section being used by Paul in New Orleans. About to go on tour with bluesman Buddy Brown, English quickly found a replacement before getting on a flight to NOLA that night. Dorsey and Joe knew each other from the latter's days with the Jam Factory, a Syracuse-based rock-and-brass ensemble purported to be the next Blood, Sweat, and Tears. After relocating to Georgia, the band morphed into Tall Dogs Orchestra of Macon. They soon gained a reputation as one the hottest and tightest ensembles on the road.

Ever the professional, English slid easily into Wings, finishing *Venus and Mars*' remaining tracks as well as other material released sporadically (if at all) in the coming years. The next big challenge was learning Macca's back catalog for upcoming swings through the U.K. beginning in September, followed by Australia through November. English's years of road experience made throwing him into the deep end an entirely canny move. He quickly mastered the material, adding his own firepower to past studio creations like "Hi Hi Hi" as well as the current album's "Rock Show" without overpowering them.

Hot off the heels of these dates, Wings headed into the studio to generate some fresh product to tour upon in America. Within their catalog, *At the Speed of Sound* stands as the equivalent of CCR's *Mardi Gras*: an attempt at band democracy that resulted in one of their weaker efforts. As Creedence had done, each member of the band got a turn in the lead vocal spotlight, a risky move for someone of Paul's stature. (Of the guest singers, only Linda's "Cook of the House" is a real embarrassment—a song *Rolling Stone* called a "celebration of scatterbrained wife-in-kitchen coziness.")

Unlike John Fogerty's band, however, McCartney didn't allow his fellows the rope to hang themselves; his *own* songwriting was the real issue. Two gonzo singles notwithstanding, Macca compositions like "Warm and Beautiful" and "Must Do Something About It" were apparently tossed off simply to fill space on an LP, recalling *Red Rose Speedway* in terms of mediocrity. However—and this is a *big* however—the latter track was redeemed utterly with revelatory singing provided by the newly installed drummer. Joe English delivered a convincing R&B vocal that raised the song above the sum of its parts. The real shame is that never again—not on the subsequent tour, nor on the following album, *London Town*—was Joe singled out for the attention he deserved—to Wings' detriment.

Nineteen-seventy-six's *Wings Over America* tour codified Wings Mark V as the "classic" iteration of an ever-changing band. Their state-of-the-art presentation, onstage ease with each other and with large audiences, and wealth of hits to choose from (Paul was no longer shy about presenting his Beatle past) epitomized 1970s concertgoing at its finest. Certainly Linda thought so, telling *Melody Maker* (presumably with her husband's concurrence), "I'd like to see this band carry on." Gushed Paul himself, "In ten years, I'll be looking back and remembering everything about it. . . . This wasn't just a one-time trip. . . . We'll be back."

Sadly, for not the last time, Paul's public pronouncement was dead wrong. Unexpectedly, Linda became pregnant, forcing a relaxed work schedule. Jimmy drifted into increasingly unhealthy habits, and soon Joe English was longing for home. He had seen, as John Lennon had once described the Shea Stadium experience, "the top of the mountain." But something inside was longing for a more meaningful existence, and to Joe at that moment, it meant America. Two months after Jimmy left—and just as "Mull of Kintyre / Girl's School" was released, Joe too took a hike, leaving Wings' finest lineup a memory.

After some time back in his Georgia stomping grounds with Chuck Leavell's Sea Level, a jazz-rock fusion group, English turned his back on the secular musical world. Following his wife's serious injuries in a car accident and subsequent recovery assisted through prayer, Joe became "born again." He formed the Joe English Band, one of the most successful acts within the Christian rock genre. The group recorded seven albums and toured the world before health issues forced Joe's retirement in the 1990s.

Steve Holley—Drummer (1978–1981)

Both Jimmy and Joe's successors would come, like Henry McCullough, through Denny Laine, who seemed capable of running a musicians' referral network on the side. Steve Holley happened to be a neighbor after Laine moved to Laleham, a village in Spelthorne, Surrey. The two became drinking buddies at their local; one day, at a party Denny hosted, both Holley and the McCartneys were in attendance. When no one else sat down at the kit in Laine's music room for an informal jam, Holley recognized an opportunity and took the seat, wowing both Wings men, but especially Denny, who had had no idea that his friend was a professional musician.

A musical background was Holley's birthright, as his father had been a swing-era bandleader and his mother, a singer. At an early age, drums became an obsession, and, like others in Wings, he'd started his first band before he was a teen. Once he came of age, Holley's seriousness about making music his career led him to put together a group versatile enough in an array of styles to record behind anyone. The aggregate became known as the Vapour Trails (or V.T.s). Their command of many genres got them attention from industry heavyweights, leading to an invitation from Elton John to back his protégée Kiki Dee.

Work on her 1977 self-titled album coincided with Elton's own musical reevaluation. The zenith of his mid-'70s popularity now behind him, John

Wings' final lineup recorded exactly one LP, a one-off single (shown here), and played a string of shows in Britain in 1979 before crashing and burning in the wake of the Japanese drug bust.

cast aside the musical mainstays (cowriter Bernie Taupin and musicians Nigel Olsson, Dee Murray, and Davey Johnstone) that had taken him this far in favor of some fresh talent. Holley won the drummer's slot in the new band, debuting on the 1978 album *A Single Man* (Elton's first U.S. long-player *not* to crack the Top 10). Holley also assisted Denny with five solo tunes, recorded at John's former Tittenhurst Park facility, now owned by Ringo.

His meeting with McCartney came at the same moment that Elton had invited the drummer to go on tour. After Macca requested a formal audition at the Soho offices of MPL, resulting in an on-the-spot offer, Holley was in a quandary. Ultimately, and with the greatest trepidation, he gave Elton his regrets and became Wings' fourth drummer in seven years (not counting Paul). Captain Fantastic took the spurning with good grace, later inviting a post-Wings Holley to contribute to his 1981 *Jump Up!* release.

After commencing with some film work (on a pair of songs written for— but not used in—the films *Heaven Can Wait* and *Same Time Next Year*, as well as a score composed for the animated *Rupert the Bear* project), Holley—along with Laurence Juber—got down to official Wings business with the *Back to the Egg* sessions in June 1978. Though Holley was seen miming along to Joe English's work on the music video to *London Town*'s "I've Had Enough," his formal musical introduction to the public came with the dance track "Goodnight Tonight" in March 1979.

That year saw an array of projects, including a new album, a major charitable event, and the first leg of a scheduled world tour, come to fruition, promising a grand future for the newest Wings lineup. Having seen Paul's seeming generosity with soliciting input from his bandmates in previous incarnations, it is possible that Holley and Juber thought their contributions would be welcomed. This ended up not being the case, although with Holley, a riff he dreamed up was included as the bridge to "Old Siam, Sir"—without credit, of course.

Whatever their expectations, the two men surely didn't anticipate things ending so ingloriously. The hubris built up over nearly two decades of superstardom brought things crashing down in January 1980 with Paul's drug bust in Japan. Wings Mark VI (or VII, depending on how one counts them) never toured outside the U.K. and only ever recorded one album together. After *Back to the Egg*, they mostly worked on bringing years' worth of shelved tracks up to snuff for a compilation album, *Cold Cuts*, that was never issued.

The final reckoning came in early 1981. Though material that would end up on *Tug of War* had been rehearsed, word was that George Martin, on board to produce the project, had no interest in putting his time into a Wings album. Whether this was a commentary on his opinion of Laine,

Holley, and Juber, or merely an estimate of the esteem he had for Paul, is not known; what is known is that in February, Steve and Laurence quit, perhaps choosing to jump rather than be pushed out of a project that had deemed them redundant. Having seen their Wings career already sidetracked once in favor of *McCartney II*, the two men saw little reason to suffer a second humiliation.

Holley's session career resumed where it had left off—working on an Elton John album. Though Wings may have been his highest-profile gig, he's hardly been a slouch, putting down drums for the New York sessions of Julian Lennon's *Valotte* album in 1984, as well as working with Ian Hunter and Joe Cocker. In 2003, Holley released his long-awaited solo debut album, *The Reluctant Dog*, showcasing his songwriting *and* singing. The tour de force, described in one review as "brilliant work," offers a fine display of what Wings Mark VI might have become, had true democracy been allowed to flower.

Laurence Juber—Guitarist (1978–1981)

Undoubtedly the most dedicated studio professional of all the Wings men, Laurence Juber actually studied music at London University, having divined at an early age that his life's goal was to become a session guitarist. As a youth, his tastes tended to run more toward Hendrix and jazz fusion then pop; consequentially, he never saw the Beatles perform. (Contrary to internet-driven myth, Juber was never a member of the 1960s Oregon psychedelic band Afterglow.)

Having mastered sight-reading as well as a variety of styles, LJ—as he is called—found work in film, in television, and on a plethora of recording projects ranging from pop vocals (Rosemary Clooney) to French disco. Six degrees of Beatles being what it is, LJ could not help his proximity to others within the ex-Fabs' orbit: he worked on the 1977 James Bond film, *The Spy Who Loved Me*—which featured Ringo's wife-to-be, Barbara Bach—as well as the first Alan Parsons Project album, *Tales of Mystery and Imagination*, in 1976. (Parsons, of course, began his career as an engineer at EMI on *Abbey Road* before working with Paul on the first two Wings albums.)

LJ had actually crossed paths with Macca in the studio well before officially being considered to replace Jimmy McCulloch. But, as he had done with others, Denny Laine proved the catalyst for bringing Juber into the band. LJ had been part of the house band on *The David Essex Show* in England, which Denny guested on in 1977. The two bonded well, and when Paul decided that it was time to go guitarist shopping again, he had his management call Juber with an invitation to a "jam" with Denny Laine—that, incidentally, Paul and Linda would be attending. (Even at this late a date, the McCartneys had a hard time calling an audition what it was.) Much to LJ's relief, no Wings tunes were performed, as he had only the barest familiarity with their work.

Being the quick study that he was, LJ mastered their repertoire in no time while making his mark on the edgier sound Paul was seeking for *Back to the Egg*. As he has stated in numerous interviews, the supreme highlight of his Wings tenure came at very nearly its tail end. At the conclusion of the Rockestra set at the Concert for Kampuchea, the gathered ensemble closed the evening with "Let It Be." The song had been part of Wings' set for the past month on their U.K. dates, but now, onstage with some of the biggest names in rock (which included Pete Townshend, John Bonham, Dave Edmunds, and Gary Brooker, among others), LJ suddenly found himself starstruck. Came the guitar solo and, for a moment doubting his own legitimacy, he rapidly glanced around, saw that everyone was deferring to *him*, and tore into it with all the emotion he could muster. Given to understatement, he observed later: "It was quite a remarkable experience."

Though Wings folded not long after, it wasn't the end of LJ's contributions to ex-Fab projects. He did manage to squeeze in some work on Ringo's 1981 *Stop and Smell the Roses* album. In 1987, his film soundtrack work saw him enlisted to contribute to the George Harrison-produced bomb *Shanghai Surprise*. (Whatever else can be said about the Madonna-starring vehicle, the soundtrack is impeccable.)

Today LJ is as busy as ever, between session work and his own albums of exquisitely produced fingerstyle acoustic music, thirteen in number as of this writing. While thematically they range from jazz to pop to folk to holiday music, it is perhaps 2000's *LJ Plays the Beatles* collection that has drawn the most attention. (Said Macca when learning of its existence: "Where's *Wings*?" LJ obliged him five years later with an assortment of *their* work, entitled *One Wing*.)

As an added footnote, a unique pop culture regurgitation came about when Juber cocomposed music to two TV spinoff musicals, *Gilligan's Island: The Musical*, and *A Very Brady Musical*. To those readers wondering how the English Juber found himself drawn into two very American properties, look no further than his wife, the former Hope Schwartz. The daughter of Brady Bunch creator Sherwood Schwartz, she appeared in the series several times, once as Jenny Wilton in "The Slumber Caper" (an episode originally airing on John Lennon's thirtieth birthday) and twice as Greg's date Rachel (most memorably seen with Bobby's frog atop her head at the drive-in).

Now living in L.A., Juber can be seen fairly regularly as a guest at the Fest for Beatles Fans.

Denny Lane—Guitarist (1971–1981)

Of all the musicians to pass through Wings over the years, singer/guitarist Denny Laine was the one constant outside of the McCartneys. Born Brian Hines in Birmingham, he began playing in public at the age of eleven, a serious student of jazz guitarist Django Reinhardt. On July 5, 1963, he first crossed paths professionally with Paul McCartney, as his group, the Diplomats, appeared on a bill headlined by the Beatles at the Plaza Ballroom in Old Hill.

The following year, Laine formed the Moody Blues. The quintet scored a #1 hit in England with their second single, a cover of Bessie Banks's "Go Now," putting them into the Beatles' orbit. *The Magnificent Moodies* album arrived in July 1965, but the hits soon dried up and Denny grew restless. Despite playing support on the Fabs' U.K. tours and Brian Epstein taking over their management, the Moody Blues' best days seemed behind them. Denny quit in 1966, a year before the band retooled and recorded their monster *Days of Future Passed* album.

In subsequent years, Laine drifted between gigs, first forming the Electric String Band, a precursor to Jeff Lynne's Electric Light Orchestra that featured amplified violin and cello. (ELO's drummer Bev Bevan had in fact played with Denny in the Diplomats.) Though garnering good reviews opening for Jimi Hendrix, the band fell apart. (One song, Denny's "Say You Don't Mind," became a hit in 1972 for ex-Zombies singer Colin Blunstone.) Laine followed this with stints in Ginger Baker's Airforce and an outfit called Balls, but these too went nowhere.

In 1970, he turned up in the studio-only exploitation band the Magic Christians. There Laine took his first shot at a McCartney tune on "Come and Get It" for Commonwealth United Records. (It's not known whether or not he actually listed this credit when applying for the open position with Wings a year later; Paul might not have been pleased at his being part of a project calculated to encroach on Apple's record sales.)

The next year, he began work on his first solo release (eventually issued in 1973 as *Ahh . . . Laine*). The album's launch was shelved when, out of the blue, Paul McCartney rang him up. As he told it after Wings was formed, Macca had been shopping for a multi-instrumentalist, someone as comfortable on guitar—lead, rhythm, or bass—as he was on keyboards, and who could provide a male harmony. He also expressed admiration for Laine as a songwriter (though Laine's apparent lack of ego couldn't have hurt).

Laine joined in time for the recording of *Wild Life* and 1972's hit-and-run university tour. As the band began to jell, he and Paul began sharing composing credits, beginning with "No Words" on *Band on the Run*. (A Laine composition, "I Would Only Smile," was recorded by the pre-Lagos Wings, but only released in 1980 as a solo Denny Laine track on *Japanese Tears*.) Occasionally Denny would take the lead vocal on a song written by Paul (e.g., "I Lie Around," "The Note You Never Wrote"), but for the most part he was content to play Larry Fine to Macca's Moe, adding support where needed but never asserting himself as a dominant personality.

His loyalty in the face of two defections proved reason enough for Paul to reward Denny with something denied the others: a share in *Band on the Run*'s profits. As newer members joined (thereby increasingly Laine's seniority), he began to receive a bigger share of the spotlight. Paul's "Spirits of Ancient Egypt," sung by Denny, is commonly thought to be Laine's own composition, so identified with it did he become through his reading during the Wings over the World tour. (He also sang lead on Paul Simon's "Richard Cory," the Moodies' hit "Go Now," plus his own "Time to Hide"—but not on any Beatles songs.) This triumph was followed by a side project, an album's worth of Buddy Holly covers entitled *Holly Days*, released in 1977.

Perhaps the high-water mark of his Wings career came during the *London Town* sessions. Laine cowrote five of the album's fourteen tracks and sang lead on two, "Children Children" and "Deliver Your Children." (Despite the recurrence of the word "children" in the titles, the two songs had nothing in common thematically.) More importantly, Laine was co-credited on the campfire sing-along "Mull of Kintyre." The idiosyncratic anthem to McCartney's Scottish retreat shattered the U.K. singles sales record held since 1963 by "She Loves You" (while dying a death in America). The achievement would, alas, be bested in 1984 by Band Aid's "Do They Know It's Christmas?," another holiday season release.

As members came and went, the Laine-McCartney axis might have tightened, but beneath the surface lay a brittle subtext. Rapport between Linda and Laine's wife Jo Jo never evolved beyond frosty. As for himself, having had a taste of what touring at its best had to offer, Laine was eager to repeat the experience, with the long-delayed entry into Japan finally within reach. But Paul's staggeringly foolish drug bust in January 1980 all but destroyed the band, irreparably straining relations. In response to the events, Denny wrote "Japanese Tears," a song commenting on the disappointment of the canceled tour, releasing it as a single that spring as Paul put Wings on hiatus to work on *McCartney II*.

Later in the year, Wings reconvened to tidy up some heretofore unreleased tracks for the long-promised *Cold Cuts* collection. Following the departure of Juber and Holley, Laine assisted on what would eventually become *Tug of War*, but on April 27, 1981—while the remaining ex-Beatles gathered to attend Ringo's wedding to Barbara Bach—Denny officially turned in his notice, simultaneously ending Wings. In the wake of John's death, Paul—out of safety concerns—had decided to make touring a thing of the past; as far as Denny was concerned, a studio-bound band was no band at all.

To hear Paul tell it, it was a mutual decision: "If we're going to pick it up again we should just be loose enough to come together again or not. . . . I hate the pressure of a group." In any event, it would be years before Denny Laine mounted a proper tour or even got any new material released, as the *Japanese Tears* album was cobbled together from tracks cut over a period of years. In the meantime, he sold out his one ace in the hole—his half of the royalties to "Mull of Kintyre"—for a one-time payout of £135,000. Through debts and a divorce settlement, by 1986 he was bankrupt.

Today, Laine has successfully retained his stature among fans. In 1995, he first appeared as a guest at the Chicago Beatlefest; his 2008 return alongside some ex-bandmates prompted rumors that he, Lawrence Juber, and Denny Seiwell might work on putting together some sort of Wings reunion. While Paul and Denny appear to have patched up any differences, Macca has expressed no interest in reheating that particular soufflé. With Linda gone, who could blame him?

15

Now What Can Be Done for You

Some Notable Guest Appearances

During the Beatle years, the individual Fabs occasionally appeared on the recordings of other artists, especially after Apple started up. Once the group ended and the four of them escaped the confines of Abbey Road's number two studio, the opportunity to participate in the larger recording community began in earnest, especially in America, where all the ex-Fabs spent a great deal of time. Nineteen-seventy-four would be something of a watershed year, with more collaborating taking place than at any other time, while the prospects for the former Fabs to work together had also never been better.

With Ringo maintaining the least prolific recording career (at least initially), it isn't surprising that he was generally available to sit in throughout the decade, recording with Harry Nilsson, Stephen Stills, and Peter Frampton, among others, all of whom returned the favor. Less expected is how little Paul guested throughout the decade, concentrating mostly on building Wings. John's collaboration on projects not of his own (or Yoko's) making was also unanticipated, as he had rarely displayed such interest in the past. As for George, he lived up to his own reputation as willing and able to play with anyone, any time.

Though far from complete, here is a rundown of some of the more notable outside recording gigs featuring the ex-Fabs as sidemen.

George on Badfinger's "Day After Day" (Single—Released November 10, 1971)

In May 1971, George commenced production duties for Badfinger at the familiar confines of EMI's Abbey Road studios. Having heard the tapes the band had recorded with Geoff Emerick at the helm, he already had a sense of what songs he wanted to revisit first. But upon Pete Ham's presentation of

Even by the standards of rock and roll's dark side, the story of Badfinger was stunningly tragic. Despite high hopes for their future, these Beatle protégés ended up as a brutal cautionary tale.

an as-yet-unrecorded composition, George was struck by the song's obvious commercial appeal. Four days into the sessions, the recording of "Day After Day" began.

A girlfriend of Pete's named Beverley Ellis had inspired the song. (She likewise provided inspiration for other Ham tunes, including "I Miss You" and "Song for a Lost Friend.") Already built into the song's DNA was a slide guitar motif, an effect that Badfinger had not yet used on a record. Proximity to George Harrison during the *All Things Must Pass* sessions may have influenced the notion, but it may also have been an attempt calculated to engage George's interest. If so, the ploy worked.

As originally planned, Pete and guitarist Joey Molland were to play the song's slide guitar embellishments in unison throughout. But George— unable to resist the compelling melody line—asked if *he* could play the slide part with the song's author, and Joey graciously stepped aside. The ex-Fab and Pete Ham spent several laborious hours working out the arrangement so as not to step on each other, though as engineer Richard Lush noted, there *were* easier ways to achieve the desired sound.

The collaboration had the effect of bonding the two men. While George already respected the individuals in Badfinger as musicians, he and Pete seemed to share a musical understanding and trust beyond this. Not long after, it was Pete Ham whom George asked to duet with him onstage before tens of thousands at the Bangladesh event, notably without the benefit of a formal rehearsal. Later, Ham provided uncredited assistance to George on the *Living in the Material World* album.

Once that element of the song was perfected and committed to tape, George had another card to play: visiting session man extraordinaire Leon Russell. The veteran multi-instrumentalist listened to it once, then laid down an exquisite piano line on the second pass. Simple but elegant, this last piece of business proved the icing on the cake: "Day After Day" reached #4 on *Billboard*'s chart (#1 in *Cashbox*) and was certified gold in March 1972.

The band themselves were of two minds about the success. While appreciative of the ex-Fab's support and grateful to have scored another hit, they were less enamored of the resulting sound, feeling it presented *George's* vision of Badfinger, not their own. (They also recognized the futility of attempting to replicate his arrangement while playing live.) Still, given the whirlwind of activity that 1971 brought—George producing *Straight Up*, the Concert for Bangladesh, the *Imagine* sessions—any complaints they harbored were tempered by recognition of their privileged position at Apple. That too would pass.

George on Cheech and Chong's "Basketball Jones" (Single—Released September 29, 1973)

Sometime after he arrived in Los Angeles to work on the *Ringo* album, George found himself drawn into the least likely of sessions. The comedy duo of Rich Marin and Tommy Chong, on a roll following the release of their first two albums, were at work on a third, entitled *Los Cochinos*, when unexpected inspiration came their way. Through the hubris of their producer, Lou Adler, and a perfect storm of show business proximity, an ad hoc all-star cast was assembled to back Cheech and Chong on a song parodying a long-forgotten hit.

In late 1972, an R&B ensemble from Chicago called Brighter Side of Darkness scored with a catchy but slight tune called "Love Jones." The rich comedic possibilities offered by a band featuring a twelve-year-old lead singer were too good to pass up, and Cheech Marin soon found the perfect way to satirize the recording. His epiphany came during a wild car ride with Jack Nicholson to a Lakers game, when in a falsetto he began singing, "I got a *basketball* jones." The remainder of the lyric was sketched out and demoed, and when the time came to record the tune, the resourceful Mr. Adler began talent scouting at A&M's recording facilities.

He quickly rounded up a stellar backing, comprised of George's usual crew: himself on lead guitar, Klaus Voormann on bass, Billy Preston on organ, Nicky Hopkins on piano, and Jim Keltner on percussion, along with the added attractions of Carole King, saxophonist Tom Scott, drummer Jimmy Karstein, and, as cheerleaders, the Blossoms (featuring Spector alumna Darlene Love and former Mama Michelle Phillips).

On the album, the track segues out of a skit satirizing ABC's *Wide World of Sports*, as an NBA star player gets interviewed. Using basketball as his meta-philosophy ("I need someone to set a pick for me at the free-throw line of life"), "Tyrone" (Cheech) tells his story, punctuating his narrative with an infectious chorus. The song builds, "Hey Jude"–style, as teammates, coaches, the cheerleaders, and the crowd are invited to sing along.

At a time when comedians regularly enjoyed hit albums, it wasn't all that unusual for Cheech and Chong to score a charting single (peaking at #15) with the resulting track. The song's popularity was further boosted by an animated video, produced by Ralph Bakshi of *Fritz the Cat* fame. What *was* unusual—at least on the surface—was George's involvment with a duo specializing in adolescent stoner humor. For an artist who'd already issued two albums' worth of weighty offerings, "Basketball Jones" was quite a departure. What it *did* publicly present was a side familiar to George's intimates: the

At a time when *comedians* could still score the occasional hit single, an ex-Beatle's participation on a Cheech and Chong recording was still pretty exceptional.

devotee of madcap absurdist humor. This aspect of his personality would find full voice as he began collaborating with members of Monthy Python, beginning with *The Rutles* and later as producer of the HandMade film *Life of Brian.*

John on Harry Nilsson's *Pussy Cats*—Released August 19, 1974

Nilsson's place on the oldies airwaves is assured. Three Dog Night's recording of "One" is the best-known of his oft-recorded compositions; conversely, his two best-known singles—"Everybody's Talkin'" and "Without You"—were written by others. His place in rock *lore* is something else, however. Known for his unpredictable career path, legendary self-abuse, and guilt by association during the simultaneously most notorious and most fruitful period of John Lennon's life, Nilsson is widely regarded as a sad figure: an enormously gifted man who took his talents lightly and never fulfilled his considerable promise. That's the conventional view, at least, but to aficionados, Nilsson's idiosyncratic releases offer rewarding listening to those of more mature tastes.

Though John and Harry had a nodding acquaintance going back to the Beatles years, not until the ex-Fab went west in the fall of 1973 did the two reenter each other's orbits full force. Until then, it was Ringo who palled around with Nilsson, beginning in spring 1972 when both George and the Ringed One contributed to Harry's *Son of Schmilsson* album. The following year, the favor was reciprocated on the *Ringo* album, when Harry added backing vocals to "You're Sixteen." The two, both going though hard times personally (both were estranged from their respective spouses) while enjoying a creative high, became inseparable. After working in the ill-starred *Son of Dracula* film together (see chapter 8), they headed out to Los Angeles with Keith Moon in tow, soon joining forces with the similarly liberated John. They shared the same emotional boat; their time together was summed up by Lennon in 1980: "It was 'let's all drown ourselves together'."

Following the infamous Troubadour incident of March 12, 1974, John realized that only way to avoid a further downward spiral was to throw himself into work. Perhaps inspired by his new best friend's thus far half-baked stab at cutting an oldies album, Harry suggested *that* as a path to pursue, with *John* at the board. Lacking the will to start a new album himself with one "half finished" (though in reality, much of it was beyond saving), John agreed to produce Harry, but wasn't so keen on the oldies concept, feeling that Harry's original material would be a better investment of their time. (They compromised by making it a half-and-half mix.) With a task before them, they rounded up the usual suspects for support (Ringo, Klaus, Keltner, Moon, Jesse Ed Davis), embarking on a project they called *Strange Pussies*.

While nominally possessing a mission and a goal, the sessions brought the musicians only a small step closer to normalcy, given the array of temptations surrounding them in the City of Angels. For one, the substance abuse hardly slowed down at all. (Paul McCartney, who happened to be in town and turned up at the studio for a visit, reported being offered angel dust by Harry one afternoon: "He said, 'It's elephant tranquilizer.' I said, 'Is it fun?' He thought for about half a minute. 'No,' he said. I said, 'Well, you know what, I won't have any.' He seemed to understand. But that's how it was there.")

Complicating matters further was Harry's physical state of being. Early on in the sessions, he began routinely spitting up blood. The multi-octave voice he'd deployed so effortlessly on "Without You" was eroding to a world-weary rasp. Given the amount of cigarettes, liquor, and drugs beings consumed, it was easy to ascribe his deterioration to simple wear and tear that would clear up over time. (The resulting smoky effect actually enhanced the material, or so he rationalized.) In fact, it was worse than he realized: a doctor informed him that he'd ruptured a vocal cord and recommended rest. Terrified that John would shut down the project if he knew, Nilsson concealed the news for as long as he could.

At last recognizing that they were getting nowhere fast, John relocated the project to New York's Record Plant in April, where he felt it would be easier to stay out of trouble. Indeed, results began taking shape. A raucous cover of Dylan's "Subterranean Homesick Blues" was the first track completed. John described it later as "really mad . . . A lot of edits in it, which I still hear." (When discussing the song on the radio, he challenged listeners to spot the splices and "win an invisible T-shirt.") Other covers included the Drifters' "Save the Last Dance for Me," a number nearly included on an early draft of the Beatles' *Let It Be*. Featuring a slowed tempo and a vocal that wrung every last drop of angst out of the Doc Pomus tune, it was originally sung by Ben. E. King, just like "Stand by Me," later famously cut by John.

Jimmy Cliff's "Many Rivers to Cross" proved to be an ideal opening number, capturing the album's subtext of desperation and dissipation in a production that evoked Lennon even more than it did Nilsson: the anguished vocal (which bore not a little resemblance to "Mother" in places), the Spector-like slathering of brass and strings, and, not least, a string arrangement that portended "#9 Dream." Fans expecting to hear the Nilsson of the Top 40 were stunned, to say the least. The original tunes may likewise have struck listeners as painfully bleak (a mood underscored by the condition of his pipes), but they surely rank as among his most succinct ruminations on romantic discord and mortality ever recorded. "Don't Forget Me" and "Old Forgotten Soldier" were particularly poignant, especially in retrospect, since both composer and performer were taken prematurely.

The album, renamed *Pussy Cats* (by an unamused RCA), wasn't exactly a runaway smash upon its summer 1974 release. It peaked at #60 (probably going that high on the strength of John's name and face on the cover art) and spawned no hit singles. Yet it stands today as a fascinating chapter in the development of both men's artistic lives: a sort of missing link between *Rock 'n' Roll* and *Walls and Bridges*. While certainly not to everyone's taste (though it does grow on one with repeated listenings), it is a challenging work, representing a brave attempt to channel each man's respective demons into art, and is therefore not to be dismissed lightly.

Though the two never again collaborated as closely, they did share one co-songwriting credit: on "Old Dirt Road," released on *Walls and Bridges*. Having already invoked the old Sons of Pioneers record "Cool Water" in the lyric, John asked Harry for an "Americanism" (while simultaneously sitting at a piano and discussing business with "a couple of suits"—talk about

Virtually a companion work to John's *Walls and Bridges*, Nilsson's *Pussy Cats* featured cover art that unsubtly captured the party atmosphere of the recording sessions (note message beneath the table). As heard in this quadraphonic version, the enhanced ambience allowed listeners to practically smell the puke.

multitasking). Harry came up with "trying to shovel smoke with a pitchfork in the wind," delighting John, who pushed him for more. Harry eventually recorded his own version for his 1980 *Flash Harry* album.

Following John's return to Yoko in early 1975, the two kindred spirits saw each other less and less, though Harry was clearly not far from John's mind, as he evoked him numerous times over the course of his 1980 *Playboy* interview ("God bless you, Harry, wherever you are"). Ringo stayed tight with Nilsson, serving as best man at Harry's wedding in 1976. (That same year, his . . . *That's the Way It Is* LP opened and closed with a cover of George's "That Is All" from *Living in the Material World*.) The two would cowrite a song for *Flash Harry* (entitled "How Long Can Disco On"), while Harry would contribute heavily to Ringo's *Stop and Smell the Roses* album in 1981. Had he been one for live appearances, Harry might have joined Ringo's traveling road show of the 1990s, but his overtaxed heart finally gave out in January 1994. Nilsson was fifty-two.

John on Mick Jagger's "Too Many Cooks" (Recorded Spring 1974)

When not stirring up trouble in nightclubs during the fabled "Lost Weekend," John logged an awful lot of studio hours. Perhaps recognizing that the path to salvation lay in work, he kept up the pace, moving quickly from one project to another. Not long after completing work on *Pussy Cats* with Harry Nilsson, what had been intended as nothing more than a freeform jam night (featuring the "Jim Keltner Orchestra"—as named by Lennon, an ensemble featuring Keltner, Nilsson, Al Kooper, Jesse Ed Davis, Jack Bruce, Bobby Keys, and Trevor Lawrence on sax) actually resulted in a viable recording, featuring none other than Mick Jagger on lead vocals.

"Too Many Cooks (Spoil the Soup)" was, all Willie Dixon speculation notwithstanding, the debut single of Motown's Holland-Dozier-Holland protégés, 100 Proof Aged in Soul. Issued in 1969, it peaked at #24 on the soul charts while most white record buyers remained blissfully unaware of its existence. Not so Jagger and company; with Lennon producing (or, as he self-deprecatingly described his production efforts, "sitting behind the desk"), a suitably funky take was captured, replete with horns and an outstanding Jagger vocal. Given the typical chemical state of some participants during that time, it's a minor miracle that something of value was captured at all.

It's impossible to hear this song without recognizing the care that was put into producing and arranging the recording; this wasn't simply a tossed-off jam. Indeed, speculation at the time held that it would be issued as a single on Apple. But instead, extra-musical issues, largely involving record labels and securing the necessary permissions for all involved, led to the track's abandonment.

By the time the session was recalled by Jagger decades later, no one knew if a releasable tape even survived. According to Mick, one master known to have existed was destroyed in a fire; another was unceremoniously trashed by an ex-wife (he didn't say which one). But still another was found in the possession of May Pang, who kept it underneath her bed. She lent it to Jagger, who then released it to near universal acclaim on his 2007 solo compilation.

Prior to its resurfacing, "Too Many Cooks" was the object of much speculation, some calling it a Jagger-Lennon duet (which would have been fascinating), others suggesting that Ringo was on drums. That neither canard was true doesn't much matter, for the recording's quality is itself enough reason to justify all the interest.

George on Ronnie Wood's "Far East Man" (From the album *I've Got My Own Album to Do*—Released September 13, 1974)

George's avid musical networking began in earnest with Apple's start-up, both as he recruited musicians for the label's roster and later as he became a part of the non-Beatle rock community. Through his travels to the States and his penchant for jamming with friends and friends of friends, his circle grew to encompass artists that inhabited separate worlds as the Beatles ruled their ever-expanding bubble.

One musician with whom he developed a rapport was guitarist/bassist Ronnie Wood, a journeyman of considerable personal charm. Wood began his career in 1964 as part of a group called the Birds (not surprisingly, given his avian features). From there, he was recruited as bassist with the Jeff Beck Group, placing him in contact with the first of two significant long-term musical partners, singer Rod Stewart. (The second was Rolling Stone Keith Richards, who formally began working with Wood in 1975.) Together, Stewart and Wood went on to spearhead the revamped Small Faces, dropping "small" along the way.

During the early '70s, an informal musical round robin came into being, with some of rock's elite hanging out and playing for fun during their down time. Clapton, Harrison, Gary Wright, Ronnie Lane, assorted Rolling Stones, Klaus Voormann, Billy Preston et al. were part of an informal grouping that assisted each other on recordings or even wrote tunes together. Beginning in 1972, Wood's home in Richmond, the Wick, became a favored gathering place for the ensemble.

It was a T-shirt worn by Wood, commemorating Faces' Far East tour, that triggered George's initial burst of inspiration for their one and only joint-credited composition. "Far East Man" presented an exploration of a slow soul groove—not a sound usually associated with either guitarist—and lyrics offering a rumination on letting a friend down (interestingly, as in the fall of 1973, Wood made full use of George's house, studio, and wife, in roughly that order).

Two versions were recorded. The first was issued on Ronnie's solo debut in September; three months later, George followed with his own slightly tweaked treatment on *Dark Horse*. In a way, Wood's version is more Harrisonian, featuring George's slide guitar and backing vocals prominently. But by the time he got around to cutting it himself, George's voice was shot—perversely giving the vocals a resemblance to Wood's. Nonetheless, it remains one of the highlights on a rather challenging album for Harrison fans.

George expressed the wish (on the actual recording, in fact) that Frank Sinatra record the song. There was no chance of that happening, despite Sinatra's famously praising George's "Something" as "Lennon-McCartney's greatest love song." The ex-Beatles seemed to share a Sinatra fixation, as three of the four had tunes they thought would work for Ol' Blue Eyes. For John, it was the *Walls and Bridges* closer, "Nobody Loves You (When You're Down and Out)"—for Paul it was a song called "Suicide" (unreleased, but for a snatch of it heard at the end of *McCartney*'s "Hot as Sun/Glasses" medley).

Though Ronnie never again worked formally with George, in 1979 Ringo sat in for a video shoot on "Buried Alive," a track from Wood's third solo album, *Gimme Some Neck*. The following year, the two laid down some tracks for Ringo's *Can't Fight Lightning* project; after some major revamping, the album was released as *Stop and Smell the Roses* in 1981 with the Starkey/Wood composition "Dead Giveaway."

George on Ravi Shankar's *Shankar Family and Friends*— Released September 20, 1974

As discussed in *Fab Four FAQ*, George was able to leverage his position as a Beatle to gain an audience with the world's foremost sitar maestro. Luckily, the two most unlikely of characters, literally worlds apart in background, connected instantly, forging a friendship that lasted until death. The fruits of that pairing impacted the world in ways both large and small: the introduction of Ravi's instrument to rock audiences led to the West's embrace of world music, while the Bangladesh benefit paved the way for increased rock star activism for worthy causes.

Actual musical collaboration between the two was rather sparse, however. It isn't hard to read George's reticence to appear in the same recording studio as the master as reflexive deference; after all, during their first one-on-one sit-down, George committed the faux pas of setting down his instrument

GEORGE HARRISON 1974 RAVI SHANKAR

ALL PROCEEDS FROM THE SALE OF THIS PROGRAM WILL GO TO THE APPALACHIAN REGIONAL HOSPITALS INC.

By inviting Ravi Shankar's world-class Indian troupe into what audiences expected to be a standard rock show in 1974, George pushed the boundaries of his art while alienating many who simply didn't get what they'd come for: the second coming of Beatle George.

and *stepping over it* to answer the phone, earning a stern rebuke for his blasphemy from his teacher in the form of a whack on the leg. Over time, he cultivated a deep humility regarding his sitar skills, recognizing that he could never truly earn his position as a Shankar sideman. Still, he did gain Ravi's respect with his sincerity, self-effacement, and command of millions of fans, many of whom would doubtless pick up on any Shankar offerings that happened to be issued on the Apple label.

The first of these came in the wake of the Bangladesh catastrophe. Just off the heels of George's "Bangla-Desh" single came Ravi's "Joi Bangla" ("Victory to Bangladesh") EP. Like his protégé's offering, it was earmarked to raise funds for the cause. George acted as producer, rather than musician, on the release, but once his benefit duties and work on *Living in the Material World* subsided, he was eager to give some musical interaction with Ravi another shot. The opportunity came when he made his mentor one of the first signings to Dark Horse: before his own follow-up album was finished, George produced *two* with Ravi.

Shankar Family and Friends was a deliberate attempt to fuse a Western pop sensibility to the classical Indian idiom. The first side featured a series of succinct tunes, not at all resembling Shankar's past work. Singer Lakshmi Shankar (a sister-in-law to Ravi) remains one of the world's foremost Hindustani singers; she provided the lead vocal on "I Am Missing You" ("you" being Lord Sri Krishna), a pop/Indian delicacy that led off the album and was issued as a single. (In a year that saw "The Lord's Prayer" by Sister Janet Mead become a surprise smash, expectations for the Shankar and family recording to compete in the Top 40 weren't as misplaced as they seemed.) Abetting Ravi's handpicked crew of India's finest classical musicians on side one were George, Ringo (as Billy Shears), Klaus Voormann, Billy Preston, Jim Keltner, and Tom Scott.

The second side contained a full-length suite, "Dream, Nightmare, and Dawn (Music for a Ballet)." (Ravi Shankar, it should be noted, began his career as a *dancer* in Paris during the 1930s.) Thematically, it was broken into several intervals; one passage, the dynamic "Dispute and Violence," was one of the more exciting pieces performed on the subsequent *Dark Horse* tour. Taken as a whole, *Shankar Family and Friends* represented a fine effort to present the public with a sort of halfway point between East and West with an emphasis on accessibility to rock music fans. While not exactly "selling out," Ravi himself was of two minds about the approach, remaining quite sensitive to charges that he was abandoning his classical roots for the rewards of superstardom.

To counter any taint, a second Dark Horse release was laid down with help from George, *Ravi Shankar's Music Festival from India*. It marked a return to the "pure" classical style Shankar had built his career upon, with extended ragas and no direct Western influence or concessions to AM radio. The release served as a further sampling for those who hadn't picked up on his two Apple LPs, the *Raga* soundtrack (1971) and his collaboration with sarod master Ali Akbar Khan, *In Concert—1972* (released in 1973). It weighed upon Ravi that he was inadvertently diluting his art through all this mingling with Western pop stars; therefore he was careful not to stray too far from the reservation, as it were.

The first of the two Dark Horse releases was showcased on the tour of the same name. Though the *Dark Horse* album was not yet in stores when the tour commenced, George still offered up a sampling of it live, along with some back catalog solo material and—begrudgingly—some Beatles songs. Though a relative newcomer to the world of rock, Ravi was an old hand in show business and knew how to read an audience. It was therefore largely through his influence that George performed any Fab material at all, as he strove mightily to resist being seen as "Beatle George." Explained Ravi: "At the rehearsal . . . it took about two hours and eighteen songs before George would do a Beatles song. He's matured so much in so many years. That's the problem with all the artists. . . . People expect him to be what he was ten years ago."

George set out to present an unheard-of mixture of classical Indian music, featuring the top musicians of the genre (albeit performing truncated "highlights" from their normal material), coupled with his own outfit, largely comprised of Tom Scott's L.A. Express, who brought a jazz-funk dynamic to the table. As conceived, the concerts would then close with both ensembles on stage, performing "I Am Missing You" in an attempt to "blow the roof off this place"—a notion George actually exhorted his audience to achieve by chanting "together purely for one minute."

Sadly, George's ambitions to enlighten the masses far outstripped the sensibilities of a mid-'70s rock audience. Mostly, they came not to reach a higher state of consciousness—they had already taken care of *that*—but to *rock* and to see, if not "Beatle George," at least a reasonable facsimile of the by-now legendary Concert for Bangladesh. What they got was neither, and it vexed some of them. For Ravi, facing crowds that were mostly indifferent if not outright hostile became too much of a strain, and following the Chicago stop he was rushed to the hospital for what was believed to be a heart attack. It actually turned out to be something more along the lines of stress-induced indigestion.

In retrospect, while the *Dark Horse* tour might be considered a noble failure, there *were* a number of fans who were tuned in to what was being attempted. They went away ecstatic, conscious that they'd just witnessed something so uplifting that it could never be repeated. George had arranged to have some shows filmed and recorded—one must therefore hope that one day the Harrison estate will see fit to issue some form of record from the much-maligned tour to share with fans what some participants, including drummer Jim Keltner and bassist Willie Weeks, recall as the highlight of their careers.

The what-ifs are worth considering: if George had gone on tour with perhaps a stronger, more listener-friendly album (say *Thirty-Three & 1/3*, for instance), hadn't gone on the road with his voice shot, had been more receptive to meeting fans halfway with Beatle material, and hadn't been in such a bad place psychologically, he might very well have achieved his aim to blow people's minds. The goodwill generated could very well have put him on a completely different career path. (Lamented Keltner: "If George had toured all the time, he would've had it down, man . . . he broke all the rules in a beautiful way.")

Ravi and George, while remaining as close as ever personally, went their separate ways professionally in the wake of the tour. Not until 1997's well-received *Chants of India* did they work together musically; four years later, George edited and penned a foreword to Ravi's second memoir, *Raga Mala*, published just a month before he succumbed to cancer. A year later, Ravi was on hand at London's Royal Albert Hall to pay tribute to his fallen friend, composing two classical pieces (entitled "Sharve Shaam" and "Arpan") at the Concert for George. Daughter Anoushka, herself a respected artist, conducted the Indian orchestra, as the frail eighty-two-year-old sat on the stage beside Olivia.

Just a word in passing about Ravi's complicated love life, since there may be readers wondering how it all fits together. Here's the quick version: at twenty-one, he married Annapurna Devi, the daughter of composer Allauddin Khan. Though the marriage was doomed early on, only decades later did they divorce. After fathering two children with Annapurna during the 1940s, Ravi took up with dancer Kamala Shastri. As his "wife," she became his romantic mainstay for over thirty years until 1981. In 1972, he met Sukanya Rajan, an eighteen-year-old tanpura player. Though both were married (Ravi to Annapurna—*still*), in 1978, the two began making time off and on in England.

Meanwhile, back in the States, New York concert promoter Sue Jones and Ravi hooked up around 1977. (Marveled Ravi: "It was like having a girl in every port.") In March 1979, Sue gave birth to Ravi's daughter, a girl she named Geetali. Two years later, Sukanya too gave birth to a daughter fathered by Ravi; this one was named Anoushka (Russian for "Ann"). It was around this time that Kamala left him. Clearly, the maestro had some deciding to do. His divorce from Annapurna *finally* came through, after which—in 1989—he decided to marry Sukanya. Though he and Sue Jones had split in 1986, things had stayed cordial—until now. She moved to Texas, cutting him off from his daughter. Geetali grew up there, and at sixteen she legally changed her name from Geetali Norah Jones Shankar to the shortened version by which she's known to the world today.

By all accounts, things are great these days between Norah, her dad, and the half-sister she did not grow up with. Says Ravi, "I am amazed myself."

Paul on Rod Stewart's "Mine for Me" (From the Album *Smiler*—Released October 4, 1974)

Though they had at least a passing acquaintance going back to the 1960s, Rod Stewart and Paul McCartney tended to operate in different circles throughout the '70s. A cover of Paul's "Maybe I'm Amazed" featured on

Rod's second Faces LP, the aptly titled *Long Player*, very likely got his attention in 1971. (Interestingly, the single release was a studio recording, but the accompanying album contained a *live* version, recorded at Phil Graham's Fillmore East.)

Not until 1974 did the ex–Jeff Beck Group singer and the ex-Fab actually find the opportunity to work together, on a Macca tune expressly written for Stewart entitled "Mine for Me." (Paul later admitted to lifting a lick from *Band on the Run*'s "Mrs. Vandebilt," but, given the new setting, it's scarcely noticeable.) The ballad, one of only five original tracks on Stewart's *Smiler* album, elicited perhaps one of the singer's finer vocal efforts on an LP that received a critical lambasting in American for being so utterly formulaic. (Mostly due to the by-numbers retreading of old ground: a Chuck Berry cover, a Sam Cooke cover, a Bob Dylan cover, and a gender-reworked version of Aretha Franklin's "Natural Woman.")

Commented Paul: "It's nice to write for someone like Rod, because he's got such a distinctive voice—you can hear him singing it as you are doing it." Featuring the McCartneys on backing vocals—adding a touch of Wings-like appeal during a year when Paul could do no wrong—"Mine for Me" was issued as a single in the U.S.

Despite the quality of the recording, it barely scraped into the Hot 100, peaking at #91 before coming to a screeching halt.

Of late, Rod hadn't had much luck in the American single charts; since 1971's #1 with "Maggie Mae," he only managed to make it to the Top 20 just once, with 1972's "You Wear It Well" (twice if you count Faces' "Stay with Me.") The drought would end with "Tonight's the Night (Gonna Be Alright)" a year and a half later.

Not long after *Smiler*'s release, "Mine for Me" provided an opportunity for a *really* rare occurrence: an onstage guest appearance. On November 27, Stewart appeared with the Faces at South London's Odeon Cinema, with the Macs in attendance. Relaxing during a backstage visit before the show, Paul made merry with the generous alcohol supply, not anticipating in a million years what would come during the ensuing set: as Rod began introducing the band's unexpected performance of "Mine for Me," he told the assembled multitudes, "Now my brother and sister are coming out to sing a song with me."

Watching from the wings, the slightly more sober Linda noted, "That's us!" and pulled her husband by the hand onto the stage. Initially mortified, Paul later admitted that his "inner ham" quickly surfaced and he turned in a suitably cheery performance. (By the sheerest coincidence, John's walk-on with Elton John came the following night in New York City.)

John on Elton John's "Lucy in the Sky with Diamonds" b/w "One Day at a Time" (Single—Released November 18, 1974)

The Beatles' connection to the former Reginald Dwight began via their music publisher, Dick James. Barely out of his teens, the young Elton had at least a nodding acquaintance with John Lennon as a staff songwriter at Dick James Music, where he distinguished himself by taking home acetates of the Fabs' publishing demos to study at night. Later, after Elton's first album spawned the hit "Your Song" in 1970, John praised him in the infamous *Lennon Remembers* interview as one of the few artists whom he reckoned was doing something new. (Likewise, George Harrison sent the rising star a congratulatory telegram after his album cracked the Top 20.)

Lennon and Elton ran into each other again in the studio in 1973, but not until Apple's Tony King made a point of formally introducing them the following year did a friendship take hold. Elton lent his by then considerable star appeal to a pair of tracks on John's *Walls and Bridges*: "Whatever Gets You Through the Night" and "Surprise, Surprise (Sweet Bird of Paradox)"; afterward, Lennon felt duty bound to repay the favor.

The time came in July 1974. Hot off the heels of *Caribou*, the follow-up to his hugely successful *Goodbye Yellow Brick Road* album, word got back to John that Elton was planning on recording a cover of "Lucy in the Sky with Diamonds." Being too shy to personally ask, Elton made his case to John via surrogates that he would be honored by the composer's presence during his recording. Lennon wasn't anticipating an actual supporting role, but soon found himself drafted into providing back-up vocals and guitar. (To his embarrassment, John couldn't remember the chords and had to be reminded what they were by Elton's guitarist, Davey Johnstone. Considering he'd only ever played the song enough times to demo and record it over seven years earlier, he had nothing to be ashamed of.)

Caribou Studios were located near Nederland, Colorado. Elton had named his current album after the facility, which had been built by producer James William Guercio (renowned for a series of brass-based acts, such as the Buckinghams; Blood, Sweat, and Tears; and Chicago) in 1972. Other acts recording at Caribou Ranch included Joe Walsh, Rick Derringer, and, that very year, Badfinger. Never having spent much time out Rocky Mountain way, John took advantage of the oxygen tanks the studio provided for those unaccustomed to the thin air at such a high elevation.

While Elton had a pretty good sense of how he wanted his arrangement of "Lucy" to unfold, John did get some input on his own composition: the recording's reggae-tinged interlude was his idea. (As a result, the final recording offered the credit "featuring the reggae guitars of Dr. Winston

LUCY IN THE SKY
WITH DIAMONDS
The Elton John Band

This single is NOT available on any Elton John album

Long smitten with the Beatles, by 1974 Elton John was a big enough star to tackle a cover without diminishing himself. Having the song's author perform on the track was a nice bonus.

O. Boogie.") The finished track, a sprawling six minutes plus in length, was issued as a stand-alone between-projects single.

While he had John at his disposal, Elton announced his intent to tackle another Lennon tune, this one a solo track from the *Mind Games* album. "One Day (at a Time)" was a not-bad soft pop number that strayed as deep into McCartney territory as anything John recorded after 1969. What distinguishes the song from his entire recorded output is the falsetto he sings it in—reportedly suggested by Yoko. (While many find this vocal approach appalling, it should be remembered that the couple were on the verge of separating and she may have been attempting to humiliate him.)

In any event, Elton's version—with John again sitting in—offers a rare example of a cover that *bettered* the original. Thankfully, he skipped the airy vocals and turned in a worthy performance. The recording backed "Lucy" as a flip side (and today both tracks can be found as bonus material on the CD issue of *Captain Fantastic and the Brown-Dirt Cowboy*); issued in November 1974, by January the release was topping the charts, a milestone that John himself had only *just* reached, at long last.

John on David Bowie's "Fame" and "Across the Universe" (From the album *Young Americans*—Released March 7, 1975)

On paper, the notion of John Lennon befriending, then collaborating with the '70s alien-*cum*-gender-bender *artiste*, the former Ziggy Stardust, seemed unlikely, if not absurd. But for all his trés cool posturing, David Bowie was a Beatles fan, and thrilled to meet Lennon at a Los Angeles party hosted by Elizabeth Taylor in 1974. The two shared familiar haunts in both L.A. and New York City, and a friendship developed between the two legends within their respective circles.

Despite John's flippant dismissal of the glam rock scene that Bowie embodied during his early successes in the decade ("It's just rock and roll with lipstick on it"), and his on-air joke at Bowie's expense (reading a commercial for a club offering a "ladies night" during a disc jockeying session, Lennon observed, "Good! Bowie can get in"), the two would converse at length on the conundrum of fame—how attaining it obsessed you when you lacked it and what a burden it was when you achieved it.

Nearing completion of what would become the *Young Americans* album, Bowie invited Lennon to hang out after the sessions moved to New York from Philadelphia. Already permeated with a blue-eyed soul vibe, the release marked a decided step away from the glam of *Diamond Dogs* on the Thin White Duke's last studio outing. Like Elton John before him, Bowie was determined to remake a Lennon Beatles classic, in this case, "Across the Universe," for inclusion on the album. (He had already referenced Lennon's Beatle work in the title cut, with his backing singers crying out, "I heard the news today, oh boy!") In a childlike plea for approval, he requested John's presence as if to secure his blessing.

While John dutifully played guitar and sang backing vocals on Bowie's version (which notably omitted the "jai guru dev a om" refrain), serendipitous circumstance resulted in a second track that landed the latter his first American #1 hit single. Given the chance to jam, John would always revert to the '50s-era songs of his youth, warning the studio players around him that he really didn't know anything released after 1963. It so happened that

Bowie guitarist Carlos Alomar had been playing around with a riff inspired by the Flares' 1961 hit, "Foot-stomping."

As Alomar tinkered, Lennon—as was his wont—yelled out whatever came into his head. His repeated shout of "aim!" caught Bowie's ever-attentive ears the way it fell into place against the melody. With the addition of an "f" before it—Bowie has contradicted himself as to whose idea it was—the whole idea of the song as a vehicle for commenting on the topic suggested itself. The singer quickly sat down to scribble down some lyrics, tapping his recollection of the conversations that he and John had had on the subject, while Lennon worked out a chord arrangement to support Alomar's guitar line.

"Fame" came together quickly, with John supplying backing vocals, acoustic guitar, and backward piano. With so obviously commercial a track now in the can, material slated for *Young Americans* was bumped to accommodate the addition (resurrected later as bonus material on the CD reissue). Upon release in August 1975, it rocketed to #1 for two *non*consecutive weeks (disrupted in between by John Denver's "Calypso"). Not until 1983 would Bowie score his second—and last—chart-topper, "Let's Dance."

To those interested in exploring the Lennon-Bowie connection further, consider this: John's apparent fly-by contribution to Bowie's "Golden Years," released on November 17, 1975. The song, recorded only a month earlier in Hollywood, was the first single to be released from the upcoming *Station to Station* album. Yet another dance groove workout (like much of *Young Americans*), it was created at a time when John's recording days were conspicuously on indefinite sabbatical

The falsetto "angel" at 0:32 bears no resemblance to the ones at 1:06 and 2:22. What it *does* sound uncannily like is Dr. Winston O'Boogie himself—judge with your own ears. In October 1975, when the song was recorded, John was savoring the birth of Sean and his own immigration case victory. The last thing he would have preoccupied himself with was lending a hand to Bowie on a song that scarcely required his presence. And yet . . . there it is.

The most likely explanation is that the sound bite was "flown in" from another existing piece of tape. No one connected with the recording has confirmed this; Bowie himself, seconded by Carlos Alomar, recalled nearly nothing of the sessions, having been enshrouded in a cocaine-induced haze at the time. If this speculation is correct, then "Golden Years" bears an off-the-books contribution from John Lennon that has gone unreported in every single published discography.

16

I'm Tired of Waking Up on the Floor

1975

For a man on the verge of taking himself out of the game, John Lennon maintained a pretty high profile this year. Despite the only new original material he issued consisting of a single non-album B-side ("Move Over Ms. L"), Lennon appeared on the airwaves and in person fairly regularly. Then there were further collaborations; David Bowie had risen from obscure Brit journeyman musician (sharing a birth name with a famous Monkee at that) to sustaining a string of Top 40 singles in America by 1974. As the New Year dawned, he found himself enjoying the same largesse that Elton John had bestowed on Lennon when the latter helped him craft a smash single, "Fame," which hit #1 that fall.

John had already begun composing new material for the follow-up to his chart-topping *Walls and Bridges*. A handful of new songs had already been demoed: one of them, "Tennessee," was a paean to the playwright Williams (not the state). It would emerge years later, completely reworked, as one of the components making up "Watching the Wheels." Also on the itinerary was a visit with the McCartneys in New Orleans, where work on *Venus and Mars* was about to resume. On the eve of releasing the troubled *Rock 'n' Roll* album, John and May had begun house hunting in Montauk in East Hampton, Long Island. Away from the nonstop party atmosphere of L.A., John's urge to move forward musically and personally seemed heightened.

But any future plans he'd sketched out were put on hold forever after a phone call from Yoko brought John back to the Dakota at the end of January. She told him that she'd found a hypnotist who could cure his smoking; just as he'd left Yoko eighteen months earlier, so Lennon departed from May with assurances that he'd be back in time for dinner. He wasn't. Not long after, Yoko found she was pregnant and John moved back in with her. When asked by the press what brought about the events, Lennon had a ready line: "The separation didn't work out."

WF&L

HELPING HAND
MARATHON

FEATURING
SPECIAL
GUEST STAR

JOHN
LENNON
(In Person)

Plus Many Other Recording Stars
LIVE - From WFIL/WPVI Parking Area
MEET WFIL AND WPVI PERSONALITIES
★ FREE ENTERTAINMENT   ★ FREE REFRESHMENTS
Starting 6 P.M. Friday May 16
and continuing until midnight
Sunday May 18, 1975 and . . . IT'S ALL FREE
WF&L CITY LINE AVENUE & MONUMENT ROAD
PHILADELPHIA

Just on the verge of sitting out the year musically, John still appeared regularly in public for charitable events, such as this one in Philadelphia.

The reunited Lennons appeared in public at the Grammys on March 1, where John was coupled with a different Paul—the one who sang with Garfunkel—to act as presenter for Record of the Year. Their pairing, alongside host Andy Williams, was played strictly for laughs, ending with Olivia Newton-John's award for "I Honestly Love You" accepted in her absence by Art Garfunkel. Deadpanned John: "Where's Linda? Too subtle, that. . . .")

Meanwhile, back in New Orleans, work proceeded on Wings' follow-up to their blockbuster, *Band on the Run*, recorded over nearly a year and a half earlier. After Wings experienced a false start with drummer Geoff Britton, Joe English settled in and was eventually invited to join permanently. The group was in for a big year, with a full-scale arena tour of the U.K., Australia, and Japan. (This last leg was dropped after Japanese government officials barred McCartney's entry, citing his drug busts. Macca was confident that he'd win them over someday, drug use or not.)

The product of their labors was issued with a splash in late May. *Venus and Mars,* sporting an attractive cover shot by Linda of yellow and red billiard balls, was a well-executed collection of songs that flowed seamlessly together. For the first time on a Wings album (the "Paul McCartney and . . ." had been dropped after two albums), junior members of the band were afforded a lead vocal, in this case Denny ("Spirits of Ancient Egypt," a Paul composition) and Jimmy ("Medicine Jar"). Securing a foothold in the marketplace was the sunny single "Listen to What the Man Said," a track whose effortless charm belied the amount of work that had gone into getting it right. The song went to #1 in July; it also marked the last of what had been Paul's eight-single streak of Top 10 hits in the U.S., although he would regain his footing with the next album.

Venus and Mars was launched at a party held in Long Beach aboard the permanently docked Queen Mary. Attendees included Bob Dylan, Gregg Allman and Cher, Derek Taylor, the New Orleans funk band the Meters, as well as Mal Evans and George Harrison. The latter's appearance was notable in that only rarely did George socialize with Paul after their split. It may have helped that Olivia, his new squeeze, was a California girl, giving the couple a reason to be in town. Though memories of the highs and lows of the *Dark Horse* tour were still fresh, George was not much inclined to be looking back in the spring of 1975. His hands were as full as ever with the start-up of Dark Horse. Other acts signed to the label included ex-Wings guitarist Henry McCullough, the American soul group the Stairsteps, and Jiva, a white funk band.

George owed one more release to EMI before he could commence recording for his own label. He might have been happier to wait until he was a little more prepared to reenter the studio, but the opening created when

Ringo too was temporarily absenting himself from the recording studio in 1975, taking a role in Ken Russell's follow-up to *Tommy*, *Lisztomania*, a bio-fantasy on Franz Liszt starring Roger Daltrey.

Splinter were unable to use time that had been booked for them at A&M's West Coast facility gave him a window to knock out his obligation early. Though committed to getting that final album off his to-do list, George was hard-pressed to come up with enough material to fill the grooves. Moreover, his mood had not lifted all that much from the rather dour funk he'd been in last time around. As a result, listeners found the overall tone of *Extra Texture (Read All About It)* to be largely melancholy, leavened by sporadic bitterness.

Luckily, he had at least one ace in the commercial hole: a track left over from the Ronnie Spector sessions, the Motown-esque "You." Recorded four years earlier, and in a key a little bit higher than might have been preferable, the song did have the virtue of being infectious. Despite the passage of time, a light dusting of synthesized strings from David Foster brought it sufficiently up to date, where it peaked at #20. On this, his penultimate Apple single, George noted the pending demise of his record company by featuring an apple core on the label—as he did also on the parent LP itself.

The album was the last long-player of new material issued on Apple before the label rose from the dead in the 1990s. Two best-of collections were also issued that year: John's *Shaved Fish,* a set collating stray singles, and Ringo's *Blast from Your Past.* Sporting a strawberry-red apple label, the solid (if brief) compilation marked the Ringed One's departure from EMI, his musical home from day one. Despite his streak of hit singles, the company declined to offer him a substantial renewal, and so Ringo ended up signing with Atlantic in the U.S. and Canada and Polydor elsewhere. The three-record deal was commemorated with a bacchanalian celebration held in Amsterdam the following spring, where Ringo was photographed lying on the floor at the feet of several semi-nude women.

The fact that he'd sought a record deal with an established company at all was slightly curious, in light of the fact that Ringo had followed George into the custom label business himself, establishing Ring O'Records—a name suggested by John. The imprint's history is a rather convoluted one, involving several name changes (before settling on the moniker it's now known for) and a rather freeform approach to marketing itself. (The start-up as "Ring O'Records" was announced in April 1975, two months after an album and single had already dropped in America.) Capitol handled distribution.

Whereas Dark Horse ultimately ended up as an outlet for George's releases and nothing more, Ring O'Records could not even claim that distinction. The drummer never appeared on his own label, though his music did: Startling Music was a track-for-track remake of the 1973 *Ringo* album, as arranged for synthesizer by engineer/producer/musician David Hentschel, assisted by one Phil Collins on drums. Other acts on the label included studio sax whiz Bobby Keys and British novelty singer Colonel Doug Bogie. Suffice to say the record charts on both sides of the Atlantic stayed blissfully unviolated by any of the company's offerings before Ringo grew tired of the enterprise and shut it down in 1978.

From a musical perspective, Ringo's year was about as uneventful as John's—in fact, more so. He would not reenter the recording studio at all in 1975, instead spending time either filming or promoting his most recent release. In February and March, he found himself before the cameras for *Tommy* director Ken Russell in the rock and roll biopic/fantasy *Lisztomania,* starring the Who's Roger Daltrey as classical composer Franz Liszt. (Ringo played the Pope.) On April 28—just days after the shocking news that Badfinger's Pete Ham had committed suicide—he plugged *Goodnight Vienna* with a memorable appearance on *The Smothers Brothers Show*, performing "No No Song."

That same night, John appeared on *Tomorrow* with Tom Snyder. Lacking any particular project to plug, the freewheeling conversation covered the Beatles' history, drug use, and Lennon's current immigration dilemma. He hadn't yet announced his time-out from recording; as such, his spring schedule remained full with public goings-on, including his second appearance on the air for Philadelphia's WFIL Radio Helping Hand Marathon in May. Over the course of fifty-six hours, John answered phones, solicited money for the charity, and met with fans—briefly—in the parking lot as he entered and exited the building. The fact that a celebrity of his stature was willing to give so freely of his time was mind-blowing even then. (He also enjoyed a brief stint as a weatherman on the station's TV affiliate, filling in for the regular meteorologist in his typical jocular fashion.)

John and Paul were both taped—separately—in 1975, talking about their Beatle past by Tony Palmer as part of his *All You Need Is Love* documentary. This miniseries, covering the history of twentieth-century popular music, aired in America on PBS stations in early 1978; episode 14, entitled "Mighty Good," presented the Beatles' story with many rare clips and newsreel footage. Similarly chronicling the Fabs on television was a special hosted by David Frost, airing on May 21. As part of ABC's late-night lineup, *A Salute to the Beatles* was pretty low-rent by most standards, but still, featuring interviews with George Martin, Mal Evans, and star of the day David Essex, it was a treat for fans too young to have experienced the phenomenon firsthand.

Onstage for what ended up being his last performance before a live audience, John was among the entertainers starring in *A Salute to Sir Lew*, a variety special (taped in April for broadcast in June) honoring Lew Grade, the head of the EMI entertainment conglomerate. Though not exactly enjoying the warmest of relations with the mogul, John agreed to take part on his terms, fronting an eight-piece band dubbed "Etcetera" for the occasion; their actual name was BOMF (for "Band of . . ." you know what). To subtly make known Lennon's feelings toward Grade, all of the musicians were garbed with a mask affixed to the back of their heads, thus making themselves two-faced.

John ripped through a raucous, high-voltage version of "Slippin' and Slidin'" from the slow-selling *Rock 'n' Roll* album, followed by "Stand by Me," which as a single had peaked at #20. Resplendent in a red leather suit and chewing gum throughout, he appeared energized, although performing on a small stage before a group of tuxedoed and gowned attendees must have seemed surreal, more like an industry gathering (which it essentially was) than an actual concert. He closed the set with "Imagine," handicapped by a freshly broken guitar string. John's final shot at working an audience was rather curious in retrospect. The mismatch between his act and the setting must have been somewhat jarring (while undoubtedly a better fit for Paul).

As for Macca, the Wings tour of the U.K. and Australia had been a smashing success, showing beyond doubt that the group was ready for the big time: an arena tour of America. With the band firing on all cylinders and a solid body of solo work to draw from, Paul was at last comfortable enough to do something he hadn't done before: perform a handful (five) of Beatles classics live. Learning from George's experience a year earlier, Paul was prepared to give the people what they wanted in the way they expected to hear it. The table had now been set for the last full-scale blast of Beatlemania.

Autumn brought with it cause for double celebration, as two ongoing issues before the Lennons came to a climax. First, the hard-fought battle to stay in the U.S. was finally won when Judge Irving Kaufman (the same jurist who had sent the Rosenbergs to their deaths) ruled in John's favor, bringing an end to the war waged by Nixon's minions against the outspoken ex-Beatle. As though this weren't enough, two days later, on John's thirty-fifth birthday, Yoko gave birth to Sean, the couple's first child (after several unsuccessful attempts). With the curtain coming down on their longtime legal battle, his record contract fulfilled, and the opportunity to at last take his parental duties seriously, John concluded that the time had finally come for a professional time-out.

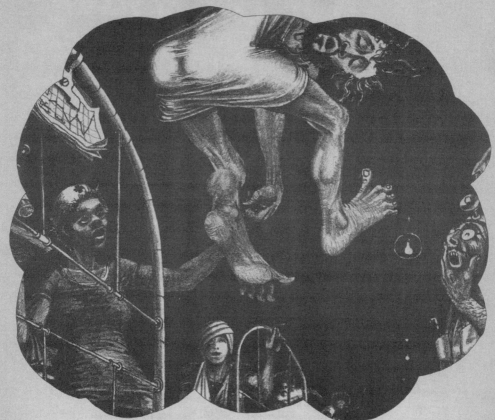

"OH MY MY" 1872

SOON TO BE RINGO'S THIRD #1 GOLD SINGLE... FROM HIS PLATINUM ALBUM

RINGO (SWAL-3413)

PRODUCED BY RICHARD PERRY

Though this ad's prediction of a third #1 was not to be, Apple's crowing over Ringo's success was completely justified. Shown here is one of Klaus Voormann's wonderful illustrations included with the album.

17

And You Better Believe It, Baby!

Their #1's

n the United States between 1964 and 1970, the Beatles collectively racked up twenty #1 hits. Separately, they managed to amass *thirteen* chart toppers between the years 1970 and 1980, a pretty impressive run. Some observations can be drawn from this data: first, it was clearly Paul who ran away with the hit singles derby (though quantity doesn't always equal quality). Second, George's momentum coming out of the Beatles was enough to launch a double-sided hit—something none of his fellow ex-Fabs would achieve.

Ringo, of whom little was expected, scored big with a pair of #1's from his self-same titled album, making him the group's true dark horse. But perhaps the most striking statistic: John, despite getting into the solo sweepstakes ahead of all of his bandmates, took the longest to actually land a #1. Further, "Whatever Gets You Through the Night" would be his only American #1 enjoyed during his lifetime—not even the much-loved "Imagine" made it this high. (It stalled at #3, the same week that Cher's "Gypsies, Tramps, and Thieves" took top honors. As with comedy and so much else in life, timing is everything.)

George Harrison: "My Sweet Lord" / "Isn't It a Pity"
December 26, 1970–January 16, 1971

Well before what became his first true solo album was a glimmer in his mind's eye, George began crafting tunes that would become essential components of *All Things Must Pass*. The title track, along with "Let It Down," "Hear Me Lord," and "Isn't It a Pity," was premiered during the *Let It Be* sessions; "Wah-Wah," "I'd Have You Anytime," and "Art of Dying" were among other tunes written well before *Abbey Road* was recorded.

As his Beatle career wound down and he produced and wrote for other acts, George continued stockpiling compositions for himself. By the time the Beatles (minus John) entered the studio in January 1970 to record "I Me Mine," he was doubtless aware that the likelihood of another group album had all but slipped away. Liberated from the need to write songs that would fit the Fab format, he began working on a song that captured the spiritual milieu that had been seeping into the Top 40.

By the end of 1970, songs like Norman Greenbaum's "Spirit in the Sky" and Pacific Gas and Electric's "Are You Ready?" as well as the rock opera *Jesus Christ Superstar* had made expressing one's religious preferences in a rock setting socially acceptable, even hip. But the tune that directly inspired George wasn't even a pop song as such, though it became a worldwide smash in 1969. "Oh Happy Day" was the first hymn to cross over into the secular charts during the rock era. Edwin Hawkins, a California choir leader, had put together a funky arrangement that transformed the seventeenth-century devotional into an uplifting paean to the Almighty that you could groove to.

Recognizing the scanning similarity between "Hallelujah" and "Hare Krishna," George set about creating a vehicle that wedded the two seemingly incompatible devotions to a backbeat while evoking the elements that made the Edwin Hawkins track a hit. What he overlooked was a shopworn underpinning that he would pay dearly for. Still, if getting the Lord into *Billboard*'s Hot 100 was worth anything, George succeeded beyond anyone's expectations. (In his infamous *Rolling Stone* interview, John Lennon—something less than a fan of the song—opined that there *must* be a God, hearing "Oh my Lord" every time he turned on the radio.)

The recording itself typified Spector's approach to the project: layer as many instruments playing the same part on top of each other as you can, and upon this foundation, add ornamental flourishes like George's slide guitar and vocal lines. Supporting the denseness were three quarters of Badfinger, strumming away on acoustic guitars, as well as the heretofore unknown "George O'Hara-Smith Singers." This latter ensemble featured two charter members: George and Phil Spector, who through generous overdubbing fleshed out nearly an entire choir from their own two voices, as well as those of keyboardist Bobby Whitlock, Eric Clapton, and a pair of mysterious vocalists George identified (doubtless facetiously) as "Cyril" and "Betty."

"Isn't It a Pity" was issued on the flip without being designated a B-side. This sprawling, majestic lament was actually penned back in 1966, but was apparently rejected by the Beatles. *All Things Must Pass* was replete with songs that easily could be interpreted as commentary on the Beatles' breakup; though this particular song predated the events of 1969–1970, the subtext isn't diminished in the least.

The song received much airplay in 1971, recalling the equally expansive "Hey Jude." That the single issue of "Isn't It a Pity" clocked in at exactly one second less than Paul's tune is no accident; the recording also featured some "na-na na na"s buried in its lengthy coda. (Hardcores will recall that George's proposed contribution to "Hey Jude"—a guitar line echoing each vocal phrase—was shot down by Paul, leading to not a little antipathy.)

George actually chose to reprise "Isn't It a Pity" in a stripped-down version near the end of *All Things Must Pass*. In lesser hands, this might have seemed self-indulgent, but in George's, it acts as a bookend to a nearly completed journey. His standing among the public following the Fabs' breakup was such that people were willing to believe his sad song *could* make it better.

The double A-sided single displaced Smokey Robinson and the Miracles' "Tears of a Clown" atop *Billboard*'s Hot 100. That song, cowritten with Stevie Wonder, had originally been issued as an album track in 1967, but exploded when relaunched in America after hitting #1 in the U.K. George was an admirer of Smokey's smooth vocal stylings and evocative songwriting, going so far as to pen *two* tribute songs, *Extra Texture*'s "Ooh Baby (You Know That I Love You)" and *Thirty-Three & 1/3*'s "Pure Smokey."

After enjoying a four-week run at #1, George's debut single was displaced by Tony Orlando and Dawn's second single, "Knock Three Times." Having fulfilled its brief to cleanse the public's palate of religiosity, "Knock" gave way to even more wholesome sounds, the Osmond Brothers' "One Bad Apple."

Paul and Linda McCartney: "Uncle Albert / "Admiral Halsey" September 4, 1971

For his first post-Beatles single, Paul released "Another Day," a song recorded in New York during the *Ram* sessions. Credited to Paul and Linda McCartney (as was *Ram*), the song introduced his brand to the marketplace, being a catchy but innocuous trifle, produced with care and not outstaying its welcome on the airwaves before reaching the finish. Lacking the gravitas of either John or George's recent work, it scarcely hinted at the somewhat more challenging material recorded during the same sessions.

In England, *Ram*'s stately album closer "Back Seat of My Car" was chosen as the follow-up single, while the Buddy Holly–inspired rocker "Eat at Home" was issued in Europe. The next U.S. single was the far more ambitious "Uncle Albert / Admiral Halsey." Fans in America hungry to relive the fab days of *Abbey Road* were thrilled with Paul's efforts, as its pastiche of distinct musical segments recalled the side two suite that marked the Beatles' last recorded collaboration.

GEORGE HARRISON
MY SWEET LORD
ISN'T IT A PITY

Number one for a month in America (and five weeks in Britain), George's "My Sweet Lord" had become so tainted by litigation that in 1975, he performed a parody version of it on TV as part of Eric Idle's *Rutland Weekend Television*.

As was often the case with some of Paul's best compositions, "Albert" isn't really about anything in particular, but instead is a series of random images put together in a musically logical fashion. This impressionistic approach called for precision in both arrangement and pacing, in much the way a film director sets a series of moods. Each musical vignette was memorable in its own right—freewheeling as the imagery was, Paul's execution was characteristically disciplined.

For example, the thunderclaps and drizzling sound following the line "I believe I'm gonna rain," came when Paul had legendary recording engineer Armin Steiner (Motown, the Wrecking Crew, Jackie Lomax) go out into a storm and capture the sounds he needed—at the edge of a cliff. Despite his drive for perfection, however, Macca was flexible enough to allow the occasional "oops" onto a finished track. At 1:20 into the song, the engineer charged with applying the filter that turned Paul's vocals into a telephone speaker jumped the gun, accidentally filtering Paul's last oral approximation of an English telephone ring.

For most, the breathtaking "hands across the water" segment was the highlight of the track, recalling the Beatles at their best with its energy and unfathomable catchiness. Despite receiving what would become routine drubbing from the critics, "Uncle Albert / Admiral Halsey" proved greater than the sum of its parts, deservedly becoming the first of six #1 singles of the decade.

The song it bumped, "How Can You Mend a Broken Heart?," came from the Bee Gees, who were enjoying *their* first U.S. #1. The Brothers Gibb's chart dominance of the decade didn't really take hold until 1975's "Jive Talkin'" from the *Main Course* album. Terminating "Albert"'s one-week reign atop the Hot 100 was Donny Osmond's "Go Away Little Girl," for those whom Paul had shortchanged on the bubble gum—at least this time.

Paul McCartney and Wings: "My Love" June 2, 1973–June 23, 1973

Given his business travails of the last several years—a period that saw Northern Songs change hands, Apple's decay, and the disintegration of his last band—Paul finally had something to feel good about. "My Love," the latest of a series of musical valentines to the Lovely Linda, became his first wholly owned composition. The song was one of a handful of newly minted originals performed in Wings' live set from the very first, one that Apple promotions manager Pete Bennett was certain would be a #1 record in the States from the moment he heard it.

Fronting a performing unit with barely a year's worth of collective playing experience, Paul demonstrated a certain amount of brio in choosing to record this track live in the studio *simultaneously* with a full orchestra. The slightest performance breakdown would have necessitated considerable time and expense to fix, given the bill for musician's scale. As it happened, Wings lead guitarist Henry McCullough had a last-second curve ball to pitch as the recording commenced.

Rather than playing the guitar part worked out in advance, Henry had a new approach to his solo that he wanted to try. (With a platoon of classically trained musicians awaiting their cue, he picked an odd time to go off the reservation.) To Paul's credit, he acquiesced, giving McCullough leave to lay down what is surely his shining legacy.

Henry's elegantly emotional, pitch-perfect lead gave Paul's otherwise possibly too sweet song the edge that it needed, elevating it beyond typical middle-of-the-road fodder. This signature solo later became the source of some rather spirited disagreement between the two men: Henry was of the opinion that a guitar solo should be a unique, spontaneous experience at every performance, whereas Paul came from the "give the people what they want" school of showbiz, demanding that Henry re-create the recording at every gig. Their philosophic disagreement paved the way for McCullough's eventual departure.

"My Love" represented the highlight of *Red Rose Speedway*, the second straight album's worth of mediocrity from Wings. Their moniker was modified to "Paul McCartney and Wings" beginning with this release, in the hopes that *Wild Life*'s anemic sales could be ascribed to the public's not realizing who the band were, rather than the cringe-inducing material contained within its sleeve.

The tune knocked the Edgar Winter Group's "Frankenstein" from its perch atop the *Billboard* chart. This synthesizer-based instrumental, a dazzling display of 1973 state-of-the-art techno wizardry, was so named for the fact that it was literally assembled piecemeal from sections of a studio jam, stitched together. The fact that the *Red Rose Speedway* album itself made it to the top slot—however briefly—was remarkable, given that Paul was competing against his past with the release of the Beatles compilations *1962–1966* and *1967–1970* a mere three weeks before. Competition was also coming from another familiar quarter in the form of *Living in the Material World*, the long-anticipated follow-up to *All Things Must Pass*.

George Harrison: "Give Me Love (Give Me Peace on Earth)" June 30, 1973

Though most of the sibling rivalry issues within the Beatles came between John and Paul, the happenstance of "My Love" being knocked from *Billboard*'s top slot by "Give Me Love" must have been particularly galling to the former's creator. As evidence that his former junior partner had eclipsed him not only in acclaim, but in sales as well, George's success must have been an especially bitter pill for Macca to swallow, though publicly he praised the tune.

"Give Me Love" was both the leadoff track and single from *Living in the Material World*, an album well past due as far as the much of the public was concerned. In the two long years since George had last released any new material, the public's tastes had shifted. Increasingly, the cachet of being an

Returning to the standard-writing form he'd first perfected with "Yesterday" in 1965, Paul's single release of "My Love" featured a contrasting flip side, "The Mess," a boogie jam recorded onstage that showed Wings flexing their musical muscle.

ex-Beatle had diminished, with first Paul, then John issuing subpar albums that would have challenged even the most devout fans. By 1973, merely being a former Fab wasn't enough to guarantee a hit record. A release's own merits—or at least a hit single—were necessary to give it legs.

Happily for George, *Living in the Material World* possessed at least the latter. Harrison, by this time, dispensed with the services of Phil Spector, and his approach resulted in considerable breathing room, with layers of echo, reverb, and dozens of instrumental overlays stripped away. Instead of the grand array of musicians he'd used on *All Things Must Pass* (including Eric Clapton and his Dominoes), George relied upon a core group of stalwarts like Ringo, Klaus Voormann, Jim Keltner, Nicky Hopkins, and Gary Wright.

Known to have taken part in sessions held at Apple Studios was Badfinger's Pete Ham; if his work made it to the final release, he is uncredited. However, several musicians verified to have contributed to *All Things Must Pass* went without credit even on the 2001 reissue, notably Peter Frampton. Given that George and Pete played the unison slide guitars on Pete's "Day After Day," it isn't beyond probability that Pete assisted with the harmony slide parts on "Give Me Love."

The song, a further enunciation of George's spiritual goals, featured some impossibly compelling slide work that doubled as his other voice—a sound joyous yet keening, often at the same time. George's prolonged "om"s similarly engaged the ear, as one rooted for the heavy smoker to sustain them for nearly twelve bars at a time.

While not as overtly religious (or litigious, for that matter) as "My Sweet Lord," "Give Me Love" cloaked philosophical concerns inside a thoroughly commercial package that easily found a place in the marketplace alongside secular offerings. Though the song topped the chart for one week only (and in fact switched slots with "My Love" in some markets), it would have been interesting to know George's reaction upon being bumped by, of all people, Billy Preston.

For the first time in several years too busy with his own project to work with George, Billy served up his own meta-philosophical statement, framed in a funky setting. "Will It Go Around in Circles?" provided Billy with his first *vocal* hit record (and first of two #1's), following the Grammy-winning, synth-driven instrumental "Outta Space" from his A&M debut the year before. The two men would resume their musical partnership in time for the 1974 *Dark Horse* tour.

Ringo Starr: "Photograph" November 24, 1973

For nearly as long as he'd been attempting to write songs, Ringo had been able to count on George for a little assistance in taking his musical ideas and making them presentable. Graphic evidence was on display in *Let It Be*: as Ringo submitted his rough draft of "Octopus's Garden," George stepped up and showed him how to go from the bridge back to the home key. Ringo was never bashful about acknowledging his musical debt: "I only know three chords and he'd stick four more in, and they'd all think I was a genius."

"It Don't Come Easy" has George's fingerprints all over it, but it is entirely likely that the latter shunned any co-crediting for the song. He was less modest two years later (or perhaps Ringo insisted) for their first publicly credited collaboration, "Photograph." Here, the musical alchemy forged between the two ex-Fabs and producer Richard Perry reaches its zenith.

Distinctly reminiscent of a Phil Spector production (complete with orchestration, brass, and castanets) without being suffocating, the song fully played to Ringo's strengths: cast in the key of D major, it featured a Harrison harmony vocal and a bittersweet subject matter aptly suited to the Ringed One's characteristic facial expression. *Sounding* like an oldie without actually *being* an oldie (at the time of its release), the song proved to be exactly the right thing at the right time, capitalizing on the year's nostalgia craze while at the same time sounding fresh.

To this point, Ringo had issued two concept albums: one of big band–era pop, the other of straight country—not exactly calculated to rock the *Crawdaddy* crowd. Ringo already had two well-received singles under his belt when he released "Photograph." This song did a good job of setting the table for the upcoming *Ringo* album, raising interest in a full album's worth of Startling Music. Once word got out as to his former bandmates' involvement, a juggernaut was launched.

For better or worse, Ringo Starr was now a viable recording artist. Most stunning of all was the fact that his album was outselling the latest offerings by John, Paul, and George.

(After "Photograph" reached the top slot, John was prompted to fire off a telegram to his ex-drummer: "Congratulations! How dare you?" Before signing off, Lennon added, "How about writing me a song?")

Ringo's successful chart run also came at the expense of ex-Temptations singer Eddie Kendricks, who was experiencing his first and only #1 solo hit since leaving the group two years earlier. "Keep On Truckin'," a musical evocation of an old R. Crumb cartoon, is seldom heard on oldies radio today (and never without a good reason). Ringo was in turn shoved aside by the Carpenters, with their excursion into country pop, "Top of the World."

Ringo Starr: "You're Sixteen" January 26, 1974

The ascent of the siblings Carpenter represented only a minor speed bump for the Ringed One in his campaign to upstage his fellow ex-Fabs. Before "Photograph" had even receded from the Top 10, Apple—wishing to strike while the fire was hot—issued a second single, Ringo's inspired remake of the 1961 Johnny Burnette song "You're Sixteen (You're Beautiful, and You're Mine)." What followed set a standard as yet unmatched by any of his Beatle peers: a *second* #1 single from the same album.

"You're Sixteen" was composed by Richard and Robert Sherman, who first struck rock and roll gold with Mouseketeer Annette Funicello's 1958 hit, "Tall Paul." The brothers later gained considerable renown from their film scores, often—but not always—for Walt Disney's studio. *Mary Poppins, The Jungle Book*, and *Chitty Chitty Bang Bang* were among their credits—they also penned the migraine-inducing jingle "It's A Small World." (Their "Let's Get Together" from *The Parent Trap* featured a "yeah, yeah, yeah" refrain in December 1961—nearly two years before "She Loves You.")

Apparently, the notion of a thirty-two-year-old ex-Beatle luring a girl half his age into his car caused hardly a stir among the record-buying public, who gamely accepted the premise and gave Ringo his second straight #1. As of 1973, no other ex-Beatle had scored back-to-back chart-toppers.

The recording featured Ringo and John's drinking buddy, Harry Nilsson, on backing vocals, along with Paul and Linda. Having already completed most of the album in Los Angeles with input from John and George, Ringo was careful not to exclude Paul from the proceedings. "You're Sixteen" was completed in England with Paul contributing what to this day much of the world believes to be a kazoo on instrumental break. It isn't—it's simply Paul's verbal approximation of a sax solo, but seemingly no one believes this.

Ringo's exercise in nostalgia knocked Al Wilson's "Show and Tell" from the #1 slot. Wilson's sole chart-topper, the tune was remake of a Johnny Mathis album track. Ringo, in turn, would be displaced by an even longer backward glance: "The Way We Were" by Barbara Streisand.

Paul McCartney and Wings: "Band on the Run" June 8, 1974

By late 1973, Paul's stint in the proverbial desert was about to end. Having finally pulled together an album that fans *and* critics alike agreed was worthy of his reputation, he was ready to reassert himself before the public. Perhaps unsure of whether he had the goods or not, Capital took no chances in America, adding the freestanding single "Helen Wheels" to the *Band on the Run* album for extra value, against Paul's wishes.

For his part, Macca preferred to issue no singles at all from the album, Beatles-style. But his notions of marketing were behind the times; with little to prod the public to buy his album, he was at last forced to goose things along by issuing "Jet" as a single. It was a wise choice, for *Band on the Run* had been slipping down the charts. Peaking at #7, "Jet" sparked renewed interest in the album, driving it to #1 by April 1974.

With the public now taking a second look at his offering, Paul spent considerable time choosing a second track to issue. There was no shortage of possibilities: the catchy but slight "Mrs. Vandebilt"; the Plastic Ono Band-esque "Let Me Roll It"; the Denny Laine co-composition, "No Words"; even "Bluebird," which would have evoked his similarly named "White Album" track from six years before. (The precision and second-guessing involved in issuing singles was evident with the decision to release "Jet" with *two* different B-sides: "Let Me Roll It" and "Mamunia.")

The album's title track became the choice, though not without some misgivings. As the album opener, the track clocked in at 5:10, a bit on the lengthy side, even from the man who gave the world all seven-plus minutes of "Hey Jude." But judiciously pruned down to a more reasonable 3:50, the song would work just fine as an AM radio sampler of the greater whole.

Like "Uncle Albert," "Band on the Run" was a song comprised of tableaus, expertly stitched together and paced to peak at the right moments. Though the album was only ostensibly conceptual—much like *Sgt. Pepper's* nearly seven years earlier—there were loose motifs of escape and freedom scattered throughout, nowhere more evident than in this song.

Given the rather harrowing experience of making the album (two band members quit, Paul became mysteriously ill, and he and Linda were robbed at knifepoint), it isn't surprising that Paul purposely explored the outsider theme: the figure apart from society and banished to the underground served as an apt metaphor for McCartney's rather diminished rock and roll status, having fallen from the heights of Beatlemania, while pointing the way to a future resurrection once freed from his confinement ("If we ever get out of here"—a phrase borrowed from George coming during an interminable business meeting).

Both the song and the album *Band on the Run* indeed gave new life to Paul's fortunes, validating his long-shrouded talents. He was now on track to overtake his former partners, eventually surpassing them, for the role of ex-Beatle Most Likely to Succeed, having snatched the crown from George. The title was codified in two years' time with the Wings Over America tour sealing the deal.

"Band on the Run" toppled Ray Stevens' execrable topical novelty, "The Streak," which had mysteriously clung to the top slot for three straight weeks. (The recent streaking incident at the Oscars on April 2 may have fueled the public's interest.) Paul's own streak ended after one week, terminated by that rarest of things, an anti-war bubblegum song. Bo Donaldson and the Heywoods' "Billy Don't Be a Hero," a cover of a U.K. hit by Paper

Lace, stayed at #1 for *two* weeks. But Paul undoubtedly took comfort in the long view, recognizing that rock's highway is littered with one- and two-hit wonders.

John Lennon with the Plastic Ono Nuclear Band: "Whatever Gets You Through the Night" November 16, 1974

In the nearly three years after he released "Happy Xmas (War Is Over)," John watched as his next two singles fell short of the Top 10, one of them missing the Top 40 entirely. "Mind Games," intended as a return to the pop form he'd mastered in the previous decade ("Love is the answer…") peaked at #18, bested even by the political screeds "Give Peace a Chance" (#14) and "Power to the People" (#11). It was therefore with great trepidation that John approached the selection of a single to help sell *Walls and Bridges* to the masses.

No longer trusting his own judgment, he put it to those around him to divine the album's strongest chart contender. A consensus formed around "Whatever Gets You Through the Night," a song Lennon initially dismissed as little more than a throwaway. As first conceived, the tune was modeled after George McCrae's fluke summer smash, "Rock Your Baby." (*That* recording had been a serendipitous accident when the journeyman singer happened into a recording studio where Harry Casey—of in K.C. and the Sunshine Band fame—had completed what had been intended as an instrumental demo. Obligingly laying down a scratch vocal, McCrae made the song a monster as it went on to sell over eleven million copies worldwide.)

Over time, John tweaked the song, eventually speeding it up to the tempo familiar today. (At one point, the arrangement featured an electric sitar, a hopelessly outdated effect by 1974.) The opening burst of saxophone gave it a New York sound that eventually would be aped by *Saturday Night Live*'s theme. Lyrically, the starting point came from John catching a late-night sermon by millionaire evangelist Reverend Ike. It dealt with alcoholism, and the phrase "whatever gets you through the night" caught his ear.

Elton John, the biggest superstar of the day, had been a friend and admirer of John's for some time. In the midst of his own heavy touring and recording schedule, the planets came into alignment and he was able to squeeze in a visit to John during the *Walls and Bridges* sessions in New York. Always anxious to receive feedback from a peer, John gave Elton a listen to the work in progress. The latter asked if he could contribute to one track in particular: "Whatever Gets You Through the Night." Somewhat surprised, John asked why and Elton noted that it gave him the most space to do his thing.

As it happened, Elton's commercial instincts were spot on. The addition of his manic piano, exuberant harmony vocal, and overall star power gave the track the lift it needed to make it a standout tune within the collection of mostly introspective songs. He and John famously wagered on the song's fate in the marketplace; Elton won, and the rest is rock lore.

For all of the airplay it's received over the last thirty-plus years, the song supplanted by "Whatever," Bachman Turner Overdrive's stuttering "You Ain't Seen Nothing Yet," was #1 for one week only. That it was released *at all* was a freak occurrence, being laid down as a one-off joke directed at Randy

John Lennon's mini-set with Elton John, showcasing the former's recent #1 single, "Whatever Gets You Through the Night," was professionally recorded, while long-rumored video documentation has yet to surface.

28th November 1974...

Bachman's stammering brother, but BTO's producer felt it had a sparkle the rest of the album lacked.

John's long-anticipated first #1 was in turn shoved aside by a one-hit wonder, Billy Swan's rockabilly showcase, "I Can Help." Swan was better known as a behind-the-scenes professional, penning songs like Clyde McPhatter's "Lover Please" and producing hits like Tony Joe White's "Polk Salad Annie." "I Can Help," a song that at the time was mistaken by many for a Ringo Starr recording, would eventually be recorded (but not released—by court order) by Richie Snare in the 1980s.

Wings: "Listen to What the Man Said" July 19, 1975

It was a far happier Paul McCartney who ventured into the studio with Wings' latest incarnation to record the follow-up to their barn-burning *Band on the Run* album. Having at last scored big with critics and fans alike, Macca had finally paved the way to producing a live performance–friendly album that would make a suitable vehicle for playing arenas—*American* arenas.

Though *that* tour was still an album away, Paul was again moved to find an exotic locale to lay down tracks. This time, perhaps to get reacquainted with what the States had to offer, he brought Wings Mark V to New Orleans, just in time for Mardi Gras. In a rather ironic twist, the local flavor evoked by "Listen to What the Man Said" arrived through trial and error only after the band left town.

The song was a sunny, piano-based bounce, sporting Macca's typically innocuous lyrics (though, as in much of George's work, the "man" in question could just as easily be the Almighty as a more earthly entity, which Paul freely admitted). But despite its creator's view that the song was a surefire hit, something in Wings' approach left its composer feeling a certain lack. He brought in ex-Traffic member Dave Mason to augment the track with a guitar overdub, but the results still missed the mark.

After the band decamped to Los Angeles, someone had the bright notion of reaching out to saxophonist Tim Scott; after all, it was his town. By 1975, Scott had already distinguished himself as a studio ace as well as the illustrious bandleader of L.A. Express. (It was his horn that had brought Carole King's "Jazzman" to life the year before.) Perhaps having a passing acquaintance with Scott through ex-bandmates Ringo and George, Paul summoned him.

On his first crack at the song, Scott laid down a spirited, lively embellishment that could not be bettered (though they tried, without success). The sound of the soprano sax—an uncommon rock voice that would become the basis of Kenny G's career—recalled the work of New Orleans' own Sydney

Bechet from a generation earlier. Scott's horn proved exactly the tonic the song needed, giving Paul his fourth U.S. #1.

Wings' feat came at the expense of the Captain and Tennille's month-long reign atop the charts. "Love Will Keep Us Together," their debut single, was a dual triumph, putting the husband-and-wife act on the map while consolidating the comeback of early '60s crooner Neil Sedaka, who penned the tune. (Largely forgotten is the earlier, somewhat less successful cover of the song by, of all people, Wilson Pickett.)

Paul, in turn, would be bested by a direct portent of the paradigm shift underway in Top 40 tastes. Van McCoy's "The Hustle" signaled disco's ascendancy at the expense of pop/rock and the by-then largely played-out singer-songwriter heyday. Opportunities for an ex-Beatle to again top the charts were fast becoming increasingly scarce.

Wings: "Silly Love Songs" June 12, 1976–July 3, 1976

With a pair of solid albums beneath his belt to support his first post-Beatles American tour, along with the moxie that comes with achieving every goal you've ever set for yourself, Paul took a moment to address what clearly had been nagging at him: the all-too-dismissive critics. No less an authority than his former partner, John Lennon, had told him directly that his solo oeuvre consisted of "pizza and fairytales"—a description that Paul briefly considered for the basis of a song.

Long past the point of striving to be the outré artiste, attending "happenings" in London and hanging out with heavy scene makers, Paul was increasingly at ease with projecting a "cozy domesticity" narrative to the public, no matter how uncool. Still, the barbs flung his way must have stung, prompting him to pen this defensive retort: "Some people want to fill the world with silly love songs / What's wrong with that?"

Propelled by a sinewy, in-your-face bass line, "Silly Love Songs" did nothing to endear Mr. Thumbs Aloft to rock's cutting-edge critics. Macca pushed back lyrically with stunning smugness—"Well here I go AGAAAIN!"—before giving way to the very banal sentiments he'd long been accused of trafficking in. ("I love you's," noted *Rolling Stone*, were rammed home "with the insistence of phonetics instructors.") But the song's very resonance with the public must have been validation enough: five weeks in the top slot (interrupted for two weeks by another '60s survivor, Diana Ross with "Love Hangover," before regaining supremacy).

The song also demonstrated Paul's willingness to accommodate current fancies, being marketed as a dance record, though certainly not as overt as the typical offerings of the day. (It was in fact issued in a twelve-inch extended "disco" format.) "Silly Love Songs" toppled the Sylvers' "Boogie Fever" from #1, in a year that saw other veteran acts like the Four Seasons and Paul Simon similarly score big with songs showing a willingness to meet the public halfway ("December 1963 (Oh What a Night)" and "Fifty Ways to Leave Your Lover," respectively).

But after months of danceable tunes topping the charts, the record-buying public took a bubblegum breather in July with a slice of pure pop saccharine. Starland Vocal Band's paean to daytime nasty, "Afternoon Delight," at last bested Wings, propelling the squeaky-clean showbiz professionals to a summer replacement TV variety show. That's how it worked in those days, folks.

Wings: "With a Little Luck" May 20, 1978–May 27, 1978

The *London Town* sessions stretched out for over a year, making it the longest in-production album yet released by Paul McCartney. As had been the custom since *Band on the Run*, new surroundings for the recording were sought; this time, the musicians boarded the yacht *Fair Carol*, moored in Watermelon Bay off the U.S. Virgin Islands. In May 1977, work was commenced on a raft of tracks (pun unintended), all of which were completed back in the U.K. later in the year. Given Linda's pregnancy and collective exhaustion in the wake of their triumphant Wings over the World tour of the year before, the band were certainly entitled to work at their leisure.

Though their thunderous live shows had defined Wings as a muscular performing unit, with little exception, *London Town* marked a retreat to a softer rock sound. Uninterested in pursuing the current dance genre and incapable of producing credibly edgy material to compete with the punks, McCartney and company took the safest path, a middle ground that steered clear of experimentation. Where fans witnessing their powerful live presence might have expected some studio encapsulation of the same, the album offered none, instead serving up an array of stylistic exercises that seemed more calculated than inspired.

The gossamer-thin "With a Little Luck" was designated as leadoff single. Bereft of guitars, heavy percussion, brass—anything remotely rock-like—the song made its point in the first line or two, then proceeded to restate it endlessly, sometimes with fey observations thrown in: "The willow turns his back on inclement weather . . ." (For those looking hard enough, the lyrics offer an inherent contradiction: is it the determined or the fortunate that "make this whole damn thing work out"?)

Clocking in at a far too generous 5:45, "With a Little Luck" was issued to radio stations in an edited-down form, much to the song's benefit. Trimmed of some of its synthesized onanism, the song worked in much the same way as any other jingle—it stuck in listeners' heads and subliminally compelled them to go out and buy the product. For proof of this, note that the single held sway at #1 for two straight weeks and enjoys heavy adult contemporary airplay to this very day.

Occupying the top of the *Billboard* charts prior to the Wings single was Yvonne Elliman's "If I Can't Have You," spawned by the powerhouse *Saturday Night Fever* soundtrack. Penned by the Bee Gees, the song was the third of *four* #1's contained on the release (not counting 1975's "Jive Talkin'"). Following Paul atop the charts was an even older act, '50s crooner Johnny Mathis, described by the author of *The 1950s' Most Wanted* as "adding his voice of reason to Deniece Williams' caterwauling" on "Too Much Too Little Too Late."

Sadly for Wings, the success of "With a Little Luck" went unmatched by the follow-up releases: the faux-rocker "I've Had Enough" or the album's title track. The *London Town* album, though perhaps marginally better than *At the Speed of Sound*, peaked at #2 before fading away, long since superseded by any of three McCartney greatest hits collections. The departure of guitarist Jimmy McCulloch and drummer Joe English during the album's recording put the core threesome essentially back to square one—exactly where they'd been four years earlier at the outset of recording *Band on the Run*.

Paul McCartney: "Coming Up" June 28, 1980–July 12, 1980

Wings' down period didn't last for long. By spring 1978, session drummer Steve Holley and guitarist Laurence Juber had been brought into the group, restoring the band's live performance capabilities. Thoroughly intrigued by punk's primal energy (via daughter Heather, by now in her mid-teens), if not its fashion, Macca was ready to rock again.

To reinforce his commitment to relevancy, former Beatles engineer and current hot producer Chris Thomas (Pretenders, Pete Townshend) was brought aboard—the first outsider at the helm since the one-off "Live and Let Die" with George Martin. The disco-*cum*-flamenco single "Goodnight Tonight" and the album that followed, *Back to the Egg*, served as the public's introduction to Wings' latest incarnation (Mark VI, for those keeping score).

Originally conceived as a thematic work, adhering to something akin to a "band on the run," *Back to the Egg*'s concept ended up being scrapped, probably resulting in a stronger album. But neither the album nor its two singles, "Arrow Through Me" and "Getting Closer," made it to the Top 5—a major disappointment considering there was a new producer, a new label (Columbia), and a new band.

Still, Wings soldiered on, gearing up by the end of 1979 for a new world tour, commencing in the U.K. The set list for the shows performed that November and December was retooled from the last go-round, featuring "new" Beatles songs, some recent Wings material, and an as-yet-unreleased composition called "Coming Up."

As it happened, the world tour fell apart following Paul's Japan pot bust (see chapter 31 for details), and Wings, likewise, not long after. But in the spring of 1979, before these events played out, Paul set to work on some home recordings, his first one-man-band project since the Beatles' breakup and the *McCartney* album. The tracks he laid down were not intended for public release—at least initially—and most of them were flat-out experimental electronic doodlings far removed from the typical Wings fare.

Perhaps the most commercially viable of the tracks was "Coming Up." With an insistent chorus, R&B-style guitar fills, and inherent catchiness, it stood out among the mostly forgettable remaining recordings. Once fate forced Paul's hand and Wings' plans for 1980 went awry, Macca decided to issue what might charitably be described as a companion album to George's 1969 *Electronic Sound*, dubbing the collection *McCartney II*.

"Coming Up" was issued as the album's first single in both the U.K. and America. Having failed to make *Back to the Egg* the chart-topper Paul felt it deserved to be, Columbia did him the favor of putting the live Wings version of "Coming Up" on the flip, perhaps recognizing that listeners in the States might not be all that receptive to hearing Paul's electronically processed vocals over a brittle synthesized musical bedding.

Their instincts proved correct. Once DJs realized that they had a choice between the bizarre A-side and the rocking B-side, it was no contest—Wings' version got the airplay and the song rocketed to the top of the charts. This put Columbia in a quandary: the public was gobbling up a single that *wasn't on the album it was intended to promote!* For North American record buyers only, the problem was solved by packaging a one-sided seven-inch pressing of the song with the *McCartney II* package (and announcing its presence via a sticker on the shrinkwrap). Thus, in the most singular ad hoc marketing of Paul's entire career, were fans forced to buy an album few loved to get a song that they did. Or they could just buy the single and bypass the LP entirely.

The live version was recorded on December 17, 1979 in Glasgow, Scotland—Wings' penultimate concert. The entire set had been taped professionally with an eye to possibly issue another live album; though widely bootlegged, this intriguing document of the band's final incarnation remains sadly unreleased. For the single release, "Coming Up" was augmented with a few overdubs, chiefly on the horn section. (Fans who actually listened to the entire 45 were treated to an apparently spontaneous crowd reaction to the song following its conclusion: as one, the audience begin chanting, "Paul McCartney!"—egged on by Steve Holley, who began banging out a "let's go" beat.)

As a coda to Wings' chart career, "Coming Up" brought things to a worthy finish (though, interestingly, the "free" copies packaged with *McCartney II* credited Paul McCartney alone). It ruled the roost for three solid weeks, displacing the even more successful last gasp of disco dominance, "Funky Town" by Lipps Inc. Following Wings atop the charts was Billy Joel with his rootsy (for Billy Joel) nod to New Wave, "It's Still Rock and Roll to Me."

John Lennon: "(Just Like) Starting Over" December 27, 1980–January 24, 1981

In the more than six years since John Lennon had last offered new original material to the public, the marketplace had undergone a sea change. He had sat out the years when disco ruled, though he himself was not averse to it and had actually shown a feel for dance music, both with "Beef Jerky" on *Walls and Bridges* and "Fame," his collaboration with David Bowie. Disco played itself out, and as radio became increasingly balkanized, unifying factors of the past no longer held. As Ringo could attest by this time, the days of an ex-Beatle producing hits at will were long gone.

The rise of punk and its more commercial stepbrother, New Wave, could have been expected to provide a receptive opening for John to reenter the record industry. Many of the most successful artists of the era, those of a generation that grew up listening to the Beatles, regarded Lennon as their spiritual godfather: an artist who paved the way for brutal honesty, topical concerns, edgy experimentation, *and* commercial appeal. Elvis Costello was perhaps his likeliest heir—an assessment Paul would later concur with.

Despite all claims to the contrary, John had been far from inactive musically during the so-called househusband years. His assertion that he had never taken his guitar off the wall was pure self-generated myth, as revealed by countless hours of tapes that surfaced after his death. What *is* true is that while on a spring 1980 trip to Bermuda, his marketing instincts were reawakened upon hearing popular artists in clubs whose work echoed his own—and, more importantly, Yoko's—from years before.

In what was probably the most widely anticipated and chased-after record deal in years, John and Yoko signed a contract with the newly minted Geffen Records, largely on the basis of a pledge of personal attention (and the fact that David Geffen shrewdly made his offer without asking to hear their new work first). The deal could hardly have been much of a risk; in the years since John had removed himself from the limelight, demand for any new Lennon product had only grown, a fact of which the artist himself was keenly aware.

To all appearances, John consciously chose to pick up exactly where he'd left off. His last American chart single had been the oldie "Stand by Me," back in March of 1975. The most deliberately retro Lennon track on *Double Fantasy*, "(Just Like) Starting Over," was chosen to reintroduce him to the marketplace. The song's theme was equally apt as a way of framing his musical rebirth: with the tiny "wishing bell" serving as intro to both the album and song, John was purposely echoing the funereal bells that tolled the opening to "Mother" on *Plastic Ono Band*. Things had come full circle, y'see?

The song itself was constructed from a pair of unfinished Lennon compositions, "My Life" and "Don't Be Crazy." Only on the last day of rehearsals was the finished song introduced—both producer Jack Douglas and John himself agreed that *this* was the only suitable opening to the album. John described his performance on the track as "Elvis Orbison," a channeling of his teenage heroes that helped him reclaim his musical mojo. (One captured bit of studio chatter reveals him dedicating the song "to Gene and Eddy and Elvis . . . and Buddy!") Despite the self-conscious affectation, the track works, if only because of the obvious joy Lennon projects in recapturing the sounds that inspired him in the first place.

The public's anticipation of the first newly recorded Lennon single in years recalled similar expectations back in the '60s when the latest Beatles record was about to drop. Pre-orders were sizable as Geffen put considerable effort into trumpeting the return of the forgotten Beatle (while not putting it quite that way—directly, anyway). In October, the single was released in advance of the album; an occurrence hyped by radio stations around the country as an *event*.

Not surprisingly, "Starting Over" did well upon its initial release, rising to the Top 10 within weeks. It's tempting to conclude that the considerable chart success enjoyed by the song—dwarfing every other solo Beatle single—was solely due to public grief over John's death, but this isn't necessarily so. The week before he was murdered, the song was #3 on the charts, as Kenny Rogers' "Lady" was in its *sixth* week at #1. It surely would have become John's second solo #1 on its own merit, but the events of December 8 were a guarantee.

Massive public grieving kept the song at the top for five weeks straight before it gave way to Blondie's "The Tide Is High." Interestingly, the far darker "I'm Losing You" had been slated as a follow-up single before John's death (a sticker on *Double Fantasy*'s shrinkwrap declared "Including the hits . . .") but this was shelved as eerily inappropriate. Instead, the pure pop of "Woman," then "Watching the Wheels," served to sustain John's comeback album.

It's worth observing that the megahit exactly ten years earlier, at the close of 1970, had been George's "My Sweet Lord." That *these* two ex-Beatles bookended the decade is a point that is as stunning as it is poignant.

18

And When the Cupboard's Bare

Their Worst-Charting Singles

Most of what comprises a hit record is timing—encompassing both what the competition is up to in a given week and exactly where the public's head is at. Tastes change capriciously; typically, a major act charting poorly in the single charts has little to do with its artistic or aesthetic merit. Today, the FM airwaves are glutted with songs that were overlooked upon their initial release but found an afterlife within the "classic rock" format.

During their heyday, the Beatles issued a seemingly endless string of singles that routinely placed in the upper reaches of the chart, rarely peaking lower than #5 in the Top 10. But after their split, goodwill alone wasn't enough to guarantee chart success. (Only George seems to have been revered by the public initially as a solo artist, but, as he quickly discovered, all things must pass.)

Newer and fresher acts built upon the Fabs' foundation, overshadowing the familiar, while of the four ex-bandmates, only Paul and Ringo consciously tailored their material to the dictates of the marketplace—with disparate results. (Worth noting is that Paul *never* placed any designated A-side outside the U.S. Top 40 during the 1970s—not even dubious offerings like "Mary Had a Little Lamb" and "Give Ireland Back to the Irish." Whatever else may have been going on, his name *always* assured him airplay.)

Traditionally, a "hit" record is one that breaches the Top 40, assuring some level of AM airplay. By the former Beatles' own standards, releases like John's "Cold Turkey," Ringo's "(It's All Down to) Goodnight Vienna," George's "Ding Dong; Ding Dong," and Paul's "Letting Go" might have been considered flops, though they peaked at #30, #31, #36, and #39, respectively. The following is a rundown of singles that charted outside the Top 40, or, in some instances, didn't chart at all. In most cases, the quality of the tracks far outstripped their public performance.

RINGO STARR
Beaucoups of Blues

The Everyman soulfulness inherent in Ringo's voice lent itself quite readily to the country music idiom. *Beaucoups of Blues* remains a largely overlooked triumph that cries out for a sequel.

Ringo Starr: "Beaucoups of Blues"—Released October 5, 1970

During the recording of *All Things Must Pass*, George summoned legendary pedal steel guitar player Pete Drake over from America. (Drake is not to be confused with "Sneaky Pete" Kleinow, *another* legendary pedal steel player who worked with John on *Mind Games* as well as *Ringo's Rotogravure*.) Ringo, on hand for the sessions, sent his car to pick up the Nashville-based musician from the airport. During the ride in, Drake was astonished to notice the Ringed One's rather expansive collection of country music tapes.

When asked about this, Starr confessed that he'd always been a huge C&W fan; what's more, he harbored a secret dream of recording an all-country album. But he doubted he'd ever find the time he'd needto put a band together, find some songs, and lay down the tracks.

Nonsense, Drake assured him: "I did *Nashville Skyline* in two days!" Although somewhat skeptical (Ringo was sure that the Bob Dylan album featuring "Lay Lady Lay" must have taken *at least* four days), Drake won him over, with a promise to set up everything—songs, musicians, production—and complete the work in a week. All Starr had to do was show up; he could even leave his kit at home.

In June, Ringo traveled to Tennessee. After selecting songs penned with him in mind by the cream of Nashville's finest, he sat back as Drake (abetted by Elvis's own Scotty Moore, who engineered) laid down the tracks, which featured the Jordanaires on backing vocals and future country rock fiddler Charlie Daniels. Then, over the course of three days, the cowboy from Liverpool swiftly tracked his leads, completing the project in time to beat George to the marketplace.

Beaucoups of Blues was met with no little skepticism from fans, the critics, and Ringo's ex-bandmates, who after all may have felt slightly sensitive to the possibility of collateral derision after his earlier long-player's worth of music, *Sentimental Journey*. But upon listening, they were won over by the utter suitability of his talents to the material. Affirmed John (with faint praise): "I didn't feel as embarrassed as I did about his first one." Even *Rolling Stone* declared *Beaucoups of Blues* "a real winner."

Adhering to country tradition, the songs mined topics ranging from drunkenness to adultery, suicide to war. With such an upbeat array of subject matter, the ideal single was hard to divine—ultimately the title song's slow waltz was issued. It would have taken a miracle to get this track into the Top 40, not because of any lack but because it was so purely a country recording.

The same week that the Partridge Family was topping the charts with "I Think I Love You," "Beaucoups of Blues" peaked at #69. (Collector's note: the single came in a picture sleeve displaying the album cover artwork. East Coast pressings printed the incorrect Apple catalog number, 1826—an error omitted on other versions, which ran Capitol's number 2969. While both versions are scarce, the correct version is even rarer.)

Though not a blockbuster, *Beaucoups of Blues* remains Ringo's justifiable pride. The real shame is that in the forty years since its release, he hasn't seen fit to revisit the genre—at least for an entire long-player's worth.

John Lennon / Plastic Ono Band: "Mother"—Released December 28, 1970

By the time he commenced recording *Plastic Ono Band*, John Lennon had released three singles—"Give Peace a Chance," "Cold Turkey," and "Instant Karma"—all of which had done respectably in the marketplace, especially the last one, which had parked at the #3 slot for three weeks (at the same time that "Let It Be" was sliding into first). Typically, he preferred issuing songs *composed* for the singles market, as opposed to releasing album tracks, feeling strongly that they were distinct entities.

Still, he realized that the commercially challenging yet artistically satisfying album he was about to drop needed *some* way of announcing its presence to record buyers. For that reason, he recognized that a track would have to be pulled to represent *Plastic Ono Band* in the charts, if only as advertising and not to compete with the Jackson Five and Creedence Clearwater Revival per se.

John knew that "Love" was probably the most traditionally commercial song on the record, but that it was also the least typical, offering no lyrical bile. Most of the remaining material was either too idiosyncratic ("Well Well Well"), too potentially offensive to delicate sensibilities ("God"), or simply unsuitable for airplay ("Working Class Hero"). Instead, he chose the opening track, "Mother," to be the album's calling card for Top 40 listeners.

The song was trimmed down from its album length of 5:34 to 3:55 (deleting the opening bells and fading the chilling "Mama don't go—daddy come home!" refrain early). Interestingly, the single was issued only in mono, a fact that must have pleased the old-school purist Phil Spector immensely. The picture sleeve, which reproduced the album cover, is a highly coveted collectible today.

Continuing the trend begun with the Plastic Ono Band's "Give Peace a Chance" in the summer of 1969, the B-side featured a Yoko track from her companion album. For that segment of the public that views her work as ear-splitting yammering, "Why" can safely be ignored; for those whose tastes are more open-minded, the song offers a fascinating slice of proto-punk, with Klaus Voormann and Ringo's cooking rhythm section and the most adventurous Lennon guitar playing ever recorded. As John himself was quick to observe, it takes a close listen to discern where his playing ends and her voice begins.

With its downbeat theme of childhood abandonment and gut-wrenching "primal scream" coda, the song didn't have a chance of placing anywhere near the Top 10. Indeed, it topped out at #43 during the same two-week stretch that "My Sweet Lord" slid from #2 to #3 on its way down.

John Lennon / Plastic Ono Band with Elephant's Memory and Invisible Strings: "Woman Is the Nigger of the World"— Released April 24, 1972

Thoroughly absorbing every political cause around him as he acclimated himself to his New York surroundings, by 1972 John was ready to address feminism head-on (although a verse in "Power to the People" did ask his "comrades and brothers" if they were right with their women). In an interview with the British women's journal *Nova*, published three years earlier, Yoko summarized her views on how male society regarded females with the comment "Woman is the nigger of the world." (Actual copies of the issue are hard to come by today, so it's difficult to judge the context of *John's* statement on the cover of the same issue: "I've been black, been a Jew, been a woman. . . .")

In any event, John found his wife's choice of words captivating enough years later to implement them as a hook, building a song around them by offering a litany of injustices inflicted by men upon the females in their lives. A certain amount of overkill informs John's intents, coming from someone who indeed had much to atone for in his treatment of women during his pre-Yoko years. But by using such a highly charged word to make his point (as had Yoko), he had to have known that he was setting himself up as a provocateur who would turn off many who might otherwise benefit from his argument.

John at least made the effort to run the song by some civil rights leaders, including comedian/activist Dick Gregory. Word was that they understood where he was coming from, using "nigger" as a metaphor for anyone oppressed or defined by others. (Less clear is if John sought similar support from actual women.) As with "The Ballad of John and Yoko," which used the word "Christ" rather too casually for some folks' taste, airplay would be an issue, as most radio stations around the country would balk at playing any record containing the N-word in any context, much less in its title. But without the support of radio, the song was lost in the marketplace, peaking at #57 (the same week the charts were topped by—of all things—Sammy Davis Jr.'s rendition of "The Candy Man.")

It's a shame that all the controversy spoiled the chance to enjoy what may be one of John's most impassioned vocal performances. Phil Spector pulled out all the stops, providing a Wagnerian wash of sound, magnifying the otherwise unremarkable backing with the enhancing charms of strings and placing Stan Bronstein's lead sax front and center. Had John used the music, with its dramatic shifts in rhythm and dynamics, to any other end, it surely would he ranked among his greatest recordings.

JET

EX-BEATLE TELLS
HOW BLACK
STARS CHANGED
HIS LIFE

YOKO ONO

DICK GREGORY

JOHN LENNON

Not a complete fool, John tried to inoculate himself against charges of racism for
his feminist manifesto, "Woman Is the Nigger of the World," by giving interviews to
African-American forums like *Jet* magazine.

George Harrison: "This Guitar (Can't Keep from Crying)"— Released December 8, 1975

A confluence of circumstance dictated that George rush into the studio a mere five months after the release of *Dark Horse* to begin a new album. Part of the urgency came from the desire to fulfill his EMI commitment, which would free him to begin the Dark Horse deal with A&M. Another factor was the fact that Bob Purvis of Splinter had been laid low with a bout of hay fever. With studio time booked and paid for, George and A&M were loath to let it go to waste. Lastly, with the unaccustomed criticism of his last LP and tour still ringing in his ears, George had every reason to clear the air in advance of launching the Dark Horse label.

With a leftover Ronnie Spector track, "You," designated as the leadoff single for what became the *Extra Texture* album, George was hard-pressed to come up with some worthy material. Convinced that the Krishna devotionals populating his releases weren't cutting it, he came up with one comedy number ("His Name Is Legs"), one Smokey Robinson tribute ("Ooh Baby"), a raft of romantic and philosophical ruminations, and this, a sequel of sorts to one of his more enduring Beatles tracks.

Somewhat to his surprise, George learned that "While My Guitar Gently Weeps" had become a radio staple in the States. (His undervaluing of the track may have stemmed from his fellow Fabs' initial apathy when the song was cut, forcing the recruitment of Eric Clapton to complete the recording.) "This Guitar (Can't Keep from Crying)" was a similarly minor-key, introspective piece; it otherwise bore no resemblance to its progenitor.

The song featured George playing acoustic and electric guitars, as well as a synthesized ARP keyboard bass, while pal Gary Wright handled the ARP strings. Fulfilling the Clapton role was Jesse Ed Davis, while Jim Keltner provided percussion. Though the net result was a fine track, featuring what may be one of George's finest vocal performances, the lyrics may have rubbed some the wrong way—especially critics.

An air of defensiveness, bordering on arrogance, was doubtless in reaction to the drubbing he'd gotten in his last go-round. "Thought by now you knew the score," George mused, before observing, "but you missed the point just like before"—not exactly an endearing sentiment. Also working against the song were the prevailing musical trends. With songs like the Bee Gees' "Nights on Broadway," K.C. and the Sunshine Band's "That's the Way I Like It," and Silver Convention's "Fly Robin Fly" on the charts (the latter tune at #1), anything not explicitly danceable was going to be a tough sell.

But the biggest hurdle to the single's success was Apple itself. Running on fumes by now, the label issued "This Guitar" as its final release prior to its reconstitution in the 1990s. Most of its staff long since departed, the office was reduced to a royalty-collecting facility, its days as an active record company well past, even on behalf of the ex-Fabs. There was no promotion, no tour, not even a music video, and so the song was allowed to rot on the vine. It did not chart.

Ringo Starr: "Hey! Baby"—Released November 22, 1976

Upon Apple's demise, Ringo took bids from several record companies before signing a deal with the legendary R&B label Atlantic. By this time featuring a number of rock acts (including Led Zeppelin), the label boasted the talents of a fine in-house production staff, spearheaded by Arif Mardin, the Turkish expat who had enjoyed considerable success behind the board with acts like the Young Rascals, Dusty Springfield, and the Bee Gees.

That the label was prepared to spend a bundle to promote the Ringed One was never in doubt. Ads were bought, videos were produced, and a generally high level of quality marked Atlantic's handling of their prized ex-Beatle. What seemed to be overestimated was the public esteem for Ringo as a top-tier recording artist. Though much loved as a charming persona who occasionally made some entertaining records, the Ringed One was overstaying his welcome.

By the time this superior recording was issued, the nostalgia craze was long over. The novelty of Ringo's recorded work featuring an ex-Fab and star-studded supporting cast was likewise wearing thin (John and Paul duly appear on *Rotogravure*—barely—and George not at all), but another aspect also seems to have worked against him.

While possessing a canny ear and a knack for creating some sublime pop records, Mardin didn't really seem to get a handle on the drummer's most appealing attributes in the same way that Richard Perry had done. Both *Ringo* and *Goodnight Vienna* were successful in part because of the attention to quirky detail found within the grooves. Perry created a virtual party around the star, projecting fun and atmosphere. In lesser hands—such as those behind Keith Moon's *Two Sides of the Moon*, for example—who apparently sought to document the actual party, the results fall flat.

Ringo's Atlantic releases featured technical perfection, superb musicianship, and a distinct anonymity, such that almost *any* singer could have been slotted over the backings and material. What might have *seemed* a wise move—keeping the artist contemporary by steering him in a dance club direction—came off as lacking credibility (ironically, since by all accounts, Ringo was the best dancer of the Fabs and an avid club-goer).

Over the long haul, "Hey! Baby" seems to have gained traction within Ringo's oeuvre, having twice been compiled in "best of" collections. The same week the single peaked at #74, the charts were topped by Mary McGregor's long-forgotten soaper, "Torn Between Two Lovers." Delayed vindication is an apt assessment of this single; the same could not be said of future Ringo releases.

Ringo Starr: "Wings"—Released August 25, 1977

No, the first single taken from *Ringo the 4th* had absolutely *nothing* to do with his ex-bandmate's chart-dominating group—really. Instead, it was a well-crafted piece of adult contemporary pop, something of a departure from Starr's usual approach. In the past, he'd scored well with oldies ("You're Sixteen," "Only You"), oldies-*sounding* songs ("Photograph," "A Dose of Rock and Roll"), and novelty material ("No No Song"). "Wings" marked a decided change of direction, in an album that was the Ringed One's least Beatle-like yet—not surprisingly, since it featured absolutely no Fab involvement.

Also absent was the usual cadre of friends: no Klaus, no Keltner, no Harry. Instead, a band of seasoned professionals did the heavy lifting. Past Paul/John/Yoko guitarist David Spinozza helped out, as did future *Double Fantasy* bassist Tony Levin. (Most of Levin's professional renown comes from his superlative work with Peter Gabriel, as well as a latter-day version of King Crimson.)

Perhaps the biggest break from tradition was Ringo's own creative input as songwriter.

A smooth adult contemporary ballad, *Ringo the 4th*'s lead-off single might have scored higher had singer Melissa Manchester's presence on the track been played up.

Given his instrumental limitations, a collaborator was often used to translate his musical ideas. Starting with *Ringo*, the artist's working relationship with Vini Poncia usually resulted in a track or two per release. On *Ringo the 4th*, the Ringed One came up with six co-compositions—more than half the album.

What his words conveyed was nothing less than a description of the romantic travails and alcohol-fueled existence his life had become. His "life of the party" public image masked a deep-seated unhappiness as well as a growing dependence on drink. As a comedown from the heights of Beatlemania, it would be difficult to expect any less—all four suffered the effects to various degrees. Still, the malady meant that, more than ever, his judgment suffered as he placed himself in the hands of those who may not have truly understood his gifts.

Ringo the 4th was an album that divided Starr's base. Fans either gamely accepted "Ringo being Ringo" or they rejected utterly the disco trappings that reduced him to guest starring on his own record. For the public at large, the decision to forgo purchasing the work of a once charming but now old-news ex-drummer was easy. Flying in the face of heavy promotion, "Wings" failed to chart at all, while *Ringo the 4th* peaked at #162—a dismal showing bested even by John and Yoko's experimental *Two Virgins*.

As a snapshot of where the public's tastes lay, Emotions' "Best of My Love" was topping the charts the week "Wings" was issued. This popular dance track may have influenced Atlantic's choice for a second single.

Ringo Starr: "Drowning in the Sea of Love"—Released October 18, 1977

On paper, the notion of Ringo Starr tackling a Gamble and Huff Philly soul tune sounds ludicrously comic—on vinyl even more so. But his recording of the Joe Tex classic still has its fans; whether out of genuine appreciation or for its inherent camp value is hard to discern. Ringo caught the disco wave in a big way with this release, which Atlantic saw fit to issue as a twelve-inch single as well. Neither iteration caught on in the marketplace, creating an instant collectible. (So badly has the recording dated that it's twice been passed over for inclusion on Ringo's post-Apple compilation releases.)

Underscoring the high hopes held for this song's success was the music video it spawned. Given the trajectory of Ringo's life at the time, it is a fascinating document. He appears as both a tuxedo-clad disco crooner and a morose barfly—simultaneously capturing both of the drummer's current, disparate personas. The clip, complete with video-friendly blonde backup singers (unconvincingly standing in for Bette Midler and Melissa

Manchester, who sang on the actual record), evoked the desperate dissipation later explored by Nicholas Cage in *Leaving Las Vegas*, making for some uncomfortable viewing.

Disappointment with the performance of this song generally and *Ringo the 4th* specifically led to the label dropping Ringo after only two of the three contracted albums had been released. While business-wise, the artist rebounded quickly—signing to the Portrait division of CBS—his musical fortunes did not improve. (For those keeping score, Debby Boone's megahit, "You Light Up My Life," was in its first of *ten* straight weeks at the top of the charts when Ringo's single was released. Hence, the failure of "Drowning in a Sea of Love" can't entirely be ascribed to public distaste for ill-conceived pop.)

Ringo Starr: "Lipstick Traces (On a Cigarette)"—Released April 18, 1978

Much like George's *Extra Texture* and John's *Mind Games*, *Bad Boy* was an album created with undue haste, seemingly to wash away the stench of what had preceded it. (Only *Sentimental Journey* and *Beaucoups of Blues* were issued in such rapid succession, but they at least were *concept* projects.) If this assessment is correct, *Bad Boy* failed in its mission, for, while avoiding the more obvious lapses on *Ringo the 4th*, it fell into others.

Stung by the utter failure of his last album, Ringo and his handlers reassessed. The disco lounge motif was dropped, while what seemed to have worked best in the past was revisited—minus the famous friends. *Bad Boy* was built implementing the tried-and-true formula of oldies and contemporary pop (with a recasting of "A Mouse Like Me" thrown in as a finale). The songwriting dominance Ringo had enjoyed on his last album was reeled in; though the crash and burn of his last Atlantic release could hardly be blamed on the Starkey-Poncia songwriting per se, Portrait was taking no chances.

There are no credited guest musicians on the album; instead, players like Dr. John and Lon Van Eaton were listed pseudonymously as "Git-tar" and "Push-a-lone." Hopes were high that the disc, released concurrently with the highly publicized *Ringo* television special (which featured three *Bad Boy* songs), could get Ringo back on the commercial track. 'Twas not to be—the album peaked at #129 and slid away as rapidly as it appeared.

Chosen as leadoff single in this exercise in futility was Bennie Spellman's "Lipstick Traces (on a Cigarette)," a minor hit from 1962. Penned by Allen Toussaint (a Ringo favorite) under the pseudonym "Naomi Neville," the song was well suited to the Ringed One's strengths. Where the concept went wrong was with the highly polished, *au courant* production, which swamped the lead vocals with faceless backings and charmless instrumental support. Had he cut the tune circa 1974 with his usual crew and Richard Perry behind the board, there *might* have been a chance for some personality to shine through. As it was, "Lipstick Traces" failed to chart, immediately leading to some serious buyer's remorse at the offices of Portrait Records.

Saturday Night Fever's dominance was in full swing at the time of Ringo's release, as the Bee Gees' "Night Fever" enjoyed eight straight weeks atop the charts, followed by Yvonne Elliman's "If I Can't Have You" (which in turn was bumped by Wings' "With a Little Luck"). Despite doing everything right from a marketing perspective, Ringo was a man out of time by early 1978—perhaps a little help from the Brothers Gibb would have made a difference. (*That* act, however, was knee-deep in a misstep of its own: a feature-length cinematic treatment of the *Sgt. Pepper* album, proving that poor judgment was hardly in short supply.)

Ringo Starr: "Hear on My Sleeve"—Released July 6, 1978

On the eve of Ringo's thirty-eighth birthday, "Heart on My Sleeve" was released in an attempt to resuscitate *Bad Boy*. Like the previous offering and its parent album, it was doomed to oblivion, despite the television exposure given the song on the *Ringo* special. The tune itself had been a hit single in England in 1976, rising to #6, as performed by its writers, Gallagher and Lyle. Benny Gallagher and Graham Lyle had a Beatle connection, having been signed by Apple in 1968 as songwriters for the label. They penned a string of tunes for Mary Hopkin, including "Sparrow," "International," and "The Fields of St. Etienne" before moving on to a career as a performing duo.

Ringo's version, inoffensive as it was, just didn't click with American record buyers, coming as it did around the same time the Rolling Stones successfully parlayed a dance-flavored composition onto the airwaves. "Miss You," the leadoff single from the *Some Girls* album, marked the debut of Ronnie Wood as full-time Stones guitarist as well as the band's commercial resurgence. (In England, the romantic ballad "Tonight" was issued from *Bad Boy*, complete with a not-bad video. It too failed to chart.)

In 1978, echoes of the 1960s—when adroitly presented—could still make their mark on contemporary audiences. Unfortunately, Ringo's days of effortless hit-making had come and gone. Portrait canceled their deal halfway through the production of the 1980 follow-up, *Can't Fight Lightning*, and the decade ended with Ringo's commercial recording career down but not out.

George Harrison: "Love Comes to Everyone"—Released May 11, 1979

In the wake of George's image rehabilitation and Dark Horse / A&M lawsuit, he produced a pair of well-received albums: 1976's *Thirty-Three & 1/3* and 1979's eponymous follow-up. The latter release featured the irresistibly catchy single "Blow Away," which became Harrison's highest-charting single in five years, peaking at #16 on the Hot 100 and #2 on the Adult Contemporary chart. Offering a stark contrast to the prevailing punk and disco dominance of the era, George seemed to have found a comfortable niche for himself in light rock—an arena increasingly populated with Wings songs.

George Harrison was undoubtedly the most relaxed-sounding album ever cut by the artist. Happily married and thoroughly enjoying his first (and only) experience of fatherhood with Dhani's birth a year earlier, George had spent the last couple of years on an extended holiday, traveling or indulging a newfound passion for Formula One racing. All inclinations toward preaching momentarily held in check, he was content on his new release to extol the virtues of love, Olivia, and psychedelic mushrooms, in various measures.

Personnel on the home-recorded release included most of the *Thirty-Three & 1/3* crew: Willie Weeks, Andy Newmark, Emil Richards, and Gary Wright, with the addition of ex-Traffic singer Steve Winwood, who would score major solo success with 1981's *Arc of a Diver* album. Eric Clapton, months away from his nuptials to the former Pattie Boyd Harrison, made what amounted to a drive-by cameo, playing lead guitar on the album opener (albeit the song's *intro* only), thereby effecting, along with Winwood, a Blind Faith semi-reunion.

"Love Comes to Everyone" was a melodic, gentle slice of commercial pop, managing to sound at once contemporary and idiosyncratically Harrison. Propelled by a subdued dance beat, the song became a radio favorite in the wake of the success of "Blow Away." But by the time George and/or Warner Brothers took notice and issued the song in single form, their window had closed and the song failed to chart at all. It was a baffling commercial failure, but as George was by this time no longer living or dying by the critical or chart reaction to his offerings, he barely seemed to notice. (The single's picture sleeve is highly prized, being extremely hard to come by.)

With his path in the marketplace cleared by the success of "Blow Away," one would have expected George's equally fine follow-up single to similarly chart with a bullet. Except—it didn't.

In England, "Faster" was issued as a follow-up, along with an accompanying video and a picture disc iteration. Though designated as a fund-raiser for the Gunnar Nilsson (no relation to Harry) Cancer Fund, it too failed to chart, though the markedly different music scene in the U.K. may have had something to do with that. (Meanwhile, back in the States, the pop ballad "Reunited" by Peaches and Herb topped the charts.)

No longer feeling any particular competitive urge, George waited two years before his next single release. Issued in the spring of 1981, it rocketed to #2 on the charts. Sadly, it would be his elegy to his recently taken ex-bandmate, "All Those Years Ago," featuring contributions from Ringo, Paul, and Linda. It was a record that George undoubtedly wished he had never had to make.

Paul McCartney: "Waterfalls"—Released June 13, 1980

With "Coming Up (Live at Glasgow)" topping the charts and ostensibly promoting a concurrent album on which it did not appear, Columbia records was in a quandary. Clearly, something was needed to salvage Paul McCartney's second underperformer in a row on their label, but *McCartney II* wasn't exactly designed for easy listening. Too many of the tracks were simply self-indulgent electronic experiments that didn't easily lend themselves to radio play, at least not in the Top 40. The sole exception was "Waterfalls," an uncharacteristically plaintive ballad played on a Fender Rhodes and featuring light synthesized orchestration. One of Paul's most poignant performances, its failure to generate any American radio attention is astonishing.

While lyrically the song doesn't exactly plumb the depths of Macca's soul (offering such cautions as avoiding polar bears, motor cars in motion, and the title phenomena), it is his *delivery* that makes the recording so compelling. On "Waterfalls," Paul reveals himself to be a man who fears the loss of love above all. Explaining his need for it "every minute of the day," you cannot doubt him when he opines that "it wouldn't be the same if you ever should decide to go away." In light of his premature loss of Linda eighteen years later, hearing him sing those words leaves little doubt as to how truly bereft he would become.

John happened to catch the song on the radio that fateful summer. When asked what he thought of Paul's current music, he observed that he thought his former partner sounded depressed. In hindsight, he realized that he'd only heard the one track and later amended his opinion accordingly, admitting that his judgment had been premature. (Privately, he cited "Coming Up" as an impetus to resume his recording career, while publicly he merely declared it a "good piece of work.")

It's not clear why U.S. radio station programmers were so resistant to adding "Waterfalls" to their playlists. It wasn't as though morose ballads were suddenly out of fashion, as evidenced by the success of acts like Christopher Cross and Air Supply at the time. Possibly it was simply that, to program-mers, it didn't sound enough like a Paul McCartney record, being somewhat downbeat. The song never even made it into *Billboard*'s Hot 100, reaching a "bubbling under" peak of #106—Ringo's turf. In the U.K., however, the song readily found a place alongside the era's mix of so-called New Wave acts and disco divas, peaking at #9.

That TLC's 1995 hit by the same name as his 1980 non-starter shared some common elements with his own work, including lyrical similarities, did not escape Macca's attention.

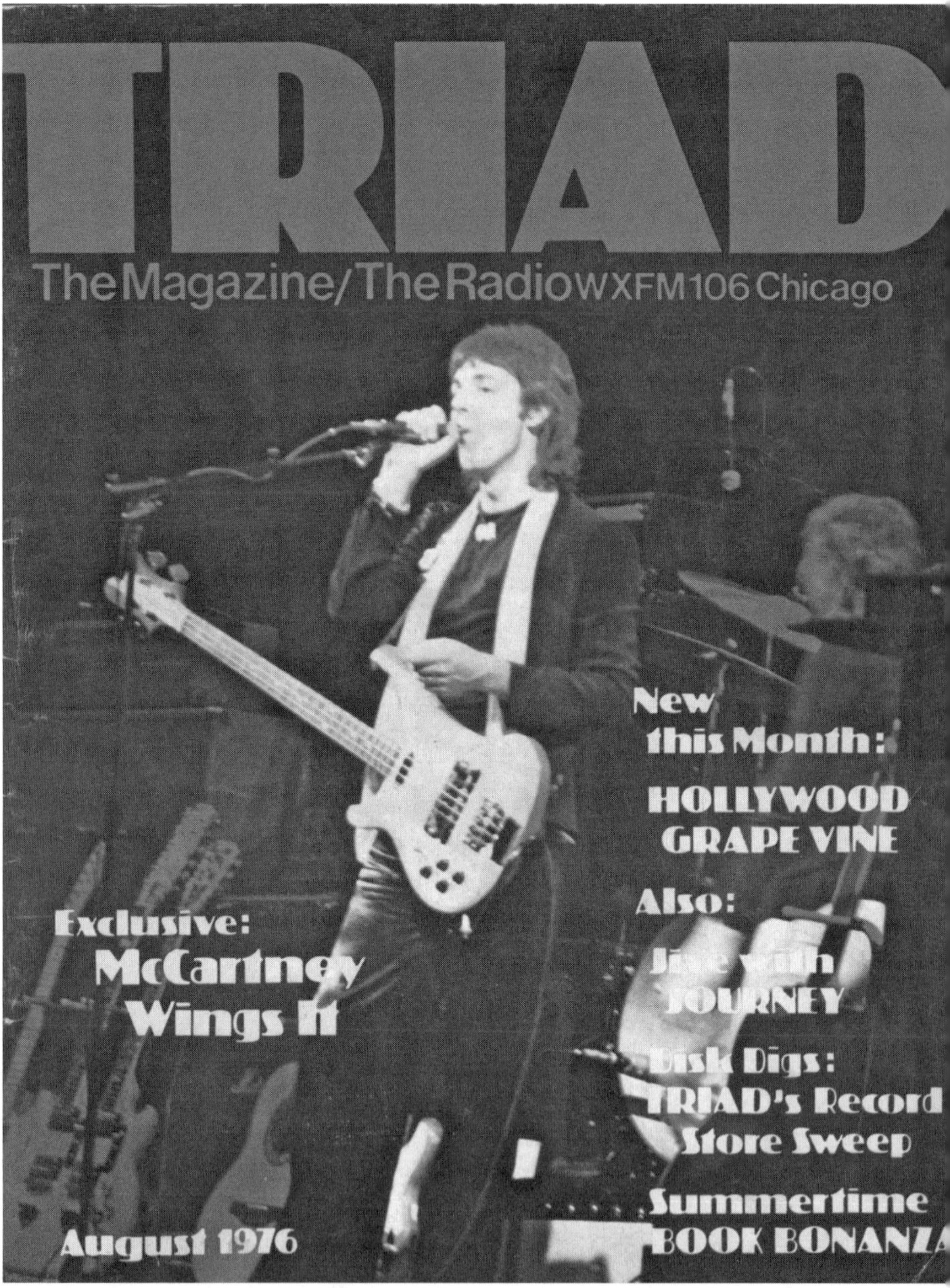

TRIAD

The Magazine/The Radio WXFM 106 Chicago

New
this Month:
HOLLYWOOD
GRAPE VINE

Also:

Jive with
JOURNEY

Disk Digs:
TRIAD's Record
Store Sweep

Summertime
BOOK BONANZA

Exclusive:
McCartney
Wings It

August 1976

Fans in attendance at Wings' 1976 American tour were treated to a thoroughly seasoned group of professionals firing on all cylinders and showcasing a powerful array of material, recent and vintage.

19

Somebody's Ringing the Bell

1976

For Beatle people, America's bicentennial year began on a note of tragedy. Estranged from his wife and family and unable to gain any traction professionally, former roadie and Beatle insider Mal Evans fell into despondency. Mal's efforts to combat his depression ended horrifically after he allegedly barricaded himself in a bedroom of his Los Angeles apartment on January 4; in a blaze of gunfire, Mal was shot by the police who were trying to prevent him from hurting others—or himself. (His death came on the eve of the publication of his memoirs, based upon his personal diaries. Neither the diaries nor the manuscript has ever surfaced publicly.) Other deaths this year would include both John and Paul's fathers, within a fortnight of each other, in the spring.

Fortunately, most of the rest of the year was much more positive. Lennon's lawsuit against Morris Levy over the unauthorized issue of his oldies albums as *Roots* a year earlier began in January, but before month's end, a mistrial was declared after Levy's attorney was caught in open court foolishly displaying a copy of *Two Virgins* within the sight of the jury. Also in court was George. A month after his six-figure settlement offer for "damages" in the "My Sweet Lord" / "He's So Fine" case was rejected, he too found himself before a judge as the infringement case moved forward, five years after being filed. The effect the action had on his songwriting was evident in interviews he gave at the time, citing the paranoia he felt every time he began composing.

As the build-up to the late-spring Wings Over America tour began, there were some with the means to make things happen who believed a tour by Paul and his sidemen , while all well and good, would fall far short of being an "event." What they had in mind, and were determined to see realized, was a full-blown reunion of all four ex-Beatles for a live concert. Bill Sargent was a pioneer in closed-circuit TV broadcasts of sporting events and Broadway shows. Fans would pay to see happenings in movie theaters across the country via a satellite feed (as with 1964's *T.A.M.I. Show*), thereby accommodating what would undoubtedly be an unprecedented demand.

He'd conceived the idea virtually as soon as the Beatles had split up in 1970, but not until 1974 did he actually put an offer on the table: $10 million. The figure represented an opening bid for their services and was duly ignored. In January 1976, he raised it to $30 million and, again drawing no notice, boosted it a month later to $50 million. This rounded figure caught the media's attention, at last fulfilling Sargent's bid to generate publicity whether the actual concert came off or not. In a nutshell, earning the $50 million would entail all four getting together to perform (at a locale of their choosing) for a minimum of twenty minutes, with Sargent securing all rights in perpetuity. If they fulfilled the absolute lowest requirement, it worked out to a payday of $625,000 per minute, per man. His target date was before the bicentennial: Sunday, July 4, 1976.

Though practically impossible to wrap one's mind around, Sargent's offer now had the ex-Fabs' attention. Reports indicated that the four actually did discuss the offer amongst themselves, without coming to any firm conclusion. Ultimately, an insurmountable distaste for Sargent and his spectacle-seeking style (around the same time of the Beatle reunion proposal, Sargent announced plans to stage a "Death Match" between Australian Wally Gibbins and a shark) pushed them away from seriously entertaining the deal. As George put it, "My suggestion was that (Sargent) fight the shark and the winner could promote the Beatles' concert."

There was no denying that the prospect of the four ex-Fabs getting together was very much in the air throughout 1976, perversely as Paul was preparing to launch the culmination of his solo act across the U.S. Even the normally contrary heard-but-not-seen John Lennon was mellowing, quoted in a *People* magazine cover story as musing, "I always felt that splitting up was a mistake in many ways" ("the dream is over" notwithstanding). Whatever his thoughts on the matter, it's certain that he was afforded the chance to air them when Paul and Linda showed up on his doorstep on Saturday, April 24. With *Wings at the Speed of Sound* topping the U.S. album charts, Paul was certainly in a strong position to drive the decision, had he wanted to.

The occasion was auspicious for the two men to be in each other's company, as this was the fabled evening when Lorne Michaels made his tongue-in-cheek pitch to reunite the group for the sum of $3,000 on *Saturday Night Live*. That the two ex-Fabs were receiving the offer in real time on live TV and were just minutes away from the SNL set staggers belief, but there it was; yet, despite the seemingly perfect alignment of the stars, they did not take the bait. Instead, the two men parted awkwardly the following day (see chapter 32), never to share each other's presence again. (George saw John for the last time in December 1974 at the *Dark Horse* end-of-tour party.)

Beyond Paul's mounting a major cross-country U.S. tour in May and June, there was another engine driving Beatlemania that year. The Beatles' contractual obligations to EMI were fulfilled, and the record company was now free to repackage Beatle-era material as they saw fit with no say from the artists themselves (though as a courtesy to their top money spinners, they may have at least clued them in as to their intentions). In March, the Fabs' original twenty-two singles were relaunched in England (having never actually gone out of print) in brand new picture sleeves, along with a "new" one, "Yesterday" (backed with "I Should Have Known Better"). At one point, all the singles were simultaneously in the Top 100; "Yesterday" itself peaked at #8.

No matter what else might be said about them, the "Red" and "Blue" album collections conspicuously lacked any cover tunes. Fan favorites like "Twist and Shout" and "Roll Over Beethoven" were absent, as were a handful of originals like "I Saw Her Standing There" that could be considered essential. To that end, EMI assembled a thematically linked collection on the rather indistinct concept of "rock and roll," meaning up-tempo material, wrapped it in a sleeve evoking the 1950s, and called it *Rock 'n' Roll Music*. The inclusion of "I'm Down" for the first time on an LP at least gave the set some purpose for existing, but the ex-Fabs themselves were reportedly horrified, not least because of the "cheap" design that clearly was designed to cash in on any lingering nostalgia for the *Happy Days* era.

To promote the release, two singles were issued from it, one for each side of the Atlantic. In the U.K., "Back in the U.S.S.R." / "Twist and Shout" made it to #18 on the charts; in America, it was essentially a two-sided Paul release: "Got to Get You into My Life," backed with "Helter Skelter." As the singer of both tracks crisscrossed the country, "Got to Get You into My Life" peaked at #7—not bad for a ten-year-old track. The selection of "Helter Skelter" was no accident; a TV miniseries of the same name, based on Vincent Bugliosi's best-selling book on the Manson Family murders, aired on consecutive nights in April. The film featured replications of Beatles songs by a Los Angeles group called Silverspoon, whose members included the sons of Carol Burnett and Rosemary Clooney. (Capitol could have chosen "Helter Skelter" for the A-side, but that might have been crass.)

Also released that year was the single from 1968's "White Album" that never was: "Ob-la-di Ob-la-da." Whether as a cynical ploy to stroke Paul or simply to push the former group's back catalog, the record, backed in the U.S. by John's "Julia," peaked at #49 late in the year.

Rock 'n' Roll Music might have hit the top spot on the album chart had it not been blocked by, of all things, *Wings at the Speed of Sound*, which in turn was buoyed by the likewise chart-topping single "Silly Love Songs." (And a good thing, too, given Paul's fear of his new music being overshadowed by his old.) Wings' sojourn across America began in Ft. Worth on May 3. The PR machine had been stoked with care, and expectations had built to a fever pitch by the time the opening notes to "Venus and Mars / Rock Show" were plucked out on a dry ice–enshrouded Texas stage. With demand for tickets running high, shows were added on off-days throughout the tour, which ended up as the success story of the year. (Ringo and George are known to have attended the May 9 Maple Leaf Gardens show in Toronto, but, oddly, John is believed to have missed out on Paul's tour completely.) Paul had learned a thing or two from George's road show, and the pacing, staging, and crowd-pleasing presentation were finely attuned, maximizing the bliss factor while dampening any clamoring for the Beatles to reunite.

Still, the offers were far from over. In September, Sid Bernstein—the man who had singlehandedly invented arena rock by booking the Beatles to play Shea Stadium in 1965—ran a full-page ad in the New York City newspapers, soliciting the ex-Fabs to get together for a one-night-only gig that could pull in over $200 million with box office receipts, a double-live album, and film rights. Lest waving cash under their collective nose was not enough of an incentive, Bernstein framed his offer as an opportunity to contribute to charity on a grand scale, with revenue generated going toward "feeding and educating the orphan children of the needy nations." If Bernstein thought an appeal to their altruism was the way to go, then he had badly misread their feelings on the subject. Said George, "It was cute the way the ad in the Times tried to put the responsibility for saving the world on our shoulders." Again, an outside attempt to push the four together was—unsurprisingly—rebuffed.

Particularly resentful of the distraction was Ringo, who had at last returned to recording for the first installment of his new record deal. Given that the Bernstein offer came just as he was giving a round of interviews to promote his first all-new album in two years, the Beatle hype wasn't exactly welcome. *Ringo's Rotogravure* kept to the formula of mixing ex-Fabs with guest stars, in this case including Peter Frampton and Eric Clapton. His ex-bandmates each contributed: John with "Cookin' (in the Kitchen of Love)," Paul with "Pure Gold," and George with the dramatic ballad "I'll Still Love You." The latter musician did not appear, as he was busy getting his own record together, but John did, and—though unplanned—Paul and Linda's drop-in visit lasted long enough for the couple to contribute some backing vocals. Though a solid effort, the record, as good as it was, barely

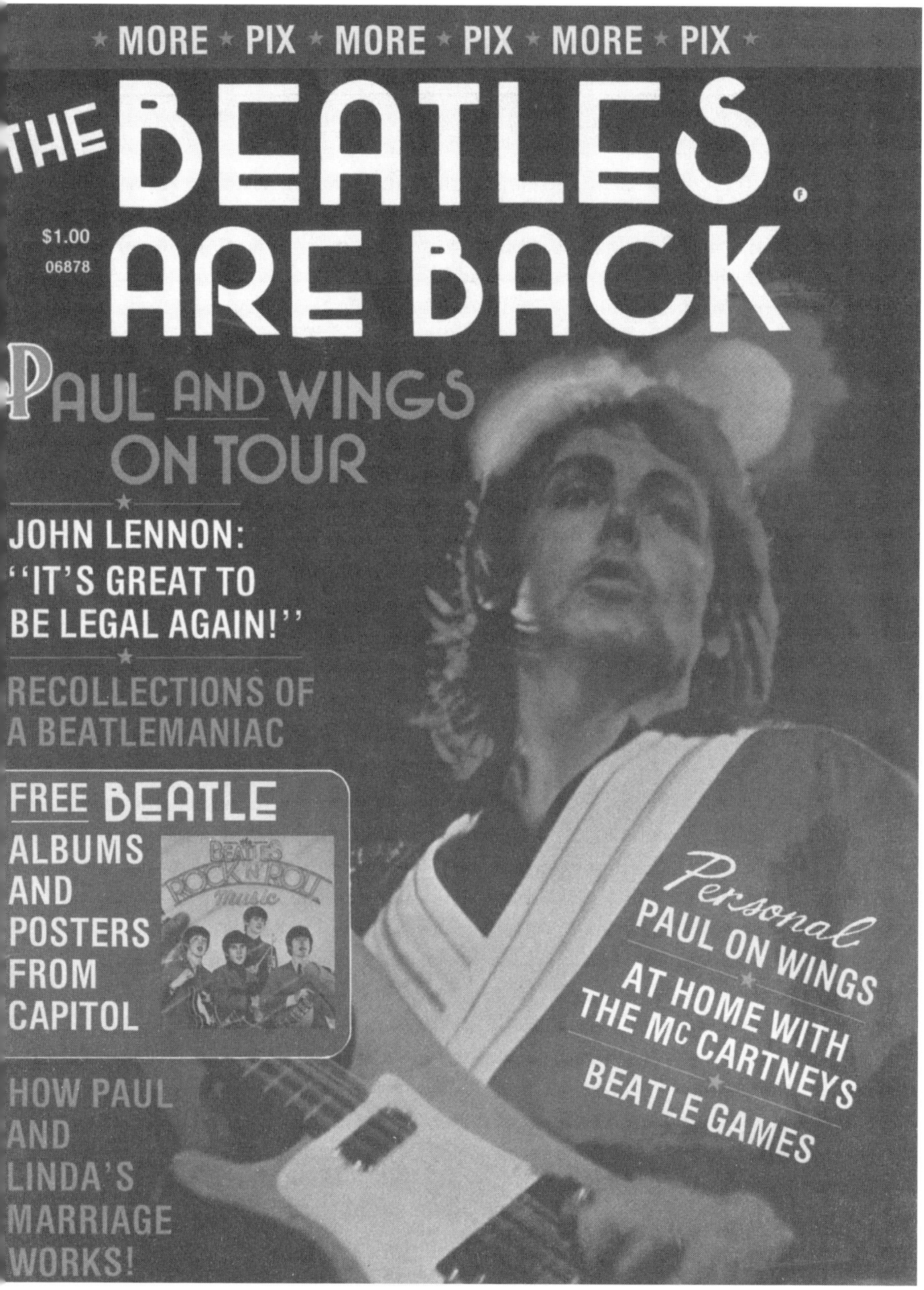

MORE PIX MORE PIX MORE PIX
THE BEATLES ARE BACK
$1.00
06878
PAUL AND WINGS ON TOUR
JOHN LENNON: "IT'S GREAT TO BE LEGAL AGAIN!"
RECOLLECTIONS OF A BEATLEMANIAC
FREE BEATLE ALBUMS AND POSTERS FROM CAPITOL
HOW PAUL AND LINDA'S MARRIAGE WORKS!
Personal
PAUL ON WINGS
AT HOME WITH THE MC CARTNEYS
BEATLE GAMES

Newsstand specials like this recalled similar ones issued during the Beatles' heyday. *The Beatles Are Back*, published quarterly throughout the late '70s, featured archival and contemporary images as well as increasingly fanciful content, including a story describing a "merger" between the ex-Fabs and the Who (as the "Super Beatles").

made the Top 30, echoing the performance of the first single, "A Dose of Rock 'n' Roll."

Ringo had had a rough year, splitting from Nancy Andrews for seven months before reconciling with her, during which time he'd shaved his head "in a fit of lethargy," to borrow John's words from another situation. Increasingly, he was making his home in Monte Carlo as a tax exile, and bouncing from one party to the next as he attempted to cope with a multitude of demons through less than healthy means.

Still, the Beatle buzz kept up, furthered satirically that autumn when *Saturday Night Live* entered its second season, hosted on October 2 by Python alumnus Eric Idle. The gag on this evening returned to the offer for the group to reunite on the show (by now swollen to $3,200). Instead of sending the group over from England, Idle was said to have spent the money and offered a video clip of the Rutles instead. Thus the "Pre-Fab Four" made their debut on American television with a clip of "I Must Be In Love." An actual Beatle finally made it to their stage in November, when George appeared, demanding all of the promised fee.

Looking tanned, fit, and rested, George was back after having spent quite some time in the rock and roll wilderness. (The "My Sweet Lord" verdict was a semi-vindication after the court found him guilty of "subconscious" infringement.) His sudden visibility and regained sense of humor (as further expressed in the musical videos shown that evening) came just in time, as *Thirty-Three & 1/3* was easily his strongest collection in years. "This Song," a catchy, tongue-in-cheek response to the "My Sweet Lord" litigation, was a welcome return to the secular world, while "Crackerbox Palace" tapped his inner Python to express the absurdities of life with a light heart. The album might have performed better in the charts had Capitol not punitively issued *The Best of George Harrison* nearly simultaneously. This compilation was drawn from both solo and Beatle-era Harrisongs, further annoying George.

Also creating probably something less than satisfaction in the collective ex-group was a one-of-a-kind film that opened late in the year. *All This and World War II* was a bizarre documentary of sorts, highlighting the course of the Second World War cinematically via newsreel footage and clips from period films, all to the strains of Beatles music, as performed by a host of contemporary stars ranging from Peter Gabriel to Keith Moon. Though the film died a quick death in theaters, the soundtrack is not bad, resulting in yet one more quirky artifact of the '70s.

With George back on track (despite lawsuit troubles), Ringo holding his own, and John enjoying the cozy domesticity for which he'd once ridiculed Paul, 1976 closed with the issue of *Wings Over America*, a three-disc souvenir of what had been for Paul, a very good year.

20

So *Sgt. Pepper* Took You By Surprise

Latter-Day Beatlemania

At the time of the public announcement of the Beatles' disbanding in 1970, their position at the top of rock's hierarchy was under serious threat: newer bands that expanded the outer limits of the genre were louder, heavier, poppier, sweeter, or more experimental. Of course, none of these acts embodied *all* of the qualities that had made the Fabs so appealing, but the divergence between the million-selling *singles* of the day and the *albums* underscored the variance within rock's audience that the Beatles had once bridged so effortlessly. In 1970, for example, while LPs from Led Zeppelin, Santana, and Chicago dominated the year's sales, Top 40 best-sellers that year included the Carpenters' "Close to You," "Raindrops Keep Falling on My Head" by B. J. Thomas, and pretty much anything by the Jackson Five.

But even though the public initially seemed to have moved on from the rampant Beatlemania of the '60s, the following decade saw a resurgent longing for what had been. Maybe it was the absence of an all-in-one unifying act; perhaps it was purely nostalgia from aging Baby Boomers, longing for simpler joys in the face of their complicated transition into adulthood. (Still another reason might have been the discovery by younger boomers of their older siblings' record collections.)

Whatever the cause, above the unceasing clamor for a reunion were a couple of major spikes in Beatlemania Mark II. The first came in 1974, the tenth anniversary of the band's American debut. Interest in anything Beatle-connected ran high, with fans drawing further joy from Paul finally enjoying the success of a decent album; Ringo following up a blockbuster with more of the same; John dueting with Elton John, the biggest act of the day; and George going out on tour.

Another outbreak came in 1978, as their collective career passed even further into history. A pair of Hollywood films capitalized on the Fabs' past, as did a television satire—more or less sanctioned by the former

POLITICS: THE MINISTRY OF GEORGE C. WALLACE

ROLLING STONE

ISSUE NO. 172   OCTOBER 24, 1974   75¢ UK25p

The Texas Rangers:
Last Gasp of Frontier Justice
By J. Anthony Lukas

Lily Tomlin
Jive Times: Part Two
By David Felton

Strange Rumblings in Pepperland

Paul Anka
Sings for
Lovers Only

Grassroots efforts at commemorating the Beatles and organizing fan gatherings were given cover-story attention in *Rolling Stone*, following the success of the first Beatlefest. John Lennon himself sanctioned Mark Lapidos's pioneering event.

Beatles—while "an incredible simulation" of their act did boffo business on Broadway.

The following is a rundown of the various ways the public's appetite for all things Fab was fed throughout the decade.

Joe Pope's *Strawberry Fields Forever* (1972)

In 1972, a rather singular Beatlemaniac by the name of Joe Pope launched *Strawberry Fields Forever*, possibly the first American fanzine. (Others that followed during the decade included Barb Fenick's *The Write Thing*, Bill King's enduring *Beatlefan*, and the short-lived *Paperback Writer* and *Imagine* 'zines.) Pope lived in Boston; just out of college and in no hurry to begin a "straight" career, he realized that there was no comprehensive forum for hardcores like himself to keep up with the doings of the ex-Fabs and also—in this pre-internet/Facebook/Twitter age—to build a network with like-minded fans.

Pope determined that he could create a sustaining publication with twenty-five subscribers; an ad placed in *Rolling Stone*'s classifieds reached twice that goal the first time it ran. *Strawberry Fields Forever* was compiled via a thorough combing of the press for any tidbits of news floating about. (In addition, Pope wrote snarky gossip items under the handle Abbey Rodent.) In the tradition of the Beatles' own official fan club of the 1960s, *Strawberry Fields Forever* issued annual Christmas flexidiscs containing rare recordings that few fans had heard.

Pope also pioneered the field of collecting Beatle memorabilia, using his own considerable expertise to determine what the going rates for collectibles really were. As his success grew, it became obvious that a vast but largely unserved constituency existed; the next logical step was for these fans from around the country to get together and celebrate en masse. To that end, Pope organized what he called the Magical Mystery Tour: the first nationally advertised Beatles fan convention. (Original plans called for an *actual* bus tour before the idea was scrapped.) The event took place at Boston's Bradford Hotel on July 26–28, 1974, and largely adhered to the template for all that followed.

Magical Mystery Tour featured a flea market of memorabilia and vinyl, as well as guest speakers (former NYC DJ Murray the K, a.k.a. the Fifth Beatle; Allan Williams, a.k.a. the Man Who Gave the Beatles Away); live music (the inimitable David Peel entertained guests in the lobby); trivia contests; and, best of all, screenings of Fab movies and "promo films." (For most, it was their first viewing of *Magical Mystery Tour*, the film, as well as *The Beatles in Tokyo*—a real treat for Beatle-starved attendees.) As Barb Fenick, who was there, later recalled, "We sang ourselves hoarse."

The success of the event prompted Pope to repeat it twice more in the years that immediately followed before Mark Lapidos's grander, flashier, and "official" conventions became the gold standard. Pope's service to the fans did not diminish, however; in 1977, fans were stunned at the release of the "Deccagone" singles: colored vinyl 45 rpm editions of the Decca audition tracks, often read about but never before accessible.

Pope continued to publish *Strawberry Fields Forever*, though as the years went on, issues became more sporadic. He also started a "Beatlephone" hotline that fans could call to hear recorded messages of the latest Beatle news.

A much loved and charismatic fellow, Pope succumbed to cancer in 1999.

John, Paul, George, Ringo . . . and Bert (Opened May 1974)

From *Sgt. Pepper's* onward, there's been an irresistible urge among some creative folk to implement the Beatles' music as the building blocks in the construction of some sort of story. From *Yellow Submarine* to *Across the Universe*, the results have been predictably mixed, but possibly the most artful use to date sprang from the imagination of Liverpool's Willy Russell, who used the Beatles' songs to tell their story—sort of.

As a Scouser, Russell had the Liverpudlian dialogue and outlook on life down cold. *John, Paul, George, Ringo . . . and Bert* was a work commissioned by the suitably named Everyman Theatre. Through the voice of the fictitious Bert McGhee, an "original" member of the Quarry Men who got the boot early on (due to musical ineptitude), the story of the Fabs' rise to fame was presented with an astonishing authenticity that resonated with anyone familiar with the particulars of their history.

In the setup to the narrative, Bert, who reckons himself the biggest Beatles fan in the world, is accosted by a leather-clad teen demanding money to go see his favorite punk band. Bert instead tries to show him that the greatest band in the world is performing right there—that night! (They are standing outside a venue where Wings is advertised, but a delusional Bert reads the marquee as "Beatles.") The teen scoffs, deriding Beatles as something that his grandfather used to talk about. But after Bert shows him a picture of the group from the Hamburg era, the youth recognizes their kinship with his punks, thus setting the table for their story to be recounted through flashback.

One of the musical's most striking innovations was the insertion of the Beatles' music not as straightforward musical accompaniment but as a device to comment upon or advance the plot. Thus it is Brian Epstein who sings "Anytime at All" as he pledges his support for the group; later, he sings "I Need You" after the boys announce their retirement from live

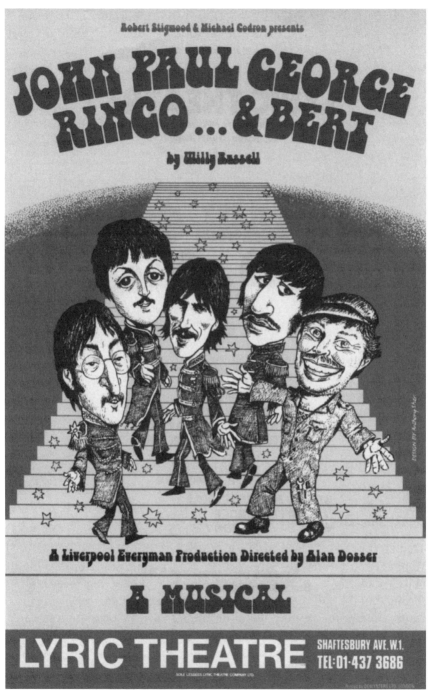

This entertaining musical comedy by Willy Russell creatively nailed the Fabs' story in its own way just as Eric Idle would do later with the Rutles.

appearances. (Bert performs "I'm a Loser" while mourning their breakup.) Also worth noting was the fanciful insertion of Adolf Hitler into the plot, circa 1960: rather than evil incarnate, he was portrayed as a heavy-handed German taskmaster that worked the boys to the limit of their endurance—for their own good, of course.

John, Paul, George, Ringo . . . and Bert drew great reviews and enjoyed sold-out performances during its initial eight-week run before heading to London. There, it was given a heavily hyped launch, courtesy of producer Robert Stigwood. As discussed in *Fab Four FAQ,* impresario Stigwood lost out on an opportunity to co-manage the Fabs; as a consolation, he instead built the Bee Gees into big stars. But the Beatle fixation never completely went away, and in August 1974 Stigwood was able to act upon it by bringing the Merseyside production to the Lyric Theatre in London's West End.

Among the show's non-fans was George Harrison. Persuaded to attend a performance by Derek Taylor, he left at the intermission after noticeably cringing throughout. (He also pulled the rights for the use of his "Here Comes the Sun," which was then replaced by "Good Day Sunshine.") As Taylor later noted, George wasn't a fan of his own history even "while it was happening." (George characterized Allan Williams' account of their early days in *The Man Who Gave the Beatles Away*—a work John purportedly loved—as "stupid.") Paul too expressed concerns, having seen an excerpt on the telly that seemed to suggest that *he* had been responsible for the group's demise—a sensitive issue. Later, Willy Russell mollified him with the explanation that what he'd seen had been taken out of context.

Once control of the Beatles' publishing transferred to Michael Jackson and Sony, the price of staging *John, Paul, George, Ringo . . . and Bert* became too cost-prohibitive for most theaters, making it a rarely seen production; more's the pity.

Beatlefest Begins (September 7–8, 1974)

That Mark Lapidos's life trajectory changed forever when the sounds of "I Want to Hold Your Hand" first reached his ears in the winter of 1964 hardly makes him unique. A strange alchemy was at work, one that affected lives throughout the country all at once. What *is* remarkable is what came next: by the time of the Beatles' debut on the *Ed Sullivan Show* not long after, it's doubtful that anyone—sixteen-year-old Mark included—could have predicted that what emanated from the flickering screen was no less than a glimpse into his future livelihood.

Lapidos ended up in the record industry, albeit at the retail end: at Sam Goody's Garden State Plaza store, in Paramus, New Jersey. Given Lapidos's *idée fixe,* anything remotely Beatle-related was prominently displayed, given in-store spins, and kept in plentiful supply. By 1973, he was assistant manager at the Radio City store. Though his position had changed, his obsession did not: when *Living in the Material World,* George's follow-up to *All Things Must Pass,* was about to drop, Mark rushed a copy of the "Give Me Love" single over to the store's audio department, dropped it on a turntable, cranked the volume, and proceeded to play both sides. The unamused department manager concluded the performance by breaking the disc in two. (Lapidos made him pay for it.)

That same year, renewed interest in the Fabs was sparked in part by the release of the two double-album compilations. Capitol stoked the fire by promoting their back catalog in anticipation of 1974's tenth anniversary of the Beatles' arrival in America with plenty of in-store displays and posters. Given his natural bent and professional environment, it didn't take long for the wheels to begin turning in Mark's head for a proper commemoration. By February, his concept for an actual Beatles fan convention began taking shape.

Though Joe Pope had been planning along similar lines up in Boston, what made the difference was Lapidos's determination to secure an official sanction. Serendipitously, at a Central Park March of Dimes event with John Lennon in attendance, Mark ran into a fellow who had given the ex-Fab and Harry Nilsson a ride to their Times Square hotel. (In a crowd of over 100,000, the two were distinguished by their "Beatles 10th Anniversary" shirts, though, unlike his fellow fan's, Mark's had not come from Lennon himself.) The Samaritan kindly slipped Lapidos Lennon's room number at the Pierre; summoning all the moxie he could muster, Mark headed over.

It was Sunday, April 28, 1974. Answering the door was Harry Nilsson, who admitted the enterprising young man. Introducing himself, Lapidos ran through his pitch. John listened politely before responding with the deathless words: "I'm all for it. I'm a Beatles fan, too." With any number of other issues on his plate (the immigration fight, Nilsson's *Pussy Cats* album, assorted lawsuits), the ex-Fab was astonishingly receptive; another year earlier or later and it might have been a different story entirely.

Further upping the ante, Lennon arranged through Tony King for Apple to send some promo films to the fest; he also solicited his fellow ex-Fabs to contribute items for auction to raise money for the charity of his choice, New York's Phoenix House, a drug rehab center. (George donated a tabla used on *Sgt. Pepper*; Ringo, a signed pair of drumsticks; John and Paul each a signed guitar.) John toyed with the idea of showing up himself to person-ally present the winning bidder with his instrument, but, after hearing of the four thousand attendees, opted to stay away. (He instead dispatched

May Pang to do some buying on his behalf, instructing her to pick up any bootlegs she could find for his collection, as well as *all* copies of *Two Virgins*, which he desperately wanted to take out of circulation.)

Now "legit," Lapidos put together the $8,000 necessary to book facilities at midtown's Commodore Hotel (now the Grand Hyatt), as well as another $1,000 for the services of Murray the K to act as MC. Promoter Sid Bernstein was the first guest speaker, while a Canadian act called Liverpool signed on as the first house band. (Not to be confused with the venerable group of the same name that's performed since 1979; Abbey Rhode did the honors from 1976 to 1978.) Dubbed *Beatlefest,* the gathering was heavily promoted on radio and in print ads. (Lapidos even instructed store staff to slip flyers into the bags of record buyers.)

Ten dollars bought fans two days' worth of Beatle heaven on that post–Labor Day weekend. All the elements of the fest that have now become part of the infrastructure—the flea market, the art displays, the guest speakers, the charity auctions—were present. A staple then (but no longer) was the ballroom screenings of the Fab films, including the seldom-seen Shea Stadium concert (which elicited screams) as well as *Let It Be* (which drew hisses at the appearance of Yoko or Linda).

Surprising everyone but Mark Lapidos was the youth of so many of the attendees: some of the most overwrought displays of emotion that weekend came from fans too young to have experienced Beatlemania firsthand. That thousands showed up to celebrate an act that had passed into history was astonishing, no less so then to the house organ of the counterculture, *Rolling Stone* magazine. (They devoted a cover story to the phenomenon a month later.) Feeling thoroughly vindicated, Lapidos quit his job not long after and began planning future fests, expanding into Los Angeles in 1976 and Chicago a year later.

Through the years, the fest's guest list has run like a Who's Who of Beatledom. While none of the Fabs themselves (nor Neil Aspinall) ever attended, any number of intimates did, giving the enterprise tacit Fab approval: Mal Evans, Cynthia Lennon, Mike McCartney, Pete Shotton (as well as the other surviving Quarry Men), Alf Bicknell, Sam Leach, Alistair Taylor, Peter Asher, Ken Mansfield, Klaus Voormann, Astrid Kirchherr, Jurgen Vollmer, Billy Preston, Pattie Boyd, May Pang, Nancy Andrews, Harry Nilsson, Donovan, Gerry Marsden, Billy J. Kramer, Ronnie Spector, Norman "Hurricane" Smith, Geoff Emerick, Victor Spinetti, Tony Bramwell, Tony Barrow, Ray Coleman, Neil Innes, Geoffrey Ellis, Louise Harrison, Robert Freeman, Denis O'Dell, Walter Shenson—the list goes on and on. For most fans, this is the closest they will ever get to legend.

A full-time business nowadays, the *Fest for Beatles Fans* (as it's now called) rolls on with no signs of slowing down. True, the bootleg vendors have been banished and most prices are no longer the bargain they once were, but there is still no better place for the average Beatles geek to feel such a sense of community for two or three weekends a year.

For that, we can thank the vision of Mark—and Carol—Lapidos, who have given the fans a place to go—as well as the Beatles themselves.

Sgt. Pepper's Lonely Hearts Club Band on the Road (Opened November 16, 1974)

Tom O'Horgan was a director of both film (1974's *Rhinoceros*, starring *The Producers*' costars, Zero Mostel and Gene Wilder) and theater (*Hair, Jesus Christ Superstar*). His signature brand was spectacle, sensorially bombarding audiences with sounds and images that served to overpower whatever linear narrative might have originally existed within the material. He pioneered nudity on the Great White Way; he also eschewed scripts in order to free his thespians to improvise. The results, while momentarily novel, embodied a sort of "professional anarchy," with the attendant mixed results.

O'Horgan proved ahead of the curve when it came to packaging '60s nostalgia. Before the decade was properly dead and buried, he began work on a re-presentation of the Beatles' music, chiefly but not exclusively drawn from their best-known album, *Sgt. Pepper's Lonely Hearts Club Band*. Along with tunes from *Abbey Road* and assorted singles, a narrative of sorts was pulled out of thin air.

The "plot," such as it was, concerned one Billy Shears (played by Ted Neeley, the eternal Jesus of *Superstar* renown), an aspiring rock musician bedeviled by the very forces of "evil" (embodied by Maxwell's Silver Hammermen) inherent within the industry. Other characters contrived from the Beatles' music include Strawberry Fields, Billy's lover; Lucy, a malevolent temptress; the lovely Rita; and Sgt. Pepper himself. Visually, the show resembled a live-action version of *Yellow Submarine*, featuring grotesque costumes, oversized props, and a pair of giant puppets for "When I'm Sixty-four" that groped each other. (Further stirring the pot, soft discs were tossed at the audience from the stage.)

Reviews ran the gamut from lukewarm to scathing. Though the show's off-Broadway opening at the Beacon Theatre was a much-hyped event (present were John, May Pang, and Mick Jagger), audiences noticeably shrank as the run extended. Despite this, *On the Road* ran briefly on Broadway before closing for good; most amazingly of all, it went on to provide the basis for one of the most lambasted cinematic creations of the decade (see below).

All This and World War II (Directed by Susan Winslow)— Released November 12, 1976

Credit for what is surely one of the more mind-blowing Beatles-related concepts appears on the soundtrack album to the film *All This and World War II* as follows: "Based on a dream by Russ Regan." Regan was a record exec; he asserts to this day that the claim is true, and that he really did have a dream wherein newsreel footage of the Good War was synched to a Beatles soundtrack.

Released by Twentieth Century-Fox, *All This and World War II* was an impressionistic journey, falling somewhere between straight documentary and pop culture kitsch. Its nearest antecedent was Australian director Philippe Mora's depiction of the Great Depression via newsreels and clips from popular films, 1975's *Brother Can You Spare a Dime?*—not surprisingly, since *All This and World War II*'s eventual director was Susan Winslow, a researcher on the Mora film. Raw material for *this* project was culled from

At once the most creative and bizarre attempt at fusing Beatles music with film, *All This and World War II* remains a surreal gem ahead of its time.

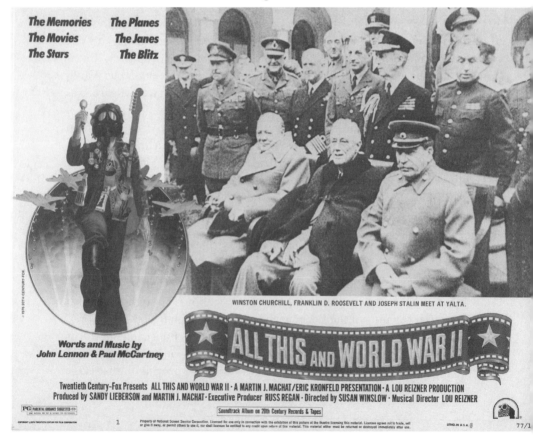

the Fox Movietone vault, along with feature film properties ranging from 1939's *Charlie Chan's City in Darkness* to 1970's *Tora! Tora! Tora!*

All This and World War II begins with Neville Chamberlain's "Peace for Our Time" announcement of the pre-war Munich Agreement (to the strains of Gabriel's "Strawberry Fields Forever": "Living is easy with eyes closed") and ends with, of course, the atomic bombing of Japan to—what else?— "The End," performed by the London Symphony Orchestra. (Over the end credits was a last-minute addition that didn't make the album: Apple artists Hot Chocolate Band's reggaefied remake of "Give Peace a Chance," likely suggested by John Lennon himself, who had been brought into the loop on the work in progress by Tony Bramwell.)

The resulting album was a selection of pleasing covers (Elton John's "Lucy in the Sky with Diamonds," though not commissioned for the project, was nonetheless included) and charming novelties (Keith Moon's take on "When I'm Sixty-four") that made an intriguing compilation even without the movie—which is how most people stumbled upon the baffling package.

The film itself barely lasted two weeks in theaters upon its November 1976 release. Despite some of the clever juxtapositions—Hitler at Berchtesgarden, his mountain retreat, as "The Fool on the Hill" plays; Status Quo's "Getting Better" as Americans join the war—the film was savaged by critics (as taste-less) and ignored by filmgoers. In retrospect, it's easy to see that the pre-sentation probably hindered efforts at clicking with audiences. A unique concept such as this would likely have fared better had it been marketed as an art film, coming from a tiny independent, rather than as the latest major studio extravaganza.

The Rutles: *All You Need Is Cash* (Aired March 22, 1978)

This spot-on parody of the Beatles' career came about through a serendipi-tous convergence of events, culminating with ex-Monty Python member Eric Idle's guest hosting *Saturday Night Live* on April 23, 1977. In that episode, a satirical telethon held to raise money in aid of the sinking British Empire featured, as entertainment, ex-Bonzo Dog Band singer/songwriter Neil Innes, billed as Ron Nasty from the Rutles. He performed a piano-based composition, "Cheese and Onions," that so out-Lennoned Lennon that it was actually bootlegged and issued on an under-the-counter Beatles release.

To backtrack: SNL producer Lorne Michaels' famous come-on to the ex-Fabs to reunite on his show first aired on April 24, 1976. Six months later, Eric Idle hosted; a bit suggesting that he'd conned Michaels out of his money by claiming he could get the Beatles but instead substituting the Rutles aired, along with the first video clip of the "Pre-Fab Four" for the song "I Must Be in Love." This *Hard Day's Night*-like promo was created for Idle's U.K. series at the time, *Rutland Weekend Television*, though it had not yet aired.

Positive reaction from both Rutle airings on SNL spurred Michaels to propose the possibility of fleshing out the concept into a full-blown film. Idle, who had been preparing to pitch the idea to the BBC, jumped at the chance to secure an American-sized budget and, presumably, a New World-sized audience for the project. Innes was commissioned to crank out a couple of dozen Beatle-like compositions, and, with SNL shorts filmmaker Gary Weiss codirecting, *All You Need Is Cash* went into production.

Several Python (and subsequent spinoffs) alumni starred, including Michael Palin as "Eric Manchester" (the Derek Taylor stand-in); also cast were many SNL actors: Gilda Radner, John Belushi (as "Ron Decline"—their latter-day manager); Dan Aykroyd (a chain-smoking Dick Rowe substitute); and Bill Murray as—what else?—Bill Murray the K. Special guest cameos (as themselves) included Paul Simon, Mick Jagger (wife Bianca also appeared, though *not* as herself), and Scaffold/GRIMM member Roger McGough. Appearing as the Rutles themselves were Innes; Eric Idle as Dirk McQuickly; Beach Boy backing musician Rikki Fataar, who, without a single line of dialogue throughout, portrayed "the Quiet One," Stig O'Hara; and John Halsey as "the Noisy One," Barry Wom (née Barrington Womble).

The biggest coup was George Harrison's cameo as a reporter, shown interviewing Manchester outside the offices of Rutle Corps as thieves make off with everything not nailed down—including his microphone. On the eve of the production of the Python film *Life of Brian*, it marked George's second public appearance in support of a Python-esque project, having already guested on *Rutland Weekend Television*. His involvement gave the enterprise the appearance of an official Fab endorsement, though the reaction from his former bandmates was mixed: John is said to have loved it unequivocally; Ringo, in parts; and Paul was, at the time at least, somewhat wary of the whole idea (though Linda thought it was a riot). Until the Beatles' *Anthology* came into being in the 1990s, Harrison recommended that anyone interested in their story check out the Rutles instead.

All the comedic takes on real-life Beatle history aside, it is Neil Innes's music that sustained the whole package. Innes, who of course as a member of the Bonzos had appeared in *Magical Mystery Tour* and, further, enjoyed the hit "I Am the Urban Spaceman" courtesy of Paul McCartney's production ten years earlier, had thoroughly absorbed every nuance of the Fabs' music. For that reason, the songs he composed were strikingly familiar but just short of plagiarism—except, perhaps for the "Get Back" pastiche, "Get

Up and Go." Lennon himself privately warned Innes that this song might have strayed too far into infringement territory; for that reason, it was cut from the soundtrack LP.

Lennon's friendly advice notwithstanding, Lew Grade's ATV, then still in control of the Fabs' copyrights, weren't sensitive to such good intentions and claimed—successfully—a piece of the action. Credits for the songs now read "Lennon-McCartney-Innes," thereby costing Neil a considerable portion of his royalties. (As the ex-Fabs never owned their own publishing, there was little they themselves could do rectify the iniquity. Eric Idle suggested to Neil that he put out an album called *The Best of Lennon-McCartney-Innes*.)

Given all of the talent, wit, and yes, love put into the effort, *All You Need Is Cash*—which NBC switched from its intended Saturday late-night time slot to prime time—bombed utterly in the ratings, coming in dead last. It is largely through the video release that the film found a considerable fan base, one that prompted Innes and company (minus Idle, who was busy with *Spamalot*) to revisit his parodic altar ego and issue *Archaeology* as a Rutles counterpoint to the Beatles' *Anthology* in 1996. Wary of going to the well once too often, Innes was reassured by George: "I don't call every eighteen years milking it!"

The Rutles (l-r: Eric Idle, John Halsey, Ricky Fataar, Neil Innes) sprang from the mind of ex–Monty Python member and George Harrison buddy Eric Idle. Neil Innes's spot-on score, skirting infringement laws, was the icing on the cake.

I Wanna Hold Your Hand (Directed by Robert Zemeckis)— Released April 21, 1978

Just one month after *The Rutles* died a lonely death on American network television, the directorial debut of Steven Spielberg protégé Robert Zemeckis appeared in theaters. *I Wanna Hold Your Hand* (retitled from *Beatlemania*, concurrently in use on Broadway) told the story of six New Jersey teenagers who, by hook or by crook, were determined to finagle a ticket to the Beatles' American television debut on the *Ed Sullivan Show*, in a deft blending of history and fiction that soon became Zemeckis' stock-in-trade.

When remembered at all, *I Wanna Hold Your Hand* is considered an "A-plus B movie"—damning faint praise for a charming but overlooked film. Without actually showing a Beatle (not directly, anyway—newsreel footage is used to depict the real deal, while stand-ins in longshot are otherwise employed), the movie's brilliance is that *they're not missed*. While Beatles music is played throughout, the central subject of *I Wanna Hold Your Hand* is the hysteria that greeted the Fabs upon their first U.S. visit and all the lives it impacted on the East Coast. Scenes familiar to latter-day Beatles geeks, shown endlessly in documentaries, are fleshed out, depicted in loving detail and given humanity. Those screamers were all real people with real lives— this is their story. (The little-remembered Beatle haters are also shown; the obscuring haze of nostalgia makes it easy to forget that not everyone was captivated by the Beatles' arrival on these shores.)

Zemeckis is best known for some of the blockbusters he directed beginning in the '80s: 1984's *Romancing the Stone*; the *Back to the Future* series; 1988's *Who Framed Roger Rabbit*; and in 1994, for better or worse, *Forrest Gump*. *I Wanna Hold Your Hand* displays ingredients evident in later releases: misunderstood teens up against authority figures, slapstick sight gags, real-life history imposed upon ordinary people. (There's even a scene depicting a clock tower and a lightning storm: shades of *Back to the Future*.) Given Zemeckis' evident talent, it's somewhat surprising to find how poorly received the movie was in 1978, but, as the director is quick to point out on the commentary track of the DVD, distribution problems ruined the film's chance to find its audience.

Though perhaps overly broad for some tastes, *I Wanna Hold Your Hand* nonetheless contains fine performances from Nancy Allen (*Carrie, Blow Out*), Theresa Saldana (*Raging Bull*—she would suffer a brutal stalker attack in 1982, but recovered), and the late Wendie Jo Sperber (Linda McFly in *Back to the Future*). Murray the K, whose career had been revitalized of late, appeared as himself. Factual liberties taken were slight: the Beatles opened *and* closed the *Ed Sullivan Show*; the *Meet the Beatles!* albums shown throughout the film bear the color scheme from a post-1964 issue; a photo from *A Hard Day's Night* is shown before the film had been shot. Minor points aside, *I Wanna Hold Your Hand* is eminently enjoyable and a minor treasure.

To most Americans in 1964 (and indeed ever after), the Beatles were an abstraction; as George held, the Fabs were an excuse for Americans to go mad. *I Wanna Hold Your Hand* is a pleasing telling of what that seismic cultural event was like for those who missed it the first time. (The film was produced in thirty-eight days on a relative shoestring. The next Beatles-related cinematic project released that year proved conclusively that budget and time don't always translate into enduring art.)

Sgt. Pepper's Lonely Hearts Club Band (Directed by Michael Schultz)—Released July 24, 1978

By 1978, both the Bee Gees and Peter Frampton had achieved their career peaks. The Brothers Gibb had broken through big in 1975 with *Main Course*, an album that simultaneously spawned three hit singles—"Nights on Broadway," "Fanny (Be Tender with My Love)," and "Jive Talkin'"—and introduced Barry Gibb's falsetto, an effect the trio would flog to death in the ensuing years. This was followed by *Children of the World*, featuring the hardcore disco of "You Should Be Dancing."

Lest anyone wonder where all this was going, the mega-success of *Saturday Night Fever* two years later typed the brothers for life as bare-chested, gold-chained, leisure suit–clad divos, their gleaming white dentistry contrasting with their Miami tans. Whatever else they now were, they had successfully managed to make themselves anathema to true rockers. (True, they had been middle-of-the-road balladeers prior to their reinvention, but at least they hadn't been despised and mocked.)

Peter Frampton had secured his rocker bona fides during his Humble Pie years. Though his breakthrough *Frampton Comes Alive* album wasn't nearly as incendiary as Pie's *Fillmore* live set, he'd managed to hold on to his base despite the rather obvious efforts to promote him through his looks. Nineteen seventy-seven's *I'm in You* disappointed some, but still managed to reach #2 and go platinum. Thus the stage was set for the project that, through the hubris of Robert Stigwood, managed to burn nearly everyone involved in it.

As discussed above, there were two Beatles-related theatrical properties playing before audiences in 1974: Willy Russell's *John, Paul, George, Ringo . . . and Bert* and Tom O'Horgan's *Sgt. Pepper's Lonely Hearts Club Band on the Road*. Both shows had been produced by Stigwood: one had scored rave reviews; the other hadn't. Logic dictated that Stigwood would bring to the big screen the artistically *successful* production—except, he didn't.

Instead, Willy Russell's show was cast aside and *Sgt. Pepper's Lonely Hearts Club Band on the Road* was retooled and given a lavish budget, fleshing out the "plot" and introducing characters not present in the play: among them, Mr. Kite (as played by the venerable George Burns, fresh off his comeback success as the Almighty in *Oh God!*); Mr. Mustard, played by English comedian Frankie Howerd; and, as Dr. Maxwell Edison, the rising-star-of-the-moment, comedian Steve Martin in his big-screen debut. (Though his maniacal, over-the-top performance was a highlight, Martin scarcely acknowledges his role in the film today.)

Also appearing in the film were Billy Preston as the second coming of Sgt. Pepper himself; shock rocker Alice Cooper (on furlough from rehab) as the evil Sun King; and Aerosmith, cannily cast as the Future Villain Band. (KISS had been the first choice, but they wisely declined, instead choosing to film their own project, *KISS Meets the Phantom of the Park*.) On the set, the band butted heads with the film's director after being told that Steven Tyler would be killed in a fistfight by Peter Frampton—a prospect that Tyler and company asserted was extremely dubious, to say the least. Instead, the action was amended to have him die by accident after a fall.

But what of the film itself? *Sgt. Pepper's Lonely Hearts Club Band* falls into the "so bad, it's good" category today, having achieved a semi-respectable camp classic status. At the time of its release, however, it was a travesty beyond measure, grossing barely half of its costs during its brief theatrical run. Critics savaged the film and all involved, calling it "quite possibly the silliest movie ever conceived" (and this was one of the kinder reviews). Having worked his film-producing magic on the back-to-back smashes *Saturday Night Fever* and *Grease*, Stigwood understandably felt that he could make *Pepper* "this generation's *Gone With the Wind*." But the sheer ill-conception of the project was evident from the start, given the *ten* rejected scripts and dismissal of the first director in favor of Michael Schultz (*Cooley High, Car Wash*), who had never directed a musical before.

As the Bee Gees complained later, their casting as the Hendersons—Billy Shears' childhood friends who alongside him now made up the new Sgt. Pepper's LHCB—meant that they were given little to do, since Frampton received the lion's share of the action (including a love interest: newcomer Sandy Farina, whose subsequent film output was exactly zero). Having been suckered in by Stigwood on the premise that *they* were the stars, the Gibbs got a sense of things after filming began and desperately tried to pull out, to no avail. As for Frampton: as one critic noted, the only future Hollywood held for him would have to be in a remake of the *Tammy* series—in the starring role.

To examine the storyline is really sort of beside the point, but for anyone curious: Heartland U.S.A. was an idyllic community where the grandson of the late Sgt. Pepper resided. Pepper's band kept people going during the trauma of numerous wars, but tradition held that so long as his magical instruments stayed in Heartland, humanity would live in eternal bliss. In short order, the band is lured to L.A. by evil record industry people who seduce Billy Shears and his fellows, while in their absence Heartland is overrun by Mean Mr. Mustard and his minions, who steal the magical instruments. Following too many fatuous plot twists to mention, order is restored by Billy Preston (who, for the second time in a Beatle-related movie, performs "Get Back" from a rooftop, this time as a weather vane.) An array of far too many people who should have known not to get anywhere near this film then join the cast to sing the title song—the end.

For a large segment of the public, classic Beatle material performed by anyone but the Fabs themselves is blasphemy; that said, the Gibbs held their own. Robin Gibb's take on "Oh! Darling" is hardly an embarrassment, while the collaboration between the brothers and Frampton on "Getting Better" comes perilously close to jelling. Wisely, none of the leads, except for the Longest-Working Man in Showbiz, George Burns, utters a word of dialogue. (Burns, though, was given leave to recite "Fixing a Hole," complete with soft-shoe routine.)

Perhaps the most interesting part of the film (to contemporary audiences) is the onscreen time capsule seen reprising "Sgt. Pepper's." During the closing theme, scores of contemporary or otherwise unaccounted-for celebs with no connection to the film whatsoever seem to have wandered in at random to join the ensemble. Two were Beatle intimates (Jackie Lomax and Donovan); among the others who rued the day they ever showed up on the set were George Benson, Jack Bruce, Keith Carradine, Carol Channing, Rick Derringer, Leif Garrett, Etta James, John Mayall, Wilson Pickett, Bonnie Raitt, Helen Reddy, Seals and Croft, Connie Stevens, Frankie Valli, big band-era singer Margaret Whiting, and Heart's Wilson sisters.

Stigwood's record label, RSO, was quite eager to broadcast the fact that the soundtrack album had shipped triple platinum (platinum being one million units). Less touted were the triple platinum returns. It should be noted that the recordings contained within the two discs were not really what could be called proper Beatles covers per se, in that they were "performances" cued to onscreen action. George Martin was called in to produce the thankless mess, a prospect he resisted until 1) a big ol' pile of money was waved under his nose—more than he'd ever made on a film project before, and 2) his wife pointed out that if he did turn it down, someone else would do it with possibly less reverence than he—and then how would he live with himself?

So it was that ten years after he had all but abandoned the helm during the "White Album" sessions did George Martin receive his comeuppance, laying down tracks with some Jeff Beck sidemen, plus—curiously—session drummer extraordinaire Bernard Purdie, who infamously soiled his reputation by claiming to have replaced Ringo's drum parts on early Beatles records. Two acts in the film shrewdly passed on Martin's services: Aerosmith and pop soulsters Earth, Wind, and Fire. Perhaps it is not a coincidence that their "Come Together" and "Got to Get You into My Life" respectively are the release's strongest tracks, surviving any taint from the accompanying film. An older but wiser Martin was left to lament his involvement over a glass of claret, hoping that the bridge between himself and Macca hadn't been burned irrevocably.

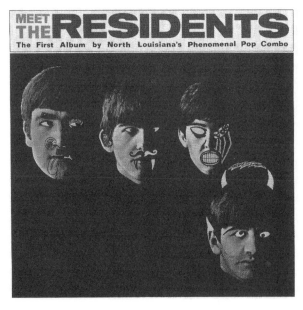

Mystery enshrouds The Residents, an experimental outfit whose 1974 LP, *Meet the Residents*, satirized the Fabs' American debut. Threat of legal action from Capitol forced a re-design while creating an instant rarity.

21

Made Me Wish That I'd Stayed Home

The Ex-Fabs on Television

D uring the 1960s, there was no shortage of Beatles to be found on American television, either as a group in performance mode (*The Ed Sullivan Show, Around the Beatles, Shindig!, The Beatles at Shea Stadium*) or in pairs or singly as interviewees (*The Tonight Show*, as one example). By the time of their breakup, their musical act was largely limited to pre-taped appearances (on shows like the *Smothers Brothers Comedy Hour*), isolating them further from their audience.

During the solo years, the ex-Fabs' TV time crept upward, though less often as performers. Sometimes, talk show appearances led to a song or two, but considering the array of outlets available on American television, it is somewhat surprising that they didn't take full advantage of presenting their music live (ABC's *In Concert*; NBC's *Midnight Special*; CBS's *Don Kirshner's Rock Concert*).

As the former bandmates' individual identities emerged, it was clear that John (usually alongside Yoko) favored forums allowing a platform for expounding his worldviews, with music almost an afterthought. While it isn't surprising that George generally shunned the opportunity to bloviate in public, it is unfortunate that he didn't parlay his 1974 tour into some sort of televised showcase.

Even less explicable was Paul's passing up the opportunities to present Wings, a steadily employed touring act. He did showcase his newest incarnation (by video) to the American public on *The Flip Wilson Show* in 1972, where they were shown performing "Mary Had a Little Lamb" (of all things), but it's his self-named 1973 television special that is most remembered: a bizarre hodgepodge of old-school showbiz that did him no good at all. Not until 1979 did he put together a concert film for television, though by the time it aired, the chance to see Wings play live in America was gone forever.

The rather outré "Gotta Sing, Gotta Dance" number from the *James Paul McCartney* special was actually written for (but never used by) model/actress Twiggy, an aficionado of 1930s Busby Berkley–type musicals.

Not surprisingly, Ringo preferred comedic appearances. At least twice he turned up on network sketch comedy shows; still, while ultimately he was blessed with a full-length comedy special, it came four years too late to do his recording career any good.

John and Yoko on *The Dick Cavett Show*—September 11, 1971; September 24, 1971; May 11, 1972

Nowadays, late-night talk shows bear little resemblance to those of the '60s and '70s. Today's shows are tightly programmed affairs, combining recurring shtick with an endless parade of celebs pushing product. Back in the day, they ran longer (ninety minutes versus the current sixty), with fewer commercials, and offered genuine unscripted conversation, usually without talking points. One master of the medium was Dick Cavett, a former stand-up comedian who'd made a name for himself in the business as a writer for Jack Paar and fellow Nebraskan Johnny Carson. In early 1969, he took over the time slot on ABC formerly occupied by Rat Packer Joey Bishop. Though his ratings scarcely posed a threat to his former employer on NBC, Cavett did manage to carve a niche for himself as television's most erudite talk show host of the day.

Barely a week after stepping off the proverbial boat that landed them in America to stay, the Lennons paid a visit to Cavett's show for an appearance that went so well that the tape was kept rolling. In addition to the initial episode (which aired three days later), leftover material was squirreled away for use in a future broadcast. Cavett possessed a natural rapport with rock stars, something completely unsuggested by his soft-spoken, intellectual manner. (Episodes featuring doomed stars Jimi Hendrix and Janis Joplin, while obvious period pieces, make fascinating viewing today in large part because of his intelligent questioning.) The DVD reissue of the Lennon shows offers a marvelous opportunity to catch John and Yoko in peak form just a year after the Fabs' split.

Cavett's forum proved the ideal setting for the couple. He facilitated their conceptual art leanings with demonstrations framed before Middle America as quirky but harmless fun (for example, when they listened to each other with a stethoscope, or when May Pang and another Lennon-Ono employee came onstage in black bags), all the while engaging in snappy repartee. On this last score, Lennon gave as good as he got, occasionally sending one-liners flying right over his host's head. ("Ella Fitzgerald, dear Watson," John says at one point in response to Cavett's Nigel Bruce impression before explaining that it was a pun on "elementary." Sometimes the reverse was true, as when Cavett facetiously asked Yoko if her "Bottoms" film would be shown at the Cannes film festival.) Better still, Cavett scored points with Yoko's husband by treating her with respect and inclusiveness, stopping short of unctuous sycophancy.

Not unexpectedly, John dominated the conversation with a sort of nervous chatter while Yoko spoke demurely when at all, at least initially. (As with much vintage television viewed today, it's somewhat jarring to observe the casual chain-smoking the couple—but not Cavett—indulged in.) Despite having already met several days before at the Lennons' St. Regis Hotel suite (where Cavett was dragooned into appearing in their *Imagine* video project), the two parties took a while to find a mutual comfort level with each other on camera.

One icebreaker came with an anecdote relating to Betty Rollin, a journalist later known for her breast cancer memoir, *First You Cry*. In response to a question about whether Yoko kept in touch with her classmates at New York's Sarah Lawrence College, John seized the opening to declare that "one of them was a 'snide'." Further elaboration revealed that a rather unflattering depiction of Yoko had appeared in an early 1969 *Look* magazine article—this after Yoko had obligingly cooked her old friend a meal, not long after suffering a miscarriage. Following this setup, John repeatedly burst out with "Betty Rollin's legs!," apparently achieving a measure of revenge. (Poker-faced, Cavett noted that he hadn't noticed anything unusual "when I was married to her.")

Attentive viewers of the DVD will note that, somewhat ahead of accepted protocol, the Lennons squandered nary an opportunity to promote product at every turn, including each of their respective albums, *Imagine* and *Fly*; a Yoko art retrospective; as well as the reissue of her 1964 book, *Grapefruit*. (George dryly mocked their shameless self-promotion when he appeared on the same program weeks later. Shilling the "Happy Xmas" single on their behalf, he noted: "There was one thing they forgot to plug.")

While John and Yoko performed no live music during their 1971 appearance, promo films for "Imagine" (in rough cut form) and Yoko's "Mrs. Lennon" were aired. John later explained that he hadn't had time to put together and rehearse a band, but that "next year" he would be on tour and would play for Cavett then. They also excerpted clips from Yoko's film *Fly*, showing said insect crawling about a woman's nude body, accompanied by some of Yoko's guttural tones (which provoked giggles from the audience), as well as John's *Erection*. (Note: This was *not* the infamous study of John's male member—*that* film was entitled *Self Portrait* and was made around the time, as he himself noted, that he was being "a real prick." No, this film was a time-lapsed view of the construction of London's International Hotel in Kensington, utilizing stills shot by *Abbey Road* cover photographer, the late Iain MacMillan.)

John was as good as his word when he returned with Yoko to Cavett's set the following May, Elephant's Memory in tow. In the eight months since their previous appearance, things had changed—not entirely for the better. Having fallen in with the Rubin-Hoffman crowd, Lennon had made himself a target of the Nixon administration, which was now moving to forcibly eject him from the country. The interview tone was decidedly less jocular than before, as the talk turned to the couple's ongoing persecution, manifested by phone taps and public surveillance. They also discussed the custody fight with Yoko's ex. As Kyoko was currently "whereabouts unknown," Yoko displayed a photo to solicit the public's help in finding her. Perhaps on the advice of network attorneys, ABC censored the image.

Also running afoul of the network was the song that John chose to perform that evening. While Yoko's "We're All Water"—the finale to the newly released *Some Time in New York City* album—raised no eyebrows, John's "Woman Is the Nigger of the World" predictably did. ABC wanted it cut completely from the broadcast on the grounds of "taste," but to his credit, Cavett stood his ground, pointing out the ludicrousness of having a former Beatle on your show and then *not* showing him sing. A clumsy compromise was hammered out, wherein Cavett was forced to tape a pre-performance disclaimer, essentially apologizing for the use of the "N-word" in the song. Ironically, the complaints Cavett received were *not* for John's performance but for the *disclaimer*.

For all his trouble in giving the Lennons a platform, Cavett would himself learn the cost of earning the president's antipathy. Years later, he discovered that not only had the administration been monitoring his program, but he and every single staffer on the show was being audited by the IRS, courtesy of the Nixon administration.

George Harrison on *The Dick Cavett Show*—November 23, 1971

Not to be outdone by the John and Yoko dog and pony show, George appeared on Cavett's program just ten weeks later, offering himself as a TV host's worst nightmare. "There's not much to say these days," he laconically announced at the outset, doubtlessly striking panic into the heart of the normally unflappable Cavett. Of course, he was merely playing up his deadpan image, for once he got going, George found he had *plenty* to talk about on topics ranging from relations with his fellow ex-Fabs to troubles getting the Bangladesh concert album released to drug use among pop stars. But for the moment, he contented himself watching Cavett squirm: "*You* just talk and *I'll* watch."

Just before coming on the set, George sat in as slide player in the group Wonderwheel, fronted by Harrison pal Gary Wright (and also featuring a pre-Foreigner Mick Jones). After performing the very un-"Dreamweaver"-like "Two-Faced Man," the band disappeared behind a curtain and George sat down. It's very telling that he handed over the national exposure on

Cavett's show to an essentially unknown act (who could have used the opportunity) rather than reprise the glory of the Bangladesh concert for himself. So as not to completely disappoint, he allowed a clip of "Bangla-Desh" from the recent concert and one from *Raga*, an Apple Films documentary on Ravi Shankar, to be shown.

Perhaps now having been placed in the Beatle orbit, Cavett seemed more at ease with his guest at the start, a disposition that George was quick to undermine, dismissing American television as a commercial-laden "load of rubbish." While the personalities on display between the Lennon and Harrison shows could not have been more different—George's laid-back cool to John's high-strung hyperactivity—both men shared a gift for candor and quick wit. (As far back as the Hamburg days, outsiders were struck by the barrage of one-liners triggered whenever the group was together.)

By way of making conversation, Cavett invoked the earlier visit from the Lennons, off-handedly mentioning that Yoko had occupied the very chair where George was now seated. Without missing a beat, George leaped up

Prior to George coming out to chat with Dick Cavett, the host recognized the audience member who'd correctly answered the most Beatles trivia questions he'd tossed out. The winner? May Pang.

and gave it a quick exam, drawing his first round of laughter from the audience. One gets the sense in seeing him interact with Cavett that a smile or a laugh was never far beneath the surface of his outwardly inscrutable facade. Also issued on DVD, the program is fascinating for the glimpse it affords of George as others knew him: with TV interviews so rare (he usually submitted to radio or print chats), he's seen "unplugged"—essentially engaged in agendaless and uncontrived conversation, displaying what other forms of expression failed to convey about his dry, self-deprecating manner.

Once the conversation got rolling, George was quite frank in discussing all topics put to him. In response to Cavett's probing, he dismissed any hint of animosity between himself and John, noting that they'd seen each other the night before at *Raga*'s premier. But he did note the suppressive nature, for him at least, of being a Beatle; while not physically "strapped down," he was restricted to a two-song-per-LP quota, resulting in a backlog of material. He also held forth on drug use, specifically disavowing responsibility for turning youth on to bad habits while the press reported this private pursuit. (He cited heroin as an especially dangerous high, unsurprisingly given his proximity to both John Lennon *and* Eric Clapton, users whom he did not identify by name.)

His candor was further displayed when he related to Cavett how, in the process of organizing the distribution of funds raised through the Bangladesh concert, it became difficult to decide which charitable pipeline to use. The American Red Cross was no good, he asserted, because in time of disaster, they distributed funds to affected *white* areas while blacks in need were ignored—or so he'd heard. This damning accusation left Cavett momentarily speechless, though George did point out that he'd heard bad things about *everyone* and that maybe it was best just to do nothing. (He was equally outspoken on the troubles he'd had getting Capitol to distribute the concert album for cost, vowing he'd put it out himself and then company president Bhaskar Menon could sue *him*.)

For the show's last segment, Ravi Shankar—ostensibly the subject of the evening's promotion—came on. Cavett asked him about the apparent link between Indian music and drug use, something decried by both Shankar and George (though the maestro was quick to point out that he didn't hold his protégé *personally* responsible for Western youth's misguided habits). The segment ended with Cavett mentioning the three LP releases the visit was intended to draw attention to: the soundtrack to *Raga*, issued by Apple; Ravi's collaboration with conductor Andre Previn (then married to the Fabs' meditation buddy, Mia Farrow), *Concerto for Sitar and Orchestra*; and the as-yet-unreleased *Concert for Bangla Desh*. Apparently feeling that Cavett hadn't adequately displayed the album jackets, George seized them and made sure they appeared on camera, commenting, "I learned a lot of things from the Lennons."

John and Yoko on *The David Frost Show*—January 13, 1972

Taped just days after the *Free John Sinclair* event in Ann Arbor, this December 1971 David Frost program captured the Lennons in full ideological flower. They'd been hard at work since the release of *Imagine,* composing topical songs on issues they'd taken up since landing in New York City months earlier, all of which ended up immortalized on their ill-fated *Some Time in New York City* album the following spring. The occasion of this broadcast offered the first opportunity outside Crisler Stadium or the Apollo Theater for John to gauge the public's reaction to his new direction.

Frost had enjoyed a casual friendship with the Beatles going back some years; it was on his show that clips of "Hey Jude" and "Revolution" had aired back in 1968, followed by a John and Yoko appearance one year later. Furthermore, he was a host who courted controversy, creating a contrast to most talk shows of the day. He therefore was probably quite pleased to host the Lennons and offer them a public forum to discuss their outspoken views.

Tapings were held in a Broadway theater, with tickets distributed daily. This assured an audience mix of native New Yorkers and tourists, the young and the old. By appearing before an arguably broader range of viewers than Cavett's—one not likely to have been following events in the rock world very closely—John was essentially test marketing his new, overtly political message. Surrounding himself with the likes of Jerry Rubin and David Peel meant that the cachet he might still have possessed as the beloved mop-top who had sung on *The Ed Sullivan Show* nearly eight years before was going to be put to the test.

That test would come after a performance of the newly penned "Attica State," a song commemorating the prison uprising that had occurred in September. After four days of rioting, Governor Nelson Rockefeller had enraged many by approving the use of state troopers to settle the standoff violently, resulting in over forty deaths on both sides. John, accompanied by an acoustic outfit featuring the same merry band of street players that had supported him at the Sinclair event, ran through the tune while one of the group sat behind him tossing paper airplanes into the audience.

No sooner had the performance ended than the trouble began. Obvious shouts of disapproval came from the balcony, catching the attention of Frost and the Lennons as the applause died down. Two of the hecklers, a man and woman—both approximately in their forties—were beckoned down by the host to join them at the front of the stage for a discussion. After a pair of chairs in the front row was vacated, the two were seated. The gist of their beef with the song was that John was "glorifying" criminals, taking their side rather than acknowledging the prison personnel and hostages whose lives had been lost. Not so, John was quick to correct them; his song decried the brutality on *both* sides, claiming the line "forty-three more widowed wives" referred to *all* the casualties.

But the couple didn't buy it. As locals, they were accustomed to the violence of New York life and they were appalled at the slightest sympathy for those whose existence made their every day a trial. "I feel like *I'm* in prison," cried the woman at one point. The man asserted, "You wouldn't be singing about the people who ended up in jail for mugging you!" It was clear that they were not crackpots; they probably spoke for a good portion of the audience, and it's a shame that Frost abandoned his responsibilities as facilitator to manage what might have been an enlightening discussion. Instead, the tone grew increasingly heated, fueled in no small part by Yoko's repeated interruptions of both the couple and her husband to inject quasi-philosophical blather into the proceedings. "Can you say you've never done anything wrong in your life?" she asked rhetorically, seemingly equating jaywalking with assault and battery.

For his part, John attempted to offer a big-picture look at the problem of crime in society, asserting that those behind bars had never had a chance in life. "Only a small minority (of inmates) are actually barmy enough to have to be restrained," he pointed out. "Let's make it human for them while they're in there." In fact, the song contained one pearl of wisdom in its conclusion—"Fear and hatred clouds our judgment / free us all from endless night"—but the insistent chorus proclaiming "We're all mates with Attica State" buried this subtlety, enraging those like the folks plucked from the audience. In the end, John grew weary of defending himself and moved on, singing "John Sinclair" and a snippet of "Luck of the Irish" while Yoko made the case for studio production with an unplugged performance of "Sisters O Sisters."

With that, the Lennons' segment concluded, but not before leaving a departing gift: the national television debut of imminent Apple signing David Peel and the Lower East Side, who performed a little ditty entitled "The Hippie from New York City." The song was a tongue-in-cheek response to country and western star Merle Haggard's "Okie from Muskogee," a 1969 crossover hit. Haggard's song was in fact *a send-up* of reactionary sentiments against the country's youth (despite being embraced by the very people he was parodying), a distinction of which Peel's audience remained largely unaware.

John and Yoko on *The Mike Douglas Show*—February 14–18, 1972

As if the Frost experience hadn't been fulfilling enough, John and Yoko decided one month later to take on a week's worth of afternoon broadcasting time in what is recalled as possibly the most subversive hijacking of a daytime talk show ever. Mike Douglas was a Philadelphia-based television host and onetime big band singer. His show's unique format was built on choosing guests to *co*-host alongside him for the week, allowing them in turn to take up the spotlight and invite guests of their own to appear. Despite his white-bread image as the epitome of establishment entertainment, Douglas was a shrewd operator who sought to enlighten as much as to entertain, hosting for example Martin Luther King, who appeared in 1967 to discuss his opposition to the Vietnam War—heady stuff for what was regarded as a diversion for housewives.

Show producer Michael Krauss—perhaps in response to the David Frost debacle, perhaps not—had the grand idea of inviting the former Fab onto the show as co-host (along with Yoko, naturally). While Douglas was an unabashed Beatles fan, it took some selling for him to accept that the program wouldn't be turned into an avant-garde "happening" or a re-creation of *Live Peace in Toronto*'s second side. John's guest "wish list" also gave Douglas pause: when told that the Lennons wanted to invite the Chicago Seven on, he thought they were kidding. They weren't.

John saw the proposition as a golden opportunity to reach beyond his established fan base and indoctrinate those most in need of, as he saw it, having their eyes opened: the housewives and schoolkids of America (two huge demographics for the afternoon program and, one might assume, a more natural fit for Paul or Ringo). If he could convince them that change was not a scary thing and that the people leading the way toward a more perfect union were not the unwashed, America-hating thugs that the media portrayed them as, it would be an effort well spent.

Douglas wasn't particularly worried about any untoward outbursts blemishing the sanctity of his program—after all, airing the shows on tape (a policy instituted after a 1965 show when Zsa Zsa Gabor called Morey Amsterdam a "son of a bitch" on live TV) would prevent that. A bigger concern was alienating his viewership. Group W, the Westinghouse holding that produced the show, were naturally concerned about skittish advertisers. But a compromise of sorts mollified everyone: John could bring on the likes of Jerry Rubin, Bobby Seale, and George Carlin, but Douglas was given leave for in-show counter-programming with guests of his own, including U.S. Surgeon General Jesse Steinfeld—essentially, a representative of the Nixon administration—as well as old-school comedian Louis Nye. An understanding was reached, not least thanks to the personal rapport established between Lennon and Douglas.

Logistics were also an issue. With John's schedule in flux, five shows fulfilling a week's worth had to be taped one at a time *per week* instead of back to back; a less than ideal situation, as Douglas felt it stymied the momentum. But this was worked through, as was an issue concerning musical airtime. As originally framed,

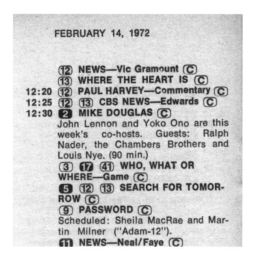

John was to perform three songs and Yoko one, *each day*; in fact when the tape was set to roll, John offered one and Yoko three. Executive producer Woody Fraser had to pull the couple aside and clarify the deal: "[Yoko] did not take kindly to this."

Eventually, the week saw John and Yoko perform two songs apiece: he played both sides of his last solo single, "It's So Hard" and "Imagine," while she performed "Midsummer New York" from *Fly* and "Sisters O Sisters." Together, they sang a lovely (and self-censored) acoustic version of "Luck of the Irish." Video clips from the *Imagine* film also aired: "Oh My Love," "How," "Crippled Inside," and Yoko's "Mrs. Lennon." But the most widely anticipated musical event of the week was the pairing of John with his idol, Chuck Berry.

By most accounts, the two had never met before. But despite his new-found political activism and seeming indifference to the past, John remained an admitted fool for rock and roll generally and Chuck Berry's brand in particular: "When I hear good rock, the caliber of Chuck Berry, I just fall apart—I have no other interest in life." His nervousness at performing with the man who, even more directly than Elvis, had helped chart his musical course was quite evident. As such, their opening number, "Memphis," was plagued by musical miscues over who was singing which vocal line: Chuck sang above where the lead normally fell, while John sang *below* it. Adding to the spirited but ragged merriment was Yoko, who added her banzai bleating on the second verse. (A lesser man would have gotten angry, or otherwise nonverbally cued his disapproval at her marring the historic occasion. But Berry, whose back was to the interloper, merely opened his eyes wide in a sort of "what the hell was *that?*" feigned astonishment.) Their subsequent take on "Johnny B. Goode" (wherein Yoko confined herself to a small drum) went more smoothly.

For Mike Douglas, this was the week's highlight. Less so was his run-in with Jerry Rubin on day two. Normally an affable, open-minded man, Douglas made no bones about his distaste for a guest he disclaimed in his introduction as an invitee of the Lennons. Very quickly he became outraged by Rubin's casual on-air denigration of the president. The sharp exchanges between the two ("Why are you so bitter about a country that affords you the opportunity to get on national television and say these things?" "Because I know what it does to Indians, blacks, and Vietnamese, and I know what it's doing to me for saying these things!" Point: Rubin) threatened to upset the harmony.

Further escalation was arrested by John, who tamped things down by taking "some of the sting out and adding a little humor to help keep things cool." It was John's levelheaded sense of fairness and innate empathy that most impressed Douglas. "He was as joyful a guest as we ever had . . . with a genuine compassion for other people and respect for other philosophies." On the other hand, Douglas clearly had to call upon every ounce of diplomacy he could muster in expressing his regard for Yoko: "She was strange and she could be difficult, but she was a powerful character. . . ." Douglas also reported finding some of her conceptual art pieces baffling.

One was the famous "mend piece," wherein a teacup was broken at the beginning of the week. Each day, it was glued back together, a piece at a time, until by the end of Friday's show it was whole again. Another was the "love calls," which entailed phoning strangers selected at random and telling whoever picked up, "I love you." As aired, the shtick culminated with a woman from Seattle thanking guest Nye for his call ("and you have a nice day!"), but according to the show's bandleader, Joe Darnell, it took *many* such calls to find recipients who didn't hang up or utter an expletive. By the end of the week, Douglas found himself wondering what *was* and *wasn't* art by the Lennons' standards. Describing a made-to-order dressing room the couple used while on set that was "trashed beyond recognition" by the taping's end, he later noted: "It may have been one of those 'performance art' things and we just didn't get it."

Among other guests invited onto the show were consumer advocate Ralph Nader, who discussed politics (and was urged by John to run for president); the gospel-soul group the Chambers Brothers ("Time Has Come Today"), who performed a pair of stirring songs on the first day; Chicago Seven defendant and Black Panther leader Bobby Seale, who relieved Douglas by coming off as an eminently levelheaded and articulate spokesperson for neighborhood self-empowerment; and comedian George Carlin.

Just completing his transformation from suit-and-tie, Brylcreemed, rather conventional coffeehouse comedian to denim-clad, ponytailed, bearded counterculture darling, he'd guested on the Douglas show before and thus was a known quantity. His album *AM/FM* had just been released; a year later it would earn him a Grammy.

For all the airtime given the Lennons, their actual talk time was limited within the mix of other guests and music, including their host's. (Douglas kicked off the week singing "Michelle," a Paul song, and followed it on Tuesday by performing "With a Little Help," a *largely*-Paul song. That same day, Jerry Rubin guested; the next day, as though making a musical retort, Mike opened with "I Whistle a Happy Tune" from *The King and I.* He abandoned the Lennon-McCartney songbook thereafter.) But the studio's small confines forced intimacy, with the public seated even closer to the stage than in other television forums. John and Yoko were close enough to look the audience in the eye, an element to the proceedings that John, for all his nervousness, seemed to thrive on.

The historic week of shows garnered Douglas higher-than-usual ratings as thousands of new viewers tuned in, including the young-adult demographic that had largely eluded him thus far. (He would report getting the thumbs-up when out in public from people who wouldn't have given him the time of day before the Lennons' visit.) For John, the experiment showed that presenting his message in a friendly setting and balancing his challenging pronouncements with lightness could be an effective way to reach people on their own terms. He promised Douglas that he and Yoko would return one day.

In the fall of 1980, Douglas renewed the invitation upon John's resumption of musical activity. Though at first agreeing, John had to beg off when work on *Double Fantasy* commanded more time than he'd planned. He promised that in December, when Douglas would be broadcasting from Hawaii, that he'd bring the family and make a return visit.

James Paul McCartney—April 16, 1973

If one judges Paul McCartney's first excursion into prime-time entertainment as the out-of-court settlement that it was, then one can easily overlook its many lapses into irretrievably anti-rock schlock. But it was Paul's name, not Wings', on the resulting "special," begging the question: was the show intended to promote the new act, or simply to indulge Macca's all-around entertainer ambitions? If the latter, *James Paul McCartney* goes a long way toward explaining why the Beatles *had* to break up.

Each of Paul's former bandmates had, by this time, taken on far more serious (or at least artier) film projects, ranging from John's *Imagine* long-form video to Ringo's work in *Blindman* and *That'll Be the Day* to George's behind-the-scenes work on the *Concert for Bangla Desh* film, presaging his future pursuits as a producer. Though he would eventually produce several Wings documentaries, released (*Wings over the World, Rock Show, Wingspan*) and unreleased (*One Hand Clapping*), as well as a slew of music videos, with *James Paul McCartney* Paul was making his first try at a major TV project outside of the Beatles.

If small screen entertainment wasn't enough, Beatle fans could take in this latter-day edition of *The Beatles: Away with Words.* Boasting dazzling visuals and a world class sound system, the multimedia roadshow wowed audiences across America in the late seventies.

Being produced for the boob tube necessarily entailed a certain amount of recalibrating one's sights to reach the targeted audience. But the show seemed to deliberately ignore Paul's existing rock audience, seeking instead to reach either prepubescent females or adults well past the age of buying Beatles records. *James Paul McCartney* offered something for everyone *but* readers of *Rolling Stone* and *Crawdaddy*: pastoral interludes, a Liverpool travelogue, pub sing-alongs, and a song-and-dance number better suited to a seniors' cruise ship than to a thirty year-old rock icon whose peers were issuing some of their best work. Only near the end does the show allow us a glimpse into Wings' fast-developing stage act that, alas, falls short of the heights they would reach three years on.

Not all of the blame can be laid at Paul's feet. The show was produced and directed by a couple of television veterans: Dwight Hemion, whose career had actually included some well-received productions (Frank Sinatra's *A Man and His Music* specials), and Gary Smith, an award-winning director whose work typically shunned anything remotely cutting-edge, encompassing acts like Petula Clark, Burt Bacharach, and Steve and Eydie. That the resulting McCartney showcase resembled much of the era's typical low- to middlebrow fare is therefore not surprising.

Few of Paul's truly outstanding compositions were properly presented. "Uncle Albert," offered up in a bizarre sequence involving white-collar workers, actually stopped short just at the most interesting part: the "Admiral Halsey" segment. "Mary Had a Little Lamb," on the other hand, is shown in all its somnambulant glory. Paul and Linda were given a vignette that served to remind us of their respective pasts: his as an accomplished tune-smith ("Blackbird," "Heart of the Country," the not-yet-issued "Bluebird," "Michelle") and hers (while looking hotter than she typically allowed herself to) as an adoring shutterbug. "Live and Let Die," a worthy new composition, is given its own "let's go the movies" segment that climaxes with a stock villain (fresh from tying the ingénue to the train tracks, no doubt) blowing up Paul's piano. Really.

Before descending into an all-too-cute segment depicting the English public butchering Beatles songs, the show invited viewers into a "typical" Liverpool pub. Within the smoke can be spotted Gerry Marsden ("and here I'll stay"), as well as Paul's dad. Once Macca's capacity for glad-handing is hammered home, the room is taken over by glass-wielding patrons laying waste to "Pack Up Your Troubles in Your Old Kit Bag"—the very sort of entertainment that the Beatles had been invented to eradicate. Just when one thinks things have bottomed out, the floor drops further, with a faux Busby Berkeley musical number, "Gotta Sing, Gotta Dance." Complete with hermaphroditic tap dancers, canned applause, and falling confetti, it's the sort of cringe-inducing milieu that would have killed a lesser talent's career dead.

By the time the in-concert climax arrives, it's too late. "The Mess" tries mightily to raise the adrenaline level but merely comes off as sub–bar band noisemaking. "Maybe I'm Amazed" hadn't yet been honed to its apex, as it would be by the time of *Wings Over America*, though it tries. Even the usually reliable "Long Tall Sally" seems forced, as though the band were auditioning for a reality talent show. If this segment was intended to truly show off what Wings could do, then the band must surely have been conscious of their shortcomings alongside virtually any other recording act of the day. When Henry McCullough buries his head in his hands during the solo finale of "Yesterday," one feels his pain.

John Lennon on *Tomorrow*—April 28, 1975

Television viewers on this night were in for a treat: a post-Beatles twofer. At 8 p.m., those with their sets tuned to NBC saw the penultimate episode of the briefly revived *Smothers Brothers Show*, starring a beardless Ringo singing his latest single, "No No Song," live. (At the end of the performance/skit, he was "arrested" by a cop played by one Bob Einstein, real-life brother of comedian Albert Brooks and known better as Super Dave Osborne.) Hours later, late-night viewers of the same network could catch John's last-ever television interview on *Tomorrow*.

Commencing in 1973, this late-night talk show (so named as the third of NBC's trio of weekday staples, following *The Today Show* and *The Tonight Show*) was hosted by the affable Tom Snyder. His distinctive laugh, garrulous manner, chain-smoking, and ability to switch from giddy to grave on a dime made him a easy target for parody, notably by Dan Aykroyd on *Saturday Night Live*. Despite being frequently uninformed (on this evening, for instance, he thought that Ringo's "Oh My My" was an oldies remake), he nonetheless managed to elicit often-candid responses from his guests.

This evening's interview, taped on April 7, was the first in memory that didn't feature Yoko at John's side, although they were reunited and with child at the time. In direct contrast to his habit, John didn't have a project to push. (Though his appearance onstage for the Lew Grade tribute—his last ever—was recorded on April 18, it would not air in America till June 13). Instead, the ninety minutes were devoted to a freewheeling discussion, largely on the Beatles but also touching on his battle with the INS.

Immediately noticeable was John's low-key demeanor. Unlike other television appearances discussed in this chapter, Lennon was notably subdued; gone was the manic persona he'd projected in his radio appearances in recent months, as he attempted to answer Snyder's questions thoughtfully (whenever allowed to without disruption), seemingly on guard against saying anything that could be used against him later. He did speak frankly about sex and drugs, topics the host seemed unduly fascinated with, as well as his relations with the other ex-Fabs. (Conspicuously absent was any talk of the "Lost Weekend" or his relationship with May Pang.)

For the final segment, attorney Leon Wildes came on and discussed Lennon's status in the immigration case. As elsewhere throughout the interview, it's evident that Snyder has little familiarity with the details, though in giving Lennon and Wildes this platform to air their side of things, he probably helped them out a great deal. No music was performed, and were it not for the fact that John never again gave a televised interview, this particular one would probably draw little notice. But it's all we have; the evening after John's death, Snyder reran it, also giving airtime to Jack Douglas and rock journalist Lisa Robinson.

It's now available on DVD, along with interviews with Paul and Ringo. The latter's interview came in 1981 to promote *Stop and Smell the Roses*, while Paul's was recorded in December 1979 during Wings' final tour, just after the Cincinnati Who concert tragedy, which took the lives of eleven fans. (Macca weighed in on the need for more entrances to stadiums.) Neither interview is nearly as interesting as John's, though each contains a music video: "Spin It On" from Wings and Ringo's "Wrack My Brain," penned by George.

A Salute to the Beatles—May 21, 1975

Largely forgotten today, this sixty-minute special was the closest thing fans had to a *Beatles Anthology*-style documentary during the '70s. Hosted by David Frost for ABC's late-night *Wide World of Entertainment*, the show was in some ways a blueprint for the Rutles film that followed three years later, with Eric Idle aping Frost's mannerisms and speech pattern to a T. Clearly put together on a tiny budget (the show was populated with archival news footage and very little actual Beatles music beyond *A Hard Day's Night* clips), it nonetheless offered a modicum of satiation to Fab-starved audiences longing to revisit their past or younger viewers for whom the group existed only on record or in books.

The documentary traced the band's trajectory nearly to day one, with loads of newsreel footage depicting the first wave of Beatlemania in England in full bloom. (Its airing of the now-familiar clip of their 1962 Cavern Club performance of "Some Other Guy" may well have been the first time America audiences saw the Fabs this early on.) All of the career milestones are enumerated—their conquering of America (with a clip from the Beatles'

Saturday morning cartoon thrown in), the MBEs, the "bigger than Jesus" flap—while the death of Brian Epstein portends their eventual decline and breakup. (Oddly, their musical achievements seem to be completely ignored—apparently fitting news footage was hard to come by.)

An astonishingly youthful-looking George Martin supplied background discussion throughout via interview segments, as did Derek Taylor, Peter Brown, and the doomed Mal Evans (who claimed, rather bizarrely, that Paul had told him that "Let It Be" was inspired by *him*—instead of "Mother Mary," the song might have evoked "Brother Malcolm." His upcoming memoir was mentioned, then titled *200 Miles to Go*).

The group's infatuation with the Maharishi and the rise and fall of Apple were shown. The special then devoted time to the "now" (at least a couple of years out of date), showing them as accomplished individuals in their post-Beatles careers: Paul was seen rehearsing Wings ("Give Ireland Back to the Irish," from 1972) while John was depicted being interviewed by future confidant Elliot Mintz. A clip from 1973's *That'll Be the Day* framed Ringo's solo years in terms of a film career, not a musical one, while George was completely slighted, with no clips of his music or recent tour.

The special ended with a 1964 film (aired in America in early 1965) of the Fabs on *Shindig!* performing "Boys," gently playing upon the nostalgia

Ringo Starr, George Harrison and Mark Twain!

9PM TONIGHT!
"RINGO"
Art Carney
Vincent Price
Carrie Fisher
Angie Dickinson
George narrates Ringo's version of Twain's "The Prince and the Pauper"— featuring Ringo's Beatle and post-Beatle hits!

MUSICAL SPECIAL!

2, 3, 41

already felt for the innocent days of the '60s. While staggeringly incomplete and almost naïve in its approach to its subjects, *A Salute to the Beatles* was charming as an early expression of post-Beatles longing. A DVD reissue might not make much business sense, but would certainly be appreciated as a quaint period piece.

Ringo (The "Ognir Rrats" Special)—April 26, 1978

High hopes were held by NBC for their one shot at showcasing a former Beatle in a star-studded one-hour prime-time special. To begin with, there was a new album of product tied in, Ringo's Portrait debut, *Bad Boy.* The producers managed to rope in some of the biggest names of the day to costar. Also, Ringo—bolstered by the participation of George, who appeared as the show's narrator—dutifully hit the promotional trail, giving airtime to Phil Donahue and Mike Douglas as well as print interviews. In the end, however, the show failed to find its audience, finishing near the bottom in the prime-time ratings—ironically, just as *The Rutles* had done one month earlier. The best analysis seemed to be that, in the face of disco, punk, and a *Charlie's Angels* rerun, Ringo's time as front-page news had passed.

The story, a melding of *The Prince and the Pauper* and *A Hard Day's Night*, centered on one Ognir Rrats, a luckless scruff struggling to make a living in Los Angeles peddling maps of the stars' homes to tourists ("Watch where they live and see how they died"). Bullied by neighborhood toughs as well as an abusive father (played with scene-stealing panache by comic actor Art Carney), Ognir found the one bright spot in his life to be his devoted girlfriend, Marquine, played by Carrie Fisher. (The twenty-one-year-old was fresh off the heels of *Star Wars* and just months away from the infamous made-for-TV *Star Wars Holiday Special.*) Ognir laments the lot he's been given while daydreaming of a starry future.

Meanwhile, superstar singer/drummer Ringo Starr (impersonated with uncanny precision by Richard Starkey) is, as his Beatle counterpart was fourteen years earlier, chafing at the restrictions that stardom has placed upon him. Television's John Ritter, riding high at the time with *Three's Company*, plays Starr's slave-driving manager, hustling him from one chore to another with no time off in between. A chance encounter between Starr and Rrats leads inescapably to the two switching identities ("for just a few hours") with predictable complications ensuing.

As expected, Ringo acquitted himself well in the dual role. (The effect of the two look-alikes interacting was seamless; technology had greatly improved in the dozen years since *The Patty Duke Show* aired.) The show's wry comedy suited him far better than his next major role, 1981's broad, lowbrow *Caveman*. Providing the story's setup, George comes off as a slightly Pythonized version of himself—unsurprisingly, given his affinity for the British comedy troupe. When questioned at the end about the story's hackneyed plot, he deadpans, "What do you want from me? . . . I'm not Mark Twain."

Also populating the cast were faces familiar to anyone alive in 1978. Angie Dickinson, star of NBC's *Police Woman* (as Sgt. "Pepper" Anderson) reprised her role, busting Ringo for grand theft auto. Gothic horror icon Vincent Price portrayed a creepy shrink, Dr. Nancy, hired by Marty Flash (Ritter) to cure "Ringo" of his delusion that he's really Ognir. Also seen in a brief cameo (as a nun) was Lois January, a veteran B-movie actress. Despite her unfamiliar name, millions of viewers of 1939's *The Wizard of Oz* know her face: she's the heavily rouged Emerald City woman seen near the end, whose cat draws Toto's attention and leads to Dorothy being stranded.

Appearing as himself was Mike Douglas. When Ognir finds himself unexpectedly dragged onto Douglas's show—live—he proceeds to unnerve the host while delivering a Pete Best–like assault on the drum kit. (Lamented the real Ringo, watching from Ognir's house: "He's going to ruin my reputation!") Ringo had appeared on Douglas's real-life show the week before in a bit of cross-promotion that sadly failed to generate many additional viewers. That, and an appearance on *Phil Donahue* that aired the same day, marked the first solo sit-down television interviews Ringo had done, underscoring the promotional commitment being poured into both his new album and the TV special.

Just by virtue of the sheer number of tunes squeezed into the show's fifty-two minutes, *Ringo* was calculated to delight any fan. He's shown performing (briefly) "I'm the Greatest" in the studio, as well as a snippet of "A Dose of Rock and Roll." "It Don't Come Easy" is heard in the background at one point, while George Martin's "Yellow Submarine in Pepperland" was utilized to represent *that* warhorse during an elaborate dance sequence. (The only Ringo-ism missing was Martin's instrumental take on "This Boy.") Carrie Fisher added sultry vocal support on a duet of "You're Sixteen," complete with an animated visual, while "With a Little Help" was performed complete with state-of-the-art visual effects (e.g., dry ice).

The story's climax came with a satellite broadcast concert finale, featuring Ringo's Roadside Attraction in musical support: Keith Allison, Dee Murray, Dr. John, and Lon Van Eaton. Three *Bad Boy* numbers were performed: "Heart on My Sleeve," "Hard Times," and—what was described as "Ringo's 'My Way'"—"A Man Like Me." The first two songs particularly benefited from the live setting, possessing an edgy grit absent on the record.

If

'The Birth of the Beatles'

In the wake of 1979's highly successful TV biopic *Elvis*, directed by John Carpenter and starring Kurt Russell, Dick Clark Productions quickly produced a follow-up on (naturally) the Beatles. Focusing on their early years, *Birth of the Beatles* credited Pete Best as a consultant (while using little actual input from him).

outtakes from this sequence exist, they could make for excellent bonus material on a DVD reissue.

Ringo was/is an entertaining effort and not the turkey some claim it is. Given the array of talent involved, it could hardly be otherwise. But it was definitely out of time, as so much of Starr's post-Apple work was. Had his career caught fire earlier in the decade—say, had he and Richard Perry gotten together in 1971 instead of 1973—his path might have achieved a higher trajectory and the accompanying work might have reached a wider audience. Reissuing this film on DVD would be a good start toward reassessing a body of work that wasn't as unremittingly awful as *Rolling Stone* would have had you believe.

Wings over the World—March 16, 1979

Not to be confused with *Rockshow* (1980), a straightforward concert film, this made-for-television look back at the 1976 tour was actually as much a Wings documentary as a performance vehicle. Though over half a million people had the privilege of witnessing the group at the zenith of their powers onstage that year, millions more did not. When the expected victory lap did not materialize in 1977, anticipation for the inevitable film version was heightened.

Soon after the tour ended, Paul set to work on producing the vinyl iteration of the Wings Over America shows, getting the three-record set on store shelves by year's end. It took more time, however, to get the documentary fully prepared, owing in large part to his dissatisfaction with the sound. He and Chris Thomas spent a considerable amount of time in post-production attempting to remedy the problems to their satisfaction. By the time they'd finished and the film was ready for broadcast, a couple of years had passed. Hence, in the spring of 1979, CBS aired a state-of-the-art presentation of a band that no longer existed.

That aside, *Wings over the World* is a fascinating document, both of the tour and of Macca and company. Along with numerous (albeit shortened) performance clips shot at Seattle's Kingdome on June 10, 1976, footage from some 1975 shows (Scotland and Australia) was thrown in, mostly as passing vignettes that included plenty of backstage goings-on. Paul is shown as insufferably hammy (as was to be expected), but also as a man very much in command of his environment and the consummate professional throughout. Any fan watching this film today will immediately be struck by how rock solid the playing—horn section and all—was, and by the crowd-pleasing power, even today, of Paul's presentation, complete with lasers and flash pots.

Also of interest are the archival clips depicting Wings' early rehearsals. Clearly, Paul was driving home the point of how far his band had come in four years from rough renditions of "Lucille" to fully integrated performances of new hits like "Silly Love Songs." Not altogether unexpectedly, the band's individual members are afforded little opportunity to shine in the spotlight, although Denny gets his star turn on "Go Now." (Their *versatility* is displayed, as Laine and McCulloch are shown alternating on piano, bass, and even marching tom-tom.)

The golden era of concertgoing is also glimpsed, with footage of thousands lined up outside the Kingdome hours before show time, some having camped out overnight. Elsewhere, numerous celebs, including Micky Dolenz, Chevy Chase, and Jack Nicholson (with Anjelica Huston) are seen arriving for the final show of the North American tour at the Forum in L.A. (As an added attraction, Ringo makes a cameo appearance backstage, clowning it up with Paul before Wings head back out on stage to encore with "Soily.")

Though currently unavailable as a *legitimate* release, *Wings over the World* is worth seeing, as a souvenir of both a band and an era. While Paul has shown a decided reticence toward reissuing much of anything depicting his post-Beatles incarnation, this document would go a long way toward reminding the public of his considerable achievements. It's a keeper.

22

No Matter Where You Roam, Know Our Love Is True

1977

With John's low profile being both unexpected and seemingly out of character, it wouldn't have taken much for conspiratorially minded Beatles fans to look for a meaning beyond his simple statement that he was intending to take time off to raise his son. The "answer," at least to some, was given widespread credence in early 1977 when disc jockeys and journalists began to pick up on the "clues" littering an LP issued the previous summer on Capitol. Bearing a slightly psychedelic cover, it was credited to Klaatu and bore no other crediting whatsoever.

Inside the jacket was a collection of tunes bearing a superficial resemblance to the Fabs' work circa 1967—some more than others. Vocally, the songs were Beatlesque in only the vaguest of ways, but still, it was enough for fans of a certain disposition to embrace the biggest Beatle hoax since Paul had shuffled off this mortal coil. That so many would embrace the meme that the Beatles had secretly reunited and were issuing an album under a pseudonym seems ridiculous now, as it did to most then. But coming off a year that saw so much pressure for the four to get back together, that an otherwise anonymous act with pop leanings would be mistaken for the Fabs wasn't entirely beyond reason—was it?

(As for the hapless trio of Canadian studio musicians who in no way were responsible for spreading the mass delusion, the story rebounded against them once the truth came out, and their return to obscurity thereafter was assured.)

The year began with word of a settlement being reached in the ongoing lawsuit between Allen Klein and Apple. Though viewed as a victory for the ex-Fabs in that they'd freed themselves of ABKCO's tentacles, the outcome left the McCartneys less impressed, since some of the payout owed to Klein

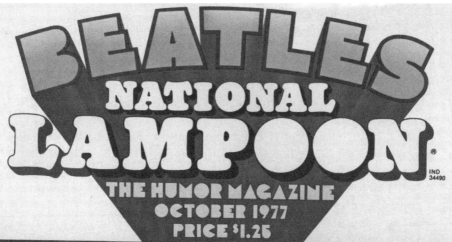

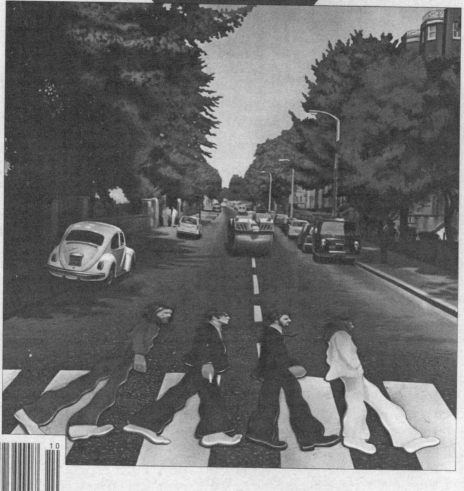

No icon was too big to savage in the pages of *National Lampoon*, including the Beatles.
In the October 1977 issue, no avenue of ridicule was left unexplored.

came from monies generated by Paul—who hadn't even accepted the managerial arrangement in the first place. Still, it seemed as though yet one more obstruction to the four making music together was gone. (As for Klein, in October he was indicted for income tax evasion.)

Rock's biggest story of 1977 was the death of Elvis in August. (Ringo's former sidekick, Marc Bolan, was killed in a car wreck a month later.) Conversely, it was the quietest year of the decade in ex-Fab terms, so far as new material went. John, of course, had taken his leave of the business. George, after a flurry of activity promoting *Thirty-Three & 1/3* upon its release, composed exactly no new songs during the entire year, instead taking a break of his own. He and Olivia did some traveling, first to India, then to Mexico; later, they would join up with Ringo in Monte Carlo in time for the Grand Prix. George had become quite an aficionado of car racing, particularly Formula One. Jackie Stewart, perhaps the best known of the champion racers on this side of the Atlantic, would later tell of how astonished he was at the depth of knowledge the ex-Beatle possessed on racing. (He in turn would impress George with his ability to recite, chapter and verse, every detail of the Beatles' career.)

After a world tour that began in late 1975, climaxed across America in spring 1976, and ended in late summer in the U.K., Paul too was ready for a well-deserved break. Ever the workaholic, he didn't refrain from recording, just from touring and releasing albums. A number of projects that had been sitting around saw issue during this time, including Thrillington, the instrumental treatment of *Ram* that he'd commissioned back in 1971. (Having gone to a great deal of trouble to actually plant press releases detailing the comings and goings of socialite/bandleader Percy "Thrills" Thrillington—a man who never was—he quietly shelved the whole curious enterprise when he decided to form Wings instead.) Another was the collection of Buddy Holly songs that he'd produced for Denny Laine, called *Holly Days*. Paul had acquired the publishing to Holly's work from producer Norman Petty; he also had instituted a weeklong celebration of the late singer's music during the first week of September, commemorating Holly's birthday. Also released after years of being hinted at was Linda's first solo track, "Seaside Woman," a pop-reggae tune cut years before. Coinciding with the work slowdown was news that Linda was with child; Paul's first son, James, was born in September.

Only Ringo recorded and issued an album that year; in retrospect, perhaps he should have followed the prevailing trend and taken a break himself. Released in September, *Ringo the 4th* jarred many fans with its departure from his established pattern of constructing long-players with the assistance of a platoon of guests and ex-bandmates. But, given the underperformance of his previous effort, a paradigm shift was deemed necessary. The only trouble was, with the move away from Starr's musical roots and embrace of current tastes, the results not only didn't jell, but came off to many fans as a personal affront and a sellout. The absolute nadir of Ringo's recording career came during this period, which saw his fortunes sink startlingly low.

Still, he did continue to find film work, though of decidedly uneven quality. This year's projects included a role in the camp comedy *Sextette* as one of aging '30s film star Mae West's ex-husbands. (Costarring Keith Moon, Alice Cooper, and a youngish Timothy Dalton, the movie was released to general displeasure the following year.) More satisfying was his appearance as himself in *The Kids Are Alright*, a fan-directed documentary on the Who. Goblet in hand, Ringo appeared on camera alongside the group's rapidly deteriorating drummer in scenes filmed in Malibu. (A fascinating outtake from the film—sans Ringo—depicted Moon taking a stab at—or perhaps a bludgeon to—the Beatles' "I Saw Her Standing There.")

Ringo also busied himself by taking on his first project marketed more or less exclusively to kids. *Scouse the Mouse*, conceived by actor Donald Pleasence, told the tale of a Liverpool rodent who travels to America in pursuit of a showbiz career. A sort of antecedent of *An American Tail*, the story made it only as far as the stage, as the planned animated film was never made. The album was issued in England by year's end (though not here), featuring the drummer crooning such tunes as "Living in the Pet Shop" and "A Mouse Like Me." As someone who one day would tackle the role of Mr. Conductor on *Shining Time Station* (a Thomas the Tank-Engine spinoff), Ringo found in Scouse an early clue to his new direction.

Despite the almost total lack of musical output from the ex-Fabs in 1977, the year was hardly a total loss for fans. Indeed, the former collective was represented by two much-anticipated releases of previously unheard material—a boon that would never again be repeated until the issue of the first Anthology set in 1995. The first came with concert recordings long known to exist: the Hollywood Bowl shows. The 1964 date had been bootlegged as early as 1971, when a copy leaked out after Phil Spector gave it a listen (at Apple's request) to determine whether it was salvageable. (Not previously booted were the 1965 shows, featuring a slightly different set list.)

The resulting composite, *The Beatles at the Hollywood Bowl*, proved to be exactly what the fans desired, being both a new listening experience and a graphic depiction of times gone by, when the world seemed a bit more innocent. The album jumped on the charts and reached #2 in America. More astonishing was its performance in the mother country, where it made it to the very top. England was in the throes of punk in 1977, with acts like the Sex Pistols, the Damned, the

8XT-11542

PROGRAM 1
Calling Occupants
True Life Hero (part 1)
PROGRAM 2
True Life Hero (concl.)
Little Neutrino

℗ 1976 Capitol Records, Inc.

PROGRAM 3
Sub-Rosa Subway
California Jam
Doctor Marvello (part 1)
PROGRAM 4
Doctor Marvello (concl.)
Anus Of Uranus
Sir Bodsworth Rugglesby III

ALL RIGHTS RESERVED.
UNAUTHORIZED DUPLICATION IS A VIOLATION OF APPLICABLE LAWS

EIGHT-TRACK CARTRIDGE MUST NOT BE LEFT EXPOSED TO DIRECT
SUNLIGHT. REMOVE FROM PLAYER WHEN NOT IN USE.
CARTRIDGE 3¾ MANUFACTURED BY CAPITOL RECORDS, INC.,
A SUBSIDIARY OF CAPITOL INDUSTRIES-EMI,
IPS INC., HOLLYWOOD AND VINE STREETS.
HOLLYWOOD, CALIFORNIA. FACTORIES: LOS ANGELES, CALIFORNIA; JACKSONVILLE,
ILLINOIS; WINCHESTER, VIRGINIA. PRINTED IN U.S.A.
Capitol®

Though perhaps the British knew better ("Deaf idiot journalist starts Beatle rumour," ran the headline in *New Musical Express*), American DJs fanned the "Klaatu-is-the-Beatles" flames while Capitol Records maintained a respectful silence.

Stranglers, and the Clash dominating the youth culture. That recordings made over a decade before could captivate so many when current tastes lay in another direction was amazing, though when one considers the release from a purely musical perspective, the trashing drums, vocal screams, and warp-speed tempos had much in common with the music of the day.

Even more "punk" was the other unreleased live set issued almost simultaneously. Onetime Beatles "manager" Allan Williams had uncovered a reel-to-reel recording made in Hamburg of the group at the tail end of their club days; its actual date, if Williams knew it, he deemed it in his interest to keep secret for proprietary reasons. (If it could be proved that the tapes had been made after the group signed with EMI in 1962—as was the case—then Williams would have no ownership claim.) Word of the tapes' existence had been bandied about in the press at least as far back as 1973 (Williams tried to peddle them to George, who offered him uncut rubies from an Indian mine in exchange for them; Williams rebuffed the offer but took the rubies anyway), but it seems that only on the eve of their release as a double album on Lingasong did EMI finally take notice and go to court to get an injunction, to no avail.

The court ruled that EMI had protested too little, too late, and in May, *Live! at the Star-Club in Hamburg, Germany, 1962* hit stores. Fans at last got to hear with their own ears what the excitement was about regarding the Beatles' fabled club days. Though the sound left much to be desired, the energy came through loud and clear, as did the freewheeling nature of the sets. (Though regarded as considerably tidied up one year after the advent of Brian Epstein, the band captured here was still a long way off from the neatly suited, unison-bowing act seen on the Ed Sullivan Show fourteen months later.) Indeed, with their raucous guitars, freeform starts and stops, and hyperkinetic drumming, the Star Club tapes were revelatory, showcasing a band not very far removed from the youth of England currently banging away in clubs, both in feel and in attitude.

The bounty of "new" Beatle product hadn't yet been played out with the twin live sets. In October, EMI issued what amounted to a companion album to the previous year's rocker collection: a double-album repackaging of Beatles ballads entitled *Love Songs*. Operating with little sign of slowing down reissue-wise, the set was a deliberate calculation for the upcoming Christmas market, featuring a dignified faux-leather, gold-embossed gatefold and a calligraphed libretto inside. Despite much marketing muscle expended to push the package, sales fizzled, and the album peaked at #24. Its relative "failure" gave EMI pause, suggesting that perhaps the public was not going to be blindly accepting of just any old attempt to resell them what they already owned. (Plans to issue "Girl," backed with "You're Going to Lose That Girl," as a single were canceled.)

One could attempt to make the connection between the taste being cultivated for a Beatles concert experience by this year's two live sets and the stunning success on Broadway of the first full-scale attempt at a re-creation of the group in performance mode, but that might be stretching things a bit. It was merely a matter of good timing that *Beatlemania* opened on Broadway in May, causing an immediate sensation. Billed as "Not the Beatles, but an incredible simulation" (lest anyone think otherwise), the show offered the novelty of experiencing the Fabs as they might have staged some of their more complex music, had they never stopped touring. It ran for another two years before being shut down by an injunction by the group themselves, who weren't particularly thrilled at seeing their brand co-opted—just in case they might want to use it again themselves.

On the subject of live performances, John Lennon, all but officially retired, spent much of the summer in Japan, after studying the language at his local Berlitz school at Rockefeller Center. All later claims to the contrary, his muse was alive and well, with compositions flowing sporadically from his pen, such as the one composed in the Land of the Rising Sun celebrating his newfound ability to come and go internationally as he pleased: "Free as a Bird." The occasion of his last public performance came quite serendipitously, according to Elliot Mintz, who joined the Lennons on their trip. In their rather spacious suite in the Hotel Okura, John happened to be singing "Jealous Guy," accompanying himself on guitar, when a Japanese couple entered the room, apparently by accident, and seated themselves. They only departed after several minutes, when no one arrived to take their drink order while John continued his performance. Little could they have known what they were witnessing.

Paul had been doing some recording for the next Wings release throughout the year, beginning in the spring. Given his penchant for exotic locales, this time out he set up the band on a yacht in the British Virgin Islands. The relaxed, vacation-like setting proved well suited to Linda in her pregnancy, while likewise fostering an atmosphere conducive to continuous partying for Jimmy McCulloch. Long a simmering issue, things finally came to a head, and in September the guitarist turned in his notice. Drummer Joe English followed suit not long after, once again reducing Wings to a trio. And, just as had occurred the last time Macca found himself in similar straits, a blockbuster record lay straight ahead.

23

I Won't Do You No Harm

The Best Unsung John

N owadays, the Lennon legend looms large. Given the nature of his passing, Yoko's stirring of the pot with periodic reissues and product, and the attraction of his rebellious spirit resonating with each successive generation, that iconic status isn't likely to fade anytime soon. Worth noting, however, is that in his own lifetime, John wasn't always accorded the benefit of doubt, even by some of his biggest fans. The political activism and self-referential slant that typified his work grew tiresome to some, so much so that even some of his most enthusiastic boosters were ready to call BS on new releases. (*Rolling Stone*'s Jon Landau, attempting to make sense of *Mind Games*, suggested that "perhaps Lennon's didacticism, preaching and banality are part of the mind game of the album's title.")

All hyperbolic overkill aside, even the most ill-conceived efforts had some gems amid the dross. This and the three similar chapters to follow will offer a look at each ex-Fab and some overlooked tracks that tended to be overshadowed by either the big singles that their parent albums spawned or the overall perception of mediocrity associated with a particular release. These songs offer proof that, no matter how flawed in execution or how forgotten by radio station programmers the balance of an LP might be, each former Beatle could usually be counted on to deliver at least a few gems per release. (As criteria for narrowing things down, no singles are included.)

"New York City"

It's probably safe to say that John did himself no favors by setting the table for the *Some Time in New York City* release by issuing "Woman Is the Nigger of the World" as an advance single. The crossing-the-line use of such an incendiary word, no matter how worthy the sentiment, proved too alienating to the very allies he needed: radio station programmers, journalists, and mainstream fans. Thus, by the time the album actually appeared, the newest

Paul Krassner Bugs James McCord

CRAWDADDY

DELL 04079-34
U.K. 40p.

1974 March 75¢

JOHN LENNON:
"Our Year is '74"

Exciting New Fiction by Harlan Ellison
Dave Mason Remembers

The same month John made headlines for a drunken free-for-all with Harry Nilsson at the Troubadour, *Crawdaddy* ran an optimistic interview where he rightly predicted better things to come that year.

offering from the Lennons was doomed to be a tough sell—and that was *before* anyone heard a note of it.

By fusing a collection of reactionary sentiments to the commercial poison that was his wife, John all but guaranteed that he would gain no new fans while seriously diminishing his standing among the old ones. The same characteristically impulsive nature that made him such a larger-than-life figure to many also resulted in the occasional misstep, no more so than on the follow-up to the much-loved *Imagine* LP. Had maintaining his audience and taking them with him on his musical journey been his mission, he might have fared better if he'd preceded the LP's release with the issue of "New York City" as leadoff single.

This thundering slice of rock 'n' boogie has often been compared to his "Ballad of John and Yoko." While true that both songs were quite literal musical diaries, the earlier cut, though not without charm, does not rock nearly as convincingly as this one, which features plenty of guitars, piano, sax, and a particularly spirited Lennon vocal. Without being overtly political, "New York City" offers an impressionistic glimpse into the locale and the people John and Yoko met upon their arrival, while summing up why they wanted to stay: "Nobody here to bug us, hustle us, or shove us."

Though the commercial failures of both "Woman Is the Nigger of the World" and *Some Time in New York City* doomed any possibility of a follow-up single ("Luck of the Irish" was considered—briefly—but ultimately kiboshed, doubtlessly for the better), "New York City" was given a prominent one-time-only showcase, as set opener at the Madison Square Garden One to One concerts held in August 1972.

"John Sinclair"

As discussed in the concert chapter of this book, the criminal case against former MC5 manager John Sinclair for possession of two joints was a cause of the day among leftists. Given the severity of his sentence, it was not an unworthy one, and John quickly fell in with a crowd determined to draw attention to his plight. While he could have marched in the street and protested along with the others, Lennon recognized that his gifts as a songwriter with a built-in constituency might do some good. He therefore put his talents to work in the name of creating something lasting that would get the word out and rally the public to the cause.

"John Sinclair" was built around a singular lick, played with a slide by John on a Dobro. The resulting sound gave the song a folkie-bluesy cast, after the style of past troubadours reporting on contemporary events. The lyrics succinctly summed up the case ("in the stir for breathing air") while appealing to the public for support. Beyond a doubt, the song's main claim to memorability was one that either attracted or repelled listeners: an eight-bar repeat of the words "got to," as in "set him free," that served as a refrain. Composed mere weeks after Bill Withers' "Ain't No Sunshine" (with its twenty-six-times repeat of "I know") was a smash hit, John recognized a compelling hook when he heard one and wasn't shy about aping it.

He also may have been taking a page from Bob Dylan, who had recently chronicled the story of a notable prisoner in song. His single "George Jackson," which told the story of the Black Panther leader gunned down at San Quentin in August, was issued not long before John debuted "John Sinclair" at the Ten for Two rally in Ann Arbor in December 1971. Where Lennon may have erred, though, was in preserving the song in the lasting medium of an LP. Unlike Dylan, who restricted his release to a single (to this day it has not seen release on an American album, though it's available on iTunes), John's decision to include such a dated subject on his album (Sinclair was released three days after the Ann Arbor show) essentially underscored the album's transient themes. Buyers needed no further incentive to discard the set the same way they would a day-old newspaper.

"Tight A$"

When he wasn't composing universal anthems or apologies to his wife, John Lennon could be counted on to turn in the occasional rocker. With "Tight A$," he doesn't disappoint: this Carl Perkins-*cum*-Doug Sahm number was one of the highlights of *Mind Games*, sounding like something John could have recorded in 1964 had it only been written. It stands as a throwback to the kind of material the Beatles tapped regularly in their club days, possessing an unmistakably American-sounding flavor, sung by an Englishman.

Lyrically, the song wasn't "about" anything in particular, merely being a return to the sort of writing he'd once engaged in regularly when a string of words that scanned nicely was enough. The pros he'd assembled to record the song—Jim Keltner, session guitarist David Spinozza (who turns in an excellent rockabilly solo), and Gordon Edwards on bass—chugged along tightly; in fact, the finished master was edited down from one of several takes that ran longer as the band hit their groove.

"Out the Blue"

Every one of John's solo albums (save *Some Time in New York City*) contained some standard-worthy ballad: *Plastic Ono Band* had "Love," *Imagine* had

"Oh My Love," *Walls and Bridges* had "Bless You," and *Double Fantasy* had "Woman." Possibly the most overlooked of the lot was *Mind Games'* "Out the Blue." Coming when the couple was on the brink of splitting, this statement of romantic destiny stands as one of John's finest performances.

From a gently picked acoustic opening, the song explodes into a piano-based gospel number, complete with choired vocal backings and a touch of pedal steel for color. Rather than being swamped by the rush of sound,

The flip side of the "Mind Games" single, the raucous "Meat City" contained a curious vocal drop-in at 0:31. Played backwards, it was a voice saying, "Check the album." The same passage on the *Mind Games* LP version said, "Fuck a pig."

John's vocal manages to stay atop the waves, projecting genuine tenderness and gratitude for "life's energy" (well, it was the year of the OPEC embargo).

It may have been the idiosyncratic quality of the song's lyric that stopped other artists from rushing to cover it. "Like a U.F.O. you came to me," John sang, never realizing that in one year's time he would actually spot a possible visitor from another world, hovering in the sky above his New York City apartment. (At that particular moment, though, he was with *another* love. And naked.)

Whatever the state of his marriage, "Out the Blue" stands as one of John's finest love songs. Its inclusion on the 2005 *Working Class Hero* collection may give hope to its eventual rediscovery by the masses.

"Slippin' and Slidin'"

The oldies project that John struggled with for well over a year did not exactly pay off in dividends as expected. For all of the squandered energy and expense, it ended up being his slowest seller this side of *Some Time in New York City*, though it eventually went gold. That said, it also contained some fine music, as evidenced by the Top 20 single, "Stand by Me." For most of the public, however, their exposure to the album's contents began and ended with that one song.

Perhaps the *Rock 'n' Roll* album's strongest rocker, "Slippin' and Slidin'" came *this close* to being issued as a follow-up to "Stand by Me," making it as far as the promo pressing stage before Apple pulled the plug.

It was unfortunate that Apple was on life support by the time of *Rock 'n' Roll*'s release, for plans to issue a second single from the album ended up being scrapped. "Slippin' and Slidin'" made it as far as the promo pressing stage before the plug was pulled. It was a real shame, because John's recording stands as perhaps his most ferocious reading on the entire album, besting in terms of sheer exuberance versions cut by both of his heroes, Little Richard and Buddy Holly.

The former's recording was issued in 1956 as the flip side of "Long Tall Sally," a tune that for years served as an excuse for Paul to trot out his Little Richard impression. Buddy Holly recorded the song amongst a clutch of other tunes in his New York City apartment just weeks before his ill-fated jaunt with the Winter Dance Party; with overdubs, it was released posthumously. (Holly recorded the song in both a fast and an eerily slow version. It's been surmised that the slow take was done as a joke, intended to produce a "Chipmunks"-style recording when sped up to normal tempo. Despite this, many fans prefer the slow take as is.)

John's version thumps along magnificently, powered by Ken Ascher's pounding piano and Bobby Key's wailing sax. Maybe it was the timing in the market, and record company execs were afraid that the window for an oldies remake had closed by the time of *Rock 'n' Roll*'s issue, but John didn't give up on promoting the song, producing a video clip at the Record Plant for airing on England's *Old Grey Whistle Test* TV show, as well as performing the song live on 1975's *Salute to Sir Lew* broadcast.

"Bring It on Home to Me / Send Me Some Lovin'"

Perhaps as a ploy to squeeze as many titles onto the vinyl as possible, *Rock 'n' Roll* was bracketed by two medleys, one each per side. The fusing of "Ready Teddy" and "Rip It Up" represented the rocker side of things, while ballads were conjoined to produce the unique but utterly fitting juxtaposition of Sam Cooke and Little Richard found on the flip. "Bring It On Home" was a hit for Cooke in early summer 1961, peaking at #13 on the pop charts. Evidently the song made a big impression on both John and Paul: Paul would record it for his 1988 Russian-only oldies release, while—in addition to tackling it on *Rock 'n' Roll*—John invoked it on "Remember" back on his debut LP. ("If you ever change your mind. . . .")

"Send Me Some Lovin'" was a rare non–rave up from the former Richard Penniman. Cowritten by Lloyd Price's brother Leo, the song was also covered by Buddy Holly that same year for the *"Chirping" Crickets* LP. John was doubtlessly familiar with both versions. (In fact, he even throws a Holly "hiccup" into his reading.) As this recording originated with the second round of oldies sessions held in late 1974, credit must go to him for the masterstroke of combining the two songs.

In addition to John's impassioned lead, Klaus Voormann also weighed in with a rare vocal cameo, contributing the response voice on "Bring It On Home." All in all, a great performance that stands as one of the album's highlights.

"I'm Losing You"

While thoroughly adept at crafting exquisite love songs, politically charged sing-alongs, and ballsy rockers, John may have produced his best work when he was offering candid glimpses into his own troubled psyche. In direct contrast to Yoko's efforts at mining the apparent discontent within her marriage, nearly all of John's material on *Double Fantasy* offered up romantic idealism or optimism for the future. The lone exception was the grittiest tune in the rather slick collection, "I'm Losing You," slated for release as a follow-up to "(Just Like) Starting Over." His death, however, prevented his strongest performance on the LP to be called out for the return to form that it was.

The song was sparked during the summer sojourn to Bermuda, arising from John's frustrating inability to reach Yoko by phone. From this momentary irritation, he channeled his annoyance into a deeper exploration of his marriage. Asserting from the outset his sense that his relationship appears to be foundering, he acknowledges past hurts inflicted while at the same time expressing resentment that he isn't allowed to live them down: "Do you still have to carry that cross?" This candid admission carries more weight than his usual lyrical acts of contrition, signifying a return to the potent self-examinations that had given *Plastic Ono Band* and *Walls and Bridges* such depth.

Jack Douglas evidently recognized the song as warranting a different approach from most of the rest of the compositions, for it was on this track that he suggested bringing in the heavy hitters from Cheap Trick. By all accounts, John was delighted with the results, which underscored the song's inherent Plastic Ono Band qualities, but, as discussed in chapter 6, their take was dropped in favor of a remake. Still, as issued, "I'm Losing You" packs an emotional wallop on an album largely bereft of such drama.

"Beautiful Boy (Darling Boy)"

In complete contrast to the previous entry, John offered up this gentle lullaby to Sean Ono Taro Lennon. The song drew much notice as a rare glimpse into John Ono Lennon's paternal side—an aspect of his personality that didn't manifest itself much between the ages of twenty-two and thirty-four. But credit must be given for his efforts at self-improvement; recognizing his failures at the first go-round, he went to the other extreme twelve years later, suspending his career to become the full-time parent he hadn't been the first time (or had ever experienced, to be completely fair).

The production of the song certainly bears the marks of its compositional origins in Bermuda during John's final summer. There are the sound of waves permeating the track, as well as a Caribbean steel drum and lyrical allusions to "sailing away." (Interesting that John would muse upon his son's future when he was "out on the ocean"—was this in subtle contrast to his father, Freddie, the merchant seaman who (according to popular lore at least) was most certainly not thinking about *his* son while over the bounding main?

One cannot help but be moved by the recording, especially if one is a parent. The song proved captivating to most everyone who heard it, including Yoko, who was motivated to write a follow-up song for the album that included both of her "boys," and Paul, himself the father of a male child at long last. In 1982 in an appearance on the BBC's long-running *Desert Island Discs*, he chose "Beautiful Boy (Darling Boy)" as his top pick to possess when shipwrecked. (The emotion that the song stirred in him is quite obvious when he is seen discussing it.) Indeed, the song's tearjerking qualities were employed to effective, if heavyhanded use, in the 1994 film, *Mr. Holland's Opus.*

Here's a parting observation: for many people, the most striking component of the song is a particular line that resonated mightily with the public after the events of 1980. Not "every day in every way it's getting better and better," which actually dates back to the nineteenth century (for those keeping score, that quote is generally attributed to French psychologist Émile Coué, who, contrary to popular irony, did not die a suicide), but "life is what happens to you while you're busy making other plans." Following the release of *Double Fantasy*, that quote was widely assumed to be a final Lennonism and began turning up on posters, coffee mugs, and greeting cards with abandon. In fact, the phrase had already been in play for many years, attributed to a number of people but believed to have originated with *Mary Worth* cartoonist Allen Saunders, who is credited with those words in a 1957 *Reader's Digest* article.

January 17, 1977 ▪ 50¢

14227

Dory Previn
smiles again

The women in
Gary Gilmore's
tormented life

Gstaad: where
the stars ski

People weekly

RINGO

His tax exile,
his new fiancée,
his rap on a
Beatle reunion

The photo shoot for this 1977 *People* cover story saw Ringo donning a fez, covering up, Nancy Andrews said later, a bad hair day.

24

It's Guaranteed to Keep You Alive

The Best Unsung Ringo

Perhaps because so little was expected from a Ringo Starr solo recording career, exceeding expectations was only one well-crafted album away. That album came in 1973, and for a brief shining moment, the Ringed One was demonstrably the most popular ex-Beatle in the world. With the help of one canny producer (who also happened to be a hot property at the time), *Ringo* had the effect of carving out a market niche for the drummer as the lovable uncle who provided a good time, even if he wasn't the best singer in the room. So long as the public was willing to play along, his successful chart career was assured.

But in an extremely cutthroat business, sustaining one's position at the top was even harder than getting there. So it was for Ringo, who saw his commercial prospects suffer a decline over the course of several ensuing releases. Accelerating the process were his own personal issues; as he coped with a broken marriage and the loss of his long-term day job, turning to assorted nefarious substances for their dubious assistance, a detachment from the process of recording diminished the former Fab to virtually a cipher on his own albums.

That said, he *was* a show business professional. In retrospect, it's startling to note the degree of unduly heavyhanded slamming he endured from critics for virtually every post-Apple release. (To quote *Rolling Stone* in 1978: "To say that *Bad Boy* is a very bad record almost misses the point. . . .") But upon giving his works a fresh listen, one finds that even when his talents were ill-used on his later long-players, he never fell so far as to phone it in. There is, at bare minimum, a certain amount of energy, enthusiasm, and likeability to be found within even the most challenging releases—if not by the general public, at least for Ringo's fans. Here are some examples.

"ONLY YOU"
THE FIRST SINGLE FROM

RINGO STARR'S

GOODNIGHT VIENNA

Produced by RICHARD PERRY

(1876)

The *Goodnight Vienna* cover art motif was drawn from the sci-fi classic *The Day the Earth Stood Still* (1951), with Ringo as Klaatu. The suit he donned for photos and the promotional video was designed by rock costumer Ola Hudson, mother of renowned guitarist Slash.

"Occapella"

If not quite perceived as the equal of *Ringo*, it's only because *Goodnight Vienna* came second. Both albums largely worked from the same template of celebrity pals custom-crafting material for the Ringed One. Under Richard Perry's astute production, a second LP's worth of what sounded like fun emerged, with the self-effacing Starr being the sun around whom the planets orbited. It was a good formula, playing to Ringo's strengths as a personality rather than as a serious singer per se. Where it went awry in subsequent releases was when producers forgot to allow the quirks to come through and surrounded him with faceless gloss that reduced him to guesting on his own albums.

While *Goodnight Vienna* lacked the usual allotment of ex-Fab support (George and Paul were absent on this release), John's presence as songwriter (the title track), arranger ("Only You"), and supporting player (guitar on "Call Me"), along with the addition of Elton John (on the breezy "Snookeroo") and the stepped-up contributions of Dr. John (born Mac Rebennack, Jr., he'd scored a hit of his own with "Right Place, Wrong Time" the year before), made their input unnecessary. Like its predecessor, *Goodnight Vienna* also spawned three U.S. hit singles, though none went to #1.

"Occapella" kept the party going in the wake of the opening "Goodnight Vienna." Penned by Ringo favorite Allen Toussaint, this blast of New Orleans funk was not, of course, sans instruments, but came with full-blown brass and some lively ivory-tinkling, courtesy of the Doctor. It's a joyful celebration of music and life, complete with a vocalizing interlude and some scatting by Rebennack. (So evocative of the Big Easy is the track that one expects to hear "Love that chicken at Popeye's" at any moment.)

Dr. John enjoyed a close friendship and a solid musical relationship with the former Fab. He would contribute to several Ringo albums (*Ringo's Rotogravure* and *Bad Boy*, in addition to *Goodnight Vienna*) as well as appear on the inaugural All-Starr tour in 1989, performing "Iko Iko."

"Easy for Me"

Sometimes there was a fine line between the songwriting styles of Randy Newman and Harry Nilsson. (It's no coincidence that one of Nilsson's most satisfying early albums consisted entirely of Newman compositions.) Both men possessed an acute sense of drama, as well as irony. Also, both had a talent for composing melodies that seemed as though they had been plucked from some obscure 1930s musical. All of these qualities are on display in this number, the haunting and lush—but not overly so—"Easy for Me." (Oddly, when Nilsson recorded it himself a year later for the *Duit on Mon Dei* album, it was retitled "*Easier* for Me.")

On piano was one Lincoln Mayorga, a virtuoso of no little renown. (There were doubtless some purchasers of *Goodnight Vienna* who assumed that the credit was simply a goofy pseudonym for *somebody*.) Mayorga entered the public's awareness as the musical director/arranger for the Four Preps ("26 Miles (Santa Catalina)") and as charter member of the Piltdown Men, an instrumental group, in the early 1960s before segueing into a distinguished career as a concert pianist/session player. His elegant keyboard work here proved a good fit for Ringo's crooning voice (last heard to good effect on "Good Night").

Between the album's up- and mid-tempo offerings, "Easy for Me" stands as a poignant reminder of the melancholy aspect of Ringo's public persona. Singing Nilsson's rather existential lyrics ("How could reason hope to find us hiding in the Milky Way without a star to shine the way?") worked far better than one would have had reason to suspect, resulting in a lovely but overlooked recording within Richie Snare's canon.

"Gave It All Up"

In the hands of most, this maudlin, yet ultimately optimistic little number from *Ringo the 4th* might have generated little more than snickers from the cognoscenti. But in a setting full of pathos custom-tailored for Ringo's whipped-dog persona, "Gave It All Up" reeks of authenticity. Embellished by a bluesy harmonica just a-wailin' away, this Poncia-Starkey original offers the tale of a ne'er-do-well who has had to make certain hard choices, for good or ill. Luckily, the bad decisions seemed to have taught valuable lessons, for by the end, the former bad boy is redeemed by love. Trite, perhaps, but such is the basis of entire genres of music enjoyed by millions. Ringo is well cast in his own composition, while Mardin's production—for once on this record—is exactly spot on.

"It's No Secret"

Another unheralded gem among *Ringo the 4th*'s overlooked offerings was this light but utterly contemporary-sounding soft rock track. Featuring a subtle synthesizer embellishment, well-balanced backing vocals, and an R&B feel, "It's No Secret" afforded Ringo the chance to acquit himself well as a vocalist in yet another self-penned (with Poncia) tune. While certainly a departure from the sort of Beatle-y material that had been his Top 40 bread and butter, it made for a nice attempt to expand his musical palette. Of course, the song was only ever familiar to his hardcore constituency, but for anyone seeking to create a good Ringo mix disc, it makes for a worthy addition.

"Who Needs a Heart"

In 1976, during his round of interviews for *Ringo's Rotogravure*, Richie Snare had an idea for taking his act on the road. "It's a Rotogravure [sic], right, of a crowd of artists and we go out and the audience doesn't have to put up with me for two hours . . . with things coming in and out . . . other artists. I can't mention them because I'm still talking to them now, so I may go

Issued as a single in Europe, this *Ringo's Rotogravure* track spawned a memorable video, commemorating the shaved-head look he sported in the summer of 1976.

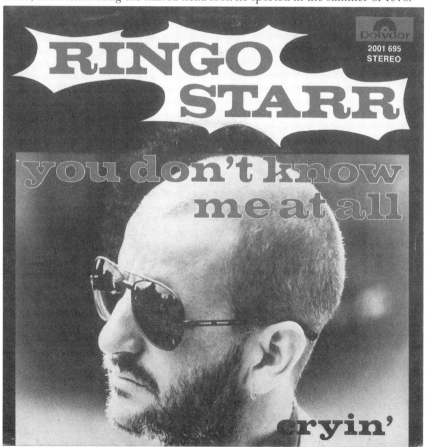

out next year if we get it together." History records that he did not "get it together," though his description of the ideal performing ensemble sounded remarkably like the All-Starr Band that finally debuted in 1989—twelve years later

One year and one record label later, Ringo put together a rock-solid outfit he dubbed "Ringo's Roadside Attraction." Again, one could infer that a tour was in the offing, if just from their name (and from the concurrent *Ringo* TV special, which featured a concert sequence), but again, it didn't happen. Still, the outfit backed him on the uneven *Bad Boy*, a collection that kicked off with this rocker. It isn't hard to imagine "Who Needs a Heart" as a set-opener. It's a solid, pounding piece of work, with an assured vocal (as well as a call-and-response), an engaging Van Eaton guitar solo, and a swagger absent from most of his material.

The song was one of only two Poncia-Starkey compositions on *Bad Boy*, the other being "Old Time Relovin'." The partnership ended with this release, but not for lack of decent tunes.

"Hard Times"

Another solid rocker from the Portrait release, this one was accorded the honor of a live performance in the *Ringo* ("Ognir Rrats") special. The song was penned by Peter Skellern, a well-known singer/songwriter in early-'70s Britain but virtually unheard of on this side of the pond. He'd had a Top 5 single there with "You're a Lady" in 1972; three years later, he was joined in the studio by one George Harrison on a song called "Make Love Not War" for his *Hard Times* album. It may have been this Hari Georgeson connection that caught Ringo's ear; in any case, something inspired him to bring the title track into his own album project three years later.

(In the early '80s, Skellern formed a group with Apple alumna Mary Hopkin and Andrew Lloyd Weber's brother Julian called Oasis—further evidence that the better-known act of the same name could not contrive a single original idea from day one.)

Powered by Dr. John's piano, a breezy horn section, and Lon Van Eaton's slide guitar, the track made for a nice up-tempo album cut, but on the *Ringo* special, it killed. Onstage and before an audience, Ringo's Roadside Attraction gave the tune a spirited reading that offered a glimpse into what might have been, had the Ringed One actually acted upon the show's premise and performed concerts at the time.

"Tonight"

Despite the fact that it was rapidly sliding toward irrelevancy, *Bad Boy* was given another shot at connecting with the public by the issue of another single, though not in the States. A romantic ballad, "Tonight" had originally been recorded by the revamped Small Faces the year before. It was cowritten by journalist / friend of the band John Pidgeon and keyboardist Ian McLagan, who sang lead. (Ringo would return the favor of the song by playing on McLagan's solo album, *Troublemaker*, a year later.)

Part and parcel of the promotion was the production of a music video. Though a thirty-minute film in collaboration with Australian director Christian Topp was planned, utilizing songs from *Bad Boy*, only one clip was ever completed: the one for "Tonight." It was filmed in July 1978 in a chateau on the French Riviera and costarred Nancy Andrews. For that alone it's significant, as perhaps the only readily accessible glimpse of Starr and Andrews together on film. They are shown dancing; with Nancy a ghostlike figure that Ringo is uncertain is anything more than a mirage.

The song did not chart in the U.K., through no fault of its own, marking the end of Ringo's ill-fated Polydor deal. (Interestingly, the song *did* generate some American airplay, notably on Los Angeles radio stations.)

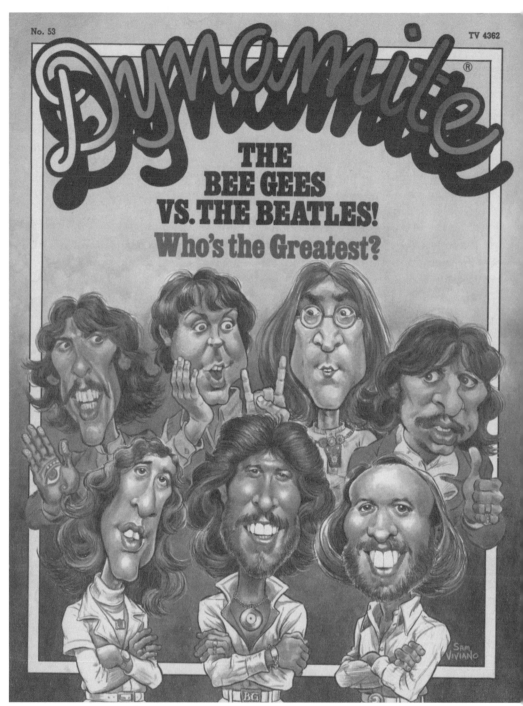

Dynamite

THE BEE GEES VS. THE BEATLES!
Who's the Greatest?

A popular kids' magazine of the day, *Dynamite* stirred debate among those breath-lessly looking for the next Beatles by wondering in print whether the Bee Gees' recent string of chart successes meant that the Fabs were passé.

25

My Desire Is Always to Be Here

1978

In August 1977, Denny Laine and Paul composed a campfire sing-along-style song on acoustic guitars. Inspired by the beauty and tranquility of the McCartneys' remote Scottish farm on the Kintyre peninsula, "Mull of Kintyre" sounded as though it could have been recorded in any year since the invention of the phonograph, complete with bagpipes and an ever-swelling mass of singers on the choruses. In short, it was—on paper at least—not the stuff with which hit singles are made, least of all in 1977–78 Britain, where if a tune was neither nihilistic and abrasive nor funky and danceable, it was nowhere. At least this theory held true in America, where the single was actually sublimated beneath the rocking "Girls School" flip side, which likewise failed to impress the masses.

But, entering the charts during the holiday season, the song became a monster in the British Isles. "Mull of Kintyre" hit #1 the week of December 3 and remained lodged there for the next eight weeks. ("Hey Jude" had likewise topped the U.S. charts for nine weeks.) Perhaps more significantly, it broke the record for the greatest-selling single in the U.K. to that time, held since 1963 when a cheeky quartet of Scousers set it with their fourth single, a little ditty called "She Loves You." So intense was the popularity of the song that EMI actually anticipated the one-millionth purchase, awarding the buyer—one David Ackroyd—a gold record, as well as a Christmas basket from the McCartneys (presented at MPL's Soho office by Denny Laine).

The fact that such a singularly popular tune, one that shattered a long-standing sales record on one side of the Atlantic, could stiff so badly on the other meant one thing to Paul: Capitol simply wasn't up to the task of marketing his work, all their previous success notwithstanding. (He also con-veniently ignored the song's completely idiosyncratic appeal, bagpipes not exactly being a staple of American rock radio.) Still, Macca's commerciality barometer was sensitive and he was determined to maintain his position within rock royalty, at least as far as sales were concerned. In the meantime, he kept a close eye on Capitol's handling of the new Wings album, *London Town*, released in March.

Though Wings' rocker credentials had been firmly established with the addition of the now-departed Jimmy McCulloch on guitar, as well as the band's muscular stage show, the new album continued the mellow mood encapsulated with few exceptions on *Wings at the Speed of Sound*. "With a Little Luck," the leadoff single, seemed custom-crafted for "adult contemporary" radio, being all synths and harmonies with nary a guitar to be heard. (Indeed, the term "elevator music" seemed especially fitting, as the arrangement would have required no changes at all in order to sound suitable for just such an environment.) Paul's instincts proved spot-on, as the single shot to #1, offering a two-week respite from the chart onslaught being staged by the Brothers Gibb at the time.

But subsequent "something for everyone" singles failed to click. The up-tempo rocker "I've Had Enough," seemingly calculated to reach adolescents with its put-upon narrative and gritty vocals, failed to leave much of an impression, barely scraping into the U.S. Top 30. Another single, the melodic but diaphanous title track, landed no higher than #39, an utterly dispiriting performance, while *London Town*, the album, showed little staying power: having peaked at #2, it slid down the charts as quickly as "With a Little Luck" left heavy rotation. All of which meant that, for the first time since "Love Me Do," Paul was now receptive to wooing from anyone but EMI.

Meanwhile, spring was shaping up as a flurry of activity for Ringo. His second Atlantic album, *Ringo the 4th*, had stiffed—and badly. Despite making a serious run at catching the disco wave, producer Arif Mardin mistakenly treated the ex-Fab's unique appeal as though it were interchangeable with any of the R&B-based acts currently burning up the charts. The album's poor performance gave the label an out and they dropped the drummer quickly, while overseas, his Polydor deal had one more album left. So it was that Ringo reentered the studio with inordinate haste and attempted to arrest the downward spiral before his fortunes hit bottom.

Again sidestepping the all-star/ex-bandmate formula, he began recording *Bad Boy* with a small group of capable hands, including Dr. John on keys and Lon Van Eaton on guitar, as well as engineer / ex–Paul Revere and the Raiders guitarist Keith Allison and Elton John bassist Dee Murray. Oddly, all were billed under pseudonyms, known collectively as "Ringo's Roadside Attraction.") Manning the desk was Ringo's songwriting partner, behind-the-scenes rock veteran Vini Poncia. Though Poncia was quite capable of crafting a commercially successful record (as witnessed by his work with artists ranging from Melissa Manchester to KISS), a combination of the lack of any real blockbuster material and Ringo's low commercial appeal at that

place and time doomed the project. Though the drummer set about recording some new material that summer after two singles—"Lipstick Traces" and
"Heart on My Sleeve"—tanked, Portrait dropped him and the new material
was left unreleased.

More successful, at least on an entertainment/novelty level, was the
one-hour television special aired in April. Talks about bringing the Ringed
One into a suitable television vehicle had been ongoing at least as far back
as 1974. What at last emerged was a contemporary take on Mark Twain's
"The Prince and the Pauper," concerning rock star Ringo and his look
alike, an L.A. map-seller. The two exchange places and lo—hilarity ensues!
The amount of prestige NBC attached to the production was evident,
from the casting and media blitz to the finagling of a role for George. The
resulting *Ringo*—crammed with music old and new—was a delight to fans.
Unfortunately, that base was shrinking, and what might have been a great
idea a few years earlier was sadly out of sync with current tastes, finishing
near the bottom of the week's ratings. Given the string of projects that had
gone south, Ringo was at last ready to give himself a break; he would not get
back to making music for another two years.

George, on the other hand, was newly rested and refreshed. One of the
first songs he completed following the resumption of his musical duties
was inspired by rather dreary circumstances: while puttering around his
ancient but expansive dwelling at Friar Park in the midst of a downpour,
he discovered water leaks caused by clogged gutters. The milieu mirrored
his own feelings, as he began to fear that, having shirked his day job for a
year, he had dried up as a composer. While attempting to deal with the twin
issues of water leaks and a creative dry spell, a "cheer up" tune came into
his head. Just as easily as that, on a windswept, waterlogged day, "Blow Away"
came into being.

Other tunes quickly followed, including an up-tempo rocker called
"Flying Hour" that, despite being one of his most contemporary and com-
mercial-sounding tunes, was arbitrarily deep-sixed by executives at Warners
when he presented it two years later. At this point, though, George was
feeling optimistic and upbeat. Olivia was expecting their first child, enabling
him to at last realize the dream of becoming a father that had eluded him
thus far. Sadly, George lost his own father that year, but Harold Harrison
presumably moved beyond the material world secure in the knowledge that
his youngest would soon produce an heir.

The couple spent time vacationing in Maui, where George had purchased a home. There, with inspiration from nature coming from within
and from without (he later copped to revisiting "organic" hallucinogenics
during this time), the new songs poured out. Back in England, he quickly

concluded that the chore of producing himself was not one that he was keen to take on, so the new record in the making, entitled *George Harrison*, was put together with the help of American producer Russ Titelman, a Warners staffer associated with work by Ry Cooder and Rickie Lee Jones. Having completely cut himself off from any connection to the current music scene, he believed it helpful to work with someone thoroughly steeped in such things. From this point onward, George's music would become increasingly idiosyncratic, having little to do with contemporary trends.

Adding to his responsibilities as a recording artist were the unexpected duties he took on as film producer. His friends in the Monty Python comedy troupe had their world rocked that year when funding for the follow-up to *Monty Python and the Holy Grail* was pulled by EMI at literally the last minute, out of fear of a religious backlash. Motivated by little deeper thought than a desire to see the next Python film, George reached into his rather substantial pockets to rescue the project, entitled *Life of Brian*, and so HandMade Films was born—just like that. It quickly became Britain's most successful independent film company. During its fifteen-year run with George and business partner Denis O'Brien at the helm, the company was responsible for such quality fare as *The Long Good Friday*, *Time Bandits* (with a theme—"Dream Away"—composed and performed by George), and *Withnail and I*, as well as the Madonna-Penn vehicle *Shanghai Surprise*.

On the subject of Fab-related films, 1978 produced an abundance, though the quality varied wildly. First up that year was the culmination of *Saturday Night Live* and *Rutland Weekend Television*'s collaborating on a perverse "salute" to the Beatles, in the form of their alter egos, the Rutles. *All You Need Is Cash*, featuring an ensemble cast led by Python Eric Idle, as well as Neil Innes and assorted SNL players (John Belushi, Dan Aykroyd, Gilda Radner, Bill Murray, and Al Franken) aired on March 22. Guest appearances by Mick Jagger and Paul Simon added to the project's satirical earnestness, but the cameo by George as a TV reporter gave the project the stamp of approval from the Fabs themselves. Despite the quality of the parody and spot-on take on Beatles history, the film failed to find an audience on its initial airing—perhaps viewers were distracted by the on-camera death of high-wire aerialist Karl Wallenda earlier that very day.

Opening in theaters in April was the directorial debut of Steven Spielberg protégé Robert Zemeckis, *I Wanna Hold Your Hand*. This slapstick period piece was a fun evocation of the Beatles' arrival in America for the *Ed Sullivan Show* in 1964 and starred Nancy Allen and Wendie Jo Sperber. Centering on a group of fans and their efforts to get into the venue for that first taping, the film did a great job of capturing the moment without actually showing the Beatles themselves (well, practically). Less successful

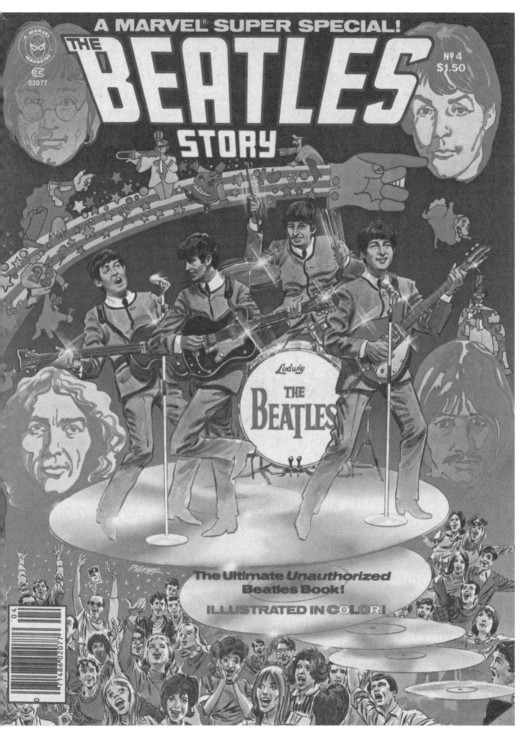

This special produced in 1978 by Marvel told the Beatles' story in what another generation would call "graphic novel" form.

artistically but more heavily hyped was the legendary film treatment of Tom O'Horgan's Broadway show, retooled as a vehicle for Peter Frampton and the Bee Gees. *Sgt. Pepper's Lonely Hearts Club Band* was expensive, bloated, and silly, bearing little in the way of coherence and certainly having nothing to do with the Fabs. Mostly, it proved to millions that entertainment mogul Robert Stigwood was indeed fallible.

In October, Paul convened a gathering of nearly two dozen peers (though no ex-Fabs) and dubbed them Rockestra. The ensemble would record a pair of tracks for his next album; sadly, Who drummer Keith Moon missed the date, having passed away a month earlier after attending Macca's third annual party honoring Buddy Holly.

As the record industry tried avoiding use of the word "recession," one novelty devised to engage the attention of at least collectors, if not the masses generally, were "picture discs"—vinyl re-pressings of albums that bore cover art or some sort of graphic beneath a layer of transparent plastic. The Beatles were not immune to this trend, and indeed Capitol issued limited-edition pressings of both *Sgt. Pepper's* and *Abbey Road* (in August and December respectively) in this format. Also, colored vinyl pressings of the "Red," "White," and "Blue" double albums (that is: *1962–1966; The Beatles,* and *1967–1970*) hit the market, pressed in the appropriate color. These items are novel collectibles today, but at the time, stacks of picture discs could readily be found at cutout prices, despite the suggestion that they would one day be valuable.

If an elaborate Broadway tribute band, collectible vinyl, and films for every taste weren't enough to satiate Beatle-starved fans, another phenomenon resurfaced that year. Earlier in the decade, a road show called *The Beatles: Away with Words* hit major cities around the country, playing mostly at small auditoriums. In a nutshell, the event was a glorified slide show (or "multimedia presentation") synching Beatles music to an array of images that essentially brought audiences on a journey through the '60s. In 1978, a newer version of the presentation came around for an encore; this time it was called *The Beatles Rise Again.* As with the earlier version, one's enjoyment may have depended upon the state of one's consciousness and how one had gone about preparing for the dazzling visuals and amplified music bombarding one's senses. As hard as it may be to imagine today, the show played to packed houses.

26

The Wonder of It All, Baby

The Best Unsung Paul

The recorded output of Sir Paul McCartney cannot be judged by the same yardstick as that of the other ex-Fabs. While John and George had something to say (more or less) each time they produced albums, and Ringo seemingly used his studio time as an excuse to hang out with friends, Paul was a compulsive recording artist, cranking out material practically nonstop from *McCartney* onward. As a result, the quality was famously uneven, ranging from the sublime highs of *Ram* and *Band on the Run* to half-baked embarrassments like *Wild Life* and *Wings at the Speed of Sound*.

His output between 1970 and 1980 (the period of releases covered in this book) was considerable: a dozen albums (including one collection and one triple live album release) and twenty-seven singles in the U.S. alone; of the latter fifty-four tracks, *twenty-one* were not released on LP initially (and out of these, only three were collated on *Wings Greatest*). All but three albums went platinum, some multiple times. In sum, whatever McCartney's standing with the critics, his work was nearly always warmly embraced by the public during the decade.

Given Paul's prodigious body of work and the attendant peaks and valleys of excellence, even the most ill-conceived albums contained some stellar material. Like his former bandmates, Macca was far too gifted a tunesmith to issue a collection *completely* lacking in merit. But in the opinion of most observers, he was led astray by a chronic inability to differentiate between quality and crap. Lacking a sounding board of the caliber of a John Lennon or a George Martin, he was left far too often without *anyone* with the clout (or the nerve) to tell him when something was simply not working.

With an abundance of tunes to choose from, it isn't hard to come up with a sampling of strong but overlooked material. As with the others' lists, nothing is included from albums ranked in this book as among the best

$1.00   MAY 31, 1976

TIME

McCartney
Comes Back

Two '60s icons intersected in 1976 when *Time* magazine commissioned a cover painting depicting Paul on tour from renowned artist Peter Max.

(see chapter 11), nor are any singles or B-sides included. One has to trim *somewhere.*

"Junk"

Aside from "Maybe I'm Amazed," "Every Night" was another *McCartney* cut that drew notice as a potential single. Eventually, it was covered by Phoebe Snow; Paul himself resurrected it to perform live (on Wings' final tour and at MTV's *Unplugged* in 1991), while radio discovered it decades later. But another "sleeper" track on the album that never quite got its due was actually one of two Beatles rejects (not counting the Quarry Men–era instrumental "Hot as Sun") dating back to the "White Album."

Composed during the trip to India in early 1968, "Junk" was originally titled "Jubilee." The wistful ballad presented an impressionistic series of ordinary items that, given the musical context, might be seen as sad reminders of happier times (in sort of a modern revisitation of the 1930s pop standard "These Foolish Things"). Following their return to England after the meditation camp, the group convened at George's home in Esher to demo their new compositions. "Junk" made it this far (the actual demo ended up being issued on *Anthology 3*) before being set aside, perhaps in favor of newer material still being composed. Had the Fabs elected to record it, it's doubtful that Paul's three bandmates would have been needed, given the simple arrangement that called for little augmentation.

It's possible that Paul thought he was a little short on material, for he included *two* versions of the song on *McCartney*, one as an instrumental ("Sing-along Junk"). His fondness for the tune is evident with its subsequent inclusion on the aforementioned *Unplugged* set, as well the 2001 *Wingspan* compilation.

"Tomorrow"

For those who appreciated the underproduction of *McCartney*, Wings' debut *Wild Life* offered more of the same, minus any material of equal weight to "Maybe I'm Amazed." The "concept" was to offer spontaneity and energy in place of the suffocating blanket of studio craft; it may also have been a reaction to the critical drubbing Paul received for his trouble in going all out on *Ram*. While the notion of producing an album quickly with a band in its formative stage wasn't necessarily as daft as it seemed in advance, it did look as though Paul was forgetting his own capabilities as a supremely gifted studio pro while taking the criticism of his detractors too seriously. The end result was a throwaway album that only further reinforced the meme that he was a musical lightweight utterly at sea without the other Fabs around him to challenge him to work at his craft.

Compositionally, *Wild Life*'s pickings were rather slim. Some cuts sounded like improvisations; others contained the germ of a good idea but either went undeveloped or got overly stretched out. Then there was this track. "Tomorrow" was a definite return to form that evoked his Beatle triumphs, or at least *McCartney*'s stronger cuts. While still a somewhat spare arrangement, the background harmonies portended what one day would be Wings' signature sound.

The song is a piano-based pop number, extolling optimism in the face of yesterday's sorrows. While "Tomorrow" doesn't come close to working itself up to the ornate level of production heard on *Ram*, it doesn't need to: the layered vocals and inventive arrangement work just fine to keep things moving along and holding the listener's interest. To cap things off, a faux-gospel coda brings the song to a close.

Issuing the song as a single might have given the album some traction with record buyers while introducing the new act. Instead, the non-album (and atypical) political tract "Give Ireland Back to the Irish" did the honors, while *Wild Life* was relegated to little more than a source of material for a stage act until newer songs replaced it—permanently.

"Dear Friend"

The *Ram* sessions in early 1971 yielded a bounty of material well beyond Paul's immediate needs. A dozen tracks would end up on the finished album; beyond this were both sides of the "Another Day" single, as well as tracks kept in reserve that would be parceled out over the next two albums. One was this song, which drew much notice upon *Wild Life*'s release by those searching for a "dear John" response to Lennon's devastating broadside on *Imagine*, "How Do You Sleep." Though "Dear Friend" actually predated Lennon's infamous character assault (and there's no reason to believe that Paul ever rewrote the words and re-recorded the vocal in response), Macca never publicly addressed the media chatter that maintained his reply came musically in the form of this gentle, conciliatory song. Indeed, Paul joined the war of words very publicly in the pages of *Melody Maker* just before the release of *Wild Life*, and his tone wasn't exactly one of "can't we all just get along?"

To his credit, Paul chose to end Wings' debut long-player with possibly the most musically developed song on the album, a bluesy, minor-key piece. "Dear Friend" begins with a sparse, almost jagged feel, featuring just Paul on piano and Denny Seiwell, whose off-and-on high-hat rhythm helps to build tension. Release came with some subtle orchestration and brass, just past the two-and-a-half-minute mark, in a marked contrast to the album's otherwise austere production values.

With a sophistication and maturity that contrasted with almost everything else around it, "Dear Friend" could've worked as is on virtually *any* Wings album, including *Band on the Run*. Despite the uneven quality of what came before it, the song gave listeners hope that, whatever else they thought about the album, future triumphs lay ahead.

"Little Lamb Dragonfly"

Much anticipated after more than a year without a new long-player in the stores (for the first time in a decade), *Red Rose Speedway* marked McCartney's return to George Martin–style production values, with orchestration, layers of instruments, and an attention to detail unseen since the critically slighted *Ram*. Unfortunately, while Paul was willing to embrace the sonic sheen of *Abbey Road*, compositionally, he was still operating on a *With the Beatles* musical level (literally titling a song "Hold Me Tight," as if to eradicate the embarrassment of a song bearing the same name that he'd written and sung—rather badly—on his former group's sophomore release).

In retrospect, it was as if all the effort Paul was putting into assembling a band and getting them road-ready was draining his compositional energies,

That Paul let McCartney go by without issuing "Maybe I'm Amazed" as a single back in 1970 dumbfounded many, but this perceived lapse was corrected when a live version from the *Wings Over America* set made the Top Ten in early 1977.

for the first couple of years of Wings' existence marked his lowest ebb as a songwriter. It is therefore unsurprising that the standout cut on *Red Rose Speedway* (aside from the singular "My Love") was a leftover from—wait for it—*Ram*, an album predating the formation of Wings.

"Little Lamb Dragonfly" is a lilting, twelve-string, acoustic-based ballad. Recording commenced in early 1971 with Hugh McCracken on guitar, but was finished up after Denny Laine joined later that year, adding backing vocals. The song, with its tone of regret and longing, has been the subject of speculation among fans for years. Some have held that it was a message to John ("Since you've gone I never know / I go on but I miss you so"). This interpretation is an odd one to square with other songs from the same sessions that seemed calculated to draw John's ire.

Others believe the song to be Paul's telling of how he came to be a vegetarian ("My heart is aching for you little lamb / I can help you out but I cannot help you in"). More likely than not, he was simply stringing together a series of phrases that scanned well and added up to whatever meaning the listener wanted to assign to them. None of this belies the fact that "Little Lamb Dragonfly" is a quietly haunting tune, one that has the power to move people without their quite understanding why.

During the 1990s, a young guitarist named Brendan Hedges made a name for himself by performing Beatles songs for commuters on Chicago's El platform. In 1995, he lost his life in a robbery. Not long after, fellow musician Eric Howell performed Paul's song before a thousand people at Beatlefest, dedicating it to Hedges. It was as poignant a reading of "Little Lamb Dragonfly" as its author could ever have wished for.

"Beware My Love"

Some of Paul's best compositions were seamlessly stitched together from fragments of musical ideas that, on their own, didn't add up to much. But when artfully assembled, the results could be amazing. "Beware My Love" is one such number. As heard on *Wings at the Speed of Sound*, the song has a distinct intro, verse, chorus, and finish that seemingly were plucked from disparate sources, yet hang together amazingly well; furthermore, the streamlined live version featured on *Wings Over America* ups the ante, bursting with energy and vocal pyrotechnics that no studio could contain.

"Beware My Love" typifies McCartney at his best, setting a mood, then taking the listener on a trip while providing no details. Exactly *what* the song is about is a mystery—as is often the case with Macca material, any message is beside the point. (With no little irony, in "Beware My Love," he sings:

"I'll leave my message in my song.") The arrangement, featuring crackling drums, a thundering bass line, and the usual creative backing vocals of Linda and Denny, seems to borrow a little drama from the Four Tops' "Reach Out (I'll Be There)" without leaving any fingerprints.

The song was the closest thing that *Speed of Sound* had to a full-blown rocker; it does indeed rock in time for the finish. But, impressive as the studio version is, it pales in comparison to the stripped-down (shortened by over a minute) concert recording issued at the end of 1976. Unleashed from the confinement of Abbey Road's number two studio, the band showed what the song was *really* about on *Wings Over America*, with Jimmy McCulloch's driving leads (complete with wah-wah), Laine's piano-pounding, and drummer Joe English inserting rolls at every turn. The resulting performance surely left the band as breathless as their audience.

"Deliver Your Children"

A multitalented instrumentalist, distinctive singer, and decent songwriter, Denny Laine operated within Wings as Paul's shadow, providing whatever was needed without really carving out a well-defined public identity. What he did, he did exceptionally well without drawing undue attention to himself. The blend of his voice with Linda's became Wings' most constant and distinguishable feature, no matter what the musical setting. Though he was "allowed" to sing lead on a few songs, not until *London Town* did he and Paul really work up any meaningful level of collaboration, with five of the album's fourteen songs (plus "Mull of Kintyre") bearing a co-credit.

The strongest of the lot was this folksy yet driving number. "Deliver Your Children," written and arranged in the style of a narrative ballad, was a seamless blending of both men's talents. The vocal was presented in tight harmony (with Paul taking the top) and featured much fingerpicking on acoustic guitars, giving it something of a "Gypsy" feel. Lyrically, the song was the rather dark tale of a man whom fortune has not smiled upon, yet very insistently declares that listeners must give their offspring "a good, good life"—failing that, "you'd better make it right."

The song was originally titled "Feel the Love"—words that appear nowhere in the lyric. Laine was also apparently involved in a custody battle with his estranged partner around the time of the *London Town* sessions, which may explain why *two* of his songs featured "children" in the title (the other being "Children, Children"). In any event, this one was a real highlight. Its selection as the B-side to the "I've Had Enough" single undoubtedly resulted in more play on jukeboxes than it ever got on the airwaves.

"So Glad to See You Here"

Paul's execution of the Rockestra concept resulted in two tracks on *Back to the Egg*: "Rockestra Theme" (naturally) and this one. The first was the simplest of songs, essentially being a recurring lick with little in the way of lyrics, save a chorus (bellowed out by all the participants): "Why haven't I had any dinner?"—a deliberate evocation of the style of the old Glenn Miller recording "Pennsylvania 6-5000." But "So Glad to See You Here" was different, being a fully sketched-out composition that took advantage of Paul's Rockestra for recording, giving the song a mammoth, larger-than-life sound.

Recognizing the reality of a musical climate in England that had embraced the raw energy of punk, Paul attempted to draw upon the genre's more compelling elements and adapt them to his purposes. In this instance, it meant capturing the gritty, full-throated vocal sound that had wowed 'em back at the Cavern and that he'd tried to channel on the Fabs' "Oh! Darling" for *Abbey Road*. On "So Glad to See You Here," his seemingly stage-blistered throat delivered a scorching lead that reminded listeners of what Macca was capable of when under optimum live conditions. The fact that he pulled it off while studio-bound is mightily impressive, as is the wall of instrumentation that he managed to master, rather than allowing it to swamp him.

As usual for Paul, the song itself spoke in lines that scanned well and evoked rather than described, in this case, the anticipation of a live act guaranteed to "knock 'em dead." What "Venus and Mars / Rock Show" only hinted at on vinyl, "So Glad to See You Here" delivered. It is too bad that the song was buried on an album that audiences avoided in droves, while its creator never thought enough of it to showcase it on the road.

"One of These Days"

McCartney II was an album released as a way of marking time after the unplanned collapse of Wings following the Japanese drug bust. (The parallels between this album and its similarly named predecessor are striking; though Paul seemed to find working by himself a reliable tonic in the wake of band breakups, *McCartney II* had in fact been recorded *before* Wings went south.) Aspiring to nothing loftier than sharing some experimenting with his fans, Paul found most reviews scathing, particularly *Rolling Stone*'s, which characterized the collection as a passable novelty while backhanding it with the damnation of "aural doodles for the amusement of very young children."

In striking contrast to what preceded it, the closing number was a gentle acoustic ballad. Though the vocals were heavily reverbed (à la Lennon), the song was otherwise bereft of the heavy electronic larking about that defined the rest of the album. Like "Waterfalls," it bore all the characteristics of having been actually composed, rather than simply improvised, then fleshed out. In fact, the song came together following a conversation Paul had with a visiting member of the Hare Krishna organization. (It is not recorded whether or not the representative was sent by George.)

The tone of the talk had been gentle and contemplative, a mood that Macca was able to sustain long enough to express with music as he worked it out in the studio. "One of These Days" was a simple expression of all the

Anonymous soundalike versions of contemporary singles, sold at a budget price, were commonplace throughout the '70s. This one, collecting Wings' hits, was actually credited, to a certain "P. K. and the Sound Explosion."

soul-satisfying things an individual might vow to do in the future, once life has stopped getting in the way. (In a way, the concept was re-presented with a romantic twist in the lovely "This One" on 1989's *Flowers in the Dirt*.) Bearing a subtle harmony from Linda, the song found a home on the least likely and most overlooked of McCartney albums, providing a suitable segue from the world of technology back into the moment.

27

I'll Try My Best to Make Everything Succeed

The Best Unsung George

George's first musical statement after the Beatles' breakup, *All Things Must Pass*, set a standard so high (much like John's *Plastic Ono Band*) that the remainder of his catalog was largely—and unfairly—judged lacking in comparison. The truth was, he issued several albums that were at least as strong, in terms of consistency, *Living in the Material World*, *Thirty-Three & 1/3*, and *George Harrison* all being top-tier.

Trouble came when the rock press afterward turned on him, in large measure chafing at the perceived humorless piety he dispensed on each album. (Said Jim Miller of *Dark Horse* in *Rolling Stone*: "His religiosity, once a spacey bauble within the Beatles' panoply, has come to resemble the obsessiveness of a zealot.") The public, meanwhile, found it hard to let go of their expectations of Beatles-like accessibility and eventually moved on, greatly reducing Harrison's standing with all but the hardcores.

But overt commerciality was a game that George grew steadily less interested in playing. The "give the people what they want" approach became something he would partake in only begrudgingly—unlike, say, Paul. That said, every one of his increasingly idiosyncratic releases had something to recommend it. Beyond the aforementioned works, here are some tracks culled from other albums, any one of which would stand up just fine on a compilation collating his "best" (if not the far-from-adequate *Let It Roll*).

"Wah-Wah"

But for his reaching his limit with Paul's tactless domination and John and Yoko's drug-addled antics, George might never have composed this stately rocker. On January 10, 1969, he left the ill-starred *Get Back* sessions

▲ 24520 OCTOBER 1971 / 75¢

CIRCUS

FREE!
HARRISON
POSTER

NEW
MOODY
BLUES
LP
PINK
FLOYD

By the fall of 1971, George's esteem in the minds of the public was probably as high as it ever got. He's shown here (with an outdated photo) on the cover of *Circus* in the wake of the triumphant Bangladesh benefit.

at Twickenham Studios—for good, as far as he was concerned. At home in Esher, he set this song to paper, a commentary on how what once had been sweet had now gone sour. (The title artifice, nominally a guitarist's effects pedal, served as synonym for "headache.") After a few days spent visiting his parents in Liverpool and collecting his thoughts, however, he agreed to return and finish the project so as not to leave his bandmates in the lurch. But, regardless of his transient Beatle concerns, striking out on his own was no longer a matter of "if" but "when."

As produced for *All Things Must Pass*, this track served as an excellent contrasting buffer between the spiritual "My Sweet Lord" and the resigned "Isn't It a Pity." "Wah-Wah" duly chugged along, powered by the rather large assembly of rockers gathered for the occasion. But not until the song's live debut at Madison Square Garden the following summer did it truly come into its own, placed in the prime slot as concert opener. Fueled by anticipatory adrenaline, the tune set off the Western half of the show in a grand fashion.

Though doubtlessly suffering from nerves, both for the auspiciousness of the occasion and the prospect of fronting a show for the first time ever, George unleashed a powerful vocal, bolstered by the non-scripted elements absent on the album version: live vocal backings, which added a gospel-esque energy to the proceedings; Billy Preston's keyboard fills; and the public debut of the "thunder and lighting" double drum team of Ringo and Keltner. Complete with a brass section and a plethora of guitarists (both electric and acoustic), the Bangladesh concert performance of "Wah-Wah" has become, through the magic of the film and soundtrack album, one of rock's transcendental moments. Not for no reason was it slotted as the group finale to 2002's *Concert for George* memorial.

"Bangla-Desh"

Unlike John, George was not a natural sloganeer. To make his points musically, he relied upon melody, harmony, dynamics, and exquisitely hooky lead guitar parts. That last element would be conspicuously downplayed on the song he composed as an appeal to the public to aid the starving masses halfway around the world. Instead, he laid out verses making the case ("It sure looks like a mess . . . I've never seen such distress") while directly asking that his listeners help "get the starving fed." Certainly, if any ex-Fab had the cachet with his fan base to solicit good works, it was the spiritual Beatle.

At Leon Russell's suggestion, George opened the song with an introductory passage drawing listeners in. After describing Ravi's entreaty, he turned the focus back to the public by acknowledging that while he himself wasn't a direct party to the suffering, he could not stand idly by. Thereupon, the band came slamming in with some dramatic piano and cymbal crashes, pivoting into a recitation of what was required. As a single, the song was possibly not the most commercial of records, but as a call to service, it could scarcely have been improved upon.

The song had only *just* been recorded by the time George and friends performed it live as the set-ender at the Bangladesh charity event. (As such, the composer needed a little prompting on the lyrics, which were taped to the floor.) In contrast to the single, the stage performance featured a double-length sax solo from Jim Horn (since George did not attempt to play the slide break featured on the single), as well as possibly Harrison's most impassioned singing.

The live performance of "Bangla-Desh" was perhaps George's high-water mark of public esteem. Afterward, though he was still much loved, his particular brand of selflessness proved to be an increasingly tough sell. August 1, 1971 marked a singular crossing of the cause with the man in a way that was impossible to surpass. Though three years later on the *Dark Horse* tour George would be bombarded with calls from fans to play the song (as they no doubt wanted to experience the magic of that earlier performance firsthand), George rather testily refused, possibly owing to the sour aftertaste that that particular charitable effort had left.

"Simply Shady"

A more disconcerting development was on full display with the album's next track. On his first two solo albums, George's compositions seldom deviated from a set paradigm, subject-wise: they either offered spiritual and philosophical guidance, or they took the form of devotionals that could as easily be about a lover as about a deity. "Simply Shady" upset the pattern by offering instead as lucid an account of his own self-defilement as could be imagined.

In a Tom Waits croak, George set about describing his fall from grace into the bottom of a bottle. Very matter-of-factly, he tells of alcohol's effects on him ("My senses took a dip") and it's not a pleasant buzz ("my madness craved for more"). What's more, he recognizes the very banality of what he's experiencing ("it's all been done and more"). Never before or since would he set to music such a devastating self-appraisal.

Everything about the track—the world-weary delivery, the muted brass, the bluesy construction—should have been unremarkable, even clichéd, given this well-trodden ground, but since this is George Harrison, it cannot help but be musically canny. The playing is sharp, the arrangement inventive. Overall, the song resembles nothing so much as the usual Lennon self-flagellation, except that George's detached delivery proves to be just as chilling in its own way as John's typical emotional approach was.

Bassist Bennett has described both "Simply Shady" and the instrumental "Hari's on Tour (Express)" as having evolved from jams (although the lyric to the former song had apparently been composed in Bombay). It has been suggested that in departing from what heretofore been his strength—the painstaking crafting of material with great attention to detail—George was abandoning what he did best, much like Paul under similar circumstances, resulting in *Wild Life*. Given the song's depiction of dissipation (without glorifying it), a looser approach is more than fitting.

"It Is He (Jai Sri Krishna)"

"My Sweet Lord" notwithstanding, George's religiosity was an aspect to his work that many fans found an increasingly heavy cross to bear. By the time some listeners plowed through the largely downbeat offerings of the *Dark Horse* album, a track bearing the name of the artist's personal savior could

Invited to the Oval Office by Jack Ford, the president's son, George exchanged buttons with the head of the free world: an "Om" for a "WIN" ("Whip Inflation Now").

not have come as welcome relief. But in fact, "It Is He (Jai Sri Krishna)," the LP's closing tune, was a joyful delight.

Bearing a refrain in the original Sanskrit, the song was a pop treatment of a "bhajan," or traditional Indian devotional. During the *All Things Must Pass* sessions, George had actually taped a bhajan entirely in this ancient language, entitled "Gopala Krishna." Built upon the riffing of his Strat (run through a Leslie speaker), this was an almost folkie-feeling recording, though its repetition and complete absence of English lyrics may have made it a nonstarter for inclusion on the record.

By the time of *Dark Horse*, however, George was ready to revisit the idea, this time including verses in his native tongue. His multitracked vocals drifted ethereally between a bed of acoustic twelve-string guitars and a flute ensemble, comprised of Jim Horn, Tom Scott, and Chuck Findley. (Interestingly, it is the one cut on the album where his voice is not a laryngitic rasp, indicating that it may have been recorded early on.)

Additionally, George commandeered a "khamak" (or "gubgubbi"), a traditional Bengali instrument constructed with two tuned strings drawn over a drum and used for rhythm. Emil Richards threw in a wobble board for good measure, while Billy Preston brought his usual fine keyboard support to yet another ex-Fab spiritual.

The song was composed in the wake of a particularly heavenly experience its author had had in India back in February, wherein a "blissed out" Hari Georgeson spent several hours in the company of like-minded devotees chanting away as the sun rose. Guru Sripad Maharaj, who'd started the bhajan, suggested to the ex-Fab that the chant might translate well into a song, and George agreed.

Had critics and a certain segment of the public not been so reflexively hostile to Harrison's Krishna paeans by this time, "It Is He" might have warranted some airplay, so unrelentingly calming yet catchy was it. But it surfaced at a time when many had grown weary of his piety, and remains yet another overlooked gem within a much-maligned release.

"The Answer's at the End"

By the time "OHNOTHIMAGEN" surfaced less than a year after his previous release, it was clear that George was still battling his demons. Though his voice was in better form than it had been on the last go-round, a cloud of gloom still hung over the proceedings. Yes, there were the echoes of his broken marriage, but now added to the mix was the critical lambasting he'd received in *Dark Horse*'s wake. What is interesting is how he chose to address what he'd been grappling with, musically. In the end, *Extra Texture* is unique within the Harrison catalog as essentially an LP-length excursion into *soul*.

Since it developed into a discernible genre in the late '50s / early '60s, soul—as an outgrowth of the blues—was the medium of choice among the oppressed to express their interactions with a world (or a romantic partner) that often misunderstood or abused them. As such, it proved the perfect format for George in his efforts to work through his many issues. Apart from the joyous "You"—a prototypical Motown pastiche—much of what follows on the album falls into a slower or darker groove. It may have been the perception that the record was a downer that put off critics and kept buyers from giving it its due.

The album's opener was followed by this song, which sonically resembled an *All Things Must Pass* outtake. "The Answer's at the End," whose title suggested a weighty *Living in the Material World* type of sermon, was in fact simply a plea not to judge our loved ones too severely for their human shortcomings. (The subject of not being so judgmental was one that would have resonated with George around this time, given the shellacking he'd been recently subjected to.)

The key message had been taken straight from the homilies of Friar Park's builder, Sir Frank Crisp, the Edwardian lawyer, horticulturist, and "microscopist." He'd had his personal words of wisdom engraved throughout the estate, so it was natural that daily exposure to them would culminate in a song one day. The particular passage that formed the basis of this track asserted that "Life is one long mystery," but if one conducted oneself with kindness and generosity, the answers to life's riddles would reveal themselves "at the end."

The song possesses a grace and majesty reminiscent of a past Harrisong, "Isn't It a Pity," which was unsurprising, considering that George drew upon Nina Simone's version of *that* composition as inspiration for *this* one. (And, as with that earlier recording, one could make the case that a little judicious pruning might have improved the song slightly.)

"Tired of Midnight Blue"

Many of the songs on *Extra Texture* were keyboard-based, giving the album as a whole a different feel from the standard guitar-drenched Harrison sound. On "Tired of Midnight Blue," the piano is front and center, ably handled by Leon Russell. (The song was originally called simply "Midnight Blue," but when Melissa Manchester's breakout single of the same name was released in the summer of 1975, George amended his title.)

This cut, an indictment of the partying lifestyle carried over from the last album, nonetheless projects a swagger noticeably absent on most of his work. It's built upon a series of seventh chords, lending the song an appropriately bluesy feel. While Russell's riffing provides the song's backbone, it's George's guitar fills that provide color within the monochrome. Further, his "blue-eyed soul" approach to the vocals here, as well as on many other *Extra Texture* tracks, conveys the right downbeat tone without sounding completely defeated. (To say "*brown*-eyed soul" doesn't make much sense, does it?)

Although both "You" and "This Guitar (Can't Keep from Crying)" were strong cuts chosen as singles, only the first was a hit. It's possible that with some promotional support, "Tired of Midnight Blue" would likewise have made a great candidate for airplay, offering another side of George beyond that of pop guru. Sadly, we'll never know, but one may hope for its rediscovery someday with inclusion on a well-conceived Harrison compilation—something *still* unrealized, *Let It Roll* notwithstanding.

"Sat Singing"

Had the final say on George's work not rested in the boardroom at Warner Brothers, Harrison not only would have gone head to head with John's comeback album, but he would have advanced his own reputation with the latest of a string of solid albums. Instead, corporate interference resulted in a work alleged to be more marketable while sacrificing the artist's original vision.

As conceived, *Somewhere in England* was a spiritually deeper album—but not impenetrably so—than George had issued in years. There were several devotional or philosophical musings, including "Writing's on the Wall." This tune, exploring the transience of life, included the observation that "death holds on to us much more with every passing hour." Had the song been in stores by December 1980—as planned—listeners would doubtless have been chilled by the song's prescience, which also included the warning that friends we thought would be around always are " . . . shot away . . . from you."

Less dark was the joyous "Sat Singing"—a description of out-of-body bliss that George experienced while meditating. (The title is a play on the Sanskrit *satsang*, which describes any session spent in the company of the highest truth or with one's holy person.) That such a sweet-sounding recording was rejected speaks volumes for the cluelessness of the record industry. While perhaps not crafted for Top 40 radio, this fusion of slide guitar, pleasing arrangement, and inspired vocal made "Sat Singing" an irresistibly compelling listening experience for those simply wishing to revel in the essence of George Harrison's unique sound.

Not hearing a "My Sweet Lord" type of blockbuster to rescue their fourth-quarter earnings, Warner Brothers handed *Somewhere in England* back to its creator, averting a head-to-head rematch in the charts between George and John a decade after their first one.

Despite its quality, the song was dropped, never to appear publicly until 1987, and only then as a bonus disc packaged within a limited-edition, leather-bound volume, entitled *Songs of George Harrison I*, an heirloom-quality item (with a price to match) from Genesis that escaped notice by most fans. For those of shallower pockets, ever-helpful bootleggers have handily issued George's version of *Somewhere in England*, a karmically justified act.

"Flying Hour"

Another *Somewhere in England* track destined for rejection was beyond argument one of the album's finest tracks. An even stronger case for the absolute idiocy of butchering the release is underscored by the cutting of "Flying Hour," a breezy tune filled to the brim with hooks. Warner's snub of the track must have seemed doubly galling, considering that the recording was a leftover from the *George Harrison* sessions, produced in early 1978 by the company's own Russ Titelman.

George was in the habit of hosting frequent jamming sessions at Friar Park with members of the "Henley Mafia": neighboring members of the rock community like Deep Purple's Jon Lord, Ten Years After's Alvin Lee, ex-Traffic drummer Jim Capaldi, and guitarist Mick Ralphs—ex–Mott the Hoople and, by the time he made the acquaintance of George, riding high with Bad Company. "Flying Hour" began as a jam with Ralphs, to which George later added lyrics. When word of the song's near-release first surfaced, Ralphs was touched to see that he'd been given a cowriter credit.

The song was a rare rocker from Hari Georgeson, complete with the requisite slide leads and a propulsive Willie Weeks bass line driving the tune along. As added embellishment: the Polymoog of Steve Winwood, last heard on "Love Comes to Everyone" and later used to great effect on his own "While You See a Chance" from 1981's *Arc of a Diver* smash. Lyrically, "Flying Hour" was almost a send-up of George's usual philosophical ruminations. Instead of extolling the next life, the song proclaims the present to be where it's at: "Right now is the one thing that I can feel, the one thing real to me."

It defies explanation that such a catchy, rocking track should have been so summarily disposed of. Eventually, it too found release on the aforementioned Genesis book set, but only in a watered down, remixed form. The reissue of Harrison's Warners work, within and outside of *The Dark Horse Years* box set, represents a major blown opportunity: instead of restoring George's vision of *Somewhere in England*, the label kept it musically as originally released, acknowledging his intentions only by offering the original cover artwork.

28

All I've Got to Be Is to Be Happy

1979

B y this time in the decade, only Paul maintained a steady schedule of producing music, planning tours, and playing the rock star game. By mid-1978 he'd reconstituted Wings with guitarist Lawrence Juber and drummer Steve Holley. The two additions made for the final incarnation of Wings, as events over the next year and a half would dictate. But this was all down the road, and as of early 1979, Paul was more intent on what his immediate future held with the advent of a new record deal.

After sixteen years with EMI, Paul went on to ink "one of the fattest royalty contracts" in record industry history with their arch-rivals, CBS/ Columbia (home of Billy Joel, Barbra Streisand, and Dylan, among many others). The label acquired the McCartney/Wings back catalog, enabling them to reissue his entire solo output. In addition to netting him beaucoup bucks, his contract, it has long been rumored, freed Paul to record with John, George, and Ringo should a reunion come to pass. The first product of the new deal was a single: the B-side, a gem entitled "Daytime Nighttime Suffering," had been recorded a year earlier, while the eventual A-side went back even farther as a solo noodling before receiving overdubs to bring it up to group and commercial speed.

The song was called "Goodnight Tonight," and unlike, say, "Silly Love Songs," a dance track masquerading as a pop tune, this one was an all-out effort to compete on the disco-dominated charts. It is therefore fair to say that the song divided Paul's fan base between those who loathed it on principle and the rest who appreciated his attempt at staying current (and relevant). (The song's insistent refrain of "don't say it" may have been a subconscious attempt to ward off derision for the experiment.) "Goodnight Tonight" was a certified smash around the world, peaking at #5 in the U.S. and Britain, but might have gone higher had it not alienated the rock audience so much. Two months after it topped out, long-suffering rock fans had their day (or night, as it were), in Chicago.

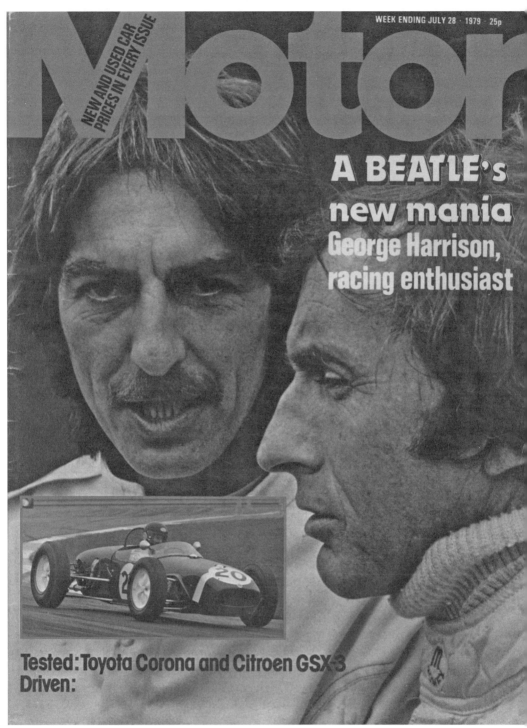

WEEK ENDING JULY 28 · 1979 · 25p

NEW AND USED CAR
PRICES IN EVERY ISSUE

Motor

A BEATLE's new mania
George Harrison, racing enthusiast

Tested: Toyota Corona and Citroen GSX-3
Driven:

Seen here with racing legend and close friend Jackie Stewart, George developed an
infatuation with high-speed Formula One racing, a seemingly incongruous contrast
with his intense spirituality. Perhaps he saw it as just one more potential way to meet
his Maker.

On Thursday, July 12 at Comiskey Park, attendees of a "Disco Demolition" rally were invited to bring their resentment-instilling records to a double-header against Detroit. Between games, the offending vinyl would be detonated in center field by rock DJ Steve Dahl, who'd spearheaded the anti-disco movement in Chicago from 97.9 FM, "the Loop" (WLUP). The lure of $0.98 admission and the chance to vent their outrage at as a cultural phenomenon that left them feeling disenfranchised (Donna Summer's "Bad Girls" was in the midst of a five-week run atop the charts) drew far more fans than either the station or the White Sox organization had bargained for. The fact that the games were sold out didn't deter the swarming masses from descending upon Thirty-fifth and Shields, where they soon began scaling walls to enter the park.

By the time a considerable amount of smoke had cleared, the second game had been forfeited because of the damage wrought upon the field by the out-of-control would-be rioters. What the whole exercise demonstrated was the intensity with which rockers felt that their entire way of life was becoming eclipsed. (What they couldn't have known was that the half-life of disco had been reached and that its cultural domination was slowly receding.) In fact, just on the horizon was an act that seemingly aped the Beatles with precision (at least in presentation) and would score a chart topper of their own that summer in a pushback to the prevailing trend. The group was the Knack, and the song bore the unlikely title "My Sharona."

As for Paul, the album he'd been working on with the final lineup had been intended as a very deliberate attempt to at least compete with (if not better) the energy of punk. *Back to the Egg* was originally conceived as a thematic song cycle, a sort of "back to our origins as a band on the road," but the concept was jettisoned early on. Instead, only the vaguest of recurring musical motifs remained, implying unity without actually delivering any particular statement. Several cuts duly rocked, such as the singles "Getting Closer" and "Spin It On," but on the whole, the album, produced by former Fab engineer and current studio hotshot Chris Thomas, was less than the sum of its parts. Reviews were largely unkind, and Macca must been mortified to find that changing labels didn't help his chart performance one bit (it peaked at #8 in the States and #6 in Great Britain).

George, meanwhile, had been biding his time in crafting a follow-up to *Thirty-Three & 1/3*'s return to commercial form. While producer Russ Titelman yielded few concessions to the marketplace, he did make sure that the material was presented as accessibly as possible without compromising George's sound too much. His approach yielded good results when the leadoff single, "Blow Away," made it into heavy rotation straight away on both rock and adult contemporary radio, peaking at #16 and #2 respectively. (It helped that the song was unrelentingly catchy.) Less explicably, the follow-up single, "Love Comes to Everyone," which seemed to have "hit" written all over it, failed to chart at all.

Still, the album carried with it the artist's pleasant buzz of contentment that came with enjoying a tranquil life while absolutely not needing to compete commercially with any other acts of the day. Unlike Paul's near-contemporaneous release, *George Harrison* was reviewed positively. Drawing particular notice from Beatles fans was the inclusion of "Not Guilty," the much-fabled outtake from the "White Album." Interest in the publicly-unheard-until-then track (coupled with a lack of any frame of reference) had resulted in helpful bootleggers offering up a Ravi Shankar track, "Frenzy and Distortion," as the lost Harrisong on bootlegs prior to.

For a year intended to be a respite from the nonstop treadmill he'd been on for at least the last five years, 1979 proved to be rather difficult for Ringo. As a child, he'd famously spent a lot of time in hospitals, owing to a variety of maladies, including a bout of pleurisy (a lung ailment) that sidelined him from keeping up scholastically with his peers. One month after he'd visited John at the Dakota (where the two were photographed together by Fred Seaman, John's newly hired gofer), Ringo fell desperately ill in Monte Carlo. A recurrence of peritonitis, an intestinal ailment he'd suffered from as a child, led to a collapse. He was rushed into emergency surgery, where the removal of five feet of intestines, by all accounts, saved the drummer's life. (Said he: "I had a good look at death's face that day.") Paul's former bandmate Jimmy McCulloch would be less fortunate later that year—and bad karma was not yet finished with the Ringed One, either. In late November, while he was staying in the Hollywood Hills home he was renting from Harry Nilsson, a fire broke out. While no one was hurt, years' worth of Beatles-era memorabilia in storage on the property was destroyed. Ringo tried desperately to rescue what he could, but unfortunately, much of it, including his gold records, were stored in the attic, where the fire seemed to have originated. By the time the flames had been extinguished, the bulk of his holdings had burned.

On a more positive note, Ringo recovered quickly from the life-saving surgery, so much so that three weeks later, on May 19, he was on hand along with George and Paul to help celebrate the wedding of Pattie Harrison to Eric Clapton. (Somewhat surprisingly, an invite to Clapton's Plastic Ono Band-mate was overlooked, probably owing to Lennon's low profile of late.) With the cream (no pun intended) of British rock in attendance—Jagger, Bowie, Elton, Jack Bruce, Denny Laine, Robert Palmer, and so forth—the inevitable jam ensued. What made it special was the three ex-Fabs sharing a public stage for the first time since playing a certain Savile Row rooftop a decade earlier. Though no one made much of the "Beatle reunion" at the moment it occurred, Clapton later expressed his regret that John hadn't been present—as did John himself.

The ex-Beatle had indeed made good on his word and kept himself increasingly out of the limelight. News of his occasional travels filtered out, such as in 1977, when he was asked in Japan for a comment on the recent death of Elvis Presley. Lennon's response—"Elvis died when he went into the army"—demonstrated that his gift for a newsworthy quote was still intact, but increasingly, many wondered in the face of the unrelenting silence if he would ever record again. *Rolling Stone* critic Dave Marsh had published "An Open Letter to John Lennon" a year earlier, wondering aloud what was going on and intimating that some sort of explanation was in order. He received a scathing slap down from John for his trouble ("I don't fucking owe anybody anything. I've done my part. It's everybody else's turn now.')

Still, when the Anglo-pop fan magazine *Trouser Press* reiterated the request for John to call a time-out to his time-out in May, he responded. On Sunday, May 27, a full-page ad ran in the *New York Times* from the Lennons, addressed to "People Who Ask Us What, When, and Why." It was vintage "johnandyoko," being equal parts childlike directness and hippie-dippy gobbledygook. In it, the couple extolled the virtues of "wishing" as a means of obtaining what one truly needs in life. As for negativity, they confided that their method of handling the anger of others was to draw a halo around said person's heads, as a reminder that "everyone has goodness inside."

Without any direct commentary on any issues in particular, they went on to note that they appreciated the "letters, telegrams, taps on the gate, or just flowers and nice thoughts" that they were bombarded with during this time: "We love you, too." But they hoped that the public would understand that their silence was "not of indifference." Of course, the real question on the public's mind was less about growing flowers or purring cats than it was—at least—when would he record again, and—at most—were there any plans to get together with the other three? On this score, the couple responded in true Zen fashion with a postscript: "We noticed three angels were looking over our shoulders when we wrote this!"

If the Lennons thought that this would in any way get the pressure for a reunion off their backs, then they were naïve beyond measure. (As for Dave Marsh, John's earlier rejoinder left him feeling "pretty small. . . . It never occurred to me . . . that my attitude reduced someone I thought I loved and admired to the status of a vending machine." But John's ad prompted "Another Open Letter to John Lennon" in *Rolling Stone*, this time with Marsh begging him not to embarrass himself by reuniting the group.) Indeed, by late summer the top-dollar offers to reunite had returned. In addition to

As the end of the decade neared, calls for the Beatles to reunite were replaced by personal appeals to John Lennon to simply emerge from his sabbatical.

Sid Bernstein, though, a new wrinkle developed: UN Secretary-General Kurt Waldheim now issued a call for the four to set aside their differences and perform in a one-off reunion to raise money to alleviate the suffering of Cambodian refugees (the "Boat People") fleeing genocide at the hands of the Khmer Rouge.

John at least asked for some specifics, while George called up Paul and asked his thoughts. The latter responded that while he wasn't against the idea in theory, just then he was rehearsing Wings for some autumn live dates in the U.K. before heading over to Japan early the next year for the long-awaited Far East tour. Ringo, already having a less than happy year, dismissed the event altogether. "They think I can just pick up the drums and drive out to Sheffield or somewhere and play. It would take us months to get an act together, even if we wanted to."

What ended up occurring was less than a reunion but certainly more than might have happened had public pressure not been brought to bear. In December, Wings headlined a four-night stand at London's Hammersmith-Odeon, anchoring an event that featured veteran acts like Queen and the Who as well as current stars like Elvis Costello, Ian Dury, and the Clash. While no former Fabs turned up—contrary to persistent rumors—the shows ended up serving a good cause while providing a stage where Paul could present his Rockestra live. (A good thing, too, as Wings' set came off as something of an under-whelming downer.) Despite the event's worthy goals, the double-album set of concert highlights as well as the accompanying film remain inexplicably out of print to this day, unlike George's Bangladesh event, which continues to raise money for the cause.

Given his contemplative, relaxed bent during this period, it was natural that George would be moved to reflect upon his body of work through the years. The resulting book, entitled *I Me Mine*, was far less of an attempt to tell his life story than it was to simply offer well-heeled fans some insight into his craft. Nonetheless, the pricey, limited-edition, hand-bound leather volume would spark controversy, both owing to the public's perception that the work amounted to an elitist-only vanity project (wrote one angry fan to a rock journal, "What ever happened to 'everywhere there's lots of piggies?'") and to the feelings of one John Lennon, who took great umbrage at what he took as an intended slight by the book's author by omitting any credit his way. Though a petty complaint, it served to underscore the existence of lingering issues among the four. As for George's book, a regular clothbound edition hit the streets the following year. (John himself was penning a rather acerbic telling of his history around that time; it would be published posthumously as *Skywriting by Word of Mouth* in 1986.)

29

You Gotta Give the Other Fellow Hell

Feuds, Fights, and Bad Behavior

The 1970s saw no shortage of sniping among the former Fabs, either privately or publicly. However, despite the extremely bitter circumstance of their breakup, for the most part things were never as intensely hostile as the public tended to imagine. By the end of 1971, it seemed that John and Paul, the former group's chief antagonists, had agreed to a cease-fire and maintained mostly cordial relations ever after. George began the decade as part of the tight-knit trio that fought their errant bassist in court, but, beginning in 1971, began having a very up-and-down relationship with John. His relations with Paul were no less volatile, if more explicable.

For his part, John's mercurial nature mandated the occasional shooting off of his mouth, but he was always quick to remind his victims not to take any bile he spewed too seriously. It is not for no reason that he, the most confrontational of the Beatles, tended to get into the most trouble. Conversely, the unflappable Ringo took pains to be fair and get along with everyone; he had no feuds to speak of and therefore is absent from this list.

Paul vs. Apple—1970/1971

The roots of Paul's legal action to dissolve the Beatles' business partnership lay in his refusal to accept Allen Klein as his manager. Thoroughly convinced of Klein's inherent shadiness while refusing to accept anyone but his in-laws to handle the group's business, he'd essentially put the band in a three-to-one standoff. Had he been capable of recognizing the bind he put the others in by insisting on the equally unacceptable Eastmans, there might have been opportunity for a third option to present itself, thereby providing a safety valve to deflate heightened inter-band tensions. But each side clung to its position, and it was this intransigence more than anything that poisoned relations.

Just before taking his estranged bandmates to court in December 1970, Paul ran this holiday greeting in the trade publications. To some, depicting himself and Linda as clowns (in a bag, no less) was a none-too-subtle provocation.

It seems remarkable in retrospect that Lennon, Harrison, and Starr were so adamant about denying Paul his freedom, seemingly to preserve a dysfunctional partnership that had long since ceased to function as a cooperative. While there was little reason to expect any new *collective* product coming into being, it is believed that Klein convinced the others that keeping Macca within the Apple stable as a company *asset* was a worthy goal, given his talents as a hit-making producer. For his part, Paul was all too aware that as any individually generated revenue was going to flow into the collective kitty per their existing agreement, it therefore would be better to simply pull out and be paid for his own labors. It was the fair thing to do, and he no more wanted to share royalties from McCartney product with the others than lay claim to monies generated by *their* work.

When pressed, John punted, telling Paul that he'd weigh in only after George and Ringo had their say. A call to George was, at least, answered with unambiguous directness. Undergoing stresses of his own (his mother's terminal illness, work on *All Things Must Pass*), he ended a phone conversation to Paul by declaring "You'll stay on the fucking label—Hare Krishna!" A face-to-face encounter between the two in New York City in early December, intended as socializing, went equally badly. The end result was that the Fabs' most adroit PR man saw no choice other than to pursue an action that he knew in advance would be a public relations disaster: take the other (ex-) Beatles to court.

This wildly unpopular (if necessary) action drew heaps of scorn from every corner, not least the public, who, being on the outside, could see no reason for the group to air their dirty linen in the full glare of a courtroom. Paul later admitted that the hirsute appearance he cultivated around this time, complete with out-of-control facial hair, was to (inwardly at least) shield himself from the derision he became acutely aware of when coming and going to the legal proceedings.

The anticipated courtroom showdown with all four in attendance never actually materialized. Mostly, Paul turned up with Linda on his arm as the others maintained an icy distance. Their say came mostly in the form of sworn depositions, notable for the downplaying of any irrevocable differences between them, *Lennon Remembers* notwithstanding. Messrs Starkey, Harrison, and Lennon met regularly with their respective legal representatives while the case was being argued in court. As the proceedings dragged on through February and into March, all three grew weary and finally George snapped. "I don't want to do it anymore—fuck it! I don't care if I'm poor, I'll give it all away."

The end of their immediate ordeal came soon enough. Paul and his attorneys were able to find an example of Klein taking a bigger commission than he'd been entitled to in the time since taking control of the

Beatles' affairs, and, having heard all sides, the court ruled in Paul's favor on March 12, calling for the appointment of a receiver to take control of the band's collective business interests until an agreement on a dissolution could be hammered out. Macca's victory did not sit well with the others: it was reported in the press that upon receiving word of the ruling, the three commandeered John's limo and headed for Paul's Cavendish Avenue digs. There, it was said, John scaled the wall and lobbed a couple of bricks through a window.

Ram vs. *Imagine*—Summer 1971

Having lost the PR war, Paul chose a very public way to satisfy his need for justice against the others generally and John specifically: on his current project, *Ram*, he threw down the gauntlet in what he thought was a very subtle manner. "Two Many People," the opening track, condemned those who were "preaching practices" while asserting, "You took your lucky break and broke it in two." (John was particularly sensitive to the perception that he was merely someone who'd lucked out by meeting Paul McCartney, rather than being a talent in his own right.) Elsewhere, the insistent refrain of "Back Seat of My Car" proclaimed, "We believe that we can't be wrong." John took the musical messages, as well as the jacket design (which featured one beetle having its way with another) as the provocations they were doubtlessly intended to be.

But being coy about his true feelings was a completely alien concept to Lennon. Knowing John as well as he did, Paul *had* to have known that some kind of retaliation was in order. It came on his next release, *Imagine*. To fans who had failed to pick up on *Ram*'s messages, "How Do You Sleep" was a stunningly direct attack. From the opening downbeat to the extended fade, the recording absolutely reeked of disdain, putting Paul down for living with "straights" who merely stroked his ego, being the tool of his controlling wife (imagine!) and having lost his musical gifts—such as they were. (John's claim that "the only thing you done was 'Yesterday'" had originally been followed by "but you probably pinched the bitch anyway"—a potentially libelous charge of plagiarism that Allen Klein talked John out of, suggesting instead the timely "and since you're gone you're just another day"—a far better line that had the virtue of being a pun on Paul's latest single.)

Indeed, penning the song's McCartney-bashing lyrics turned into a game as the song was being laid down in the studio, with John and Yoko entering into a giddy, sophomoric competition to see who could come up with the worst insults. Felix Dennis (from *Oz* magazine and later the publisher of *Maxim*) was a guest at the time of the sessions. He recollected that as ideas came, Yoko would run in with a piece of paper, share its contents with John, and then the pair would giggle like schoolkids at their own cleverness.

George, as one of the contributing musicians, was present, but so too was Ringo, who'd merely popped in for a visit. As the character assassination escalated, it became obvious to Dennis that the Ringed One was getting quite upset at the lyrical lambasting the Lennons were dishing out.

Never one to let an insult go unreturned, John took the bait offered by Paul on *Ram* with *Imagine*, responding both musically and with this satirical jab at the former album's cover art.

Finally, he reached his limit and said, "That's enough, John." According to Dennis, the final product is positively tame compared to what might have been. For his part, George limited his contribution to guitar, providing a stinging six-string rebuke that carried more weight than mere words could.

Public reaction to the song was almost entirely negative. Despite John's multiple attempts to justify the apparent overkill (variously as an attempt to write a Dylanesque accusatory song, as a way to put his sibling-rivalry resentment of Paul to good use, or as a disguised critique of himself), "How Do You Sleep" reflected badly on its creator, taking the public to a sad place that they did not want to go and dismaying critics, who thought Lennon was squandering his talents by enshrining his destructive impulses. (Said Ben Gerson in *Rolling Stone*: ". . . beyond the cruelty of it, it is offensive because it is unjust. Paul's music may be muzak to John's ears, but songs like "Oh Yoko" or "Crippled Inside" are no more consequential than anything on *McCartney* or *Ram*.")

As for the song's target, Paul was indeed hurt by the attack, but he also knew that he had invited it in the first place. (His own insults had been sparked by John's words in the *Lennon Remembers* interview, particularly where he'd been compared to Engelbert Humperdinck.) But it was not his style to return fire in kind; he was as loath as anyone to match wits in a verbal joust with his former partner. Instead he responded gently with an apparent stylistic *tribute* to John on the *Band on the Run* album, "Let Me Roll It." A Plastic Ono Band–sounding pastiche if ever was one, it featured a stark arrangement, sharp staccato guitar riffing, and a heavily reverbed vocal (complete with primal scream at the end). To anyone keeping score, Paul came out the bigger man.

(Some listeners suggested that Paul responded earlier, on the *Wild Life* album just months after *Imagine*. The song "Dear Friend," a melancholy rumination on a falling-out, contains the line "Does it really mean so much to you?" Some took this as a veiled query to John, but in fact the song was a leftover from the *Ram* sessions and therefore predated "How Do You Sleep" by some months. Another song, "Some People Never Know," mentions people who *can* sleep at night, but the context in no way suggests it is a response to John's riposte.)

John vs. Frank Zappa—1971/1972

It was a busy year for John to be picking fights with people. What transpired between him and the esteemed founder of the Mothers of Invention, though, was less a battle than simply a case of egregiously bad form. As noted in *Fab Four FAQ*, musician/conductor/social critic Frank Zappa kept a toehold in pop culture (even guesting on an episode of *The Monkees* and in their film, *Head*). Though Zappa operated in a separate world from the Fabs, he saw the Beatles phenomenon as an example of vacant idolatry.

In 1967, he went to a great deal of trouble to satirize *Sgt. Pepper*'s artwork for the Mothers' *We're Only in It for the Money*. From his perspective, the Fabs were a corporate cash cow seemingly able to summon adulation and acclaim at will—rewards that he felt were properly *his* due. What he failed to recognize was their profound daring with *Pepper*—a swan dive into the unknown that both Brian Epstein and EMI felt was a tremendous—and unnecessary—commercial risk.

For Lennon's part, he admired Zappa from afar, less for his music than for his no-bullshit disposition. In his *Rolling Stone* interview, he summed up what he believed to be Zappa's essence: "'Listen, you fuckers, this is what I did. And I don't care whether you like my attitude saying it, but . . . I'm a fuckin' artist, man.'" Upon Lennon's landing in New York City, it was probably inevitable that the two would bump into each other, if not actually collaborate. Zappa had, of course, already worked with Ringo earlier that year on *200 Motels*. Odds of him getting together with George were rather slim, though Hari Georgeson would evoke him by name in a song in 1981. As for any musical interactions with Paul, Zappa blamed him unfairly for their less than successful "negotiation" over his parody of *Pepper*'s cover—even though he was being forced to turn his own LP jacket inside out because *EMI*, and not the Beatles, owned the image.

In any event, in 1971, Zappa and the Mothers, augmented by the addition of the Turtles' former lead singers, Howard Kaylan and Mark Vollman (known professionally as Flo and Eddie), were booked to play the Fillmore East during its final month. On Saturday, June 5, John—in town to oversee some overdubs on *Imagine*—spent the day sightseeing with *Village Voice* columnist and radio show host Howard Smith. When Smith mentioned that he would be interviewing Zappa later that day, Lennon asked if he could tag along: "I really, really admire him."

With John and Yoko in tow, Smith arrived at Zappa's hotel, waking him from sleep with his knock. Zappa was polite but not particularly starstruck at the sight of his unexpected guests. While Yoko irritated him by continually suggesting that everything Zappa had done, she had done first, he found John to be surprisingly humble (an attitude described by Smith as "I may be a star but you're the real thing"). The irreverent humor both men shared made for a good bond, leading Frank to extend an invitation to come down and jam with them at the Fillmore that night. After considerable hedging from John and cajoling from Zappa ("It'll be fun!"), an agreement was struck.

Zappa's shows tended to run long, and by the time he'd completed another encore in the early morning hours of Sunday, some of the audience had began filing out. But the stage lights went on yet again and the word soon spread that "John and Yoko" were now sharing his stage, prompting attendees to come running back. Backstage, they'd discussed a rudimentary set, prompting John to confess that he really didn't know any Zappa music. But the twelve-bar basics of the Olympics' "Well" would work well enough to kick things off. John introduced the oldie—which he'd soon after lay down in the studio—as a song he used to perform at the Cavern. Bolstered by some intermittent squalling by Yoko, the ensemble delivered a fine version of the tune.

From that point on, however, things began to degenerate. John's obvious nervousness led to some clumsy fumbling with his malfunctioning amp, while Frank had to show him some of the chords to what followed. Recognizable to everyone but the Lennons, a song entitled "King Kong"— first released on Zappa's 1969 album, *Uncle Meat*—emerged from the cacophony. The tune had a readily discernible melody and structure, but John and Yoko seemed to believe that *they* had led the band through this surprisingly well-received "jam." An improvisational workout followed, punctuated by John's repeated shouts of "scumbag!" (The term was slang for a used condom, something Lennon may or may not have known, but which, under the circumstances, seemed appropriate at the time.)

The Lennon-Mothers set ended with Yoko's wailing and John's feedback on a "composition" they would later title "Au." Yoko was, at this point, fully enveloped by one of her trademark black bags. It was therefore not immediately obvious to her when the musicians—including her husband—had filed off the stage, leaving her to do her thing before whatever audience remained. Afterward, Zappa agreed to make a duplicate multitrack master of the evening's performance for John to use in any way he saw fit.

That chance came during the following year when, in need of some sort of marketing tool to help sell *Some Time in New York City*, Apple issued the recordings as one half of the "Live Jam" disc. Originally, Zappa had intended to release the tracks as one side of a *double*-record *Fillmore East—June 1971* album, but the shows emerged only two months later as a single LP. Lennon appropriated Zappa's plain, pencil-sketched cover design and augmented it with a red pen to reflect *his* take on the evening. That he in effect defaced *Zappa's* artwork to use as an inner sleeve to *his* album may have been irritating, but less so than John's careless theft of Frank's intellectual property.

"King Kong," now retitled "Jamrag" (English vernacular for a used sanitary napkin), appeared, credited as a Lennon-Ono tune. While *Some Time*

Composer/musician/iconoclast Frank Zappa drew strong reactions from the public. The infamous "Phi Zappa Krappa" poster, shot in 1967, depicted what some thought of as the artist at work.

in New York City was not one of Lennon's best-selling albums, it undoubtedly outsold most of Zappa's output; the oversight would therefore have cost him quite a pile of change. Equally galling was the mix of "Scumbag" on the Lennon album: several instruments, including some of Zappa's guitar, were mixed out, as were Flo and Eddie's improvised vocals. (Perhaps understandably, as they chanted "Now Yoko's in the scumbag . . . we're putting Yoko in a scumbag. . . .")

Zappa might have taken legal action against the Lennons, but ultimately did not, instead complaining bitterly about what had transpired whenever asked. The months following the show did not go all that well for him: in Switzerland in December, a fire at the Montreux Casino during their set (started, ironically, as they performed "King Kong") ended up destroying the band's gear. (The incident was, of course, famously chronicled in Deep Purple's "Smoke on the Water.") Then, just days later in London, a crazed attendee stormed the stage and attacked Zappa violently, throwing him ten feet down into the orchestra pit. (The song they were performing? "I Want to Hold Your Hand.")

Only in 1992, as part of his *Playground Psychotics* release, did Zappa get around to issuing his own version of the Lennon set. Most fans who have heard both prefer the Zappa mix, which features parts mixed out of John's. He did make one editorial emendation to the titles: "Au" was now retitled "A Small Eternity with Yoko Ono."

Paul vs. John in *Melody Maker*—November/December 1971

It was inevitable that the rock press, always on the lookout for the next big story, would pit the two feuding ex-Beatles against each other if given half a chance. John's musical diatribe against him meant that the next time Paul reared his head in public he'd be deluged with questions. That time came later that year as he prepared to launch Wings' first long-player. In an article for England's *Melody Maker*, he was given a platform to air his views on what was going on between him and John. He did not disappoint.

Under a headline reading "Why Lennon Is Uncool," Macca asserted that as far as "How Do You Sleep" went, it was a non-issue: "So what if I live with straights? . . . It doesn't affect him. . . . He says the only thing I did was 'Yesterday.' He knows that's wrong." His public coolness toward the blistering insult must have gotten John's goat, but no more than the praise that followed: "'Imagine,'" he went on, "is what John is really like but there was too much political stuff on the other albums. You know," he joked, "I only listen to them to see if there's something I can pinch."

He went on to tell his side of the ongoing litigation, insisting, "I just want the four of us to get together somewhere and sign a piece of paper saying it's all over. . . . That's all I want now but John won't do it. Everybody thinks I am the aggressor but I'm not, you know. I just want out." Elsewhere in the piece he repeated his wish for the Beatles to have gone back to their club roots and played under a false name, without hype (something he would soon begin doing with Wings). Instead, Paul noted, John rejected his idea and went out to do a stadium show in Toronto. "I didn't dig that at all."

It didn't take long for Lennon to respond to the red flag waved in his face. Demanding equal time, he quickly fired off a rebuttal. To his credit, he didn't go off on a wild, expletive-laden rant (although nine lines he wrote *were* deleted by the magazine to avoid any slander lawsuits). First, he addressed the assertions that *he* was blocking an easy solution to their problems. "It's all very well, playing 'simple honest ole Paul' in *Melody Maker* but you know damn well we can't just sign a bit of paper." The problem, he reiterated, was the tax liability that would hit them all upon the dissolution of Apple. "You say, 'John won't do it.' I will if you indemnify us against the tax man!"

Paul's disingenuous claim of innocence in bringing about the disunity was especially galling. "If YOU'RE not the aggressor (as you claim), who the hell took us to court and shat all over us in public?. . . Have you ever thought that you might POSSIBLY be wrong about something? . . . Good God! You must know WE'RE right about Eastman. . . . Anyway, enough of this petty bourgeois fun."

He then went on to discuss the notion of performing live again. "Whadya mean BIG THING in Toronto? It was completely spontaneous. . . . We'd never played together before . . . (I said it was daft for the Beatles to do it. I still think it's daft.) . . . It's best to just DO IT. I know you'll dig it and they don't even expect the Beatles now anyway!" He also took exception to Paul's assessment of his work. "So you think 'Imagine' ain't political? It's 'Working Class Hero' with sugar on it for conservatives like yourself!! You obviously didn't dig the words."

It was pretty clear by this time that despite feeling as though he'd been provoked, John was getting tired of the nonstop bickering. He ended his response on a conciliatory note: "No hard feelings to you either. I know basically we want the same. . . ." He ended with a series of sign-offs (including "All you need is love") before adding a P.S.: "The bit that really puzzled us was asking to meet WITHOUT LINDA AND YOKO. I thought you'd understood BY NOW that I'm JOHNANDYOKO." A follow-up face-to-face dinner in New York in early 1972 sealed the détente for the foreseeable future.

John vs. the Smothers Brothers—March 12, 1974

A sort of Leopold and Loeb symbiosis marked the friendship between John Lennon and Harry Nilsson: whenever the two were together, there was no limit to the trouble they'd get themselves into—the kind that, left to their own devices, each man would have steered clear of. Since falling into each other's orbits during the *Rock 'n' Roll* sessions of fall 1973, the two kept company in and around Los Angeles, seemingly in a competition to see who could get to the bottom of the bottle fastest. The culmination of their shenanigans was the infamous Troubadour Club incident during a set by the Smothers Brothers musical/comedy team.

Their hour-long 1960s comedy show was favored by any number of rock acts of the day, including the Doors, Jefferson Airplane, and the Turtles. The Beatles allowed their clips for "Hey Jude" and "Revolution" to air there, instead of on their usual outlet, the *Ed Sullivan Show.* In 1969, Tommy joined John at the Montreal Bed-In and contributed guitar to the recording of "Give Peace a Chance." Therefore, it could be said that a warm relationship existed between the Fabs and the Smothers Brothers; when John turned up for their engagement at L.A.'s prestigious Troubadour Club, it was expected that he was there as a friend supporting their "comeback."

Instead, it proved to be a painful night out for all concerned. John and Harry, accompanied by May Pang, were seated in the V.I.P. section of the club, where such showbiz luminaries as former Rat Packer Peter Lawford, Leonard Nimoy, Cliff Robertson, and Pam Grier were in attendance. The trouble began when Nilsson took the occasion to introduce John to Brandy Alexanders. The drink, consisting of brandy, ice cream or heavy cream, and dark crème de cacao, tasted like a milkshake to John, and he downed them accordingly. They took effect slowly, and after the first set, John and Harry began serenading the attendees with their take on Ann Peebles' "I Can't Stand the Rain."

Once Tommy and Dick were back onstage, the two songbirds were too lubricated to stop. John's telling of what came next, entertaining though it was in retrospect, was anything but at the time. He told *Playboy*'s David Sheff ". . . suddenly I was in the fourth dimension. In the fourth dimension I noticed what I'd always secretly thought, that Dickie Smothers was an asshole even though I always liked Tommy. And so that's what I said, but because I was drunk, I said it out loud." According to witnesses present, he augmented his critique with shouts of "Fuck a cow!" (In defense of their behavior, Nilsson had caught Tommy's act as a solo some time before and had come away believing that Smothers *encouraged* heckling, that he felt it enhanced his performance. It was therefore with the intention of *helping* the brothers that night that Harry egged John on.)

Lawford repeatedly (and heatedly) stage-whispered to Lennon, telling him to knock it off. This only fueled John's belligerence, as profanities began flying in all directions, disrupting the act and drawing unwanted attention from the club's attendees. Lawford then got up from his table and found the club's manager, warning that if the manager couldn't silence Lennon, he would take it upon himself to do so. Meanwhile, the Smothers Brothers' manager, Ken Fritz, decided to handle things himself, approaching John and Harry's table to make a personal appeal. This only resulted in punches—and a glass—being thrown, with more innocent bystanders getting pulled into the unfolding melee. A table overturned and slammed down on Pam Grier's toes, painfully breaking three nails, while bouncers were summoned to insure John's swift departure.

During the fracas, John's glasses came off his head (they were later retrieved by Tommy Smothers' wife, who kept them for decades as a novelty/souvenir before putting them up for auction). Now outside the club and nearly blind, he threw punches wildly, apparently striking one Brenda Perkins in the eye—she later sued for damages. (Though Lennon vehemently denied touching her, insisting that she was shaking him down for money, others believe that under the chaotic conditions, he simply didn't know that he was lashing out at a woman. In any event, he settled out of court, fearing that more litigation would adversely affect his ongoing immigration battle.)

Once sobriety and sanity returned, the two miscreants were keen to undo the damage. Two floral displays were dispatched to the club: one for the manager and staff, another for Tom and Dick, by way of regrets. ("We humbly apologize for our bad manners. Love and Tears, John and Harry.") The entire episode left John feeling deeply humiliated. For all of the carousing that had gone on since arriving on the West Coast, he had at last hit bottom. Said May with considerable understatement: "I realized that I had to work harder to clean him up." About a month later, the couple moved back to New York, where it seemed less likely that he would get into trouble.

Equally enshrined in Lennon lore is another Troubadour incident from a few days earlier, this one involving a feminine hygiene product. (In some retellings, this product is a tampon, but the more accurate version is only slightly less remarkable.) It happened that John, paying a visit to the gents' facilities, found an unused sanitary napkin. As a gag, he returned to his table with it affixed to his forehead (as May begged him to take it off)—just good clean fun, folks. The levity of the moment was enhanced when John demanded of his waitress, "Do you know who I am?" "Yeah," she retorted.

"You're the asshole with the Kotex on your forehead." Over time, the two Troubadour incidents fused, spawning the myth believed by many that John *hit* a waitress. In any event, the damage to his reputation took some time to shake off.

George vs. Paul—October 23, 1974

Bashing your quite popular ex-bandmate in public is possibly not the best way to set the tone for kicking off a full-scale North American tour. But George was nothing if not forthright when questioned, in this case at a Los Angeles press conference announcing his late-autumn tour. He was asked about a number of things not related to the current project, including the breakup of his marriage ("I'd rather [Pattie] was with [Eric] than some dope"). Inevitably, the dialogue shifted to the Fabs. In 1974, their popularity was as strong as ever, and with George about to drop a new release on the heels of John and Ringo's recent offerings, the public was *still* pining for the four to set aside their differences long enough to, in John's words, "get crucified again."

George would have none of it. "Having played with other musicians," he began, "I don't think the Beatles were even that good. It's all a fantasy, this idea of putting the Beatles back together again. The only way it will happen is if we're all broke." Throwing out that bone for the press to chew on, he went further. "Even then, I wouldn't relish playing with Paul. To play with the Beatles, I'd rather have Willie Weeks on bass than Paul McCartney. With all respect to Paul, since the Beatles I've been in a box, taking me years to be able to play with other musicians. Paul's a fine bass player but sometimes he's a bit overpowering."

Whatever gasps might have emitted from reporters at this point were stifled as George went on to single out both Ringo ("the best backbeat in the business") and John ("his new record, I think, is lovely") for special praise, though he noted—tellingly, as it happened—that he was again feeling good about the latter: "John has gone through his scene, but feels to me like he's come around." His public whipping of Paul was not yet finished, though: "I'd join a band any day with John Lennon, but I wouldn't join a band with Paul McCartney. That's not personal; it's from a musician's point of view."

Although this jaw-dropping bit of candor merely reinforced what the public was already predisposed to think—as witnessed in *Let It Be*, where the two are explicitly shown butting heads over musical issues—it was slightly jarring to see that the philosophical ex-Beatle was, after all these years, *still* holding on to his personal resentments. Still, comments suggesting that being in a band with Macca hindered his musicianship only echoed how Henry McCullough had already described *his* tenure in Wings.

John responded gently to George's outburst, telling *Rolling Stone*, "I could play with all of them. George is entitled to say that, and he'll probably change his mind by Friday. You know, we're all human. We can all change our minds." Paul, however, was understandably defensive. "I don't agree with George. I don't think that the Beatles weren't any good. I think he's quite wrong on that." He seemed initially willing to think that perhaps George's remarks had been taken out of context. But while he accepted that Willie Weeks might be more technically proficient ("[He's] a better bass player than me. . . . It doesn't make me very happy to say that"), he was unwilling to cede the point that his former band "weren't any good." The Beatles, asserted Paul, "had more of an excitement . . . more of a kind of joy. That was what people picked up on, actually."

His assessment was entirely correct, but sort of beside the point. He and George would never again share the camaraderie on record that they once had—only after John's death did any musical interaction occur. The whole episode underscored how profoundly scarred the Beatle experience had left George. Though eventually he would make peace with Paul, an undercurrent of unease always lay not far from the surface.

George vs. John—December 14 and 19, 1974

As graceless as George's comments about Paul may have seemed, his real enmity exploded upon John, outside of the public eye, during his besieged tour. A number of issues were coming to a head that month: the imminent release of *Dark Horse*, the album, which—despite his tireless efforts to prepare it in time—was still not yet in stores; Ravi Shankar's illness, which forced him to miss several shows (no loss for Lennon, who when he saw the show on December 15, noted with glee that he "didn't have to sit through Ravi's bit"); and, most ominously, the signing of the official documents marking the end of all business ties with his fellow ex-Fabs. The tour's lukewarm reception only added to George's stress. By the time he met up with John and May Pang in New York in advance of his Nassau, Long Island show, he'd reached the end of his rope.

"Tired and wiped out" was how George described himself even *before* the first concert kicked off in Vancouver. (Alone out of all the ex-Beatles, John had sent George flowers on opening night.) Now, receiving John and May at the Plaza Hotel, he unleashed a torrent of built-up frustration and anger, described by May later as of the "where were you when I needed you?" variety. Years of hurt from an array of slights, including John's stiffing him at the Bangladesh concert, came to the surface. As his rage reached its peak, George demanded to see John's eyes. Though the latter quickly switched from sunglasses to his normal prescription ones, this placating gesture was not enough; the infuriated Harrison literally tore Lennon's glasses from his face and flung them to the floor.

It must have taken almost superhuman self-control—something Lennon wasn't particularly noted for—to not respond physically. (As he told May later, "I saw George going through pain and I know what pain is about.

Whereas his rough-hewn vocals on *Dark Horse*'s title track actually enhanced the composition, George's Father Time impression really didn't help his New Year single, "Ding Dong, Ding Dong."

So I let him do it.") Instead, John remained calm and left the encounter promising that he would appear with George the following week onstage at Madison Square Garden—if he thought it might help the tour. George accepted the offer and the two parted; the next day—his rage dissipated—he embraced John and apologized profusely, explaining he was worn down and feeling ill.

The day of the New York City show, Paul, George, and John were scheduled to meet with their respective lawyers at the Plaza to sign the papers ending the partnership. (Ringo, seeking to dodge a subpoena from Allen Klein, remained in England but took part via speaker phone; his signature was already on the document.) The assembled ex-Fabs and their business representatives sat and waited around for John to show. (The McCartneys had even brought a camera to document the historic occasion.) As the minutes ticked away, the gathering began wondering aloud why John, who was but a five-minute cab ride away, had failed to arrive.

Unbeknownst to everyone, he had his reasons for balking at signing, chiefly that, as the sole ex-Beatle resident of the U.S., he would be hit with a tax burden that could run as high as a million dollars. Moreover (though he was loath to admit it), the finality of the actual lawful breakup was something John found hard to face. Rather than come to terms with his reservations, he instead dispatched a helium-filled balloon to the conference by courier, bearing a card that read, "Listen to This Balloon." For George, this was the last straw.

He picked up the phone and dialed John's number. May answered, and after asking if he wanted to talk to John, she heard George bark, "Just tell him that I started this tour on my own and I'll end it on my own" before slamming the receiver down. John was actually more relieved than upset to be uninvited, feeling his usual attack of nerves at the prospect of going out onstage without the benefit of a rehearsal for what wasn't really his type of show. Later that evening, Paul spoke with John and assured him that they would be able to come to a satisfactory solution to the stumbling block.

The next day, Lennon and McCartney visited Linda's father, John Eastman, to work out an agreement. For most of the meeting, Eastman, who had viewed John as a troublemaker since their initial contact back in 1969, attempted to leverage the recalcitrant ex-Fab by telling him how much he'd let George down and that he'd be lucky if George ever spoke to him again. The conversation went on and on along these lines until disrupted by a call from Julian, who just happened to be attending George's show that night.

May relayed the message: "All's forgiven. George loves you and wants you to come to his party tonight." Sure enough, Paul and Linda, along with John and May, met up with the Dark Horse at New York's Hippopotamus Club. A group hug was shared (egregiously undocumented on film by either Linda or May), and the former bandmates shared a final moment of camaraderie together. Unbeknownst to anyone at the time, John and George would never see each other again.

Biographer Ray Coleman quotes John as saying,

> George and I are still good pals and we always will be. . . . I was a bit nervous about going on stage, but I agreed to because it would have been mean of me not to go on with George after I'd gone on with Elton. I didn't sign the document on that day because my astrologer told me it wasn't the right day, tee hee! George was furious with me at the time because I hadn't signed it when I was supposed to, and somehow or other I was informed that I needn't bother to go to George's show. I was quite relieved . . . and I didn't want it to be a case of just John jumping up and playing a few chords. I went to see him at Nassau and it was a good show. . . . George's voice was shot but the atmosphere was good and the crowd was great. I saw George after the Garden show and we were friends again.

For his part, the exhausted and somewhat dispirited Harrison went back to England to lick his wounds. Whatever issues lingered between the two men seemed to dissipate once he removed himself from the volatile situation he'd gotten himself into.

John vs. George—Fall 1980

In the years following their collective legal dissolution, the ex-Fabs maintained their individual paths. Paul and Ringo continued their recording careers while John reunited with Yoko, took a hiatus from recording, completed the final stretch of his immigration battle, and became a full-time father. George took a brief break before starting up work on *Extra Texture*, mentored some Dark Horse acts, tended to his garden, and wooed Olivia Arias while cleaning up some bad habits. His ambitions within the rock world slowly diminished, as he—in his own way—left the entertainment rat race behind. With each release, George played the promotional game less and less, unwilling to compete and content to produce music simply for its own sake.

Thereafter, he and the near-likewise sidelined Lennon maintained only sporadic contact. Said George to *Rolling Stone* in 1979: "I get post cards from him—it sounds like the Rutles (smiling), but he keeps in touch with tapping on the table and post cards." That said, John's day-to-day life became as big a mystery to George as it was to the rest of the world. (George confided to

Songwriter magazine that same year that he wondered if John was still writing or if he'd given it up.) Unbeknownst to the world, John *was* still writing, although in a less focused way, without a contractual obligation to tailor material to.

But by 1980, his sabbatical was nearing an end. As John prepared to reenter the world of media interaction, he began shaping a meme to at once explain where he'd been and what his new message was. The narrative that emerged extolled the virtues of monogamous love, family, and working toward universal goals: "one world, one people." Explicitly absent from his talk was any stated ambition to revisit his Fab past. Indeed, his first publicly aired interview (which appeared in *Newsweek*) displayed a distaste for his former group that bordered on enmity: "I know as much about [Paul] as he does about me, which is zilch." "When I first got out of the Beatles, I thought, 'Oh great. I don't have to listen to Paul and Ringo and George.'"

The most cutting remark seemed to at once echo what the group's harshest critics opined about George and Ringo's disposability while displaying a profound ignorance about what made the Beatles what they were: "What if Paul and I got together? It would be boring. Whether George or Ringo joined in *is irrelevant* [emphasis added] because Paul and I created the music. OK?" A little context is in order: John had not *seen* either Paul or George in years—Paul since 1976, George since 1974 (though there was occasional phone contact with both, mostly over business matters).

Ringo, on the other hand, socialized regularly with the Lennons. To be so publicly dissed by one of his closest "brothers" must have hurt; it isn't hard to imagine that John, once he recognized how crass his observation looked in print, would have made amends with the Ringed One, at least. But, in a role reversal from six years earlier, George seemed to be his whipping boy of the moment. This theme was underscored in the *Playboy* interview that followed, with Hari Georgeson seemingly singled out for John's particular scorn.

Of George's singular humanitarian work, John was dismissive. Bangladesh—the moment that he'd had the opportunity to put his money where his mouth was while allowing someone else to occupy the spotlight—was described rather derisively as a con job. As for the "My Sweet Lord" lawsuit, Lennon—no stranger to plagiarism litigation himself—was equally unsympathetic: "He's smarter than that." But most of his professed hurt poured forth when he was asked point-blank by David Sheff why he seemed to be ignoring George in his Beatle talk. Here John let loose, citing the publication of *I Me Mine* as practically a deliberate provocation on George's part.

"By glaring omission . . . my influence on his life is absolutely zilch and nil . . . he remembers every two-bit sax player or guitarist he met in subsequent years. I'm not in the book." He went on to psychoanalyze his former bandmate, declaring that George possessed a daddy complex and a love-hate attitude toward him. For the record, the book was never intended to be the be-all, end-all memoir of George's Beatle years. The focus was on his songs for the most part and—for those keeping score—John's eleven mentions easily eclipsed Paul's four. (Macca was not reported to have a beef with the book.)

The whole of John's bruised feelings seemed to be a contrived resentment. It's hard to square the perception that the househusband of the Dakota, who—according to himself—had neither the time nor interest to keep up with the careers of his peers and the former Fabs would lose sleep over a perceived slight in a book that shaped few opinions. Still, his sensitivity to how his fellow ex-Fabs saw him spoke volumes, as though any posture short of blind hero worship were simply unacceptable.

Once he'd gotten that off his chest, John—to his credit—attempted to reel in his more cutting remarks (or perhaps Yoko had left the room). Displaying the self-awareness that informed his own best material, he asserted that, no matter what he was feeling today, tomorrow would likely be different: "I still love those guys. The Beatles are over but John, Paul, George, and Ringo go on. . . . I don't want to start another whole thing between me and George just because of the way I feel today."

As far as George's reaction to John's remarks goes, little is documented. It was said that a call was placed to the Dakota in the fall of 1980—a call that went unreturned. But George knew John well enough to know that, as with previous targets Paul and George Martin, John would swallow his words soon enough. Indeed, within weeks, John would give his sworn deposition in the *Beatlemania* case, asserting that the four of them were planning to reunite for a concert. Perhaps it's best to let that be the final word on a decade's worth of sibling-like squabbling.

30

Sometimes I Feel Like Going Down

Wives and Lovers

t is not the purpose of this book to traffic in tabloid-style celebrity gossip. Details of who was doing whom and when are best left to tomes penned by ex-wives or former employees. That said, the Beatles *are* history, and any personal relationships affecting their lives and influencing their art are therefore worthy of examination. So, without getting too salacious, here are some of the womenfolk who held sway with three of the former Fabs during the decade. (Once betrothed to Linda, Macca did a life-changing one-eighty and remained, till the end of her life, a one-woman man. As far as anyone knows.)

May Pang

Born to Chinese parents living in Spanish Harlem in 1950, May Pang was surrounded by a rich array of cultural and musical influences. It is therefore not surprising that once she came of age, she was drawn to the rock music industry, which by the late 1960s had become the voice of youth as well as a boundary-pushing art form. By pure chance, she discovered the Broadway office of ABKCO while interviewing elsewhere. On impulse, she applied for a job at the outfit that she knew managed both the Beatles and the Rolling Stones; much to her surprise, she was hired.

Soon, though, the daily tedium of filing copyright applications and answering the phone became too much; desiring more creative fulfillment after sixteen months in Klein's employ, May was ready to move on when out of the blue, the opportunity to work exclusively as a personal assistant to John and Yoko came along. As a fan of the Fabs generally and John in particular, she was ecstatic.

Whatever else her new job was, it was never boring. Duties ranged from picking up after them in their flat to helping secure flies for an art film of Yoko's (titled, appropriately enough, *Fly*—it consisted of fifty minutes of

75¢ MAY 1975

HIT PARADER

CDC 00045

...ILTON
...CATION

PAUL & LINDA
EXCLUSIVE INTERVIEW
WITH ROCK'S MOST
SUCCESSFUL COUPLE

DAVID BOWIE
TRYING TO SORT OUT
HIS CONFUSED IMAGE

RANDY BACHMAN
HE SAYS BTO'S LAST HIT
WAS AN ACCIDENT....

WAYNE COUNTY SAYS
THE KINKS & THE PRETTY THINGS
WERE BEHIND IT ALL

A FEW THINGS
ABOUT THE BEACH BOYS

WORDS TO THE LATEST HIT SONGS!

That Paul McCartney would eventually sustain a love relationship for thirty years was a bet no one would have taken in the mid-'60s. But Linda, who stood up to the enormous pressures he placed on her by inviting her into his post-Beatles act, truly was Paul's soul mate.

close-ups of said insect crawling about on a nude woman's body). When the couple appeared on Dick Cavett's show in September 1971, it was May who acted as a stand-in for Yoko in a black bag, as a demonstration of "bagism."

Though the position was demanding and required an almost complete subsuming of a personal life (that said, May *did* manage to date Badfinger's Pete Ham briefly), Pang was cognizant of the ringside seat to rock history she was being afforded: at the Bangladesh concert and for the recording of *Imagine* and subsequent albums, as well as the "Happy Xmas" single (she can be spotted on the single sleeve).

In 1968, the public pairing of John and Yoko upset a lot of people. Beatles fans were outraged that someone who seemingly disrupted the group's unity had entered the inner circle, encouraging John to act upon his wildest impulses. Another segment of the population despised their coupling on racial grounds, bewildered that this Englishman would cast aside his perfectly lovely blonde wife for a controlling "Dragon Lady." Still others, even within the counterculture community, objected to what they saw as the degradation of Lennon's art at the hands of a pretentious wannabe who steered him from his established path in the name of advancing her own career (notwithstanding her own pre-Lennon fame).

Thus the pressures sustained by the Lennons grew increasingly difficult to bear. Adding to their troubles was the ongoing effort from on high to kick them out of America. It is therefore not surprising that sooner or later, something had to give. Yoko has said that the tipping point that led to their eventual time-out from each other arose from an ugly incident that occurred on election night, 1972. The two were attending a party at Jerry Rubin's apartment in the Village, populated by the usual assortment of artists, intellectuals, and journalists.

At some point in the evening, the magnitude of Richard Nixon's electoral victory over George McGovern became crushingly obvious. John, an unreasonable drunk during the best of times, acted out his rage by pulling a young woman into a bedroom and having at it with her—loudly—before the stunned guests. (One sympathetic attendee sought to mask the noise by putting on a Dylan record, to no avail.) Yoko's humiliation was complete; as she later observed, "Something was lost that night for me."

While the details of this sordid incident eventually reached May's ears from Yoko herself, she nonetheless was unprepared for the bombshell her employer dropped on her in the summer of 1973, as the *Mind Games* LP began production. Explaining that she and John hadn't been getting along lately (not exactly a revelation to those close to the Lennons), Yoko suggested that her husband was newly in need of female companionship; furthermore, since he "liked" May, it wouldn't be advisable to say no should he ask her out. Coming from Yoko and couched in such terms, May knew that the "suggestion" was really an order.

To someone raised a Catholic and by reputation a bit of a Girl Scout, May was mortified. She had never viewed John as anything other than her boss and an artist whom she admired—no romantic fantasies had ever entered her mind, or so she protested. But in a battle of wills, May was no match for Mrs. Lennon—as John would have readily pointed out. As May would later divulge, the Lennons had apparently worked it out between them that the generally agreeable and accommodating twenty-two-year-old would make the perfect partner for John, given her desire to please and aversion to conflict.

Let off the leash by Yoko, John soon made his move, openly propositioning May once work on *Mind Games* resumed. It took considerable pressure before the young woman was sufficiently worn down and accepted the situation, allowing John to come "home" to her tiny studio apartment (and, truth be told, she wasn't completely averse to experiencing a man whom she did find attractive). However, May's own morality made her too ashamed to broadcast their relationship (least of all to her mother), fearing disapproval.

Some major mythmaking has taken place regarding what became known in Lennon lore as the "Lost Weekend," propagated by friendly publications, Elliot Mintz, Yoko, and John himself. In the decades since, May has made efforts through interviews and two books to set the record straight on an odyssey that John himself told journalist Larry Kane privately may have been "the happiest [he] had ever been."

After John and Yoko's reconciliation, their separation was described as commencing when Yoko "kicked him out." The reality appears to have been a mutual parting, with no particular expectation that they'd ever resume their marital relations ("We're just good friends" was how John described their relationship). Further, John was not "ordered" to L.A., as has been claimed: May says that they went on the spur of the moment upon learning that Harold Seider, John's lawyer, was flying out that very evening.

The initial escape from whatever demons plagued Lennon in New York City naturally resulted in excesses, chronicled as though the Troubadour episodes were the defining moments of his time away from Yoko. In fact, the bad press acted as a warning sign, through which John, with May's encouragement, was able to pull back from the edge of oblivion and shake off the peer pressure to party like there was no tomorrow. The couple returned to the East Coast to complete Harry Nilsson's album as well the next two of John's, visiting the West Coast thereafter usually only to work.

May provided John with nonjudgmental support while nurturing the little boy inside of him. If she lacked the acumen to play three-dimensional mental chess with him as Yoko had done, she enabled him to let down his

STAND BY ME

Words and Music by BEN E. KING and ELMO GLICK

From the album ROCK 'N' ROLL
recorded by JOHN LENNON on APPLE RECORDS

THE ABERBACH GROUP
Sole Selling Agent:
Hill and Range Songs, Inc.
241 West 72nd Street
New York, N.Y. 10023

$1.50
Distributed
by

May Pang's visit to the first Beatlefest in 1974 (at John's behest) bore unexpected fruit when she encountered Jurgen Vollmer, the Beatles' old Hamburg friend. Brought back into John's orbit, Vollmer provided wonderful period images that were used for the *Rock 'n' Roll* package.

guard and stop seeing everyone he met as a potential threat or challenger. Suddenly, old acquaintances like Mick Jagger were happily reporting that the "old John" was back, the witty, highly social friend and peer who could reminisce about the old days without stirring insecurities with his partner.

John learned to cast aside his reclusive ways and was actually empowered to interact with the world, listening to popular music of the day, walking about and experiencing life instead of hiring limos to go anywhere, and actually acknowledging fans with respect rather than disdain. Perhaps most importantly, communication with his three fellow ex-Fabs was *encouraged*, with Paul in particular. With both men questioning their own talents, the prospect of writing together again seemed tantalizingly possible for the first time since 1968—or at least since around the time John turned his back on the Beatles.

May was also instrumental in setting up extended visits with Lennon's son Julian, who hadn't seen his father in three years, owing in no small part to John's immigration issues but also traceable to poor parenting skills. Though they stayed in touch by phone and John would duly send birthday and Christmas presents, their interactions tended toward the awkward. May smoothed relations, inviting Julian to America for trips to Disneyland and extended father-son bonding. John exhibited pride in the young man his son was becoming while privately expressing regret at his lack of attention when it would have mattered most.

Regaining some of his lost confidence and energy, John plunged into work. Although *Rock 'n' Roll* was something of an albatross, it eventually was completed to his satisfaction, while *Walls and Bridges* marked a maturing of his craft that seemed to effortlessly bridge the gulf between the personal and the commercial. May was an instrumental player in both projects as coordinator (credited by John as "Mother Superior"); she even provided musical support, as part of a vocal ensemble ("The 44th Street Fairies") and as a soloist, whispering John's name on "#9 Dream." (Years later, when Yoko created a new set of music videos to accompany a repackaging of John's hits, she actually inserted footage of *herself* mouthing May's vocal.)

The album also included a song he'd written about May (whom he privately called Fung Yee, her Chinese name), "Surprise, Surprise (Sweet Bird of Paradox)." The song extolled her positive effect on him while declaring his love, intimating that what he had expected to be a mere diversion had become something more ("It's so hard to swallow when you're wrong"). Like "Whatever Gets You Through the Night," the song featured a guest harmony vocal from Elton John (who later noted that John's singular phrasing made it difficult for him to get a handle on his own part).

After the formal legal dissolution of the Beatles' partnership in December 1974, John and May began to make plans for their future. One goal on their list was a visit to New Orleans to see the McCartneys, as Paul prepared to work on *Venus and Mars*. Talk of the former partners writing some songs together was in the air; in addition to the creative benefit, it might have made a powerful negotiating card for Lennon, without a record deal, to play. (In his on-air interview with Dennis Elsas back in September, John had facetiously remarked that he and the others might end up on Dark Horse Records, a "good-looking label.")

The couple also talked of getting a home. They'd been living in an apartment (434 East Fifty-second Street) but wanted something more substantial. May found a Scottish-style cottage for sale in Montauk, near the Hamptons, where they'd been spending a lot of time with Mick Jagger. They'd fallen in love with the area, and John was adamant about living by water. But just before he put in an offer on the property, the separation ended, and on February 1, 1975, he moved back into the Dakota.

There have been conflicting narratives about how the Lennons ended up back together and what conclusions could be drawn from that development. The net effect has served to establish the enduring John & Yoko love story, a point that was hammered home with little subtlety during the round of 1980 *Double Fantasy* interviews and amplified in the wake of his murder, diminishing May Pang's role in his life. Whatever interpretation one wants to accept, John's time with May represented his most productive post-Beatles period, with two of his own albums produced, as well as Harry Nilsson's *Pussy Cats*. He contributed to Ringo's *Goodnight Vienna*, and further managed to squeeze in contributions to hit records by David Bowie and Elton John.

Yoko loyalists have met with skepticism May's assertions that John was interested in working with his former bandmates. In fact, her story of John's intent to go New Orleans to meet with Macca was verified by Derek Taylor, who received a postcard from John saying exactly that. Certainly, the four of them had their ups and downs, especially with George, but John never disputed his love for his three brothers. Doing the honorable thing by supporting a now-pregnant partner was a familiar path for John; his reuniting with Yoko may have begun as fulfilling a duty as his life's journey moved onward.

As for May, she maintains that she and John stayed in touch, enjoying physical relations as late as 1977 and contact through the summer of 1980. (Via a go-between messenger, he'd forwarded her tapes of the upcoming *Double Fantasy*.) She would marry producer Tony Visconti (The Iveys, David Bowie, T. Rex) in 1989, six years after her memoir, *Loving John*, was published. In 2007, a collection of photos, *Instamatic Karma*, was published, allowing fans to see for themselves what a miserable wreck John was during their time together. Or not.

Olivia Trinidad Arias

Maritally, professionally, and spiritually adrift in 1974, George was in serious need of healing. Pattie had left him for Eric Clapton near the end of the previous year, and though his standing with the public had slipped somewhat, he found his input welcome with an assortment of collaborators. Ten Years After's Alvin Lee found himself the recipient of George's generosity when gifted with a heretofore unreleased Harrisong, "So Sad (No Love of His Own)," a commentary on recent events.

Though as devout as always, George found that no amount of chanting or meditating could fill the void in his life. While occupying himself with Dark Horse—the album, tour, and label—George still managed to squeeze in a fling with an ex-Rod Stewart girlfriend, model Kathy Simmonds. But it would be an unassuming assistant in A&M's merchandising department who caught his attention—permanently—when she began to work with him after being hired on at the nascent Dark Horse office.

By purist standards, Friar Park, purchased by George in 1970, was an architectural monstrosity, being an undisciplined blend of styles. Built in 1890 by lawyer Frank Crisp, the 120-room Henley estate boasted caverns beneath, a state-of-the-art recording studio within, and lavish gardens lovingly restored by George.

Friar Park, Henley-on-Thames — 221

Olivia Arias was born in 1948 in Mexico City but grew up in Southern California. Like George, she studied meditation, and despite—or perhaps because of—her interest in the metaphysical, she proved to be a capable and even-tempered administrator, ably handling the routine chaos involved with setting up a record label and dealing with all manner of personalities. George began looking forward to their daily phone calls, and as his feelings grew, he had an L.A. friend check her out (not *literally* investigate her, as implied in one bio).

Soon after, George flew out to meet Olivia face to face; what ensued, improbably, was the much-fabled "love at first sight." The two became inseparable, and Olivia soon found herself thrown into the deep end of things as George set out on his ill-starred North American tour. The experience would truly test the limits of her devotion, as she accompanied an ex-Beatle who wasn't exactly at his best at that time.

The downward spiral did not end with the conclusion of the shows, but continued on into the next year as George's alcohol and cocaine abuse further compounded his demons. It was Olivia's stable, calming influence that eventually led him back to the light, pressing him to seek help through means beyond prayer. It took a little doing and a lot of support, but by 1976, despite the ongoing "My Sweet Lord" suit and litigation with Olivia's former boss, Herb Alpert, over Dark Horse issues, George had finally regained his footing. The release of *Thirty-Three & 1/3* that year saw his musical fortunes restored in a grand way, as the funny, non-preachy George reemerged, arguably for the first time in a decade.

Olivia shared in George's spiritual and lifestyle pursuits, cooking up vegetarian dishes and tending to the restoration of his beloved Friar Park gardens. In 1978, the couple were blessed by the birth of their only child, a son they named Dhani. The Harrisons indulged a love of travel, eventually purchasing homes in both Australia (on Hamilton Island) and Hawaii (in Nahiku on Maui). With George's attentions turned toward both Formula One racing and film producing, music increasingly took a back seat.

Much of the establishment press regarded the Harrisons as "reclusive," as though not partaking in the usual rock star happenings made one a hermit. But the couple enjoyed a rich social life, entertaining at Friar Park (where the public was allowed to roam around the grounds) or hanging out with friends within and outside of the rock community. (Deep Purple keyboardist Jon Lord and the aforementioned Alvin Lee were members of the self-styled "Henley Mafia," occasionally playing the local pub as the "Pishill Artists.") Neighbors regarded George as less an ex-Beatle than just another member of the community.

All of this relative tranquility changed with the murder of John Lennon in 1980. Almost overnight, Friar Park was put under lockdown, and George's visits to his local grew less frequent. Still, the need to make music beckoned, and Olivia was instrumental in getting George to accept an invitation from boyhood idol Carl Perkins to perform in a cable television concert in 1985. First *Cloud Nine*, then the *Traveling Wilburys* followed to close out the decade. Olivia tapped the latter outfit to record a special charity single to benefit Romanian orphans after the fall of the Ceausescu government in 1990.

Just as Olivia had rescued George from the perils of rock stardom at the onset of their relationship, so too did she *literally* save him from a psychotic intruder in December 1999, bashing the assailant on the head with first a poker, then a brass lamp. Thus ended their idyll, as the next crisis proved to be the cancer that would take George's life in 2001. Today, Olivia keeps the flame of their life together alive with her ongoing charitable work and the overseeing of remastered reissues of George's music.

Barbara Bach

Born Barbara Goldbach in Queens, this Austrian/Irish beauty possessed a European aura that made some believe she couldn't possibly be an American. Like Nancy Andrews, she became an Eileen Ford model while in her teens, appearing regularly on *Seventeen* and countless other magazine covers. The fast career track quickly made her worldly beyond her years; unlike others of her age group, she really didn't much care for the Beatles, being more of a Ray Charles / Bob Dylan fan. Nonetheless, she *did* attend the 1965 Beatles Shea Stadium concert—but only to chaperone her younger sister.

That same year, while traveling to a photo shoot in Italy, Barbara met an Italian businessman, Augosto Gregorini. They married three years later and produced two children before the marriage ended in 1978. In the meantime, she parlayed her stunning looks into a small-scale film career, mostly in Italian-made B-movies (bearing translated titles like "The Sensual Man" and "The Anonymous Avenger"). After moving back to the States in 1975, she was recommended by a friend of a friend to producers casting the latest 007 flick, *The Spy Who Loved Me*. At the age of thirty, Barbara Bach became a Bond girl.

After her success in the role, she was cast in the long-delayed sequel to 1961's *The Guns of Navarone* / *Force 10 from Navarone*, starring opposite Robert Shaw and Harrison Ford. Barbara might have continued in the action film idiom where she had proven successful, but longed to try her hand at something lighter. After failing to make the cut as a replacement for actress Kate Jackson on the TV series *Charlie's Angels*, she accepted roles in a pair of comedies back to back, the *Mad* magazine–produced *Up the Academy* and actor Carl Gottlieb's big-screen directorial debut, *Caveman*.

On the set in Mexico for the latter film, she met Ringo, the ensemble's lead actor, for the first time. She already knew Nancy Andrews—on hand to document the proceedings in pictures—from their Eileen Ford modeling days. Ringo ("Richard," as Barbara called him) was cast as "Atouk," the ostensible leader of the primitive pre–*Homo sapiens* clan, while Bach was "Lana," the vixen whom Atouk lusts after, despite his loyal woman, Tala (played by a pre-*Cheers* Shelley Long). Early on in the filming, Barbara commented to an interviewer about the Starr player: "He's so interesting, a very nice guy."

Before long, the on-screen chemistry became something more, and by the end of the shoot in March 1980, the two were officially coupled up. Barbara might have become simply one more in the string of flings with which Ringo indulged himself, but an unexpected trauma cemented their relationship for good. On May 19 while in England, Ringo—behind the wheel of his Mercedes 350SL—skidded on a rain-drenched street to avoid a truck, somersaulting the heavy car into two lampposts before it came to a rest.

Ringo was thrown clear, his leg injured, while Barbara was still inside beneath the crushed roof. He managed to free her (while making a return trip to retrieve his smokes). Both were so shaken by the almost-deadly experience that they vowed never to be apart again. (As a permanent reminder of the experience, Ringo had the car cubed for display as an objet d'art; he further commissioned a jeweler to set broken windshield glass into matching lockets for each of them.)

Thus began a chronicle of togetherness that has endured to this day, despite several ugly episodes. Upon receiving word of John's murder that year while on holiday, the couple—without hesitation—headed for New York and the Dakota, braving grieving throngs gathered to pay their respects. Once inside, Ringo was informed by Yoko to come up—alone. But the drummer stood his ground, telling the widow "Look, it was you who started all this. We're *both* coming in." Yoko acknowledged her faux pas; it *was* she who had penetrated the psyches of four Northern men and introduced the "man and woman as one" concept.

The unity between them eventually extended to a joint effort at rehab, initiated in 1988 when, after a particularly brutal bender, Ringo woke from a blackout to find Barbara's battered and bloody body beside him: he'd evidently beaten her and hadn't the faintest recollection of doing so. The wake-up call came in time, for the two of them were, by then, sharing a mutual love of intoxicants and little else. The cure took, and currently, the Richard-Barbara love match is on track to surpass the not-quite thirty years that Paul and Linda were husband and wife.

Fans received a delightful twofer in *Playboy*'s January 1981 issue: John's last major interview, alongside a close-up look at cover girl Barbara Bach. Though she'd starred in *The Spy Who Loved Me*, readers found photos of Honore Blackman's *Goldfinger* character throughout.

31

Why Don't We Take Off Alone

Extensive negotiations were necessary to clear away the red tape preventing Paul McCartney from entering Japan, owing to the country's strict drug laws and Macca's habit of flouting them. Having at long last gotten the green light, members of Wings were looking forward to touring the country where the sort of screaming mania the Beatles had inspired still existed (as pop-rockers Cheap Trick famously discovered in 1978). Eleven shows were scheduled for the dates running January 21 through February 2—all were sold out.

Before setting foot on Japanese soil for the first time in fourteen years, however, the McCartneys had a brief stop in New York City. Staying at the Stanhope Hotel, just across Central Park from the Dakota, Paul rang up John to explore the possibility of a get-together; as enticement, he reportedly told Yoko that he'd scored some "dynamite weed." But he never actually spoke to John, and the two did not connect. Shortly thereafter, with all the little McCartneys in tow, Paul and Linda flew into Tokyo's Narita International Airport. Upon their January 16 arrival, during the routine customs inspection in the VIP area, an official checking the very last bag discovered two plastic bags of marijuana (about the size of a football in bulk), weighing 219 grams—nearly half a pound. (A photo of Paul's face taken just before the bag was opened would have been invaluable to posterity to accompany the word "hubris" in the dictionary.)

It is doubtful that the inspector could possibly have been any more shocked than Paul himself was moments later when handcuffs were slapped on his wrists and he was whisked away to a detention center. Any wailing from Linda and the kids at that moment was surely buried beneath the sound of heavy pounding: Denny Laine's head hitting the wall, over and over. (So beside himself with anger was he at his employer's carelessness and the loss of a substantial payday that he flew off to France while Paul remained in custody, thereafter composing and recording a song called

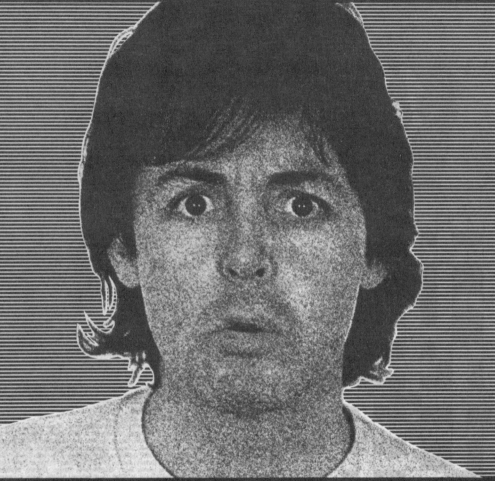

ON HIS OWN

WITH HIS NEW ALBUM

McCARTNEY II

INCLUDES THE HIT SINGLE 'COMING UP'

AVAILABLE ON CASSETTE

With Wings in tatters following his devastating Japanese drug bust, Paul marked time between projects by issuing his second one-man-band release, a decade after his first.

"Japanese Tears" describing the devastation canceling the tour wrought upon the fans—and himself.)

It has long been rumored that authorities had been tipped off to McCartney's hidden stash by Yoko Ono herself, based on the dubious concept that she had some kind of pull within Japanese officialdom—since they all know each other, you know. (Conversely, others claimed that John himself said Yoko could have gotten Paul out with just a phone call, but that he was too proud to ask for help.) In fact, as a convicted drug offender, Macca was a marked man upon entering the country, Yoko's input or not. What is beyond belief is that the richest man in rock would not have simply hired a courier to handle his personal needs, a failure that John, when he heard the news, is said to have found completely incomprehensible.

Once in stir, Paul was informed of the very egregious nature of his offense and that further, someone in his position could reasonably expect to get seven years hard labor under the current law. It was a sobering moment, no less so for the conditions he found himself in after being transferred to a four-by-eight-foot cell in the Metropolitan jail. There, prisoner #22 was denied his request of a guitar and had his wedding ring confiscated, although he was able to socialize, in a fashion: sharing jokes with his fellow inmates, and—inevitably—leading them in sing-alongs during bath time. (Though he recounted singing "Yesterday," it is unknown whether or not he attempted "Band on the Run": "Stuck inside these four walls . . .") Linda was allowed to visit on his fourth day of captivity, where she related that every piece of band equipment had been broken down and searched; furthermore, airplay of Wings songs had been banned on the radio for the next three months. They had, however, received a telegram that read in part: "Thinking of you all with love. Keep your spirits high. . . . Love, George and Olivia."

The story of Paul's unfathomably stupid act has preoccupied armchair psychologists ever since: what could he possibly have been thinking? He himself later opined that subconsciously, he must have wanted to end Wings; certainly, given Linda's increasing resistance to touring, he may have simply wanted out of his commitment. In any event, the bust cost him dearly, as his tour insurance had been allowed to lapse just before Japan, meaning that he was forced to pay the promoters out of pocket their expenses and the cost of refunding tickets—to those fans who didn't want to keep their souvenir, anyway. On January 25—on the tenth day—the prosecutor's office announced that no charges would be pressed. He was immediately transported to the airport and sent home.

In the wake of the highly embarrassing incident, the McCartneys hunkered down at their Scottish farm and reflected on their musical future.

DECEMBER 3-9, 1980

THE MORMONS' NEW MESSIAH
KOCH FOR PRESIDENT?
Joel Kotkin

$1.00

Y CENTS

SOHO NEWS

YOKO ONLY

Peter Occhiogrosso

'Those hate vibes,
they're like love
vibes, they are very
strong.
It kept me going.
When you're hated
so much, you live.
Hate was feeding
me.'

NY RIGHT: FIGHTING FOR THE SPOILS.........John Buckley

TV: BUYING AND SELLING CULTURE...............Bob Brewin

ANTHONY BURGESS BOMBS OUT.....................Don Shewey

SPOILED MOVIE BRATS...................................Veronica Geng

The very week John's life ended, this prophetically headlined issue of *Soho Weekly*
graced New York City newsstands. At last drawing praise as a musical force whose time
had come (outside the shadow of her husband), Yoko likely achieved realization of
what had been John's goal all along.

Plans for resuming the tour in America were canceled, and the only commitments still in place were for readying some archival tracks for release as part of a long-promised collection of unreleased and non-album material Paul called *Cold Cuts*. Wings duly applied themselves to the task, but it was clear that any certainty of a future was lacking. Instead of beginning work on a new project, Paul released an LP's worth of mostly electronic tunes he'd recorded by himself the previous summer, calling it *McCartney II*.

The album would spawn a #1 hit—sort of. The track "Coming Up" was issued as a single; in England, it reached #2, "as is." But the B-side featured a live version by Wings recorded in Glasgow back in December: this was the side favored by American disc jockeys, and it was this version that hit #1, creating a bit of an awkward situation as the concert recording wasn't on the album. Columbia applied a Band-Aid solution by packaging the LP with a one-sided seven-inch promo pressing.

Helping to promote the single was a video produced by Paul and Linda, featuring the couple in multiple roles simultaneously (via special effects), comprising "the Plastic Macs." Most all of the dozen characters were based on real people, such as Shadows guitarist Hank Marvin, Ron Mael of Sparks, and Paul himself, circa 1964. Though CGI has rendered the impact moot, it was a pretty big deal at the time. The McCartneys appeared on *Saturday Night Live* on May 17, as Father Guido Sarducci (Don Novello), the chain-smoking Vatican correspondent, turned up outside their residence at five in the morning to interview them before running the clip. He could not, however, stop himself from making references to marijuana use, despite having been "warned" not to talk about anything but the song. Finally, he attempted to redeem himself by asking a "journalistic" question: what kind of animal would you be if you could? After Paul answered "a koala bear," Sarducci observed, "Is that the little animal all the time, they eat eucalypse [sic] leaves, they get-a stoned all the time?"

Also honing his comedy act was Ringo. Having taken off a stress-filled year, he resumed his filmmaking career in March with the shooting of a slapstick comedy, *Caveman*. (Upon his arrival in Mexico, he found himself being strip-searched by authorities as part of the fallout from Paul's bust.) Though the film itself was a puerile farce, the redeeming aspect for Ringo was meeting—and falling in love with—actress Barbara Bach. Nancy Andrews was understandably heartbroken at the loss of her fiancé, but despite the seeming improbability of the former Bond girl falling for her legendary costar, the pairing proved to be the real thing.

Perhaps the almost deadly experience they found themselves in not long after hooking up sealed the deal. In the early morning hours of May 19 in London, the Mercedes Ringo was driving lost control and skidded into a pair of lampposts before cartwheeling off the road. He was thrown clear, but Barbara was trapped inside. Having faced death a year earlier kept him a cool customer as he pulled her from the wreckage. After treatment for minor injuries, the two flew to Los Angeles; during the flight, he proposed and she accepted. The couple would marry the next year in London, with two of Ringo's "brothers" in attendance.

Now feeling himself in a better place than he had been in for a while, Ringo—prodded by Barbara, who had missed out on his glory years—began making plans for a new album. For the first time in four years, he openly solicited assistance from his well-known friends in the business (including Harry Nilsson, Ronnie Wood, and Steven Stills) as well as the ex-Fabs. Both Paul and John responded with offers to pen material and perform; George likewise committed but had his own album to finish first. The sessions began in July in France with Paul, Linda, Laurence Juber, and Howey Casey, whereupon four tracks plus a Linda composition (not intended for the release) were cut.

Among the songs George offered up in the fall was one that Ringo eventually rejected (as the vocal key was a little high for him) after laying down the backing track; it was called "All Those Years Ago." Another was an arrangement of the old pop standard "You Belong to Me." The last was a song ripping on the record industry—a sentiment shared by both men—entitled "Wrack My Brain." Released as a single in 1981, it marked Ringo's last excursion into the Top 40 singles chart.

The song had been penned in response to the losing battle George was waging with the suits at Warners. Desperately hoping for a blockbuster to salvage their fourth-quarter earnings, they judged the self-produced effort George turned in, *Somewhere in England*, to be something less than what they'd bargained for. Though replete with a fine array of Harrisongs bearing a slightly more philosophical bent than the previous release, the album lacked a single track with "blockbuster smash" written all over it. That said, executives displayed appalling judgment in wielding the ax; at least two of the four songs dropped deserved a fair hearing and would have done the album a lot of good.

With four new replacement cuts and brand new artwork, *Somewhere in England* was eventually issued in 1981; had Warners not postponed its scheduled release, George would have found himself in the unenviable position of competing with the return of John to the recording world.

In the spring of 1980, John found himself emerging from whatever state he'd been in that had kept him largely inside and away from friends and colleagues. Though he'd managed to log some serious travel time (with stops including South Africa, Spain, and Germany), his social interactions

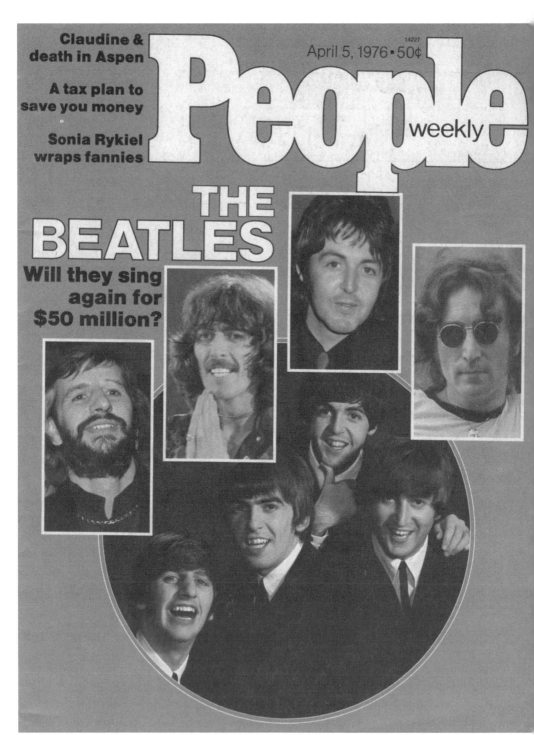

April 5, 1976 • 50¢

14227

**Claudine &
death in Aspen**

**A tax plan to
save you money**

**Sonia Rykiel
wraps fannies**

People weekly

THE
BEATLES
Will they sing
again for
$50 million?

Throughout the decade, increasingly titanic offers to reunite (as reported in *People*)
were directed toward the ex-Fabs, not all of them sincere. Paul later revealed that
fear of disappointing fans was one factor that kept the former Beatles from acting
on the invitations.

had been few and far between, limited mostly to actor Peter Boyle, his Dakota neighbor.

As if to symbolize a new beginning, John shaved off his heavy beard in April. In the months just after, he fulfilled a lifelong ambition of learning to sail when he chartered a boat and crew to take Sean and himself to Bermuda. Yoko, as always, was busy with business matters, including the record-breaking sale (over a quarter-million dollars) of a Holstein dairy cow in June. By that time, John had landed, having endured a horrific three-day storm that had imperiled the craft, forcing him to take the wheel. But to hear him tell it, at least, the experience had reawakened his creative urges. Upon hearing the B-52s channeling Yoko on "Rock Lobster" one night in a Bermuda club, John was struck with the epiphany that perhaps the world was ready for them on their own terms.

He began demoing songs in earnest: some new but others reworkings of previously composed material. After he announced his intention to record again via long-distance phone call, Yoko readied some material of her own. During their separation in 1973–74, she had recorded an album (unreleased until the 1990s), toured Japan, and played a stint at New York's Kenny's Castaways club. While at no time was her musical star in peril of eclipsing John's, it appeared that her ambitions had not diminished in six years. Despite rumors swirling that summer that she was preparing to divorce John, she told producer Jack Douglas that the pending project would be a duo. It was possible now that, with tastes in quirky pop becoming mainstream, her time had come.

Double Fantasy was recorded fairly quickly. Once the buzz that John Lennon was recording again spread around, record labels came a-calling in droves. Mogul David Geffen had just started up his own self-named label, with acts including Elton John and Donna Summer aboard. Pledging personal attention and a willingness to sign the couple without first hearing their work, he easily won the Lennons over. So began a media blitz, with print and radio interviews being given in all directions that autumn as the Lennons revamped their Bed-Peace message of a decade earlier by trumpeting their own domestic and artistic partnership as the wave of the future.

Nineteen-eighty proved to be a year that saw an unusually high mortality rate among rock musicians. Among the casualties that year were Larry Williams, the soul shouter so beloved of Lennon's youth (as a Beatle, he'd sung Williams' "Bad Boy," "Slow Down," and "Dizzy Miss Lizzie"), of a gunshot wound. AC/DC's Bon Scott and Led Zeppelin's John Bonham each succumbed to alcohol poisoning, while Joy Division's Ian Curtis and the Germs' Darby Crash were suicides. In every case that year, death came prematurely.

It's Not Like It Was Before

Some Post-Fab Socializing and Near-Reunions

All of the available evidence suggests that the last time all four Beatles were together in one place was on August 22, 1969; the occasion was their last photo shoot at Tittenhurst Park. From that point onward, three ex-Fabs at most would gather at any one time (notwithstanding the hoax that all four reunited in secret for a November 1976 recording session). Though they eventually resumed cordial relations, the split's effect of generating four separate careers made even casual get-togethers difficult.

Of course, each would assist another on recording projects from their breakup onward, but only once were three of them in the studio simultaneously—for the recording of John's "I'm the Greatest" during the *Ringo* sessions—and even that was a bit of a fluke. All four seemed to possess a certain self-consciousness about "Beatling" together that kept them from being as close as they otherwise might have been, given the enormous weight of expectations that came from being former Fabs.

Paul and John's public sniping kept them physically apart for over two years, until they decided to end the self-generated bad press over dinner in New York in early 1972. Thereafter, their contact was sporadic: only in 1974 did relations thaw to the point where they began to hang out, even making music (or something resembling it). Their second honeymoon ended when Paul overplayed his hand two years later, but it was with no small measure of gratitude that he reported that his last phone conversation with John had gone well.

Though George's relations with John and Paul had their ups and downs, each man's esteem for Ringo endured. No matter what they felt toward each other at any given time, all three made it a point to help their former drummer out whenever they could. History records the strong likelihood that early 1981 would have at least seen the foursome back together for the Ringed One's nuptials; where that might have led—if anywhere—is anyone's guess.

"I'm the Greatest" Session—March 13, 1973

Had he not bailed on an earlier commitment to appear at the Bangladesh benefit, John might have comprised one third of an ex-Fab threesome just two years after *Abbey Road* was recorded. Instead, it would be another year and a half before the same lineup would get together for a good cause, in this case to jump-start Ringo's career as a rock album artist. On tap was one of John's compositions, "I'm the Greatest"—a sort of Muhammad Ali–like bit of self-promotion that its author knew he could never get away with singing. But retooled slightly and put into the hands of the self-effacing percussionist, the braggadocio was endearing rather than off-putting.

Ensconced in producer Richard Perry's beloved Sunset Sound studios in Los Angeles, John and Ringo, accompanied by Billy Preston and Klaus Voormann, were attempting to get a handle on the not-quite-finished song. Perry, who had never met John before, was not a little starstruck. Not long before, George had been on hand to record "Photograph," "Sunshine Life for Me," and "You and Me (Babe)" for the album. For Perry, the chance to work alongside *two* ex-Fabs (albeit separately) on Ringo's album was a rare treat, even with their progress momentarily bogged down as they attempted to craft a smooth middle eight. What came next would later be recalled as one of the most delightfully surreal moments in Perry's long and colorful career.

The studio phone rang—it was George, calling to check on the session's progress. (It is not known whether or not he knew John was in the studio at that moment; it's inferred that he was merely touching base on things generally.) Stunned, Perry called out to the musicians: "George is on the phone—he wants to know if he can come down." Shouted John from the piano bench: "Tell him to get down here and help me finish this bridge!" Nearly shaking by now, Perry relayed the message. Within moments, Hari Georgeson indeed arrived and, opening his guitar case, got down to business.

Watching the three ex-Fabs at work, Perry was struck by the contagious energy generated as the musicians instinctively picked up on each other's wavelength, as though the last four years hadn't happened. Lacking any better word to describe the scene, it was "magic." Gushed Perry later, "You could really tell that they were excited. There was such a fantastic energy coming out of the room—it was really sensational!"

With George's Beatle-esque arpeggios, Billy's carnival-like organ, and John's supporting vocal, "I'm the Greatest" indeed became a worthy celebration of the musicians' collective past. Without evoking any particular song directly, it summed up the best of their sound, hitting all the right notes and offering the public a glimpse into the what-ifs, even without Paul's input. Once word of the session leaked out, the response was immediate: the press trumpeted "reunion!" while fans still going through withdrawal in the wake of the breakup were suddenly jolted by the sensation that their three-year ordeal was over and that the Beatles—well, most of them, anyway—were back in the studio.

Representatives of John, George, and Ringo were quick to downplay expectations that something profound had occurred. While John granted that the session had been enjoyable, he wasn't yet ready to cop to anything amounting to personal nostalgia, instead issuing a mock press release that read in part: "As usual, an awful lot of rumours, if not downright lies, were going on, including the possibility of impresario Allen De Klein of grABKCo playing bass for the other three in an 'as-yet-untitled' album called *I Was a Teenage Fat Cat*. Producer, Richard Perry, who planned to take the tapes along to sell them to Paul McCartney, told a friend, 'I'll take the tapes to Paul McCartney'."

Indeed, Ringo himself recognized the significance of John and George's involvement and made a point of spiriting the tapes off to England to get Paul (and Linda) into the project. For his trouble, he was rewarded with a splendid original ballad ("Six O'Clock") and a hit single ("You're Sixteen"), abetted by Macca (and Harry Nilsson). Though *Ringo* didn't exactly spark the all-out reunion that many hoped for, it certainly underscored the passing of ill will that the former group and fans had endured for too long. Indeed, it looked like the long and lonely winter had at last given way to sunshine.

John, Ringo, and Paul in Los Angeles—March–April 1974

One year after the "I'm the Greatest" session, much had happened in the careers of the ex-Fabs. Both Paul and Ringo were suddenly enjoying massive chart success and generating rave reviews (for *Band on the Run* and *Ringo*, respectively). George too had had a #1 album and single (*Living in the Material World*, "Give Me Love") during the past year, but his personal life was in upheaval while his professional fortunes were about to enter a downturn. For John, the past year had been the hardest. Still in a funk after the lambasting *Some Time in New York City* had earned him, he expected *Mind Games* was to turn things around. It didn't.

Adding to his woes was the continued courtroom battle against the department of immigration (acting at the behest of the Nixon administration), as well as his marital situation, which suffered from the aforementioned pressures as well as internal stresses resulting in a separation from Yoko. As winter 1974 turned to spring, John had further suffered the indignity of having a new album project (*Rock 'n' Roll*) seized from him by the producer, leaving it in limbo. Lastly, his unfettered acting out had culminated in the public humiliation of being tossed from a nightclub. Though enjoying a second (or third) adolescence, surrounded by his gang (Ringo, Harry, Klaus, Mal, Keith Moon, and assorted showbiz pals) and his new girl (May), he was still rudderless. Work on *Pussy Cats* at least offered a purpose, but in his own life, he still had trouble finding a direction.

It was therefore a most auspicious time for his former partner to slip back into his life. While riding high with his current album, Paul was also in a bit of a holding pattern. Wings had disintegrated beneath the weight of his own ex-Beatle baggage months earlier; the irony was that they had been formed to facilitate a return to live performances and now, with the biggest album of his solo career on his hands, Paul had no band to tour with.

He'd been in town earlier that month to attend the Grammys, where *Live and Let Die* had been nominated for Best Original Score. (It lost to Neil Diamond's long-forgotten *Jonathan Livingston Seagull* soundtrack.) Now, catching wind of John's role at the helm of Harry's new album, he and Linda paid a visit to Warner Brothers' Burbank Studios to check out the action. As

Bootlegged years after the fact (with cover art "inspired" by a 1979 U.K. compilation entitled *The Songs Lennon and McCartney Gave Away*, by way of *Revolver*), the one and only post-Beatles Lennon-McCartney studio session was something of a nonstarter.

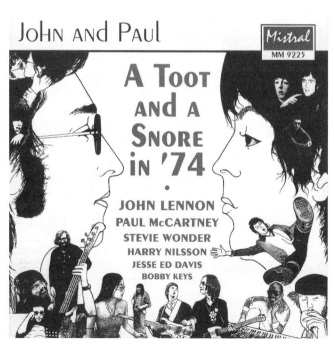

it happened, it was the first day of the *Pussy Cats* sessions, and by the time they arrived, recording had ended for the evening. Ringo, Klaus, and Keith Moon left soon after, completely missing out on the reunion that followed.

Witnesses recall being stunned when the McCartneys, with Paul sporting a modest, devil-like musketeer, entered the studio. (According to writer Christopher Sandford, he announced his presence by calling out: "Fuck me! Anyone left alive?") Onlookers awaited John's reaction; he'd been listening to playbacks in the control room and now strolled purposefully over to the Macs. Onlookers weren't sure whether there'd be a bear hug or a punch thrown. Instead there was neither: a strong handshake followed by warm greetings. Paul declared that he'd like to make some music and immediately commandeered Ringo's vacated drum kit. The tired Lennon might have demurred, but he was well aware of the numerous sets of eyes in the room "all just watching me and Paul," so he dutifully strapped on a guitar, once a bassist had been located.

What ensued was famously bootlegged on a release entitled *A Toot and a Snore in '74*. By the time the tape began rolling on the "session," Stevie Wonder, who apparently had been recording nearby, wandered in, having been tipped off to the momentous occasion. Ever the congenial host, John is heard offering the Motown legend a pick-me-up: "Do you want a snort, Steve? A toot? It's going 'round. . . ." Wonder must have declined the offer, for he seems to be the only star in the room in full command of his musicality, delivering a marvelous performance on a Fender Rhodes throughout. As Paul bangs away on the traps and occasionally chimes in on harmonies, John can be heard mostly either exhorting the musicians to settle on a song to play—one that everyone knows—and stick with it, or cussing out the engineers for an assortment of crimes, mostly concerning his headphone mix.

It would be satisfying to report that the re-pairing of John and Paul after nearly four years resulted in a return of the Beatle magic heard a year earlier on the "I'm the Greatest" session. This would be a lie, however. What the recording revealed was the sound of two former partners having a good time—more or less—in just hanging out casually, but hindered by the less than ideal circumstances (nerves, fatigue, lack of forethought) from producing anything worth hearing more than once. Moreover, as May Pang has said repeatedly through the years, the tape was *never* meant to be made public; none of the participants made any claims of greatness for what ended up recorded.

Among the tunes that were actually attempted were "Lucille"—a song expected to be Macca's forte, given his well-known Little Richard predilection—sung by John with Paul harmonizing; "Stand by Me"—sadly, a mess, especially in comparison to the hit version John would record later that year; and an improvisation featuring John's stream-of-consciousness ramblings, titled by bootleggers "Never Trust a Bugger with Your Mother." May recalls Leadbelly's "Midnight Special" also being performed: if recorded, it has not yet surfaced. All told, additional participants included May on tambourine, Linda McCartney on organ, Nilsson on vocals and piano, Jesse Ed Davis on lead guitar, sax man Bobby Keys, and engineer Ed Freeman on out-of-tune bass.

The following day, when Ringo arrived for work on Harry's album, he immediately noticed his setup was not as he'd left it and demanded to know who the culprit was. "Paul was here last night," John told him. "He played 'em." Famously fussy about his drums (they loomed large in his legend, after all), Ringo sulked. "He's always fuckin' around with me things!" (May documented the exchange, providing us with a vivid snapshot of the former Fabs' personal dynamic—it was as if they'd never left Liverpool.)

Macca was in town for at least a few more days to attend the Academy Awards on April 2—the famous "streaker" evening—to again claim an award for "Live and Let Die," should it win. (It didn't—Marvin Hamlish's recording of Scott Joplin's "The Entertainer" won for *The Sting*.) He'd also accepted an invitation by John to come visit the Santa Monica house he'd rented, ground zero for gatherings of the "Hollywood Vampires."

It was here at poolside on the sunny afternoon of April 1 that John and Paul were photographed together for the very last time. Both May and Keith Moon's gofer, Dougal Butler, captured the two ex-Beatles on film: Butler's shot also includes Linda, May, and Keith Moon, while May's featured the two men alone, talking, with Paul shading his eyes from the sun. She also got off a shot of Ringo and Paul at the piano that day, as well as one of *John* and Ringo, but alas, not one of all three together. (Nancy Andrews, well acquainted with John and May, was apparently not present and would not meet Ringo until the following month; otherwise it's quite probable that *her* camera would also have captured the rare get-together.)

John, Paul, and George in New York City—December 20, 1974

Likewise undocumented visually was the last time *these* three ex-Fabs met up in person.

The place was the trendy Club Hippopotamus, located at 405 East Sixty-second Street (near First Avenue). It had been the scene of a party on November 14, attended by John and May, Mick and Bianca, Ronnie Spector, and others, celebrating the off-Broadway opening of *Sgt. Pepper's Lonely Hearts Club Band on the Road*—an event not likely to warm the heart of

George, who'd already made known his displeasure with Willy Russell's *John, Paul, George, Ringo . . . and Bert* that same year.

This evening marked the end of the *Dark Horse* tour, which had been attended by John and May in Nassau, Long Island a week before; Paul and Linda (in an outlandish disguise, sporting Afro wigs and a fake mustache) had attended the Madison Square Garden show. By all accounts, George's dark mood swings had given way to relief at having finished the slog of the demanding tour. The stress had been especially manifest in his dealings with John of late (see chapter 29), but on this night all was well. Also attending the party were May, Olivia, Neil Aspinall, and—by some accounts—Yoko.

It was a propitious time for a Fab gathering. (Ducking a subpoena from Allen Klein, Ringo was hiding out in England.) Though literally on the verge of dissolving their legal ties as "Beatles," the four of them were closer together now than they'd been since 1968. Paul and Linda had formed the habit of dropping in on the Fifty-second Street apartment of John and May when they were in town, where evenings were spent reminiscing over a bottle of wine as John played Paul selections from his Beatles bootleg collection. Wings had been reconstituted with the additions of Jimmy McCulloch and Geoff Britton, and Paul told John of his plans to record their next album in New Orleans.

Herein lies one of the most tantalizing "what-ifs" in all of the ex-Fab saga. For years, May Pang has told interviewers, and related in her own books, how John was planning on joining Paul down in Louisiana, in advance of the *Venus and Mars* sessions, with the intent of doing some writing together. Both men were at their commercial peak at the same time, with *Band on the Run*'s runaway success coming within the same year as John scoring a #1 album *and* single with *Walls and Bridges*. But Wings wasn't exactly stable and fooled no one into believing it was a "band" and not merely Paul's hand puppet.

For his part, while John had managed to produce perhaps his strongest collection of original material since *Imagine* at least, the inspiration was beginning to wane. He had the chore of getting *Rock 'n' Roll* finished up, but after that—and with Apple shutting down—he was a free agent. Paul was likewise transitioning over to Capitol as his contractual obligations were ending. It was as if the planets were at last in alignment for those two, and possibly George and Ringo as well, to get together to do *something*.

(Lest anyone think this enticingly intriguing episode was purely a too-good-to-be-true figment of Ms. Pang's imagination, consider this: Derek Taylor received a postcard around that time from John, saying, "Going to New Orleans to see Paul." Furthermore, Art Garfunkel, whom John was friendly with, reported being quizzed by the ex-Fab about the prospect of working again with *his* Paul. Telling him, "It's a lot of fun if you can

A Central Park West landmark since its construction in the 1880s, the Dakota became the Lennons' residence in 1973. Eerily, the building pops up as the backdrop to images shot of John, Paul, and Ringo in Central Park taken upon their U.S. arrival in February 1964.

keep it on that pure musical level," Garfunkel later said that he was disappointed John hadn't followed through on his advice. As for himself, he and Mr. Simon got together that very year to record the first new Simon and Garfunkel song in half a decade, "My Little Town," scoring a Top 10 hit in the process.)

Unfortunately, the New Orleans meet-up never occurred. John moved back into the Dakota in February 1975, Yoko became pregnant, and the rest has been subject to endless speculation.

John and Paul at the Dakota—April 24 and 25, 1976

Despite the New Orleans visit having come to naught, relations between Lennon and McCartney stayed warm. On Christmas 1975, Paul and Linda charmed their way past security at the Dakota and showed up outside the Lennons' door, singing Christmas carols. The Macs got to meet Sean, and from that time forward, an awful lot of their conversation dealt with child care.

Come the following spring, Wings was at last ready (as Paul's last band had been in February 1964) to conquer the States. The Wings Over America tour was set to begin in April but, owing to guitarist Jimmy McCulloch breaking a finger, was delayed for three weeks. During the ensuing downtime, Macca headed over to the Dakota to pay his respects. As it happened, Paul had lost his father five weeks earlier; coincidentally, Freddie Lennon had succumbed to stomach cancer on April 1. Just as the two men had once bonded as youths over the loss of their mothers, they undoubtedly now had more to talk about.

The media chatter of the day concerned the increased likelihood that the Beatles would reunite, expressed in the face of Paul's massive road show. (With all the time and energy Paul had put into launching such a high-profile tour, the idea of a reunion being *more* likely instead of less sounds even stranger now than it did then, but such were the times.) Picking up on the rampant rumors was NBC's *Saturday Night Live*, a show launched the previous October that had quickly made a name for itself with its blend of subversive humor and music.

On the evening of April 24, the show was hosted by Raquel Welch, with musical guests Phoebe Snow and John Sebastian. Following the latter's performance of "Welcome Back," Lorne Michaels, the show's producer, appeared, seated at a desk. In an earnest tone, he addressed "four very special people: John, Paul, George, and Ringo—the Beatles." At the very moment he spoke these words, John and Paul were sitting together, watching—a ten-minute cab ride away. The universe could not have scripted a better scenario for what was happening.

Michaels began his pitch. "Lately, there have been a lot of rumors to the effect that the four of you might be getting back together. . . . In my book, the Beatles are the best thing that ever happened to music." He then acknowledged that there might be personal obstacles to getting together, and that other offers on the table might have been too low. Therefore, he assured the former Fabs that "the National Broadcasting Company has authorized me to offer you this . . . certified check for $3,000. . . . All you have to do is sing three Beatles songs. . . . 'She loves you, yeah, yeah, yeah.' That's $1,000 right there."

While the audience took the tongue-in-cheek offer for the satire that it was and laughed along with it, Lennon and McCartney saw an opportunity to one-up the gag: what if they hailed a taxi, showed up on the set, and claimed their half of the offer? (Meanwhile, Michaels petition continued: "You divide it up any way you want. If you want to give less to Ringo, that's up to you—I'd rather not get involved.") So it was that a once-in-a-lifetime opportunity that might have become the most talked-about moment in live television history arose—only to be cast aside. Deciding that they were too tired to follow through, John and Paul decided to simply let it be.

(Consider, too, that just days earlier, on Tuesday, April 20, George had been in New York City. He'd appeared at the Fifty-fifth Street Theater with Monty Python, and performed "The Lumberjack Song" onstage. What if he had still been in town on Saturday night? Could he have been independently tipped off to Michaels' offer, arriving at the studio to surprise the producer and all of America, but John and Paul too?)

The SNL campaign to entice the former Fabs onto the show picked up a month later. On May 22—the same day that Wings played the Boston Garden—Michaels again appeared before the cameras, this time upping the ante to a princely *$3,200* (". . . an extra fifty dollars for each of you. That's if you split it equally—I'm still not sure what your situation with Ringo is"), plus paid accommodations at Cross Town Motor Inn ("hosting New York's visitors since 1971"). The show would eventually settle on hosting George alone six months later.

In any event, that April Saturday ended well, with the McCartneys taking their leave sometime after the show ended. The following day, Paul arrived again, this time brandishing a guitar. Unfortunately, as anyone with a six-month-old can attest (and Paul himself should have known), sleep is the first casualty of parenting. He found Lennon in no mood for socializing, much less making music. Having apparently been up late with Sean, he dismissed Macca with the words "Please call before you come over. It's not 1956 and turning up at the door isn't the same anymore." Paul took the hint with something more than its intended weight and flew off to Texas to begin his tour soon after. John's telling of the incident indicated regret that he never saw Paul again after that day, but he certainly had not meant to close the door on their relationship. (A dreadful made-for-VH-1 dramatization fictionalized the visit, airing in 2000 as *Two of Us*. Starring Jared Harris and Aidan Quinn as Lennon and McCartney respectively, it was directed by *Let It Be*'s Michael Lindsay-Hogg.)

The two would have their ups and downs by phone—not surprisingly, considering John's capricious nature. Paul later recalled one conversation where, to his ears, it sounded like his former partner was affecting an "American" attitude. Not in the mood for such pretension, he slammed down the phone after telling him, "Oh, fuck off, Kojak." But memories of their final phone call proved to be of great comfort after their separation became permanent.

In 1981, the legendary Carl Perkins flew down to George Martin's studio in Montserrat to record "Get It," a song Paul had written with him in mind for a duet on *Tug of War*. Gratified by all the attention and hospitality,

Only one photo taken after 1969 containing more than two ex-Beatles is known to exist prior to "The Threetles" reuniting for *Anthology* during the 1990s. (It was shot at Eric and Patties's 1979 wedding.) This one, of Ringo with Paul and Linda, was taken backstage at Wings' final 1976 show in Los Angeles.

Perkins sat Paul and Linda down by way of thanks to play for them a song that had come to him during the night. It was called "My Old Friend." Before the tune had finished, Paul suddenly arose and left, visibly moved to the point of tears. As Carl told the story later, Linda gave the bewildered rockabilly a hug and explained that during their last conversation, John had said to Paul, "Think of me every now and then, my old friend"—the very same words that were in Carl's song.

Paul, George, and Ringo at the Wedding of Eric Clapton and Pattie Boyd—May 19, 1979

On June 9, 1977, the long-moribund Harrison-Boyd marriage was at last officially ended in London. Though Pattie and Eric had set up a household long before (as had George and Olivia), the couple had no particular plans for nuptials. When a wedding finally occurred on March 27, 1979, it was less a matter of legalizing their relationship than it was the result of Clapton's manager, Roger Forrester's, efforts to generate some good press while reconciling Pattie with her famously unfaithful lover. A fling with model Jenny McLean had enraged Pattie, who flew off to America. Forrester bet Clapton that he could get his name in the next day's papers, then announced to the press that his client was marrying Pattie Boyd. Clapton duly proposed and the two were married in Tucson.

Clapton was on the road that spring with his *Backless* tour, but he sent Pattie back to England in April, where plans were soon formed for an "official" wedding celebration at their home, Hurtwood Edge. Guests received invites that said the following:

> Hello
>
> Me and the Mrs. got married the other day but that was in America so we've decided to have a bash in my garden on Saturday, May 19th about 3:00 p.m. for all our mates here at home. If you are free, try and make it, it's bound to be a laugh.
>   . . . see you then . . .
>
> Eric and Pattie Clapton
> P.S. you don't have to bring any presents if you don't want to.

The guest list ran like a Who's Who of British rock, ranging from skiffle pioneer Lonnie Donegan to Clapton's ex-Cream bandmates, members of the Rolling Stones, and three of the ex-Beatles, including his bride's former husband. While not formally asking his musician friends to entertain, Clapton had installed a stage, complete with amps, PA, and instruments, just in case.

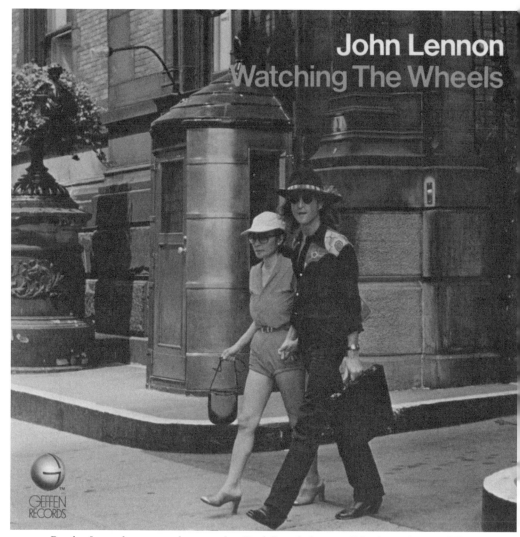

GEFFEN RECORDS

Beatles fan and amateur photographer Paul Goresh first met John by posing as a VCR repairman to gain access to the Dakota. Initially angry, John eventually warmed to him and allowed himself to be photographed. Taken very near where he later met his end, this Goresh image captured the Lennons off to the Hit Factory in August 1980.

Sure enough, soon the stage was filled with guests and an ad hoc set began blasting out. All three ex-Fabs were onstage—while no photos or recordings of the event have been made public, at least a couple of songs played that day are known: "Get Back" and "Sgt. Pepper's Lonely Heart's Club Band." Like the Lennon-McCartney jam at Burbank studios, the effort wasn't being made in the name of great music; just, as Clapton had promised, for "a laugh." (Denny Laine described their sound as "absolute rubbish.") By all accounts, though, a grand time was had by all (except perhaps Jack Bruce, who fell victim to a cruel prank by Clapton, who spread the word around to the musicians to leave the stage one by one until Bruce was by himself—humiliated).

The historic nature of the occasion—the last semi-public live performance of three quarters of the Beatles—was little noted by the participants at the time, but for Clapton was cause for regret in view of later events. John Lennon, through egregious oversight, had not been invited. According to Slowhand, John later told him that if he'd been asked, he would have come. As the bluesman reflected years later, "A great opportunity was lost for the Beatles to re-form for one last performance."

The Green-Eyed Goddamn Straight from Your Heart

The Death of John—December 8, 1980

T he promotion of John's first album of new material in over five years sparked a whirlwind of activity (though as the father of a pre-schooler, Lennon was quite accustomed to moving nonstop). This Monday saw scheduled a major radio interview, a photo shoot, and more studio work. If the grind of such a full slate of chores seemed taxing, it was belied by the energy that the revitalized ex-Beatle was happily putting into it.

Other plans lay ahead as well. On Wednesday, the couple was expected to fly to San Francisco to reignite their political activism with participation in a march for striking Japanese food workers seeking wage parity. Another trip was planned for England after the New Year. Oddly, since acquiring his "legal" status five years before, John had not bothered to squeeze in a visit to his homeland, not even to see Mimi. (Though the two maintained steady phone contact, she had never met Sean). Also looming on the agenda was work on Ringo's new album. A wedding too was on the horizon, with an ex-Fab reunion expected when the drummer tied the knot with Barbara Bach sometime in spring.

Whatever notions John had of collaborating with the ex-Fabs beyond helping out on Ringo's project would have to come after the follow-up to *Double Fantasy* was completed. *Milk and Honey* had already been started, but most of the tracks were not quite releasable just yet. Still, the album would have to be completed quickly, for John was already planning a tour—his first since the Beatles—to begin around March, covering the States, Japan, and possibly Europe. With his studio musicians "hot as shit," he was ready to put aside any reservations about performing live in order to fully realize the potential of his new songs that had only been hinted at on record. He also discussed revisiting his back catalog (among the songs he mentioned *specifically*: "I Want to Hold Your Hand") for live presentation for the first time in over a decade.

But first there was this day to get through. After a breakfast at his beloved Café La Fortuna on Seventy-first Street, John got a haircut, possibly in anticipation of photographer Annie Leibovitz's arrival that day. A favorite of the Lennons (she'd shot the photos accompanying the *Lennon Remembers* interview), she was again expecting to provide a cover image for an upcoming *Rolling Stone* piece. Several frames depicted John around the house: in a black jacket, sitting in a window frame, or in his bed, holding a guitar. Then too there were a couple of straight-on portraits (one of which graced the cover of the compilation *The John Lennon Collection*).

But the most famous image was one with Yoko. At first, Leibovitz wasn't particularly interested in photographing the two as a couple, *Double Fantasy* notwithstanding. But she acquiesced on the condition that the two pose nude, as a sort of take on *Two Virgins*, twelve years on. While John happily agreed to doff his drawers, Yoko would only go so far as removing her top, which Leibovitz observed wasn't quite the same thing. But then she had a flash of inspiration: she allowed Yoko to keep all her clothes on, while John alone got naked. He responded by lying beside his wife on the floor alongside their bed, attaching himself to her in an almost fetal position. A test Polaroid assured the three of them that they'd captured something special—John expressed his wish that this be the magazine cover image. It would be, though not in the context he'd imagined.

Before Ms. Leibovitz's departure, a team from RKO radio had arrived to conduct a lengthy interview that would be syndicated as a radio special around the world. Reinforcing the johnandyoko/househusband meme he'd first initiated in *Newsweek*, and then later expanded upon in sessions with David Sheff for *Playboy* and Andy Peebles for the BBC (just two days earlier), he boosted the husband-and-wife artistic team narrative, referred to the Beatles as old news, and expressed great optimism for the 1980s as the dawn of an era that would build upon the successes of the '60s while avoiding the excesses of the recently finished decade ("Weren't the '70s a drag?").

At around 4:30 p.m., the couple was ready to leave for the Record Plant to oversee the transferring of some *Double Fantasy* album tracks into singles, as well as to finalize mixes of Yoko's "Walking on Thin Ice," which they'd been working on over the past couple of weeks. John had apparently spent the night listening to a rough mix for hours on end at the Dakota, so entranced was he with the undeniably hypnotic recording. (Due to the fact that their limo was late, the couple ended up hitching a ride with the RKO staffers.) But before their departure, they encountered an unscheduled visitor.

Within hours of the shooting, this *New York Daily News* extra hit the streets. It was superseded by an edition proclaiming the killer's words: "I just shot John Lennon."

Paul Goresh was an amateur photographer who had ingratiated himself with the Lennons. (A shot he'd taken that summer of John and Yoko leaving the Dakota was later used on the "Watching the Wheels" single sleeve.) He would spend hours hanging around outside their residence whenever he could; on this afternoon, John wanted to see some photos Paul had taken of them the week before. Also nearby was a stranger who'd told Goresh before the Lennons came out that he'd traveled all the way from Hawaii by way of Georgia to see John. As John flipped through the photos, Paul noticed the stranger drawing nearer, to John's left, clutching a copy of *Double Fantasy.*

John took his gaze away from the pictures for a moment to ask of the silent stranger, "Do you want that signed?" The stranger nodded. John took the album, along with a pen the stranger provided, and wrote "John Lennon 1980" across Yoko's neck on the cover image. As he wrote, Paul snapped a shot, thinking at the time to minimize the stranger in the frame. The autograph's recipient was strangely silent—so much so that Paul said John exchanged glances with him as if to say, "Can't he talk?" Upon handing it back, John asked, "Is that all right?" The stranger nodded and backed away; as John stepped toward his waiting car, Paul snapped a final frame of his friend and idol about to enter it.

What John didn't know was that the stranger had earlier that day encountered his son Sean as the boy's nanny returned him home from an outing. Though only turned five recently, the boy seemed to be quite accustomed to attention from strangers; as this one knelt before him and squeezed his hand, Sean neither spoke nor freaked out.

At the Record Plant, John and Yoko listened to playbacks of the single masters. At some point in the evening, the couple, along with producer

Jack Douglas, worked on the final mix of Yoko's "Walking on Thin Ice." Perfecting the track took hours, but as they worked Douglas was documenting every word spoken by way of a surreptitious recording devise he'd installed back at the beginning of the *Double Fantasy* sessions (on the grounds that what they were doing was historic). What was recorded *that* night has long been the subject of conjecture, because afterward, Douglas erased the recording of John's last evening, describing the recordings as "painful"—"strange things were said."

As the ten o'clock hour came around, the by now mentally exhausted and famished couple recognized that, no matter what the results of the evening's work were, it was getting late—perhaps tomorrow morning at nine they could reconvene and judge their work with fresh ears. Before leaving, John signed a final autograph, this one for studio switchboard operator Rabiah Seminole. (After completing the signing, which included a self-portrait, Rabiah noted that he'd misspelled her name. "That's how it sounds to me," was his response.) Once in their limo, there was the decision to make whether to stop and have dinner at Broadway Deli, another of their regular spots. John told Yoko he'd rather go home first, since he could then say good night to Sean before it got too late.

At about 10:50 p.m., the long car glided up to the curbside in front of their residence. On other occasions, the couple would avoid any gathered throngs by having the driver pull into the building's courtyard, past the gothic arched entranceway. Paul Goresh had left a couple of hours before; no one else was apparently around to delay their plan to see Sean, having spent so many hours immersed in work apart from him. Yoko exited first. The stranger was lurking in the archway's shadow, clutching his .32 caliber Charter Arms pistol, loaded with deadly hollow-nose bullets.

As Yoko recalled later, the stranger said "Hello"—or perhaps she said it to him. Such perfunctory salutations were routine, coming reflexively as one went about one's business in public. John trailed behind, carrying a tape player and cassettes bearing the fruit of their labors. In his final moment of lucidity, he passed the stranger, his mind occupied by thoughts of seeing his boy, of "Walking on Thin Ice," of his next meal. He probably didn't notice the stranger whose album he'd signed hours earlier. Any musings engaging him at that moment were disrupted by the call of a voice: "Mr. Lennon?"

*   *   *

On *Walls and Bridges*, John sang, "Hatred and jealousy are gonna be the death of me." Mortality was a subject that he was intimately acquainted with, beginning with his Uncle George (who passed away when he was fourteen), followed by his mother (three years later) and his friend Stuart Sutcliffe (four years after that). On the occasion of that last bereavement, he advised Stuart's girlfriend Astrid that she had to make the choice whether to live or die: there was no in between.

On his final afternoon, he mused to his inquisitors from RKO radio that as an artist he was just getting started; he expected to carry on for another forty years. John had been asked to explain his thoughts on what death meant for virtually as long as he'd been famous: in 1969, he pronounced it nothing more than getting out of one car and getting into another; as for himself, he saw presenting his heavy messages with humor as a way to inoculate himself against violence, since "all the serious people get shot" (while conceding elsewhere, "I'll probably get popped off by some loony").

He never got the opportunity to engage the instrument of his destruction, but if he had, chances were good that he could have figuratively (and literally) disarmed him. Those close to Lennon were always struck by how very unstar-like he was in seeking to engage people of every stratum who happened to touch lives with him, and that he certainly didn't shy away from confrontation. Alto saxist Ron Aprea, a member of the "Little Big Horns" brass section that had worked on *Walls and Bridges*, shared late-night after-session walks with John as they made their way home. He would later recall being surprised and more than a little concerned at how the ex-Beatle eschewed the native New Yorker insularity and actually sought out people to engage: "On many occasions he would stand there or kneel down and chat with total strangers in a most casual way. I couldn't help thinking how compassionate but reckless this was."

But, as Lennon had often expressed it, he could not be what he was not. While he didn't exactly revel in hysterical attention from strangers à la *A Hard Day's Night*, his innate curiosity and desire to learn about the lives of others was his hallmark; it was also a projectable trait. There were (and are) millions around the world who felt an emotional investment in the four men who were the Beatles, feeling that they *knew* them, and moreover that the Fabs knew *them* and could understand and help them sort out their own lives. The stranger who took John Lennon's life was exceptional only in degree. More disturbed than the usual Beatles fan, this one felt personally affronted by what he perceived as Lennon's phoniness: for this, he had to die.

* * *

A police cruiser, dispatched by the Dakota's doorman, arrived within minutes. After assessing the situation, the officers decided not to wait for an ambulance, instead placing the dying musician into the car's backseat before speeding off to the emergency room. They made the short distance to Roosevelt Hospital quickly and upon their arrival hustled John inside upon a waiting gurney. As John's earthly existence slipped away, a familiar tune could be heard playing over the hospital's muzak system. It was "All My Loving"—a Paul composition, but also the very first song that John had played on American soil, in this very city, nearly seventeen years earlier. In a way, John Lennon's New York sojourn had been brought full circle.

*   *   *

Ringo was on vacation in the Bahamas with Barbara Bach when he received word of the tragedy. Barbara's daughter Francesca called with the news; it's possible that she was tipped off by any one of the millions watching ABC's *Monday Night Football*. (As it happened, an ABC producer was in the emergency room at Roosevelt Hospital when John was brought in. A quick phone call to the network resulted in sportscaster Howard Cosell, himself friendly with John, breaking the news to most of America.) Without a second thought, Ringo and Barbara booked a flight to New York. John—Ringo's "brother"—was dead, and all he could think to do was comfort the widow in person.

John's first wife, Cynthia, got the word from Maureen, Ringo's ex. The two women were quite close; just a day earlier, Cyn had arrived for a brief visit to Mo—four hours from home—while attending to some business. Sometime in the early morning hours, Ringo called Maureen with the news. Her screams woke Cynthia, who then had her own shock to face. Her first thoughts were of seventeen-year-old Julian, at home in Wales with his stepfather. Though John Twist agreed not to break the news to Julian until Cynthia returned, the local media had other ideas. Not long after he awoke, the youth learned from a glance out his window that something terrible had happened. Within hours, a strained call between Yoko and Cynthia resulted in Julian flying out to New York, too.

Paul received word of the tragedy after Yoko called his MPL office. A staffer relayed the message, which came while Linda was driving the kids to school in the morning. She returned home, still unaware, to find Paul with a bloodless look on his face, one she'd never seen before. After speaking with Yoko, Paul, who as it happened had a recording session scheduled with George Martin that day, was given the option of canceling. He couldn't: faced with feelings too deep to get any kind of handle on, he instinctively knew that the best thing for him to be doing was work. (For George Martin, also distraught, the story was the same.)

Upon leaving the facility at the end of the day, Paul—wiped out on every level—slipped a little when inanely asked his reaction to the day's news by a reporter: "It's a drag, innit?" For this momentary and very human attempt to answer the unanswerable, he was kicked around in the press for days afterward.

George likewise was compelled to channel his loss into work. He'd been awakened during the night by Olivia, who had learned of the tragedy from her sister in California. In his less than fully conscious state, George took the message as meaning John had been hurt in an accident and wasn't actually gone. Only upon waking did he absorb the full measure of the tragedy.

He might have had his own reasons for compounded grief, given the state of disunity between the two at the time. George knew John well enough and long enough to not take his rants at face value, but still, the sense that his "big brother" might have been upset with him was not a pleasant thought to dwell upon.

Drummer Dave Mattacks was in the studio that day with George, a singular experience that has never left him. He saw in George the grief and resignation that came from years of exploration into life's meaning. But any comfort that his spiritual teachings might have offered was subsumed by a greater struggle with the utter senselessness of it all. Said George: "All I ever wanted to do was play guitar in a band. And this is the result. . . ."

CASH BOX

December 20, 1980

NEWSPAPER

$2.20

John Lennon
1940 • 1980

Selected Bibliography

Source material consulted for this book runs the gamut from primary works, such as the original recordings and TV/film, to a wide array of books and period magazines. Here's a rough breakdown of what was tapped:

Books

Andrews, Nancy Lee. *A Dose of Rock 'n' Roll*. Deerfield, IL: Dalton Watson, 2008.

Badman, Keith. *The Beatles Off the Record 2: The Dream Is Over*. London: Omnibus, 2002.

Bielen, Ken, and Ben Urish. *The Words and Music of John Lennon*. Santa Barbara: Praeger, 2007.

Blaney, John. *Beatles for Sale: How Everything They Touched Turned to Gold*. New York: Jawbone Press, 2008.

Blaney, John. *Lennon and McCartney: Together Alone*. New York: Jawbone Press, 2007.

Boyd, Pattie, and Penny Junor. *Wonderful Today: The Autobiography*. London: Headline Review, 2007.

Buckley, David. *Elton: The Biography*. Chicago: Chicago Review Press, 2007.

Chapman, Graham, and Jim Yoakum. *Ojril: The Completely Incomplete Graham Chapman*. Dulles, VA: Brassey's, 2000.

Clapton, Eric. *Clapton: The Autobiography*. New York: Broadway, 2007.

DiLello, Richard. *The Longest Cocktail Party: An Insider's Diary of the Beatles, Their Million-Dollar "Apple" Empire, and Its Rise and Fall*. Chicago: Playboy Press, 1972.

Douglas, Mike, et al. *I'll Be Right Back: Memories of TV's Greatest Talk Show*. New York: Simon and Schuster, 2000.

Editors of *Goldmine*. *The Beatles Digest*. Iola, WI: Krause Publications, 2000.

Editors of *Rolling Stone*. *The Ballad of John and Yoko*. New York: Doubleday, 1982.

Editors of *Rolling Stone*. *Harrison*. New York: Simon and Schuster, 2002.

Greene, Joshua M. *Here Comes the Sun: The Spiritual and Musical Journey of George Harrison.* Hoboken, NJ: John Wiley and Sons, 2007.

Heylin, Clinton. *Bootleg: The Secret History of the Other Recording Industry.* New York: St. Martin's Press, 1996.

Huntley, Elliot J. *Mystical One: George Harrison After the Break-up of the Beatles.* Toronto: Guernica Editions, 2004.

Kane, Larry. *Lennon Revealed.* London: Running Press, 2005.

Leng, Simon. *While My Guitar Gently Weeps: The Music of George Harrison.* Milwaukee, WI: Hal Leonard, 2006.

Lennon, Cynthia. *John.* New York: Crown Publishers, 2008.

Madinger, Chip and Easter, Mark. *Eight Arms To Hold You: The Solo Beatles Compendium.* Chesterfield, MO: 44.1 Productions, 2000.

Mansfield, Ken. *The White Book: The Beatles, the Bands, the Biz: An Insider's Look at an Era.* Nashville: Thomas Nelson, 2007.

McGee, Garry. *Band on the Run: A History of Paul McCartney and Wings.* Lanham, MD: Taylor Trade, 2003.

Miles, Barry. *Paul McCartney: Many Years from Now.* New York: Henry Holt and Company, 1997.

Miles, Barry. *Zappa.* New York: Grove Press, 2004.

Norman, Philip. *John Lennon: The Life.* New York: Ecco, 2008.

Palin, Michael. *Diaries 1969–1979: The Python Years.* New York: St. Martin's Griffin, 2008.

Pang, May. *Instamatic Karma: Photographs of John Lennon.* New York: St. Martin's Press, 2008.

Pang, May, and Henry Edwards. *Loving John: The Untold Story.* New York: Warner Books, 1983.

Paytress, Mark. *Bolan: The Rise and Fall of a 20th Century Superstar.* London: Music Sales, 2007.

Ribowsky, Mark. *He's a Rebel: Phil Spector, Rock and Roll's Legendary Producer.* New York: Cooper Square Press, 1989.

Rodriguez, Robert, and Stuart Shea. *Fab Four FAQ: Everything Left to Know About the Beatles . . . and More!* New York: Hal Leonard Books, 2007.

Sandford, Christopher. *McCartney.* New York: Carroll and Graf, 2006.

Spizer, Bruce. *The Beatles Solo on Apple Records.* New Orleans: 498 Productions, 2005.

Sulpy, Doug, and Ray Schweighart. *Get Back: The Unauthorized Chronicle of the Beatles' "Let It Be" Disaster.* New York: St. Martin's Griffin, 1999.

Wiener, Jon. *Come Together: John Lennon in His Time.* New York: Random House, 1984.

Magazines

The vintage periodicals depicted in this book were all reviewed for their contemporaneous reporting. Additionally, some modern-day publications carried excellent interviews and articles. Here they are in list form:

Beatlefan (1978–present)
Billboard (1968–1981)
Circus (1969–1981)
Crawdaddy (1970–1977)
Creem (1970–1980)
Disc (1971–1973)
Discoveries (1995–2000)
Goldmine (1988–present)
Hit Parader (1970–1980)
Melody Maker (1969–1980)
Modern Drummer (1981–1987)
Mojo (1995–present)
Musician (1980–1984)
National Lampoon (1973–1977)
New Musical Express (1970–1980)
People (1975–1988)
Playboy (January 1981)
Rolling Stone (1969–present)
Song Hits (1977–1981)
Trouser Press (1977–1981)
Uncut (2000–present)

Websites

There are any number of Beatle-related websites out there, of course, but there were a few key solo reference ones I found myself returning to over and over again. Given the transient nature of the Internet, however, I won't enshrine them here. Instead, I urge you to bookmark *these* two sites:

www.fabfourfaq2.com
www.fabfourfaq.com

Also, look for *Fab Four FAQ 2.0* on Facebook. At each of these sites, you'll find updates, links, and news; and at the first, a forum for us to keep the conversation going. Hope you come by soon!

Lastly, for readers of this book who wish to see or hear some of the material described in this book, I invite you to visit YouTube. Some accommodating folks have posted a wealth of music, including hard-to-find recordings as well as TV appearances and videos. Some of what you'll *read* about here you'll be able to *see* there.

Index